THRILLING

ALIEN INVASION

SHORT STORIES

ANTHOLOGY OF NEW & CLASSIC TALES

Foreword by Patrick Parrinder

FLAME TREE PUBLISHING

TALES

This is a FLAME TREE Book

Publisher & Creative Director: Nick Wells
Project Editor: Laura Bulbeck
Editorial Board: Gillian Whitaker, Josie Mitchell, Catherine Taylor

Special thanks to Joanne Li and the editors of *Science Fiction World Magazine*,
and Xie Zhaoli for her co-ordination in Beijing.

Publisher's Note: Due to the historical nature of the classic text, we're aware that there may be some language used which has the potential to cause offence to the modern reader. However, wishing overall to preserve the integrity of the text, rather than imposing contemporary sensibilities, we have left it unaltered.

FLAME TREE PUBLISHING
6 Melbray Mews, Fulham,
London SW6 3NS, United Kingdom
www.flametreepublishing.com

First published 2018

18 20 22 21 19
3 5 7 9 10 8 6 4 2

ISBN: 978-1-78664-768-9

The cover image is created by Flame Tree Studio
based on artwork by Slava Gerj and Gabor Ruszkai.

A copy of the CIP data for this book is available from the British Library.

Printed and bound in China

And Coming Soon
FLAME TREE PRESS | FICTION WITHOUT FRONTIERS
New and original writing in Horror, Crime, SF and Fantasy

THRILLING

ALIEN INVASION

SHORT STORIES

ANTHOLOGY OF NEW & CLASSIC TALES

Foreword by Patrick Parrinder

FLAME TREE PUBLISHING

TALES

Contents

Foreword: Alien Invasion Short Stories

'They were the most mortifying sight I ever beheld.'
Jonathan Swift, Gulliver's Travels, Part 3, Chapter 10

GIANT CREEPY-CRAWLIES, groping tentacles, blobs, parasites, slimy-scaled vampires: many of us, when we think of alien invaders, will call up a host of computer-enhanced images from Hollywood cinema. The movie industry owes a big debt to the bug-eyed monsters of 1930s science-fiction magazine covers, and, before them, to the octopoid Martians of H.G. Wells's *The War of the Worlds*. Wells's Martian invaders, however stomach-churning, come to Earth in very small numbers; it is their technological firepower that turns them into a marauding army. One of Wells's presumed sources was a highly realistic narrative of future war, George Chesney's *The Battle of Dorking*. Here the invaders are the German soldiers who had swept across France in the Franco-Prussian War of 1870–71. Chesney's novel, intended as a wake-up call to the British, is unlike most of the stories in this book in that it contains nothing truly fantastic or grotesque. It does, however, remind us of the variety of meanings we attach to the term 'alien' and, for that matter, to the idea of invasion.

In legal language an alien is simply an outsider, usually the citizen of another country. Yet the notion that, to be properly called alien, a thing must also be non-human is at least as old as the Roman playwright Terence, who famously declared that *Homo sum, humani nihil a me alienum puto*: I am a man, and I consider nothing human alien to me. But what is it, exactly, to be human? The 'most mortifying sight' that Swift's hero Lemuel Gulliver beholds on his extensive travels is that of subtly altered human beings.

If the alien is (in some sense, at least) the non-human, then a truly alien entity is not merely different from us, but something we can barely describe, let alone understand. In the stories of H.P. Lovecraft and others, the alien is an insoluble mystery, something whose nature can only be guessed at. Often such a mystery is associated with particular, remote places on Earth, with regions that only an intrepid (and, usually, white male) explorer would be foolish enough to enter. Can these alien presences be called invaders, or is it, rather, *their* domains – their privacy, we might say – that we, as readers, are intruding upon? Invasion is not always a military phenomenon, however hostile the aliens may be. Austin Hall's Martians, in 'The Man Who Saved the Earth', manage to devastate our planet without landing on it or, indeed, launching spaceships at all. And if super-intelligent beings do arrive here in gigantic spaceships they might have come on a diplomatic mission, or be stopping off on a much longer journey. Or could they just come here to laugh at us? In Voltaire's satire 'Micromégas', the two visiting giants, confronted by human self-importance, are reduced to the 'inextinguishable laughter' that Homer once said belonged to the gods. We like to think of imaginary aliens as monsters and devils, but they can also be disturbingly like gods.

Patrick Parrinder
President, H.G. Wells Society

Publisher's Note

Visitors from other planets have long fascinated us. H.G. Wells's *The War of the Worlds* spawned a huge wave of speculative fiction, but the roots of such fears run deep in our literature, with themes of invasion stretching back to writers such as Voltaire and Jonathan Swift. Of course not all invaders are 'extra-terrestrial' even if they might still be described as alien. In searching back through the origins of the alien invasion genre, we have chosen to include George Chesney's *The Battle of Dorking* (in which Britain is invaded by a German-speaking country), an alarmist novella which had clear influences on later SF stories; as well as a couple of tales from the Irish *Book of Invasions* – just one example we could have included from various cultures' mythological traditions, which show just how much fear of the 'other' has always pervaded. Of course there's some good old traditional interplanetary invasions in here too – from some lesser known early pulp stories to the ever-masterful Wells and Lovecraft.

We had a fantastic number of contemporary submissions, and have thoroughly enjoyed delving into authors' imaginations of just how the discovery of another species might go. From acts of aggression to silent infiltration or peaceful interactions, each story reminds us we're a tiny speck in this gargantuan universe. We're also thrilled to be extending our own horizons, including our first story from a modern Chinese author, courtesy of the popular Chinese monthly *SFWorld*. Making the final selection is always a tough decision, but ultimately we chose a collection of stories we hope sit alongside each other and with the classic fiction, to provide a fantastic *Alien Invasion* book for all to enjoy.

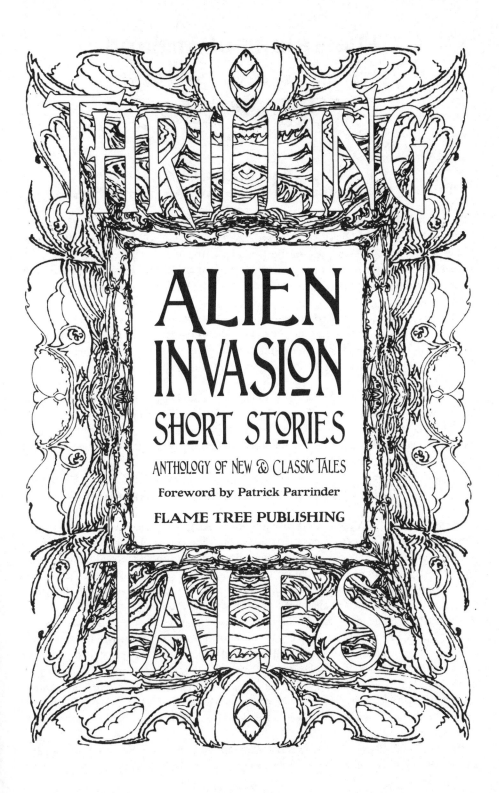

THRILLING

ALIEN INVASION

SHORT STORIES

ANTHOLOGY OF NEW & CLASSIC TALES

Foreword by Patrick Parrinder

FLAME TREE PUBLISHING

TALES

The Taking of Ireland

Retold Tales from The Book of Invasions

Introduction
Tales of the Tuatha Dé Danann and the Early Milesians

THE STORIES included here are based on tales selected from the *Book of Invasions*, otherwise known as *Lebor Gabála Érenn* (*The Book of the Taking of Ireland*). The tale below begins after the conquest of the Fir Bolg by the Tuatha Dé Danann, the god-like race, whose name translates as 'the people of the god whose mother is Dana'. Two of the most outstanding stories have been chosen here, each of which has an especially powerful narrative impact.

The Tuatha Dé Danann are recorded as having originally travelled to Erin from the northern islands of Greece around 2000 BC. They possessed great gifts of magic and druidism and they ruled the country until their defeat by the Milesians, when they were forced to establish an underground kingdom known as the Otherworld or the Sidhe, meaning Hollow Hills.

Lugh (pronounced 'Lu', 'gh' is silent, as in English) of the Long Arm, who also appears later in the Ulster Cycle as Cúchulainn's divine father, emerges as one of the principal heroes of the Tuatha Dé Danann who rescues his people from the tyranny of the Fomorians. The Quest of the Children of Tuirenn, together with the sorrowful account of Lir's children, are undoubtedly two of the great epic tales of this cycle.

The Quest of the Children of Tuirenn

NUADA OF THE SILVER HAND rose to become King of the Tuatha Dé Danann during the most savage days of the early invasions. The Fomorians, a repulsive band of sea-pirates, were the fiercest of opponents who swept through the country destroying cattle and property and imposing tribute on the people of the land. Every man of the Tuatha Dé Danann, no matter how rich or poor, was required to pay one ounce of gold to the Fomorians and those who neglected to pay this tax at the annual assembly on the Hill of Uisneach were maimed or murdered without compassion. Balor of the Evil Eye was leader of these brutal invaders, and it was well known that when he turned his one glaring eyeball on his foes they immediately fell dead as if struck by a thunderbolt. Everyone lived in mortal fear of Balor, for no weapon had yet been discovered that could slay or even injure him. Times were bleak for the Tuatha Dé Danann and the people had little faith in King Nuada who appeared powerless to resist Balor's tyranny and oppression. As the days passed by, they yearned for a courageous leader who would rescue them from their life of wretched servitude.

The appalling misery of the Tuatha Dé Danann became known far and wide and, after a time, it reached the ears of Lugh of the Long Arm of the fairymounds, whose father was

Cian, son of Cainte. As soon as he had grown to manhood, Lugh had proven his reputation as one of the most fearless warriors and was so revered by the elders of Fairyland that they had placed in his charge the wondrous magical gifts of Manannan the sea-god which had protected their people for countless generations. Lugh rode the magnificent white steed of Manannan, known as Aenbarr, a horse as fleet of foot as the wailing gusts of winter whose charm was such that no rider was ever wounded while seated astride her. He had the boat of Manannan, which could read a man's thoughts and travel in whatever direction its keeper demanded. He also wore Manannan's breast-plate and body armour which no weapon could ever pierce, and he carried the mighty sword known as 'The Retaliator' that could cut through any battle shield.

The day approached once more for the People of Dana to pay their annual taxes to the Fomorians and they gathered together, as was customary, on the Hill of Uisneach to await the arrival of Balor's men. As they stood fearful and terrified in the chill morning air, several among them noticed a strange cavalry coming over the plain from the east towards them. At the head of this impressive group, seated high in command above the rest, was Lugh of the Long Arm, whose proud and noble countenance mirrored the splendour of the rising sun. The King was summoned to witness the spectacle and he rode forth to salute the leader of the strange army. The two had just begun to converse amiably when they were interrupted by the approach of a grimy-looking band of men, instantly known to all as Fomorian tax-collectors. King Nuada bowed respectfully towards them and instructed his subjects to deliver their tributes without delay. Such a sad sight angered and humiliated Lugh of the Long Arm and he drew the King aside and began to reproach him:

"Why do your subjects bow before such an evil-eyed brood," he demanded, "when they do not show you any mark of respect in return?"

"We are obliged to do this," replied Nuada. "If we refuse we would be killed instantly and our land has witnessed more than enough bloodshed at the hands of the Fomorians."

"Then it is time for the Tuatha Dé Danann to avenge this great injustice," replied Lugh, and with that, he began slaughtering Balor's emissaries single-handedly until all but one lay dead at his feet. Dragging the surviving creature before him, Lugh ordered him to deliver a stern warning to Balor:

"Return to your leader," he thundered, "and inform him that he no longer has any power over the People of Dana. Lugh of the Long Arm, the greatest of warriors, is more than eager to enter into combat with him if he possesses enough courage to meet the challenge."

Knowing that these words would not fail to enrage Balor, Lugh lost little time preparing himself for battle. He enlisted the King's help in assembling the strongest men in the kingdom to add to his own powerful army. Shining new weapons of steel were provided and three thousand of the swiftest white horses were made ready for his men. A magnificent fleet of ships, designed to withstand the most venomous ocean waves, remained moored at port, awaiting the moment when Balor and his malicious crew would appear on the horizon.

The time finally arrived when the King received word that Balor's fierce army had landed at Eas Dara on the northwest coast of Connacht. Within hours, the Fomorians had pillaged the lands of Bodb the Red and plundered the homes of noblemen throughout the province. Hearing of this wanton destruction, Lugh of the Long Arm was more determined than ever to secure victory for the Tuatha Dé Danann. He rode across the plains of Erin back to his home to enlist the help of Cian, his father, who controlled all the armies of the fairymounds. His two uncles, Cu and Cethen, also offered their support and the three brothers set off in different directions to round up the remaining warriors of Fairyland.

Cian journeyed northwards and he did not rest until he reached Mag Muirthemne on the outskirts of Dundalk. As he crossed the plain, he observed three men, armed and mailed, riding towards him. At first he did not recognize them, but as they drew closer, he knew them to be the sons of Tuirenn whose names were Brian, Iucharba and Iuchar. A long-standing feud had existed for years between the sons of Cainte and the sons of Tuirenn and the hatred and enmity they felt towards each other was certain to provoke a deadly contest. Wishing to avoid an unequal clash of arms, Cian glanced around him for a place to hide and noticed a large herd of swine grazing nearby. He struck himself with a druidic wand and changed himself into a pig. Then he trotted off to join the herd and began to root up the ground like the rest of them.

The sons of Tuirenn were not slow to notice that the warrior who had been riding towards them had suddenly vanished into thin air. At first, they all appeared puzzled by his disappearance, but then Brian, the eldest of the three, began to question his younger brothers knowingly:

"Surely brothers you also saw the warrior on horseback," he said to them. "Have you no idea what became of him?"

"We do not know," they replied.

"Then you are not fit to call yourselves warriors," chided Brian, "for that horseman can be no friend of ours if he is cowardly enough to change himself into one of these swine. The instruction you received in the City of Learning has been wasted on you if you cannot even tell an enchanted beast from a natural one."

And as he was saying this, he struck Iucharba and Iuchar with his own druidic wand, transforming them into two sprightly hounds that howled and yelped impatiently to follow the trail of the enchanted pig.

Before long, the pig had been hunted down and driven into a small wood where Brian cast his spear at it, driving it clean through the animal's chest. Screaming in pain, the injured pig began to speak in a human voice and begged his captors for mercy:

"Allow me a dignified death," the animal pleaded. "I am originally a human being, so grant me permission to pass into my own shape before I die."

"I will allow this," answered Brian, "since I am often less reluctant to kill a man than a pig."

Then Cian, son of Cainte, stood before them with blood trickling down his cloak from the gaping wound in his chest.

"I have outwitted you," he cried, "for if you had killed me as a pig you would only be sentenced for killing an animal, but now you must kill me in my own human shape. And I must warn you that the penalty you will pay for this crime is far greater than any ever paid before on the death of a nobleman, for the weapons you shall use will cry out in anguish, proclaiming your wicked deed to my son, Lugh of the Long Arm."

"We will not slay you with any weapons in that case," replied Brian triumphantly, "but with the stones that lie on the ground around us." And the three brothers began to pelt Cian with jagged rocks and stones until his body was a mass of wounds and he fell to the earth battered and lifeless. The sons of Tuirenn then buried him where he had fallen in an unmarked grave and hurried off to join the war against the Fomorians.

With the great armies of Fairyland and the noble cavalcade of King Nuada at his side, Lugh of the Long Arm won battle after battle against Balor and his men. Spears shot savagely through the air and scabbards clashed furiously until at last, the Fomorians could hold out no longer. Retreating to the coast, the terrified survivors and their leader boarded their vessels and sailed as fast as the winds could carry them back through the northern mists towards their own depraved land. Lugh of the Long Arm became the hero of his people and they presented him with the finest trophies of valour the kingdom had to offer, including a golden war chariot, studded with precious jewels which was driven by four of the brawniest milk-white steeds.

When the festivities had died down somewhat, and the Tuatha Dé Danann had begun to lead normal lives once more, Lugh began to grow anxious for news of his father. He called several of his companions to him and appealed to them for information, but none among them had received tidings of Cian since the morning he had set off towards the north to muster the armies of the fairymounds.

"I know that he is no longer alive," said Lugh, "and I give you my word that I will not rest again, or allow food or drink to pass my lips, until I have knowledge of what happened to him."

And so Lugh, together with a number of his kinsmen, rode forth to the place where he and his father had parted company. From here, the horse of Manannan guided him to the Plain of Muirthemne where Cian had met his tragic death. As soon as he entered the shaded wood, the stones of the ground began to cry out in despair and they told Lugh of how the sons of Tuirenn had murdered his father and buried him in the earth. Lugh wept bitterly when he heard this tale and implored his men to help him dig up the grave so that he might discover in what cruel manner Cian had been slain. The body was raised from the ground and the litter of wounds on his father's cold flesh was revealed to him. Lugh rose gravely to his feet and swore angry vengeance on the sons of Tuirenn:

"This death has so exhausted my spirit that I cannot hear through my ears, and I cannot see anything with my eyes, and there is not one pulse beating in my heart for grief of my father. Sorrow and destruction will fall on those that committed this crime and they shall suffer long when they are brought to justice."

The body was returned to the ground and Lugh carved a headstone and placed it on the grave. Then, after a long period of mournful silence, he mounted his horse and headed back towards Tara where the last of the victory celebrations were taking place at the palace.

Lugh of the Long Arm sat calmly and nobly next to King Nuada at the banqueting table and looked around him until he caught sight of the three sons of Tuirenn. As soon as he had fixed his eye on them, he stood up and ordered the Chain of Attention of the Court to be shaken so that everyone present would fall silent and listen to what he had to say.

"I put to you all a question," said Lugh. "I ask each of you what punishment you would inflict upon the man that had murdered your father?"

The King and his warriors were astonished at these words, but finally Nuada spoke up and enquired whether it was Lugh's own father that had been killed.

"It is indeed my own father who lies slain," replied Lugh "and I see before me in this very room the men who carried out the foul deed."

"Then it would be far too lenient a punishment to strike them down directly," said the King. "I myself would ensure that they died a lingering death and I would cut off a single limb each day until they fell down before me writhing in agony."

Those who were assembled agreed with the King's verdict and even the sons of Tuirenn nodded their heads in approval. But Lugh declared that he did not wish to kill any of the Tuatha Dé Danann, since they were his own people. Instead, he would insist that the perpetrators pay a heavy fine, and as he spoke he stared accusingly towards Brian, Iuchar and Iucharba, so that the identity of the murderers was clearly exposed to all. Overcome with guilt and shame, the sons of Tuirenn could not bring themselves to deny their crime, but bowed their heads and stood prepared for the sentence Lugh was about to deliver.

"This is what I demand of you," he announced.

> *"Three ripened apples*
> *The skin of a pig*
> *A pointed spear*
> *Two steeds and a chariot*
> *Seven pigs*
> *A whelping pup*
> *A cooking spit*
> *Three shouts on a hill.*

"And," Lugh added, "if you think this fine too harsh, I will now reduce part of it. But if you think it acceptable, you must pay it in full, without variation, and pledge your loyalty to me before the royal guests gathered here."

"We do not think it too great a fine," said Brian, "nor would it be too large a compensation if you multiplied it a hundredfold. Therefore, we will go out in search of all these things you have described and remain faithful to you until we have brought back every last one of these objects."

"Well, now," said Lugh, "since you have bound yourselves before the court to the quest assigned you, perhaps you would like to learn more detail of what lies in store," And he began to elaborate on the tasks that lay before the sons of Tuirenn.

"The apples I have requested of you," Lugh continued, "are the three apples of the Hesperides growing in the gardens of the Eastern World. They are the colour of burnished gold and have the power to cure the bloodiest wound or the most horrifying illness. To retrieve these apples, you will need great courage, for the people of the east have been forewarned that three young warriors will one day attempt to deprive them of their most cherished possessions.

"And the pig's skin I have asked you to bring me will not be easy to obtain either, for it belongs to the King of Greece who values it above everything else. It too has the power to heal all wounds and diseases.

"The spear I have demanded of you is the poisoned spear kept by Pisar, King of Persia. This spear is so keen to do battle that its blade must always be kept in a cauldron of freezing water to prevent its fiery heat melting the city in which it is kept.

"And do you know who keeps the chariot and the two steeds I wish to receive from you?" Lugh continued.

"We do not know," answered the sons of Tuirenn.

"They belong to Dobar, King of Sicily," said Lugh, "and such is their unique charm that they are equally happy to ride over sea or land, and the chariot they pull is unrivalled in beauty and strength.

"And the seven pigs you must gather together are the pigs of Asal, King of the Golden Pillars. Every night they are slaughtered, but every morning they are found alive again, and any person who eats part of them is protected from ill-health for the rest of his life.

"Three further things I have demanded of you," Lugh went on. "The whelping hound you must bring me guards the palace of the King of Iruad. Failinis is her name and all the wild beasts of the world fall down in terror before her, for she is stronger and more splendid than any other creature known to man.

"The cooking-spit I have called for is housed in the kitchen of the fairywomen on Inis Findcuire, an island surrounded by the most perilous waters that no man has ever safely reached.

"Finally, you must give the three shouts requested of you on the Hill of Midcain where it is prohibited for any man other than the sons of Midcain to cry aloud. It was here that my father received his warrior training and here that his death will be hardest felt. Even if I should one day forgive you of my father's murder, it is certain that the sons of Midcain will not."

As Lugh finished speaking, the children of Tuirenn were struck dumb by the terrifying prospect of all that had to be achieved by them and they went at once to where their father lived and told him of the dreadful sentence that had been pronounced on them.

"It is indeed a harsh fine," said Tuirenn, "but one that must be paid if you are guilty, though it may end tragically for all three of you." Then he advised his sons to return to Lugh to beg the loan of the boat of Manannan that would carry them swiftly over the seas on their difficult quest. Lugh kindly agreed to give them the boat and they made their way towards the port accompanied by their father. With heavy hearts, they exchanged a sad farewell and wearily set sail on the first of many arduous journeys.

"We shall go in search of the apples to begin with," said Brian, and his command was answered immediately by the boat of Manannan which steered a course towards the Eastern World and sailed without stopping until it came to rest in a sheltered harbour in the lands of the Hesperides. The brothers then considered how best they might remove the apples from the garden in which they were growing, and it was eventually decided among them that they should transform themselves into three screeching hawks.

"The tree is well guarded," Brian declared, "but we shall circle it, carefully avoiding the arrows that will be hurled at us until they have all been spent. Then we will swoop on the apples and carry them off in our beaks."

The three performed this task without suffering the slightest injury and headed back towards the boat with the stolen fruit. The news of the theft had soon spread throughout the kingdom, however, and the king's three daughters quickly changed themselves into three-taloned ospreys and pursued the hawks over the sea. Shafts of lightning lit up the skies around them and struck the wings of the hawks, scorching their feathers and causing them to plummet towards the waters below. But Brian managed to take hold of his druidic wand and he transformed himself and his brothers into swans that darted below the waves until the ospreys had given up the chase and it was safe for them to return to the boat.

After they had rested awhile, it was decided that they should travel on to Greece in search of the skin of the pig.

"Let us visit this land in the shape of three bards of Erin," said Brian, "for if we appear as such, we will be honoured and respected as men of wit and wisdom."

They dressed themselves appropriately and set sail for Greece composing some flattering verses in honour of King Tuis as they journeyed along. As soon as they had landed, they made their way to the palace and were enthusiastically welcomed as dedicated men of poetry who had travelled far in search of a worthy patron. An evening of drinking and merry-making followed; verses were read aloud by the King's poets and many ballads were sung by the court musicians. At length, Brian rose to his feet and began to recite the poem he had written for King Tuis. The King smiled rapturously to hear himself described as 'the oak among kings" and encouraged Brian to accept some reward for his pleasing composition.

"I will happily accept from you the pig's skin you possess," said Brian, "for I have heard that it can cure all wounds."

"I would not give this most precious object to the finest poet in the world," replied the King, "but I shall fill the skin three times over with red gold, one skin for each of you, which you may take away with you as the price of your poem."

The brothers agreed to this and the King's attendants escorted them to the treasure-house where the gold was to be measured out. They were about to weigh the very last share when Brian suddenly snatched the pig's skin and raced from the room, striking down several of the guards as he ran. He had just found his way to the outer courtyard when King Tuis appeared before him, his sword drawn in readiness to win back his most prized possession. Many bitter blows were exchanged and many deep wounds were inflicted by each man on the other until, at last, Brian dealt the King a fatal stroke and he fell to the ground never to rise again.

Armed with the pig's skin that could cure their battle wounds, and the apples that could restore them to health, the sons of Tuirenn grew more confident that they would succeed in their quest. They were determined to move on as quickly as possible to the next task Lugh had set them and instructed the boat of Manannan to take them to the land of Persia, to the court of King Pisar, where they appeared once more in the guise of poets. Here they were also made welcome and were treated with honour and distinction. After a time, Brian was called upon to deliver his poem and, as before, he recited some verses in praise of the King which won the approval of all who were gathered. Again, he was persuaded to accept some small reward for his poem and, on this occasion, he requested the magic spear of Persia. But the King grew very angry at this request and the benevolent attitude he had previously displayed soon turned to open hostility:

"It was most unwise of you to demand my beloved spear as a gift," bellowed the King, "the only reward you may expect now is to escape death for having made so insolent a request."

When Brian heard these words he too was incensed and grabbing one of the three golden apples, he flung it at the King's head, dashing out his brains. Then the three brothers rushed from the court, slaughtering all they encountered along the way, and hurried towards the stables where the spear of Pisar lay resting in a cauldron of water. They quickly seized the spear and headed for the boat of Manannan, shouting out their next destination as they ran, so that the boat made itself ready and turned around in the direction of Sicily and the kingdom of Dobar.

"Let us strike up a friendship with the King," said Brian, "by offering him our services as soldiers of Erin."

And when they arrived at Dobar's court they were well received and admitted at once to the King's great army where they won the admiration of all as the most valiant defenders of the realm. The brothers remained in the King's service for a month and two weeks, but during all this time they never once caught a glimpse of the two steeds and the chariot Lugh of the Long Arm had spoken of.

"We have waited long enough," Brian announced impatiently. "Let us go to the King and inform him that we will quit his service unless he shows us his famous steeds and his chariot."

So they went before King Dobar who was not pleased to receive news of their departure, for he had grown to rely on the three brave warriors. He immediately sent for his steeds and ordered the chariot to be yoked to them and they were paraded before the sons of Tuirenn. Brian watched carefully as the charioteer drove the steeds around in a circle and as they came towards him a second time he sprung onto the nearest saddle and seized the reins. His two brothers fought a fierce battle against those who tried to prevent them escaping, but it was not long before they were at Brian's side, riding furiously through the palace gates, eager to pursue their fifth quest.

They sailed onwards without incident until they reached the land of King Asal of the Pillars of Gold. But their high spirits were quickly vanquished by the sight of a large army guarding the harbour in anticipation of their arrival. For the fame of the sons of Tuirenn was widespread by this time, and their success in carrying away with them the most coveted treasures of the world was well known to all. King Asal himself now came forward to greet them and demanded to know why they had pillaged the lands of other kings and murdered so many in their travels. Then Brian told King Asal of the sentence Lugh of the Long Arm had pronounced upon them and of the many hardships they had already suffered as a result.

"And what have you come here for?" the King enquired.

"We have come for the seven pigs which Lugh has also demanded as part of that compensation," answered Brian, "and it would be far better for all of us if you deliver them to us in good will."

When the King heard these words, he took counsel with his people, and it was wisely decided that the seven pigs should be handed over peacefully, without bloodshed. The sons of Tuirenn expressed their gratitude to King Asal and pledged their services to him in all future battles. Then Asal questioned them on their next adventure, and when he discovered that they were journeying onwards to the land of Iruad in search of a puppy hound, he made the following request of them:

"Take me along with you," he said "for my daughter is married to the King of Iruad and I am desperate, for love of her, to persuade him to surrender what you desire of him without a show of arms."

Brian and his brothers readily agreed to this and the boats were made ready for them to sail together for the land of Iruad.

When they reached the shores of the kingdom, Asal went ahead in search of his son-in-law and told him the tale of the sons of Tuirenn from beginning to end and of how he had rescued his people from a potentially bloody war. But Iruad was not disposed to listen to the King's advice and adamantly refused to give up his hound without a fight. Seizing his weapon, he gave the order for his men to begin their attack and went himself in search of Brian in order to challenge him to single combat. A furious contest ensued between the two and they struck each other viciously and angrily. Eventually, however, Brian succeeded in overpowering King Iruad and he hauled him before Asal, bound and gagged like a criminal.

"I have spared his life," said Brian, "perhaps he will now hand over the hound in recognition of my clemency."

The King was untied and the hound was duly presented to the sons of Tuirenn who were more than pleased that the battle had come to a swift end. And there was no longer any bitterness between Iruad and the three brothers, for Iruad had been honestly defeated and had come to admire his opponents. They bid each other a friendly farewell and the sons of Tuirenn took their leave of the land of the Golden Pillars and set out to sea once again.

Far across the ocean in the land of Erin, Lugh of the Long Arm had made certain that news of every success achieved by the sons of Tuirenn had been brought to his attention. He was fully aware that the quest he had set them was almost drawing to a close and became increasingly anxious at the thought. But he desired above everything else to take possession of the valuable objects that had already been recovered, for Balor of the Evil Eye had again reared his ugly head and the threat of another Fomorian invasion was imminent. Seeking to lure the sons of Tuirenn back to Erin, Lugh sent a druidical spell after the brothers, causing them to forget that their sentence had not yet been fully completed. Under its influence, the sons of Tuirenn entertained visions of the heroic reception that awaited them on the shores of the Boyne and their hearts were filled with joy to think that they would soon be reunited with their father.

Within days, their feet had touched on Erin's soil again and they hastened to Tara to the Annual Assembly, presided over by the High King of Erin. Here, they were heartily welcomed by the royal family and the Tuatha Dé Danann who rejoiced alongside them and praised them for their great courage and valour. And it was agreed that they should submit the tokens of their quest to the High King himself who undertook to examine them and to inform Lugh of the triumphant return of the sons of Tuirenn. A messenger was despatched to Lugh's household and within an hour he had arrived at the palace of Tara, anxious to confront the men he still regarded as his enemies.

"We have paid the fine on your father's life," said Brian, as he pointed towards the array of objects awaiting Lugh's inspection.

"This is indeed an impressive sight," replied Lugh of the Long Arm, "and would suffice as payment for any other murder. But you bound yourselves before the court to deliver everything asked for and I see that you have not done so. Where is the cooking-spit I was promised? And what is to be done about the three shouts on the hill which you have not yet given?"

When the sons of Tuirenn heard this, they realized that they had been deceived and they collapsed exhausted to the floor. Gloom and despair fell upon them as they faced once more the reality of long years of searching and wandering. Leaving behind the treasures that had hitherto protected them, they made their way wearily towards their ship which carried them swiftly away over the storm-tossed seas.

They had spent three months at sea and still they could not discover the smallest trace of the island known as Inis Findcurie. But when their hopes had almost faded, Brian suggested that they make one final search beneath the ocean waves and he put on his magical water-dress and dived over the side of the boat. After two long weeks of swimming in the salt water, he at last happened upon the island, tucked away in a dark hollow of the ocean bed. He immediately went in search of the court and found it occupied by a large group of women, their heads bent in concentration, as they each embroidered a cloth of gold. The women appeared not to notice Brian and he seized this opportunity to move forward to where the cooking-spit rested in a corner of the room. He had just lifted it from the hearth when the women broke into peals of laughter and they laughed long and heartily until finally the eldest of them condescended to address him:

"Take the spit with you, as a reward for your heroism," she said mockingly, "but even if your two brothers had attended you here, the weakest of us would have had little trouble preventing you from removing what you came for."

And Brian took his leave of them knowing they had succeeded in humiliating him, yet he was grateful, nonetheless, that only one task remained to be completed.

They lost no time in directing the boat of Manannan towards their final destination and had reached the Hill of Midcain shortly afterwards, on whose summit they had pledged themselves to give three shouts. But as soon as they had begun to ascend to the top, the guardian of the hill, none other than Midcain himself, came forward to challenge the sons of Tuirenn:

"What is your business in my territory," demanded Midcain.

"We have come to give three shouts on this hill," said Brian, "in fulfilment of the quest we have been forced to pursue in the name of Lugh of the Long Arm."

"I knew his father well," replied Midcain, "and I am under oath not to permit anyone to cry aloud on my hill."

"Then we have no option but to fight for that permission," declared Brian, and he rushed at his opponent with his sword before Midcain had the opportunity to draw his own, killing him with a single thrust of his blade through the heart.

Then the three sons of Midcain came out to fight the sons of Tuirenn and the conflict that followed was one of the bitterest and bloodiest ever before fought by any group of warriors. They battled with the strength of wild bears and the ruthlessness of starving lions until they had carved each other to pieces and the grass beneath their feet ran crimson with blood. In the end, however, it was the sons of Tuirenn who were victorious, but their wounds were so deep that they fell to the ground one after the other and waited forlornly for death to come, wishing in vain that they still had the pig skin to cure them.

They had rested a long time before Brian had the strength to speak, and he reminded his brothers that they had not yet given the three shouts on the Hill of Midcain that Lugh had demanded of them. Then slowly they raised themselves up off the ground and did as they had been requested, satisfied at last that they had entirely fulfilled their quest. And after this, Brian lifted his wounded brothers into the boat, promising them a final glimpse of Erin if they would only struggle against death a brief while longer.

And on this occasion the boat of Manannan did not come to a halt on the shores of the Boyne, but moved speedily overland until it reached Dun Tuirenn where the dying brothers were delivered into their father's care. Then Brian, who knew that the end of his life was fast approaching, pleaded fretfully with Tuirenn:

"Go, beloved father," he urged, "and deliver this cooking-spit to Lugh, informing him that we have completed all the tasks assigned us. And beg him to allow us to cure our wounds with the pig skin he possesses, for we have suffered long and hard in the struggle to pay the fine on Cian's murder."

Then Tuirenn rode towards Tara in all haste, fearful that his sons might pass away before his return. And he demanded an audience with Lugh of the Long Arm who came out to meet him at once and graciously received the cooking-spit presented to him.

"My sons are gravely ill and close to death," Tuirenn exclaimed piteously. "I beg you to part with the healing pig skin they brought you for one single night, so that I may place it upon their battle wounds and witness it restore them to full health."

But Lugh of the Long Arm fell silent at this request and stared coldly into the distance towards the Plain of Muirthemne where his father had fallen. When at length he was ready to give Tuirenn his answer, the expression he wore was cruel and menacing and the tone of his voice was severe and merciless:

"I would rather give you the expanse of the earth in gold," said Lugh, "than hand over any object that would save the lives of your sons. Let them die in the knowledge that they have achieved something good because of me, and let them thank me for bringing them renown and glory through such a valorous death."

On hearing these words, Tuirenn hung his head in defeat and accepted that it was useless to bargain with Lugh of the Long Arm. He made his way back despondently to where his sons lay dying and gave them his sad news. The brothers were overcome with grief and despair and were so utterly devastated by Lugh's decision that not one of them lived to see the sun set in the evening sky. Tuirenn's heart was broken in two and after he had placed the last of his sons in the earth, all life departed from him and he fell dead over the bodies of Brian, Iucharba and Iuchar. The Tuatha Dé Danann witnessed the souls of all four rise towards the heavens and the tragic tale of the sons of Tuirenn was recounted from that day onwards throughout the land, becoming known as one of the Three Sorrows of Story-Telling.

The Tragedy of the Children of Lir

DURING THE GREAT BATTLE of Tailtiu that raged on the plain of Moytura, the Tuatha Dé Danann were slain in vast numbers and finally defeated by a race of Gaelic invaders known as the Milesians. Following this time of wretched warring, Erin came to be divided into two separate kingdoms. The children of Miled claimed for themselves all the land above ground, while the Tuatha Dé Danann were banished to the dark regions below the earth's surface. The Danann gods did not suffer their defeat easily, and immediately set about re-building an impressive underground kingdom worthy of the divine stature they once possessed. Magnificent palaces, sparkling with jewels and precious stones, were soon erected and a world of wondrous beauty and light was created where once darkness had prevailed. Time had no meaning in this new domain and all who lived there remained eternally beautiful, never growing old as mortals did above ground.

The day approached for the Tuatha Dé Danann to choose for themselves a King who would safeguard their future peace and happiness. The principle deities and elders of the people gathered together at the Great Assembly and began deliberating on their choice of leader. Lir, father of the sea-god, Manannan mac Lir, had announced his desire to take the throne, but so too had Bodb the Red, son of the divinity Dagda, lord of perfect knowledge. It came to pass that the People of Dana chose Bodb the Red as their King and built for him a splendid castle on the banks of Loch Dearg. The new ruler made a solemn pledge to his people, promising to prove himself worthy of the great honour bestowed on him. Before long, the People of Dana began to applaud themselves on their choice. Their lives were happy and fulfilled and their kingdom flourished as never before.

Only one person in the entire land remained opposed to the new sovereign. Lir was highly offended that he had not been elected by the People of Dana. Retreating to his home at Sídh Fionnachaidh, he refused to acknowledge Bodb the Red, or show him any mark of respect. Several of the elders urged the King to gather his army together and march to Armagh where Lir could be punished for this insult, but Bodb the Red would not be persuaded. He desired more than anything to be reconciled to every last one of his subjects and his warm and generous spirit sought a more compassionate way of drawing Lir back into his circle.

One morning, the King received news that Lir's wife had recently passed away, leaving him grief-stricken and despondent. Many had tried, but none had yet managed to improve Lir's troubled heart and mind and it was said that he would never recover from his loss. Bodb the Red immediately sent a message to Lir, inviting him to attend the palace. Deeply moved by the King's forgiveness and concern, Lir graciously accepted the invitation to visit Loch Dearg. A large banquet was prepared in his honour and four shining knights on horseback were sent forth to escort the chariot through the palace gates. The King greeted Lir warmly and sat him at the royal table at his right hand. The two men began to converse as if they had always been the closest of friends, and as the evening wore on it was noticed by all that the cloud of sorrow had lifted from Lir's brow. Presently, the King began to speak more earnestly to his friend of the need to return to happier times.

"I am sorely grieved to hear of your loss," he told Lir, "but you must allow me to help you. Within this court reside three of the fairest maidens in the kingdom. They are none other than my foster-daughters and each is very dear to me. I give you leave to take the one you most admire as your bride, for I know that she will restore to your life the happiness you now lack."

At the King's request, his three daughters entered the hall and stood before them. Their beauty was remarkable indeed, and each was as fair as the next. Lir's eyes travelled from one to the other in bewilderment. Finally, he settled on the daughter known as Aeb, for she was the eldest and deemed the wisest of the three. Bodb the Red gave the couple his blessing and it was agreed that they should be married without delay.

After seven days of glorious feasting and celebrating, Aeb and Lir set off from the royal palace to begin their new life together as husband and wife. Lir was no longer weighted down by sorrow and Aeb had grown to love and cherish the man who had chosen her as his bride. Many years of great joy followed for them both. Lir delighted in his new wife and in the twin children she bore him, a boy and a girl, whom they named Aed and Fionnguala. Within another year or two, Aeb again delivered of twins, two sons named Fiachra and Conn, but the second birth proved far more difficult and Aeb became gravely ill. Lir watched over her night and day. Yet despite his tender love and devotion, she could not be saved and his heart was again broken in two. The four beautiful children Aeb had borne him were his only solace in this great time of distress. During the worst moments, when he thought he would die of grief, he was rescued by their image and his love for them was immeasurable.

Hearing of Lir's dreadful misfortune, King Bodb offered him a second foster-daughter in marriage. Aeb's sister was named Aoife and she readily agreed to take charge of Lir's household and her sister's children. At first, Aoife loved her step-children as if they were her very own, but as she watched Lir's intense love for them increase daily, a feeling of jealousy began to take control of her. Often Lir would sleep in the same bed chamber with them and as soon as the children awoke, he devoted himself to their amusement, taking them on long hunting trips through the forest. At every opportunity, he kissed and embraced them and was more than delighted with the love he received in return. Believing that her husband no longer felt any affection for her, Aoife welcomed the poisonous and wicked thoughts that invaded her mind. Feigning a dreadful illness, she lay in bed for an entire year. She summoned a druid to her bedside and together they plotted a course to destroy Lir's children.

One day Aoife rose from her sickbed and ordered her chariot. Seeking out her husband in the palace gardens, she told him that she would like to take the children to visit her father, King Bodb. Lir was happy to see that his wife had recovered her health and was quick to encourage the outing. He gathered his children around him to kiss them goodbye, but Fionnguala refused her father's kiss and drew away from him, her eyes brimming with tears.

"Do not be troubled, child," he spoke softly to her, "your visit will bring the King great pleasure and he will prepare the most fleet-footed horses for your speedy return".

Although her heart was in turmoil, Fionnguala mounted the chariot with her three brothers. She could not understand her sadness, and could not explain why it deepened with every turning of the chariot wheels as they moved forward, away from her father and her beloved home at Sídh Fionnachaidh.

When they had travelled some distance from Lir's palace, Aoife called the horses to a halt. Waking the children from their happy slumber, she ordered them out of the chariot and shouted harshly to her manservants:

"Kill these monstrous creatures before you, for they have stolen the love Lir once had for me. Do so quickly, and I shall reward you as you desire."

But the servants recoiled in horror from her shameful request and replied resolutely:

"We cannot perform so terrible an evil. A curse will surely fall on you for even thinking such a vile thing."

They journeyed on further until they approached the shores of Loch Dairbhreach. The evening was now almost upon them and a bank of deep crimson cloud hung lazily on the horizon above the shimmering lake. Weary starlings were settling in their nests and owls were preparing for their nocturnal watch. Aoife now sought to kill the children herself and drew from her cloak a long, pointed sabre. But as she raised her arm to slay the first of them, she was overcome by a feeling of maternal sympathy and it prevented her completing the task. Angry that she had been thwarted once more, she demanded that the children remove their garments and bathe in the lake. As each one them entered the water, she struck them with her druid's wand and they were instantly transformed into four milk-white swans. A death-like chill filled the air as she chanted over them the words the druid had taught her:

> "Here on Dairbhreach's lonely wave
> For years to come your watery home
> Not Lir nor druid can now ye save
> From endless wandering on the lonely foam."

Stunned and saddened by their step-mother's cruel act of vengeance, the children of Lir bowed their heads and wept piteously for their fate. Fionnguala eventually found the courage to speak, and she uttered a plea for lenience, mindful of her three brothers and of the terrible tragedy Lir would again have to suffer:

"We have always loved you Aoife," she urged, "why have you treated us in this way when we have only ever shown you loyalty and kindness?"

So sad and helpless were Fionnguala's words, so soft and innocent was her childlike voice, that Aoife began to regret what she had done and she was suddenly filled with panic and despair. It was too late for her to undo her druid's spell, and it was all she could do to fix a term to the curse she had delivered upon the children:

"You will remain in the form of four white swans," she told them, "until a woman from the south shall be joined in marriage to a man from the north, and until the light of Christianity shines on Erin. For three hundred years you will be doomed to live on Loch Dairbhreach, followed by three hundred years on the raging Sea of Moyle, and a further three hundred years on Iorras Domhnann. I grant you the power of speech and the gift of singing, and no music in the world shall sound more beautiful and pleasing to the ear than that which you shall make."

Then Aoife called for her horse to be harnessed once more and continued on her journey to the palace of Bodb the Red, abandoning the four white swans to their life of hardship on the grey and miserable moorland lake.

The King, who had been eagerly awaiting the arrival of his grandchildren, was deeply disappointed to discover that they had not accompanied his daughter.

"Lir will no longer entrust them to you," Aoife told him, "and I have not the will to disobey his wishes."

Greatly disturbed by this news, the King sent a messenger to Lir's palace, demanding an explanation for his extraordinary behaviour. A strange sense of foreboding had already entered Lir's soul and, on receiving the King's message, he became tormented with worry for his children's safety. He immediately called for his horse to be saddled and galloped away into the night in the direction of Loch Dearg. Upon his arrival at Bodb's palace, he was met by one of Aoife's servants who could not keep from him the terrible tale of his wife's treachery. The King was now also informed and Aoife was ordered to appear before them both. The evil expression in his daughter's eye greatly enraged the King and his wand struck violently, changing Aoife into a demon, destined to wander the cold and windy air until the very end of time.

Before the sun had risen the next morning, an anguished party had set off from the palace in search of Lir's children. Through the fog and mist they rode at great speed until the murky waters of Loch Dairbhreach appeared before them in the distance. It was Lir who first caught a glimpse of the four majestic white swans, their slender necks arched forwards towards the pebbled shore, desperately seeking the warm and familiar face of their father. As the swans swam towards him, they began to speak with gentle voices and he instantly recognized his own children in the sad, snow-white creatures. How Lir's heart ached at this woeful sight, and how his eyes wished to disbelieve the sorrowful scene he was forced to witness. He began to sob loudly and it seemed that his grief would never again be silenced.

"Do not mourn us, father," whispered Fiachra comfortingly, "your love will give us strength in our plight and we shall all be together one day."

A beautiful, soothing music now infused the air, miraculously lifting the spirits of all who heard it. After a time, Lir and his companions fell into a gentle, peaceful sleep and when they awoke they were no longer burdened by troubles. Every day, Lir came to visit his children and so too did the Men of Erin, journeying from every part to catch even a single note of the beautiful melody of the swans.

Three hundred years passed pleasantly in this way, until the time arrived for the Children of Lir to bid farewell to the People of Dana and to move on to the cold and stormy Sea of Moyle. As the stars faded and the first rays of sunlight peered through the heavens, Lir came forward to the shores of the lake and spoke to his children for the very last time. Fionnguala began to sing forlornly of the grim and bitter times which lay ahead and as she sang she spread her wings and rose from the water. Aed, Fiachra and Conn joined in her song and then took to the air as their sister had done, flying wearily over the velvet surface of Loch Dairbhreach towards the north-east and the raging ocean:

"Arise, my brothers, from Dairbhreach's wave,
On the wings of the southern wind;
We leave our father and friends today
In measureless grief behind.
Ah! Sad the parting, and sad our flight.
To Moyle's tempestuous main;
For the day of woe
Shall come and go
Before we meet again!"

Great was the suffering and hardship endured by the swans on the lonely Sea of Moyle, for they could find no rest or shelter from the hissing waves and the piercing cold of the wintry gales. During that first desolate winter, thick black clouds perpetually gathered in the sky, causing the sea to rise up in fury as they ruptured and spilled forth needles of icy rain and sleet. The swans were tossed and scattered by storms and often driven miles apart. There were countless nights when Fionnguala waited alone and terrified on the Rock of Seals, tortured with anxiety for the welfare of her brothers. The gods had so far answered her prayers and they had been returned to her on each occasion, drenched and battered. Tears of joy and relief flowed freely from her eyes at these times, and she would take her brothers under her wing and pull them to her breast for warmth.

Three hundred years of agony and misery on the Sea of Moyle were interrupted by only one happy event. It happened that one morning, the swans were approached by a group of horsemen while resting in the mouth of the river Bann. Two of the figures introduced themselves as Fergus and Aed, sons of Bodb the Red, and they were accompanied by a fairy host. They had been searching a good many years for the swans, desiring to bring them happy tidings of Lir and the King. The Tuatha Dé Danann were all now assembled at the annual Feast of Age, peaceful and happy, except for the deep sorrow they felt at the absence of the four children of Lir. Fionnguala and her brothers received great comfort from this visit and talked long into the evening with the visitors. When the time finally came for the men to depart, the swans felt that their courage had been restored and looked forward to being reunited with the People of Dana sometime in the future.

When at last their exile had come to an end on the Sea of Moyle, the children of Lir made ready for their voyage westwards to Iorras Domhnann. In their hearts they knew they were travelling from one bleak and wretched place to another, but they were soothed by the thought that their suffering would one day be over. The sea showed them no kindness during their stay at Iorras Domhnann, and remained frozen from Achill to Erris during the first hundred years. The bodies of the swans became wasted from thirst and hunger, but they weathered the angry blasts of the tempests and sought shelter from the driving snow under the black, unfriendly rocks, refusing to give up hope. Each new trial fired the desire within them to be at home once again, safe in the arms of their loving father.

It was a time of great rejoicing among Lir's children when the three hundred years on Iorras Domhnann finally came to an end. With hearts full of joy and elation, the four swans rose ecstatically into the air and flew southwards towards Sídh Fionnachaidh, their father's palace. But their misery and torment was not yet at an end. As they circled above the plains of Armagh, they could not discover any trace of their former home. Swooping closer to the ground, they recognized the familiar grassy slopes of their childhood, but these were now dotted with stones and rubble from the crumbling castle walls. A chorus of wailing and sorrow echoed through the ruins of Lir's palace as the swans flung themselves on the earth, utterly broken and defeated. For three days and three nights they remained here until they could bear it no longer. Fionnguala led her brothers back to the west and they alighted on a small, tranquil lake known as Inis Gluare. All that remained was for them to live out the rest of their lives in solitude, declaring their grief through the saddest of songs.

On the day after the children of Lir arrived at Inis Gluare, a Christian missionary known as Chaemóc was walking by the lakeside where he had built for himself a small church. Hearing the haunting strains floating towards him from the lake, he paused by the water's edge and prayed that he might know who it was that made such stirring music. The swans then revealed themselves to him and began to tell him their sorry tale. Chaemóc bade them come ashore and he joined the swans together with silver chains and took them into his home where he tended them and provided for them until they had forgotten all their suffering. The swans were his delight and they joined him in his prayers and religious devotions, learning of the One True God who had come to save all men.

It was not long afterwards that Deoch, daughter of the King of Munster, came to marry Lairgnéan, King of Connacht, and hearing of Chaemóc's four wonderful swans, she announced her desire to have them as her wedding-present. Lairgnéan set off for Inis Gluare intent on seizing the swans from Chaemóc. Arriving at the church where they were resting, their heads bowed in silent prayer, he began to drag them from the altar. But he had not gone more than four paces when the plumage dropped from the birds and they were changed back into their human form. Three withered old men and a white-faced old woman now stood before Lairgnéan and he turned and fled in horror at the sight of them.

For the children of Lir had now been released from Aoife's curse, having lived through almost a thousand years, to the time when her prophecy came to be fulfilled. Knowing that they had little time left to them, they called for Chaemóc to baptize them and as he did so they died peacefully and happily. The saint carried their bodies to a large tomb and Fionnguala was buried at the centre, surrounded by her three beloved brothers. Chaemóc placed a large headstone on the mound and he inscribed it in oghram. It read: 'Lir's children, who rest here in peace at long last'.

A House of Her Own

Bo Balder

AOIFE WAS ONLY ELEVEN when she caught the little house in the forest. She surprised it as it drank from a puddle, half-hidden under a writhing tree root as large as her own body. Fast as an eel, she snaked her hand around it and held on tight. It was no bigger than a strawberry, all soft and furry and yellow. Even in the gloom of the giant, bad-tempered trees, it shone like a candle flame.

"House," she whispered, "you're mine now."

It couldn't answer back yet, but she knew it understood.

She showed her catch to Mama. Mama hugged her and told the big house they lived in what Aoife had found.

House spoke from the walls. "Good girl. Show it to me, little one. Let me see if it's the right kind."

Aoife clenched her fist tighter around the little house until it squirmed against the pressure. Sometimes the big hice didn't approve of the little ones, for reasons no human could guess at. She didn't plan on letting anything happen to her house.

"It's mine, Big House. None of your business."

The floor shook with deep laughter, a sound so resonant it made Aoife a little sick to her stomach. Mama's house was a good provider and kept them all warm and well fed, but it had a mean streak. It liked to make the little girls stumble, or scare them by dousing the glow of its walls unexpectedly.

"House –" Mama said in a tight voice.

"Hush, dear," it said. "If little Aoife already loves it that much, I'm sure it's the right kind of little house."

Aoife didn't think she'd ever met the wrong kind of house. And she was certain she'd know it if she did. Her downy pet felt just right.

You weren't supposed to give hice names. If Mama stood out on the square and said, "House," every house in the village knew exactly who she was talking to. But Aoife gave hers a secret name anyway. She called it Mine.

* * *

Mama was having another baby. It was a good time to be out of the house. Its walls strummed with tension as Mama screamed. It was busy cooling and warming the birthing room as Mama's needs fluctuated. Aoife and her sisters sat around the fire pit in the middle of the village, watching the house colors ebb and flow, and all the other hice standing cool and grey-brown and unconcerned. Aoife felt safe, surrounded by the village of hice. Nothing bad would happen here.

"What if it's a boy again?" Ho asked. "What's Mama gonna do?"

"Nothing she can do," Biri, the eldest, said. "House is gonna do what it's gonna do."

Aoife didn't like her tone of voice.

While Biri spoke, she fondled the feeler her little house had put on her leg. That house wasn't so little anymore – it was as tall as Biri and about four times as wide and deep. Biri longed to strike out on her own, but as Mama said, not until you can stand up and lay down in your house. "Hurry up and grow, you," Biri whispered to it and it glowed pink with pleasure. It was a light tan, no longer the bright yellow of childhood.

Aoife cradled her house in her lap. It had grown to about the size of her head, but it was still small enough to carry around. If it wanted, it could make legs and waddle after her, but not quickly. Funny how girls grew faster than hice when they were little, and then when the girls were grown, the hice overtook them.

"She's at it longer than last time," Biri said.

What she didn't say, but they all heard, even little Koori: what if something goes wrong? They would have nowhere to stay. If a mama died, her house upped and went to plant itself in the forest, taking the body with it. None of them had hice that were big enough to live in, although maybe Biri could cram into hers.

Biri's house cooed. Biri stood up. "It wants to forage," she said. "See you later."

The three girls watched her go, between the hice, toward the veldt. They all thought the same thing. *Eat, Biri's house, eat! Grow big enough to take care of us!*

A young man slipped out of the men's lodge and headed after Biri. It was the new boy, just come in from the Exchange. Ho elbowed Aoife in the side and sniggered. Aoife wondered why.

A rumbling sounded overhead. Aoife craned her neck, scanning the green sky for thunderclouds. No thunderheads, but one long, thin, white cloud streaking across the sky, hurtling toward them.

"What's that?" Aoife said.

Ho stood up, hindered by the house clenching its feelers around her in fear. "I don't know!"

The three girls huddled together. As much as they wanted to run home, they couldn't go inside House while Mama was birthing. It wouldn't let them in. They watched as the cloud trail sped closer and closer. It ended with a bang that shook the ground. Behind the farthest hice, black clouds boiled up.

* * *

By the time the strange women in white suits entered the village, the adult women had gathered in the square, and the men and girls sent away. Aoife and her sisters pretended to leave but hid behind a stand of trees. At first, the strangers didn't look like people at all, but then Aoife noticed the frozen water glistening before their faces, and behind it eyes and noses like people.

"Something something!" the front woman shouted. She had a deep voice like a man. Maybe she intended to speak true words, but nothing other than garble came out.

Mama's sister Noriko, pregnant belly thrust out proudly, lifted a hand. "Greetings. What manner of women are you? From what village?"

The white-clad women conferred amongst themselves. Did they even understand true speech? Hadn't their mothers taught them?

The first woman lifted her head-covering. She had a beard and bushy eyebrows. When she spoke again in that deep, rumbling voice, she changed into a man before Aoife's eyes. A man who spoke like a leader? Had these people lost their great women?

Noriko scratched her head. "You are hard to understand, mistress. Speak slower, if you will."

Aoife guffawed. Noriko hadn't yet seen he wasn't a woman! "It's a man!" she called out. "Look at his beard!"

Ho pinched Aoife into silence.

Noriko hummed and hawed. "Are you a man? We already had our man exchange a couple of weeks ago. Are you lost?"

Aoife got bored with the grown-up talk and wandered off to catch bugs for Mine. Later that evening, she snuck back to the village square where now only the elders and the strange visitors – mostly men, she thought, from their beards and wide shoulders and deep voices – sat around the fire and talked. Hoping for a scrap of food – Mama's house was still sealed and Mama would spank her if she raided the gardens – she crept up behind the man who'd spoken to Noriko earlier. She settled in cross-legged, petting Mine in her lap.

Beard sounded like a man who was fast using up his patience. "Like I said, we're from Earth, your home planet, looking for lost colonies. The wars are over, the star lanes are safe again, and we're here to do a census, a genetic assay."

Noriko poked around in the fire, which didn't need any poking. "I don't really get where you're from. But new blood in the exchange would be good. Maybe we can escort you to the exchange house at Mountainfoot?"

The man sighed. "Do you have any memories of not being from this place? Tales your grandmothers told?"

Several women nodded. "The First Woman and her house, you mean?"

"Maybe," the man said. "Can you tell it to me?"

The women burst into laughter. "That's not a tale for men's ears! If you've forgotten it from when your mama told you, we're not going to repeat it."

"Men's ears? So where are all the men?"

Aoife wished Mama wasn't still birthing, or that Biri had returned from her foraging. What if Biri had been burnt in that streak of fire?

One of the strange men leaned back and stretched. He caught sight of Aoife huddling in the dark, stroking Mine's dome.

"Hey there," he said. "What a cute toy you have. He looks a bit like a baby duck, only bigger."

Aoife didn't know what a duck was, but he sounded friendly. He talked funny, yet she understood most of it. "It's not a toy. It's my house."

The man smiled. "He doesn't look like a house to me." He gestured to the dim shapes of the hice standing around the square, almost invisible in the dusk. "Not that those are very big, mind."

Aoife gaped. "They're all grown. A mama and lots of kids can live in there. Are your hice bigger?"

"Lots bigger. We build them from stone or wood or brick. What are yours made of? Mud? Moss?"

"I don't know what they're made of," Aoife said. "They just grow that way."

A sudden ruckus drew them back to the circle.

Biri leaned exhaustedly on her house, soot-smudged even in the flickering firelight. She must have been close to the black smoke. Behind her, an equally blackened young man tried to back away from the women's eyes.

"What in God's name is that!" the man said.

Nobody paid him any attention.

He turned to Aoife. "What is that ugly critter with the girl? Something native?"

"It's just her house. Look at her! She's all dirty and burnt from the thing that fell from the sky."

"You mean our ship?" the man asked.

"Ship?"

"Like a house in the sky or on water."

"If it's your house, you should have been more careful where you went and not burnt people," Aoife said and ran away. Now Biri was here, they could go and see if Mama was done birthing yet. Aoife was cold and hungry.

* * *

Mama, looking very tired, had two babies in her lap. That was odd. One was a boy. Aoife sucked on her teeth and cuddled Mine harder. What would House do?

Mama's face turned distant, a sign House was talking to her. Aoife wished Mine was old enough to do that.

Mama's eyes rolled back down and a flush blossomed on her drawn cheeks. "House says he's talked to the others and I can keep the boy. You're going to have a brother!"

Aoife lifted up the baby's blanket. He had a little thing between his legs, just like her sisters had told her he would. Not really interesting – if Mine wanted it could make a bigger feeler to put in her even now. She'd often watched Biri and her house playing and couldn't imagine what a real boy could do better. Maybe she'd find out when she was bigger and visited the men's lodge. There had to be a reason why Biri and that boy had met up in the veldt.

She set Mine in the crook of her elbow. It was growing so fast that it was getting hard to carry him. But she wanted to get out to the veldt without anybody making her weed or feed the eels, so she sneaked from house to house until she was in the open. The women's fields looked green, and sometimes reddish. The mamas always said they could eat house food if they had to, but that it never tasted the way it should. So they stubbornly grew their own, against the hice grumbling about it.

The veldt was cool yellow, with flashes of blue like Mama's eyes.

She put Mine down so it could sink feelers into the ground for bugs. Later, when it was big, it would root permanently and snack on the skin cells and waste of the people who lived inside it. She hunkered low, taking a few steps whenever Mine moved. Its baby-yellow was starting to shade into the yellow grasses of the veldt.

She crawled over to it and lay down on her back, shading her eyes. Grey clouds drifted across the green sky.

A thumping sounded. She tensed. The men were supposed to take care of the veldt beasts, but maybe they'd missed one. She slung a hand toward Mine. She bet it could sting a veldt beast to death, some day.

But no – voices rang out. Male voices. Aoife grabbed Mine and crawled nearer. What were they up to?

"Careful, we don't know what they can do. They must have some kind of defense!"

"We got it, we got it! Tighten the rope!"

That sounded like men hunting, even if it was the strange men. Aoife almost went back to her daydream spot, but the tone of their voices caught her attention. They sounded afraid but fascinated. And disgusted, maybe? What had they caught?

"God, doesn't that turn your stomach? They're so ugly and the smell is just awful," a woman's voice said. Aoife hadn't realized some of the strange men were women. Why hadn't they taken charge?

She inched forward. Mine wormed himself from under her armpit and padded ahead.

Someone grunted, torn slashes of sound, a girl. What were they doing? Aoife became scared. She should sneak away and get help from the village. She pawed at Mine but it didn't react. If it wanted to stay, then so must she.

Under the cover of the tussling and shouting, she crawled further forward. If Mine dared, so would she. Between stalks of bluish grass, she caught glimpses of the strange men fighting a young woman called Salome and her house. They were tearing them apart from each other, ripping the house's feeler out of Salome's body. The girl kicked and screamed, the crazed house whipped needle-stingers around. Too bad it wasn't old enough to sting to death.

Very unwise of these men to interfere between woman and house. Aoife wasn't sure if she felt scorn for their stupidity or sadness for the pain Salome and her house must be suffering. She stuffed her hand in her mouth to keep herself from crying out.

"What the hell was that thing doing?'

"Kill it! It's raping the girl!"

A great foot swung down from the sky and near trampled Mine. Aoife tugged it backwards. She didn't want Mine to be handled by these men, who didn't appear to know how men ought to act.

She waited for a long time as the scuffling and shouting died down.

Her heart beat in her ears, the only sound in the whole wide world. She crawled forward to a rough circle of trampled grass. Salome and her house, as well as the strangers, had gone. Mine was sampling the ground. A drop of blood hung on a blade of scythe grass. A feeler drew it inside Mine's body.

Blood? Had they hurt Salome?

"We have to get home!" she hissed to Mine. "We have to tell House and Mama! These are bad men."

"Are we really?" a male voice said and a heavy hand landed on her shoulders.

Mine wriggled out of her grip and rolled away into the grass.

The bearded man turned her body toward his. His hands were large and hot, his face flushed. "Don't fight, we're here to help you."

Aoife let her mouth hang open. Her brain whispered directions. *Look stupid. Look childish.* It helped that she really wasn't sure what was going on. "Help us how?"

He looked left and right. Who did he think might be watching? The women, the hice, his own people?

"We're just here to count the population and do a tax inventory. We'll set up a government, build roads, hospitals, schools. We'll help against the critters. I can't just stand idly by and watch women being used by aliens."

"You mean the hice?" she asked.

"Yes, I mean the houses." He stood frowning down at her. "Where's your pet? Is he really a young one of those big houses you live in?"

She stayed silent. Maybe she could even squeeze a tear or two out of her eyes.

"I wanna go to my mama," she said and quivered her lip.

His face softened. He reached out a hand as if to stroke her head, but stopped short of touching her. "Do you want to save your mama and her friends?"

Aoife nodded.

"Go tell her to stay away from the house creatures, okay? We'll get you out of here and eventually you'll live in a real house with no aliens around. Your mama could be free and happy, you'd get an education."

She nodded again. She swooped up Mine and ran off, choosing the highest patches of bluegrass to cut through for cover.

She found Mama tying up vines in the bean yard, moving slowly, newborns on her back.

"Mama!" she tried to yell, but only panting and squeaking emerged.

Mama looked up and must have seen something on Aoife's face because she moved out from the beans double-quick.

"What is it, Aoife? Where's your house? Did you lose it?"

That would have been even worse than her actual news. But Mine had just hidden in a patch of yellow weed.

Aoife puffed until she could speak. "The strange men want to steal us and take us to their village. And kill the young hice. They already hurt Salome and her house."

"What!" Mama grew dark in the face and then ashen. Her hands fisted. "Men," she breathed between clenched teeth. "Maybe the hice were right. Maybe we should kill all the men."

"We wouldn't get any babies," Aoife said.

"Never mind that now. Oh, what a day. Old Imoh died, so her house is pulling up roots and going to live in the forest. We really could have used their advice. And my breasts hurt."

Mama's shirt was wet with milk.

"Why are you out here – I thought you were tired?"

"House was fussing," Mama said distractedly. "Never mind that, either. Oh, I can't think straight when I breastfeed. We have to talk to the other women."

Aoife could have told her that, but kept her mouth shut.

Mama dragged her back to the village. Aoife could barely keep a grip on Mine. Mama put her hand on the first house at the edge of the fields. The hice could send each other messages faster than women could run. The house would scent the urgency in Mama's sweat and tell the others.

Both babies were wailing by the time they reached Mama's house. Mama unslung them and gave one to Aoife to rock while she fed the other. "House, we're in danger. What can we do?"

House rumbled, as always when it wanted to speak with its voice. To warm up the tubes, get air flowing around the vocal cords in the walls.

"They are your species, Minny. What do you want us to do with them?"

Mama frowned while she rocked the suckling baby. The faraway look in her eyes sharpened as the milk was drawn from her breast. "Imprison them. Maybe Imoh's house can be persuaded to stay a bit before it uproots?"

House gargled. "A man in a house? Imoh's house won't like that. It'll eat them."

"Can't you ask it to wait?"

The floors shuddered. "Imoh's dead. Her house is already changing. I could keep from eating them, I've already got a boy in me so my inner walls are immune to man scent."

Mama's face scrunched up. "Oh, do we have to? I'm already so tired."

"The other hice agree. The young ones won't have the self-control. Imoh's house isn't responding anymore. I think it has started migrating."

"It should have kept Imoh alive a little longer," Mother grumbled and switched babies with Aoife.

The baby burped against Aoife's shoulder, its dark curly head sweaty from the hard work of nursing. It smelled deliciously of milk and baby skin, and less deliciously of poop. People always smelled better than hice, no matter how hard the hice tried.

She whispered to Mine, "When you are grown, I want you to smell like this baby, or like my own hair. Not like Big House." Mine kissed her cheek with its feeler.

She had to change the baby. Hice ate the used nappy leaves and poo. She stripped nappy leaves off House's wall, keeping an ear cocked to listen to the conversation. Mine nibbled on her heels, talking to House with one small feeler in the floor.

Mama and House took their time about their discussion. Aoife couldn't understand why they didn't get up to do something about the strange men *now*.

"We can lengthen your lives, but not indefinitely," House said.

"I know, I know." Mama sighed. "Are the young women out there yet?"

House boomed. A patch of wall turned dark blue, a color Aoife had never seen House wear before.

"They're attacking," it shouted, forgetting all about modulating its voice for human ears. "They damaged my walls!"

Mama plucked the protesting baby off her breast and put it in its cot. She ignored the wailing, milk still seeping from her breast. "Aoife, put the babies in the closet and warn your sisters."

Aoife pulled her eating knife from her girdle and did as Mama said. Biri and her house stumbled out, Biri flushed and heavy-eyed from play.

"The strangers are attacking House," Aoife said. "Go out and kill them."

"Can my house sting them?" asked Biri.

"Yes," Mama snapped. In one hand she held her scythe, in the other a heavy wooden grain pestle. "Stun them if possible."

"Where's Koori and Ho?"

Aoife found Koori cowering in her room. "Stay here," she said. "We're fighting. Where's Ho?"

"She went out to play with Mariah," Koori said, shaking as if it was her fault.

Aoife's heart thundered. It might have been Ho out there in the fields, taken by the men. What if they'd killed her house? Now she was getting mad.

The house boomed again and another patch of dark blue bloomed on the opposite wall. Mine shivered in her arms, as if it was feeling House's pain.

"We go out now," Mama said. "Keep your weapons down, they might not attack us. They want to steal us, right, Aoife? That means they want us unharmed."

House opened its sphincter door.

"Stand down!" a male voice yelled. "They're coming out."

"Mama," Aoife whispered, "pretend you want to be stolen."

Mama nodded.

They stepped outside, Mama, Biri, Aoife, their hands down at their sides, their little hice behind them. Aoife worried someone would step on Mine.

"Don't shoot, it's the women! Ma'am, are you all right?"

"Why did you hurt our House?" Mama asked and kept walking toward the three men with black things in their gloved hands. "You could have killed us. The babies."

The lead man threw a look to the smaller man on the right. "Our apologies, ma'am. My colleagues will escort you to the ship while we take care of the aliens."

"He means the hice," Aoife said.

Beard smiled down at her. "We've talked before, eh?"

Aoife kept walking, trying to look as scared and childish as she could.

When she was close enough, she stabbed upward with her eating knife and got him in the groin. Beard screamed loudly. The other men turned toward him. A loud bang rang out.

Biri went down without a sound. A fountain of blood spurted from her neck.

"Jesus fuck you killed a child!"

"They attacked first! That little one stabbed Klaus."

Biri's house threw itself onto her. Holes appeared in the big house, accompanied by loud bangs. The bangs were coming from the sticks.

"Kill that ugly critter – it's raping her right now!"

While the strangers were yelling at each other, mother bashed a skull in. Other women helped, even a few men with hunting bows. The women had brought weapons and hit the strangers until they stopped banging. The strangers didn't look used to fighting, they only wanted to hurt the hice.

Aoife remembered to breathe. She loosened her clutch on Mine, who was busy absorbing Beard's blood from her arms. Biri was dead. Biri! Now she would never live in her own house with her own children. The feeling sank like a stone to just below her heart. It hurt.

Some of the strange men were dead, as they deserved. A few had only been wounded and lay moaning and bleeding. Noriko was dead, others were being tended by their hice.

One of their own men had keeled over. Maybe he'd been too old for fighting.

Mama took charge, wild-eyed and leaking breast-milk. The women dragged the strangers inside Mama's house, even though it was indigo-blotched and shuddering. It declared itself still able to not eat the men. Mama fed dead Beard to it, to speed up its healing.

A strange quiet descended on the village. It was midday, a time for working outdoors and chatting with other women, courting men, playing. Instead, everyone crept inside their hice, shaken, waiting for the return of normal life.

Aoife, her sisters and Mama sat vigil around Biri's body and her stunned house. It would consume her and then drag itself into the forest to find its mother tree and gift itself back into her soil. They wept as much for the house as for Biri. Just like her, it would never reach maturity, never plant, nurture children, or become a mother tree at the end of its cycle.

Mama nursed one baby, patting its tiny back in a slow, slow rhythm. It was supposed to soothe the baby, but it soothed everyone. Except Aoife. Her house grazed the soles of her feet and it made her twitchy.

"What are we going to do with the strangers?" Aoife asked finally, when she couldn't stand the silence one moment longer. Ho was older, but she and her house were wrapped tightly around each other, dumb and frozen with grief.

"I don't know," Mama said. "I wanted to ask them where they came from, what that thing is that fell from the sky, why they wanted to steal us away from our hice."

"But not anymore?"

"No," Mama answered. "At first I thought they might become our neighbors or friends. Now I see these people will never be that. But I won't do anything hasty. Tomorrow when everyone is rested from the fight, I'll talk to the women and the grown hice. See what they think."

"I think we should let the house squash them to a pulp," Aoife said. "And then eat it."

Mama ruffled her hair. "It's a good thing you are not a grown woman yet. A person's life is not to be taken lightly."

"But they tried to take our lives. They deserve to have theirs taken."

"Shush," Mama said. "You are a child and your opinion doesn't yet matter. Watch and learn from our decisions."

Late that night, when everyone had retreated to their chambers – even Biri's body had been dragged into her room by her sorrowing, quivering house – Aoife snuck out to the dining room. She rapped on the wall where she knew the men to be imprisoned.

"House," she said, "make me a hole. I want to talk to them."

House rumbled. It had regained its normal tone of voice. That meant it must be mostly healed. "Why? Your mama forbade it."

"I want to understand," she said. "Why they did what they did."

House thought. "Curiosity about strange creatures is a good thing," it said. "If we didn't possess it, the humans would never have become our partners. You are so much more interesting than the *iwah* we lived with before. Curiosity should be rewarded."

It made a small hole in the wall.

"Make it bigger? I can hardly see," Aoife said.

The house didn't answer. Mine spit on the sides of the little hole and made it part.

Aoife pulled herself up and wriggled inside. House rumbled but didn't do anything to stop her and Mine.

The floor was packed with strange men lying supine. The house had grown bands to restrain them.

Aoife poked the nearest man. "Wake up."

He opened his eyes, groggily, and tried to sit, but the house flesh over his chest prevented him. It was the man she'd talked to by the fire.

"What? Who? Huh?"

Aoife smiled at his fuzziness. That gave her the advantage.

His pupils shrank as the house walls grew brighter.

"Why did you try to steal us? Didn't you think that would make us angry?"

He blinked. "What's your name? Mine is Jonah."

Aoife poked him again. "My name is none of your business. Tell me why."

"You remind me of my niece," he said. His face twisted. "We just wanted to help you. Haven't you wondered why there are so few men in the village? Maybe these aliens kill them to keep you for themselves."

"Just like you were planning to," Aoife said. And of course the hice culled the men. You just didn't need that many.

She inched closer. "You should have asked us. Why didn't you?"

He hesitated. "You've been…isolated for so long. Become primitive. We didn't think you'd understand the scope of the decision."

It was as she'd thought. Aoife bent forward and slit his throat with her small eating knife. He burbled and fell still.

The house hummed in surprise but didn't intervene.

Aoife crept among the sleeping men and cut all their throats, even the one that was a woman.

For Biri. For her sad, lonely house.

For all these cautious grown-up women. Someone needed to make the hard decisions.

Sin Nombre

Jennifer Rachel Baumer

"IT'S ME," CJ told the scanner, so tired she couldn't focus on the machine's inability to distinguish all the 'me's in the building or the fact that, if the building did know who she was, it probably wouldn't let her in.

She hadn't observed any of the protocols. What was the point? Constantly washing, standing under sprayers, being scrubbed down in her suit, out of her suit, in her skivvies – she no longer had any residual embarrassment, just thick exhaustion that made her eyes burn and made the suit heavier than ever.

Bio-level 4. In a city. It wasn't possible to contain everything. The human population hadn't been sent away because there was no away to go to. So she worked around them, pretending a barrier existed between her potential as a vector and their potential as victims.

The west coast virus carried a 50 percent kill rate. It hadn't been identified as aerosolized yet; that made stupid people overconfident and overconfident people even more stupid.

It made Dr. Cynthia Jones tired.

She finally remembered just to thump the scanner with her fist, the way her stepson showed her. The stupid thing responded to violence and so did the scanner. No, no, she wasn't going to think like that anymore. Kev was Kyle's son and she loved Kyle. She slugged the scanner, which blinked. The door to the downtown Reno once-luxury condominiums slid open grudgingly about six inches. CJ stuck her hand in and shoved it all the way open.

The elevator was down. She didn't know why she even tried it anymore. If it ever sent a car and opened to her, she'd run in terror. Anyway, power had been iffy ever since everything went to hell and everyone started to die. Ever since the lights appeared in the summer evening skies, moving too fast for the fastest military jet to intercept.

Everything was weird and iffy and wrong, and everyone still alive was busy learning new skills.

Kyle had designed the reconversion of the downtown casino to condos they now inhabited as the virus crisis went on and on. They'd taken the penthouse. Twenty stories up. CJ took a breath, realized she still wore her hood and face mask, and was too tired to take them off. She clumped up the stairs in her spacesuit and stood staring at the front door until she had the energy to enter. Nothing would ever make her admit it, but it had been pleasant when Kev had run away at the start of the crisis. A lot of teenagers had, run away and come home days later. The news reported it all with a kind of world-weary cynicism, a kind of 'and in addition to everything else, this is just what we needed' attitude. The trend had passed.

CJ let herself into the condo.

"Ahh, the crusader, home from the holy war."

"Give it a rest, Kev," Kyle said without looking up from his laptop and then, catching sight of her when he did, "You're still suited."

CJ touched the mike at her throat. "Thought I'd save time. Sleep in it. For the few hours I have."

"Too tired to get out?"

"Couldn't get the back zipper and there were no cute guys to assist me."

"The cute guys are all dead," Kyle said. "The zipper is on the front. And it's Velcro. You wanted me to do it. Come here."

Kev made a loud retching sound and slammed out of the apartment.

"He forgot his respirator," CJ said, staring at the door.

"He'll be all right. It's calming down and no one knows for sure it's airborne."

"Is that enough for you?"

He didn't answer right away. No one knew how the contagion spread, only the results. But it started in the East, along with the lights in the night sky. So people fled West, until the new strain started. Suits were now more to protect anyone who might be able to find a cure than anything else.

Anything could be lurking on her suit.

"Has to be enough, doesn't it?" he said.

* * *

The man on the table might be forty. Virile, dark, once-handsome. The man on the table was in his forties, virile, dark, covered in blood. Blood jetted from his nose and mouth. Blood leaked from his ears, ran down his face in streams from burst capillaries. Blood-red eyes rolled as he thrashed, blind, terrified and screaming. Hands reached to pull him down. Restraints clicked around his wrists. Someone wound towels around his hands so he wouldn't scratch anyone. Seizures bent him. Medics shouted for vaccines, IV liquids, anything. Blood streamed as the patient twisted and dropped back to the table.

CJ shot up from sleep. "No one is bleeding out."

Beside her Kyle stirred in the pre-dawn grayness. "You're exhausted. Try to sleep."

He was too. Even architects were hard-pressed, redesigning quick fixes to turn every empty house into multifamily homes for refugees. Or into triage units. Into quarantine facilities and level 4 bio safety labs. Into morgues.

Just like veterinarians could be pressed into service in a hot zone.

"I was dreaming," she said and stared at her hands in the dim light of the bedroom. In the dream her hands had been covered in blood.

"You were dreaming about the Midwest."

She made a face. "I was dreaming about a guy –"

"I know."

"It's not Ebola, Lassa, a known hemorrhagic fever. I'm not that kind of a doctor and people keep dying, but they're not bleeding and it's not Hanta and it's not –"

"It's not morning. You get to sleep a while longer. I love you."

"How do I sleep?"

He rolled her over onto her side and put his arms around her. "You close your eyes and you just do. Because you can't help anyone this way. The crisis is over."

She started to respond, but he was exhausted too. He'd been asleep. She'd said it all before.

She squeezed his arms where they crossed around her and listened to him slide back to sleep, and thought what she would have said.

The crisis is just getting started. Eighty percent along the eastern seaboard. Fifty to seventy percent throughout the Midwest. And whatever this is throughout the west where everyone came because there was no HF. They came here to breathe and I think breathing is killing them.

Your son, she might have continued, is out there protesting in favor of the viruses. One more of the New Lifers, the Viruses Have Rights contingency. Only this time the fruitcakes can kill us. All they need to do is make friends with the enemy and it will travel through the world at the speed of light.

But she didn't think it. She slept.

* * *

In the morning there were more bodies in the Northern Nevada valleys. CJ didn't want to see them. The director of the crisis team was excited.

"A family." He seemed unaware he was talking about their deaths. He'd peered too long into the mystery. "You need to go to Wadsworth."

You know I'm a veterinarian, right? She had never meant to work with humans.

That kind of responsibility, being the hope of dying people, it made her unable to remember a damned thing.

But too many people had died this summer.

The summer the lights came.

…Why did she always think of both things? Virus and lights. She was as bad as the New Lifers.

On the drive along I-80 she saw a herd of wild horses. The temperature was already rising and the world smelled of sage.

And smoke, from funerary fires. Illegal and insane while the virus was unknown, but how could you stop people from honoring their dead? Wadsworth appeared, a wide spot in the road. She hadn't been given directions. She couldn't miss it. True. Ambulance, helicopter, EMTs and sheriff's deputies surrounded an angry family that didn't want to let their loved ones go. The small, paint-peeling house was the scene of the only action in Wadsworth aside from a ruffled crow the size of a cat tearing at something in an oil-sheened puddle at the edge of the road. As CJ drove past she saw the crow clutched a wriggling, white-bellied mouse in one talon and she shuddered.

Ubiquitous protestors. Of course. Just beyond range of anyone wanting to throw something at them, or arrest them under the new laws for interfering with medics. They carried poorly or creatively spelled signs about the right of *all* life. They themselves might be breeding new life; none of them looked particularly clean. The signs claimed viruses had a right to life.

Viruses can do good.

…No.

What about medically designed smart viruses?

Not the same thing.

Viruses know how to PARTY.

CJ didn't know what to make of that one. She scanned the group to make certain Kev wasn't there and got out of the car.

"You a relative?" one of the deputies asked.

"I'm a – doctor," she said, and held up her kit with mask, gloves and coat, and tried not to hope this was the time the officer would say, *No, you aren't, you're an imposter,* and refuse her entry.

He didn't.

The interior was shadowy and stuffy, even with the windows open. If whatever had killed them was airborne, it was already released into the world.

No one went in with her. As if they were safer outside in the scrub grass front yard. The ambulance waited to transport bodies. The helicopter pilot smoked a cigarette. The sheriff's deputies repeated, "We're sorry for your loss. Please move back behind the yellow tape. You'll be notified when you can claim the bodies."

CJ forced herself over the threshold.

The family lay inside the cramped living room, the only things out of place in an otherwise spotless dark space.

They'd died without fanfare, probably within minutes of each other. CJ thought the teenaged girls died last; both had fallen while reaching out to their parents, who lay slumped together on the couch. Even in the shadowy living room she could see their faces were cyanotic. They'd suffocated in a room full of air.

Outside, the protestors shouted.

Yes, CJ thought. *Viruses are alive. There are smart viruses. Created to penetrate and consume unhealthy cells. Before theoretically they themselves die. And we know everything always goes according to plan.*

But this doesn't seem like anything of ours.

They called it Sin Nombre. Without name. Not without suffering. Victims died of pulmonary failure, lungs filled with fluid, drowning in the hot, dry desert air. It was a hantavirus, rodent-borne and aerosolized, and it thrived in conditions like this – dry, hot, full of mice.

In 1993, the Four Corners outbreak showed more cases in clean homes than in those that weren't. People in clean homes swept, disturbing dust and dirt impregnated with rodent droppings and urine. The carrier was the white-bellied deer mouse, cute, friendly, fond of people and their food.

Which told her nothing. Time after time the virus was stained and observed. Each time it resisted becoming anything anyone could understand. If it was hanta, it was a new strain. If it was Sin Nombre, the unnamed virus from the 90s, it was a strain. CDC, USAMRIID, state and county public health, veterinarians pulled into service – everyone left alive was working together.

And a lot of them weren't. Alive. Early on they just used masks and goggles. Later they moved to bio safety level 4 labs. Negative pressure labs. Full spacesuits. Nothing worked – researchers died.

Viruses always searched for hosts. Just not like this. This seemed intentional.

In the dim stillness of the living room, edge of vision, CJ saw something move. "You're getting jumpy."

Past the family on the couch, across the dining room, a lace-covered window showed patches of desert-empty backyard. Maybe she saw a bird out there, or an EMT. Or a bereaved family member trying to break in.

Or more of the lights in the sky, the ones that showed up just before the heat wave. Whatever. She was here for samples. CJ knelt, gathering her swabs and hypos, the log she needed to fill out. It seemed likely the virus couldn't be identified because it was mutating so quickly, jumping from form to form and host to host. Samples meant... – Something in the living room moved. On the couch. Like...the father.

CJ's heart hammered. She stayed still, scalpel in hand, watching the bodies.

That was when one of the girls on the floor moved, hand scrabbling on the carpet as if to pull herself closer to her parents.

CJ screamed. She ran for the door before she understood. They'd made a mistake. Not everyone in the family was dead. They'd checked the others, not the girl. Made an assumption. Been too afraid, desperate to get out. The fear of contagion did that.

She bolted anyway. Paramedics were equipped for the living. CJ had tools for the dead. She managed a professional front, walking the instant she was outside, over to the knot of officials watching the house, avoiding the cameras and eyes of those outside it and the furious words of the bereaved family.

"They're not dead," she told the first paramedic she reached.

"What?"

"Alive. At least one is. She – moved. You need to go in there."

He looked at her, wide-eyed and disbelieving. Unwilling. She couldn't blame him.

"Please. Just go in there."

She turned her back to the house. She'd left her gear inside and held only a roll of gauze. An EMT came over and bagged it, traded her for a paper cup of coffee in her gloved hands. It felt wonderful despite the gathering warmth of the morning. She faced west, watching the mountains, until slowly her attention moved from the Sierra to the treetops to the knot of protestors in the street. Young, punky, death-positive, carrying signs. One of them read 'REV-olution.' That made no sense. The next read 'R-EVOLUTION.' She frowned, and read in no particular order.

'Evolve and die.'

'Bottoms up, food chain.'

'The ones left behind are always afraid.'

'Only human arrogance states only humans have right to life.'

Right to life. Kev believed that, if he didn't just use it to get under her skin. Right to life for everything.

She thought of the family inside, parents drowning, girls reaching, left alone because everyone was too afraid.

She thought of thousands in the East and across the heartlands, bleeding out from arenavirus, identifiable and still unstoppable.

Right to life. This wasn't a game for children, racing across the world to protest at every tragedy, holding signs that spouted nonsense.

Rage gathered. CJ balled her fists and started forward. Instantly the EMT barred her path. "Not worth it," he said. He redirected her, hands on her shoulders. "Sit. Have you eaten today? We've got some protein bars."

She focused. "No. Thanks. Sorry."

"Nah. They're a pain. Like it's a game. Like they're immortal. Like their signs are counterculture and shocking."

She met his eyes. He was older than she was. Older than most EMTs, a fine net of crows' feet beside greenish eyes. "What do you think?"

"I think they might be right."

Right about what, she wanted to ask, but before she could, the other medic came out of the house, shaking his head. One hand went to his throat, checked its own movement, and shoved his hair back instead. He came over to where CJ sat on the back of the ambulance, cradling the coffee.

"They're dead," and before she could say anything, "but it's creepy in there. I don't wonder you thought you saw someone move. Did you get what you needed or do you need to do more? I'd like to bag-and-tag."

She swallowed hard at that. He accepted her as a fellow professional. That's what was done with bodies beyond the reach of antibiotics or immune serum.

"I'll get my samples," she said, and handed him the cup.

* * *

The family lay in the same positions. She'd expected them to have been moved. It wasn't a crime scene; someone could have moved them into less traumatic positions.

Like who? There had only been CJ, and the first responder, already out again, and the EMT, who clearly had wanted out.

And there were changes. She saw one girl's hand was moved. Maybe he checked her pulse, then laid her arm back down awkwardly beside her body. CJ didn't feel braver, but she herself had done more.

Maybe it was too overwhelming for everyone. Maybe when it was all over she'd have a nice, long breakdown. Meanwhile, she needed blood, saliva and hair. Probably. No telling what she'd want to look at, since nothing ever revealed a damn thing anyway.

She still wanted to apologize when she drew blood, but that was silly. She could poke around as long as she wanted for the mother's veins and no one would ever –

"I think she's dead," a voice behind her said.

CJ jerked, hands flying. The needle jabbed through the dead woman's arm, through thin tissue and out the other side, missing her left index finger by the width of the needle itself. She felt it slide by. She *did not* feel a short, sharp pain. She was saved the 30-second decision of whether to cut off her own finger or risk invasion by the virus.

The voice was a girl's.

The girl was sitting up behind her, looking on curiously.

"I'm – are you –" CJ gave up and just stared.

The girl was maybe 14, Kev's age. Black hair, roundish face, still a little baby fat. Pretty. And dead. "Are you –" she tried again.

"Dead?" the girl asked.

Nod. She was already backing away from the mother, her eyes locked on the girl. As she moved she looked for the other girl, found her still face down, some distance from her sister, but starting to move.

"More or less," the animate girl answered, her head cocked at CJ. "Do I frighten you?"

CJ stopped moving. Thought about it. No one had done anything. It was just unexpected. But dead was supposed to be dead. The EMTs said they were dead. Now one of them was talking to her.

"More or less."

That elicited a smile from the girl, mocking and cocky, but no more so than Kev's average smirk. *What are you?* She stopped herself from asking. "What's your name?"

Another smile, this one actively unpleasant. Her eyes met CJ's as she rose easily to her feet.

"I am without name." She looked past CJ, out to the street. "It's not what you think it is. Or at least, it doesn't end there. Everyone thinks this is the end. For you, it is. For us, it's the beginning. Those left behind when the new order comes in always panic. It's natural. But we're as old as you are. We've been around as long. It's only recently you've set us free."

CJ opened her mouth again. She was dizzy. The house was too hot. Panicky heartbeats struck her ribs. This time she would ask, *What are you?*

Behind her, the door opened. "What's taking so – oh, my god."

She heard something fall just before the EMT stood beside her.

"She was dead."

"Still is," CJ said, and wasn't contradicted.

"But what –?"

"You need to tell them," the girl with no name said. "Tell them the future has come calling."

The door banged behind them as the EMT dragged CJ to the porch.

They stopped on the steps, facing a sea of waiting faces. Cameras. Signs. The world stared back at them.

"They're alive," CJ said.

The EMT looked at her. She couldn't see any reason to keep that a secret. But she capped the hypo and tucked it into her back pocket without fanfare, hoping no one noticed. That she kept secret.

The yellow tape around the scene came down. Sheriff's deputies, unprepared for this, tried to push back against the surging crowd. Neighbors, relatives, press and protestors, a tide of hot bodies, tablets, phones, microphones pushed forward, everyone asking questions at once. CJ took a step back and bumped into the front door. The EMT cursed, once, then managed to look stoic.

Over the crowd, CJ could see the helicopter blades start to turn, lazily at first, then faster, and the high pitched whine of the engine kicked up. Over the confusion of voices she heard commands being given, saw deputies spreading out, surrounding the house, and thought, *Shouldn't they wait to see if maybe it wasn't all just a ghastly mistake and the family never was dead?*

The sheriff pushed his way through the crowd to them. "Military is demanding to see you. They're alive?" He gestured at the front door as if she might not know who he meant.

The EMT said something about movement, muscle contractions. His eyes were dazed. CJ touched his wrist, as if they'd known each other forever. "One of the girls is up and talking. One is coming to. Maybe not dead? That make the most sense, doesn't it?"

The sheriff stared at her. "Ma'am, nothing has made sense in this country in months. The house is going to be sealed until we figure out who's in charge and –"

"They haven't done anything wrong," CJ said softly.

"No, ma'am," the sheriff said with a tangible lack of sincerity. "Public safety. They could still be contagious."

And having them in that flimsy house will certainly be enough to prevent contagion.

"Meanwhile, the military infectious disease folk want to see you. The chopper's winding up." He motioned her to precede him and took a step.

CJ didn't move. "My kit is still inside. I need it. And I'm not going anywhere in a helicopter. Where is it they want to meet?"

He looked at her as if she were simple. "There's a temporary command post set up in Reno."

"Reno is 20 minutes from here. I'll drive." When he didn't stop staring at her but looked mutinous and stubborn, she said, "Am I being arrested for something?"

"No, ma'am."

She wished he'd stop calling her ma'am.

"I'll drive. Where to?"

"County public health."

She was crisis-team-based there anyway. They had an electron microscope there. "Want to come with?" she asked the EMT.

"I like helicopters," he said and she didn't know if he really did or if he was simply cooperating the way she wasn't. He looked kind of avid about the chopper. CJ wanted time to think. She didn't think she'd get it at a USAMRIID base.

* * *

The minute she drove onto I-80 she called Kyle's cell, but instead of Kyle, Kev answered. She didn't want to waste her drive talking to Kev. Why wasn't he out protesting something, anyway?

"Nah. He forgot his cell. Like always. He's out turning some building into some other building." He sounded bored and belligerent.

Damn it. She took a chance. "Look, Kev, I need you to tell him something."

Silence. Then, "That's *not* my name."

She took a breath. "Kevin, then."

"Whatever." He'd never offer anything up front. She sighed. "I'm very likely going to be arrested for disobeying a direct military command." No idea if she could really be commanded by military – she was a normal civilian. No idea if they could arrest her for not coming when they called. The point was to impress Kevin.

"Cool."

"Can you please have Kyle call me? If he can't reach me in a reasonable amount of time, I'm probably at public health." Because if they did arrest her, they'd probably only take her where they wanted her in the first place.

"Got it," Kev said, and he sounded like he really did. And then, without warning, he voluntarily spoke to her. "Have you figured it out yet?"

Please, no more Kevin riddles.

"Have I figured what out yet?" The road in front of her was clear. Where I-80 out of Reno used to be jammed in every direction, the traffic was now in fits and starts, military carriers, huge refrigerated trucks carrying things she didn't like to speculate on, scared families crossing each other's paths as they looked for somewhere safer in a world that no longer offered safer places.

"What's going on."

"Have *you*?" She didn't want to hear more placard slogans. She didn't even know if Kev believed or simply wanted to annoy.

"Change," he said promptly. "If everyone would just calm down, it's not that bad."

"People are dying," CJ said. Her cell fluttered, going through a canyon near the power plant. For once she didn't want to lose the connection.

"Not permanently."

She blinked. The road in front of her was empty. She sped up. She thought of the girl in the house in Wadsworth. Alive. Again?

"Not everything that's living is human," said Kev. "Those left behind are always afraid." Her phone went dead. He'd probably hung up on her. It was the most Kevin had said to her since she'd married his father.

Those left behind are always afraid. The girl in the house said the same thing. So did one of Kev's signs. So maybe it was nothing more than teenagers making a craze out of the insanity, turning a virus into a *cause celebre*.

Not everything that's alive is human.

In the wake of the viruses. Viruses were alive.

"That doesn't make sense," she said aloud. Because she needed to hear it out loud. Because she needed to deny it. Because viruses on Earth didn't reanimate.

She'd been heading to public health, hoping something would make sense before she got there. So far her thoughts had just gone round and round.

She bypassed the Wells Avenue exit to public health. Just in case someone saw her. She took the next exit by the University, turned around, took I-80 East again, connected with the interchange, headed south to her own practice. Every lab in the city had been seized by the remaining researchers, but no one had thought of her little one-person veterinary practice. It wasn't state of the art.

But it had a lab.

* * *

Her techs had been in every day, caring for the animals. Otherwise, the place was empty, just the dogs making a racket and the cats sounding like parrots in their rage. But all the animals had food and water.

"You're all fine, you big babies," she said, and let the boarded basset twins out to hang out under her feet while the clinic cat perched at her computer. She didn't have an electron microscope. She sent virus samples out.

So what did she know?

She started making a list.

The eastern seaboard and much of the Midwest had been devastated by an arenavirus causing hemorrhagic fever with an eighty percent mortality rate.

People had headed west before anyone could think to set up barriers or stop them. Before quarantines were imposed. Before common sense took effect, which still hadn't.

Then the summer hit and the West exploded into a virus with no name, one that looked like a member of the hantavirus family but refused to admit it in any experiment. So people in the West started dying.

Or disappearing and reappearing, she thought suddenly and wrote that down. Like Kev. Like a good many adolescents and young adults listed as missing.

Everything that's living isn't necessarily human.

Everything has a right to life.

Those left behind are always afraid.

A virus without name. Close to Sin Nombre in effects. People found drowned in open air, their lungs filled with fluids. A virus without name and a girl, who had been dead, standing and saying, "I am without name."

Tell them the future has come calling.

The lights in the sky at the beginning of summer.

"You're over-tired. You're insane."

She turned off the laptop and sat, thinking. She turned it back on and waited impatient for virus checkers to do their stuff.

Virus checkers, she thought, amused, and brought up Google.
She typed in 'smart viruses.'

* * *

The military never came. Maybe they had too much else to do. Maybe they were too old. The people surviving, by and large, were under 30. Or 20. She'd find out. It was strange to realize she was no longer part of the equation, that all those eons of evolution had suddenly bypassed her and left her behind. She wondered what relationships would be like, what thought processes would be. The kids seemed cocky as ever but there was never any way of knowing what went on inside a teenage mind and less chance of it now.

On her way back to the condo she went by the Public Health Administration complex and dropped off the syringe of blood she'd taken from the dead woman in Wadsworth. There didn't seem to be any point in using the electron microscope to look at the viruses in the sample. The virus had resisted being identified this long and whatever she saw now she wouldn't understand.

She thought about the family in the white house in Wadsworth and wondered that the parents had still been dead while the daughters had been moving, talking. Laughing. The next generation always bypassed the ones in front of it, but she'd be annoyed if she had to die and stay dead just because she was over 30.

"Just barely over 30," CJ said aloud, and laughed. The woman who collected the syringe and logged it extensively on a clipboard gave her a funny look. "Inside joke," CJ said, which didn't get her a better reception. After all, she was alone.

Probably.

* * *

"It's me," she told the scanner at the door to the condos and then she slugged it for good measure. She'd go upstairs, see if Kyle was home, talk to Kev. No, that wasn't his name anymore. She didn't think it was because he wanted to be Kevin. She thought he didn't expect to be called anything. The future didn't have a name or shape, it was all just possibilities.

She hit the button for the elevator and it opened. "Just kidding," CJ said when the power flickered. She turned for the stairs and as she pulled the door open, the puncture wound on her left index finger began to throb.

The Battle of Dorking

Reminiscences of a Volunteer

George Chesney

YOU ASK ME TO TELL YOU, my grandchildren, something about my own share in the great events that happened fifty years ago. 'Tis sad work turning back to that bitter page in our history, but you may perhaps take profit in your new homes from the lesson it teaches. For us in England it came too late. And yet we had plenty of warnings, if we had only made use of them. The danger did not come on us unawares. It burst on us suddenly, 'tis true; but its coming was foreshadowed plainly enough to open our eyes, if we had not been wilfully blind. We English have only ourselves to blame for the humiliation which has been brought on the land. Venerable old age! Dishonourable old age, I say, when it follows a manhood dishonoured as ours has been. I declare, even now, though fifty years have passed, I can hardly look a young man in the face when I think I am one of those in whose youth happened this degradation of Old England – one of those who betrayed the trust handed down to us unstained by our forefathers.

What a proud and happy country was this fifty years ago! Free-trade had been working for more than a quarter of a century, and there seemed to be no end to the riches it was bringing us. London was growing bigger and bigger; you could not build houses fast enough for the rich people who wanted to live in them, the merchants who made the money and came from all parts of the world to settle there, and the lawyers and doctors and engineers and other, and trades-people who got their share out of the profits. The streets reached down to Croydon and Wimbledon, which my father could remember quite country places; and people used to say that Kingston and Reigate would soon be joined to London. We thought we could go on building and multiplying for ever.

'Tis true that even then there was no lack of poverty; the people who had no money went on increasing as fast as the rich, and pauperism was already beginning to be a difficulty; but if the rates were high, there was plenty of money to pay them with; and as for what were called the middle classes, there really seemed no limit to their increase and prosperity. People in those days thought it quite a matter of course to bring a dozen of children into the world – or, as it used to be said, Providence sent them that number of babies; and if they couldn't always marry off all the daughters, they used to manage to provide for the sons, for there were new openings to be found in all the professions, or in the Government offices, which went on steadily getting larger. Besides, in those days young men could be sent out to India, or into the army or navy; and even then emigration was not uncommon, although not the regular custom it is now. Schoolmasters, like all other professional classes, drove a capital trade. They did not teach very much, to be sure, but new schools with their four or five hundred boys were springing up all over the country.

Fools that we were! We thought that all this wealth and prosperity were sent us by Providence, and could not stop coming. In our blindness we did not see that we were merely a big workshop, making up the things which came from all parts of the world; and that if other nations stopped sending us raw goods to work up, we could not produce them ourselves. True, we had in those days an advantage in our cheap coal and iron; and had we taken care not to waste the fuel, it might have lasted us longer. But even then there were signs that coal and iron would soon become cheaper in foreign parts; while as to food and other things, England was not better off than it is now. We were so rich simply because other nations from all parts of the world were in the habit of sending their goods to us to be sold or manufactured; and we thought that this would last for ever. And so, perhaps, it might have lasted, if we had only taken proper means to keep it; but, in our folly, we were too careless even to insure our prosperity, and after the course of trade was turned away it would not come back again.

And yet, if ever a nation had a plain warning, we had. If we were the greatest trading country, our neighbours were the leading military power in Europe. They were driving a good trade, too, for this was before their foolish communism (about which you will hear when you are older) had ruined the rich without benefiting the poor, and they were in many respects the first nation in Europe; but it was on their army that they prided themselves most. And with reason. They had beaten the Russians and the Austrians, and the Prussians too, in bygone years, and they thought they were invincible.

Well do I remember the great review held at Paris by the Emperor Napoleon during the great Exhibition, and how proud he looked showing off his splendid Guards to the assembled kings and princes. Yet, three years afterwards, the force so long deemed the first in Europe was ignominiously beaten, and the whole army taken prisoners. Such a defeat had never happened before in the world's history; and with this proof before us of the folly of disbelieving in the possibility of disaster merely because it had never fallen upon us, it might have been supposed that we should have the sense to take the lesson to heart.

And the country was certainly roused for a time, and a cry was raised that the army ought to be reorganised, and our defences strengthened against the enormous power for sudden attacks which it was seen other nations were able to put forth. And a scheme of army reform was brought forward by the Government. It was a half-and-half affair at best; and, unfortunately, instead of being taken up in Parliament as a national scheme, it was made a party matter of, and so fell through. There was a Radical section of the House, too, whose votes had to be secured by conciliation, and which blindly demanded a reduction of armaments as the price of allegiance. This party always decried military establishments as part of a fixed policy for reducing the influence of the Crown and the aristocracy. They could not understand that the times had altogether changed, that the Crown had really no power, and that the Government merely existed at the pleasure of the House of Commons, and that even Parliament-rule was beginning to give way to mob-law.

At any rate, the Ministry, baffled on all sides, gave up by degrees all the strong points of a scheme which they were not heartily in earnest about. It was not that there was any lack of money, if only it had been spent in the right way. The army cost enough, and more than enough, to give us a proper defence, and there were armed men of sorts in plenty and to spare, if only they had been decently organised. It was in organisation and forethought that we fell short, because our rulers did not heartily believe in the need for preparation. The fleet and the Channel, they said, were sufficient protection. So army reform was put off to some more convenient season, and the militia and volunteers were left untrained as before, because to call them out for drill would 'interfere with the industry of the country.'

We could have given up some of the industry of those days, forsooth, and yet be busier than we are now. But why tell you a tale you have so often heard already?

The nation, although uneasy, was misled by the false security its leaders professed to feel; the warning given by the disasters that overtook France was allowed to pass by unheeded. We would not even be at the trouble of putting our arsenals in a safe place, or of guarding the capital against a surprise, although the cost of doing so would not have been so much as missed from the national wealth. The French trusted in their army and its great reputation, we in our fleet; and in each case the result of this blind confidence was disaster, such as our forefathers in their hardest struggles could not have even imagined.

I need hardly tell you how the crash came about. First, the rising in India drew away a part of our small army; then came the difficulty with America, which had been threatening for years, and we sent off ten thousand men to defend Canada – a handful which did not go far to strengthen the real defences of that country, but formed an irresistible temptation to the Americans to try and take them prisoners, especially as the contingent included three battalions of the Guards. Thus the regular army at home was even smaller than usual, and nearly half of it was in Ireland to check the talked-of Fenian invasion fitting out in the West. Worse still – though I do not know it would really have mattered as things turned out – the fleet was scattered abroad: some ships to guard the West Indies, others to check privateering in the China seas, and a large part to try and protect our colonies on the Northern Pacific shore of America, where, with incredible folly, we continued to retain possessions which we could not possibly defend. America was not the great power forty years ago that it is now; but for us to try and hold territory on her shores which could only be reached by sailing round the Horn, was as absurd as if she had attempted to take the Isle of Man before the independence of Ireland. We see this plainly enough now, but we were all blind then.

It was while we were in this state, with our ships all over the world, and our little bit of an army cut up into detachments, that the Secret Treaty was published, and Holland and Denmark were annexed. People say now that we might have escaped the troubles which came on us if we had at any rate kept quiet till our other difficulties were settled; but the English were always an impulsive lot: the whole country was boiling over with indignation, and the Government, egged on by the press, and going with the stream, declared war. We had always got out of scrapes before, and we believed our old luck and pluck would somehow pull us through.

Then, of course, there was bustle and hurry all over the land. Not that the calling up of the army reserves caused much stir, for I think there were only about 5000 altogether, and a good many of these were not to be found when the time came; but recruiting was going on all over the country, with a tremendous high bounty, 50,000 more men having been voted for the army. Then there was a Ballot Bill passed for adding 55,500 men to the militia; why a round number was not fixed on I don't know, but the Prime Minister said that this was the exact quota wanted to put the defences of the country on a sound footing. Then the shipbuilding that began! Ironclads, despatch-boats, gunboats, monitors – every building-yard in the country got its job, and they were offering ten shillings a-day wages for anybody who could drive a rivet. This didn't improve the recruiting, you may suppose. I remember, too, there was a squabble in the House of Commons about whether artisans should be drawn for the ballot, as they were so much wanted, and I think they got an exemption. This sent numbers to the yards; and if we had had a couple of years to prepare instead of a couple of weeks, I daresay we should have done very well.

It was on a Monday that the declaration of war was announced, and in a few hours we got our first inkling of the sort of preparation the enemy had made for the event which they had really brought about, although the actual declaration was made by us. A pious appeal to the God of battles, whom it was said we had aroused, was telegraphed back; and from that moment all communication with the north of Europe was cut off. Our embassies and legations were packed off at an hour's notice, and it was as if we had suddenly come back to the middle ages. The dumb astonishment visible all over London the next morning, when the papers came out void of news, merely hinting at what had happened, was one of the most startling things in this war of surprises. But everything had been arranged beforehand; nor ought we to have been surprised, for we had seen the same Power, only a few months before, move down half a million of men on a few days' notice, to conquer the greatest military nation in Europe, with no more fuss than our War Office used to make over the transport of a brigade from Aldershot to Brighton – and this, too, without the allies it had now. What happened now was not a bit more wonderful in reality; but people of this country could not bring themselves to believe that what had never occurred before to England could ever possibly happen. Like our neighbours, we became wise when it was too late.

Of course the papers were not long in getting news – even the mighty organisation set at work could not shut out a special correspondent; and in a very few days, although the telegraphs and railways were intercepted right across Europe, the main facts oozed out. An embargo had been laid on all the shipping in every port from the Baltic to Ostend; the fleets of the two great Powers had moved out, and it was supposed were assembled in the great northern harbour, and troops were hurrying on board all the steamers detained in these places, most of which were British vessels. It was clear that invasion was intended. Even then we might have been saved, if the fleet had been ready. The forts which guarded the flotilla were perhaps too strong for shipping to attempt; but an ironclad or two, handled as British sailors knew how to use them, might have destroyed or damaged a part of the transports, and delayed the expedition, giving us what we wanted, time. But then the best part of the fleet had been decoyed down to the Dardanelles, and what remained of the Channel squadron was looking after Fenian filibusters off the west of Ireland; so it was ten days before the fleet was got together, and by that time it was plain the enemy's preparations were too far advanced to be stopped by a coup-de-main.

Information, which came chiefly through Italy, came slowly, and was more or less vague and uncertain; but this much was known, that at least a couple of hundred thousand men were embarked or ready to be put on board ships, and that the flotilla was guarded by more ironclads than we could then muster. I suppose it was the uncertainty as to the point the enemy would aim at for landing, and the fear lest he should give us the go-by, that kept the fleet for several days in the Downs; but it was not until the Tuesday fortnight after the declaration of war that it weighed anchor and steamed away for the North Sea. Of course you have read about the Queen's visit to the fleet the day before, and how she sailed round the ships in her yacht, and went on board the flag-ship to take leave of the admiral; how, overcome with emotion, she told him that the safety of the country was committed to his keeping. You remember, too, the gallant old officer's reply, and how all the ships' yards were manned, and how lustily the tars cheered as her Majesty was rowed off. The account was of course telegraphed to London, and the high spirits of the fleet infected the whole town. I was outside the Charing Cross station when the Queen's special train from Dover arrived, and from the cheering and shouting which greeted her Majesty as she drove away, you might have supposed we had already won a great victory. The leading journal, which had gone in strongly for the army reduction carried out during the session, and had been nervous and desponding in tone during the past fortnight, suggesting all sorts of compromises as a way of getting out of the war, came out in a very jubilant form next morning.

Panic-stricken inquirers, it said, *ask now, where are the means of meeting the invasion? We reply that the invasion will never take place. A British fleet, manned by British sailors whose courage and enthusiasm are reflected in the people of this country, is already on the way to meet the presumptuous foe. The issue of a contest between British ships and those of any other country, under anything like equal odds, can never be doubtful. England awaits with calm confidence the issue of the impending action.*

Such were the words of the leading article, and so we all felt. It was on Tuesday, the 10th of August, that the fleet sailed from the Downs. It took with it a submarine cable to lay down as it advanced, so that continuous communication was kept up, and the papers were publishing special editions every few minutes with the latest news. This was the first time such a thing had been done, and the feat was accepted as a good omen. Whether it is true that the Admiralty made use of the cable to keep on sending contradictory orders, which took the command out of the admiral's hands, I can't say; but all that the admiral sent in return was a few messages of the briefest kind, which neither the Admiralty nor any one else could have made any use of. Such a ship had gone off reconnoitring; such another had rejoined – fleet was in latitude so and so. This went on till the Thursday morning. I had just come up to town by train as usual, and was walking to my office, when the newsboys began to cry, "New edition – enemy's fleet in sight!"

You may imagine the scene in London! Business still went on at the banks, for bills matured although the independence of the country was being fought out under our own eyes, so to say, and the speculators were active enough. But even with the people who were making and losing their fortunes, the interest in the fleet overcame everything else; men who went to pay in or draw out their money stopped to show the last bulletin to the cashier. As for the street, you could hardly get along for the crowd stopping to buy and read the papers; while at every house or office the members sat restlessly in the common room, as if to keep together for company, sending out some one of their number every few minutes to get the latest edition. At least this is what happened at our office; but to sit still was as impossible as to do anything, and most of us went out and wandered about among the crowd, under a sort of feeling that the news was got quicker at in this way.

Bad as were the times coming, I think the sickening suspense of that day, and the shock which followed, was almost the worst that we underwent. It was about ten o'clock that the first telegram came; an hour later the wire announced that the admiral had signalled to form line of battle, and shortly afterwards that the order was given to bear down on the enemy and engage. At twelve came the announcement, "Fleet opened fire about three miles to leeward of us" – that is, the ship with the cable. So far all had been expectancy, then came the first token of calamity. "An ironclad has been blown up" – "the enemy's torpedoes are doing great damage" – "the flag-ship is laid aboard the enemy" – "the flag-ship appears to be sinking" – "the vice-admiral has signalled to" – there the cable became silent, and, as you know, we heard no more till, two days afterwards, the solitary ironclad which escaped the disaster steamed into Portsmouth.

Then the whole story came out – how our sailors, gallant as ever, had tried to close with the enemy; how the latter evaded the conflict at close quarters, and, sheering off, left behind them the fatal engines which sent our ships, one after the other, to the bottom; how all this happened almost in a few minutes. The Government, it appears, had received warnings of this invention; but to the nation this stunning blow was utterly unexpected. That Thursday I had to go home early for regimental drill, but it was impossible to remain doing nothing, so when that was over I went up to town again, and after waiting in expectation of news which never came, and missing the midnight train, I walked home.

It was a hot sultry night, and I did not arrive till near sunrise. The whole town was quite still – the lull before the storm; and as I let myself in with my latch-key, and went softly up-stairs to my room to avoid waking the sleeping household, I could not but contrast the peacefulness of the morning – no sound breaking the silence but the singing of the birds in the garden – with the passionate remorse and indignation that would break out with the day. Perhaps the inmates of the rooms were as wakeful as myself; but the house in its stillness was just as it used to be when I came home alone from balls or parties in the happy days gone by.

Tired though I was, I could not sleep, so I went down to the river and had a swim; and on returning found the household was assembling for early breakfast. A sorrowful household it was, although the burden pressing on each was partly an unseen one. My father, doubting whether his firm could last through the day; my mother, her distress about my brother, now with his regiment on the coast, already exceeding that which she felt for the public misfortune, had come down, although hardly fit to leave her room. My sister Clara was worst of all, for she could not but try to disguise her special interest in the fleet; and though we had all guessed that her heart was given to the young lieutenant in the flag-ship – the first vessel to go down – a love unclaimed could not be told, nor could we express the sympathy we felt for the poor girl. That breakfast, the last meal we ever had together, was soon ended, and my father and I went up to town by an early train, and got there just as the fatal announcement of the loss of the fleet was telegraphed from Portsmouth.

The panic and excitement of that day – how the funds went down to 35; the run upon the bank and its stoppage; the fall of half the houses in the city; how the Government issued a notification suspending specie payment and the tendering of bills – this last precaution too late for most firms, Graham & Co. among the number, which stopped payment as soon as my father got to the office; the call to arms, and the unanimous response of the country – all this is history which I need not repeat. You wish to hear about my own share in the business of the time. Well, volunteering had increased immensely from the day war was proclaimed, and our regiment went up in a day or two from its usual strength of 600 to nearly 1000. But the stock of rifles was deficient. We were promised a further supply in a few days, which however, we never received; and while waiting for them the regiment had to be divided into two parts, the recruits drilling with the rifles in the morning, and we old hands in the evening.

The failures and stoppage of work on this black Friday threw an immense number of young men out of employment, and we recruited up to 1400 strong by the next day; but what was the use of all these men without arms? On the Saturday it was announced that a lot of smooth-bore muskets in store at the Tower would be served out to regiments applying for them, and a regular scramble took place among the volunteers for them, and our people got hold of a couple of hundred. But you might almost as well have tried to learn rifle-drill with a broom-stick as with old brown bess; besides, there was no smooth-bore ammunition in the country. A national subscription was opened for the manufacture of rifles at Birmingham, which ran up to a couple of millions in two days, but, like everything else, this came too late.

To return to the volunteers: camps had been formed a fortnight before at Dover, Brighton, Harwich, and other places, of regulars and militia, and the headquarters of most of the volunteer regiments were attached to one or other of them, and the volunteers themselves used to go down for drill from day to day, as they could spare time, and on Friday an order went out that they should be permanently embodied; but the metropolitan volunteers were still kept about London as a sort of reserve, till it could be seen at what point the invasion would take place. We were all told off to brigades and divisions. Our brigade consisted of the 4th Royal Surrey Militia, the 1st Surrey Administrative Battalion, as it was called, at Clapham, the 7th Surrey Volunteers at Southwark, and ourselves; but only our battalion and the militia were quartered in the same place, and the whole brigade had merely two or three afternoons together at brigade exercise in Bushey Park before the march took place. Our brigadier belonged to a line regiment in Ireland, and did not join till the very morning the order came. Meanwhile, during the preliminary fortnight, the militia colonel commanded.

But though we volunteers were busy with our drill and preparations, those of us who, like myself, belonged to Government offices, had more than enough of office work to do, as you may suppose. The volunteer clerks were allowed to leave office at four o'clock, but the rest were kept hard at the desk far into the night. Orders to the lord-lieutenants, to the magistrates, notifications, all the arrangements for cleaning out the workhouses for hospitals – these and a hundred other things had to be managed in our office, and there was as much bustle indoors as out. Fortunate we were to be so busy – the people to be pitied were those who had nothing to do.

And on Sunday (that was the 15th August) work went on just as usual. We had an early parade and drill, and I went up to town by the nine o'clock train in my uniform, taking my rifle with me in case of accidents, and luckily too, as it turned out, a mackintosh overcoat. When I got to Waterloo there were all sorts of rumours afloat. A fleet had been seen off the Downs, and some of the despatch-boats which were hovering about the coasts brought news that there was a large flotilla off Harwich, but nothing could be seen from the shore, as the weather was hazy. The enemy's light ships had taken and sunk all the fishing-boats they could catch, to prevent the news of their whereabouts reaching us; but a few escaped during the night and reported that the Inconstant frigate coming home from North America, without any knowledge of what had taken place, had sailed right into the enemy's fleet and been captured. In town the troops were all getting ready for a move; the Guards in the Wellington Barracks were under arms, and their baggage-waggons packed and drawn up in the Bird-cage Walk. The usual guard at the Horse Guards had been withdrawn, and orderlies and staff-officers were going to and fro.

All this I saw on the way to my office, where I worked away till twelve o'clock, and then feeling hungry after my early breakfast, I went across Parliament Street to my club to get some luncheon. There were about half-a-dozen men in the coffee-room, none of whom I knew; but in a minute or two Danvers of the Treasury entered in a tremendous hurry. From him I got the first bit of authentic news I had had that day. The enemy had landed in force near Harwich, and the metropolitan regiments were ordered down there to reinforce the troops already collected in that neighbourhood; his regiment was to parade at one o'clock, and he had come to get something to eat before starting. We bolted a hurried lunch, and were just leaving the club when a messenger from the Treasury came running into the hall.

"Oh, Mr. Danvers," said he, "I've come to look for you, sir; the secretary says that all the gentlemen are wanted at the office, and that you must please not one of you go with the regiments."

"The devil!" cried Danvers.

"Do you know if that order extends to all the public offices?" I asked.

"I don't know," said the man, "but I believe it do. I know there's messengers gone round to all the clubs and luncheon-bars to look for the gentlemen; the secretary says it's quite impossible any one can be spared just now, there's so much work to do; there's orders just come to send off our records to Birmingham to-night."

I did not wait to condole with Danvers, but, just glancing up Whitehall to see if any of our messengers were in pursuit, I ran off as hard as I could for Westminister Bridge, and so to the Waterloo station.

The place had quite changed its aspect since the morning. The regular service of trains had ceased, and the station and approaches were full of troops, among them the Guards and artillery. Everything was very orderly: the men had piled arms, and were standing about in groups. There was no sign of high spirits or enthusiasm. Matters had become too serious. Every man's face reflected the general feeling that we had neglected the warnings given us, and that now the danger so long derided as impossible and absurd had really come and found us unprepared. But the soldiers, if grave, looked determined, like men who meant to do their duty whatever might happen.

A train full of guardsmen was just starting for Guildford. I was told it would stop at Surbiton, and, with several other volunteers, hurrying like myself to join our regiment, got a place in it. We did not arrive a moment too soon, for the regiment was marching from Kingston down to the station. The destination of our brigade was the east coast. Empty carriages were drawn up in the siding, and our regiment was to go first. A large crowd was assembled to see it off, including the recruits who had joined during the last fortnight, and who formed by far the largest part of our strength. They were to stay behind, and were certainly very much in the way already; for as all the officers and sergeants belonged to the active part, there was no one to keep discipline among them, and they came crowding around us, breaking the ranks and making it difficult to get into the train.

Here I saw our new brigadier for the first time. He was a soldier-like man, and no doubt knew his duty, but he appeared new to volunteers, and did not seem to know how to deal with gentlemen privates. I wanted very much to run home and get my greatcoat and knapsack, which I had bought a few days ago, but feared to be left behind; a good-natured recruit volunteered to fetch them for me, but he had not returned before we started, and I began the campaign with a kit consisting of a mackintosh and a small pouch of tobacco.

It was a tremendous squeeze in the train; for, besides the ten men sitting down, there were three or four standing up in every compartment, and the afternoon was close and sultry, and there were so many stoppages on the way that we took nearly an hour and a half crawling up to Waterloo. It was between five and six in the afternoon when we arrived there, and it was nearly seven before we marched up to the Shoreditch station. The whole place was filled up with stores and ammunition, to be sent off to the east, so we piled arms in the street and scattered about to get food and drink, of which most of us stood in need, especially the latter, for some were already feeling the worse for the heat and crush.

I was just stepping into a public-house with Travers, when who should drive up but his pretty wife? Most of our friends had paid their adieus at the Surbiton station, but she had driven up by the road in his brougham, bringing their little boy to have a last look at papa.

She had also brought his knapsack and greatcoat, and, what was still more acceptable, a basket containing fowls, tongue, bread-and-butter, and biscuits, and a couple of bottles of claret – which priceless luxuries they insisted on my sharing.

Meanwhile the hours went on. The 4th Surrey Militia, which had marched all the way from Kingston, had come up, as well as the other volunteer corps; the station had been partly cleared of the stores that encumbered it; some artillery, two militia regiments, and a battalion of the line, had been despatched, and our turn to start had come, and long lines of carriages were drawn up ready for us; but still we remained in the street.

You may fancy the scene. There seemed to be as many people as ever in London, and we could hardly move for the crowds of spectators – fellows hawking fruits and volunteers' comforts, newsboys and so forth, to say nothing of the cabs and omnibuses; while orderlies and staff-officers were constantly riding up with messages. A good many of the militiamen, and some of our people too, had taken more than enough to drink; perhaps a hot sun had told on empty stomachs; anyhow, they became very noisy. The din, dirt, and heat were indescribable.

So the evening wore on, and all the information our officers could get from the brigadier, who appeared to be acting under another general, was, that orders had come to stand fast for the present. Gradually the street became quieter and cooler. The brigadier, who, by way of setting an example, had remained for some hours without leaving his saddle, had got a chair out of a shop, and sat nodding in it; most of the men were lying down or sitting on the pavement – some sleeping, some smoking. In vain had Travers begged his wife to go home. She declared that, having come so far, she would stay and see the last of us. The brougham had been sent away to a by-street, as it blocked up the road; so he sat on a doorstep, she by him on the knapsack. Little Arthur, who had been delighted at the bustle and the uniforms, and in high spirits, became at last very cross, and eventually cried himself to sleep in his father's arms, his golden hair and one little dimpled arm hanging over his shoulder.

Thus went on the weary hours, till suddenly the assembly sounded, and we all started up. We were to return to Waterloo. The landing on the east was only a feint – so ran the rumour – the real attack was on the south. Anything seemed better than indecision and delay, and, tired though we were, the march back was gladly hailed. Mrs. Travers, who made us take the remains of the luncheon with us, we left to look for her carriage; little Arthur, who was awake again, but very good and quiet, in her arms.

We did not reach Waterloo till nearly midnight, and there was some delay in starting again. Several volunteer and militia regiments had arrived from the north; the station and all its approaches were jammed up with men, and trains were being despatched away as fast as they could be made up. All this time no news had reached us since the first announcement; but the excitement then aroused had now passed away under the influence of fatigue and want of sleep, and most of us dozed off as soon as we got under way. I did, at any rate, and was awoke by the train stopping at Leatherhead. There was an up-train returning to town, and some persons in it were bringing up news from the coast. We could not, from our part of the train, hear what they said, but the rumour was passed up from one carriage to another. The enemy had landed in force at Worthing. Their position had been attacked by the troops from the camp near Brighton, and the action would be renewed in the morning. The volunteers had behaved very well. This was all the information we could get. So, then, the invasion had come at last. It was clear, at any rate, from what was said, that the enemy had not been driven back yet, and we should be in time most likely to take a share in the defence.

It was sunrise when the train crawled into Dorking, for there had been numerous stoppages on the way; and here it was pulled up for a long time, and we were told to get out and stretch ourselves – an order gladly responded to, for we had been very closely packed all night. Most of us, too, took the opportunity to make an early breakfast off the food we had brought from Shoreditch. I had the remains of Mrs. Travers's fowl and some bread wrapped up in my waterproof, which I shared with one or two less provident comrades. We could see from our halting-place that the line was blocked with trains beyond and behind. It must have been about eight o'clock when we got orders to take our seats again, and the train began to move slowly on towards Horsham. Horsham Junction was the point to be occupied – so the rumour went; but about ten o'clock, when halting at a small station a few miles short of it, the order came to leave the train, and our brigade formed in column on the highroad. Beyond us was some field-artillery; and further on, so we were told by a staff-officer, another brigade, which was to make up a division with ours. After more delays the line began to move, but not forwards; our route was towards the north-west, and a sort of suspicion of the state of affairs flashed across my mind. Horsham was already occupied by the enemy's advanced-guard, and we were to fall back on Leith Common, and take up a position threatening his flank, should he advance either to Guildford or Dorking. This was soon confirmed by what the colonel was told by the brigadier and passed down the ranks; and just now, for the first time, the boom of artillery came up on the light south breeze. In about an hour the firing ceased. What did it mean? We could not tell.

Meanwhile our march continued. The day was very close and sultry, and the clouds of dust stirred up by our feet almost suffocated us. I had saved a soda-water-bottleful of yesterday's claret; but this went only a short way, for there were many mouths to share it with, and the thirst soon became as bad as ever. Several of the regiment fell out from faintness, and we made frequent halts to rest and let the stragglers come up. At last we reached the top of Leith Hill. It is a striking spot, being the highest point in the south of England. The view from it is splendid, and most lovely did the country look this summer day, although the grass was brown from the long drought. It was a great relief to get from the dusty road on to the common, and at the top of the hill there was a refreshing breeze. We could see now, for the first time, the whole of our division. Our own regiment did not muster more than 500, for it contained a large number of Government office men who had been detained, like Danvers, for duty in town, and others were not much larger; but the militia regiment was very strong, and the whole division, I was told, mustered nearly 5000 rank and file. We could see other troops also in extension of our division, and could count a couple of field-batteries of Royal Artillery, besides some heavy guns, belonging to the volunteers apparently, drawn by carthorses.

The cooler air, the sense of numbers, and the evident strength of the position we held, raised our spirits, which, I am not ashamed to say, had all the morning been depressed. It was not that we were not eager to close with the enemy, but that the counter-marching and halting ominously betokened a vacillation of purpose in those who had the guidance of affairs. Here in two days the invaders had got more than twenty miles inland, and nothing effectual had been done to stop them. And the ignorance in which we volunteers, from the colonel downwards, were kept of their movements, filled us with uneasiness. We could not but depict to ourselves the enemy as carrying out all the while firmly his well-considered scheme of attack, and contrasting it with our own uncertainty of purpose. The very silence with which his advance appeared to be conducted filled us with mysterious awe.

Meanwhile the day wore on, and we became faint with hunger, for we had eaten nothing since daybreak. No provisions came up, and there were no signs of any commissariat officers. It seems that when we were at the Waterloo station a whole trainful of provisions was drawn up there, and our colonel proposed that one of the trucks should be taken off and attached to our train, so that we might have some food at hand; but the officer in charge, an assistant-controller I think they called him – this control department was a newfangled affair which did us almost as much harm as the enemy in the long-run – said his orders were to keep all the stores together, and that he couldn't issue any without authority from the head of his department. So we had to go without. Those who had tobacco smoked – indeed there is no solace like a pipe under such circumstances. The militia regiment, I heard afterwards, had two days' provisions in their haversacks; it was we volunteers who had no haversacks, and nothing to put in them.

All this time, I should tell you, while we were lying on the grass with our arms piled, the General, with the brigadiers and staff, was riding about slowly from point to point of the edge of the common, looking out with his glass towards the south valley. Orderlies and staff-officers were constantly coming, and about three o'clock there arrived up a road that led towards Horsham a small body of lancers and a regiment of yeomanry, who had, it appears, been out in advance, and now drew up a short way in front of us in column facing to the south. Whether they could see anything in their front I could not tell, for we were behind the crest of the hill ourselves, and so could not look into the valley below; but shortly afterwards the assembly sounded. Commanding officers were called out by the General, and received some brief instructions; and the column began to march again towards London, the militia this time coming last in our brigade.

A rumour regarding the object of this counter-march soon spread through the ranks. The enemy was not going to attack us here, but was trying to turn the position on both sides, one column pointing to Reigate, the other to Aldershot; and so we must fall back and take up a position at Dorking. The line of the great chalk-range was to be defended. A large force was concentrating at Guildford, another at Reigate, and we should find supports at Dorking. The enemy would be awaited in these positions. Such, so far as we privates could get at the facts, was to be the plan of operations. Down the hill, therefore, we marched.

From one or two points we could catch a brief sight of the railway in the valley below running from Dorking to Horsham. Men in red were working upon it here and there. They were the Royal Engineers, some one said, breaking up the line. On we marched. The dust seemed worse than ever. In one village through which we passed – I forget the name now – there was a pump on the green. Here we stopped and had a good drink; and passing by a large farm, the farmer's wife and two or three of her maids stood at the gate and handed us hunches of bread and cheese out of some baskets. I got the share of a bit, but the bottom of the good woman's baskets must soon have been reached. Not a thing else was to be had till we got to Dorking about six o'clock; indeed most of the farm-houses appeared deserted already.

On arriving there we were drawn up in the street, and just opposite was a baker's shop. Our fellows asked leave at first by twos and threes to go in and buy some loaves, but soon others began to break off and crowd into the shop, and at last a regular scramble took place. If there had been any order preserved, and a regular distribution arranged, they would no doubt have been steady enough, but hunger makes men selfish; each man felt that his stopping behind would do no good – he would simply lose his share; so it ended by almost the whole regiment joining in the scrimmage, and the shop was cleared out in a couple of minutes; while as for paying, you could not get your hand into your pocket for the crush. The colonel tried in vain to stop the row; some of the officers were as bad as the men.

Just then a staff-officer rode by; he could scarcely make way for the crowd, and was pushed against rather rudely, and in a passion he called out to us to behave properly, like soldiers, and not like a parcel of roughs. "Oh, blow it, governor," said Dick Wake, "you aren't a-going to come between a poor cove and his grub." Wake was an articled attorney, and, as we used to say in those days, a cheeky young chap, although a good-natured fellow enough. At this speech, which was followed by some more remarks of the sort from those about him, the staff-officer became angrier still. "Orderly," cried he to the lancer riding behind him, "take that man to the provostmarshal. As for you, sir," he said, turning to our colonel, who sat on his horse silent with astonishment, "if you don't want some of your men shot before their time, you and your precious officers had better keep this rabble in a little better order;" and poor Dick, who looked crestfallen enough, would certainly have been led off at the tail of the sergeant's horse, if the brigadier had not come up and arranged matters, and marched us off to the hill beyond the town.

This incident made us both angry and crestfallen. We were annoyed at being so roughly spoken to: at the same time we felt we had deserved it, and were ashamed of the misconduct. Then, too, we had lost confidence in our colonel, after the poor figure he cut in the affair. He was a good fellow, the colonel, and showed himself a brave one next day; but he aimed too much at being popular, and didn't understand a bit how to command.

To resume: We had scarcely reached the hill above the town, which we were told was to be our bivouac for the night, when the welcome news came that a food-train had arrived at the station; but there were no carts to bring the things up, so a fatigue-party went down and carried back a supply to us in their arms – loaves, a barrel of rum, packets of tea, and joints of meat – abundance for all; but there was not a kettle or a cooking-pot in the regiment, and we could not eat the meat raw. The colonel and officers were no better off. They had arranged to have a regular mess, with crockery, steward, and all complete, but the establishment never turned up, and what had become of it no one knew.

Some of us were sent back into the town to see what we could procure in the way of cooking utensils. We found the street full of artillery, baggage-waggons, and mounted officers, and volunteers shopping like ourselves; and all the houses appeared to be occupied by troops. We succeeded in getting a few kettles and saucepans, and I obtained for myself a leather bag, with a strap to go over the shoulder, which proved very handy afterwards; and thus laden, we trudged back to our camp on the hill, filling the kettles with dirty water from a little stream which runs between the hill and the town, for there was none to be had above. It was nearly a couple of miles each way; and, exhausted as we were with marching and want of rest, we were almost too tired to eat. The cooking was of the roughest, as you may suppose; all we could do was to cut off slices of the meat and boil them in the saucepans, using our fingers for forks. The tea, however, was very refreshing; and, thirsty as we were, we drank it by the gallon.

Just before it grew dark, the brigade-major came round, and, with the adjutant, showed our colonel how to set a picket in advance of our line a little way down the face of the hill. It was not necessary to place one, I suppose, because the town in our front was still occupied with troops; but no doubt the practice would be useful. We had also a quarter-guard, and a line of sentries in front and rear of our line, communicating with those of the regiments on our flanks. Firewood was plentiful, for the hill was covered with beautiful wood; but it took some time to collect it, for we had nothing but our pocket-knives to cut down the branches with.

So we lay down to sleep. My company had no duty, and we had the night undisturbed to ourselves; but, tired though I was, the excitement and the novelty of the situation made sleep difficult. And although the night was still and warm, and we were sheltered by the woods, I soon found it chilly with no better covering than my thin dust-coat, the more so as my clothes, saturated with perspiration during the day, had never dried; and before daylight I woke from a short nap, shivering with cold, and was glad to get warm with others by a fire. I then noticed that the opposite hills on the south were dotted with fires; and we thought at first they must belong to the enemy, but we were told that the ground up there was still held by a strong rear-guard of regulars, and that there need be no fear of a surprise.

At the first sign of dawn the bugles of the regiments sounded the reveillé, and we were ordered to fall in, and the roll was called. About twenty men were absent, who had fallen out sick the day before; they had been sent up to London by train during the night, I believe. After standing in column for about half an hour, the brigademajor came down with orders to pile arms and stand easy; and perhaps half an hour afterwards we were told to get breakfast as quickly as possible, and to cook a day's food at the same time. This operation was managed pretty much in the same way as the evening before, except that we had our cooking pots and kettles ready.

Meantime there was leisure to look around, and from where we stood there was a commanding view of one of the most beautiful scenes in England. Our regiment was drawn up on the extremity of the ridge which runs from Guildford to Dorking. This is indeed merely a part of the great chalk-range which extends from beyond Aldershot east to the Medway; but there is a gap in the ridge just here where the little stream that runs past Dorking turns suddenly to the north, to find its way to the Thames. We stood on the slope of the hill, as it trends down eastward towards this gap, and had passed our bivouac in what appeared to be a gentleman's park. A little way above us, and to our right, was a very fine country-seat to which the part was attached, now occupied by the headquarters of our division. From this house the hill sloped steeply down southward to the valley below, which runs nearly east and west parallel to the ridge, and carries the railway and the road from Guildford to Reigate; and in which valley, immediately in front of the chateau, and perhaps a mile and a half distant from it, was the little town of Dorking, nestled in the trees, and rising up the foot of the slopes on the other side of the valley which stretched away to Leith Common, the scene of yesterday's march.

Thus the main part of the town of Dorking was on our right front, but the suburbs stretched away eastward nearly to our proper front, culminating in a small railway station, from which the grassy slopes of the park rose up dotted with shrubs and trees to where we were standing. Round this railway station was a cluster of villas and one or two mills, of whose gardens we thus had a bird's-eye view, their little ornamental ponds glistening like looking-glasses in the morning sun. Immediately on our left the park sloped steeply down to the gap before mentioned, through which ran the little stream, as well as the railway from Epsom to Brighton, nearly due north and south, meeting the Guildford and Reigate line at right angles. Close to the point of intersection and the little station already mentioned, was the station of the former line where we had stopped the day before. Beyond the gap on the east (our left), and in continuation of our ridge, rose the chalk-hill again. The shoulder of this ridge overlooking the gap is called Box Hill, from the shrubbery of boxwood with which it was covered. Its sides were very steep, and the top of the ridge was covered with troops.

The natural strength of our position was manifested at a glance; a high grassy ridge steep to the south, with a stream in front, and but little cover up the sides. It seemed made for a battle-field. The weak point was the gap; the ground at the junction of the railways and the roads immediately at the entrance of the gap formed a little valley, dotted, as I have said, with buildings and gardens. This, in one sense, was the key of the position; for although it would not be tenable while we held the ridge commanding it, the enemy by carrying this point and advancing through the gap would cut our line in two. But you must not suppose I scanned the ground thus critically at the time.

Anybody, indeed, might have been struck with the natural advantages of our position; but what, as I remember, most impressed me, was the peaceful beauty of the scene – the little town with the outline of the houses obscured by a blue mist, the massive crispness of the foliage, the outlines of the great trees, lighted up by the sun, and relieved by deep-blue shade. So thick was the timber here, rising up the southern slopes of the valley, that it looked almost as if it might have been a primeval forest. The quiet of the scene was the more impressive because contrasted in the mind with the scenes we expected to follow; and I can remember, as if it were yesterday, the sensation of bitter regret that it should now be too late to avert this coming desecration of our country, which might so easily have been prevented. A little firmness, a little prevision on the part of our rulers, even a little common-sense, and this great calamity would have been rendered utterly impossible. Too late, alas! We were like the foolish virgins in the parable.

But you must not suppose the scene immediately around was gloomy: the camp was brisk and bustling enough. We had got over the stress of weariness; our stomachs were full; we felt a natural enthusiasm at the prospect of having so soon to take a part as the real defenders of the country, and we were inspirited at the sight of the large force that was now assembled. Along the slopes which trended off to the rear of our ridge, troops came marching up – volunteers, militia, cavalry, and guns; these, I heard, had come down from the north as far as Leatherhead the night before, and had marched over at daybreak. Long trains, too, began to arrive by the rail through the gap, one after the other, containing militia and volunteers, who moved up to the ridge to the right and left, and took up their position, massed for the most part on the slopes which ran up from, and in rear of, where we stood. We now formed part of an army corps, we were told, consisting of three divisions, but what regiments composed the other two divisions I never heard.

All this movement we could distinctly see from our position, for we had hurried over our breakfast, expecting every minute that the battle would begin, and now stood or sat about on the ground near our piled arms. Early in the morning, too, we saw a very long train come along the valley from the direction of Guildford, full of redcoats. It halted at the little station at our feet, and the troops alighted. We could soon make out their bear-skins. They were the Guards, coming to reinforce this part of the line. Leaving a detachment of skirmishers to hold the line of the railway embankment, the main body marched up with a springy step and with the band playing, and drew up across the gap on our left, in prolongation of our line. There appeared to be three battalions of them, for they formed up in that number of columns at short intervals.

Shortly after this I was sent over to Box Hill with a message from our colonel to the colonel of a volunteer regiment stationed there, to know whether an ambulance-cart was obtainable, as it was reported this regiment was well supplied with carriage, whereas we were without any: my mission, however, was futile. Crossing the valley, I found a scene of great confusion at the railway station. Trains were still coming in with stores, ammunition, guns, and appliances of all sorts, which were being unloaded as fast as possible; but there were scarcely any means of getting the things off. There were plenty of waggons of all sorts, but hardly any horses to draw them, and the whole place was blocked up; while, to add to the confusion, a regular exodus had taken place of the people from the town, who had been warned that it was likely to be the scene of fighting. Ladies and women of all sorts and ages, and children, some with bundles, some empty-handed, were seeking places in the train, but there appeared no one on the spot authorised to grant them, and these poor creatures were pushing their way up and down, vainly asking for information and permission to get away.

In the crowd I observed our surgeon, who likewise was in search of an ambulance of some sort: his whole professional apparatus, he said, consisted of a case of instruments. Also in the crowd I stumbled upon Wood, Travers's old coachman. He had been sent down by his mistress to Guildford, because it was supposed our regiment had gone there, riding the horse, and laden with a supply of things – food, blankets, and, of course, a letter. He had also brought my knapsack; but at Guildford the horse was pressed for artillery work, and a receipt for it given him in exchange, so he had been obliged to leave all the heavy packages there, including my knapsack; but the faithful old man had brought on as many things as he could carry, and hearing that we should be found in this part, had walked over thus laden from Guildford. He said that place was crowded with troops, and that the heights were lined with them the whole way between the two towns; also, that some trains with wounded had passed up from the coast in the night, through Guildford. I led him off to where our regiment was, relieving the old man from part of the load he was staggering under.

The food sent was not now so much needed, but the plates, knives, and drinking-vessels, promised to be handy – and Travers, you may be sure, was delighted to get his letter; while a couple of newspapers the old man had brought were eagerly competed for by all, even at this critical moment, for we had heard no authentic news since we left London on Sunday. And even at this distance of time, although I only glanced down the paper, I can remember almost the very words I read there. They were both copies of the same paper: the first, published on Sunday evening, when the news had arrived of the successful landing at three points, was written in a tone of despair. The country must confess that it had been taken by surprise. The conqueror would be satisfied with the humiliation inflicted by a peace dictated on our own shores; it was the clear duty of the Government to accept the best terms obtainable, and to avoid further bloodshed and disaster, and avert the fall of our tottering mercantile credit.

The next morning's issue was in quite a different tone. Apparently the enemy had received a check, for we were here exhorted to resistance. An impregnable position was to be taken up along the Downs, a force was concentrating there far outnumbering the rash invaders, who, with an invincible line before them, and the sea behind, had no choice between destruction or surrender. Let there be no pusillanimous talk of negotation, the fight must be fought out; and there could be but one issue. England, expectant but calm, awaited with confidence the result of the attack on its unconquerable volunteers. The writing appeared to me eloquent, but rather inconsistent. The same paper said the Government had sent off 500 workmen from Woolwich, to open a branch arsenal at Birmingham.

All this time we had nothing to do, except to change our position, which we did every few minutes, now moving up the hill farther to our right, now taking ground lower down to our left, as one order after another was brought down the line; but the staff-officers were galloping about perpetually with orders, while the rumble of the artillery as they moved about from one part of the field to another went on almost incessantly. At last the whole line stood to arms, the bands struck up, and the general commanding our army corps came riding down with his staff. We had seen him several times before, as we had been moving frequently about the position during the morning; but he now made a sort of formal inspection. He was a tall thin man, with long light hair, very well mounted, and as he sat his horse with an erect seat, and came prancing down the line, at a little distance he looked as if he might be five-and-twenty; but I believe he had served more than fifty years, and had been made a peer for services performed when quite an old man. I remember that he had more decorations than there was room for on the breast of his coat, and wore them suspended like a necklace round his neck. Like all the other generals, he was dressed in blue, with a cocked-hat and feathers – a bad plan, I thought, for it made them very conspicuous.

The general halted before our battalion, and after looking at us a while, made a short address: We had a post of honour next her Majesty's Guards, and would show ourselves worthy of it, and of the name of Englishmen. It did not need, he said, to be a general to see the strength of our position; it was impregnable, if properly held. Let us wait till the enemy was well pounded, and then the word would be given to go at him. Above everything, we must be steady. He then shook hands with our colonel, we gave him a cheer, and he rode on to where the Guards were drawn up.

Now then, we thought, the battle will begin. But still there were no signs of the enemy; and the air, though hot and sultry, began to be very hazy, so that you could scarcely see the town below, and the hills opposite were merely a confused blur, in which no features could be distinctly made out. After a while, the tension of feeling which followed the general's address relaxed, and we began to feel less as if everything depended on keeping our rifles firmly grasped: we were told to pile arms again, and got leave to go down by tens and twenties to the stream below to drink. This stream, and all the hedges and banks on our side of it, were held by our skirmishers, but the town had been abandoned. The position appeared an excellent one, except that the enemy, when they came, would have almost better cover than our men.

While I was down at the brook, a column emerged from the town, making for our position. We thought for a moment it was the enemy, and you could not make out the colour of the uniforms for the dust; but it turned out to be our rearguard, falling back from the opposite hills which they had occupied the previous night. One battalion, of rifles, halted for a few minutes at the stream to let the men drink, and I had a minute's talk with a couple of the officers. They had formed part of the force which had attacked the enemy on their first landing. They had it all their own way, they said, at first, and could have beaten the enemy back easily if they had been properly supported; but the whole thing was mismanaged. The volunteers came on very pluckily, they said, but they got into confusion, and so did the militia, and the attack failed with serious loss. It was the wounded of this force which had passed through Guildford in the night. The officers asked us eagerly about the arrangements for the battle, and when we said that the Guards were the only regular troops in this part of the field, shook their heads ominously.

While we were talking, a third officer came up; he was a dark man with a smooth face and a curious excited manner. "You are volunteers, I suppose," he said, quickly, his eye flashing the while. "Well, now, look here; mind I don't want to hurt your feelings, or to say anything unpleasant, but I'll tell you what; if all you gentlemen were just to go back, and leave us to fight it out alone, it would be a devilish good thing. We could do it a precious deal better without you, I assure you. We don't want your help, I can tell you. We would much rather be left alone, I assure you. Mind I don't want to say anything rude, but that's a fact." Having blurted out this passionately, he strode away before any one could reply, or the other officers could stop him. They apologised for his rudeness, saying that his brother, also in the regiment, had been killed on Sunday, and that this, and the sun, and marching, had affected his head.

The officers told us that the enemy's advanced-guard was close behind, but that he had apparently been waiting for reinforcements, and would probably not attack in force until noon. It was, however, nearly three o'clock before the battle began. We had almost worn out the feeling of expectancy. For twelve hours had we been waiting for the coming struggle, till at last it seemed almost as if the invasion were but a bad dream, and the enemy, as yet unseen by us, had no real existence. So far things had not been very different, but for the numbers and for what we had been told, from a Volunteer review on Brighton Downs. I remember that these thoughts were passing through my mind as we lay down in groups on the grass, some smoking, some nibbling at their bread, some even asleep, when the listless state we had fallen into was suddenly disturbed by a gunshot fired from the top of the hill on our right, close by the big house. It was the first time I had ever heard a shotted gun fired, and although it is fifty years ago, the angry whistle of the shot as it left the gun is in my ears now. The sound was soon to become common enough.

We all jumped up at the report, and fell in almost without the word being given, grasping our rifles tightly, and the leading files peering forward to look for the approaching enemy. This gun was apparently the signal to begin, for now our batteries opened fire all along the line. What they were firing at I could not see, and I am sure the gunners could not see much themselves. I have told you what a haze had come over the air since the morning, and now the smoke from the guns settled like a pall over the hill, and soon we could see little but the men in our ranks, and the outline of some gunners in the battery drawn up next us on the slope on our right. This firing went on, I should think, for nearly a couple of hours, and still there was no reply. We could see the gunners – it was a troop of horse-artillery – working away like fury, ramming, loading, and running up with cartridges, the officer in command riding slowly up and down just behind his guns, and peering out with his field-glass into the mist. Once or twice they ceased firing to let their smoke clear away, but this did not do much good.

For nearly two hours did this go on, and not a shot came in reply. If a battle is like this, said Dick Wake, who was my next-hand file, it's mild work, to say the least. The words were hardly uttered when a rattle of musketry was heard in front; our skirmishers were at it, and very soon the bullets began to sing over our heads, and some struck the ground at our feet. Up to this time we had been in column; we were now deployed into line on the ground assigned to us. From the valley or gap on our left there ran a lane right up the hill almost due west, or along our front. This lane had a thick bank about four feet high, and the greater part of the regiment was drawn up behind it; but a little way up the hill the lane trended back out of the line, so the right of the regiment here left it and occupied the open grass-land of the park. The bank had been cut away at this point to admit of our going in and out.

We had been told in the morning to cut down the bushes on the top of the bank, so as to make the space clear for firing over, but we had no tools to work with; however, a party of sappers had come down and finished the job. My company was on the right, and was thus beyond the shelter of the friendly bank. On our right again was the battery of artillery already mentioned; then came a battalion of the line, then more guns, then a great mass of militia and volunteers and a few line up to the big house. At least this was the order before the firing began; after that I do not know what changes took place.

And now the enemy's artillery began to open; where their guns were posted we could not see, but we began to hear the rush of the shells over our heads, and the bang as they burst just beyond. And now what took place I can really hardly tell you. Sometimes when I try and recall the scene, it seems as if it lasted for only a few minutes; yet I know, as we lay on the ground, I thought the hours would never pass away, as we watched the gunners still plying their task, firing at the invisible enemy, never stopping for a moment except when now and again a dull blow would be heard and a man fall down, then three or four of his comrades would carry him to the rear. The captain no longer rode up and down; what had become of him I do not know. Two of the guns ceased firing for a time; they had got injured in some way, and up rode an artillery general. I think I see him now, a very handsome man, with straight features and a dark mustache, his breast covered with medals. He appeared in a great rage at the guns stopping fire.

"Who commands this battery?" he cried.

"I do, Sir Henry," said an officer, riding forward, whom I had not noticed before.

The group is before me at this moment, standing out clear against the background of smoke, Sir Henry erect on his splendid charger, his flashing eye, his left arm pointing towards the enemy to enforce something he was going to say, the young officer reining in his horse just beside him, and saluting with his right hand raised to his busby. This for a moment, then a dull thud, and both horses and riders are prostrate on the ground. A round-shot had struck all four at the saddle-line. Some of the gunners ran up to help, but neither officer could have lived many minutes.

This was not the first I saw killed. Some time before this, almost immediately on the enemy's artillery opening, as we were lying, I heard something like the sound of metal striking metal, and at the same moment Dick Wake, who was next me in the ranks, leaning on his elbows, sank forward on his face. I looked round and saw what had happened; a shot fired at a high elevation, passing over his head, had struck the ground behind, nearly cutting his thigh off. It must have been the ball striking his sheathed bayonet which made the noise. Three of us carried the poor fellow to the rear, with difficulty for the shattered limb; but he was nearly dead from loss of blood when we got to the doctor, who was waiting in a sheltered hollow about two hundred yards in rear, with two other doctors in plain clothes, who had come up to help. We desposited our burden and returned to the front. Poor Wake was sensible when we left him, but apparently too shaken by the shock to be able to speak. Wood was there helping the doctors. I paid more visits to the rear of the same sort before the evening was over.

All this time we were lying there to be fired at without returning a shot, for our skirmishers were holding the line of walls and enclosures below. However, the bank protected most of us, and the brigadier now ordered our right company, which was in the open, to get behind it also; and there we lay about four deep, the shells crashing and bullets whistling over our heads, but hardly a man being touched. Our colonel was, indeed, the only one exposed, for he rode up and down the lane at a footpace as steady as a rock; but he made the major and adjutant dismount, and take shelter behind the hedge, holding their horses. We were all pleased to see him so cool, and it restored our confidence in him, which had been shaken yesterday.

The time seemed interminable while we lay thus inactive. We could not, of course, help peering over the bank to try and see what was going on; but there was nothing to be made out, for now a tremendous thunderstorm, which had been gathering all day, burst on us, and a torrent of almost blinding rain came down, which obscured the view even more than the smoke, while the crashing of the thunder and the glare of the lightning could be heard and seen even above the roar and flashing of the artillery. Once the mist lifted, and I saw for a minute an attack on Box Hill, on the other side of the gap on our left. It was like the scene at a theatre – a curtain of smoke all round and a clear gap in the centre, with a sudden gleam of evening sunshine lighting it up. The steep smooth slope of the hill was crowded with the dark-blue figures of the enemy, whom I now saw for the first time – an irregular outline in front, but very solid in rear: the whole body was moving forward by fits and starts, the men firing and advancing, the officers waving their swords, the columns closing up and gradually making way.

Our people were almost concealed by the bushes at the top, whence the smoke and their fire could be seen proceeding: presently from these bushes on the crest came out a red line, and dashed down the brow of the hill, a flame of fire belching out from the front as it advanced. The enemy hesitated, gave way, and finally ran back in a confused crowd down the hill. Then the mist covered the scene, but the glimpse of this splendid charge was inspiriting, and I hoped we should show the same coolness when it came to our turn. It was about this time that our skirmishers fell back, a good many wounded, some limping along by themselves, others helped. The main body retired in very fair order, halting to turn round and fire; we could see a mounted officer of the Guards riding up and down encouraging them to be steady.

Now came our turn. For a few minutes we saw nothing, but a rattle of bullets came through the rain and mist, mostly, however, passing over the bank. We began to fire in reply, stepping up against the bank to fire, and stooping down to load; but our brigade-major rode up with an order, and the word was passed through the men to reserve our fire. In a very few moments it must have been that, when ordered to stand up, we could see the helmet-spikes and then the figures of the skirmishers as they came on: a lot of them there appeared to be, five or six deep I should say, but in loose order, each man stopping to aim and fire, and then coming forward a little. Just then the brigadier clattered on horseback up the lane. "Now, then, gentlemen, give it them hot!" he cried; and fire away we did, as fast as ever we were able. A perfect storm of bullets seemed to be flying about us too, and I thought each moment must be the last; escape seemed impossible, but I saw no one fall, for I was too busy, and so were we all, to look to the right or left, but loaded and fired as fast as we could.

How long this went on I know not – it could not have been long; neither side could have lasted many minutes under such a fire, but it ended by the enemy gradually falling back, and as soon as we saw this we raised a tremendous shout, and some of us jumped up on the bank to give them our parting shots. Suddenly the order was passed down the line to cease firing, and we soon discovered the cause; a battalion of the Guards was charging obliquely across from our left across our front. It was, I expect, their flank attack as much as our fire which had turned back the enemy; and it was a splendid sight to see their steady line as they advanced slowly across the smooth lawn below us, firing as they went, but as steady as if on parade. We felt a great elation at this moment; it seemed as if the battle was won.

Just then somebody called out to look to the wounded, and for the first time I turned to glance down the rank along the lane. Then I saw that we had not beaten back the attack without loss. Immediately before me lay Bob Lawford of my office, dead on his back from a bullet through his forehead, his hand still grasping his rifle. At every step was some friend or acquaintance killed or wounded, and a few paces down the lane I found Travers, sitting with his back against the bank. A ball had gone through his lungs, and blood was coming from his mouth. I was lifting him up, but the cry of agony he gave stopped me. I then saw that this was not his only wound; his thigh was smashed by a bullet (which must have hit him when standing on the bank), and the blood streaming down mixed in a muddy puddle with the rain-water under him.

Still he could not be left here, so, lifting him up as well as I could, I carried him through the gate which led out of the lane at the back to where our camp hospital was in the rear. The movement must have caused him awful agony, for I could not support the broken thigh, and he could not restrain his groans, brave fellow though he was; but how I carried him at all I cannot make out, for he was a much bigger man than myself; but I had not gone far, one of a stream of our fellows, all on the same errand, when a bandsman and Wood met me, bringing a hurdle as a stretcher, and on this we placed him.

Wood had just time to tell me that he had got a cart down in the hollow, and would endeavour to take off his master at once to Kingston, when a staff-officer rode up to call us to the ranks. "You really must not straggle in this way, gentlemen," he said; "pray keep your ranks." "But we can't leave our wounded to be trodden down and die," cried one of our fellows. "Beat off the enemy first, sir," he replied. "Gentlemen, do, pray, join your regiments, or we shall be a regular mob."

And no doubt he did not speak too soon; for besides our fellows straggling to the rear, lots of volunteers from the regiments in reserve were running forward to help, till the whole ground was dotted with groups of men. I hastened back to my post, but I had just time to notice that all the ground in our rear was occupied by a thick mass of troops, much more numerous than in the morning, and a column was moving down to the left of our line, to the ground before held by the Guards.

All this time, although the musketry had slackened, the artillery-fire seemed heavier than ever; the shells screamed overhead or burst around; and I confess to feeling quite a relief at getting back to the friendly shelter of the lane. Looking over the bank, I noticed for the first time the frightful execution our fire had created. The space in front was thickly strewed with dead and badly wounded, and beyond the bodies of the fallen enemy could just be seen – for it was now getting dusk – the bear-skins and red coats of our own gallant Guards scattered over the slope, and marking the line of their victorious advance.

But hardly a minute could have passed in thus looking over the field, when our brigade-major came moving up the lane on foot (I suppose his horse had been shot), crying, "Stand to your arms, volunteers! They're coming on again;" and we found ourselves a second time engaged in a hot musketry-fire. How long it went on I cannot now remember, but we could distinguish clearly the thick line of skirmishers, about sixty paces off, and mounted officers among them; and we seemed to be keeping them well in check, for they were quite exposed to our fire, while we were protected nearly up to our shoulders, when – I know not how – I became sensible that something had gone wrong.

"We are taken in flank!" called out some one; and looking along the left, sure enough there were dark figures jumping over the bank into the lane and firing up along our line. The volunteers in reserve, who had come down to take the place of the Guards, must have given way at this point; the enemy's skirmishers had got through our line, and turned our left flank. How the next move came about I cannot recollect, or whether it was without orders, but in a short time we found ourselves out of the lane, and drawn up in a straggling line about thirty yards in rear of it – at our end, that is, the other flank had fallen back a good deal more – and the enemy were lining the hedge, and numbers of them passing over and forming up on our side. Beyond our left a confused mass were retreating, firing as they went, followed by the advancing line of the enemy.

We stood in this way for a short space, firing at random as fast as we could. Our colonel and major must have been shot, for there was no one to give an order, when somebody on horseback called out from behind – I think it must have been the brigadier – "Now, then, volunteers! Give a British cheer, and go at them – charge!" and, with a shout, we rushed at the enemy. Some of them ran, some stopped to meet us, and for a moment it was a real hand-to-hand fight. I felt a sharp sting in my leg, as I drove my bayonet right through the man in front of me. I confess I shut my eyes, for I just got a glimpse of the poor wretch as he fell back, his eyes starting out of his head, and, savage though we were, the sight was almost too horrible to look at. But the struggle was over in a second, and we had cleared the ground again right up to the rear hedge of the lane.

Had we gone on, I believe we might have recovered the lane too, but we were now all out of order; there was no one to say what to do; the enemy began to line the hedge and open fire, and they were streaming past our left; and how it came about I know not, but we found ourselves falling back towards our right rear, scarce any semblance of a line remaining, and the volunteers who had given way on our left mixed up with us, and adding to the confusion.

It was now nearly dark. On the slopes which we were retreating to was a large mass of reserves drawn up in columns. Some of the leading files of these, mistaking us for the enemy, began firing at us; our fellows, crying out to them to stop, ran towards their ranks, and in a few moments the whole slope of the hill became a scene of confusion that I cannot attempt to describe, regiments and detachments mixed up in hopeless disorder. Most of us, I believe, turned towards the enemy and fired away our few remaining cartridges; but it was too late to take aim, fortunately for us, or the guns which the enemy had brought up through the gap, and were firing point-blank, would have done more damage. As it was, we could see little more than the bright flashes of their fire. In our confusion we had jammed up a line regiment immediately behind us, which I suppose had just arrived on the field, and its colonel and some staff-officers were in vain trying to make a passage for it, and their shouts to us to march to the rear and clear a road could be heard above the roar of the guns and the confused babel of sound.

At last a mounted officer pushed his way through, followed by a company in sections, the men brushing past with firm-set faces, as if on a desperate task; and the battalion, when it got clear, appeared to deploy and advance down the slope. I have also a dim recollection of seeing the Life Guards trot past the front, and push on towards the town – a last desperate attempt to save the day – before we left the field. Our adjutant, who had got separated from our flank of the regiment in the confusion, now came up, and managed to lead us, or at any rate some of us, up to the crest of the hill in the rear, to re-form, as he said; but there we met a vast crowd of volunteers, militia, and waggons, all hurrying rearward from the direction of the big house, and we were borne in the stream for a mile at least before it was possible to stop.

At last the adjutant led us to an open space a little off the line of fugitives, and there we re-formed the remains of the companies. Telling us to halt, he rode off to try and obtain orders, and find out where the rest of our brigade was. From this point, a spur of high ground running off from the main plateau, we looked down through the dim twilight into the battle-field below. Artillery-fire was still going on. We could see the flashes from the guns on both sides, and now and then a stray shell came screaming up and burst near us, but we were beyond the sound of musketry.

This halt first gave us time to think about what had happened. The long day of expectancy had been succeeded by the excitement of battle; and when each minute may be your last, you do not think much about other people, nor when you are facing another man with a rifle have you time to consider whether he or you are the invader, or that you are fighting for your home and hearths. All fighting is pretty much alike, I suspect, as to sentiment, when once it begins. But now we had time for reflection; and although we did not yet quite understand how far the day had gone against us, an uneasy feeling of self-condemnation must have come up in the minds of most of us; while, above all, we now began to realise what the loss of this battle meant to the country. Then, too, we knew not what had become of all our wounded comrades. Reaction, too, set in after the fatigue and excitement. For myself, I had found out for the first time that beside the bayonet-wound in my leg, a bullet had gone through my left arm, just below the shoulder, and outside the bone. I remember feeling something like a blow just when we lost the lane, but the wound passed unnoticed till now, when the bleeding had stopped and the shirt was sticking to the wound.

This half-hour seemed an age, and while we stood on this knoll the endless tramp of men and rumbling of carts along the downs besides us told their own tale. The whole army was falling back. At last we could discern the adjutant riding up to us out of the dark. The army was to retreat and take up a position on Epsom Downs, he said; we should join in the march, and try and find our brigade in the morning; and so we turned into the throng again, and made our way on as best we could.

A few scraps of news he gave us as he rode alongside of our leading section; the army had held its position well for a time, but the enemy had at last broken through the line between us and Guildford, as well as in our front, and had poured his men through the point gained, throwing the line into confusion, and the first army corps near Guildford were also falling back to avoid being outflanked. The regular troops were holding the rear; we were to push on as fast as possible to get out of their way, and allow them to make an orderly retreat in the morning. The gallant old lord commanding our corps had been badly wounded early in the day, he heard, and carried off the field. The Guards had suffered dreadfully; the household cavalry had ridden down the cuirassiers, but had got into broken ground and been awfully cut up. Such were the scraps of news passed down our weary column. What had become of our wounded no one knew, and no one liked to ask. So we trudged on.

It must have been midnight when we reached Leatherhead. Here we left the open ground and took to the road, and the block became greater. We pushed our way painfully along; several trains passed slowly ahead along the railway by the roadside, containing the wounded, we supposed – such of them, at least, as were lucky enough to be picked up. It was daylight when we got to Epsom. The night had been bright and clear after the storm, with a cool air, which, blowing through my soaking clothes, chilled me to the bone. My wounded leg was stiff and sore, and I was ready to drop with exhaustion and hunger. Nor were my comrades in much better case; we had eaten nothing since breakfast the day before, and the bread we had put by had been washed away by the storm: only a little pulp remained at the bottom of my bag. The tobacco was all too wet to smoke. In this plight we were creeping along, when the adjutant guided us into a field by the roadside to rest awhile, and we lay down exhausted on the sloppy grass. The roll was here taken, and only 180 answered out of nearly 500 present on the morning of the battle. How many of these were killed and wounded no one could tell; but it was certain many must have got separated in the confusion of the evening.

While resting here, we saw pass by, in the crowd of vehicles and men, a cart laden with commissariat stores, driven by a man in uniform. "Food!" cried some one, and a dozen volunteers jumped up and surrounded the cart. The driver tried to whip them off; but he was pulled off his seat, and the contents of the cart thrown out in an instant. They were preserved meats in tins, which we tore open with our bayonets. The meat had been cooked before, I think; at any rate we devoured it.

Shortly after this a general came by with three or four staff-officers. He stopped and spoke to our adjutant, and then rode into the field. "My lads," said he, "you shall join my division for the present: fall in, and follow the regiment that is now passing." We rose up, fell in by companies, each about twenty strong, and turned once more into the stream moving along the road; – regiments' detachments, single volunteers or militiamen, country people making off, some with bundles, some without, a few in carts, but most on foot; here and there waggons of stores, with men sitting wherever there was room, others crammed with wounded soldiers. Many blocks occurred from horses falling, or carts breaking down and filing up the road.

In the town the confusion was even worse, for all the houses seemed full of volunteers and militiamen, wounded or resting, or trying to find food, and the streets were almost choked up. Some officers were in vain trying to restore order, but the task seemed a hopeless one. One or two volunteer regiments which had arrived from the north the previous night, and had been halted here for orders, were drawn up along the roadside steadily enough, and some of the retreating regiments, including ours, may have preserved the semblance of discipline, but for the most part the mass pushing to the rear was a mere mob. The regulars, or what remained of them, were now, I believe, all in the rear, to hold the advancing enemy in check. A few officers among such a crowd could do nothing.

To add to the confusion, several houses were being emptied of the wounded brought here the night before, to prevent their falling into the hands of the enemy, some in carts, some being carried to the railway by men. The groans of these poor fellows as they were jostled through the street went to our hearts, selfish though fatigue and suffering had made us.

At last, following the guidance of a staff-officer who was standing to show the way, we turned off from the main London road and took that towards Kingston. Here the crush was less, and we managed to move along pretty steadily. The air had been cooled by the storm, and there was no dust. We passed through a village where our new general had seized all the public-houses, and taken possession of the liquor; and each regiment as it came up was halted, and each man got a drink of beer, served out by companies. Whether the owner got paid, I know not, but it was like nectar.

It must have been about one o'clock in the afternoon that we came in sight of Kingston. We had been on our legs sixteen hours, and had got over about twelve miles of ground. There is a hill a little south of the Surbiton station, covered then mostly with villas, but open at the western extremity, where there was a clump of trees on the summit. We had diverged from the road towards this, and here the general halted us and disposed the line of the division along his front, facing to the south-west, the right of the line reaching down to the water-works on the Thames, the left extending along the southern slope of the hill, in the direction of the Epsom road by which we had come. We were nearly in the centre, occupying the knoll just in front of the general, who dismounted on the top and tied his horse to a tree. It is not much of a hill, but commands an extensive view over the flat country around; and as we lay wearily on the ground we could see the Thames glistening like a silver field in the bright sunshine, the palace at Hampton Court, the bridge at Kingston, and the old church tower rising above the haze of the town, with the woods of Richmond Park behind it.

To most of us the scene could not but call up the associations of happy days of peace – days now ended and peace destroyed through national infatuation. We did not say this to each other, but a deep depression had come upon us, partly due to weakness and fatigue, no doubt, but we saw that another stand was going to be made, and we had no longer any confidence in ourselves. If we could not hold our own when stationary in line, on a good position, but had been broken up into a rabble at the first shock, what chance had we now of manoeuvring against a victorious enemy in this open ground? A feeling of desperation came over us, a determination to struggle on against hope; but anxiety for the future of the country, and our friends, and all dear to us, filled our thoughts now that we had time for reflection. We had had no news of any kind since Wood joined us the day before – we knew not what was doing in London, or what the Government was about, or anything else; and exhausted though we were, we felt an intense craving to know what was happening in other parts of the country.

Our general had expected to find a supply of food and ammunition here, but nothing turned up. Most of us had hardly a cartridge left, so he ordered the regiment next to us, which came from the north and had not been engaged, to give us enough to make up twenty rounds a man, and he sent off a fatigue-party to Kingston to try and get provisions, while a detachment of our fellows was allowed to go foraging among the villas in our rear; and in about an hour they brought back some bread and meat, which gave us a slender meal all round. They said most of the houses were empty, and that many had been stripped of all eatables, and a good deal damaged already.

It must have been between three and four o'clock when the sound of cannonading began to be heard in the front, and we could see the smoke of the guns rising above the woods of Esher and Claremont, and soon afterwards some troops emerged from the fields below us. It was the rear-guard of regular troops. There were some guns also, which were driven up the slope and took up their position round the knoll. There were three batteries, but they only counted eight guns amongst them. Behind them was posted the line; it was a brigade apparently of four regiments, but the whole did not look to be more than eight or nine hundred men. Our regiment and another had been moved a little to the rear to make way for them, and presently we were ordered down to occupy the railway station on our right rear.

My leg was now so stiff I could no longer march with the rest, and my left arm was very swollen and sore, and almost useless; but anything seemed better than being left behind, so I limped after the battalion as best I could down to the station. There was a goods shed a little in advance of it down the line, a strong brick building, and here my company was posted. The rest of our men lined the wall of the enclosure. A staff-officer came with us to arrange the distribution; we should be supported by line troops, he said; and in few minutes a train full of them came slowly up from Guildford way. It was the last; the men got out, the train passed on, and a party began to tear up the rails, while the rest were distributed among the houses on each side. A sergeant's party joined us in our shed, and an engineer officer with sappers came to knock holes in the walls for us to fire from; but there were only half-a-dozen of them, so progress was not rapid, and as we had no tools we could not help.

It was while we were watching this job that the adjutant, who was as active as ever, looked in, and told us to muster in the yard. The fatigue-party had come back from Kingston, and a small baker's hand-cart of food was made over to us as our share. It contained loaves, flour, and some joints of meat. The meat and the flour we had not time or means to cook. The loaves we devoured; and there was a tap of water in the yard, so we felt refreshed by the meal. I should have liked to wash my wounds, which were becoming very offensive, but I dared not take off my coat, feeling sure I should not be able to get it on again. It was while we were eating our bread that the rumour first reached us of another disaster, even greater than that we had witnessed ourselves. Whence it came I know not; but a whisper went down the ranks that Woolwich had been captured. We all knew that it was our only arsenal, and understood the significance of the blow. No hope, if this were true, of saving the country. Thinking over this, we went back to the shed.

Although this was only our second day of war, I think we were already old soldiers so far that we had come to be careless about fire, and the shot and shell that now began to open on us made no sensation. We felt, indeed, our need of discipline, and we saw plainly enough the slender chance of success coming out of troops so imperfectly trained as we were; but I think we were all determined to fight on as long as we could. Our gallant adjutant gave his spirit to everybody; and the staff-officer commanding was a very cheery fellow, and went about as if we were certain of victory. Just as the firing began he looked in to say that we were as safe as in a church, that we must be sure and pepper the enemy well, and that more cartridges would soon arrive.

There were some steps and benches in the shed, and on these a part of our men were standing, to fire through the upper loop-holes, while the line soldiers and others stood on the ground, guarding the second row. I sat on the floor, for I could not now use my rifle, and besides, there were more men than loop-holes. The artillery fire which had opened now on our position was from a longish range; and occupation for the riflemen had hardly begun when there was a crash in the shed, and I was knocked down by a blow on the head. I was almost stunned for a time, and could not make out at first what had happened. A shot or shell had hit the shed without quite penetrating the wall, but the blow had upset the steps resting against it, and the men standing on them, bringing down a cloud of plaster and brickbats, one of which had struck me.

I felt now past being of use. I could not use my rifle, and could barely stand; and after a time I thought I would make for my own house, on the chance of finding some one still there. I got up therefore, and staggered homewards. Musketry fire had now commenced, and our side were blazing away from the windows of the houses, and from behind walls, and from the shelter of some trucks still standing in the station. A couple of field-pieces in the yard were firing, and in the open space in rear of the station a reserve was drawn up. There, too, was the staff-officer on horseback, watching the fight through his field-glass. I remember having still enough sense to feel that the position was a hopeless one. That straggling line of houses and gardens would surely be broken through at some point, and then the line must give way like a rope of sand.

It was about a mile to our house, and I was thinking how I could possibly drag myself so far when I suddenly recollected that I was passing Travers's house – one of the first of a row of villas then leading from the Surbiton station to Kingston. Had he been brought home,

I wonder, as his faithful old servant promised, and was his wife still here? I remember to this day the sensation of shame I felt, when I recollected that I had not once given him – my greatest friend – a thought since I carried him off the field the day before. But war and suffering make men selfish. I would go in now at any rate and rest awhile, and see if I could be of use.

The little garden before the house was as trim as ever – I used to pass it every day on my way to the train, and knew every shrub in it – and ablaze with flowers, but the hall-door stood ajar. I stepped in and saw little Arthur standing in the hall. He had been dressed as neatly as ever that day, and as he stood there in his pretty blue frock and white trousers and socks showing his chubby little legs, with his golden locks, fair face, and large dark eyes, the picture of childish beauty, in the quiet hall, just as it used to look – the vases of flowers, the hat and coats hanging up, the familiar pictures on the walls – this vision of peace in the midst of war made me wonder for a moment, faint and giddy as I was, if the pandemonium outside had any real existence, and was not merely a hideous dream.

But the roar of the guns making the house shake, and the rushing of the shot, gave a ready answer. The little fellow appeared almost unconscious of the scene around him, and was walking up the stairs holding by the railing, one step at a time, as I had seen him do a hundred times before, but turned round as I came in. My appearance frightened him, and staggering as I did into the hall, my face and clothes covered with blood and dirt, I must have looked an awful object to the child, for he gave a cry and turned to run toward the basement stairs. But he stopped on hearing my voice calling him back to his god-papa, and after a while came timidly up to me. Papa had been to the battle, he said, and was very ill: mamma was with papa: Wood was out: Lucy was in the cellar, and had taken him there, but he wanted to go to mamma.

Telling him to stay in the hall for a minute till I called him, I climbed up-stairs and opened the bedroom-door. My poor friend lay there, his body resting on the bed, his head supported on his wife's shoulder as she sat by the bedside. He breathed heavily, but the pallor of his face, the closed eyes, the prostrate arms, the clammy foam she was wiping from his mouth, all spoke of approaching death. The good old servant had done his duty, at least – he had brought his master home to die in his wife's arms. The poor woman was too intent on her charge to notice the opening of the door, and as the child would be better away, I closed it gently and went down to the hall to take little Arthur to the shelter below, where the maid was hiding. Too late! He lay at the foot of the stairs on his face, his little arms stretched out, his hair dabbled in blood. I had not noticed the crash among the other noises, but a splinter of a shell must have come through the open doorway; it had carried away the back of his head. The poor child's death must have been instantaneous. I tried to lift up the little corpse with my one arm, but even this load was too much for me, and while stooping down I fainted away.

When I came to my senses again it was quite dark, and for some time I could not make out where I was; I lay indeed for some time like one half asleep, feeling no inclination to move. By degrees I became aware that I was on the carpeted floor of a room. All noise of battle had ceased, but there was a sound as of many people close by. At last I sat up and gradually got to my feet. The movement gave me intense pain, for my wounds were now highly inflamed, and my clothes sticking to them made them dreadfully sore.

At last I got up and groped my way to the door, and opening it at once saw where I was, for the pain had brought back my senses. I had been lying in Travers's little writing-room at the end of the passage, into which I made my way. There was no gas, and the drawing-room door was closed; but from the open dining-room the glimmer of a candle feebly lighted up the hall, in which half-a-dozen sleeping figures could be discerned, while the room itself was crowded with men. The table was covered with plates, glasses, and bottles; but most of the men were asleep in the chairs or on the floor, a few were smoking cigars, and one or two with their helmets on were still engaged at supper, occasionally grunting out an observation between the mouthfuls.

"*Sind wackere Soldaten, diese Englischen Freiwilligen*," said a broad-shouldered brute, stuffing a great hunch of beef into his mouth with a silver fork, an implement I should think he must have been using for the first time in his life.

"*Ja, ja*," replied a comrade, who was lolling back in his chair with a pair of very dirty legs on the table, and one of poor Travers's best cigars in his mouth; "*Sie so gat laufen können.*"

"*Ja wohl*," responded the first speaker; "*aber sind nicht eben so schnell wie die Französischen Mobloten.*"

"*Gewiss*," grunted a hulking lout from the floor, leaning on his elbow, and sending out a cloud of smoke from his ugly jaws; "*und da sind hier etwas gute Schützen.*"

"*Hast recht, lange Peter*," answered number one; "*wenn die Schurken so gut exerciren wie schützen könnten, so waren wir heute nicht hier!*"

"*Recht! Recht!*" said the second; "*Das exerciren macht den guten Soldaten.*"

What more criticisms on the shortcomings of our unfortunate volunteers might have passed I did not stop to hear, being interrupted by a sound on the stairs. Mrs. Travers was standing on the landing-place; I limped up the stairs to meet her. Among the many pictures of those fatal days engraven on my memory, I remember none more clearly than the mournful aspect of my poor friend, widowed and childless within a few moments, as she stood there in her white dress, coming forth like a ghost from the chamber of the dead, the candle she held lighting up her face, and contrasting its pallor with the dark hair that fell disordered round it, its beauty radiant even through features worn with fatigue and sorrow. She was calm and even tearless, though the trembling lip told of the effort to restrain the emotion she felt.

"Dear friend," she said, taking my hand, "I was coming to seek you; forgive my selfishness in neglecting you so long; but you will understand" – glancing at the door above – "how occupied I have been."

"Where," I began, "is –" "My boy?" she answered, anticipating my question. "I have laid him by his father. But now your wounds must be cared for; how pale and faint you look! – Rest here a moment," – and, descending to the dining-room, she returned with some wine, which I gratefully drank, and then, making me sit down on the top step of the stairs, she brought water and linen, and cutting off the sleeve of my coat, bathed and bandaged my wounds.

'Twas I who felt selfish for thus adding to her troubles; but in truth I was too weak to have much will left, and stood in need of the help which she forced me to accept; and the dressing of my wounds afforded indescribable relief. While thus tending me, she explained in broken sentences how matters stood. Every room but her own, and the little parlour into which with Wood's help she had carried me, was full of soldiers. Wood had been taken away to work at repairing the railroad, and Lucy had run off from fright; but the cook had stopped at her post, and had served up supper and opened the cellar for the soldiers' use: she herself did not understand what they said, and they were rough and boorish, but not uncivil. I should now go, she said, when my wounds were dressed, to look after my own home, where I might be wanted; for herself, she wished only to be allowed to remain watching there – glancing at the room where lay the bodies of her husband and child – where she would not be molested.

I felt that her advice was good. I could be of no use as protection, and I had an anxious longing to know what had become of my sick mother and sister; besides, some arrangement must be made for the burial. I therefore limped away. There was no need to express thanks on either side, and the grief was too deep to be reached by any outward show of sympathy.

Outside the house there was a good deal of movement and bustle; many carts going along, the waggoners, from Sussex and Surrey, evidently impressed and guarded by soldiers; and although no gas was burning, the road towards Kingston was well lighted by torches held by persons standing at short intervals in line, who had been seized for the duty, some of them the tenants of neighbouring villas. Almost the first of these torch-bearers I came to was an old gentleman whose face I was well acquainted with, from having frequently travelled up and down in the same train with him. He was a senior clerk in a Government office, I believe, and was a mild-looking old man with a prim face and a long neck, which he used to wrap in a white double neckcloth, a thing even in those days seldom seen. Even in that moment of bitterness I could not help being amused by the absurd figure this poor old fellow presented, with his solemn face and long cravat doing penance with a torch in front of his own gate, to light up the path of our conquerors. But a more serious object now presented itself, a corporal's guard passing by, with two English volunteers in charge, their hands tied behind their backs. They cast an imploring glance at me, and I stepped into the road to ask the corporal what was the matter, and even ventured, as he was passing on, to lay my hand on his sleeve.

"*Auf dem Wege, Spitzbube!*" cried the brute, lifting his rifle as if to knock me down. "Must one prisoners who fire at us let shoot," he went on to add; and shot the poor fellows would have been, I suppose, if I had not interceded with an officer, who happened to be riding by.

"Herr Hauptmann," I cried, as loud as I could, "is this your discipline, to let unarmed prisoners be shot without orders?"

The officer, thus appealed to, reined in his horse, and halted the guard till he heard what I had to say. My knowledge of other languages here stood me in good stead, for the prisoners, northcountry factory hands apparently, were of course utterly unable to make themselves understood, and did not even know in what they had offended. I therefore interpreted their explanation: they had been left behind while skirmishing near Ditton, in a barn, and coming out of their hiding-place in the midst of a party of the enemy, with their rifles in their hands, the latter thought they were going to fire at them from behind. It was a wonder they were not shot down on the spot. The captain heard the tale, and then told the guard to let them go, and they slunk off at once into a by-road. He was a fine soldier-like man, but nothing could exceed the insolence of his manner, which was perhaps all the greater because it seemed not intentional, but to arise from a sense of immeasurable superiority.

Between the lame freiwilliger pleading for his comrades, and the captain of the conquering army, there was, in his view, an infinite gulf. Had the two men been dogs, their fate could not have been decided more contemptuously. They were let go simply because they were not worth keeping as prisoners, and perhaps to kill any living thing without cause went against the hauptmann's sense of justice. But why speak of this insult in particular? Had not every man who lived then his tale to tell of humiliation and degradation? For it was the same story everywhere. After the first stand in line, and when once they had got us on the march, the enemy laughed at us. Our handful of regular troops was sacrificed almost to a man in a vain conflict with numbers; our volunteers and militia, with officers who did not know their work, without ammunition or equipment, or staff to superintend, starving in the midst of plenty, we had soon become a helpless mob, fighting desperately here and there, but with whom, as a manoeuvring army, the disciplined invaders did just what they pleased.

Happy those whose bones whitened the fields of Surrey; they at least were spared the disgrace we lived to endure. Even you, who have never known what it is to live otherwise than on sufferance, even your cheeks burn when we talk of these days; think, then, what those endured who, like your grandfather, had been citizens of the proudest nation on earth, which had never known disgrace or defeat, and whose boast it used to be that they bore a flag on which the sun never set! We had heard of generosity in war; we found none; the war was made by us, it was said, and we must take the consequences. London and our only arsenal captured, we were at the mercy of our captors, and right heavily did they tread on our necks.

Need I tell you the rest? – Of the ransom we had to pay, and the taxes raised to cover it, which keep us paupers to this day? – The brutal frankness that announced we must give place to a new naval Power, and be made harmless for revenge? – The victorious troops living at free quarters, the yoke they put on us made the more galling that their requisitions had a semblance of method and legality? Better have been robbed at first hand by the soldiery themselves, than through our own magistrates made the instruments for extortion. How we lived through the degradation we daily and hourly underwent, I hardly even now understand. And what was there left to us to live for? Stripped of our colonies; Canada and the West Indies gone to America; Australia forced to separate; India lost for ever, after the English there had all been destroyed, vainly trying to hold the country when cut off from aid by their countrymen; Gibraltar and Malta ceded to the new naval Power; Ireland independent and in perpetual anarchy and revolution.

When I look at my country as it is now – its trade gone, its factories silent, its harbours empty, a prey to pauperism and decay – when I see all this, and think what Great Britain was in my youth, I ask myself whether I have really a heart or any sense of patriotism that I should have witnessed such degradation and still care to live!

France was different. There, too, they had to eat the bread of tribulation under the yoke of the conqueror! Their fall was hardly more sudden or violent than ours; but war could not take away their rich soil; they had no colonies to lose; their broad lands, which made their wealth, remained to them; and they rose again from the blow. But our people could not be got to see how artificial our prosperity was – that it all rested on foreign trade and financial credit; that the course of trade once turned away from us, even for a time, it might never return; and that our credit once shaken might never be restored. To hear men talk in those days, you would have thought that Providence had ordained that our Government should always borrow at three per cent, and that trade came to us because we lived in a foggy little island set in a boisterous sea.

They could not be got to see that the wealth heaped up on every side was not created in the country, but in India and China, and other parts of the world; and that it would be quite possible for the people who made money by buying and selling the natural treasures of the earth, to go and live in other places, and take their profits with them. Nor would men believe that there could ever be an end to our coal and iron, or that they would get to be so much dearer than the coal and iron of America that it would no longer be worth while to work them, and that therefore we ought to insure against the loss of our artificial position as the great centre of trade, by making ourselves secure and strong and respected. We thought we were living in a commercial millennium, which must last for a thousand years at least.

After all the bitterest part of our reflection is, that all this misery and decay might have been so easily prevented, and that we brought it about ourselves by our own shortsighted recklessness. There, across the narrow Straits, was the writing on the wall, but we would not choose to read it. The warnings of the few were drowned in the voice of the multitude. Power was then passing away from the class which had been used to rule, and to face political dangers, and which had brought the nation with honour unsullied through former struggles, into the hands of the lower classes, uneducated, untrained to the use of political rights, and swayed by demagogues; and the few who were wise in their generation were denounced as alarmists, or as aristocrats who sought their own aggrandisement by wasting public money on bloated armaments. The rich were idle and luxurious; the poor grudged the cost of defence. Politics had become a mere bidding for Radical votes, and those who should have led the nation stooped rather to pander to the selfishness of the day, and humoured the popular cry which denounced those who would secure the defence of the nation by enforced arming of its manhood, as interfering with the liberties of the people.

Truly the nation was ripe for a fall; but when I reflect how a little firmness and self-denial, or political courage and foresight, might have averted the disaster, I feel that the judgment must have really been deserved. A nation too selfish to defend its liberty, could not have been fit to retain it. To you, my grandchildren, who are now going to seek a new home in a more prosperous land, let not this bitter lesson be lost upon you in the country of your adoption. For me, I am too old to begin life again in a strange country; and hard and evil as have been my days, it is not much to await in solitude the time which cannot now be far off, when my old bones will be laid to rest in the soil I have loved so well, and whose happiness and honour I have so long survived.

The Thing from – 'Outside'

George Allan England

THEY SAT ABOUT their camp-fire, that little party of Americans retreating southward from Hudson Bay before the on-coming menace of the great cold. Sat there, stolid under the awe of the North, under the uneasiness that the day's trek had laid upon their souls. The three men smoked. The two women huddled close to each other. Fireglow picked their faces from the gloom of night among the dwarf firs. A splashing murmur told of the Albany River's haste to escape from the wilderness, and reach the Bay.

"I don't see what there was in a mere circular print on a rock-ledge to make our guides desert," said Professor Thorburn. His voice was as dry as his whole personality. "Most extraordinary."

"*They* knew what it was, all right," answered Jandron, geologist of the party. "So do I." He rubbed his cropped mustache. His eyes glinted grayly. I've seen prints like that before. That was on the Labrador. And I've seen things happen, where they were."

"Something surely happened to our guides, before they'd got a mile into the bush," put in the Professor's wife; while Vivian, her sister, gazed into the fire that revealed her as a beauty, not to be spoiled even by a tam and a rough-knit sweater. "Men don't shoot wildly, and scream like that, unless –"

"They're all three dead now, anyhow," put in Jandron. "So they're out of harm's way. While we – well, we're two hundred and fifty wicked miles from the C.P.R. rails."

"Forget it, Jandy!" said Marr, the journalist. "We're just suffering from an attack of nerves, that's all. Give me a fill of 'baccy. Thanks. We'll all be better in the morning. Ho-hum! Now, speaking of spooks and such –"

He launched into an account of how he had once exposed a fraudulent spiritualist, thus proving – to his own satisfaction – that nothing existed beyond the scope of mankind's everyday life. But nobody gave him much heed. And silence fell upon the little night-encampment in the wilds; a silence that was ominous.

Pale, cold stars watched down from spaces infinitely far beyond man's trivial world.

Next day, stopping for chow on a ledge miles upstream, Jandron discovered another of the prints. He cautiously summoned the other two men. They examined the print, while the women-folk were busy by the fire. A harmless thing the marking seemed; only a ring about four inches in diameter, a kind of cup-shaped depression with a raised center. A sort of glaze coated it, as if the granite had been fused by heat.

Jandron knelt, a well-knit figure in bright mackinaw and canvas leggings, and with a shaking finger explored the smooth curve of the print in the rock. His brows contracted as he studied it.

"We'd better get along out of this as quick as we can," said he in an unnatural voice. "You've got your wife to protect, Thorburn, and I – well, I've got Vivian. And –"

"*You* have?" nipped Marr. The light of an evil jealously gleamed in his heavy-lidded look. "What you need is an alienist."

"Really, Jandron," the Professor admonished, "you mustn't let your imagination run away with you."

"I suppose it's imagination that keeps this print cold!" the geologist retorted. His breath made faint, swirling coils of vapor above it.

"Nothing but a pot-hole," judged Thorburn, bending his spare, angular body to examine the print. The Professor's vitality all seemed centered in his big-bulged skull that sheltered a marvellous thinking machine. Now he put his lean hand to the base of his brain, rubbing the back of his head as if it ached. Then, under what seemed some powerful compulsion, he ran his bony finger around the print in the rock.

"By Jove, but it is cold!" he admitted. "And looks as if it had been stamped right out of the stone. Extraordinary!"

"Dissolved out, you mean," corrected the geologist. "By cold."

The journalist laughed mockingly.

"Wait till I write this up!" he sneered. "Noted Geologist Declares Frigid Ghost Dissolves Granite!"

Jandron ignored him. He fetched a little water from the river and poured it into the print.

"Ice!" ejaculated the Professor. "Solid ice!"

"Frozen in a second," added Jandron, while Marr frankly stared. "And it'll never melt, either. I tell you, I've seen some of these rings before; and every time, horrible things have happened. Incredible things! Something burned this ring out of the stone – burned it out with the cold interstellar space. Something that can import cold as a permanent quality of matter. Something that can kill matter, and totally remove it."

"Of course that's all sheer poppycock," the journalist tried to laugh, but his brain felt numb.

"This something, this Thing," continued Jandron, "is a Thing that can't be killed by bullets. It's what caught our guides on the barrens, as they ran away – poor fools!"

A shadow fell across the print in the rock. Mrs. Thorburn had come up, was standing there. She had overheard a little of what Jandron had been saying.

"Nonsense!" she tried to exclaim, but she was shivering so she could hardly speak.

That night, after a long afternoon of paddling and portaging – laboring against inhibitions like those in a nightmare – they camped on shelving rocks that slanted to the river.

"After all," said the Professor, when supper was done, "we mustn't get into a panic. I know extraordinary things are reported from the wilderness, and more than one man has come out, raving. But we, by Jove! with our superior brains – we aren't going to let Nature play us any tricks!"

"And of course," added his wife, her arm about Vivian, "everything in the universe is a natural force. There's really no super-natural, at all."

"Admitted," Jandron replied. "But how about things *outside* the universe?"

"And they call you a scientist?" gibed Marr; but the Professor leaned forward, his brows knit.

"Hm!" he grunted. A little silence fell.

"You don't mean, really," asked Vivian, "that you think there's life and intelligence – Outside?"

Jandron looked at the girl. Her beauty, haloed with ruddy gold from the firelight, was a pain to him as he answered:

"Yes, I do. And dangerous life, too. I know what I've seen, in the North Country. I know what I've seen!"

Silence again, save for the crepitation of the flames, the fall of an ember, the murmur of the current. Darkness narrowed the wilderness to just that circle of flickering light ringed by the forest and the river, brooded over by the pale stars.

"Of course you can't expect a scientific man to take you seriously," commented the Professor. "I know what I've seen! I tell you there's Something entirely outside man's knowledge."

"Poor fellow!" scoffed the journalist; but even as he spoke his hand pressed his forehead.

"There are Things at work," Jandron affirmed, with dogged persistence. He lighted his pipe with a blazing twig. Its flame revealed his face drawn, lined. "Things. Things that reckon with us no more than we do with ants. Less, perhaps."

The flame of the twig died. Night stood closer, watching.

"Suppose there are?" the girl asked. "What's that got to do with these prints in the rock?"

"*They*," answered Jandran, "are marks left by one of those Things. Footprints, maybe. That Thing is near us, here and now!"

Marr's laugh broke a long stillness.

"And you," he exclaimed, "with an A.M. and a B.S. to write after your name,"

"If you knew more," retorted Jandron, "you'd know a devilish sight less. It's only ignorance that's cock-sure."

"But," dogmatized the Professor, "no scientist of any standing has ever admitted any outside interference with this planet."

"No, and for thousands of years nobody ever admitted that the world was round, either. What I've seen, I know."

"Well, what *have* you seen?" asked Mrs. Thorburn, shivering.

"You'll excuse me, please, for not going into that just now."

"You mean," the Professor demanded, dryly, "if the – hm! – this suppositious Thing wants to –?"

"It'll do any infernal thing it takes a fancy to, yes! If it happens to want us –"

"But what *could* Things like that want of us? Why should They come here, at all?"

"Oh, for various reasons. For inanimate objects, at times, and then again for living beings. They've come here lots of times, I tell you," Jandron asserted with strange irritation, "and got what They wanted, and then gone away to – Somewhere. If one of Them happens to want us, for any reason, It will take us, that's all. If It doesn't want us, It will ignore us, as we'd ignore gorillas in Africa if we were looking for gold. But if it was gorilla-fur we wanted, that would be different for the gorillas, wouldn't it?"

"What in the world," asked Vivian, "could a – well, a Thing from Outside want of *us?*"

"What do men want, say, of guinea-pigs? Men experiment with 'em, of course. Superior beings use inferior, for their own ends. To assume that man is the supreme product of evolution is gross self-conceit. Might not some superior Thing want to experiment with human beings?

"But how?" demanded Marr,

"The human brain is the most highly-organized form of matter known to this planet. Suppose, now –"

"Nonsense!" interrupted the Professor. "All hands to the sleeping-bags, and no more of this. I've got a wretched headache. Let's anchor in Blanket Bay!"

He, and both the women, turned in. Jandron and Marr sat a while longer by the fire. They kept plenty of wood piled on it, too, for an unnatural chill transfixed the night-air. The fire burned strangely blue, with greenish flicks of flame.

At length, after vast acerbities of disagreement, the geologist and the newspaperman sought their sleeping-bags. The fire was a comfort. Not that a fire could avail a pin's weight against a Thing from interstellar spacs, but subjectively it was a comfort. The instincts of a million years, centering around protection by fire, cannot be obliterated.

After a time – worn out by a day of nerve-strain and of battling with swift currents, of flight from Something invisible, intangible – they all slept.

The depths of space, star-sprinkled, hung above them with vastness immeasurable, cold beyond all understanding of the human mind.

Jandron woke first, in a red dawn.

He blinked at the fire, as he crawled from his sleeping-bag. The fire was dead; and yet it had not burned out. Much wood remained unconsumed, charred over, as if some gigantic extinguisher had in the night been lowered over it.

"*Hmmm!*" growled Jandron. He glanced about him, on the ledge. "Prints, too. I might have known!"

He aroused Marr. Despite all the jourelist's mocking hostility, Jandron felt more in common with this man of his own age than with the Professor, who was close on sixty.

"Look here, now!" said he. "*It* has been all around here. See? It put out our fire – maybe the fire annoyed *It*, some way – and *It* walked round us, everywhere." His gray eyes smouldered. "I guess, by gad, you've got to admit facts, now!"

The journalist could only shiver and stare.

"Lord, what a head I've got on me, this morning!" he chattered. He rubbed his forehead with a shaking hand, and started for the river. Most of his assurance had vanished. He looked badly done up.

."Well, what say?" demanded Jandron. "See these fresh prints?"

"Damn the prints!" retorted Marr, and fell to grumbling some unintelligible thing. He washed unsteadily, and remained crouching at the river's lip, inert, numbed.

Jandron, despite a gnawing at the base of his, brain, carefully examined the ledge. He found prints scattered everywhere, and some even on the river-bottom near the shore. Wherever water had collected in the prints on the rock, it had frozen hard. Each print in the river-bed, too, was white with ice. Ice that the rushing current could not melt.

"Well, by gad!" he exclaimed. He lighted his pipe and tried to think. Horribly afraid – yes, he felt horribly afraid, but determined. Presently, as a little power of concentration came back, he noticed that all the prints were in straight lines, each mark about two feet from the next.

"*It* was observing us while we slept," said Jandron.

"What nonsense are you talking, eh?" demanded Marr. His dark, heavy face sagged. "Fire, now, and grub!"

He got up and shuffled unsteadily away from the river. Then he stopped with a jerk, staring.

"Look! Look a' that axe!" he gulped, pointing.

Jandron picked up the axe, by the handle, taking good care not to touch the steel. The blade was white-furred with frost. And deep into it, punching out part of the edge, one of the prints was stamped.

"This metal," said he, "is clean gone. It's been absorbed. The Thing doesn't recognize any difference in materials. Water and steel and rock are all the same to It."

"You're crazy!" snarled the journalist. "How could a Thing travel on one leg, hopping along, making marks like that?"

"It could roll, if it was disk-shaped. And –"

A cry from the Professor turned them. Thorburn was stumbling toward them, hands out and tremulous.

"My wife –!" he choked.

Vivian was kneeling beside her sister, frightened, dazed.

"Something's happened!" stammered the Professor. "Here – come here –!"

Mrs. Thorburn was beyond any power of theirs, to help. She was still breathing; but her respirations were stertorous, and a complete paralysla had stricken her. Her eyes, half-open and expressionless, showed pupils startlingly dilated. No resources of the party's drug-kit produced the slightest effect on the woman.

The next half-hour was a confused panic, breaking camp, getting Mrs. Thorburn into a canoe, and leaving that accursed place, with a furious energy of terror that could no longer reason. Up-stream, ever up against the swirl of the current the party fought, driven by horror. With no thought of food or drink, paying no heed to landmarks, lashed forward only by the mad desire to be gone, the three men and the girl flung every ounce of their energy into the paddles. Their panting breath mingled with the sound of swirling eddies. A mist-blurred sun brooded over the northern wilds. Unheeded, hosts of black-flies sang high-pitched keenings all about the fugitives. On either hand the forest waited, watched.

Only after two hours of sweating toil had brought exhaustion did they stop, in the shelter of a cove where black waters circled, foam-flecked. There they found the Professor's wife – she was dead.

Nothing remained to do but bury her. At first Thorburn would not hear of it. Like a madman he insisted that through all hazards he would fetch the body out. But no – impossible. So, after a terrible time, he yielded.

In spite of her grief, Vivian was admirable. She understood what must be done. It was her voice that said the prayers; her hand that – lacking flowers – laid the fir boughs on the cairn. The Professor was dazed past doing anything, saying anything.

Toward mid-afternoon, the party landed again, many miles up-river. Necessity forced them to eat. Firs would not burn. Every time they lighted it, it smouldered and went out with a heavy, greasy smoke. The fugitives ate cold food and drank water, then shoved off in two canoes and once more fled.

In the third canoe, hauled to the edge of the forest, lay all the rock-specimens, data and curios, scientific instruments. The party kept only Marr's diary, a compass, supplies, fire-arms and medicine-kit.

"We can find the things we've left – sometime," said Jandron, noting the place well. "Sometime – after *It* has gone,"

"And bring the body out," added Thorburn. Tears, for the first time, wet his eyes. Vivian said nothing. Marr tried to light his pipe. He seemed to forget that nothing, not even tobacco, would burn now.

Vivian and Jandron occupied one canoe. The other carried the Professor and Marr. Thus the power of the two canoes was about the same. They kept well together, up-stream.

The fugitives paddled and portaged with a dumb, desperate energy. Toward evening they struck into what they believed to be the Mamattawan. A mile up this, as the blurred sun faded beyond a wilderness of ominous silence, they camped. Here they made determined efforts to kindle fire. Not even alcohol from the drug-kit would start it. Cold, they mumbled a little food; cold, they huddled into their sleeping-bags, there to lie with darkness leaden on their fear. After a long time, up over a world void of all sound save the river-flow, slid an amber moon notched by the ragged tops of the conifers. Even the wail of a timber-wolf would have come as welcome relief; but no wolf howled.

Silence and night enfolded them. And everywhere they felt that *It* was watching.

Foolishly enough, as a man will do foolish things in a crisis, Jandron laid his revolver outside his sleeping-bag, in easy reach. His thought – blurred by a strange, drawing headache – was:

"If *It* touches Vivian, I'll shoot!"

He realized the complete absurdity of trying to shoot a visitant from interstellar space; from the Fourth Dimension, maybe. But Jandron's ideas seemed tangled. Nothing would come right. He lay there, absorbed in a kind of waking nightmare. Now and then, rising on an elbow, he hearkened; all in vain. Nothing so much as stirred.

His thought drifted to better days, when all had been health, sanity, optimism; when nothing except jealousy of Marr, as concerned Vivian, had troubled him. Days when the sizzle of the frying-pan over friendly coals had made friendly wilderness music; when the wind and the northern star, the whirr of the reel, the whispering vortex of the paddle in clear water had all been things of joy. Yes, and when a certain happy moment had, through some word or look of the girl, seemed to promise his heart's desire. But now –

"Damn it, I'll save *her*, anyhow!" he swore with savage intensity, knowing all the while that what was to be, would be, unmitigably. Do ants, by any waving of antenna, stay the down-crushing foot of man?

Next morning, and the next, no sign of the Thing appeared. Hope revived that possibly It might have flitted away elsewhere; back, perhaps, to outer space. Many were the miles the urging paddles spurned behind. The fugitives calculated that a week more would bring them to the railroad. Fire burned again. Hot food and drink helped, wonderfully. But where were the fish?

"Most extraordinary," all at once said the Professor, at noonday camp. He had become quite rational again. "Do you realize, Jandron, we've seen no traces of life in some time?"

The geologist nodded. Only too clearly he had noted just that, but he had been keeping still about it.

"That's so, too!" chimed in Marr, enjoying the smoke that some incomprehensible turn of events was letting him have. "Not a muskrat or beaver. Not even a squirrel or bird."

"Not so much as a gnat or black-fly!" the Professor added. Jandron suddenly realized that he would have welcomed even those.

That afternoon, Marr fell into a suddenly vile temper. He mumbled curses against the guides, the current, the portages, everything. The Professor seemed more cheerful. Vivian complained of an oppressive headache. Jandron gave her the last of the aspirin tablets; and as he gave them, took her hand in his.

"I'll see *you* through, anyhow," said he, "I don't count, now. Nobody counts, only you!"

She gave him a long, silent look. He saw the sudden glint of tears in her eyes; felt the pressure of her hand, and knew they two had never been so near each other as in that moment under the shadow of the Unknown.

Next day – or it may have been two days later, for none of them could be quite sure about the passage of time – they came to a deserted lumber-camp. Even more than two days might have passed; because now their bacon was all gone, and only coffee, tobacco, beef-cubes and pilot-bread remained. The lack of fish and game had cut alarmingly into the duffle-bag. That day – whatever day it may have been – all four of them suffered terribly from headache of an odd, ring-shaped kind, as if something circular were being pressed down about their heads. The Professor said it was the sun that made his head ache. Vivian laid it to the wind and the gleam of the swift water, while Marr claimed it was the heat. Jandron wondered at all this, inasmuch as he plainly saw that the river had almost stopped flowing, and the day had become still and overcast.

They dragged their canoes upon a rotting stage of fir-poles and explored the lumber-camp; a mournful place set back in an old 'slash,' now partly overgrown with scrub poplar, maple and birch. The log buildings, covered with tar-paper partly torn from the pole roofs, were of the usual North Country type. Obviously the place had not been used for years. Even the landing-stage where once logs had been rolled into the stream had sagged to decay.

"I don't quite get the idea of this," Marr exclaimed. "Where did the logs go to? Downstream, of course. But *that* would take 'em to Hudson Bay, and there's no market for spruce timber or pulpwood at Hudson Bay." He pointed down the current.

"You're entirely mistaken," put in the Professor. "Any fool could see this river runs the other way. A log thrown in here would go down toward the St. Lawrence!"

"But then," asked the girl, "why can't we drift back to civilization?" The Professor retorted:

"Just what we *have* been doing, all along! Extraordinary, that I have to explain the obvious!" He walked away in a huff,

"I don't know but he's right, at that," half admitted the journalist. "I've been thinking almost the same thing, myself, the past day or two – that is, ever since the sun shifted."

"What do you mean, shifted?" from Jandron, "You haven't noticed it?"

"But there's been no sun at all, for at least two days!"

"Hanged if I'll waste time arguing with a lunatic!" Marr growled. He vouchsafed no explanation of what he meant by the sun's having "shifted," but wandered off, grumbling.

"What *are* we going to do?" the girl appealed to Jandron. The sight of her solemn, frightened eyes, of her palm-outward hands and (at last) her very feminine fear, constricted Jandron's heart.

"We're going through, you and I," he answered simply. "We've got to save them from themselves, you and I have."

Their hands met again, and for a moment held. Despite the dead calm, a fir-tip at the edge of the clearing suddenly flicked aside, shrivelled as if frozen. But neither of them saw it.

The fugitives, badly spent, established themselves in the 'bar-room' or sleeping-shack of the camp. They wanted to feel a roof over them again, if only a broken one. The traces of men comforted them: a couple of broken peavies, a pair of snowshoes with the thongs all gnawed off, a cracked bit of mirror, a yellowed almanac dated 1899.

Jandron called the Professor's attention to this almanac, but the Professor thrust it aside.

"What do *I* want of a Canadian census-report?" he demanded, and fell to counting the bunks, over and over again. His big bulge of his forehead, that housed the massive brain of him, was oozing sweat. Marr cursed what he claimed was sunshine through the holes in the roof, though Jandron could see none; claimed the sunshine made his head ache.

"But it's not a bad place," he added. "We can make a blaze in that fireplace and be comfy. I don't like that window, though."

"What window?" asked Jandron. "Where?"

Marr laughed, and ignored him. Jandron turned to Vivian, who had sunk down on the 'deacon-seat' and was staring at the stove.

"*Is* there a window here?" he demanded. "Don't ask me," she whispered. "I – I don't know."

With a very thriving fear in his heart, Jandron peered at her a moment. He fell to muttering:

"I'm Wallace Jandron. Wallace Jandron, 37 Ware Street, Cambridge, Massachusetts. I'm quite sane. And I'm going to stay so. I'm going to save her! I know perfectly well what I'm doing. And I'm sane. Quite, quite sane!"

After a time of confused and purposeless wrangling, they got a fire going and made coffee. This, and cube bouillon with hardtack, helped considerably. The camp helped, too. A house, even a poor and broken one, is a wonderful barrier against a Thing from – Outside.

Presently darkness folded down. The men smoked, thankful that tobacco still held out. Vivian lay in a bunk that Jandron had piled with spruce boughs for her, and seemed to sleep. The Professor fretted like a child, over the blisters his paddle had made upon his hands. Marr laughed, now and then; though what he might be laughing at was not apparent. Suddenly he broke out:

"After all, what should It want of us?"

"Our brains, of course," the Professor answered, sharply.

"That lets Jandron out," the journalist mocked. "But," added the Professor, "I can't imagine a, Thing callously destroying human beings. And yet –"

He stopped short, with surging memories of his dead wife.

"What was it," Jandron asked, "that destroyed all those people in Valladolid, Spain, that time so many of 'em died in a few minutes after having been touched by an invisible Something that left a slight red mark on each? The newspapers were full of it."

"Piffle!" yawned Marr.

"I tell you," insisted Jandron, "there are forms of life as superior to us as we are to ants. We can't see 'em. No ant ever saw a man. And did any ant ever form the least conception of a man? These Things have left thousands of traces, all over the world. If I had my reference-books –"

"Tell that to the marines!"

"Charles Fort, the greatest authority in the world on unexplained phenomena," persisted Jandron, "gives innumerable cases of happenings that science can't explain, in his *Book of the Damned*. He claims this earth was once a No-Man's land where all kinds of Things explored and colonized and fought for possession. And he says that now everybody's warned off, except the Owners. I happen to remember a few sentences of his:

> "*In the past, inhabitants of a host of worlds have dropped here, hopped here, wafted here, sailed, flown, motored, walked here; have come singly, have come in enormous numbers; have visited for hunting, trading, mining. They have been unable to stay here, have made colonies here, have been lost here.*"

"Poor fish, to believe that!" mocked the journalist, while the Professor blinked and rubbed his bulging forehead.

"I *do* believe it!" insisted Jandron. "The world is covered with relics of dead civilizations, that have mysteriously vanished, leaving nothing but their temples and monuments."

"Rubbish!"

"How about Easter Island? How about all the gigantic works there and in a thousand other places! – Peru, Yucatan and so on – which certainly no primitive race ever built?"

"That's thousands of years ago," said Marr, "and I'm sleepy. For heaven's sake, can it!"

"Oh, all right. But *how* explain things, then!"

"What the devil could one of those Things want of our brains?" suddenly put in the Professor. "After all, what?"

"Well, what do we want of lower forms of life? Sometimes food. Again, some product or other. Or just information. Maybe *It* is just experimenting with us, the way we poke an ant-hill. There's always this to remember, that the human brain-tissue is the most highly-organized form of matter in this world."

"Yes," admitted the Professor, "but what –?"

"*It* might want brain-tissue for food, for experimental purposes, for lubricant – how do I know?"

Jandron fancied he was still explaining things; but all at once he found himself waking up in one of the bunks. He felt terribly cold, stiff, sore. A sift of snow lay here and there on the camp floor, where it had fallen through holes in the roof.

"Vivian!" he croaked hoarsely. "Thorburn! Marr!"

Nobody answered. There was nobody to answer. Jandron crawled with immense pain out of his bunk, and blinked round with bleary eyes. All of a sudden he saw the Professor, and gulped.

The Professor was lying stiff and straight in another bunk, on his back. His waxen face made a mask of horror. The open, staring eyes, with pupils immensely dilated, sent Jandron shuddering back. A livid ring marked the forehead, that now sagged inward as if empty.

"*Vivian!*" croaked Jandron, staggering away from the body. He fumbled to the bunk where the girl had lain. The bunk was quite deserted.

On the stove, in which lay half-charred wood – wood smothered out as if by some noxious gas – still stood the coffee-pot. The liquid in it was frozen solid. Of Vivian and the journalist, no trace remained.

Along one of the sagging beams that supported the roof, Jandron's horror-blasted gaze perceived a straight line of frosted prints, ring-shaped, bitten deep.

"Vivian! Vivian!"

No answer.

Shaking, sick, gray, half-blind with a horror not of this world, Jandron peered slowly around. The duffle-bag and supplies were gone. Nothing was left but that coffee-pot and the revolver at Jandron's hip.

Jandron turned, then. A-stare, his skull feeling empty as a burst drum, he crept lamely to the door and out – out into the snow.

Snow. It came slanting down. From a gray sky it steadily filtered. The trees showed no leaf. Birches, poplars, rock-maples all stood naked. Only the conifers drooped sickly-green. In a little shallow across the river snow lay white on thin ice.

Ice? Snow? Rapt with terror, Jandron stared. Why, then, he must have been unconscious three or four weeks? But how –?

Suddenly, all along the upper branches of trees that edged the clearing, puffs of snow flicked down. The geologist shuffled after two half-obliterated sets of footprints that wavered toward the landing.

His body was leaden. He wheezed, as he reached the river. The light, dim as it was, hurt his eyes. He blinked in a confusion that could just perceive one canoe was gone. He pressed a hand to his head, where an iron band seemed screwed up tight, tighter.

"Vivian! Marr! Halloooo!"

Not even an echo. Silence clamped the world; silence, and a cold that gnawed. Everything had gone a sinister gray.

After a certain time – though time now possessed neither reality nor duration – Jandron dragged himself back to the camp and stumbled in. Heedless of the staring corpse he crumpled down by the stove and tried to think, but his brain had been emptied of power. Everything blent to a gray blur. Snow kept slithering in through the roof.

"Well, why don't you come and get me. Thing?" suddenly snarled Jandron. "Here I am. Damn you, come and get me!"

Voices. Suddenly he heard voices. Yes, somebody was outside, there. Singularly aggrieved, he got up and limped to the door. He squinted out into the gray; saw two figures down by the landing. With numb indifference he recognized the girl and Marr.

"Why should they bother me again?" he nebulously wondered. Can't they go away and leave me alone?" He felt peevish irritation.

Then, a modicum of reason returning, he sensed that they were arguing. Vivian, beside a canoe freshly dragged from thin ice, was pointing; Marr was gesticulating. All at once Marr snarled, turned from her, plodded with bent back toward the camp.

"But listen!" she called, her rough-knit sweater all powdered with snow. "*That's* the way!" She gestured downstream.

"I'm not going either way!" Marr retorted. "I'm going to stay right here!" He came on, bareheaded. Snow grayed his stubble of beard; but on his head it melted as it fell, as if some fever there had raised the brain-stuff to improbable temperatures. "I'm going to stay right here, all summer." His heavy lids sagged. Puffy and evil, his lips showed a glint of teeth. "Let me alone!"

Vivian lagged after him, kicking up the ash-like snow. With indifference, Jandron watched them. Trivial human creatures!

Suddenly Marr saw him in the doorway and stopped short. He drew his gun; he aimed at Jandron.

"*You* get out!" he mouthed. "Why in — can't you stay dead?"

"Put that gun down, you idiot!" Jandron managed to retort. The girl stopped and seemed trying to understand. "We can get away yet, if we all stick together."

"Are you going to get out and leave me alone?" demanded the journalist, holding his gun steadily enough.

Jandron, wholly indifferent, watched the muzzle. Vague curiosity possessed him. Just what, he wondered, did it feel like to be shot?

Mart pulled trigger.

Snap!

The cartridge missed fire. Not even powder would burn.

Marr laughed, horribly, and shambled forward. "Serves him right!" he mouthed, "He'd better not come back again!"

Jandron understood that Marr had seen him fall. But still he felt himself standing there, alive. He shuffled away from the door. No matter whether he was alive or dead, there was always Vivian to be saved.

The journalist came to the door, paused, looked down, grunted and passed into the camp. He shut the door. Jandron heard the rotten wooden bar of the latch drop. From within echoed a laugh, monstrous in its brutality.

Then quivering, the geologist felt a touch on his arm.

"Why did you desert us like that?" he heard Vivian's reproach. "Why?"

He turned, hardly able to see her at all.

"Listen," he said, thickly. "I'll admit anything. It's all right. But just forget it, for now. We've got to get out o' here. The Professor is dead, in there, and Marr's gone mad and barricaded himself in there. So there's no use staying. There's a chance for us yet. Come along!"

He took her by the arm and tried to draw her toward the river, but she held back. The hate in her face sickened him. He shook in the grip of a mighty chill.

"Go, with – you?" she demanded.

"Yes, by God!" he retorted, in a swift blaze of anger, "or I'll kill you where you stand. *It* shan't get you, anyhow!"

Swiftly piercing, a greater cold smote to his inner marrows. A long row of the cup-shaped prints had just appeared in the snow beside the camp. And from these marks wafted a faint, bluish vapor of unthinkable cold.

"What are you staring at?" the girl demanded. "Those prints! In the snow, there – see?" He pointed a shaking finger.

"How can there be snow at this season?"

He could have wept for the pity of her, the love of her. On her red tam, her tangle of rebel hair, her sweater, the snow came steadily drifting; yet there she stood before him and prated of summer. Jandron heaved himself out of a very slough of down-dragging lassitudes. He whipped himself into action.

"Summer, winter – no matter!" he flung at her. "You're coming along with me!" He seized her arm with the brutality of desperation that must hurt, to save. And murder, too, lay in his soul. He knew that he would strangle her with his naked hands, if need were, before he would ever leave her there, for *It* to work Its horrible will upon.

"You come with me," he mouthed, "or by the Almighty –!"

Marr's scream in the camp, whirled him toward the door. That scream rose higher, higher, even more and more piercing, just like the screams of the runaway Indian guides in what now appeared the infinitely long ago. It seemed to last hours; and always it rose, rose, as if being wrung out of a human body by some kind of agony not conceivable in this world. Higher, higher –

Then it stopped.

Jandron hurled himself against the plank door. The bar smashed; the door shivered inward.

With a cry, Jandron recoiled. He covered his eyes with a hand that quivered, claw-like.

"Go away, Vivian! Don't come here – don't look –"

He stumbled away, babbling.

Out of the door crept something like a man. A queer, broken, bent over thing; a thing crippled, shrunken and flabby, that whined.

This thing – yes, it was still Marr – crouched down at one side, quivering, whimpering. It moved its hands as a crushed ant moves its antennae, jerkily, without significance.

All at once Jandron no longer felt afraid. He walked quite steadily to Marr, who was breathing in little gasps. From the camp issued an odor unlike anything terrestrial. A thin, grayish grease covered the sill.

Jandron caught hold of the crumpling journalist's arm. Marr's eyes leered, filmed, unseeing. He gave the impression of a creature whose back has been broken, whose whole essence and energy have been wrenched asunder, yet in which life somehow clings, palpitant. A creature vivisected.

Away through the snow Jandron dragged him. Marr made no resistance; just let himself be led, whining a little, palsied, rickety, shattered. The girl, her face whitely cold as the snow that fell on it, came after.

Thus they reached the landing at the river.

"Come, now, let's get away!" Jandron made shift to articulate. Marr said nothing. But when Jandron tried to bundle him into a canoe, something in the journalist revived with swift, mad hatefulness. That something lashed him into a spasm of wiry, incredibly venomous resistance. Slavers of blood and foam streaked Marr's lips. He made horrid noises, like an animal. He howled dismally, and bit, clawed, writhed and grovelled! He tried to sink his teeth into Jandron's leg. He fought appallingly, as men must have fought in the inconceivably remote days even before the Stone Age. And Vivian helped him. Her fury was a tiger-cat's.

Between the pair of them, they almost did him in. They almost dragged Jandron down – and themselves, too – into the black river that ran swiftly sucking under the ice. Not till Jandron had quite flung off all vague notions and restraints of gallantry; not until he struck from the shoulder – to kill, if need were – did he best them.

He beat the pair of them unconscious, trussed them hand and foot with the painters of the canoes, rolled them into the larger canoe, and shoved off. After that, the blankness of a measureless oblivion descended.

Only from what he was told, weeks after, in the Royal Victoria Hospital at Montreal, did Jandron ever learn how and when a field-squad of Dominion Foresters had found them drifting in Lake Moosawamkeag. And that knowledge filtered slowly into his brain during a period inchoate as Iceland fogs.

That Marr was dead and the girl alive – that much, at all events, was solid. He could hold to that; he could climb back, with that, to the real world again.

Jandron climbed back, came back. Time healed him, as it healed the girl. After a long, long while, they had speech together. Cautiously he sounded her wells of memory. He saw that she recalled nothing. So he told her white lies about capsized canoes and the sad death – in realistically-described rapids – of all the party except herself and him.

Vivian believed. Fate, Jandron knew, was being very kind to both of them.

But Vivian could never understand in the least why, her husband, not very long after marriage, asked her not to wear a wedding-ring or any ring whatever.

"Men are so queer!" covers a multitude of psychic agonies.

Life, for Jandron – life, softened by Vivian – knit itself up into some reasonable semblance of a normal pattern. But when, at lengthening intervals, memories even now awake – memories crawling amid the slime of cosmic mysteries that it is madness to approach – or when at certain times Jandron sees a ring of any sort, his heart chills with a cold that reeks of the horrors of Infinity.

And from shadows past the boundaries of our universe seem to beckon Things that, God grant, can never till the end of time be known on earth.

The Man who Saved the Earth

Austin Hall

Chapter I
The Beginning

EVEN THE BEGINNING. From the start the whole thing has the precision of machine work. Fate and its working – and the wonderful Providence which watches over Man and his future. The whole thing unerring: the incident, the work, the calamity, and the martyr. In the retrospect of disaster we may all of us grow strong in wisdom. Let us go into history.

A hot July day. A sun of scant pity, and a staggering street; panting thousands dragging along, hatless; fans and parasols; the sultry vengeance of a real day of summer. A day of bursting tires; hot pavements, and wrecked endeavor, heartaches for the seashore, for leafy bowers beside rippling water, a day of broken hopes and listless ambition.

Perhaps Fate chose the day because of its heat and because of its natural benefit on fecundity. We have no way of knowing. But we do know this: the date, the time, the meeting; the boy with the burning glass and the old doctor. So commonplace, so trivial and hidden in obscurity! Who would have guessed it? Yet it is – after the creation – one of the most important dates in the world's history.

This is saying a whole lot. Let us go into it and see what it amounts to. Let us trace the thing out in history, weigh it up and balance it with sequence.

Of Charley Huyck we know nothing up to this day. It is a thing which, for some reason, he has always kept hidden. Recent investigation as to his previous life and antecedents have availed us nothing. Perhaps he could have told us; but as he has gone down as the world's great martyr, there is no hope of gaining from his lips what we would so like to know.

After all, it does not matter. We have the day – the incident, and its purport, and its climax of sequence to the day of the great disaster. Also we have the blasted mountains and the lake of blue water which will ever live with his memory. His greatness is not of warfare, nor personal ambition; but of all mankind. The wreaths that we bestow upon him have no doubtful color. The man who saved the earth!

From such a beginning, Charley Huyck, lean and frail of body, with, even then, the wistfulness of the idealist, and the eyes of a poet. Charley Huyck, the boy, crossing the hot pavement with his pack of papers; the much treasured piece of glass in his pocket, and the sun which only he should master burning down upon him. A moment out of the ages; the turning of a straw destined to out-balance all the previous accumulation of man's history.

The sun was hot and burning, and the child – he could not have been more than ten – cast a glance over his shoulder. It was in the way of calculation. In the heyday of childhood he was not dragged down by the heat and weather: he had the enthusiasm of his half-score of years and the joy of the plaything. We will not presume to call it the spirit of the scientist, though it was, perhaps, the spark of latent investigation that was destined to lead so far.

A moment picked out of destiny! A boy and a plaything. Uncounted millions of boys have played with glass and the sun rays. Who cannot remember the little, round-burning dot in the palm of the hand and the subsequent exclamation? Charley Huyck had found a new toy, it was a simple thing and as old as glass. Fate will ever be so in her working.

And the doctor? Why should he have been waiting? If it was not destiny, it was at least an accumulation of moment. In the heavy eye-glasses, the square, close-cut beard; and his uncompromising fact-seeking expression. Those who knew Dr. Robold are strong in the affirmation that he was the antithesis of all emotion. He was the sternest product of science: unbending, hardened by experiment, and caustic in his condemnation of the frailness of human nature.

It had been his one function to topple over the castles of the foolish; with his hard-seeing wisdom he had spotted sophistry where we thought it not. Even into the castles of science he had gone like a juggernaut. It is hard to have one's theories derided – yea, even for a scientist – and to be called a fool! Dr. Robold knew no middle language; he was not relished by science.

His memory, as we have it, is that of an eccentric. A man of slight compassion, abrupt of manner and with no tact in speaking. Genius is often so; it is a strange fact that many of the greatest of men have been denied by their follows. A great man and laughter. He was not accepted.

None of us know today what it cost Dr. Robold. He was not the man to tell us. Perhaps Charley Huyck might; but his lips are sealed forever. We only know that he retired to the mountain, and of the subsequent flood of benefits that rained upon mankind. And we still denied him. The great cynic on the mountain. Of the secrets of the place we know little. He was not the man to accept the investigator; he despised the curious. He had been laughed at – let be – he would work alone on the great moment of the future.

In the light of the past we may well bend knee to the doctor and his protégé, Charley Huyck. Two men and destiny! What would we be without them? One shudders to think. A little thing, and yet one of the greatest moments in the world's history. It must have been Fate. Why was it that this stern man, who hated all emotion, should so have unbended at this moment? That we cannot answer. But we can conjecture. Mayhap it is this: We were all wrong; we accepted the man's exterior and profession as the fact of his marrow.

No man can lose all emotion. The doctor, was, after all, even as ourselves – he was human. Whatever may be said, we have the certainty of that moment – and of Charley Huyck.

The sun's rays were hot; they were burning; the pavements were intolerable; the baked air in the canyoned street was dancing like that of an oven; a day of dog-days. The boy crossing the street; his arms full of papers, and the glass bulging in his little hip-pocket.

At the curb he stopped. With such a sun it was impossible to long forget his plaything. He drew it carefully out of his pocket, lay down a paper and began distancing his glass for the focus. He did not notice the man beside him. Why should he? The round dot, the brownish smoke, the red spark and the flash of flame! He stamped upon it. A moment out of boyhood; an experimental miracle as old as the age of glass, and just as delightful. The boy had spoiled the name of a great Governor of a great Stata; but the paper was still salable. He had had his moment. Mark that moment.

A hand touched his shoulder. The lad leaped up.

"Yessir. *Star* or *Bulletin*?"

"I'll take one of each," said the man. "There now. I was just watching you. Do you know what you were doing?"

"Yessir. Burning paper. Startin' fire. That's the way the Indians did it."

The man smiled at the perversion of fact. There is not such a distance between sticks and glass in the age of childhood.

"I know," he said – "the Indians. But do you know how it was done; the why – why the paper began to blaze?"

"Yessir."

"All right, explain."

The boy looked up at him. He was a city boy and used to the streets. Here was some old highbrow challenging his wisdom. Of course he knew.

"It's the sun."

"There," laughed the man. "Of course. You said you knew, but you don't. Why doesn't the sun, without the glass, burn the paper? Tell me that."

The boy was still looking up at him; he saw that the man was not like the others on the street. It may be that the strange intimacy kindled into being at that moment. Certainly it was a strange unbending for the doctor.

"It would if it was hot enough or you could get enough of it together."

"Ah! Then that is what the glass is for, is it?"

"Yessir."

"Concentration?"

"Con— I don't know, sir. But it's the sun. She's sure some hot. I know a lot about the sun, sir. I've studied it with the glass. The glass picks up all the rays and puts them in one hole and that's what burns the paper.

"It's lots of fun. I'd like to have a bigger one; but it's all I've got. Why, do you know, if I had a glass big enough and a place to stand, I'd burn up the earth?"

The old man laughed. "Why, Archimedes! I thought you were dead."

"My name ain't Archimedes. It's Charley Huyck."

Again the old man laughed.

"Oh, is it? Well, that's a good name, too. And if you keep on you'll make it famous as the name of the other." Wherein he was foretelling history. "Where do you live?"

The boy was still looking. Ordinarily he would not have told, but he motioned back with his thumb.

"I don't live; I room over on Brennan Street."

"Oh, I see. You room. Where's your mother?"

"Search me; I never saw her."

"I see; and your father?"

"How do I know. He went floating when I was four years old."

"Floating?"

"Yessir – to sea."

"So your mother's gone and your father's floating. Archimedes is adrift. You go to school?"

"Yessir."

"What reader?"

"No reader. Sixth grade.

"I see. What school?"

"School Twenty-six. Say, it's hot. I can't stand here all day. I've got to sell my papers."

The man pulled out a purse.

"I'll take the lot," he said. Then kindly: "My boy, I would like to have you go with me."

It was a strange moment. A little thing with the fates looking on. When destiny plays she picks strange moments. This was one. Charley Huyck went with Dr. Robold.

Chapter II
The Poison Pall

WE ALL OF US REMEMBER that fatal day when the news startled all of Oakland. No one can forget it. At first it read like a newspaper hoax, in spite of the oft-proclaimed veracity of the press, and we were inclined to laughter. 'Twixt wonder at the story and its impossibilities we were not a little enthused at the nerve of the man who put it over.

It was in the days of dry reading. The world had grown populous and of well-fed content. Our soap-box artists had come to the point at last where they preached, not disaster, but a full-bellied thanks for the millennium that was here. A period of Utopian quietness – no villain around the corner; no man to covet the ox of his neighbor.

Quiet reading, you'll admit. Those were the days of the millennium. Nothing ever happened. Here's hoping they never come again. And then:

Honestly, we were not to blame for bestowing blessing out of our hearts upon that newspaperman. Even if it were a hoax, it was at least something.

At high noon. The clock in the city hall had just struck the hour that held the post 'twixt a.m. and p.m., a hot day with a sky that was clear and azure; a quiet day of serene peace and contentment. A strange and a portent moment. Looking back and over the miracle we may conjecture that it was the clearness of the atmosphere and the brightness of the sun that helped to the impact of the disaster. Knowing what we know now we can appreciate the impulse of natural phenomena. It was *not* a miracle.

The spot: Fourteenth and Broadway, Oakland, California.

Fortunately the thousands of employees in the stores about had not yet come out for their luncheons. The lapse that it takes to put a hat on, or to pat a ribbon, saved a thousand lives. One shudders to think of what would have happened had the spot been crowded. Even so, it was too impossible and too terrible to be true. Such things could not happen.

At high noon: Two street-cars crossing Fourteenth on Broadway – two cars with the-same joggle and bump and the same aspect of any of a hundred thousand at a traffic corner. The wonder is – there were so few people. A Telegraph car outgoing, and a Broadway car coming in. The traffic policeman at his post had just given his signal. Two automobiles were passing and a single pedestrian, so it is said, was working his way diagonally across the corner. Of this we are not certain.

It was a moment that impinged on miracle. Even as we recount it, knowing, as we do, the explanation, we sense the impossibility of the event. A phenomenon that holds out and, in spite of our findings, lingers into the miraculous. To be and not to be. One moment life and action, an ordinary scene of existent monotony; and the next moment nothing. The spot, the intersection of the street, the passing street-cars, the two automobiles, pedestrian, the policeman – non-existent! When events are instantaneous reports are apt to be misleading. This is what we find.

Some of those who beheld it, report a flash of bluish white light; others that it was of a greenish or even a violet hue; and others, no doubt of stronger vision, that it was not only of a predominant color but that it was shot and sparkled with a myriad specks of flame and burning.

It gave no warning and it made no sound; not even a whir. Like a hot breath out of the void. Whatever the forces that had focused, they were destruction. There was no Fourteenth and Broadway. The two automobiles, the two street-cars, the pedestrian, the policeman had been whiffed away as if they had never existed. In place of the intersection of the thoroughfares was a yawning gulf that looked down into the center of the earth to a depth of nausea.

It was instantaneous; it was without sound; no warning. A tremendous force of unlimited potentiality had been loosed to kinetic violence. It was the suddenness and the silence that belied credence. We were accustomed to associate all disaster with confusion; calamity has an affinity with pandemonium, all things of terror climax into sound. In this case there was no sound. Hence the wonder.

A hole or bore forty feet in diameter. Without a particle of warning and without a bit of confusion. The spectators one and all aver that at first they took it for nothing more than the effect of startled eyesight. Almost subtle. It was not until after a full minute's reflection that they became aware that a miracle had been wrought before their faces. Then the crowd rushed up and with awe and now awakened terror gazed down into that terrible pit.

We say 'terrible' because in this case it is an exact adjective. The strangest hole that man ever looked into. It was so deep that at first it appeared to have no bottom; not even the strongest eyesight could penetrate the smoldering blackness that shrouded the depths descending. It took a stout heart and courage to stand and hold one's head on the brink for even a minute.

It was straight and precipitous; a perfect circle in shape; with sides as smooth as the effect of machine work, the pavement and stone curb had been cut as if by a razor. Of the two street cars, two automobiles and their occupants there was nothing. The whole thing so silent and complete. Not even the spectators could really believe it.

It was a hard thing to believe. The newspapers themselves, when the news came clamoring, accepted it with reluctance. It was too much like a hoax. Not until the most trusted reporters had gone and had wired in their reports would they even consider it. Then the whole world sat up and took notice.

A miracle! Like Oakland's *Press* we all of us doubted that hole. We had attained almost everything that was worth the knowing; we were the masters of the earth and its secrets and we were proud of our wisdom; naturally we refused such reports all out of reason. It must be a hoax.

But the wires were persistent. Came corroboration. A reliable news-gathering organization soon was coming through with elaborate and detailed accounts of just what was happening. We had the news from the highest and most reputable authority.

And still we doubted. It was the story itself that brought the doubting; its touch on miracle. It was too easy to pick on the reporter. There might be a hole, and all that; but this thing of no explanation! A bomb perhaps? No noise? Some new explosive? No such thing? Well, how did we know? It was better than a miracle.

Then came the scientists. As soon as could be men of great minds had been hustled to the scene. The world had long been accustomed to accept without quibble the dictum of these great specialists of fact. With their train of accomplishments behind them we would hardly be consistent were we to doubt them.

We know the scientist and his habits. He is the one man who will believe nothing until it is proved. It is his profession, and for that we pay him. He can catch the smallest bug that ever crawled out of an atom and give it a name so long that a Polish wrestler, if he had to bear it, would break under the burden. It is his very knack of getting in under that has given us our civilization. You don't baffle a scientist in our Utopia. It can't be done. Which is one of the very reasons why we began to believe in the miracle.

In a few moments a crowd of many thousands had gathered about the spot; the throng grew so dense that there was peril of some of them being crowded into the pit at the center. It took all the spare policemen of the city to beat them back far enough to string ropes from the corners. For blocks the streets were packed with wondering thousands. Street traffic was impossible. It was necessary to divert the cars to a roundabout route to keep the arteries open to the suburbs.

Wild rumors spread over the city. No one knew how many passengers had been upon the street cars. The officials of the company, from the schedule, could pick the numbers of the cars and their crews; but who could tell of the occupants?

Telephones rang with tearful pleadings. When the first rumors of the horror leaked out every wife and mother felt the clutch of panic at her heartstrings. It was a moment of historical psychology. Out of our books we had read of this strange phase of human nature that was wont to rise like a mad screeching thing out of disaster. We had never had it in Utopia.

It was rumbling at first and out of exaggeration; as the tale passed farther back to the waiting thousands it gained with the repetition. Grim and terrible enough in fact, it ratioed up with reiteration. Perhaps after all it was not psychology. The average impulse of the human mind does not even up so exactly. In the light of what we now know it may have been the poison that had leaked into the air; the new element that was permeating the atmosphere of the city.

At first it was spasmodic. The nearest witnesses of the disaster were the first victims. A strange malady began to spot out among those of the crowd who had been at the spot of contact. This is to be noticed. A strange affliction which from the virulence and rapidity of action was quite puzzling to the doctors.

Those among the physicians who would consent to statement gave it out that it was breaking down of tissue. Which of course it was; the new element that was radiating through the atmosphere of the city. They did not know it then.

The pity of it! The subtle, odorless pall was silently shrouding out over the city. In a short time the hospitals were full and it was necessary to call in medical aid from San Francisco. They had not even time for diagnosis. The new plague was fatal almost at conception. Happily the scientists made the discovery.

It was the pall. At the end of three hours it was known that the death sheet was spreading out over Oakland. We may thank our stars that it was learned so early. Had the real warning come a few hours later the death list would have been appalling.

A new element had been discovered; or if not a new element, at least something which was tipping over all the laws of the atmospheric envelope. A new combination that was fatal. When the news and the warning went out, panic fell upon the bay shore.

But some men stuck. In the face of such terror there were those who stayed and with grimness and sacrifice hung to their posts for mankind. There are some who had said that the stuff of heroes had passed away. Let them then consider the case of John Robinson.

Robinson was a telegraph operator. Until that day he was a poor unknown; not a whit better than his fellows. Now he has a name that will run in history. In the face of what he knew he remained under the blanket. The last words out of Oakland – his last message:

Whole city of Oakland in grip of strange madness. Keep out of Oakland –

following which came a haphazard personal commentary:

I can feel it coming on myself. It is like what our ancestors must have felt when they were getting drunk – alternating desires of fight and singing – a strange sensation, light, and ecstatic with a spasmodic twitching over the forehead. Terribly thirsty. Will stick it out if I can get enough water. Never so dry in my life.

Followed a lapse of silence. Then the last words:

I guess we're done for. There is some poison in the atmosphere – something. It has leaked, of course, out of this thing at Fourteenth and Broadway. Dr. Manson of the American Institute says it is something new that is forming a fatal combination; but he cannot understand a new element; the quantity is too enormous.
Populace has been warned out of the city. All roads are packed with refugees. The Berkeley Hills are covered as with flies – north, east, and south and on the boats to Frisco. The poison, whatever it is, is advancing in a ring from Fourteenth and Broadway. You have got to pass it to these old boys of science. They are staying with that ring. Already they have calculated the rate of its advance and have given warning. They don't know what it is, but they have figured just how fast it is moving. They have saved the city.
I am one of the few men now inside the wave. Out of curiosity I have stuck. I have a jug and as long as it lasts I shall stay. Strange feeling. Dry, dry, dry, as if the juice of one's life cells was turning into dust. Water evaporating almost instantly. It cannot pass through glass. Whatever the poison it has an affinity for moisture. Do not understand it. I have had enough –

That was all. After that there was no more news out of Oakland. It is the only word that we have out of the pall itself. It was short and disconnected and a bit slangy; but for all that a basis from which to conjecture.

It is a strange and glorious thing how some men will stick to the post of danger. This operator knew that it meant death; but he held with duty. Had he been a man of scientific training his information might have been of incalculable value. However, may God bless his heroic soul!

What we know is thirst! The word that came from the experts confirmed it. Some new element of force was stealing or sapping the humidity out of the atmosphere. Whether this was combining and entering into a poison could not be determined.

Chemists worked frantically at the outposts of the advancing ring. In four hours it had covered the city; in six it had reached San Leandro, and was advancing on toward Haywards.

It was a strange story and incredible from the beginning. No wonder the world doubted. Such a thing had never happened. We had accepted the the law of judging the future by the past; by deduction; we were used to sequence and to law; to the laws of Nature. This thing did look like a miracle; which was merely because – as usually it is with 'miracles' – we could not understand it. Happily, we can look back now and still place our faith in Nature.

The world doubted and was afraid. Was this peril to spread slowly over the whole state of California and then on to the – world. Doubt always precedes terror. A tense world waited. Then came the word of reassurance – from the scientists:

"Danger past; vigor of the ring is abating. Calculation has deduced that the wave is slowly decreasing in potentiality. It is too early yet to say that there will be recessions, as the wave is just reaching its zenith. What it is we cannot say; but it cannot be inexplicable. After a little time it will all be explained. Say to the world there is no cause for alarm."

But the world was now aroused; as it doubted the truth before, it doubted now the reassurance. Did the scientists know? Could they have only seen the future! We know now that they did not. There was but one man in all the world great enough to foresee disaster. That man was Charley Huyck.

Chapter III
The Mountain that Was

ON THE SAME DAY on which all this happened, a young man, Pizzozi by name and of Italian parentage, left the little town of Ione in Amador County, California, with a small truck-load of salt. He was one of the cattlemen whose headquarters or home-farms are clustered about the foot-bills of the Sierras. In the wet season they stay with their home-land in the valley; in the summer they penetrate into the mountains. Pizzozi had driven in from the mountains the night before, after salt. He had been on the road since midnight.

Two thousand salt-hungry cattle do not allow time for gossip. With the thrift of his race, Joe had loaded up his truck and after a running snatch at breakfast was headed back into the mountains. When the news out of Oakland was thrilling around the world he was far into the Sierras.

The summer quarters of Pizzozi were close to Mt. Heckla, whose looming shoulders rose square in the center of the pasture of the three brothers. It was not a noted mountain – that is, until this day – and had no reason for a name other than that it was a peak outstanding from the range; like a thousand others; rugged, pine clad, coated with deer-brush, red soil, and mountain miserie.

It was the deer-brush that gave it value to the Pizzozis – a succulent feed richer than alfalfa. In the early summer they would come up with bony cattle. When they returned in the fall they went out driving beef-steaks. But inland cattle must have more than forage. Salt is the tincture that makes them healthy.

It was far past the time of the regular salting. Pizzozi was in a hurry. It was nine o'clock when he passed through the mining town of Jackson; and by twelve o'clock – the minute of the disaster – he was well beyond the last little hamlet that linked up with civilization. It was four o'clock when he drew up at the little pine-sheltered cabin that was his headquarters for the summer.

He had been on the road since midnight. He was tired. The long weary hours of driving, the grades, the unvaried stress though the deep red dust, the heat, the stretch of a night and day had worn both mind and muscle. It had been his turn to go after salt; now that he was here, he could lie in for a bit of rest while his brothers did the salting.

It was a peaceful spot, this cabin of the Pizzozis; nestled among the virgin shade trees, great tall feathery sugar-pines with a mountain live-oak spreading over the door yard. To the east the rising heights of the Sierras, misty, gray-green, undulating into the distance to the pink-white snow crests of Little Alpine. Below in the canyon, the waters of the Mokolumne; to the west the heavy dark masses of Mt. Heckla, deep verdant in the cool of coming evening.

Joe drew up under the shade of the live oak. The air was full of cool, sweet scent of the afternoon. No moment could have been more peaceful; the blue clear sky overhead, the breath of summer, and the soothing spice of the pine trees. A shepherd dog came bounding from the doorway to meet him.

It was his favorite cow dog. Usually when Joe came back the dog would be far down the road to forestall him. He had wondered, absently, coming up, at the dog's delay. A dog is most of all a creature of habit; only something unusual would detain him. However the dog was here; as the man drew up he rushed out to greet him. A rush, a circle, a bark, and a whine of welcome. Perhaps the dog had been asleep.

But Joe noticed that whine; he was wise in the ways of dogs; when Ponto whined like that there was something unusual. It was not effusive or spontaneous; but rather of the delight of succor. After scarce a minute of patting, the dog squatted and faced to the westward. His whine was startling; almost fearful.

Pizzozi knew that something was wrong. The dog drew up, his stub tail erect, and his hair all bristled; one look was for his master and the other whining and alert to Mt. Heckla. Puzzled, Joe gazed at the mountain. But he saw nothing.

Was it the canine instinct, or was it coincidence? We have the account from Pizzozi. From the words of the Italian, the dog was afraid. It was not the way of Ponto; usually in the face of danger he was alert and eager; now he drew away to the cabin. Joe wondered.

Inside the shack he found nothing but evidence of departure. There was no sign of his brothers. It was his turn to go to sleep; he was wearied almost to numbness, for forty-eight hours he had not closed an eyelid. On the table were a few unwashed dishes and crumbs of eating. One of the three rifles that hung usually on the wall was missing; the coffee pot was on the floor with the lid open. On the bed the coverlets were mussed up. It was a temptation to go to sleep. Back of him the open door and Ponto. The whine of the dog drew his will and his consciousness into correlation. A faint rustle in the sugar-pines soughed from the canyon.

Joe watched the dog. The sun was just glowing over the crest of the mountain; on the western line the deep lacy silhouettes of the pine trees and the bare bald head of Heckla. What was it? His brothers should be on hand for the salting; it was not their custom to put things off for the morrow. Shading his eyes he stepped out of the doorway.

The dog rose stealthily and walked behind him, uneasily, with the same insistent whine and ruffled hair. Joe listened. Only the mountain murmurs, the sweet breath of the forest, and in the lapse of bated breath the rippling melody of the river far below him.

"What you see, Ponto? What you see?"

At the words the dog sniffed and advanced slightly – a growl and then a sudden scurry to the heels of his master. Ponto was afraid. It puzzled Pizzozi. But whatever it was that roused his fear, it was on Mt. Heckla.

This is one of the strange parts of the story – the part the dog played, and what came after. Although it is a trivial thing it is one of the most inexplicable. Did the dog sense it? We have no measure for the range of instinct, but we do have it that before the destruction of Pompeii the beasts roared in their cages. Still, knowing what we now know, it is hard to accept the analogy. It may, after all have been coincidence.

Nevertheless it decided Pizzozi. The cattle needed salt. He would catch up his pinto and ride over to the salt logs.

There is no moment in the cattle industry quite like the salting on the range. It is not the most spectacular perhaps, but surely it is not lacking in intenseness. The way of Pizzozi was musical even if not operatic. He had a long-range call, a rising rhythm that for depth and tone had a peculiar effect on the shattered stillness. It echoed and reverberated, and peeled from the top to the bottom of the mountain. The salt call is the talisman of the mountains.

Alleewahoo!"

Two thousand cattle augmented by a thousand strays held up their heads in answer. The sniff of the welcome salt call! Through the whole range of the man's voice the stock stopped in their leafy pasture and listened.

"*Alleewahoo!*"

An old cow bellowed. It was the beginning of bedlam. From the bottom of the mountain to the top and for milse beyond went forth the salt call. Three thousand head bellowed to the delight of salting.

Pizzozi rode along. Each lope of his pinto through the tall tangled miserie was accented. "*Alleewahoo! Alleewahoo!*" The rending of brush, the confusion, and pandemonium spread to the very bottom of the leafy gulches. It is no place for a pedestrian. Heads and tails erect, the cattle were stampeding toward the logs.

A few head had beat him to it. These he quickly drove away and cut the sack open. With haste he poured it upon the logs; then he rode out of the dust that for yards about the place was tramped to the finest powder. The center of a herd of salting range stock is no place for comfort. The man rode away; to the left he ascended a low knob where he would be safe from the stampede; but close enough to distinguish the brands.

In no time the place was alive with milling stock. Old cows, heifers, bulls, calves, steers rushed out of the crashing brush into the clearing. There is no moment exactly like it. What before had been a broad clearing of brownish reddish dust was trampled into a vast cloud of bellowing blur, a thousand cattle, and still coming. From the farthest height came the echoing call. Pizzozi glanced up at the top of the mountain.

And then a strange thing happened.

From what we gathered from the excited accounts of Pizzozi it was instantaneous; and yet by the same words it was of such a peculiar and beautiful effect as never to be forgotten. A bluish azure shot though with a myriad flecks of crimson, a peculiar vividness of opalescence; the whole world scintillating; the sky, the air, the mountain, a vast flame of color so wide and so intense that there seemed not a thing beside it. And instantaneous – it was over almost before it was started. No noise or warning, and no subsequent detonation: as silent as winking and much, indeed, like the queer blur of color induced by defective vision. All in the fraction of a second. Pizzozi had been gazing at the mountain. There was no mountain!

Neither were there cattle. Where before had been the shade of the towering peak was now the rays of the western sun. Where had been the blur of the milling herd and its deafening pandemonium was now a strange silence. The transparency of the air was unbroken into the distance. Far off lay a peaceful range in the sunset. There was no mountain! Neither were there cattle!

For a moment the man had enough to do with his plunging mustang. In the blur of the subsequent second Pizzozi remembers nothing but a convulsion of fighting horseflesh bucking, twisting, plunging, the gentle pinto suddenly maddened into a demon. It required all the skill of the cowman to retain his saddle.

He did not know that he was riding on the rim of Eternity. In his mind was the dim subconscious realization of a thing that had happened. In spite of all his efforts the horse fought backward. It was some moments before he conquered. Then he looked.

It was a slow, hesitant moment. One cannot account for what he will do in the open face of a miracle. What the Italian beheld was enough for terror. The sheer immensity of the thing was too much for thinking.

At the first sight his simplex mind went numb from sheer impotence; his terror to a degree frozen. The whole of Mt. Heckla had been shorn away; in the place of its darkened shadow the sinking sun was blinking in his face; the whole western sky all golden. There was no vestige of the flat salt-clearing at the base of the mountain. Of the two thousand cattle milling in the dust not a one remained. The man crossed himself in stupor. Mechanically he put the spurs to the pinto.

But the mustang would not. Another struggle with bucking, fighting, maddened horseflesh. The cow-man must needs bring in all the skill of his training; but by the time he had conquered his mind had settled within some scope of comprehension.

The pony had good reasons for his terror. This time though the man's mind reeled it did not go dumb at the clash of immensity. Not only had the whole mountain been torn away, but its roots as well. The whole thing was up-side down; the world torn to its entrails. In place of what had been the height was a gulf so deep that its depths were blackness.

He was standing on the brink. He was a cool man, was Pizzozi; but it was hard in the confusion of such a miracle to think clearly; much less to reason. The prancing mustang was snorting with terror. The man glanced down.

The very dizziness of the gulf, sheer, losing itself into shadows and chaos overpowered him, his mind now clear enough for perception reeled at the distance. The depth was nauseating. His whole body succumbed to a sudden qualm of weakness: the sickness that comes just before falling. He went limp in the saddle.

But the horse fought backward; warned by instinct it drew back from the sheer banks of the gulf. It had no reason but its nature. At the instant it sensed the snapping of the iron will of its master. In a moment it had turned and was racing on its wild way out of the mountains. At supreme moments a cattle horse will always hit for home. The pinto and its limp rider were fleeing on the road to Jackson.

Pizzozi had no knowledge of what had occurred in Oakland. To him the whole thing had been but a flash of miracle; he could not reason. He did not curb his horse. That he was still in the saddle was due more to the near-instinct of his training than to his volition.

He did not even draw up at the cabin. That he could make better time with his motor than with his pinto did not occur to him; his mind was far too busy; and, now that the thing was passed, too full of terror. It was forty-four miles to town; it was night and the stars were shining when he rode into Jackson.

Chapter IV

'Man – a Great Little Bug'

AND WHAT OF CHARLEY HUYCK? It was his anticipation, and his training which leaves us here to tell the story. Were it not for the strange manner of his rearing, and the keen faith and appreciation of Dr. Hobold there would be today no tale to tell. The little incident of the burning-glass had grown. If there is no such thing as Fate there is at least something that comes very close to being Destiny.

On this night we find Charley at the observatory in Arizona. He is a grown man and a great one, and though mature not so very far drawn from the lad we met on the street selling papers. Tall, slender, very slightly stooped and with the same idealistic, dreaming eyes of the poet. Surely no one at first glance would have taken him for a scientist. Which he was and was not.

Indeed, there is something vastly different about the science of Charley Huyck. Science to be sure, but not prosaic. He was the first and perhaps the last of the school of Dr. Robold, a peculiar combination of poetry and fact, a man of vision, of vast, far-seeing faith and idealism linked and based on the coldest and sternest truths of materialism. A peculiar tenet of the theory of Robold: 'True science to be itself should be half poetry.' Which any of us who have read or been at school know it is not. It is a peculiar theory and though rather wild still with some points in favor.

We all of us know our schoolmasters; especially those of science and what they stand for. Facts, facts, nothing but facts; no dreams or romance. Looking back we can grant them just about the emotions of cucumbers. We remember their cold, hard features, the prodding after fact, the accumulation of data. Surely there is no poetry in them.

Yet we must not deny that they have been by far the most potent of all men in the progress of civilzation. Not even Robold would deny it.

The point is this:

The doctor maintained that from the beginning the progress of material civilization had been along three distinct channels; science, invention, and administration. It was simply his theory that the first two should be one; that the scientist deal not alone with dry fact but with invention, and that the inventor, unless he is a scientist, has mastered but half his trade. "The really great scientist should be a visionary," said Robold, "and an inventor is merely a poet, with tools."

Which is where we get Charley Huyck. He was a visionary, a scientist, a poet with tools, the protégé of Dr. Robold. He dreamed things that no scientist had thought of. And we are thankful for his dreaming.

The one great friend of Huyck was Professor Williams, a man from Charley's home city, who had known him even back in the days of selling papers. They had been cronies in boyhood, in their teens, and again at College. In after years, when Huyck had become the visionary, the mysterious Man of the Mountain, and Williams a great professor of astronomy, the friendship was as strong as ever.

But there was a difference between them. Williams was exact to acuteness, with not a whit of vision beyond pure science. He had been reared in the old stone-cold theory of exactness; he lived in figures. He could not understand Huyck or his reasoning. Perfectly willing to follow as far as facts permitted he refused to step off into speculation.

Which was the point between them. Charley Huyck had vision; although exact as any man, he had ever one part of his mind soaring out into speculation. What is, and what might be, and the gulf between. To bridge the gulf was the life work of Charley Huyck.

In the snug little office in Arizona we find them; Charley with his feet poised on the desk and Williams precise and punctilious, true to his training, defending the exactness of his philosophy. It was the cool of the evening; the sun was just mellowing the heat of the desert. Through the open door and windows a cool wind was blowing. Charley was smoking; the same old pipe had been the bane of Williams's life at college.

"Then we know?" he was asking.

"Yes," spoke the professor, "what we know, Charley, we know; though of course it is not much. It is very hard, nay impossible, to deny figures. We have not only the proofs of geology but of astronomical calculation, we have facts and figures plus our sidereal relations all about us.

"The world must come to an end. It is a hard thing to say it, but it is a fact of science. Slowly, inevitably, ruthlessly, the end will come. A mere question of arithmetic."

Huyck nodded. It was his special function in life to differ with his former roommate. He had come down from his own mountain in Colorado just for the delight of difference.

"I see. Your old calculations of tidal retardation. Or if that doesn't work the loss of oxygen and the water."

"Either one or the other; a matter of figures; the earth is being drawn every day by the sun: its rotation is slowing up; when the time comes it will act to the sun in exactly the same manner as the moon acts to the earth today."

"I understand. It will be a case of eternal night for one side of the earth, and eternal day for the other. A case of burn up or freeze up."

"Exactly. Or if it doesn't reach to that, the water gas will gradually lose out into sidereal space and we will go to desert. Merely a question of the old dynamical theory of gases; of the molecules to be in motion, to be forever colliding and shooting out into variance.

"Each minute, each hour, each day we are losing part of our atmospheric envelope. In course of time it will all be gone; when it is we shall be all desert. For instance, take a look outside. This is Arizona. Once it was the bottom of a deep blue sea. Why deny when we can already behold the beginning."

The other laughed.

"Pretty good mathematics at that, professor. Only –"

"Only?"

"That it is merely mathematics."

"Merely mathematics?" The professor frowned slightly. "Mathematics do not lie, Charlie, you cannot get away from them. What sort of fanciful argument are you bringing up now?"

"Simply this," returned the other, "that you depend too much on figures. They are material and in the nature of things can only be employed in a calculation of what *may* happen in the future. You must have premises to stand on, facts. Your figures are rigid: they have no elasticity; unless your foundations are permanent and faultless your deductions will lead you only into error."

"Granted; just the point: we know where we stand. Wherein are we in error?"

It was the old point of difference. Huyck was ever crashing down the idols of pure materialism. Williams was of the world-wide school.

"You are in error, my dear professor, in a very little thing and a very large one."

"What is that?"

"Man."

"Man?"

"Yes. He's a great little bug. You have left him out of your calculation – which he will upset."

The professor smiled indulgently. "I'll allow; he is at least a conceited bug; but you surely cannot grant him much when pitted against the Universe."

"No? Did it ever occur to you, Professor, what the Universe is? The stars for instance? Space, the immeasurable distance of Infinity. Have you never dreamed?"

Williams could not quite grasp him. Huyck had a habit that had grown out of childhood. Always he would allow his opponent to commit himself. The professor did not answer. But the other spoke.

"Ether. You know it. Whether mind or granite. For instance, your desert." He placed his finger to his forehead. "Your mind, my mind – localized ether."

"What are you driving at?"

"Merely this. Your universe has intelligence. It has mind as well as matter. The little knot called the earth is becoming conscious. Your deductions are incompetent unless they embrace mind as well as matter, and they cannot do it. Your mathematics are worthless."

The professor bit his lip.

"Always fanciful," he commented, "and visionary. Your argument is beautiful, Charley, and hopeful. I would that it were true. But all things must mature. Even an earth must die."

"Not our earth. You look into the past, professor, for your proof, and I look into the future. Give a planet long enough time in maturing and it will develop life; give it still longer and it will produce intelligence. Our own earth is just coming into consciousness; it has thirty million years, at least, to run."

"You mean?"

"This. That man is a great little bug. Mind: the intelligence of the earth."

This of course is a bit dry. The conversation of such men very often is to those who do not care to follow them. But it is very pertinent to what came after. We know now, everyone knows, that Charley Huyck was right. Even Professor Williams admits it. Our earth is conscious. In less than twenty-four hours it had to employ its consciousness to save itself from destruction.

A bell rang. It was the private wire that connected the office with the residence. The professor picked up the receiver. "Just a minute. Yes? All right." Then to his companion: "I must go over to the house, Charley. We have plenty of time. Then we can go up to the observatory."

Which shows how little we know about ourselves. Poor Professor Williams! Little did he think that those casual words were the last he would ever speak to Charley Huyck.

The whole world seething! The beginning of the end! Charley Huyck in the vortex. The next few hours were to be the most strenuous of the planet's history.

Chapter V
Approaching Disaster

IT WAS NIGHT. The stars which had just been coming out were spotted by millions over the sleeping desert. One of the nights that are peculiar to the country, which we all of us know so well, if not from experience, at least from hearsay; mellow, soft, sprinkled like salted fire, twinkling.

Each little light a message out of infinity. Cosmic grandeur; mind: chaos, eternity – a night for dreaming. Whoever had chosen the spot in the desert had picked full well. Charley had spoken of consciousness. On that night when he gazed up at the stars he was its personification. Surely a good spirit was watching over the earth.

A cool wind was blowing; on its breath floated the murmurs from the village; laughter, the song of children, the purring of motors and the startled barking of a dog; the confused drone of man and his civilization. From the eminence the observatory looked down upon the town and the sheen of light, spotting like jewels in the dim glow of the desert. To the east the mellow moon just tipping over the mountain. Charley stepped to the window.

He could see it all. The subtle beauty that was so akin to poetry: the stretch of desert, the mountains, the light in the eastern sky; the dull level shadow that marked the plain to the northward. To the west the mountains looming black to the star line. A beautiful night; sweetened with the breath of desert and tuned to its slumber.

Across the lawn he watched the professor descending the pathway under the acacias. An automobile was coming up the driveway; as it drove up under the arcs he noticed its powerful lines and its driver; one of those splendid pleasure cars that have returned to favor during the last decade; the soft purr of its motor, the great heavy tires and its coating of dust. There is a lure about a great car coming in from the desert. The car stopped, Charley noted. Doubtless some one for Williams. If it were, he would go into the observatory alone.

In the strict sense of the word Huyck was not an astronomer. He had not made it his profession. But for all that he knew things about the stars that the more exact professors had not dreamed of. Charley was a dreamer. He had a code all his own and a manner of reasoning. Between him and the stars lay a secret.

He had not divulged it, or if he had, it was in such an open way that it was laughed at. It was not cold enough in calculation or, even if so, was too far from their deduction. Huyck had imagination; his universe was alive and potent; it had intelligence. Matter could not live without it. Man was its manifestation; just come to consciousness. The universe teemed with intelligence. Charley looked at the stars.

He crossed the office, passed through the reception-room and thence to the stairs that led to the observatory. In the time that would lapse before the coming of his friend he would have ample time for observation. Somehow he felt that there was time for discovery. He had come down to Arizona to employ the lens of his friend the astronomer. The instrument that he had erected on his own mountain in Colorado had not given him the full satisfaction that he expected. Here in Arizona, in the dry clear air, which had hitherto given such splendid results, he hoped to find what he was after. But little did he expect to discover the terrible thing he did.

It is one of the strangest parts of the story that he should be here at the very moment when Fate and the world's safety would have had him. For years he and Dr. Robold had been at work on their visionary projects. They were both dreamers. While others had scoffed they had silently been at their great work on kinetics.

The boy and the burning glass had grown under the tutelage of Dr. Robold: the time was about at hand when he could out-rival the saying of Archimedes. Though the world knew it not, Charley Huyck had arrived at the point where he could literally burn up the earth.

But he was not sinister; though he had the power he had of course not the slightest intention. He was a dreamer and it was part of his dream that man break his thraldom to the earth and reach out into the universe. It was a great conception and were it not for the terrible event which took his life we have no doubt but that he would have succeeded.

It was ten-thirty when he mounted the steps and seated himself. He glanced at his watch: he had a good ten minutes. He had computed before just the time for the observation. For months he had waited for just this moment; he had not hoped to be alone and now that he was in solitary possession he counted himself fortunate. Only the stars and Charley Huyck knew the secret; and not even he dreamed what it would amount to.

From his pocket he drew a number of papers; most of them covered with notations; some with drawings; and a good sized map in colors. This he spread before him, and with his pencil began to draw right across its face a net of lines and cross lines. A number of figures and a rapid computation. He nodded and then he made the observation.

It would have been interesting to study the face of Charley Huyck during the next few moments. At first he was merely receptive, his face placid but with the studious intentness of one who has come to the moment: and as he began to find what he was after – an eagerness of satisfaction. Then a queer blankness; the slight movement of his body stopped, and the tapping of his feet ceased entirely.

For a full five minutes an absolute intentness. During that time he was out among the stars beholding what not even he had dreamed of. It was more than a secret: and what it was only Charley Huyck of all the millions of men could have recognized. Yet it was more than even he had expected. When he at last drew away his face was chalk-like; great drops of sweat stood on his forehead: and the terrible truth in his eyes made him look ten years older.

"My God!"

For a moment indecision and strange impotence. The truth he had beheld numbed action; from his lips the mumbled words:

"This world; my world; our great and splendid mankind!"

A sentence that was despair and a benediction.

Then mechanically he turned back to confirm his observation. This time, knowing what he would see, he was not so horrified: his mind was cleared by the plain fact of what he was beholding. When at last he drew away his face was settled.

He was a man who thought quickly – thank the stars for that – and, once he thought, quick to spring to action. There was a peril poising over the earth. If it were to be voided there was not a second to lose in weighing up the possibilities.

He had been dreaming all his life. He had never thought that the climax was to be the very opposite of what he hoped for. In his under mind he prayed for Dr. Robold – dead and gone forever. Were he only here to help him!

He seized a piece of paper. Over its white face he ran a mass of computations. He worked like lightning; his fingers plying and his mind keyed to the pin-point of genius. Not one thing did he overlook in his calculation. If the earth had a chance he would find it.

There are always possibilities. He was working out the odds of the greatest race since creation. While the whole world slept, while the uncounted millions lay down in fond security, Charley Huyck there in the lonely room on the desert drew out their figured odds to the point of infinity.

"Just one chance in a million."

He was going to take it. The words were not out of his mouth before his long legs were leaping down the stairway. In the flash of seconds his mind was rushing into clear action. He had had years of dreaming; all his years of study and tutelage under Robold gave him just the training for such a disaster.

But he needed time. Time! Time! Why was it so precious? He must get to his own mountain. In six jumps he was in the office.

It was empty. The professor had not returned. He thought rather grimly and fleetingly of their conversation a few minutes before; what would Williams think now of science and consciousness? He picked up the telephone receiver. While he waited he saw out of the corner of his eye the car in the driveway. It was –

"Hello. The professor? What? Gone down to town? No! Well, say, this is Charley" – he was watching the car in front of the building, "Say, hello – tell him I have gone home, home! H-o-m-e to Colorado – to Colorado, yes – to the mountain – the m-o-u-n-t-a-i-n. Oh, never mind – I'll leave a note.

He clamped down the receiver. On the desk he scrawled on a piece of paper:

Ed:

Look these up. I'm bound for the mountain. No time to explain. There's a car outside. Stay with the lens. Don't leave it. If the earth goes up you will know that I have not reached the mountain.

Beside the note he placed one of the maps that he had in his pocket – with his pencil drew a black cross just above the center. Under the map were a number of computations.

It is interesting to note that in the stress of the great critical moment he forgot the professor's title. It was a good thing. When Williams read it he recognized the significance. All through their life in crucial moments he had been 'Ed.' to Charley.

But the note was all he was destined to find. A brisk wind was blowing. By a strange balance of fate the same movement that let Huyck out of the building ushered in the wind and upset calculation.

It was a little thing, but it was enough to keep all the world in ignorance and despair. The eddy whisking in through the door picked up the precious map, poised it like a tiny plane, and dropped it neatly behind a bookcase.

Chapter VI
A Race to Save the World

HUYCK WAS WORKING in a straight line. Almost before his last words on the phone were spoken he had requisitioned that automobile outside; whether money or talk, faith or force, he was going to have it. The hum of the motor sounded in his ears as he ran down the steps. He was hatless and in his shirt-sleeves. The driver was just putting some tools in the car. With one jump Charley had him by the collar.

"Five thousand dollars if you can get me to Robold Mountain in twenty hours."

The very suddenness of the rush caught the man by surprise and lurched him against the car, turning him half around. Charley found himself gazing into dull brown eyes and sardonic laughter: a long, thin nose and lips drooped at the corners, then as suddenly tipping up – a queer creature, half devil, half laughter, and all fun.

"Easy, Charley, easy! How much did you say? Whisper it."

It was Bob Winters. Bob Winters and his car. And waiting. Surely no twist of fortune could have been greater. He was a college chum of Huyck's and of the professor's. If there was one man that could make the run in the time allotted, Bob was he. But Huyck was impersonal. With the burden on his mind he thought of naught but his destination.

"Ten thousand!" he shouted.

The man held back his head. Huyck was far too serious to appreciate mischief. But not the man.

"Charley Huyck, of all men. Did young Lochinvar come out of the West? How much did you say? This desert air and the dust, 'tis hard on the hearing. She must be a young, fair maiden. Ten thousand."

"Twenty thousand. Thirty thousand. Damnation, man, you can have the mountain. Into the car."

By sheer subjective strength he forced the other into the machine. It was not until they were shooting out of the grounds on two wheels that he realized that the man was Bob Winters. Still the workings of fate.

The madcap and wild Bob of the races! Surely Destiny was on the job. The challenge of speed and the premium. At the opportune moment before disaster the two men were brought together. Minutes weighed up with centuries and hours out-balanced millenniums. The whole world slept; little did it dream that its very life was riding north with these two men into the midnight.

Into the midnight! The great car, the pride of Winter's heart, leaped between the pillars. At the very outset, madcap that he was, he sent her into seventy miles an hour; they fairly jumped off the hill into the village. At a full seventy-five he took the curve; she skidded, sheered half around and swept on.

For an instant Charley held his breath. But the master hand held her; she steadied, straightened, and shot out into the desert. Above the whir of the motor, flying dust and blurring what-not, Charley got the tones of his companion's voice. He had heard the words somewhere in history.

"Keep your seat, Mr. Greely. Keep your seat!"

The moon was now far up over the mountain, the whole desert was bathed in a mellow twilight; in the distance the mountains brooded like an uncertain slumbering cloud bank. They were headed straight to the northward; though there was a better road round about, Winters had chosen the hard, rocky bee-line to the mountain.

He knew Huyck and his reputation; when Charley offered thirty thousand for a twenty-hour drive it was not mere byplay. He had happened in at the observatory to drop in on Williams on his way to the coast. They had been classmates; likewise he and Charley.

When the excited man out of the observatory had seized him by the collar, Winters merely had laughed. He was the speed king. The three boys who had gone to school were now playing with the destiny of the earth. But only Huyck knew it.

Winters wondered. Through miles and miles of fleeting sagebrush, cacti and sand and desolation, he rolled over the problem. Steady as a rock, slightly stooped, grim and as certain as steel he held to the north. Charley Huyck by his side, hatless, coatless, his hair dancing to the wind, all impatience. Why was it? Surely a man even for death would have time to get his hat.

The whole thing spelled speed to Bob Winters; perhaps it was the infusion of spirit or the intensity of his companion; but the thrill ran into his vitals. Thirty thousand dollars – for a stake like that – what was the balance? He had been called Wild Bob for his daring; some had called him insane; on this night his insanity was enchantment.

It was wild; the lee of the giant roadster a whirring shower of gravel: into the darkness, into the night the car fought over the distance. The terrific momentum and the friction of the air fought in their faces; Huyck's face was unprotected: in no time his lips were cracked, and long before they had crossed the level his whole face was bleeding.

But he heeded it not. He only knew that they were moving; that slowly, minute by minute, they were cutting down the odds that bore disaster. In his mind a maze of figures; the terrible sight he had seen in the telescope and the thing impending. Why had he kept his secret?

Over and again he impeached himself and Dr. Robold. It had come to this. The whole world sleeping and only himself to save it. Oh, for a few minutes, for one short moment! Would he get it?

At last they reached the mountains. A rough, rocky road, and but little traveled. Happily Winters had made it once before, and knew it. He took it with every bit of speed they could stand, but even at that it was diminished to a minimum.

For hours they fought over grades and gulches, dry washouts and boulders. It was dawn, and the sky was growing pink when they rode down again upon the level. It was here that they ran across their first trouble; and it was here that Winters began to realize vaguely what a race they might be running.

The particular level which they had entered was an elbow of the desert projecting into the mountains just below a massive, newly constructed dam. The reservoir had but lately been filled, and all was being put in readiness for the dedication.

An immense sheet of water extending far back into the mountains – it was intended before long to transform the desert into a garden. Below, in the valley, was a town, already the center of a prosperous irrigation settlement; but soon, with the added area, to become a flourishing city. The elbow, where they struck it, was perhaps twenty miles across. Their northward path would take them just outside the tip where the foothills of the opposite mountain chain melted into the desert. Without ado Winters put on all speed and plunged across the sands. And then:

It was much like winking; but for all that something far more impressive. To Winters, on the left hand of the car and with the east on the right hand, it was much as if the sun had suddenly leaped up and as suddenly plumped down behind the horizon – a vast vividness of scintillating opalescence: an azure, naming diamond shot by a million fire points.

Instantaneous and beautiful. In the pale dawn of the desert air its wonder and color were beyond all beauty. Winters caught it out of the corner of his eye; it was so instantaneous and so illusive that he was not certain. Instinctively he looked to his companion.

But Charley, too, had seen it. His attitude of waiting and hoping was vigorized into vivid action. He knew just what it was. With one hand he clutched Winters and fairly shouted.

"On, on, Bob! On, as you value your life. Put into her every bit of speed you have got."

At the same instant, at the same breath came a roar that was not to be forgotten; crunching, rolling, terrible – like the mountain moving.

Bob knew it. It was the dam. Something had broken it. To the east the great wall of water fallout of the mountains! A beautiful sight and terrible; a relentless glassy roller fringed along its base by a lace of racing foam. The upper part was as smooth as crystal; the stored-up waters of the mountain moving out compactly. The man thought of the little town below and its peril. But Huyck thought also. He shouted in Winter's ear:

"Never mind the town. Keep straight north. Over yonder to the point of the water. The town will have to drown."

It was inexorable; there was no pity; the very strength and purpose of the command drove into the other's understanding. Dimly now he realized that they were really running a race against time. Winters was a daredevil; the very catastrophe sent a thrill of exultation through him. It was the climax, the great moment of his life, to be driving at a hundred miles an hour under that wall of water.

The roar was terrible, Before they were half across it seemed to the two men that the very sound would drown them. There was nothing in the world but pandemonium. The strange flash was forgotten in the terror of the living wall that was reaching out to engulf them. Like insects they whizzed in the open face of the deluge. When they had reached the tip they were so close that the outrunning fringe of the surf was at their wheels.

Around the point with the wide open plain before them. With the flood behind them it was nothing to outrun it. The waters with a wider stretch spread out. In a few moments they had left all behind them.

But Winters wondered; what was the strange flash of evanescent beauty? He knew this dam and its construction; to outlast the centuries. It had been whiffed in a second. It was not lightning. He had heard no sound other than the rush of the waters. He looked to his companion.

Hueyk nodded.

"That's the thing we are racing. We have only a few hours. Can we make it?"

Bob had thought that he was getting all the speed possible out of his motor. What it yielded from that moment on was a revelation.

It is not safe and hardly possible to be driving at such speed on the desert. Only the best car and a firm roadway can stand it. A sudden rut, squirrel hole, or pocket of sand is as good as destruction. They rushed on till noon.

Not even Winters, with all his alertness, could avoid it. Perhaps he was weary. The tedious hours, the racking speed had worn him to exhaustion. They had ceased to individualize, their way a blur, a nightmare of speed and distance.

It came suddenly, a blind barranca – one of those sunken, useless channels that are death to the unwary. No warning.

It was over just that quickly. A mere flash of consciousness plus a sensation of flying. Two men broken on the sands and the great, beautiful roadster a twisted ruin.

Chapter VII
A Riven Continent

BUT BACK TO THE WORLD. No one knew about Charley Huyck nor what was occurring on the desert. Even if we had it would have been impossible to construe connection.

After the news out of Oakland, and the destruction of Mt. Heckla, we were far too appalled. The whole thing was beyond us. Not even the scientists with all their data could find one thing to work on. The wires of the world buzzed with wonder and with panic. We were civilized. It is really strange how quickly, in spite of our boasted powers, we revert to the primitive.

Superstition cannot die. Where was no explanation must be miracle. The thing had been repeated. When would it strike again. And where?

There was not long to wait. But this time the stroke was of far more consequence and of far more terror. The sheer might of the thing shook the earth. Not a man or government that would not resign in the face of such destruction.

It was omnipotent. A whole continent had been riven. It would be impossible to give description of such catastrophe; no pen can tell it any more than it could describe the creation. We can only follow in its path.

On the morning after the first catastrophe, at eight o'clock, just south of the little city of Santa Cruz, on the north shore of the Bay of Monterey, the same light and the same, though not quite the same, instantaneousness. Those who beheld it report a vast ball of azure blue and opalescent fire and motion; a strange sensation of vitalized vibration; of personified living force. In shape like a marble, as round as a full moon in its glory, but of infinitely more beauty.

It came from nowhere; neither from above the earth nor below it. Seeming to leap out of nothing, it glided or rather vanished to the eastward. Still the effect of winking, though this time, perhaps from a distanced focus, more vivid. A dot or marble, like a full moon, burning, opal, soaring to the eastward.

And instantaneous. Gone as soon as it was come; noiseless and of phantom beauty; like a finger of the Omnipotent tracing across the world, and as terrible. The human mind had never conceived a thing so vast.

Beginning at the sands of the ocean the whole country had vanished; a chasm twelve miles wide and of unknown depth running straight to the eastward. Where had been farms and homes was nothing; the mountains had been seared like butter. Straight as an arrow.

Then the roar of the deluge. The waters of the Pacific breaking through its sands and rolling into the Gulf of Mexico. That there was no heat was evidenced by the fact that there was no steam. The thing could not be internal. Yet what was it?

One can only conceive in figures. From the shores of Santa Cruz to the Atlantic – a few seconds; then out into the eastern ocean straight out into the Sea of the Sargasso. A great gulf riven straight across the face of North America.

The path seemed to follow the sun; it bore to the eastward with a slight southern deviation. The mountains it cut like cheese. Passing just north of Fresno it seared through the gigantic Sierras halfway between the Yosemite and Mt. Whitney, through the great desert to southern Nevada, thence across northern Arizona, New Mexico, Texas, Arkansas, Mississippi, Alabama, and Georgia, entering the Atlantic at a point half-way between Brunswick and Jacksonville. A great canal twelve miles in width linking the oceans. A cataclysmic blessing. Today, with thousands of ships bearing freight over its water, we can bless that part of the disaster.

But there was more to come. So far the miracle had been sporadic. Whatever had been its force it had been fatal only on point and occasion. In a way it had been local. The deadly atmospheric combination of its aftermath was invariable in its recession. There was no suffering. The death that it dealt was the death of obliteration. But now it entered on another stage.

The world is one vast ball, and, though large, still a very small place to live in. There are few of us, perhaps, who look upon it, or even stop to think of it, as a living being. Yet it is just that. It has its currents, life, pulse, and its fevers; it is coordinate; a million things such as the great streams of the ocean, the swirls of the atmosphere, make it a place to live in. And we are conscious only, or mostly, through disaster.

A strange thing happened.

The great opal like a mountain of fire had riven across the continent. From the beginning and with each succession the thing was magnified. But it was not until it had struck the waters of the Atlantic that we became aware of its full potency and its fatality.

The earth quivered at the shock, and man stood on his toes in terror. In twenty-four hours our civilization was literally falling to pieces. We were powerful with the forces that we understood; but against this that had been literally ripped from the unknown we were insignificant. The whole world was frozen. Let us see.

Into the Atlantic! The transition. Hitherto silence. But now the roar of ten thousand million Niagaras, the waters of the ocean rolling, catapulting, roaring into the gulf that had been seared in its bosom. The Gulf Stream cut in two, the currents that tempered our civilization sheared in a second. Straight into the Sargasso Sea. The great opal, liquid fire, luminescent, a ball like the setting sun, lay poised upon the ocean. It was the end of the earth!

What was this thing? The whole world knew of it in a second. And not a one could tell. In less than forty hours after its first appearance in Oakland it had consumed a mountain, riven a continent, and was drinking up an ocean. The tangled sea of the Sargasso, dead calm for ages, was a cataract; a swirling torrent of maddened waters rushed to the opal – and disappeared.

It was hellish and out of madness; as beautiful as it was uncanny. The opal high as the Himalayas brooding upon the water; its myriad colors blending, winking in a phantasm of iridescence. The beauty of its light could be seen a thousand miles. A thing out of mystery and out of forces. We had discovered many things and knew much; but had guessed no such thing as this. It was vampirish, and it was literally drinking up the earth.

Consequences were immediate. The point of contact was fifty miles across, the waters of the Atlantic with one accord turned to the magnet. The Gulf Stream veered straight from its course and out across the Atlantic. The icy currents from the poles freed from the warmer barrier descended along the coasts and thence out into the Sargasso Sea. The temperature of the temperate zone dipped below the point of a blizzard.

The first word come out of London. Freezing! And in July! The fruit and entire harvest of northern Europe destroyed. Olympic games at Copenhagen postponed by a foot of snow. The river Seine frozen. Snow falling in New York. Crops nipped with frost as far south as Cape Hatteras.

A fleet of airplanes was despatched from the United States and another from the west coast of Africa. Not half of them returned. Those that did reported even more disaster. The reports that were handed in were appalling. They had sailed straight on. It was like flying into the sun; the vividness of the opalescence was blinding, rising for miles above them alluring, drawing and unholy, and of a beauty that was terror.

Only the tardy had escaped. It even drew their motors, it was like gravity suddenly become vitalized and conscious. Thousands of machines vaulted into the opalescence. From those ahead hopelessly drawn and powerless came back the warning. But hundreds could not escape.

"Back," came the wireless. "Do not come too close. The thing is a magnet. Turn back before too late. Against this man is insignificant."

Then like gnats flitting into fire they vanished into the opalescence.

The others turned back. The whole world freezing shuddered in horror. A great vampire was brooding over the earth. The greatness that man had attained to was nothing. Civilization was tottering in a day. We were hopeless.

Then came the last revelation; the truth and verity of the disaster and the threatened climax. The water level of all the coast had gone down. Vast ebb tides had gone out not to return. Stretches of sand where had been surf extended far out into the sea. Then the truth! The thing, whatever it was, was drinking up the ocean.

Chapter VIII
The Man who Saved the Earth

IT WAS TRAGIC; grim, terrible, cosmic. Out of nowhere had come this thing that was eating up the earth. Not a thing out of all our science had there been to warn us; not a word from all our wise men. We who had built up our civilization, piece by piece, were after all but insects.

We were going out in a maze of beauty into the infinity whence we came. Hour by hour the great orb of opalescence grew in splendor; the effect and the beauty of its lure spread about the earth; thrilling, vibrant like suppressed music. The old earth helpless. Was it possible that out of her bosom she could not pluck one intelligence to save her? Was there not one law – no answer?

Out on the desert with his face to the sun lay the answer. Though almost hopeless there was still some time and enough of near-miracle to save us. A limping fate in the shape of two Indians and a battered runabout at the last moment.

Little did the two red men know the value of the two men found that day on the desert. To them the debris of the mighty car and the prone bodies told enough of the story. They were Samaritans; but there are many ages to bless them.

As it was there were many hours lost. Without this loss there would have been thousands spared and an almost immeasurable amount of disaster. But we have still to be thankful. Charley Huyck was still living.

He had been stunned; battered, bruised, and unconscious; but he had not been injured vitally. There was still enough left of him to drag himself to the old runabout and call for Winters. His companion, as it happened, was in even better shape than himself, and waiting. We do not know how they talked the red men out of their relic – whether by coaxing, by threat, or by force.

Straight north. Two men battered, worn, bruised, but steadfast, bearing in that limping old motor-car the destiny of the earth. Fate was still on the job, but badly crippled.

They had lost many precious hours. Winters had forfeited his right to the thirty thousand. He did not care. He understood vaguely that there was a stake over and above all money. Huyck said nothing; he was too maimed and too much below will-power to think of speaking. What had occurred during the many hours of their unconsciousness was unknown to them. It was not until they came sheer upon the gulf that had been riven straight across the continent that the awful truth dawned on them.

To Winters it was terrible. The mere glimpse of that blackened chasm was terror. It was bottomless; so deep that its depths were cloudy; the misty haze of its uncertain shadows was akin to chaos. He understood vaguely that it was related to that terrible thing they had beheld in the morning. It was not the power of man. Some force had been loosened which was ripping the earth to its vitals. Across the terror of the chasm he made out the dim outlines of the opposite wall. A full twelve miles across.

For a moment the sight overcame even Huyck himself. Full well he knew; but knowing, as he did, the full fact of the miracle was even more than he expected. His long years under Robold, his scientific imagination had given him comprehension. Not puny steam, nor weird electricity, but force, kinetics – out of the universe.

He knew. But knowing as he did, he was overcome by the horror. Such a thing turned loose upon the earth! He had lost many hours; he had but a few hours remaining. The thought gave him sudden energy. He seized Winters by the arm.

"To the first town, Bob. To the first town – an aerodome."

There was speed in that motor for all its decades. Winters turned about and shot out in a lateral course parallel to the great chasm. But for all his speed he could not keep back his question.

"In the name of Heaven, Charley, what did it? What is it?"

Came the answer; and it drove the lust of all speed through Winters:

"Bob," said Charley, "it is the end of the world – if we don't make it. But a few hours left. We must have an airplane. I must make the mountain."

It was enough for Wild Bob. He settled down. It was only an old runabout; but he could get speed out of a wheelbarrow. He had never driven a race like this. Just once did he speak. The words were characteristic.

"A world's record, Charley. And we're going to win. Just watch us."

And they did.

There was no time lost in the change. The mere fact of Huyck's name, his appearance and the manner of his arrival was enough. For the last hours messages had been pouring in at every post in the Rocky Mountains for Charley Huyck. After the failure of all others many thousands had thought of him.

Even the government, unappreciative before, had awakened to a belated and almost frantic eagerness. Orders were out that everything, no matter what, was to be at his disposal. He had been regarded as visionary; but in the face of what had occurred, visions were now the most practical things for mankind. Besides, Professor Williams had sent out to the world the strange portent of Huyck's note. For years there had been mystery on that mountain. Could it be?

Unfortunately we cannot give it the description we would like to give. Few men outside of the regular employees have ever been to the Mountain of Robold. From the very first, owing perhaps to the great forces stored, and the danger of carelessness, strangers and visitors had been barred. Then, too, the secrecy of Dr. Robold – and the respect of his successor. But we do know that the burning glass had grown into the mountain.

Bob Winters and the aviator are the only ones to tell us; the employees, one and all, chose to remain. The cataclysm that followed destroyed the work of Huyck and Robold – but not until it had served the greatest deed that ever came out of the minds of men. And had it not been for Huyck's insistence we would not have even the account that we are giving.

It was he who insisted, nay, begged, that his companions return while there was yet a chance. Full well he knew. Out of the universe, out of space he had coaxed the forces that would burn up the earth. The great ball of luminous opalescence, and the diminishing ocean!

There was but one answer. Through the imaginative genius of Robold and Huyck, fate had worked up to the moment. The lad and the burning glass had grown to Archimedes.

What happened?

The plane neared the Mountain of Robold. The great bald summit and the four enormous globes of crystal. At least we so assume. We have Winter's word and that of the aviator that they were of the appearance of glass. Perhaps they were not; but we can assume it for description. So enormous that were they set upon a plain they would have overtopped the highest building ever constructed; though on the height of the mountain, and in its contrast, they were not much more than golf balls.

It was not their size but their effect that was startling. They were alive. At least that is what we have from Winters. Living, luminous, burning, twisting within with a thousand blending, iridescent beautiful colors. Not like electricity but something infinitely more powerful. Great mysterious magnets that Huyck had charged out of chaos. Glowing with the softest light; the whole mountain brightened as in a dream, and the town of Robold at its base lit up with a beauty that was past beholding.

It was new to Winters. The great buildings and the enormous machinery. Engines of strangest pattern, driven by forces that the rest of the world had not thought of. Not a sound; the whole works a complicated mass covering a hundred acres, driving with a silence that was magic. Not a whir nor friction. Like a living composite body pulsing and breathing the strange and mysterious force that had been evolved from Huyck's theory of kinetics. The four great steel conduits running from the globes down the side of the mountain. In the center, at a point midway between the globes, a massive steel needle hung on a pivot and pointed directly at the sun.

Winters and the aviator noted it and wondered. From the lower end of the needle was pouring a luminous stream of pale-blue opalescence, a stream much like a liquid, and of an unholy, radiance. But it was not a liquid, nor fire, nor anything seen by man before.

It was force. We have no better description than the apt phrase of Winters. Charley Huyck was milking the sun, as it dropped from the end of the four living streams to the four globes that took it into storage. The four great, wonderful living globes; the four batteries; the very sight of their imprisoned beauty and power was magnetic.

The genius of Huyck and Robold! Nobody but the wildest dreamers would have conceived it. The life of the sun. And captive to man; at his will and volition. And in the next few minutes we were to lose it all! But in losing it we were to save ourselves. It was fate and nothing else. There was but one thing more upon the mountain – the observatory and another needle apparently idle; but with a point much like a gigantic phonograph needle. It rose square out of the observatory, and to Winters it gave an impression of a strange gun, or some implement for sighting.

That was all. Coming with the speed that they were making, the airmen had no time for further investigation. But even this is comprehensive. Minus the force. If we only knew more about that or even its theory we might perhaps reconstruct the work of Charley Huyck and Dr. Robold.

They made the landing. Winters, with his nature, would be in at the finish; but Charley would not have it.

"It is death, Bob," he said. "You have a wife and babies. Go back to the world. Go back with all the speed you can get out of your motors. Get as far away as you can before the end comes."

With that he bade them a sad farewell. It was the last spoken word that the outside world had from Charley Huyck.

The last seen of him he was running up the steps of his office. As they soared away and looked back they could see men, the employees, scurrying about in frantic haste to their respective posts and stations. What was it all about? Little did the two aviators know. Little did they dream that it was the deciding stroke.

Chapter IX
The Most Terrific Moment in History

STILL THE GREAT BALL of Opalescence brooding over the Sargasso. Europe now was frozen, and though it was midsummer had gone into winter quarters. The Straits of Dover were no more. The waters had receded and one could walk, if careful, dry-shod from the shores of France to the chalk cliffs of England. The Straits of Gibraltar had dried up. The Mediterranean completely land-locked, was cut off forever from the tides of the mother ocean.

The whole world going dry; not in ethics, but in reality. The great Vampire, luminous, beautiful beyond all ken and thinking, drinking up our life-blood. The Atlantic a vast whirlpool.

A strange frenzy had fallen over mankind: men fought in the streets and died in madness. It was fear of the Great Unknown, and hysteria. At such a moment the veil of civilization was torn to tatters. Man was reverting to the primeval.

Then came the word from Charley Huyck; flashing and repeating to every clime and nation. In its assurance it was almost as miraculous as the Vampire itself. For man had surrendered.

To the People of the World:

The strange and terrible Opalescence which, for the past seventy hours, has been playing havoc with the world, is not miracle, nor of the supernatural, but a mere manifestation and result of the application of celestial kinetics. Such a thing always was and always will be possible where there is intelligence to control and harness the forces that lie about us. Space is not space exactly, but an infinite cistern of unknown laws and forces. We may control certain laws on earth, but until we reach out farther we are but playthings.

Man is the intelligence of the earth. The time will come when he must be the intelligence of a great deal of space as well. At the present time you are merely fortunate and a victim of a kind fate. That I am the instrument of the earth's salvation is merely chance. The real man is Dr. Robold. When he picked me up on the streets I had no idea that the sequence of time would drift to this moment. He took me into his work and taught me.

Because he was sensitive and was laughed at, we worked in secret. And since his death, and out of respect to his memory, I have continued in the same manner. But I have written down everything, all the laws, computations, formulas – everything; and I am now willing it to mankind.

Robold had a theory on kinetics. It was strange at first and a thing to laugh at; but he reduced it to laws as potent and as inexorable as the laws of gravitation.

The luminous Opalescence that has almost destroyed us is but one of its minor manifestations. It is a message of sinister intelligence; for back of it all is an Intelligence. Yet it is not all sinister. It is self-preservation. The time is coming when eons of ages from now our own man will be forced to employ just such a weapon for his own preservation. Either that or we shall die of thirst and agony.

Let me ask you to remember now, that whatever you have suffered, you have saved a world. I shall now save you and the earth.

In the vaults you will find everything. All the knowledge and discoveries of the great Dr. Robold, plus a few minor findings by myself.

And now I bid you farewell. You shall soon be free.

Charley Huyck.

A strange message. Spoken over the wireless and flashed to every clime, it roused and revived the hope of mankind. Who was this Charley Huyck? Uncounted millions of men had never heard his name; there were but few, very few who had.

A message out of nowhere and of very dubious and doubtful explanation. Celestial kinetics! Undoubtedly. But the words explained nothing. However, man was ready to accept anything, so long as it saved him.

For a more lucid explanation we must go back to the Arizona observatory and Professor Ed. Williams. And a strange one it was truly; a certain proof that consciousness is more potent, far more so than mere material; also that many laws of our astronomers are very apt to be overturned in spite of their mathematics.

Charley Huyck was right. You cannot measure intelligence with a yard-stick. Mathematics do not lie; but when applied to consciousness they are very likely to kick backward. That is precisely what had happened.

The suddenness of Huyck's departure had puzzled Professor Williams; that, and the note which he found upon the table. It was not like Charley to go off so in the stress of a moment. He had not even taken the time to get his hat and coat. Surely something was amiss.

He read the note carefully, and with a deal of wonder.

"Look these up. Keep by the lens. If the world goes up you will know I have not reached the mountain."

What did he mean? Besides, there was no data for him to work on. He did not know that an errant breeze, had plumped the information behind the bookcase. Nevertheless he went into the observatory, and for the balance of the night stuck by the lens.

Now there are uncounted millions of stars in the sky. Williams had nothing to go by. A needle in the hay-stack were an easy task compared with the one that he was allotted. The flaming mystery, whatever it was that Huyck had seen, was not caught by the professor. Still, he wondered. "If the world goes up you will know I have not reached the mountain." What was the meaning?

But he was not worried. The professor loved Huyck as a visionary and smiled not a little at his delightful fancies. Doubtless this was one of them. It was not until the news came flashing out of Oakland that he began to take it seriously. Then followed the disappearance of Mount Heckla. "If the world goes up" – it began to look as if the words had meaning.

There was a frantic professor during the next few days. When he was not with the lens he was flashing out messages to the world for Charley Huyck. He did not know that Huyck was lying unconscious and almost dead upon the desert. That the world was coming to catastrophe he knew full well; but where was the man to save it? And most of all, what had his friend meant by the words, 'look these up?'

Surely there must be some further information. Through the long, long hours he stayed with the lens and waited. And he found nothing.

It was three days. Who will ever forget them? Surely not Professor Williams. He was sweating blood. The whole world was going to pieces without the trace of an explanation. All the mathematics, all the accumulations of the ages had availed for nothing. Charley

Huyck held the secret. It was in the stars, and not an astronomer could find it. But with the seventeenth hour came the turn of fortune. The professor was passing through the office. The door was open, and the same fitful wind which had played the original prank was now just as fitfully performing restitution. Williams noticed a piece of paper protruding from the back of the bookcase and fluttering in the breeze. He picked it up. The first words that he saw were in the handwriting of Charley Huyck. He read:

In the last extremity – in the last phase when there is no longer any water on the earth; when even the oxygen of the atmospheric envelope has been reduced to a minimum – man, or whatever form of intelligence is then upon the earth, must go back to the laws which governed his forebears. Necessity must ever be the law of evolution. There will be no water upon the earth, but there will be an unlimited quantity elsewhere.

By that time, for instance, the great planet, Jupiter, will be in just a convenient state for exploitation. Gaseous now, it will be, by that time, in just about the stage when the steam and water are condensing into ocean. Eons of millions of years away in the days of dire necessity. By that time the intelligence and consciousness of the earth will have grown equal to the task.

It is a thing to laugh at (perhaps) just at present. But when we consider the ratio of man's advance in the last hundred years, what will it be in a billion? Not all the laws of the universe have been discovered, by any means. At present we know nothing. Who can tell?

Aye, who can tell? Perhaps we ourselves have in store the fate we would mete out to another. We have a very dangerous neighbor close beside us. Mars is in dire straits for water. And we know there is life on Mars and intelligence! The very fact on its face proclaims it. The oceans have dried up; the only way they have of holding life is by bringing their water from the polar snow-caps. Their canals pronounce an advanced state of cooperative intelligence; there is life upon Mars and in an advanced stage of evolution.

But how far advanced? It is a small planet, and consequently eons of ages in advance of the earth's evolution. In the nature of things Mars cooled off quickly, and life was possible there while the earth was yet a gaseous mass. She has gone to her maturity and into her retrogression; she is approaching her end. She has had less time to produce intelligence than intelligence will have – in the end – upon the earth.

How far has this intelligence progressed? That is the question. Nature is a slow worker. It took eons of ages to put life upon the earth; it took eons of more ages to make this life conscious. How far will it go? How far has it gone on Mars?

That was as far the comments went. The professor dropped his eyes to the rest of the paper. It was a map of the face of Mars, and across its center was a black cross scratched by the dull point of a soft pencil.

He knew the face of Mars. It was the Ascraeus Lucus. The oasis at the juncture of a series of canals running much like the spokes of a wheel. The great Uranian and Alander Canals coming in at about right angles.

In two jumps the professor was in the observatory with the great lens swung to focus. It was the great moment out of his lifetime, and the strangest and most eager moment, perhaps, ever lived by any astronomer. His fingers fairly twitched with tension. There before his view was the full face of our Martian neighbor!

But was it? He gasped out a breath of startled exclamation. Was it Mars that he gazed at; the whole face, the whole thing had been changed before him.

Mars has ever been red. Viewed through the telescope it has had the most beautiful tinge imaginable, red ochre, the weird tinge of the desert in sunset. The color of enchantment and of hell!

For it is so. We know that for ages and ages the planet has been burning up; that life was possible only in the dry sea-bottoms and under irrigation. The rest, where the continents once were, was blazing desert. The redness, the beauty, the enchantment that we so admired was burning hell.

All this had changed.

Instead of this was a beautiful shade of iridescent green. The red was gone forever. The great planet standing in the heavens had grown into infinite glory. Like the great Dog Star transplanted.

The professor sought out the Ascraeus Lucus. It was hard to find. The whole face had been transfigured; where had been canals was now the beautiful sheen of green and verdure. He realized what he was beholding and what he had never dreamed of seeing; the seas of Mars filled up.

With the stolen oceans our grim neighbor had come back to youth. But how had it been done. It was horror for our world. The great luminescent ball of Opalescence! Europe frozen and New York a mass of ice. It was the earth's destruction. How long could the thing keep up; and whence did it come? What was it?

He sought for the Ascraeus Lucus. And he beheld a strange sight. At the very spot where should have been the juncture of the canals he caught what at first looked like a pin-point flame, a strange twinkling light with flitting glow of Opalescence. He watched it, and he wondered. It seemed to the professor to grow; and he noticed that the green about it was of different color. It was winking, like a great force, and much as if alive; baneful.

It was what Charley Huyck had seen. The professor thought of Charley. He had hurried to the mountain. What could Huyck, a mere man, do against a thing like this? There was naught to do but sit and watch it drink of our life-blood. And then –

It was the message, the strange assurance that Huyck was flashing over the world. There was no lack of confidence in the words he was speaking. 'Celestial Kinetics,' so that was the answer! Certainly it must be so with the truth before him. Williams was a doubter no longer. And Charley Huyck could save them. The man he had humored. Eagerly he waited and stuck by the lens. The whole world waited.

It was perhaps the most terrific moment since creation. To describe it would be like describing doomsday. We all of us went through it, and we all of us thought the end had come; that the earth was torn to atoms and to chaos.

The State of Colorado was lurid with a red light of terror; for a thousand miles the flame shot above the earth and into space. If ever spirit went out in glory that spirit was Charley Huyck! He had come to the moment and to Archimedes. The whole world rocked to the recoil. Compared to it the mightiest earthquake was but a tender shiver. The consciousness of the earth had spoken!

The professor was knocked upon the floor. He knew not what had happened. Out of the windows and to the north the flame of Colorado, like the whole world going up. It was the last moment. But he was a scientist to the end. He had sprained his ankle and his face was bleeding; but for all that he struggled, fought his way to the telescope. And he saw:

The great planet with its sinister, baleful, wicked light in the center, and another light vastly larger covering up half of Mars. What was it? It was moving. The truth set him almost to shouting.

It was the answer of Charley Huyck and of the world. The light grew smaller, smaller, and almost to a pin-point on its way to Mars.

The real climax was in silence. And of all the world only Professor Williams beheld it. The two lights coalesced and spread out; what it was on Mars, of course, we do not know.

But in a few moments all was gone. Only the green of the Martian Sea winked in the sunlight. The luminous opal was gone from the Sargasso. The ocean lay in peace.

It was a terrible three days. Had it not been for the work of Robold and Huyck life would have been destroyed. The pity of it that all of their discoveries have gone with them. Not even Charley realized how terrific the force he was about to loosen.

He had carefully locked everything in vaults for a safe delivery to man. He had expected death, but not the cataclysm. The whole of Mount Robold was shorn away; in its place we have a lake fifty miles in diameter.

So much for celestial kinetics.

And we look to a green and beautiful Mars. We hold no enmity. It was but the law of self-preservation. Let us hope they have enough water; and that their seas will hold. We don't blame them, and we don't blame ourselves, either for that matter. We need what we have, and we hope to keep it.

Long as I Can See the Light

Maria Haskins

"DO YOU REMEMBER that night when we saw the light?"

She asks this as they're sitting on the balcony, and he turns to look at her. When he meets her gaze he can see the thing that lurks within her now – the presence that isn't really her – look back at him, peering out through those familiar blue eyes. A cold trickle of fear runs down his spine, and he almost gets up, he almost runs away from her again, but he has been running for so long already. He's too old to run, too tired.

What year is it? What month? He has to think about it for a while, and when he eventually remembers, he realizes that it's almost exactly forty years since he ran away from her the first time.

He inhales deeply from the cigarette, knowing it's his last smoke: a filthy, hand-rolled, slim and rather bitter stick of something that is supposed to resemble tobacco, but doesn't really. She asked him about that: where he got the cigarettes, why he started smoking. "No one smokes anymore," she said. "No one even manufactures cigarettes." And of course that's true enough. He could have told her that he picked up the habit in recent years when he lived rough in the alleys downtown. He could have told her that there are times and places and situations when sharing something, anything – even a lousy cigarette – with a stranger is a way to feel a connection, however briefly: a fragile tendril of community and communion. But in the end he said nothing at all, just shrugged.

"Do you remember?" she asks again, prodding him. As if he could forget. As if that one memory is not his everlasting, never-ending nightmare.

He remembers it very well. He remembers sitting with her, with Lisa, in the park that night, in that small suburb outside Vancouver. They sat next to each other on the blanket he had brought and spread out in the grass near the baseball field. The blanket was just for sitting on. It wasn't like he thought they'd be making out or anything like that. It wasn't like that between them, not then or ever. And that was fine, because Lisa was his friend. His best friend. His only friend, really, when he thinks about it now.

They were born the same year and grew up in the same cul-de-sac: they went to the same preschool, the same school, eventually the same high school. Through the years, Lisa stuck with him, even when other kids laughed at him, and called him crazy or stupid. The doctors and his parents used words like 'neurological disorder' instead, of course. Whatever that meant. All he knew was that he noticed some things that no one else seemed to see, and that he couldn't understand some things that others found self-evident. But Lisa never seemed to care about any of that. Lisa simply remained his friend.

The night when they saw the light, he had asked her to come with him to the park after dark, saying he wanted to show her something. Maybe she thought he'd bring his telescope and that they'd look at some planet, or the moon. They used to do that back then because they were both into science and science fiction and astronomy. He didn't tell her what he had seen in the park on the two previous nights: he just wanted her to come with him, because if she could see it, too, then it had to be real, and not all in his head. She kept asking: "What is it? What is it you want me to see?" And he remembers saying: "You'll see. It'll be worth it."

She was always kind to me, he thinks, and feels a piercing sense of guilt and loss and grief as he sucks in another puff of stinking fake tobacco.

The woman who looks like Lisa, but who has someone else or something else hidden behind her eyes and beneath the bone of her skull, is still regarding him: her face is patient, compassionate, even. It's a convincing mask, but he knows better than to trust her.

They sat side by side in the grass. It was warm and summery and early July. She looked up at the sky, and he looked up at the sky, too, when he wasn't looking at her. "Which star do you want to go to," she asked, and he laughed. They had played that game from when they were kids, picking out stars to go to, imagining the planets around those stars and the beings and creatures inhabiting those worlds. And right when he was going to answer, when he was going to tell her which star he would pick that night…there it was. It looked exactly like when he had seen it before: surfacing in the night-sky above them without warning like a gigantic metallic whale in deep ocean water, suspended between the stars. It looked close, but somehow you knew that it was far away – a shiny, luminescent metal hull, just hanging there above the Earth: terrifying, menacing, and wondrous all at once.

He heard her gasp and knew that it was real, that she could see it too, and he felt relieved. The first night he had seen it, he thought he must have imagined it, but then it had come back the second night. This was the third time he beheld it, and still his mind could barely contain the sheer mind-bending enormity of it. Everything about it – its glow, the smoothness of its surface, the magnitude of it – was utterly and undeniably alien.

Lisa looked at him with a strange expression, halfway between terror and elation, and she opened her mouth, as if to say something. Through the years he has often wondered what she was going to say, but he will never know, because in that moment the light hit her. A blinding, radiant, noiseless beam coming down from the metal hull above, lighting up her face and striking her down. She fell, fell flat on her back on the blanket.

And what did he do? He looked up and saw the ship disappear again, slipping back into the universe, unseen, while Lisa lay there, dead, on the ground. The light had killed her, that's what he assumed. So he ran. What else was there to do? It was the alien invasion. The takeover, doomsday, Armageddon, whatever you'd like to call it. He ran. And as he ran he saw the light come down again and again and again: that beam multiplying, stabbing down soundlessly, into the houses all the way down his street. Into his house, too, where his parents lived. He never saw them again. There is an almost unbearable emptiness in that thought.

He ran: crying, screaming, stumbling. He ran, wondering why it had stabbed Lisa and not him, wondering why there had been no warning, wondering how it was possible – with radar and NASA and satellites and internet – that no one knew it was there. No one but him, and he hadn't told anyone, hadn't warned anyone, not even Lisa. Instead he had brought her right to it. He ran, and kept running while the world was struck down all around him, and he kept running for forty years. Until today.

"What happened to you after that night?"

He looks at the glowing tip of the cigarette, not sure if he can, or wants to tell her. Certainly he doesn't remember all of it. He remembers running that whole night until he could go no farther. He remembers seeing people being hit, sprawling on the sidewalks, cars and trucks stopped dead on bridges and highways. He remembers looking up, but there was no sign of that massive hulk of metal up above. Still, the light struck from nowhere and everywhere.

Finally, he fell asleep in a ditch on the outskirts of Vancouver – just rolled into some bushes next to the road and passed out. When he woke up it was daylight, and everything looked normal: people walking around, buses and cars driving, everything as it should be. No dead bodies. No carnage. He couldn't understand it and stumbled through the streets, feeling half-dead and probably looking more than half crazy. Someone must have seen him and set the police on him because soon, four policemen descended. He remembers that three of them had oddly smooth, placid expressions as they looked at him, while the fourth seemed concerned and worried, asking: "What are you doing here? Are you hurt?"

Nobody else asked him that. The three other officers gazed at him silently and when he looked into their faces he saw it, saw that other presence for the first time. It – whatever it was – looked out at him through three pairs of human eyes, and he felt his heart slow and almost stop.

"Leave him," one of the three said, and the fourth policeman turned as if to question that order.

He wasn't even surprised when the light struck that fourth policeman down and he fell. He almost expected it. This time he stayed and watched: saw the man rise again after a few minutes, brush off his uniform and straighten his jacket and then turn and walk away with the others like nothing had happened.

Once the police were gone, he started running again. For days he ran and walked, stumbled and hid. He stole cars, bicycles, even a boat to get himself as far away from the city as he possibly could, heading into the northern wilderness along the pacific coast. There were less people there, more safety, he figured, but every time he met someone, he saw that other presence, that intruder, gazing out at him: every human face had become a mask with something else peeking out through the eye-sockets.

He went up the coast, farther into the wild. Life wasn't bad in the woods, along the ocean, but it was hard. He fished in the streams and ocean shallows, dug for clams and caught crabs, stole food sometimes, and went deep into the forest. A few times he was attacked, not by humans, but by bears, and cougars. He suffered through a few bouts of what might have been pneumonia over the years, and one time he almost died from an infection: a small cut on his shoulder that turned foul and black. In the end, he managed to steal some medical supplies from a truck and get rid of it, but his left arm hasn't been the same since.

How many years did he live in the wild? Almost thirty-five years it seems, though he is astounded it was that long. Some of those years, maybe most of them, he cannot remember. Amnesia or psychosis, the medical professionals might say. Post-traumatic stress. A mental breakdown. Paranoia. Whatever. His brain is like that, he knows now. Sometimes it clocks out when things get to be too much. But through it all, a part of his mind was always working away: remembering Lisa, remembering the light, remembering that night in the park, fitting the memories together with what he saw afterwards, trying to piece it all together, trying to understand what had happened to him, and to everyone else.

Even in the woods he occasionally ran into other people. Mining and logging operations seemed to be expanding every year, creeping ever farther into the wilderness. One time, he walked right into a group of workers near a hydroelectric dam. First, he thought they would kill or try to capture him, but they all just looked at him where he stood at the edge of the forest, saying nothing. Eventually they went back to their work. They were indifferent to his presence, almost as if they could not even see him, as if they knew he was not like them, as if they knew he had seen the light, but had not been touched by it.

The woods were not a bad place to be, but the years wore him down, and eventually he got sick. Sick and old. It was then that he started walking back to where he'd come from: back to the city. He was scared, but he figured he was sick and old enough that maybe no one would care.

When he came back to Vancouver five years ago, wandering across the old abandoned bridge that led into what used to be the park but was now the ever-expanding Space Hub, he could hardly believe his eyes. It was another world: brilliant lights illuminating the vessels being assembled; people crawling all over a vast expanse of metal and concrete; and all of those people working and working and working, ceaselessly, day and night. And the cars were all gone, that's something else he noticed right away: no combustion engines anymore. Just clean vehicles, quiet and efficient, running along the spotless streets. It was like arriving on another planet.

He ended up in the alleys of the Downtown Eastside. In the old days, it was a place for poor people, drug users, and misfits living precariously on the margins of society. It still is. Except now the misfits are those who have not been touched by the light. He has realized that most of them are like he is, that their minds are different somehow, deviating in minor or major ways from the norm. And he has realized that the Downtown Eastside is a pen, a ghetto, maintained to contain the dwindling number of untouched who have stubbornly refused to die.

In some ways the area has improved in the past forty years, he supposes. The alleys are cleaner, there are no drug dealers and no stores selling liquor or tobacco, and there is food and shelter for those who want it. Not that he has ever taken any charity. He knows what they are, these people who say they want to help. He has allowed them to treat his infections and illnesses, but afterwards he always goes back to the alleys. Before the light came, it was the do-gooders and religious nutters helping out the needy. Now it is the people who were stabbed by the light doing it: all of them kindly indifferent as they hand out blankets and food and medication. He knows they are not what they seem, that they want brains, souls, life force, whatever. Through the years he has told everyone he meets what he knows, yet nothing happens to him, and no one believes him. No one else can see it, no one else understands.

Suddenly he realizes that he's been talking out loud, that he has been telling her everything passing through his mind. He hears himself say:

"I slept in doorways, mostly. Scrounged food from garbage cans, ate rats."

"And then I found you."

He nods. Then she found him. Today. He figures she must have been looking for him, but he doesn't understand why. She found him sitting outside an old crumbling brick building, putting on a new pair of socks. There she was. Lisa. Not dead. Older, but much the same, even though he knows it isn't really Lisa anymore behind those eyes.

She stopped and looked at him in his filth and poverty. Looked at him like Lisa might have looked, her face soft and kind and gentle, but it was still just another mask, albeit a familiar one.

"Thomas," she said and it wasn't a question. She knew. She even touched his hand the way the real Lisa used to. She's doing it now, here on the balcony, too, squeezing his fingers lightly, smiling at him. And even though he knows it is not really Lisa, he begins to cry.

"Are you all right?"

She asks him this. As if he could be all right. She has brought him to this place, this apartment on the waterfront, with mountains on the horizon, a bird's eye view of the Space Hub, and the underwater industrial domes glinting far away in the dark ocean beyond. He has had a shower for the first time in months. She has fed him, and he is wearing the clean clothes she got for him: some kind of workman's overalls, but clean and comfortable.

His cigarette has burned out. There will be no more cigarettes for him, he is very sure of that. He looks up at the stars, though they are hard to see here because of all the lights. It is a summer night, just like the last time he sat next to her.

"Which star do you want to go to?" he asks and she sort of smiles, but he knows that the question means something else to her now than it used to do.

She starts talking. She tells him that his parents died some years before. They were good people and always missed him, she says, but they kept busy working in the space program after he disappeared. He thinks about his mother, who was an elementary school teacher, and his father, who worked his whole life at the port. He tries to imagine them working for a space program, but that is obviously impossible. Still, he cries for them, too.

"Thomas. Why do you think I brought you here?"

"To kill me. Or to take let them take me. One way or another you will destroy me."

She sighs.

"What is it you think happened when the light came? Can you tell me that?"

"I don't need to tell you. You know. Your kind knows."

"My kind? I see. But I would still like to hear you say it. Explain it to me. Explain why you ran away and kept running for forty years."

So he tells her. He tells her what he has spent so many sleepless nights and haunted days figuring out, piecing together. That something travelled across space and time in that enormous spacecraft. That it, they, came to earth and entered orbit and stabbed people's souls and hearts and minds with that light, taking them over, taking them away.

She says nothing, so he keeps talking.

"I think they wander the stars. Whether they are lost or exiled, I don't know. I think they have been traveling the galaxies for millennia. Maybe they have a goal in mind, maybe not. But they want to keep traveling, and they need resources to do so. I wonder how many worlds they've taken before this, how many worlds have been stripped of everything, just like our world is being stripped. The population taken and re-focused on one thing: producing the means for them, whoever they are, to keep going through the universe. I don't know what they are building exactly, or what they are extracting from the bottom of the ocean and the depths of earth, but I see the signs of their plan everywhere: new technology, mining, construction, space projects, everything consuming the earth. I figure after forty years they are probably almost ready to leave."

She is quiet for a moment, and then she laughs, a soft and not unpleasant sound.

"Oh, Thomas. Is that really what you think?"

He expected her to be colder and harder than this. He did not expect soft laughter, or the hand that still holds his.

"Let me tell you another story, a different story. You will probably not believe it, but I will tell it anyway. What if there were others out there, among the stars, just like you and I always hoped. What if they can indeed travel space and time, and what if they came here and saw us, watched us, watched our world, and saw us suffer through misery and war and poverty and disease and pain? And what if they realized that the reason for all that misery was locked deep inside our minds, and that we, the human beings, would never ever be free or happy or able to join this great universe as citizens until we cast off all the fears and doubts and weaknesses of our minds. What if they could cure us? Yes. Cure. Not 'take'. Not 'kill'. Not 'use'. Just free us, cure us, and then we would still be human, but stronger, and better."

She is right: he does not believe it.

"Just like that? One bright light, and then we're cured of every ill that's plagued humanity for over ten thousand years?"

She nods. He closes his eyes for a moment. It is a good story. It is a story that maybe, somewhere, he has thought of before, long before the lights came, during the nights when he and Lisa talked and watched the stars. It is not a true story, though. It can't be true. He has seen enough to know it isn't true, and he tells her that when he is able to speak again.

"What do you really know, Thomas? And what have you imagined, twisting reality to fit your own fears? Can you honestly tell me that your perception of other people, of this world, of the things around you has always been reliable?"

He knows the answer is 'no', but he doesn't want to tell her that. Instead he says:

"Why didn't the light take me that night? Why did it take you but not me?"

"It couldn't touch you, because your mind would have been…damaged. That is why some people were left out."

"But now it wants me? Are you that desperate? I guess you're running out of human bodies to do the work. I've noticed that there are fewer children. Are you really not able to breed enough new humans to meet the demand?"

She turns away. Maybe she sighs. Maybe she pretends to wipe away a tear.

"You are older. Things have changed in you. And if you can let it take you, willingly, and not be afraid, then you will be all right. I know it."

"So why not just take me? Like you were taken? Like everyone else was taken."

"Because it's better this way. No one wants to hurt you."

"Did it hurt you? When they took you?"

She still doesn't look at him, just shakes her head, gently.

"You're the one who is in pain, Thomas."

It is the truth, but he doesn't want to hear it. He looks at Lisa. She is looking at the stars now. He wonders what the thing inside her sees when it watches the night sky. Forty years is a long time. He can feel the years in his bones, feel the distances he's traveled in his sinews and joints, feel the cold nights and the biting winters in his flesh. He is scarred and weathered, aged, and diminished.

"I know what I have seen" he says, stubbornly.

"You know what I have seen?" Her eyes are suddenly strangely large and luminous in the dark. "I have seen a world without war for almost half a century. I have seen a world where human beings work together to develop the means for space travel and exploration. I have seen a world where every human being is better off than they were back then. How is that a horror story, Thomas? It is a story of salvation."

He thinks about that. He feels very old and tired and alone.

"I wish I'd gone back to see my parents, just one time."

"Why didn't you?"

"Because I knew they'd do to me what you are doing now. They would let me be taken."

"Thomas…"

"No." He tries to fight it, fight her, fight his own weakness. "Tell me what you've done to the humans. Tell me where they are. Are they still inside you? Are their minds trapped inside you? And when you're finished with this planet, will they all die then? Or will you let them go back to what they were before?"

She doesn't get angry, doesn't even raise her voice.

"Don't you want to believe it?" she asks. "That there is a better way to be human, that we are the real humans, and that you are the twisted remnant of what we no longer have to be: crippled by anxieties and fears and aggression that you don't even understand yourself. We are free. We are making this world better."

"By using up the Earth? By using up every human being in this world to leave this planet?" He is speaking louder, more desperately now, as if trying to get the words out before it's too late. "To build those damn spaceships, to take flight, to go into space again, to go out there among the stars and take another world, devour other planets and other souls and other knowledge, just to propel yourselves a little farther into eternity?"

"You know that space is where humanity is meant to go. You used to believe that, too."

"Humanity, yes. But you are not human."

She is very quiet for a very long time.

"Thomas," she says finally. "Which star do you want to go to?"

And then he cracks. It is not a violent, painful thing. Rather, it is a relief: to give up, to surrender, to no longer have to fight. The light takes him almost right away: hits him, envelops him in its blinding power. This time it shines inside him, and he feels it burn away and sizzle and destroy. And for a moment he is nothing, he is annihilated, he is dead, but there is no darkness because he is starlight, pure and everlasting, and in that radiant purity he senses something else stir inside him, someone else, an awakening presence that either comes from outside or has always been there, he isn't exactly sure.

The last thing he feels before his body is taken away from him, before the presence fully takes hold, is Lisa – or rather: the thing that is not Lisa – letting go of his hand.

The last thing he sees – as the new presence in his mind overpowers and submerges his consciousness – is a brief glimpse of the night sky: the distant stars suddenly more familiar and alluring than they have ever been before.

The last thing he thinks is: "I was right! I was right all along!" He even tries to speak, scream, shout the words, but it is not his mouth anymore.

After that, the light goes out.

Blind Jump

Suo Hefu (索何夫)

Translated by Cai Yingqian (蔡盈倩) *& Collin Kong* (孔令武)

RUMBLING AND CRACKLING – now, it was too late to do anything.

He finally came to his senses and realized what a fatal mistake he had made when the massive and billowy brown surge broke through acoustic barriers outside the campsite and started to engulf this only peaceful and safe land. He should have perceived the perilousness lurking behind this seemingly tranquil woodland and marsh two days ago, after the scout unit that had been sent out lost contact with his team; they should have been prepared for the impending danger when the missioned reconnaissance UAV first sent back signals flickering on the screen of the landing spacecraft, locating an expanse of Darkness in the distance spreading far into the sky. Yet they hadn't – half stemming from excessive arrogance, and half out of self-deception and blind optimism. For a piece of comfort and numbness, they immersed themselves in countless optimistic 'excuses' and lies, thus letting the chance of self-rescue slip through their fingers. Finally, the situation became irretrievable.

Resistance was still going on at some places nearby – just as prey falling into a predator's claws still wants to fight a desperate battle for survival, his team members didn't wish to lie on the dining-table of this Darkness either. At the former camp border, explosions and flame accompanied by cries of rage or fear incessantly lit up the great caesious sky in the wee hours of the morning. His reason pitilessly reminded him that nothing could be changed – there was a definite lack of favorable conditions surviving from the jaws of death. Fuel and ammunition carried by the exploration team were limited, with the contrast of that vivid and lively ocean containing endless power; they could drag on for another minute, hour or even a day but as for the destined forthcoming outcome, they were unable to escape.

However he knew that there was at least one thing he could do.

He dashed through a heap of litten materials and climbed over a parapet cursorily built with some empty crates, the translucent mucus left nearby which told clearly the guarders' tragedy. A lump of Darkness found him and immediately started to condense, swooping on him like an agminate shadow. However, he moved faster than his enemy – this 'shadow' trembled and convulsed in deadly fiery arms and turned into a small black blob at last, smoking thickly and acridly on the ground. It was just like a monster whose soul had been stripped from its body by the Creator, but again returned to its original state before the creation.

He had a victory – sure, only a negligible one. For the ocean they were fighting against, it could not be counted a loss to evaporate a small drop of water. Yet it at least made his plan more feasible. After thinking for a while, he dropped the drained flamethrower and turned back, rushing towards the other end of the campsite. His lander was a star hanging in the sky, but fortunately, he still had another chance – there were two usable communicators at the campsite in total, one of which had been taken from the lander after he commanded it yesterday morning.

As he rushed to the tent sheltering that communicator, a dead silence was gradually taking the place of chaos and noise around – more and more people were encircled, overwhelmed, and engulfed by the surging and acrid flood of darkness, and the glow of flame and lights faded into nothingness as well. In two hours, the first flush of dawn would pass through the near canyons and spatter itself over this heavily forested but dry lagoon. However, he knew he would never see it.

He fell down in the dark, and stumbled for the second time. While he was tripping again, a lump of cold liquid caught his heels, entangling itself with him like the legendary Norse Kraken – the one that has an appetite for sailors, and dragged him into the hungry sea behind.

He tried to resist against the overwhelming force, but in vain. A sense of despair scratched his heart and pinched his throat like claws, but in this frantic struggle, his remaining sense of rationality still allowed him to take the last correct action – he grabbed the thing hanging from his belt, pulled the pin out, and hurriedly triggered the metal pull-tab on the top before more black tentacles could control him.

To his relief, all this ended quickly at least.

Night fell.

Nothing seemed different from every day before here on this planet which would never be named 'Earth'. Located a few kilometers south of the equator, a continent that would never be named 'Australia' was taking a slow southbound journey driven by the asthenosphere in the mantle. Onto its eastern coast, the warm sea waves from the equator were pounding and smashing, delivering a great amount of water vapor to the east side of the mountain range which could be named anything but 'Great Divide'. On its innumerable sister planets, this precious precipitation had all fruited vascular plant communities with exuberant vitality. Here, by contrast, the coastline, thousands of kilometers long, was covered by a sheet of gloomy and sticky liquid, appearing in the deepest sea-like black.

Anu still stayed wide awake when the last glow of the setting sun faded from the horizon. For it, this scene was not going to make any sense. This was because not only had it experienced billions of planetary rotations in its life, but the concept of 'alternation of day and night' did not make sense at all to it – its body stretched over every piece of land and parts of it pervaded each continent. At any time, there were some parts of its body being bathed in sunlight coming from 150 million kilometers away, while others hid themselves in the low-lying night view. These sensory signals were transmitted and aggregated by biological electronic pulses at the speed of light, and then became part of Anu's incredibly complex consciousness.

In many other parallel universes – formed by accidental quantum events – that would never have been a slightest overlap with this universe, this planet had bred a rich variety of life forms – there were, of course, the same number of other parallel universes where this planet had always been a deadly cold wilderness during the five billion years since it was originally formed, or a living hell baked by the greenhouse effect. However, the situation in this universe was different from both of the above – multicellular carbon-based organisms had never held a dominant position here because of a series of accidents and coincidences within a strange combination of circumstances along the long path of life evolution, and they had even been marginalized from the entire ecosystem during nearly 100 million sidereal years. An intelligent creature will find that the planet's surface has an albedo of more than 10 percentage points lower than its peers' in countless parallel universes, if he/ she looks at it from its only satellite – most of its land except the two poles was heavily covered by trillions of thick blanket-like black slime molds and even a considerable part of shallow sea had also been invaded.

This super-giant symbiont drew heat continuously and directly from the sun and then, with this energy, combined the collected carbon with water electrolysis hydrogen into a wide variety of hydrocarbon-based compounds, to constantly repair and expand its huge body. However, it was not a sole resident in this world as in this black-untouched area, there were still remaining advanced carbon-based ecosystems through which this super Leviathan could supplement trace elements that cannot be absorbed directly from air and water, and maintain atmospheric oxygen content at a liveable level. In short, the status of this planet was like a dynamic abstract painting explicitly expressing the concept of 'terror' – the living Darkness dominated anything and everything, greedily, insensibly and irrationally and their actions were solely guided by the most basic biological instincts – swallowing, digestion, and reproduction.

Of course, objective facts tend to be quite at odds with subjective impressions. Although it was somewhat incredible, the fact was that the first ray of intellectual light had quietly appeared amid this black as early as hundreds of thousands of centuries ago. In order to be more effective in adapting to the surviving competition mechanism, the slime mold community, which had not yet become an absolutely dominant species then, tried to achieve complex physiological mechanisms that do not belong to single-celled organisms through the specificity of its certain members – they did not own a nervous system, but they could achieve a similar result by increasing the conductivity of cell sap and cell membranes in some members and arranging them in a particular pattern; they did not have any limbs, so a part of the members at the edge of the symbiont formed versatile pseudopodia; they had no eyes, ears or nose and as a result, a large number of members distributed on the surface of the community became increasingly sensitive to thermal signals, air vibration and pheromones in the surrounding environment. All these developments eventually led to the need for a unified reception and processing of information, prompting more and more slime mold communities to further integrate together. After that, Anu was born.

Although Anu's 'lifespan' had far surpassed any living body that had gone through natural evolution, Anu got this name just a few planetary days before. On that unusual day, a small group of strange objects suddenly appeared in the sky almost 10,000 meters high above the planet, plunging toward the land surface as rapidly as meteors did.

Among a total of five such objects, one unfortunately crashed into a towering mountain range and was immediately buried in a terrible landslide caused by the impact; a wobbling one toppled into an active volcano standing on the edge of the mainland and was soon burnt to ashes among molten basalt; another two went straight to an island far from the island, beyond the reach of Anu and disappeared; only the last one landed safely on the continent and eventually fell into a saline bog that had not been covered by Anu's body.

At the beginning, Anu didn't pay too much attention to these 'meteors' – yes, these objects were indeed different from those of the past; they could not only appear in the atmosphere without any warning, but also realize a substantial reduction in their own speed in the final stage of falling so as to avoid the fate of dashing to pieces. But Anu, without a Ph.D. in astronomy or any experience taking related courses, naturally failed to recognize the implication of this series of anomalies. Everything stayed unchanged until a whole planetary day after the arrival of this 'meteor'.

In the wee hours of that morning, two creatures with two legs each – or rather, two flexible and bipedal multicellular organisms with an odd-shaped endoskeleton which was mostly composed of calcium carbonate – left the 'meteor' site, rashly approached the forest belt of ferns at the edge of a swamp, and then tripped into Anu's hunting trap.

On the whole, the two creatures from that meteor were not fundamentally different from the billions of carbon-based organisms that Anu once devoured, but in the process of capturing them, their reactions were much more unexpected – instead of instinctively running away like stupid animals, the two creatures used some kind of instrument spraying high-temperature plasma, trying to defend themselves from its attacks. Although they were still doomed to be engulfed in the end, fiery flames in the previous battle had destroyed a rather large part of Anu's body – it had never encountered this before.

Anu, out of curiosity, sneakily and prudently permeated the area of that fallen meteor and suddenly launched an attack on a small group of bipedal creatures camping around it unawares. This time, it didn't directly digest these creatures as a source of carbohydrate and protein. Instead, it did its best to capture them in their full shape (of course, the process did not go off smoothly) and carried out a meticulous study on these creatures – again, this was another thing that it had never done in the past hundreds of thousands of years.

The result of this study surprised Anu. Each of these bipedal creatures was an independent individual, but they obviously possessed wisdom not inferior to Anu's – these creatures who called themselves 'human beings' could act purposefully in a planned way, could carry out organized logical thinking like it did, and could even make and use tools to compensate for their lack of flexibly structured and multifunctional limbs and organs. (The word 'tool' was borrowed from the bipedal creatures' vocabulary. Anu had no idea of it before this study).

Anu was not new to fiddling with the nervous systems of multicellular organisms for it had been treating local animals with nervous systems as its playthings, manipulating their every movement by pheromones and bioelectrical signals, to kill time during its endless years. Finally, practice showed that these experiences could also be applied to these more advanced bipedal animals. Anu gradually mastered the knack of controlling these new toys after repeated attempts, which meant that it could not only have command over their basic physiological activities with the help of well-coded bioelectrical signals, but read their memory and absorb their knowledge by analyzing the brain activity of these creatures as well. On the third day after capturing them, Anu made use of the knowledge extracted from the brain belonging to a female creature known as 'Chief Programmer', to manage the computer which was made of metal, silicide crystals and other inorganic compounds in this man-made 'meteor' – it was also a crucial turning point of its incomparably long life.

It was within just one day that this magical machine gave it knowledge more than the information it had received over the past thousand centuries. It even used the data stored on the computer to name itself – Anu, a name originating from an ancient Babylonian myth, of a very good match with its own story. Yes, it was as omnipresent, omniscient, and overweening as the Sky God imagined by the ancients and tightly held the authority of this whole world with a supreme will.

But now, it was no longer satisfied with this.

The lungs in its chest, under the exact stimulation of a series of bioelectric pulses, gradually shrank and gently squeezed out a pocket of gas from the trachea. This air flow passed through the vocal cords and nasal cavity, coordinating with several delicate movements performed by the tongue, lip, jaw and mouth, and then a string of sound waves representing special meanings were spreading by ambient air. The woman sat upright in her former position, repeating mildly a short passage in her mother tongue – the working language of the spacecraft *Good Boy-21*, just as she used to do in dozens of rehearsals.

Of course, one thing was different from the rehearsal-version – she did not turn on the video system on the communication console or the video device as required. Or if not, people who received this communication signal would see the most bizarre scene they had seen in their life – at the back of the woman's head, on both sides of her cervical spine and her back, dozens of blood vessel-like pulsating black 'ropes' penetrated her grimy sky-blue uniform and hid beneath her pale skin, looking every bit like the strings pulling a puppet – certainly, people who saw this scene would be completely right if they really thought so. Although this woman was still alive in the sense of physiology, she was not much different from lower invertebrates that could only and simply respond to the stimulus; she used to be a correspondent of the expedition, but now she lost the title, and her name. In a sense, she was now only an organ attached to another organism.... But those who talked to her could not be aware of it.

"This is *Good Boy-21*. We call any monitoring centre at the landing site." A minute after the end of the 30th call, the correspondent pushed the button at the bottom of the control panel and started to repeat exactly the same content in exactly the same calm voice. This correspondent had once been a grouch. In the past, thirty consecutive fruitless calls would have probably made her hopping mad and foul-mouthed. But Anu never knew what anxiety really was because its endless but lifeless life had cultivated in it the virtue of patience a long time ago. "The landing ground has been successfully developed with no casualties. A survey shows that the local environment is at least of B-class liveable, but the accessory cabin carrying airdrop supplies encountered a jumping failure. We need emergency support. We need emergency support. For any listener of this message, please reply as soon as possible."

No response. Only white noise, boring and monotonous, came from the speaker. However Anu still decently kept its countenance. Following this woman's eyes (It had to admit that this organ that had a very sophisticated biological structure and was capable of stereoscopic vision, was much more effective than that light-sensitive stuff adhering to its surface which could only hazily distinguish between light and shade and hardly detect different colors), it patiently observed the timer at the corner of the communication console, waiting for the minute to end. If necessary, it could repeat this process thousands of, or even tens of thousands of times – after all, a short wait now would be worth it in the end.

Time was still gently lapsing through the timer display. A few small black sticks of equal length and width continuously flashed and extinguished, forming numeral characters one after another. Among all human inventions, numbers and mathematics astonished Anu most – before it was exposed to these concepts, its understanding of this world was made up of its pure perceptual knowledge about objective reality. But now, a new bright window was opened in front its eyes (This was another concept belonging to humanity, captured from the head of its captive). This was nothing more than a negligible tiny fraction, Anu told itself. The information contained in such a small cabin had already made it so excited. What would the humanity on the world bring it?

The last two digits on the timer changed to '50', and then '51', '52', '53', '54'.... As for Anu of past, such small fine-cut bits of time (The human term used for this was 'second', which was about 86,000 times shorter than the length of a planetary day) didn't make any sense. But given the short lifespan of humans and their tight and fast lifestyle, it was not surprising that this species would create such a sophisticated timing system. The number turned to

'58' and then '59'. Anu was adept at inputting a series of electrical instruction signals into the human body it controlled, preparing for the next attempt which might still be futile....

"This is communication relay station Ω-4. We have received your request." A voice – it should be of a middle-aged woman if Anu's analysis of those humans were correct, or to be more precise, it was a recording that had been coded, restructured and selected by an A.I. working at an automated communication relay station. The moment a correspondent laid a finger on the control panel, it sounded, "There was some interference within the frequency band just now, and now a more stable one has been made available. The new communication line will be opened in 75 seconds. Please repeat your identity. Thank you."

"This is *Good Boy-21*, Landing Spacecraft *UHG-2402*. We call any monitoring centre at the landing site." The voice of that woman sounded rather clear, but Lee couldn't read the image on the screen after he tried several times. "Repeat. The landing ground has been successfully developed with no casualties. A survey shows that the local environment is at least of B-class liveable. According to the certificate of authorization by the Exploration Committee, we hereby declare that we shall enjoy the ownership and prior usufruct of all natural resources at the landing site and the surrounding areas. Please answer as soon as you hear this message."

"This is a designated Monitor, No. 4313. The signal has been received." After the third attempt to connect video signals, Lee finally found that the other party hadn't uploaded video files from the start, by checking the task manager. "The computer is confirming your identity, why don't you open the video system as required?"

"The camera of the communication station didn't work while landing due to certain... physical damage." The woman on the other side continued to speak in a leisurely manner. It sounded like a restaurant waitress checking bills for her customers rather than an explorer in a new world of unknown danger. "We currently lack effective maintenance methods, but luckily sound signals can still be transmitted."

"All right. This is Landing Spacecraft *UHG-2402*." Lee cleared his throat. He had seen a variety of bizarre accidents during the six whole years that he worked for the Jumping Monitoring Centre. But no one ever made him feel like this...this kind of uneasy. Lee was not sure how to describe his feelings, but he felt like his head was filled with something unknown, stuffing him to nervousness. "We do have records about a bunch of guys like you. Please report your identity code..."

" -4404, Chad." The woman's voice was still 'quiet' – this was the first adjective Lee could think of. He was right. There was nothing unusual in her voice but still, it sounded as if something had gone. Yet somehow, the 'missing part' always made him feel like a fish out of water.

"The identity code is correct, captain." Rolfe, Lee's assistant, rubbed his sleepy eyes and yawned. As the most junior employee in the Listening Centre, Rolfe had been treated with the most frequent night shift among all people – this situation would continue until the next simpleton who registered for Multiverse Colonisation Project but was unqualified for pioneering work, joined the monitoring team. "Let me see.... Oh yes, the spacecraft was one of five landing spacecrafts that were sent to K-59 last month, and it didn't contact us until today, for the first time." He shook his head and poured half cup of cold coffee on monitoring console into his belly, like taking medicine. "I thought those guys had already kicked the bucket."

"Apparently not yet," Lee shrugged. He knew about the world called K-59 – of all the potential destinations of the Multiverse project, it was a sister world of 'their' Earth. But they parted ways about 800 to 1,000 million years ago caused by an unsettled major quantum event. Samples of gas and water collected through exploratory micro-channels indicated that the nitrogen-oxygen atmosphere there could support living creatures like humans. And of course, the concentrations of carbon dioxide and oxygen were slightly higher, and the humidity was unduly low. But overall, that was no big deal. The DNA double helix of local organisms was mostly right-handed rather than left-handed, which was exactly the same as this world where humans are born. What was really puzzling was that the amount of biomass detected in both the collected atmosphere and water sample was surprisingly small. The experts in the analysis group didn't discover pollen or wind-borne seeds. Spores, eggs, bacteria, and other living microorganisms did exist but were limited to a certain type and number. Undoubtedly the result of single sampling is often inaccurate and the location of sea and land, climatic conditions and even some special geographical features may also affect the test result. However, this resulting data was an average value based on a continuous sampling of different latitudes but it was still so hopelessly low. This, should really count for something.

Lee could still recall it when, in the following two days, a war of words had been waged in the Project Feasibility Assessment Committee on whether K-59 was suitable for human migration. Its intensity was no less than thirty-five years ago when Professor Greunov unveiled his 'Parallel Universe Jumping Theory' at the Global Physicist Annual Meeting, or fifteen years ago when experts of the Massachusetts Institute of Technology sparked off a massive public controversy through their formal application for launching the Multiverse Colonisation Project. Fortunately (or unfortunately, depending on your attitude towards it), K-59 was finally evaluated as B-level liveable. Two hundred and twenty-five volunteers who had been longing for this for a long time, carrying their real estate ownership certificates issued by the Exploration Committee according to the *New Homestead Act*, entered into five landing spacecraft equipped with chemical energy booster rockets, and entered into this unknown world at a relatively 'safe' height of ten thousand meters.

Then we got not a single message from them.

No one was surprised at the disappearance of this expedition. Although the Multiverse Colonisation Project had been under way for ten years, the colonial activities remained extremely difficult and dangerous. As to what was revealed by Professor Greunov's formula, though it is possible to 'drill' from one side through the gap between two parallel worlds separated by certain contingencies (in fact, it was in this way that the early scientists proved the existence of those worlds), it is totally uneconomical. The energy consumption to keep the passage open will grow exponentially as time goes by. The entropy a passage needs to last for only tens of femtoseconds for very few molecules to get through is not even enough for a luminous bacterium parasitizing on an anglerfish's tentacles to radiate. However, to maintain the connection between two worlds for hundreds of milliseconds – the time a passage should last for a common launching, the energy required equals the sum of all fossil fuels burned by humankind throughout the nineteenth century, and the amount of energy a passage cost to last hours was a much more shocking amount of energy. According to the technology department, even if every single hydrogen atom in this universe were fused into an iron atom by whatever means, with all background radiation taken into account, the energy they would generate could not keep the passage that long.

Of course, it is not impossible to establish a continuous connection between two worlds; otherwise, Lee would have had to find another job. To achieve that, all you have to do is just install a passage generator in each side at the exact same coordinate, so that the space-time passage can be opened and 'stretched' from both sides rather than one side – but you should find a suitable place at first to install the equipment, and prepare a stable energy supply for it. Before these two things, however, you must safely send a team in advance to the destination – that is where problems usually occur.

"Landing Spacecraft *UHG-2404*, this is the monitoring centre. Your identity has been confirmed." Lee cleared his throat, supressed his feeling of uneasiness as much as possible, "How are you now?"

"We are not too bad," said the correspondent of the landing spacecraft with the official unemotional calm tone, "the landing spacecraft and the equipment are basically intact. The staff...a few are dead, and some injured. Local creatures are not very friendly. We have found some hydrocarbon-based slime molds and algae, and few aggressive higher animals. But generally we are good." The emotionless voice paused a bit, "Overall, it is a liveable world."

"Well, sir, seems you're losing it." Rolfe patted Lee on the shoulder, laughing, "You've bet fifty bucks that it's not liveable. Don't you regret it now."

"Don't be so impatient, lad." Lee waved his hand. What he worried about was not the two-hour salary, but some...something else. He was grasped by a sense of foreboding which was getting increasingly intense and pressing. "Where are the other landing spacecraft? Do you have any contact with them?"

"We...yes, we haven't found any other spacecraft, but probably one or more of them haven't managed to land successfully. After landing, we have seen at least a pall of smoke in the northeast."

Lee felt no surprise that some of the landing spacecraft had crashed. It is always risky to explore a new parallel world. The casualty rate of the first explorers is no less than that of five centuries ago when voyagers and sailors sailed their crude wooden ships to find the new continent. Since the space-time passage formed at an instant is full of rampageous powerful electromagnetic pulses, any electronic equipment that is more complex than an incandescent light bulb should be dismantled into parts and reassembled after arrival. That rules out the possibility of real-time reconnaissance with unmanned probes or computer-aided driving. The poor pilots had to use the most primitive mechanical transmission, like the pilots of the first half of the twentieth century did, to handle the giant cans falling down to the ground through completely manual operation. The only information they could resort to was the few scraps from the experts of the technical team from several attempts of opening mini passages. Although the entrance was set at a relatively safe altitude of ten thousand meters, in order to set aside time for staff in the landing spacecraft to react, failure was still quite common due to operational errors or merely poor luck. 'Blind Jump' – that was what the experts of the technical team called it when they referred to the multiverse colonization activities. There was, from Lee's point of view at least, absolutely no exaggeration in the slightest.

"In addition, the perimeter of the landing site has already been cleared out, and the passage generator has already been installed." The woman said continuously, "We will send you the three-dimensional coordinates right away, so that..."

"Hold on, please." After these words, Lee immediately turned off the pickup on the communication console. "This is weird," he said to Rolfe, "actually, very weird."

"Oh?"

"It's too late to get a message from them." Lee glanced at the screen beside the console, "This is very odd. I know exactly how those explorers are. Once they had landed and found they could still breathe, the first thing they would have done would have been to assemble the communication equipment and contact us, so that they could have instantly claimed the lawful ownership of the land under their feet. If I calculate it correctly, they arrived at K-59 at least…two weeks ago, right? Why are they contacting us for the first time today? Also, I don't really believe that 'certain physical damage' could cause the breakdown of video communication. As the most important equipment, the communication system has been supplied with more than one spare for its crucial parts. What is the chance that they've become a bunch of scrap all at once?" He scratched his chin. "And why are they so anxious for us to send them the passage generator? You know, the energy this thing demands to turn on is nearly as much as it would take to drain the reserve power in the superconducting battery of the spacecraft. But they should be badly in need of the power to sustain life and supply the construction equipment to build their settlement. As far as I know, only if the first solar power station starts to work will the explorers, most of them, try to open a permanent passage." And my instinct, I have a bad feeling for them…. Lee shook his head – no, it's not the right time to say it.

"Probably." Said Rolfe, "So, what would you do? Send an urgent notice to the administration committee and let them dispatch another team of idiots for further detective work?"

"Not now. Let me ask her more questions?" Lee waved his hand and turned on the pickup again, "Landing Spacecraft *UHG-2404*, this is the monitoring centre. We need more of your information. Please briefly describe all your activities within 24 hours since your entry into K-59's atmosphere, as well as your current stock of supplies and condition of your spacecraft."

The other end of the communication channel fell into silence for a few seconds, and a few seconds more. "After jumping into the atmosphere of K-59, we found an accidental leak in the liquid fuel storage equipment. Our engineer thought it was possibly caused by a defective seal. The fire that followed spread to three supply reserves – there were four in total. Only the cabin for the passage generator's parts was spared. We have lost a lot of supplies including most parts of the electronic equipment, all inflatable barracks, and more than half of various tools. We spent over ten days picking out available parts from the remains and assembling this communication equipment…" From the speaker came a sharp wheeze, which sounded somewhat like a laugh, "We've been living in the spacecraft for two weeks, and are likely to stay here for more days. The stones and woods here are not good enough to build houses, the soil is too soft to support a building of common weight, and we are short of enough equipment to build the foundation. In short, we do not lack food and energy, but necessary construction materials and equipment."

"Poor guys. How could they have been living in the spacecraft for as long as two weeks?" Rolfe muttered, "I'd rather sleep in the mud than live in the damn coffin. Do you know how terrible the air filtration system is…?"

"So, you should probably feel happy that you didn't pass the explorer's selection test." Lee glanced at his co-worker, signalled the young man to calm down. Her reply was quite reasonable, so reasonable that his suspicion seemed groundless. Still the sense of uneasiness haunted him, deep in his mind, just as it was at the beginning. "Well, Landing Spacecraft *UHG-2404*, your current situation has been confirmed." Lee took a deep breath slowly, "We will receive your three-dimensional coordinates right now, but you have to wait for some time to open the passage, because you are not the first exploration team in K-59 seeking support from us."

"Sir, what are you…" Rolfe just wanted to speak, but shut up his mouth right away at a glimpse from Lee. "There is at least one team who got in touch with us earlier, who we think are worse off than you are, so it's necessary to help them first." Lee continued, "In other words, because of the limited reserve of equipment and other supplies, we must give priority to them, contact and supply them first; and before that, I'm afraid that you have to wait for some time. Any questions?"

"Of course not." After a short while of silence, the woman's voice replied, "If we can help our companions by doing so, we are glad to keep at it longer. Over."

"Over." While turning off the communicator, Lee had a complicated smile emerging on his face, "Good luck."

The moment belonging to it is coming soon.

Anu had been devoted to the preparation for this moment in the past ten days. Under its 'guidance', the captured humans had installed the first passage generator on an open platform with parts in the spacecraft, and powered it with the superconducting battery. A few hours later, those credulous people would open from the other side the door to a new world. If everything went well, it would soon become the master of these two worlds.

For preparing this invasion, Anu spent most of its time studying and analyzing files stored in the computers of the spacecraft. If all the files were true, this invasion would not be confronted with many difficulties. That was right. Humankind, born to be a combative and brutal race, had developed extraordinary military techniques during their tens of thousands of years of existence, but all the weapons they possessed were aimed at their own kind. The innate inertial mind-set of this race could also be a major obstacle for them when reacting to any contingencies. Nevertheless, such a great creature as Anu was, it could still be mortally threatened by humans' weapons of mass destruction, but Anu was ready and there would be no chance for humankind to launch those weapons. Over the past several days, Anu had produced hundreds of billions of spores carrying its genetic information. Once the passage was open, the spores would, following the atmospheric circulation, reach every corner of the humans' world within just a few sidereal days, and take root, germinate, and become part of its body. By then, human beings should either be forced to destroy their entire world, or bend their knees to it.

Anu knew clearly that the upcoming victory would bring with it incredibly huge benefit. So far, it had only explored a small part of a human's body; once it learned how to efficiently utilize the most complicated organ, the 'brain' as it was called, this kind of creature would not simply maintain the status of being organs passively manipulated by it, instead, they would help it think! Anu was sure that only by establishing full connections to a few normally active human brains, its overall thinking ability could increase exponentially. In the world it was about to march into lived billions of individuals that could think and would become part of it. Anu could not even imagine what it would be after connecting to such a huge number of brains – in some sense, it would thereby become a real almighty and omniscient God, or a real ANU!

– The moment was coming.

When the countdown on the spacecraft's timer finally turned to zero, a message popped up on the passage generator's console, announcing that it had detected a pulse spike that did not belong to this space-time continuum system. Power in the superconducting battery pack was continuously transmitted as microwaves into the generator; the computer on the generator automatically started to capture the signal source, analyze its features, and orderly arrange a series of preparation works. After just hundreds of milliseconds, a mirror pulse had formed with exactly the same specifications within the generator's functioning scope. Air, dust, and other tiny things on the ground, boosted by the air pressure difference, started to get off the ground and flocked to a point a few meters above the ground. The point turned into a ball, the ball was getting larger and larger, with a pungent smell of ozone pervading the air, and finally the opaque ball extended its diameter equal to the height of an average adult and the core was getting dark....

Anu transported tens of millions of spores to its body part that besieged where the ball was. Following the strong airflow, the spores flocked into the centre of the passage. In just a few seconds – it took only a few seconds – the vanguard invisible to the naked eye would charge into the new world at the other end of the passage, and it, Anu, would become the master of these two worlds.

This was the closest moment towards victory for Anu.

A fiery light, without any warning, flashed on the console. All of a sudden, the air pressure difference between the two ends totally changed. The moment when Anu sent its first troop of spores into the passage, the air pressure at the other end of the passage abruptly soared over two hundred times. The high-pressure air, all at once, spewed backward and transported back Anu's vanguard that was infinitely close to its destination. What followed was a large bulk of grey dusty matter fluxing into this world with the airflow, and there came more, more and more....

A human captured by Anu – one of the operators in charge of the passage generator – suddenly fell to the ground, getting out of control and trembling. Just in tens of seconds, all his vital signs faded away, and his body fluids froze promptly because of rapid cooling, making him a frozen meat as hard as a steel. Soon, it spread to all the staff and even to Anu's body. The tens of billions of spores that Anu produced to invade the new world were all killed before they got the chance to release. The cell sap of the slime molds by which Anu's body was formed was all getting frozen, and the organelles were all pierced through by spreading ice. Soon, the area surrounding the spacecraft disappeared from Anu's vision, becoming a blind zone, a frozen blind zone even colder than absolute zero.

That was a devastating start, but it just began.

When this blind zone started to extend itself, Anu finally found the cause bringing this: the snow-like grey dust that was hurrying to devour all the heat of anything it passed by, vanishing all life in its way. Part of the 'snow', getting full with heat, turned into invisible and odorless gas rising into the atmosphere and, very soon, condensing into a solid again and falling to the ground again by the force of gravity, starting a new cycle of depriving life.

As the deadly blind zone expanded steadily to half of Anu's body, the crumble of most sensory systems pushed Anu's consciousness to the edge of collapsing. Biological instinct replaced rational thinking, and began to direct its last struggle. Anu attempted to prevent its heat from escaping by sending a signal to individual bits on its body surface to secrete a thick layer of insulating matter. Yet Anu eventually found it all in vain, no matter what, as another kind of 'snow' started to fall.

– That was Dry Ice.

Oh, Crap. It was the last thought of Anu before the collapse of its integral senses.

"See? Problem solved."

In the central monitoring room, Lee gave a very relieved stretch, crumpled the disposable coffee cup in his hand, and tossed it into the bin. For some reason, the little move made him feel so relaxed as if it was something extremely heavy and uncomfortable.

– For example, an unfamiliar parallel world with unknown dangers lurking.

Beside Lee, experts of the technical team, standing casually in groups, talked with each other, with a few of them – the minority of course – expressing their doubts in vehement voices and wording. Lee did not even notice what had they said; after all, it was over. After the extermination-like attack specially designed for a 'hostile world' with potential threats, the atmosphere of that earth would become a layer of dirty snow sticking to the ground for many years. No living thing, including all the explorers if there were any of them still alive, could live there any more, except for few Chemosynthetic bacteria that could live off the geothermal energy.

"Hey, Sir. How did you make sure the one talking to us was not a real explorer?" Rolfe patted his colleague on the shoulder, "I hadn't heard any problem...."

"That's why you'll never be an explorer. Never." Lee shrugged, "If I'm correct, you failed the last section of the explorer's selection test, right?"

"Yep! I achieved the highest level in all sections including physical fitness, knowledge level and living skills! But they, they..." When it came to his 'old story,' Rolfe was still quite indignant, "they said I lacked the 'necessary psychological quality!' But –"

"But you did lack the necessary psychological quality." Lee helped him finish the words, "Of course they would not tell you what quality it is. Because no evaluation criteria is going public, and I know well that the secrecy is indeed justified. Not the same as many people think, the qualities for an explorer do not...conform to the public values. Do you know what I mean?"

"No, I don't."

"Well." Lee thought for a moment, "Do you remember the last section of the test?"

"I'll never forget it." Rolfe subconsciously lowered his head, "We were all dumped at the deserted tiny islands in Micronesia with not even a decent tool to survive – but a radio, of course. Every ten days, teams scattered on different islands would receive random communications, and the examiners would tell us about other teams, and we had the right to apply for an airdrop of supplies or to give the opportunity to teams worse off."

"And your team was very lucky, and was always one of best condition teams."

"Yes, we...how do you know it?"

"Because all the teams were of the 'best' condition – since you couldn't verify the authenticity of the information provided by the examiner." Lee shrugged, "Survivability was not the real end of the test but kind of your uh...psychological quality that is not suitable to speak out in public. If I'm not mistaken, you hardly received any airdrop supplies, right?"

"Well, actually we had received them twice, but I left most of the opportunities to others."

"Hence you shall never be an explorer," Lee said, "because you're not selfish enough."

"What?"

"Selfishness. That's the psychological quality they really want, but also really not suitable for telling the public. People living in a civil society are naturally opposed to selfishness, because selflessness is much more beneficial for a society that generally does not lack living materials." Lee threw his hands up, "But to colonize another world or another universe is totally different. At least in the very early period, the connection between explorers and us is extremely weak. An accident, or even a tiny error, could mean they never see any of homo sapiens. Don't forget that only one fifth of the potential colonial worlds eventually established permanent contact with our world, and not all of those who were missing were dead."

"So –"

"So the colonists shouldn't be too noble. Living in the jungle as a civil man, you'd definitely be swallowed by the jungle. Only those who are selfish enough and can behave in the most cold-blooded pragmatism can most probably survive and spread the human gene. This is the precious experience that the Vikings, the Polynesians and the colonists of the new continent drew from their own experiences. That, of course, is the reason why I can make sure that the one talking to us was not a real explorer – who would attempt to convince us to deliver the supplies first to them; at least they would try every means to do so."

"Certainly," Rolfe subconsciously licked his lips, "but...but who do you think we were talking to? Or...uhm...what is it?"

"I don't know and I don't want to know." Lee shook his head, "What we only need to know is that it was a potential threat. That's enough. Don't forget that the liveable worlds can be so plenty that a world can definitely be sacrificed as long as we can eliminate a threat by doing so."

"Of course." Rolfe nodded, turned back, and walked to the exit of the monitoring room, "Good night, sir."

Home is a House That Loves You

Rachael K. Jones

BEFORE THE WAR with Apsides, I wanted to be like my Aunt Martha, who at the age of forty five stepped into an abandoned lot near Aurora's city center, buried her toes in dirt, stretched up her arms, and became a skyscraper. Her legs were steel girders, earthquake-strong, her fingers long iron spires that caught pigeons and kites. Aunt Martha, 101 floors tall, sides aglitter with splendid floor-to-ceiling windows, family's pride, city's pride. When I was sixteen, I'd race up her stairwells whenever we visited, trailing fingers along her textured oak banisters up through offices and ballrooms and apartments of Martha's design that hummed like beehives and smelled of Sumatran coffee. Martha would creak and shift and whisper back, and I knew she remembered me.

Martha was the first in my family to become a skyscraper. Mostly we became ordinary buildings. Service ran in my family. When our time came to take root, we usually carried on our lifelong vocations. My surgeon great-grandmother became the new cancer wing at the Aurora hospital, and Uncle Bert, who loved pickup basketball on the street at summer, transformed into the elementary school gymnasium when the old one grew too old to repair herself any longer.

My grandfather seized upon my pride in Aunt Martha and reflected it back as resentment. He kicked steel-toed factory boots against her red brick foundation, thumped on her drywall, gray eyes scanning and probing her structure for flaws. But he turned up nothing worth criticizing. Martha was perfection, an architectural marvel, a monument to define the horizon's boundaries for future generations. So he made up his own reasons to hate her. "Forty-five is too young to take root. Cat and Graham aren't even eighteen yet."

My father cupped an arm around five-year-old Graham's shoulder and steered him down one of Martha's grand cobblestone courtyards to muffle out the adult talk. "I think I saw a lizard crawl beneath the picnic table," he said. Graham's tears ran to hiccups. The little boy squatted down, lost to his search.

Cat, though, glowered at Grandfather, her hands twined like ivy through the fantastic brass scrollwork of her mother's fire escapes. She had caught them saying her name, and hadn't overlooked the slur against her mother. "That's ridiculous," she called after them. "Uncle Bert took root even younger."

"Bert was sick," Grandfather said. He returned Cat's pointed look. He didn't like us to bring up Uncle Bert. It was still a sensitive topic, a tooth that ached when storms blew in from the far-off ocean. When he got his diagnosis, Bert marched down to City Planning and volunteered his body to take root where needed. "Martha could have waited a few more years at least. She's all those kids had left. Selfish woman."

Cat pulled her stocking cap over her eyebrows to shield her from Grandfather's angry eyes. The adults moved on to dividing up Aunt Martha's estate.

"Those kids can't live in the house alone," said Grandfather. "I suppose we can keep her in trust for when Cat's old enough for independence." By *her*, Grandfather meant Aunt Martha's house, his older sister Angela. "She only just took root."

There was no talk of selling the house. In Aurora, nobody ever sold houses. You might sell land, but you had to wait for the building to die, or else petition City Planning.

"Cat and Graham better stay with us in that case," said Dad. "We're only a block away."

Grandfather squatted down beneath the picnic table. "How about that? You want to live with your cousins?"

"Okay," said Graham.

Grandfather pointed his chin at Cat, who was still pretending not to listen. "And you?"

Cat glanced at me, a look of anger and sadness and overwhelming pride. A soldier's eyes, where pride and loss were housemates. Those who fought in the wars with Apsides often wore that look. She nodded sharply. So it was decided like it often was in Aurora when relatives took root too young.

From that day, I worshipped Martha in the way of teenaged girls. She became my god and my morality, the name I prayed in the dark as I fell asleep. I wanted to be like her. She chose her own immortality, and didn't ask for our opinions. It took great strength of mind to stretch your body so far when you took root, and Martha brushed the sky.

* * *

People talk about what starts wars, as if by knowing we could stop it from happening again. As if all events are selected from an infinite menu. Like choice is an ocean instead of a closed set picked and guided and hedged by circumstance and history and competing wants and needs.

The truth is the people of Apsides never understood us. Not when they drove on our roads or climbed our stairs or walked our sidewalks. They never understood our city was built on service offered up by the generations before, and that we were their stewards and caretakers.

None of us could stand a tourist. They graffitied our heroes. They gouged potholes in our beloved weathermen and trod gum into our musicians, and through all of this, we forgave. We tended our broken buildings, cleaned off the insult, and we forgave, because we knew they didn't understand. Their cities were dead, and their homes did not love them. Nowhere else in the world did people take root like we did, and we did not invite outsiders in. Only Apsides, which lived on the edge of our nimbus.

But even our forgiveness had our limits. For me, it was what they did to Graham.

* * *

The seeds of collapse were sown in the years after Aunt Martha took root, when three teens on a field trip to Apsides disappeared overnight. When they were found, it was a horror of fresh asphalt for their parents. Barely old enough to take root, they couldn't become more than some access roads to line a strip mall.

The Apsides police insisted the kids must've done it on their own. Who could prove otherwise? The criminals were never caught and punished.

That marked the start of a new era. You had to be careful when you traveled abroad, because if they found out you were Aurora-born, the wrong people might force you to take root, your body used for a stranger's gain, and you helpless to stop it. And if your family somehow found out, what could they do? At that point, it was only the priest and the bulldozer, or else leave you forever in a strange city, alone among silent buildings that had no memory of birthday cake, or french kissing, or the taste of strawberry wine.

From people like that, what can you do but withdraw, hide away, deepen your reservoirs and store up flour and rice and canned black beans? What trust can there be? What commerce or cultural exchange? We shared a language, but we did not understand one another.

Our buildings whispered and creaked and groaned. Our sidewalks bent crooked in the night. The jail counseled war. Two old women on the westside became gun factories. Their grandchildren sold bullets.

Through all of it, Martha whispered to those of us who listened. *If they only understood,* she said. *If they truly understood, they would let us be. Make them understand.*

Graham, eighteen and idealistic, cut straight from his mother's brick, struck off on a road trip the day he graduated high school. The last time I saw him, his arms sunburnt and peeling where his t-shirt sleeves ended, he gave me his second-favorite baseball cap and told me to get outside more.

"You're getting paranoid in your old age," he said. I had had my daughter Cleo by then, and a son on the way, and Graham took this as proof positive I was now certified *old,* risk-averse from some parental infection he swore he would never contract.

"Not old. Just less stupid." But I cracked a sideways grin when I said it, so he hugged me. A real, tight hug, hard enough to make my shoulders ache, doled out like favors to those Graham loved enough to outstrip his machismo.

I was grateful for that hug later, when he fell out of touch entirely. He was a day or two late coming home, and we thought nothing of it. After a week, we made jokes he'd fallen in love with an Apsides girl on a beach somewhere. After a month, Cat showed up on my doorstep with a road map and a packed bag and one of the guns from the new factory.

Cat and I traced his route together, alternating the driving and sleeping so we just stopped for gas. We kept the brights on at night for signs of new construction: dirt piles, fresh asphalt, anything that could be him. We spoke to no one, lest our accents give us away. Every foreigner became a kidnapper on that trip. I touched my belly, slightly rounded, and finally understood the fear that could make a woman into a gun factory.

We found him behind a chain-link fence around a new supermarket.

He was a parking lot. Not a smooth, flat one – he'd arched up in the middle, epileptic, his painted lines radiating downhill like an infected wound. Flat as his mother was tall. It had been a violent rooting for him. I pressed my face against the sun-warmed tar and sobbed. We'd found him too late. Oh, much too late.

"Oh, Martha." A prayer, an oath, a vow. I wasn't sure which. "I am so sorry, Cat."

Cat had curled around one of the violent asphalt swells in the frozen black ocean. She whispered to her brother. Maybe he whispered back, but I didn't hear.

I gave them their privacy.

We spent the night in Graham's parking lot, the cheap streetlights flickering on whenever a squirrel climbed the fence. In the morning, new cracks spiderwebbed Graham's asphalt like shattered glass. He'd grayed like he'd aged twenty years overnight. He'd gone on.

Buildings could do this too, when they chose.

* * *

Martha collapsed the first day of the war, smashed in her knees by the missile that sent her weighted majesty crashing down into white dust, all her residents buried inside. The other skyscrapers fell, too: old Ty Markum and Joy Delgado, the soaring spires of Caroline Watts and the flat-topped garden of Delbert Hunt, giants who sheltered us, gone forever.

I was home with Cleo and Chachi, staking tomatoes in the garden while morning shaded me from the worst of the sun. I swear the world shifted deep in my bones before I heard anything. Sudden thunder shook my knees, though the sky was bright and cloudless. Black smoke rose in dark, thick braids, cutting off the skyline. Asphalt odor blew on the wind. Whenever I breathed, I gagged.

My phone rang, and I answered automatically.

"She's gone," said Cat, before I even got in *hello*.

"Oh, Cat. I'm sorry." Conversational, like we were discussing groceries. When your world goes to dust in a moment, your brain doesn't always believe it. "Where are you?"

"At work. Everyone else left. They all went home. I was supposed to go see Mom this afternoon. Meet a client in her rooftop restaurant."

"Come to my house. It's safe here. So far."

On the westside, those who survived the initial volley rooted themselves on the spot, throwing up wall after rigid wall, wrapping themselves around Aurora as far as their strength permitted. They made a half-nautilus maze just beyond the gleaming steel war machines of Apsides digging down, angling their guns up, preparing the next volley.

On the eastside, we waited and watched.

* * *

We took shelter inside Grandfather's walls, my children and Cat and Jake and me. The former mayor Ami Nguyen had fallen. She loved Aurora so much that when her time to take root came, she stretched her arms wider and wider until they became a wooden roller coaster, our outermost border. Which meant she was the first to go when the invasion began.

"What do they want?" Jake peeled red potatoes over a wooden mixing bowl. He cooked when he got nervous. The sour smell of bread yeast suffused the whole room. He came from a family of restaurants, and intended to become one himself when the time came, part of our plan from the days when we dated. I would be a skyscraper, like Martha, and he would be the restaurant crowning my summit. I would house the city, and he would feed it.

"It's finally happened. They're moving in." I pitched my voice low, so I wouldn't scare Cleo, who at four was old enough to detect fear. "They think we'll make their lives more *convenient*." Living buildings repaired themselves, lived for decades and centuries longer than the ones other cities built by hand. Our buildings responded to our needs. No collapsed roofs, or broken stairs, or subway cars stalled on overworn tracks. Rooted structures died eventually, but there was always someone to take their place, to serve in turn.

"It won't work, you know," said Jake. "They think it'll be easy, but we won't be used."

I didn't like that sharp edge in his eyes. I didn't want guns or war. I just wanted our home back. I wanted to sink my toes deep into bedrock and stand beside Aunt Martha, proud and strong, showing just how far the horizon reached by cracking it like a blue-shelled robin's egg against my peak.

I excused myself to the kitchen. Bread dough rose in a pan next to a bowl of mixed berries. I picked a couple of blackberries off the top and crushed them against the roof of my mouth. The sweet-tart taste didn't quite wash away the acrid asphalt smell clinging to my hair.

I leaned against the antique oak pantry door. "Grandfather," I whispered, "I don't know what to do." I never knew I'd miss him so much until he was gone. I even missed his anger.

He didn't reply. Grandfather had been rooted for nine years now, and didn't speak much. But that night I woke to creaking and groaning deep in the walls. Grandfather trembled, knocking pictures and mirrors askew. It began to rain outside, drumming down so hard it drowned out the distant sounds of war. The roof sprung a leak, right over our bed in the master bedroom. Suitcases clattered down out of the attic and skittered down the newly warped hallway floor until they hit our bedroom door.

We had our answer. We got up and began to pack. Chachi cried at being woken so early, but Cat rocked and hushed him asleep again. I gave Cleo a backpack to fill with her favorite things: a stuffed beaver, a plastic sword, some boardbooks pressed from the last beams of her great-grandmother.

It was much the same with our neighbors. Boards warped, door knobs rusted, stairs bowed downward. The structures of Aurora had taken counsel overnight, and we had their verdict. Our rooted families nudged us out the only way they could.

In the distance, bombs exploded against tall walls that hadn't been there the night before, human bodies holding back the invaders so we might escape. The nautilus maze had thickened inside. There wasn't much time left.

We only had so many bodies, after all.

* * *

We fled weeping. We fled into the eastern wilderness, an undeveloped, empty country of steep hills and evergreens and thick, prickly bramble. Jake and I packed the children into our car, and Cat squeezed into the backseat. We joined the slow-moving traffic wending from the city's wreckage. Eventually the jam got so bad, we parked and shut off the engine. Jake and I left Cat with the kids and approached a knot of refugees having words with a tired police officer by the roadside.

"What's the problem?"

The police officer cocked her chin eastward. "Roads aren't wide enough to handle this much traffic. It gets even worse ahead. This highway narrows to a single lane, cutting into hills and forests. People don't take that road often, unless they're visiting the ocean. It isn't very tidy out there. All granite boulders and switchbacks around rivers and lakes. Wild country."

"So what are you saying?" said Jake. He fanned himself with a baseball cap, the hot asphalt intensifying the growing heat.

The police officer sketched a phantom map in the gravel with her boot. "I don't know. But we can't get out of the city to the west, not with Apsides coming in that way. We should consolidate into fewer vehicles. Leave behind as much as we can. Save our bodies, at least."

The whole group turned as one to watch the black smoke rise in the west, a nonstop line since the first attack. It struck us all as a bad idea, but nobody had a better one.

We were halfway through the disordered and chaotic consolidation when I realized I couldn't find Jake.

"Have you seen my husband?" I asked the police officer, the other travelers, sprinted from car to car along the shoulder as the traffic began to creep along. I checked with Cat, but he wasn't in the car, either.

Then I spotted him far up the road, unlacing his shoes, stripping off his socks, and stepping barefoot onto the asphalt at the road's shoulder.

"Jake. Wait!"

I was too late. He'd already buried his toes and reached eastward. For a moment he bowed to the sun. Then he lengthened, broadened, his white t-shirt running pebbly black as he flowed down the road, faster than my eye could follow.

He transformed. He disappeared forever.

Numb, I climbed behind the wheel and began to drive. I caught Cat's eye and cut off her comment with a tiny head shake. Now wasn't the time. I gripped the steering wheel hard, dodging Cleo's questions as I nosed us into traffic. "He's in another car," I told her. It was a horrible fate for a man destined to play restaurant to my skyscraper when we took root.

Jake ran smooth and true for mile upon mile, without bump or fault. I did not change lanes.

That night, when we stopped to sleep, I lay down on the sun-warmed tar and whispered, *This wasn't our plan. You changed our plan.* True things. Bitter things. Words of blame. What I really meant was, *I love you.*

I don't know how many survived the flight from the city. Our numbers thinned as we went, lost to the necessities of survival. More roads, when the older ones ended. I said goodbye to Jake. I wanted him to speak to me, but he was a road, and roads cannot even creak and sigh like houses can. When another woman lay down and joined ends with Jake, his brand-new asphalt was already pitted and potholed, graying like he had been rooted for many decades, weeds hurrying to bury him. He'd closed the way behind us to slow any pursuit.

That was when I knew for sure our city was dead. Our beloved ghosts had fled their haunts. Without them, we had only dry rot and snapped beams and crumbling cement to return to.

Aurora had fallen.

* * *

We reached no end to sacrifice.

When the snow fell, some of us became cabins, or if we were able, hotels. The oldest and most powerful among us disappeared first. Our structures grew smaller as we traveled. Always behind us we left new walls to block the way. In the west, a black oily plume snaked upwards against the sunset.

We finally reached the ocean. Nowhere else to run except into the water, and the black smoke still persisted. No city center for me. No long, languid dance of generations racing down my stairwells. There would never be a city without these children, too young to take root, and we adults too few to hold off our pursuers.

We left the cars behind and let the children on the beach. Cat found me. We buried our feet in the sand together like we were girls again, on a holiday. The sun sank trembling at our backs and turned the ocean into tossing, broken light. It hurt my eyes to look at it.

"I tried to become a bridge," Cat said. "I tried. I did just what Mom did, but nothing happened." Her voice strangled with suppressed sobs. "I should be old enough. I'm not much younger than you."

I took her cold hand and squeezed it. "Shh, it's okay." She leaned against my shoulder, and her whole body shook. "It's too early for you, Cat. You wouldn't be able to get far, anyway. Not all the way across, not at your age."

"Do you think there's another shore at all?" She wiped ocean spray mixed with tears from her cheeks.

"I don't know. It's not on the maps."

I dug my toes a little deeper, squeezing the grit and broken shell fragments between them, and thought *bridge*.

But if I bridged the sea, I would only lead the enemy to the other side. We would never be safe so long as our own roads betrayed us.

What then? A gun factory? A house of death to wreak some last revenge? I could become a lighthouse, and wait for the enemy. I could gather them up inside me, welcome the soldiers of Apsides with warmth and shelter to drive back the ocean's storms. When they slept, I could collapse roof to floor, and take them down to the sea. Our bones could mingle and house the fish, and no one would speak the name *Aurora* ever again.

I skipped shells into the ocean. Children splashed in the shallows, chasing the tide in and out. Cleo had taken a wooden plank (a memento, perhaps, of Grandfather?) and paddled around on her belly in the shallows, her bare toes kicking and digging into the waves. I longed to gather her back into myself, a tiny thing to shelter in my belly from awful things like asphalt and smoke, that same impulse that drove every person to throw up girders and drywall when they reached maturity.

Martha a skyscraper, Graham a parking lot, and Jake an asphalt road. Three generations stepping down and down from dignity and use. We stood at the end of the Age of Cities.

My toes curled into the water, soft and yielding as silk bed sheets, but it had a weight to it, a gravity. Maybe there was more than one way. Maybe the ocean could be a home, too.

Martha, help me, I prayed. I stepped into the water. The waves licked waist-deep, chest-deep, then lapped my chin.

I reached out toward the ocean, my back lengthening, ribs bending out, vertebrae fusing and bowing at both ends. My arms lifted into masts, and my black hair snapped and spread into sails caught between my fingers. *Come with me.* I spoke as a hundred planks and a hundred iron spikes rocking in the wind. Rope ladders unspooled down my sides. I filled my belly with chocolate and oranges and Sumatran coffee, and my cabins with beds of soft down. At my bow, I shaped a figurehead in the image of Graham the day he hugged me goodbye, a road no more, carved in Martha's brick-red stone, wrapped in iron scrollwork.

It would be enough. I could carry them. I would carry them far away.

I whispered my love in swishing nets and flapping sails. Their feet trembled against my belly and my decks. Their voices reverberated in my planks. Their hands tangled in my ropes. We sailed on together.

The black smoke receded and disappeared in the night. The water went on and on for days and months. Still I reached for another shore, and longed for the comfort of skyscrapers.

Being Here

Claude Lalumière

THE NIGHT BEFORE, you and I had fought, and it had taken me forever to fall asleep. We didn't make up then, and I still regret that. We'd argued about nothing and everything – the dishes, the vacuuming, the cat litter. A stupid fight. One in which none of the important things got said, in which all the real reasons for the tension between us were carefully avoided.

Exasperated, you had turned your back to me; a snore interrupted me mid-sentence. Waking you up would only have made a bad situation worse. There was nothing I could have said at that moment that would have brought us closer. I let you sleep and tried to calm myself.

It was useless. I lay awake for hours, unable even to keep my eyes closed, until I fell from sheer exhaustion into an unrestful sleep.

I woke up at dawn, as I always did. The clock on my bedside dresser told me it was not quite six yet. I usually took advantage of the time before I woke you up at eight to go running in the park. That morning, thinking I had a choice, I decided to be lazy and stay in bed. I knew the exercise would help snap me out of my funk, but I just couldn't gather the energy to get up and start my day.

After a few minutes, it occurred to me that in the morning I always needed to pee urgently. And yet there I was, feeling absolutely no pressure on my bladder.

I wanted to enjoy a drowsy morning in bed, just rest and relax. But I couldn't get comfortable. The blankets were so heavy.

* * *

The clock read 7:12. The feeling of being trapped by the blankets was unbearable. I was getting tenser and angrier by the second. I couldn't muster the strength to get up. I liked mornings, but already I was hating this one.

The digital readout on the clock became my lifeline to sanity. That every minute a numeral changed filled me with a strange and pathetic reassurance.

Still irritated from the previous night, I wanted to shout at you to stop snoring, but, with our fight still so fresh, I knew waking you up this early would only make things worse.

Lying there, I was hypersensitive to noises I usually blanked out. The morning traffic, the creaking building, the shrill wind outside. I could make out what the neighbours were saying through the walls; they were calmly reading each other snippets from the morning paper. Everything was so loud.

And the smell! The cat litter stank like we hadn't changed it in months. Were we really that bad? The whole apartment reeked: the unwashed laundry, the sinkful of dirty dishes, the garbage. How could we have let things slide so much, I thought.

* * *

Finally, it was eight o'clock; time to wake you.

No matter how hard I tried, I couldn't push the blankets off me, I couldn't reach over and touch you. I wasn't paralyzed, though. I could move my neck, my face, and the top of my right shoulder – everything that wasn't caught under the blankets. I tried to say your name over and over again, but no sound came out of my mouth. I thought: you'll be late for work; you'll be furious with me.

And then the fact that I couldn't speak hit me, hit me much harder than being trapped in bed. I panicked, losing track of time, unable even to think, until I heard you roar my name.

But that was no roar, not really, only a mumble amplified by my hypersensitive hearing. You were finally waking up. The clock told me it was 10:34. You always mumbled my name when you were in that dozy state, rising from sleep to wakefulness. I loved that.

You turned toward me – I'd never noticed before how pungent your morning breath was – and your eyes popped open. You were looking past me at the clock. You flung out of bed, screaming my name without looking at me, shouting abuse and insults because I hadn't woken you up in time. The noise and stress combined to give me the god of all headaches.

When you got out of bed, the blankets moved enough so that my other shoulder was freed. But no more than that. I could move that shoulder again. Such frustrating relief.

Ten minutes later, you stomped back into the bedroom – your skin moist from the shower – and, still angry, shouted, "Where the fuck are you?" You turned on the light, and it was too much for my eyes. I squeezed them shut to block out the searing brightness. I mean, I tried to. My face wasn't paralyzed. I could feel my facial muscles react when I moved them – even my eyelids. But closing them didn't stop the light. While putting your clothes on, you kept shouting at me like I wasn't there.

Before slamming the front door on your way out, you had let George in from the backyard. He jumped on the bed and walked all over me. His paws were like steel girders; the bed under me gave with his every step. After a minute or so of this, he zeroed in on my crotch and kneaded it mercilessly. Purring. My life was pain. At least you had turned off the lights.

* * *

George stayed nestled on my crotch until you came back home after work. How much did he weigh? Eight pounds? Ten? Something like that. It felt like a bowling ball was crushing my pelvis.

As soon as he heard you unlock the front door, he leapt off me. He meowed to be let out. You cooed at him and opened the back door. These noises were still too loud, but by this time, having had to cope with it for a whole day, I'd become somewhat used to my newfound sensitivity. Even the light and smells, while still harsh, didn't bother me as much. In general, the pain was getting duller – an irritation instead of an assault.

After shutting the back door, you called my name. I tried to answer, but I still couldn't manage to make any sound.

I heard you pick up the phone, no doubt checking for messages. The phone hadn't rung all day. I was thankful for that bit of silence.

You swore and slammed the phone down. You turned on the TV and set the volume high. I braced myself for the pain, but I was adapting well – too well – to my condition. There was no discernible increase in my pain level.

I heard you wander through the apartment, shuffling papers, opening doors. You returned to the living room and plunked yourself down on the couch. Over the sounds of a car advertisement, I could hear you sniffle and sob. Already, I missed you so much.

* * *

You watched TV all evening, not bothering to eat. At 1:04 in the morning, you finally turned off the TV and walked into the bedroom. You looked miserable. You stared at me. In a tearful whine, you said, "Where are you?"

Desperate, I tried to channel all my strength, all my energy into screaming that I was right there, but I still failed. Couldn't you see me? It's not like I was dead. If I were, there'd be a corpse, a body.

And that's when I couldn't ignore it anymore.

I craned my neck to look down at myself, at where I felt my body squeezed into immobility by the blankets, and…and there was nothing there.

* * *

I stayed awake that whole night.

You fell asleep on your stomach, without taking your clothes off. You didn't move all night, but you snored – of course, you snored. Your left arm fell across me and crushed my chest – the part of me that still felt like a chest – until you woke up at 10:42 the next morning.

It was only after your arm had been separating my upper self from my lower for several hours that I noticed that I was no longer breathing. When I thought about it, I was pretty sure that I hadn't breathed since I'd woken up in this condition.

Whatever that was.

I listed the symptoms: I was invisible, even to myself; I didn't get hungry; I didn't need to pee or shit; I didn't get tired, but I felt a constant, numbing weakness; my senses were too acute for comfort; I wasn't breathing; blankets were too heavy for me to lift.

Like a list was going to explain everything, or anything.

And where was my body? How could I feel so much physical pain if I didn't have a body?

* * *

You rolled on your back, away from me. I felt my rib cage pop back up. Did I still have a rib cage? I looked at where I felt my body to be, and there still wasn't even the slightest hint of a shape. Was I even in there with you? Or was that sensation an illusion of some kind?

I told you, silently, that I was sorry for everything, for being so distant, for so often only pretending to listen to you, for so often having some stupid thing to do when all you wanted was to enjoy spending time with me – and in the middle of my futile apology George sat on my face.

* * *

You called in sick for the next two days. Minutes crawled by like weeks, sleepless days and nights like lifetimes.

You called my office and a few of my friends, but I could tell from your voice the emotional price you were paying for doing this. You gave that up quickly.

Couldn't you see that all my clothes were still there? My keys by the bed? Couldn't you feel that I was still there, longing for you?

Your orbit consisted of the bed, the fridge, the couch, and the toilet. The centre of your universe was the TV.

You stopped calling in sick. You just stayed home. When the phone rang, you ignored it.

* * *

A week later, your sister used her spare key to come in when you failed to respond to the doorbell. At first she was furious, yelling at you to snap out of it. Eventually, you broke down and started crying. That mollified her.

You told her that I'd vanished on you with no warning. She said she was surprised at that; she'd always thought of me as good for you.

You were an odd combination of fragile and tough, and I'd fallen in love with the intensity that accompanied that mix. You needed undivided attention to feel loved. You didn't give your trust easily, but, once you did, you trusted without question. Being with you was a heady experience that left little time or energy for anything else. I indulged like an addict: your intensity was a powerful narcotic. You had tended to attract lovers who abused your fragility, who took pleasure in shattering someone so strong who could nevertheless be so easily broken. Your sister had liked that I made you laugh, had seen how it thrilled me to have you permeate my whole world.

Eventually, life outside our bubble intruded. Friends, work, whatever. And I drifted away. I let you suffer, even though I knew you were suffering; I let my growing indifference chip away at you. And, like a coward, instead of talking to you and trying to mend the rift, I just ignored it. I ignored you.

Sex with you was so beautiful, such a complete escape, sad and hard, silly and serious, in all the best ways. How could I let anything get in the way of that? Of being close to you?

I've never wanted to comfort you as much as when I heard you tell your sister how much you'd been hurt by my disappearance. But I'd started to disappear much earlier than you were telling her, and I hated myself for that. For betraying you. For betraying myself.

* * *

Do you remember when, the week before we moved in together, you stopped by my office and took me out to lunch? Warming your hands on my cup of tea, a fleck of something green stuck between your teeth, you asked me what I needed, and we bonded because of our common goal: your happiness. When did that stop being important?

* * *

Your sister couldn't see me either. She cleaned the bathroom. After she put you in a hot bath, she turned off the TV and put on the radio instead. Classical. Worse: opera. Then, she attacked the embarrassing mess of our apartment. I'd like to say that most of it was due to your recent binge, but our place was always a disaster area.

And then she changed the bed.

The weakness disappeared when the weight of the blankets was lifted off me.

And, just like that, I was free. I was free! I danced and leapt and twirled and ran and –

And then I caught the words 'missing' and 'disappeared' on the radio news report.

There was, all around the world, an alarming increase in missing-person reports. The prime minister of Canada. The CEO of Toshiba. The US ambassador to the UN. The populations of whole villages in Africa. Hundreds of Afghan women. And so on. From the most disenfranchised to the most powerful, people everywhere were vanishing.

The news that I probably was not the only victim of this peculiar condition did not reassure me, but rather filled me with overwhelming dread. I walked into the bathroom, needing the security of your presence, and sat on the edge of the tub. You had no reaction when I reached out and stroked your face. Was I that insubstantial?

I could no longer take comfort in the slight plumpness of your cheek. To my touch, your flesh was as hard and unyielding as concrete.

* * *

When your sister left the apartment, I took advantage of the open door – all physical objects now being immovable, impassable obstacles – and left with her. I didn't follow her. I had been cooped up inside for so long. I needed the open air. I wandered and mulled over what I had heard on the news. I was already so used to the pain from the sensory overload that it was no longer even a distracting irritant.

Were all the vanished in the same situation I was? If I met another vanished person, would we see each other?

Outside I discovered that rain, even the mildest precipitation, knocked the strange substance of my nearly insubstantial body to the ground, raindrops hammering into me like nails. Yet, for all that I had some, if almost negligible, physical presence, I cast no shadow. I was truly invisible.

There were fewer and fewer people about every day. Obviously, we vanished could not perceive each other. What people were left acquired a haunted or persecuted look. They knew that their time would soon come.

Less than a week after I escaped from the apartment, civil order broke down. Vandalized and overturned police cars burned on street corners. All the stores I passed had their windows broken, their stock looted or destroyed.

The city grew quiet, as traffic dwindled away and industry stopped dead.

The silence was occasionally punctuated by bursts of gunshots and quickly silenced screams. Those sounds filled me with more dread than my inexplicable vanishing ever did. I was always careful to walk away from such noises and never discovered exactly what was happening.

Dogs wailed and wandered everywhere, searching for their vanished human companions, scavenging through garbage for food.

I saw stray cats hunt some of the smaller wildlife that was reclaiming the city. They gave the bears a wide berth, though. Often, I thought I saw George, but the cat was always gone before I could be sure.

During that time, I returned to the apartment only once. The door had been torn off. Everything had been trashed. A raccoon family was living in our bedroom. By then you must have vanished, like me. I wanted to find you, hold you. But you were beyond my reach.

* * *

I was following a bear around, excited by what would have been in normal circumstances suicidal behaviour, when a giant shadow fell over me. I looked up. Swift grey clouds covered the afternoon sky. Scraps of old newspapers were being blown every which way. There was so much wind – wild, chaotic wind. Before I could think to take cover, I was hit on all sides – by a ragged shirt, a torn magazine, a broken beer bottle, cigarette butts, gum wrappers. I was jabbed and crushed and flattened and stabbed and twisted. It hadn't hurt this much since that first morning.

The storm erupted; the sharp, heavy rain felled me, knifed through my prone body.

* * *

The storm ended; the clouds parted and revealed the moonlit sky, glittering with stars. I lay on the ground, recovering from the storm, and gazed at the sky. There were more stars visible than before: when people had vanished, so had the city lights that had made the nighttime too bright for starlight.

I stayed like that until dawn, and then someone stepped on me.

I looked around; the streets were filled with people. Naked as newborns, they walked calmly but with a sense of purpose, murmuring softly to each other, casually touching each other, sharing complicit glances.

I recognized a few faces – no-one I knew well, but people I'd seen in shops or cafés.

Still wobbly, I stood up. Was this ordeal finally over? Was I back, too? A quick test – trying in vain to see my hands or any part of my body   told me I wasn't. I tried to call out to the people around me, but I was still mute.

What about you? Could you have returned? I ran to our apartment.

* * *

When I neared home, I saw them. They were also heading there: hand in hand, smiling and laughing, so obviously deeply in love with each other.

It was you and me. More beautiful, more in love, more confident, more at peace than we'd ever been. Serene.

But it wasn't you, was it? No more than it was me. You must still be vanished like me. Neither dead nor alive. And so it must be for everyone.

Do you, like me, spend your time watching our doppelgangers? Are you frustrated at being unable to understand their language? Are you jealous at how much better they are at being us – at loving each other – than we ever were? At how much even George seems happier with them? Are you envious that all these new people have made the world a better place?

I want to end my life, but I don't think I can. I've tried jumping off roofs, but all I get out of it is more pain – never death.

Are you here with me, my love?

I long to die with you.

To be really dead. Together. Forever oblivious.

Water Scorpions

Rich Larson

"THIS IS YOU," Noel says to his new brother, holding up a writhing water scorpion by its tail. Spindly legs churn and its pincers clack, but the tail is stingerless. It is thin and stiff and hollow like a straw, so the water scorpion can breathe through it when it clings to the rusty iron bar around the inside of the pool.

Danny rocks forward on his haunches and watches through his cluster of gleaming black eyes. His body is all slippery spars and gray angles. Noel hopes he sees the resemblance to the creature dangling between his fingers.

"This is you," Danny mimics, a warbling echo that doesn't require movement from his needle-lined jaws, coming instead from the porous bulb underneath them.

Noel stands up from the pool's blue-tiled lip, keeping the water scorpion pinched between thumb and finger. He doesn't have to tell Danny to follow. Danny always follows, even when Noel stamps his feet and screams at him to go away.

He leads his brother along the concrete deck, slapping wet footprints. Danny's feet clop instead of slapping, like when their mother wears high heels. Now she sits barefoot in a dilapidated beach chair, wearing the stretchy black one-piece that hides her scar. Her eyes are on a work screen full of lab notes, but she sets down her stylus and waves and smiles when Noel and Danny pass by.

Noel lowers the water scorpion into the pocket of his trunks to shield it from view, still gripping the tail. It squirms and rasps against the fabric.

Nobody else looks up from their loungers. Nobody stares at Danny here, not even the cooks anymore. The private pool on the edge of Faya-Largeau, only hours from the Saharan crash site, was bought out by the UN specifically for its team of scientists, translators, engineers – all of them now used to seeing aliens.

Noel and Danny pass under a stucco arch, and the concrete becomes the courtyard's chipped mosaic tile, hot on Noel's feet. He does not know if it is hot on Danny's feet; Danny never jerks away from scalding sand or half-buried thorns. Not even when Noel has him walk over a spread of prickly goatheads.

Pungent eucalyptus overtakes the smell of chlorine and greasy samosas. The silvery-gray trees line a long open-air entryway. Noel leads Danny all the way to the end, into the red dust of the parking lot where the pool sounds of splashing and satellite radio and voices are muted. Danny's neck pops and swivels toward the family car where it gleams hot white in the sunlight.

"Look at this, Danny," Noel says, lifting the water scorpion from his pocket. "Watch this."

"Watch this," comes the wavery echo. He crouches obediently as Noel drops the creature into the warm sand. It makes a skittering circle, claws waving, then tries to dart away. Noel meets it with a wave of sand kicked up by the blade of his hand. The water scorpion flails and shies off, scuttles in the other direction. Noel tosses another fistful of sand.

Danny keeps watching, stone still, as Noel pours scoop after scoop of sand onto the panicking scorpion, sucking the moisture from the cracks in its keratin, battering down on its carapace, until the creature turns sluggish and can only slowly kick its legs in place.

"That's like you, if Mom didn't bring you to the pool all the time," Noel says softly. "You'd cook. You'd get all dried up and die, and after a while she'd forget you ever existed. Just like she forgot Maya."

Danny looks up at him with all of his black beetle eyes. Danny never blinks. He never smiles and never cries. He doesn't understand, not a single thing.

Noel covers the water scorpion over, heaping a burial mound. With his eyes on his work, he whispers, "I hate you."

"I hate you," Danny trills softly back.

* * *

The stork ship came down on the day Noel's sister died. He was sitting in the waiting room, watching red balloons in animated smartpaint drift across the peeling green walls, reminding him his tenth birthday wasn't far away, when the news feed sliced onto every screen in the hospital. A crumbling castle of pitted alloy and crystalline spars, falling from the sky. When the ship crash landed in the Sahara, an ocean away, an orderly gasped and bit the skin between her thumb and finger.

Noel understood it was something his xenobiologist mother would need to know about, something as important as the baby in her belly, so when she came from the examination room with her shoulders shaking, he rushed to show her the screen. She watched the crash calmly, nodded to herself as if it made perfect sense. Her eyes were shot through with pink.

Later, on the metro, she explained in her doctor voice that Maya's umbilical cord had shrunk too thin, and she'd starved, but they would still have to go back to the hospital the next day for induced labor.

"If she died, then how can you give birth to her?" Noel asked, feeling a wave of confusion, a panic aching his throat.

His mother wept then, a raw rusty sound that made other people watch her in the subway windows. Noel buried his face in the crook of her arm. The woman in front of them played the news feed at full volume on her tab, about the UN seeking to assemble a response party, to drown out the noise.

* * *

Back poolside, their mother has migrated back under the gazebo, rolling up her work screen. Noel and Danny join her in the straw shade for samosas. Iridescent green and purple swirls over Danny's body, as it always does around their mother. Noel leans back against a rust-flaking pole of the gazebo while Danny hurries to her. She strokes his jaws, an approved contact from the stork instructional transmissions, but can't resist giving a human squeeze at the end. When she motions the same for Noel he digs back against the pole, feeling it on the nodes of his spine.

"Have you been playing Marco Polo today?" she asks helplessly, trying to drop her open arms naturally to the tabletop.

"We're killing water scorpions," Noel says, just to watch her smile cloud over. "They're pests," he adds, because the clouding still hurts. "Jean says so. Says we can."

"Eat now," his mother says. "Stay in the shade for a while. You'll burn."

"Danny'll burn, you mean," Noel says. In the year since they came to Africa, leaving the flat in Montreal with the empty baby room, he's baked dark. He never burns anymore.

They eat the samosas without speaking. Noel hides the gristle with ketchup. Danny cakes them with the nutrient powder from their mother's Tupperware, which is better than when he covers them in sand. Danny can eat anything. Once, he ate half the pages from Noel's favorite paperbook comic, slow and deliberate, back when Noel was scared to put his fingers near Danny's teeth. Their mother thought he confused it with the paper-wrapped spearmint gum she'd given him a day before.

"I have to go back on-site for a few hours," she says, zipping her swim bag. "Will the pair of you be all right until supper? Jean is in the clubhouse."

"Jean is in the clubhouse," Danny echoes, a high sweet distortion of their mother's voice. His bony head swivels toward the stucco entrance.

She smiles. "That's right. Noel, watch out for your brother."

She gives them francs so they can buy Fanta and credit for Noel's tab so he can play netgames. When she leaves, Danny's skin fades back to slippery gray.

* * *

They'd been in Chad for three months already when Noel's mother told him about Danny. He'd spent the day, like most, climbing trees, hurling a mangy tennis ball against the concrete wall of the house, and watching procedurally generated cartoons instead of doing Skype school.

The first weeks had been the exciting ones, with his mother coming home with stories each night about the team cleaving their way inside the ship to find the stork adults (Gliese-876s, back then, after their star system) dead and decaying, bonded by bone and neurocable to the ship's navigation equipment, rot seeping slowly outward. Noel had liked hearing about the low keening sound that made some of the other xenobiologists and one of the soldiers vomit, about the dissolving corpses in the dark swampy corridors.

He'd even liked hearing about the warm red amniotic pool where they found the babies who'd been remade, as best the storks' genelabs could achieve, in humanity's image, swapping vestigial wings and spiny shells for bipedalism and articulated necks. Babies who grew to child size with slender limbs and overlarge heads, features vaguely neotenized either by chance, a side-effect of the gene alterations that saved them from the ship-wide plague, or by design, like a cuckoo trying to slip its eggs in.

But now his mother wanted to bring one home.

"Danyal," she said, pulling herself up to the Formica countertop beside him. "The government still wants them all to have Arabic names. But we call him Danny."

Noel spooned yogurt into his ceramic bowl, listening to a breathless story about the one stork baby who wouldn't socialize with his siblings, who aced cognition tests and mimicked speech and followed her tirelessly through the lab.

"He's sort of imprinted," she said, with the fragile smile Noel had learned to cherish these past three months, learned to cup in his hands like a brittle bird. He felt the question coming before it reached her lips.

"What if he stays with us?" she asked. "He's not doing well at the center. And you always wanted a brother."

The word felt like a glass shard in his gut, but he kept his face blank, how he'd learned from watching her. Noel had wanted a brother. It was true. It gnawed at him. Maybe if he'd wanted a sister more, she wouldn't have died. They wouldn't have had to cut her out of his mother's belly. Maybe he hadn't wished hard enough.

"For just a little while," his mother said, smile already moving to slip away.

Noel couldn't say no.

* * *

Noel and Danny are swimming circles around the bobbing, plastic-coated lifeguard, making it spin in place like a sprinkler. No matter how hard Noel kicks, Danny is still quicker. They don't notice the weather turning until the stacks of rust-red cloud wall off the sun. Noel comes up for air in a sudden dusk and the smell of cool wet dirt itches inside his nose. The deserted pool deck is strangely still. Then all at once the trees frenzy, a ripple of whipping branches, and the dust storm the weather probes missed sweeps down over them.

Noel barely has time to pull up his goggles before the stinging sand slaps across his face. He throws out a hand for the lifeguard's orange floaters but finds Danny's slick hard skin instead and flinches away. But Danny's hands clamp to him, and then his legs, and Noel's chest seizes with a sudden panic: Danny is drowning him. Then Danny vanishes, slides past, and Noel thrashes blindly after him until he rams against the metal bar of the edge.

Someone heaves him up and out of the water; sand pelts his bare back and shoulders. "Inside, *vas-y*," Jean's voice booms in his ear. The big man has already draped a protective beach towel over Danny's head, and now grips Noel's arm.

"My tab," Noel says automatically, looking to where the table should have been visible, not looking at Danny.

"I have it. *Dépêche-toi, hein?*"

Jean ushers them back across the slippery deck, through a battering cloud of red dust, into the clubhouse. He puts his shoulder into the door to close it behind them. Noel claws sand out of his hair while Danny struggles out of the orange towel. The barrage has left small red welts on his gray skin.

"Wash out your eyes at the sink," Jean says, pointing to the concrete basin back behind the bar. The clubhouse is dark except for one flickering fluorescent tube in the ceiling and the glow of a plasma screen hooked to the wall. The few UN workers who didn't leave earlier now slouch to the sunken couches, mumbling bitterly about cell signals lost, windows left wide open, faulty weather probes.

"I had my goggles," Noel says, tapping one lens.

"Wash the rest of you," Jean says curtly. "Then help the stork."

Noel goes to the basin and splashes cold chemical-tanged water over his skinny arms, his chest, his face, rinsing away the dust stuck to his wet skin. When he straightens up, Danny is standing directly behind him. The sight jolts him.

"Don't do that," Noel hisses.

Danny says nothing, washing himself in silence. Someone brings two bottles of wine from the kitchen, and someone else finds a preset film on the television, something with arctic explorers on shifting glaciers, and everyone settles in to wait out the storm. Jean clears Noel a space on the far end of the couch, pulls his unharmed tab out of his pocket.

Noel keeps his head bent over the small screen when Danny slips away to the kitchen, but he still sees it happen.

* * *

Danny had lived with them for a week when Noel tried to show him Maya's picture. He took the Polaroid from his mother's closet, where she kept an album in case digital storage somehow disappeared, which to Noel sounded like the sun somehow going out. It showed Maya's small face in black-and-white, the face he remembered as scrunched and dead purple.

With the photo clutched to his chest, Noel went to the living room where Danny was playing. Their mother called it playing, but Danny mostly stared at the old die-cast Hot Wheels and Lego kits, except for the time Noel left and came back to find the plastic blocks built into a twisting Fibonacci spire. Now, Danny was crouched on the rug, holding a chewed yellow Mac truck in his spidery hands.

"This is the sister Mom lost," Noel said, extending the photo. "We lost. The one I told you about."

Danny gave him a gleaming black stare.

Noel had tried to teach him words, in English, in French, sometimes in the Arabic he picked up from the response center guard. *Car. Voiture. Sayara.* He'd guided Danny to the porch one morning to warble a near-indiscernible "I love you" to their mother. That had made her happy for an entire day.

"This is Maya," Noel said, shaking the photo slightly between his fingers.

Danny took it, gently, then eased upright, clicking and clacking, and walked away. Noel blinked. He followed Danny into the kitchen, past the fridge where he'd scrawled *Bienvenue Danyal* and then *Welcome Danny* the day Noel's mother brought him back from the response center, savoring the static crackle under his fingertip and the electricity of anticipation.

Danny opened the sink cupboard, looked back at him, and slipped the photo neatly into the garbage. As his new brother walked back out of the kitchen, Noel wanted desperately to hit him, to stop him, to make him understand, but he just stood digging crescents in his palms with the ragged edges of his nails.

He realized that he hated Danny. Danny, who was here because Noel's sister was *not,* who secreted his strange fluids on the concrete floor, who made a low keening screech in the night, who'd shredded Noel's book. Maybe his sister was *not* because Danny was *here.*

As soon as he'd fished Maya's photo out of the trash and put it back in its album, Noel went to his tab. It only took a simple question: *are storks bad.* The nets were inundated with vitriolic conspiracy rants and he read them now, one after another, even though he didn't understand some words. He read how the stork babies secreted a mind-altering pheromone like the ones that bonded pregnant mothers to their newborns.

"There is no pheromone, Noel," his mother told him that night, when he said, voice shaking, that they needed to wear masks around Danny. "Is that what's upset you? It's just a myth."

Noel knew better. Danny was making her forget.

* * *

On the screen, an explorer stuck in an ice crevasse takes the pickaxe to his trapped arm. The adults groan or stammer laughs, gesticulating with tumblers of sloshing wine.

Noel makes himself watch the axe thwack, the blood trickle and steam, until the man's arm tears away. Then he slides from the couch into his chunky plastic flip-flops, and goes to the kitchen to find a Fanta.

He expects Danny to be there, because Danny doesn't like crowds of people unless their mother is nearby, but the kitchen is empty. A forgotten pot of coagulating spaghetti bubbles on the burner. The lime green radio built into the counter stutters static from the storm. Noel looks to the heavy back door and sees a wash of red sand around it.

Danny is outside. Noel finds a crate of lukewarm Fanta in the corner and tugs one free, replaces it with a handful of francs. He searches slowly for a bottle opener while he thinks of what might happen. Danny's skin is soft. Danny doesn't breathe well in Harmattan season. Stupid of him, to go out in the storm.

Noel knows in his hot angry gut that his mother will blame him if Danny is hurt. He could tell Jean to go look, but Jean would pick him up and bring him back without a flicker of irritation on his face. If Noel finds him alone, he can punish him for being so stupid, so selfish. Nobody will notice bruises among the welts.

Noel has never hit Danny before. The thought of it unsettles his stomach, but he loops it through his head as he sets the Fanta aside, pulls someone's track jacket from the hooks on the wall. By the time he wrestles his way out of the door, a brief shriek of wind that the adults won't notice with the volume up, he thinks he knows how it will feel.

Outside, the dust flies like shrapnel. Noel hides his face in the peaked hood of the jacket and wishes he'd brought his goggles. The transplanted eucalyptus trees are lurching with the wind, near cracking, as he battles his way into the courtyard. Sand peppers his exposed calves and feet like a thousand tiny wasps.

Through the maelstrom, Noel catches a flash of angular silhouette: Danny, hobbling away toward the parking lot, through the archway of thrashing trees. Noel opens his mouth to shout and ends up chewing sand. He pulls the hood tighter and follows Danny, eyes squeezed to slits, fists clenched inside the balled up ends of his sleeves.

By the time he fights his way to the end of the tile and scuttles down the worn steps into the lot, Danny is sitting where they buried the water scorpion. His head is bent against the wind and his overlong arms envelop his knees, compacting him. Waves of dust belt across him, rocking him back and forth.

"What are you doing?" Noel demands, fists still clenched, chest still scalding. The wind scours his words away, but Danny notices him. He looks up with all of his glittering black eyes. Then he reaches into the dirt and pours a handful over his head. The puff of dust is nothing in the storm, but Noel understands. He understands even before Danny's thin distorted voice slides under the windy howl.

"This is you," Danny says, shaking another handful of dust. "Watch this."

Noel's stomach plummets. He reaches for his anger. "Get up," he shouts. "You'll get us in trouble. You'll get me in trouble." He tries to kick at him and loses his flip flop. "Come back inside!" His eyes are stinging from sand and now tears, sliding thick down his grimy cheeks. "Come on," he pleads. He tries to haul Danny up by the shoulder, but his hand's shrugged off.

Noel feels a panic welling inside, panic for Danny's face crumpled purple, for a grave dug with one shovel. "Stay, then," he hollers. "Stay and get sand in your lungs and die."

Danny's head cocks up at the last word. He considers the sand trickling through his fingers. "This is Maya," he says.

Noel doesn't realize he's no longer standing until his kneecaps scrape the dirt. "I'm sorry," he says, crawling forward, face level with Danny's. "Danny. Sorry. It wasn't your fault. It's not your fault." He goes to drape his arms over Danny, but is shoved off. "Come inside," Noel begs.

Danny turns away. Another billow of dust blasts across them; Danny takes the brunt of it and every bit of him wilts. As the wind roars louder, Noel strips off his jacket and pulls it over their heads like a tarp. Danny stiffens, then allows it.

Their breath is hot underneath the nylon. Noel feels his skin press against Danny's clammy back. He feels the puckered marks left by flying sand.

"Not your fault," Noel mutters. The storm dances all around them.

He waits, and waits, for the echo.

The Shadow over Innsmouth

H.P. Lovecraft

Chapter I

DURING the winter of 1927–28 officials of the Federal government made a strange and secret investigation of certain conditions in the ancient Massachusetts seaport of Innsmouth. The public first learned of it in February, when a vast series of raids and arrests occurred, followed by the deliberate burning and dynamiting – under suitable precautions – of an enormous number of crumbling, worm-eaten, and supposedly empty houses along the abandoned waterfront. Uninquiring souls let this occurrence pass as one of the major clashes in a spasmodic war on liquor.

Keener news-followers, however, wondered at the prodigious number of arrests, the abnormally large force of men used in making them, and the secrecy surrounding the disposal of the prisoners. No trials, or even definite charges were reported; nor were any of the captives seen thereafter in the regular gaols of the nation. There were vague statements about disease and concentration camps, and later about dispersal in various naval and military prisons, but nothing positive ever developed. Innsmouth itself was left almost depopulated, and it is even now only beginning to show signs of a sluggishly revived existence.

Complaints from many liberal organizations were met with long confidential discussions, and representatives were taken on trips to certain camps and prisons. As a result, these societies became surprisingly passive and reticent. Newspaper men were harder to manage, but seemed largely to cooperate with the government in the end. Only one paper – a tabloid always discounted because of its wild policy – mentioned the deep diving submarine that discharged torpedoes downward in the marine abyss just beyond Devil Reef. That item, gathered by chance in a haunt of sailors, seemed indeed rather far-fetched; since the low, black reef lay a full mile and a half out from Innsmouth Harbour.

People around the country and in the nearby towns muttered a great deal among themselves, but said very little to the outer world. They had talked about dying and half-deserted Innsmouth for nearly a century, and nothing new could be wilder or more hideous than what they had whispered and hinted at years before. Many things had taught them secretiveness, and there was no need to exert pressure on them. Besides, they really knew little; for wide salt marshes, desolate and unpeopled, kept neighbors off from Innsmouth on the landward side.

But at last I am going to defy the ban on speech about this thing. Results, I am certain, are so thorough that no public harm save a shock of repulsion could ever accrue from a hinting of what was found by those horrified men at Innsmouth. Besides, what was found might possibly have more than one explanation. I do not know just how much of the whole tale has been told even to me, and I have many reasons for not wishing to probe deeper. For my contact with this affair has been closer than that of any other layman, and I have carried away impressions which are yet to drive me to drastic measures.

It was I who fled frantically out of Innsmouth in the early morning hours of July 16, 1927, and whose frightened appeals for government inquiry and action brought on the whole reported episode. I was willing enough to stay mute while the affair was fresh and uncertain; but now that it is an old story, with public interest and curiosity gone, I have an odd craving to whisper about those few frightful hours in that ill-rumored and evilly-shadowed seaport of death and blasphemous abnormality. The mere telling helps me to restore confidence in my own faculties; to reassure myself that I was not the first to succumb to a contagious nightmare hallucination. It helps me, too, in making up my mind regarding a certain terrible step which lies ahead of me.

I never heard of Innsmouth till the day before I saw it for the first and – so far – last time. I was celebrating my coming of age by a tour of New England – sightseeing, antiquarian, and genealogical – and had planned to go directly from ancient Newburyport to Arkham, whence my mother's family was derived. I had no car, but was travelling by train, trolley and motor-coach, always seeking the cheapest possible route. In Newburyport they told me that the steam train was the thing to take to Arkham; and it was only at the station ticket-office, when I demurred at the high fare, that I learned about Innsmouth. The stout, shrewd-faced agent, whose speech shewed him to be no local man, seemed sympathetic toward my efforts at economy, and made a suggestion that none of my other informants had offered.

"You could take that old bus, I suppose," he said with a certain hesitation, "but it ain't thought much of hereabouts. It goes through Innsmouth – you may have heard about that – and so the people don't like it. Run by an Innsmouth fellow – Joe Sargent – but never gets any custom from here, or Arkham either, I guess. Wonder it keeps running at all. I s'pose it's cheap enough, but I never see mor'n two or three people in it – nobody but those Innsmouth folk. Leaves the square – front of Hammond's Drug Store – at 10 a.m. and 7 p.m. unless they've changed lately. Looks like a terrible rattletrap – I've never been on it."

That was the first I ever heard of shadowed Innsmouth. Any reference to a town not shown on common maps or listed in recent guidebooks would have interested me, and the agent's odd manner of allusion roused something like real curiosity. A town able to inspire such dislike in its neighbors, I thought, must be at least rather unusual, and worthy of a tourist's attention. If it came before Arkham I would stop off there and so I asked the agent to tell me something about it. He was very deliberate, and spoke with an air of feeling slightly superior to what he said.

"Innsmouth? Well, it's a queer kind of a town down at the mouth of the Manuxet. Used to be almost a city – quite a port before the War of 1812 – but all gone to pieces in the last hundred years or so. No railroad now – B. and M. never went through, and the branch line from Rowley was given up years ago.

"More empty houses than there are people, I guess, and no business to speak of except fishing and lobstering. Everybody trades mostly either here or in Arkham or Ipswich. Once they had quite a few mills, but nothing's left now except one gold refinery running on the leanest kind of part time.

"That refinery, though, used to be a big thing, and old man Marsh, who owns it, must be richer'n Croesus. Queer old duck, though, and sticks mighty close in his home. He's supposed to have developed some skin disease or deformity late in life that makes him keep out of sight.

Grandson of Captain Obed Marsh, who founded the business. His mother seems to've been some kind of foreigner – they say a South Sea islander – so everybody raised Cain when he married an Ipswich girl fifty years ago. They always do that about Innsmouth people, and folks here and hereabouts always try to cover up any Innsmouth blood they have in 'em. But Marsh's children and grandchildren look just like anyone else far's I can see. I've had 'em pointed out to me here – though, come to think of it, the elder children don't seem to be around lately. Never saw the old man.

"And why is everybody so down on Innsmouth? Well, young fellow, you mustn't take too much stock in what people here say. They're hard to get started, but once they do get started they never let up. They've been telling things about Innsmouth – whispering 'em, mostly – for the last hundred years, I guess, and I gather they're more scared than anything else. Some of the stories would make you laugh – about old Captain Marsh driving bargains with the devil and bringing imps out of hell to live in Innsmouth, or about some kind of devil-worship and awful sacrifices in some place near the wharves that people stumbled on around 1845 or thereabouts – but I come from Panton, Vermont, and that kind of story don't go down with me.

"You ought to hear, though, what some of the old-timers tell about the black reef off the coast – Devil Reef, they call it. It's well above water a good part of the time, and never much below it, but at that you could hardly call it an island. The story is that there's a whole legion of devils seen sometimes on that reef – sprawled about, or darting in and out of some kind of caves near the top. It's a rugged, uneven thing, a good bit over a mile out, and toward the end of shipping days sailors used to make big detours just to avoid it.

"That is, sailors that didn't hail from Innsmouth. One of the things they had against old Captain Marsh was that he was supposed to land on it sometimes at night when the tide was right. Maybe he did, for I dare say the rock formation was interesting, and it's just barely possible he was looking for pirate loot and maybe finding it; but there was talk of his dealing with demons there. Fact is, I guess on the whole it was really the Captain that gave the bad reputation to the reef.

"That was before the big epidemic of 1846, when over half the folks in Innsmouth was carried off. They never did quite figure out what the trouble was, but it was probably some foreign kind of disease brought from China or somewhere by the shipping. It surely was bad enough – there was riots over it, and all sorts of ghastly doings that I don't believe ever got outside of town – and it left the place in awful shape. Never came back – there can't be more'n 300 or 400 people living there now.

"But the real thing behind the way folks feel is simply race prejudice – and I don't say I'm blaming those that hold it. I hate those Innsmouth folks myself, and I wouldn't care to go to their town. I s'pose you know – though I can see you're a Westerner by your talk – what a lot our New England ships used to have to do with queer ports in Africa, Asia, the South Seas, and everywhere else, and what queer kinds of people they sometimes brought back with 'em. You've probably heard about the Salem man that came home with a Chinese wife, and maybe you know there's still a bunch of Fiji Islanders somewhere around Cape Cod.

"Well, there must be something like that back of the Innsmouth people. The place always was badly cut off from the rest of the country by marshes and creeks and we can't be sure about the ins and outs of the matter; but it's pretty clear that old Captain Marsh must have brought home some odd specimens when he had all three of his ships in commission back in the twenties and thirties. There certainly is a strange kind of streak in the Innsmouth folks today – I don't know how to explain it but it sort of makes you crawl. You'll notice a little in Sargent if you take his bus. Some of 'em have queer narrow heads with flat noses and bulgy, starry eyes that never seem to shut, and their skin ain't quite right. Rough and scabby, and the sides of the necks are all shriveled or creased up. Get bald, too, very young. The older fellows look the worst – fact is, I don't believe I've ever seen a very old chap of that kind. Guess they must die of looking in the glass! Animals hate 'em – they used to have lots of horse trouble before the autos came in.

"Nobody around here or in Arkham or Ipswich will have anything to do with 'em, and they act kind of offish themselves when they come to town or when anyone tries to fish on their grounds. Queer how fish are always thick off Innsmouth Harbour when there ain't any anywhere else around – but just try to fish there yourself and see how the folks chase you off! Those people used to come here on the railroad – walking and taking the train at Rowley after the branch was dropped – but now they use that bus.

"Yes, there's a hotel in Innsmouth – called the Gilman House – but I don't believe it can amount to much. I wouldn't advise you to try it. Better stay over here and take the ten o'clock bus tomorrow morning; then you can get an evening bus there for Arkham at eight o'clock. There was a factory inspector who stopped at the Gilman a couple of years ago and he had a lot of unpleasant hints about the place. Seems they get a queer crowd there, for this fellow heard voices in other rooms – though most of 'em was empty – that gave him the shivers. It was foreign talk he thought, but he said the bad thing about it was the kind of voice that sometimes spoke. It sounded so unnatural – slopping like, he said – that he didn't dare undress and go to sleep. Just waited up and lit out the first thing in the morning. The talk went on most all night.

"This fellow – Casey, his name was – had a lot to say about how the Innsmouth folk watched him and seemed kind of on guard. He found the Marsh refinery a queer place – it's in an old mill on the lower falls of the Manuxet. What he said tallied up with what I'd heard. Books in bad shape, and no clear account of any kind of dealings. You know it's always been a kind of mystery where the Marshes get the gold they refine. They've never seemed to do much buying in that line, but years ago they shipped out an enormous lot of ingots.

"Used to be talk of a queer foreign kind of jewelry that the sailors and refinery men sometimes sold on the sly, or that was seen once or twice on some of the Marsh women-folks. People allowed maybe old Captain Obed traded for it in some heathen port, especially since he always ordered stacks of glass beads and trinkets such as seafaring men used to get for native trade. Others thought and still think he'd found an old pirate cache out on Devil Reef. But here's a funny thing. The old Captain's been dead these sixty years, and there's ain't been a good-sized ship out of the place since the Civil War; but just the same the Marshes still keep on buying a few of those native trade things – mostly glass and rubber gewgaws, they tell me. Maybe the Innsmouth folks like 'em to look at themselves – Gawd knows they've gotten to be about as bad as South Sea cannibals and Guinea savages.

"That plague of '46 must have taken off the best blood in the place. Anyway, they're a doubtful lot now, and the Marshes and other rich folks are as bad as any. As I told you, there probably ain't more'n 400 people in the whole town in spite of all the streets they say there are. I guess they're what they call 'white trash' down South – lawless and sly, and full of secret things. They get a lot of fish and lobsters and do exporting by truck. Queer how the fish swarm right there and nowhere else.

"Nobody can ever keep track of these people, and state school officials and census men have a devil of a time. You can bet that prying strangers ain't welcome around Innsmouth. I've heard personally of more'n one business or government man that's disappeared there, and there's loose talk of one who went crazy and is out at Danvers now. They must have fixed up some awful scare for that fellow.

"That's why I wouldn't go at night if I was you. I've never been there and have no wish to go, but I guess a daytime trip couldn't hurt you – even though the people hereabouts will advise you not to make it. If you're just sightseeing, and looking for old-time stuff, Innsmouth ought to be quite a place for you."

And so I spent part of that evening at the Newburyport Public Library looking up data about Innsmouth. When I had tried to question the natives in the shops, the lunchroom, the garages, and the fire station, I had found them even harder to get started than the ticket agent had predicted; and realized that I could not spare the time to overcome their first instinctive reticence. They had a kind of obscure suspiciousness, as if there were something amiss with anyone too much interested in Innsmouth. At the Y.M.C.A., where I was stopping, the clerk merely discouraged my going to such a dismal, decadent place; and the people at the library shewed much the same attitude. Clearly, in the eyes of the educated, Innsmouth was merely an exaggerated case of civic degeneration.

The Essex County histories on the library shelves had very little to say, except that the town was founded in 1643, noted for shipbuilding before the Revolution, a seat of great marine prosperity in the early 19th century, and later a minor factory center using the Manuxet as power. The epidemic and riots of 1846 were very sparsely treated, as if they formed a discredit to the county.

References to decline were few, though the significance of the later record was unmistakable. After the Civil War all industrial life was confined to the Marsh Refining Company, and the marketing of gold ingots formed the only remaining bit of major commerce aside from the eternal fishing. That fishing paid less and less as the price of the commodity fell and large-scale corporations offered competition, but there was never a dearth of fish around Innsmouth Harbour. Foreigners seldom settled there, and there was some discreetly veiled evidence that a number of Poles and Portuguese who had tried it had been scattered in a peculiarly drastic fashion.

Most interesting of all was a glancing reference to the strange jewelry vaguely associated with Innsmouth. It had evidently impressed the whole countryside more than a little, for mention was made of specimens in the museum of Miskatonic University at Arkham, and in the display room of the Newburyport Historical Society. The fragmentary descriptions of these things were bald and prosaic, but they hinted to me an undercurrent of persistent strangeness. Something about them seemed so odd and provocative that I could not put them out of my mind, and despite the relative lateness of the hour I resolved to see the local sample – said to be a large, queerly-proportioned thing evidently meant for a tiara – if it could possibly be arranged.

The librarian gave me a note of introduction to the curator of the Society, a Miss Anna Tilton, who lived nearby, and after a brief explanation that ancient gentlewoman was kind enough to pilot me into the closed building, since the hour was not outrageously late. The collection was a notable one indeed, but in my present mood I had eyes for nothing but the bizarre object which glistened in a corner cupboard under the electric lights.

It took no excessive sensitiveness to beauty to make me literally gasp at the strange, unearthly splendour of the alien, opulent phantasy that rested there on a purple velvet cushion. Even now I can hardly describe what I saw, though it was clearly enough a sort of tiara, as the description had said. It was tall in front, and with a very large and curiously irregular periphery, as if designed for a head of almost freakishly elliptical outline.

The material seemed to be predominantly gold, though a weird lighter lustrousness hinted at some strange alloy with an equally beautiful and scarcely identifiable metal. Its condition was almost perfect, and one could have spent hours in studying the striking and puzzlingly untraditional designs – some simply geometrical, and some plainly marine – chased or moulded in high relief on its surface with a craftsmanship of incredible skill and grace.

The longer I looked, the more the thing fascinated me; and in this fascination there was a curiously disturbing element hardly to be classified or accounted for. At first I decided that it was the queer other-worldly quality of the art which made me uneasy. All other art objects I had ever seen either belonged to some known racial or national stream, or else were consciously modernistic defiances of every recognized stream. This tiara was neither. It clearly belonged to some settled technique of infinite maturity and perfection, yet that technique was utterly remote from any – Eastern or Western, ancient or modern – which I had ever heard of or seen exemplified. It was as if the workmanship were that of another planet.

However, I soon saw that my uneasiness had a second and perhaps equally potent source residing in the pictorial and mathematical suggestion of the strange designs. The patterns all hinted of remote secrets and unimaginable abysses in time and space, and the monotonously aquatic nature of the reliefs became almost sinister. Among these reliefs were fabulous monsters of abhorrent grotesqueness and malignity – half ichthyic and half batrachian in suggestion – which one could not dissociate from a certain haunting and uncomfortable sense of pseudomemory, as if they called up some image from deep cells and tissues whose retentive functions are wholly primal and awesomely ancestral. At times I fancied that every contour of these blasphemous fish-frogs was over-flowing with the ultimate quintessence of unknown and inhuman evil.

In odd contrast to the tiara's aspect was its brief and prosy history as related by Miss Tilton. It had been pawned for a ridiculous sum at a shop in State Street in 1873, by a drunken Innsmouth man shortly afterward killed in a brawl. The Society had acquired it directly from the pawnbroker, at once giving it a display worthy of its quality. It was labeled as of probable East-Indian or Indochinese provenance, though the attribution was frankly tentative.

Miss Tilton, comparing all possible hypotheses regarding its origin and its presence in New England, was inclined to believe that it formed part of some exotic pirate hoard discovered by old Captain Obed Marsh. This view was surely not weakened by the insistent offers of purchase at a high price which the Marshes began to make as soon as they knew of its presence, and which they repeated to this day despite the Society's unvarying determination not to sell.

As the good lady shewed me out of the building she made it clear that the pirate theory of the Marsh fortune was a popular one among the intelligent people of the region. Her own attitude toward shadowed Innsmouth – which she never seen – was one of disgust at a community slipping far down the cultural scale, and she assured me that the rumours of devil-worship were partly justified by a peculiar secret cult which had gained force there and engulfed all the orthodox churches.

It was called, she said, 'The Esoteric Order of Dagon', and was undoubtedly a debased, quasi-pagan thing imported from the East a century before, at a time when the Innsmouth fisheries seemed to be going barren. Its persistence among a simple people was quite natural in view of the sudden and permanent return of abundantly fine fishing, and it soon came to be the greatest influence in the town, replacing Freemasonry altogether and taking up headquarters in the old Masonic Hall on New Church Green.

All this, to the pious Miss Tilton, formed an excellent reason for shunning the ancient town of decay and desolation; but to me it was merely a fresh incentive. To my architectural and historical anticipations was now added an acute anthropological zeal, and I could scarcely sleep in my small room at the 'Y' as the night wore away.

Chapter II

SHORTLY BEFORE TEN the next morning I stood with one small valise in front of Hammond's Drug Store in old Market Square waiting for the Innsmouth bus. As the hour for its arrival drew near I noticed a general drift of the loungers to other places up the street, or to the Ideal Lunch across the square. Evidently the ticket-agent had not exaggerated the dislike which local people bore toward Innsmouth and its denizens. In a few moments a small motor-coach of extreme decrepitude and dirty grey colour rattled down State Street, made a turn, and drew up at the curb beside me. I felt immediately that it was the right one; a guess which the half-illegible sign on the windshield – *Arkham-Innsmouth-Newb'port* – soon verified.

There were only three passengers – dark, unkempt men of sullen visage and somewhat youthful cast – and when the vehicle stopped they clumsily shambled out and began walking up State Street in a silent, almost furtive fashion. The driver also alighted, and I watched him as he went into the drug store to make some purchase. This, I reflected, must be the Joe Sargent mentioned by the ticket-agent; and even before I noticed any details there spread over me a wave of spontaneous aversion which could be neither checked nor explained. It suddenly struck me as very natural that the local people should not wish to ride on a bus owned and driven by this man, or to visit any oftener than possible the habitat of such a man and his kinsfolk.

When the driver came out of the store I looked at him more carefully and tried to determine the source of my evil impression. He was a thin, stoop-shouldered man not much under six feet tall, dressed in shabby blue civilian clothes and wearing a frayed golf cap. His age was perhaps thirty-five, but the odd, deep creases in the sides of his neck made him seem older when one did not study his dull, expressionless face. He had a narrow head, bulging, watery-blue eyes that seemed never to wink, a flat nose, a receding forehead and chin, and singularly undeveloped ears. His long thick lip and coarse-pored, greyish cheeks seemed almost beardless except for some sparse yellow hairs that straggled and curled in irregular patches; and in places the surface seemed queerly irregular, as if peeling from some cutaneous disease. His hands were large and heavily veined, and had a very unusual greyish-blue tinge. The fingers were strikingly short in proportion to the rest of the structure, and seemed to have a tendency to curl closely into the huge palm. As he walked toward the bus I observed his peculiarly shambling gait and saw that his feet were inordinately immense. The more I studied them the more I wondered how he could buy any shoes to fit them.

A certain greasiness about the fellow increased my dislike. He was evidently given to working or lounging around the fish docks, and carried with him much of their characteristic smell. Just what foreign blood was in him I could not even guess. His oddities certainly did not look Asiatic, Polynesian, Levantine or negroid, yet I could see why the people found him alien. I myself would have thought of biological degeneration rather than alienage.

I was sorry when I saw there would be no other passengers on the bus. Somehow I did not like the idea of riding alone with this driver. But as leaving time obviously approached I conquered my qualms and followed the man aboard, extending him a dollar bill and murmuring the single word 'Innsmouth.' He looked curiously at me for a second as he returned forty cents change without speaking. I took a seat far behind him, but on the same side of the bus, since I wished to watch the shore during the journey.

At length the decrepit vehicle started with a jerk, and rattled noisily past the old brick buildings of State Street amidst a cloud of vapour from the exhaust. Glancing at the people on the sidewalks, I thought I detected in them a curious wish to avoid looking at the bus – or at least a wish to avoid seeming to look at it. Then we turned to the left into High Street, where the going was smoother; flying by stately old mansions of the early republic and still older colonial farmhouses, passing the Lower Green and Parker River, and finally emerging into a long, monotonous stretch of open shore country.

The day was warm and sunny, but the landscape of sand and sedge-grass, and stunted shrubbery became more and desolate as we proceeded. Out the window I could see the blue water and the sandy line of Plum Island, and we presently drew very near the beach as our narrow road veered off from the main highway to Rowley and Ipswich. There were no visible houses, and I could tell by the state of the road that traffic was very light hereabouts. The weather-worn telephone poles carried only two wires. Now and then we crossed crude wooden bridges over tidal creeks that wound far inland and promoted the general isolation of the region.

Once in a while I noticed dead stumps and crumbling foundation-walls above the drifting sand, and recalled the old tradition quoted in one of the histories I had read, that this was once a fertile and thickly-settled countryside. The change, it was said, came simultaneously with the Innsmouth epidemic of 1846, and was thought by simple folk to have a dark connection with hidden forces of evil. Actually, it was caused by the unwise cutting of woodlands near the shore, which robbed the soil of the best protection and opened the way for waves of wind-blown sand.

At last we lost sight of Plum Island and saw the vast expanse of the open Atlantic on our left. Our narrow course began to climb steeply, and I felt a singular sense of disquiet in looking at the lonely crest ahead where the rutted road-way met the sky. It was as if the bus were about to keep on in its ascent, leaving the sane earth altogether and merging with the unknown arcana of upper air and cryptical sky. The smell of the sea took on ominous implications, and the silent driver's bent, rigid back and narrow head became more and more hateful. As I looked at him I saw that the back of his head was almost as hairless as his face, having only a few straggling yellow strands upon a grey scabrous surface.

Then we reached the crest and beheld the outspread valley beyond, where the Manuxet joins the sea just north of the long line of cliffs that culminate in Kingsport Head and veer off toward Cape Ann. On the far misty horizon I could just make out the dizzy profile of the Head, topped by the queer ancient house of which so many legends are told; but for the moment all my attention was captured by the nearer panorama just below me. I had, I realized, come face to face with rumour-shadowed Innsmouth.

It was a town of wide extent and dense construction, yet one with a portentous dearth of visible life. From the tangle of chimney-pots scarcely a wisp of smoke came, and the three tall steeples loomed stark and unpainted against the seaward horizon. One of them was crumbling down at the top, and in that and another there were only black gaping holes where clock-dials should have been. The vast huddle of sagging gambrel roofs and peaked gables conveyed with offensive clearness the idea of wormy decay, and as we approached along the now descending road I could see that many roofs had wholly caved in. There were some large square Georgian houses, too, with hipped roofs, cupolas, and railed 'widow's walks.' These were mostly well back from the water, and one or two seemed to be in moderately sound condition. Stretching inland from among them I saw the rusted, grass-grown line of the abandoned railway, with leaning telegraph-poles now devoid of wires, and the half-obscured lines of the old carriage roads to Rowley and Ipswich.

The decay was worst close to the waterfront, though in its very midst I could spy the white belfry of a fairly well preserved brick structure which looked like a small factory. The harbour, long clogged with sand, was enclosed by an ancient stone breakwater; on which I could begin to discern the minute forms of a few seated fishermen, and at whose end were what looked like the foundations of a bygone lighthouse. A sandy tongue had formed inside this barrier and upon it I saw a few decrepit cabins, moored dories, and scattered lobster-pots. The only deep water seemed to be where the river poured out past the belfried structure and turned southward to join the ocean at the breakwater's end.

Here and there the ruins of wharves jutted out from the shore to end in indeterminate rottenness, those farthest south seeming the most decayed. And far out at sea, despite a high tide, I glimpsed a long, black line scarcely rising above the water yet carrying a suggestion of odd latent malignancy. This, I knew, must be Devil Reef. As I looked, a subtle, curious sense of beckoning seemed superadded to the grim repulsion; and oddly enough, I found this overtone more disturbing than the primary impression.

We met no one on the road, but presently began to pass deserted farms in varying stages of ruin. Then I noticed a few inhabited houses with rags stuffed in the broken windows and shells and dead fish lying about the littered yards. Once or twice I saw listless-looking people working in barren gardens or digging clams on the fishy-smelling beach below, and groups of dirty, simian-visaged children playing around weed-grown doorsteps. Somehow these people seemed more disquieting than the dismal buildings, for almost every one had certain peculiarities of face and motions which I instinctively disliked without being able to define or comprehend them. For a second I thought this typical physique suggested some picture I had seen, perhaps in a book, under circumstances of particular horror or melancholy; but this pseudo-recollection passed very quickly.

As the bus reached a lower level I began to catch the steady note of a waterfall through the unnatural stillness. The leaning, unpainted houses grew thicker, lined both sides of the road, and displayed more urban tendencies than did those we were leaving behind, The panorama ahead had contracted to a street scene, and in spots I could see where a cobblestone pavement and stretches of brick sidewalk had formerly existed. All the houses were apparently deserted, and there were occasional gaps where tumbledown chimneys and cellar walls told of buildings that had collapsed. Pervading everything was the most nauseous fishy odour imaginable.

Soon cross streets and junctions began to appear; those on the left leading to shoreward realms of unpaved squalor and decay, while those on the right shewed vistas of departed grandeur. So far I had seen no people in the town, but there now came signs of a sparse habitation – curtained windows here and there, and an occasional battered motorcar at the curb. Pavement and sidewalks were increasingly well-defined, and though most of the houses were quite old – wood and brick structures of the early 19th century – they were obviously kept fit for habitation. As an amateur antiquarian I almost lost my olfactory disgust and my feeling of menace and repulsion amidst this rich, unaltered survival from the past.

But I was not to reach my destination without one very strong impression of poignantly disagreeable quality. The bus had come to a sort of open concourse or radial point with churches on two sides and the bedraggled remains of a circular green in the centre, and I was looking at a large pillared hall on the right-hand junction ahead. The structure's once white paint was now gray and peeling and the black and gold sign on the pediment was so faded that I could only with difficulty make out the words 'Esoteric Order of Dagon'. This, then was the former Masonic Hall now given over to a degraded cult. As I strained to decipher this inscription my notice was distracted by the raucous tones of a cracked bell across the street, and I quickly turned to look out the window on my side of the coach.

The sound came from a squat stone church of manifestly later date than most of the houses, built in a clumsy Gothic fashion and having a disproportionately high basement with shuttered windows. Though the hands of its clock were missing on the side I glimpsed, I knew that those hoarse strokes were tolling the hour of eleven. Then suddenly all thoughts of time were blotted out by an onrushing image of sharp intensity and unaccountable horror which had seized me before I knew what it really was. The door of the church basement was open, revealing a rectangle of blackness inside. And as I looked, a certain object crossed or seemed to cross that dark rectangle; burning into my brain a momentary conception of nightmare which was all the more maddening because analysis could not shew a single nightmarish quality in it.

It was a living object – the first except the driver that I had seen since entering the compact part of the town – and had I been in a steadier mood I would have found nothing whatever of terror in it. Clearly, as I realised a moment later, it was the pastor; clad in some peculiar vestments doubtless introduced since the Order of Dagon had modified the ritual of the local churches. The thing which had probably caught my first subconscious glance and supplied the touch of bizarre horror was the tall tiara he wore; an almost exact duplicate of the one Miss Tilton had shown me the previous evening. This, acting on my imagination, had supplied namelessly sinister qualities to the indeterminate face and robed, shambling form beneath it. There was not, I soon decided, any reason why I should have felt that shuddering touch of evil pseudo-memory. Was it not natural that a local mystery cult should adopt among its regimentals an unique type of head-dress made familiar to the community in some strange way – perhaps as treasure-trove?

A very thin sprinkling of repellent-looking youngish people now became visible on the sidewalks – lone individuals, and silent knots of two or three. The lower floors of the crumbling houses sometimes harboured small shops with dingy signs, and I noticed a parked truck or two as we rattled along. The sound of waterfalls became more and more distinct, and presently I saw a fairly deep river-gorge ahead, spanned by a wide, iron-railed highway bridge beyond which a large square opened out. As we clanked over the bridge I looked out on both sides and observed some factory buildings on the edge of the grassy bluff or part way down. The water far below was very abundant, and I could see two vigorous sets of falls upstream on my right and at least one downstream on my left. From this point the noise was quite deafening. Then we rolled into the large semicircular square across the river and drew up on the right-hand side in front of a tall, cupola crowned building with remnants of yellow paint and with a half-effaced sign proclaiming it to be the Gilman House.

I was glad to get out of that bus, and at once proceeded to check my valise in the shabby hotel lobby. There was only one person in sight – an elderly man without what I had come to call the 'Innsmouth look' – and I decided not to ask him any of the questions which bothered me; remembering that odd things had been noticed in this hotel. Instead, I strolled out on the square, from which the bus had already gone, and studied the scene minutely and appraisingly.

One side of the cobblestoned open space was the straight line of the river; the other was a semicircle of slant-roofed brick buildings of about the 1800 period, from which several streets radiated away to the southeast, south, and southwest. Lamps were depressingly few and small – all low-powered incandescents – and I was glad that my plans called for departure before dark, even though I knew the moon would be bright. The buildings were all in fair condition, and included perhaps a dozen shops in current operation; of which one was a grocery of the First National chain, others a dismal restaurant, a drug store, and a wholesale fish-dealer's office, and still another, at the eastward extremity of the square near the river an office of the town's only industry – the Marsh Refining Company. There were perhaps ten people visible, and four or five automobiles and motor trucks stood scattered about. I did not need to be told that this was the civic centre of Innsmouth. Eastward I could catch blue glimpses of the harbour, against which rose the decaying remains of three once beautiful Georgian steeples. And toward the shore on the opposite bank of the river I saw the white belfry surmounting what I took to be the Marsh refinery.

For some reason or other I chose to make my first inquiries at the chain grocery, whose personnel was not likely to be native to Innsmouth. I found a solitary boy of about seventeen in charge, and was pleased to note the brightness and affability which promised cheerful information. He seemed exceptionally eager to talk, and I soon gathered that he did not like the place, its fishy smell, or its furtive people. A word with any outsider was a relief to him. He hailed from Arkham, boarded with a family who came from Ipswich, and went back whenever he got a moment off. His family did not like him to work in Innsmouth, but the chain had transferred him there and he did not wish to give up his job.

There was, he said, no public library or chamber of commerce in Innsmouth, but I could probably find my way about. The street I had come down was Federal. West of that were the fine old residence streets – Broad, Washington, Lafayette, and Adams – and east of it were the shoreward slums. It was in these slums – along Main Street – that I would find the old Georgian churches, but they were all long abandoned. It would be well not to make oneself too conspicuous in such neighbourhoods – especially north of the river since the people were sullen and hostile. Some strangers had even disappeared.

Certain spots were almost forbidden territory, as he had learned at considerable cost. One must not, for example, linger much around the Marsh refinery, or around any of the still used churches, or around the pillared Order of Dagon Hall at New Church Green. Those churches were very odd – all violently disavowed by their respective denominations elsewhere, and apparently using the queerest kind of ceremonials and clerical vestments. Their creeds were heterodox and mysterious, involving hints of certain marvelous transformations leading to bodily immortality – of a sort – on this earth. The youth's own pastor – Dr. Wallace of Asbury M.E. Church in Arkham – had gravely urged him not to join any church in Innsmouth.

As for the Innsmouth people – the youth hardly knew what to make of them. They were as furtive and seldom seen as animals that live in burrows, and one could hardly imagine how they passed the time apart from their desultory fishing. Perhaps – judging from the quantities of bootleg liquor they consumed – they lay for most of the daylight hours in an alcoholic stupor. They seemed sullenly banded together in some sort of fellowship and understanding – despising the world as if they had access to other and preferable spheres of entity. Their appearance – especially those staring, unwinking eyes which one never saw shut – was certainly shocking enough; and their voices were disgusting. It was awful to hear them chanting in their churches at night, and especially during their main festivals or revivals, which fell twice a year on April 30th and October 31st.

They were very fond of the water, and swam a great deal in both river and harbour. Swimming races out to Devil Reef were very common, and everyone in sight seemed well able to share in this arduous sport. When one came to think of it, it was generally only rather young people who were seen about in public, and of these the oldest were apt to be the most tainted-looking. When exceptions did occur, they were mostly persons with no trace of aberrancy, like the old clerk at the hotel. One wondered what became of the bulk of the older folk, and whether the 'Innsmouth look' were not a strange and insidious disease-phenomenon which increased its hold as years advanced.

Only a very rare affliction, of course, could bring about such vast and radical anatomical changes in a single individual after maturity – changes invoking osseous factors as basic as the shape of the skull – but then, even this aspect was no more baffling and unheard-of than the visible features of the malady as a whole. It would be hard, the youth implied, to form any real conclusions regarding such a matter; since one never came to know the natives personally no matter how long one might live in Innsmouth.

The youth was certain that many specimens even worse than the worst visible ones were kept locked indoors in some places. People sometimes heard the queerest kind of sounds. The tottering waterfront hovels north of the river were reputedly connected by hidden tunnels, being thus a veritable warren of unseen abnormalities. What kind of foreign blood – if any – these beings had, it was impossible to tell. They sometimes kept certain especially repulsive characters out of sight when government and others from the outside world came to town.

It would be of no use, my informant said, to ask the natives anything about the place. The only one who would talk was a very aged but normal looking man who lived at the poorhouse on the north rim of the town and spent his time walking about or lounging around the fire station. This hoary character, Zadok Allen, was 96 years old and somewhat touched in the head, besides being the town drunkard. He was a strange, furtive creature who constantly looked over his shoulder as if afraid of something, and when sober could not be persuaded to talk at all with strangers. He was, however, unable to resist any offer of his favorite poison; and once drunk would furnish the most astonishing fragments of whispered reminiscence.

After all, though, little useful data could be gained from him; since his stories were all insane, incomplete hints of impossible marvels and horrors which could have no source save in his own disordered fancy. Nobody ever believed him, but the natives did not like him to drink and talk with strangers; and it was not always safe to be seen questioning him. It was probably from him that some of the wildest popular whispers and delusions were derived.

Several non-native residents had reported monstrous glimpses from time to time, but between old Zadok's tales and the malformed inhabitants it was no wonder such illusions were current. None of the non-natives ever stayed out late at night, there being a widespread impression that it was not wise to do so. Besides, the streets were loathsomely dark.

As for business – the abundance of fish was certainly almost uncanny, but the natives were taking less and less advantage of it. Moreover, prices were falling and competition was growing. Of course the town's real business was the refinery, whose commercial office was on the square only a few doors east of where we stood. Old Man Marsh was never seen, but sometimes went to the works in a closed, curtained car.

There were all sorts of rumors about how Marsh had come to look. He had once been a great dandy; and people said he still wore the frock-coated finery of the Edwardian age curiously adapted to certain deformities. His son had formerly conducted the office in the square, but latterly they had been keeping out of sight a good deal and leaving the brunt of affairs to the younger generation. The sons and their sisters had come to look very queer, especially the elder ones; and it was said that their health was failing.

One of the Marsh daughters was a repellent, reptilian-looking woman who wore an excess of weird jewellery clearly of the same exotic tradition as that to which the strange tiara belonged. My informant had noticed it many times, and had heard it spoken of as coming from some secret hoard, either of pirates or of demons. The clergymen – or priests, or whatever they were called nowadays – also wore this kind of ornament as a headdress; but one seldom caught glimpses of them. Other specimens the youth had not seen, though many were rumoured to exist around Innsmouth.

The Marshes, together with the other three gently bred families of the town – the Waites, the Gilmans, and the Eliots – were all very retiring. They lived in immense houses along Washington Street, and several were reputed to harbour in concealment certain living kinsfolk whose personal aspect forbade public view, and whose deaths had been reported and recorded.

Warning me that many of the street signs were down, the youth drew for my benefit a rough but ample and painstaking sketch map of the town's salient features. After a moment's study I felt sure that it would be of great help, and pocketed it with profuse thanks. Disliking the dinginess of the single restaurant I had seen, I bought a fair supply of cheese crackers and ginger wafers to serve as a lunch later on. My program, I decided, would be to thread the principal streets, talk with any non-natives I might encounter, and catch the eight o'clock coach for Arkham. The town, I could see, formed a significant and exaggerated example of communal decay; but being no sociologist I would limit my serious observations to the field of architecture.

Thus I began my systematic though half-bewildered tour of Innsmouth's narrow, shadow-blighted ways. Crossing the bridge and turning toward the roar of the lower falls, I passed close to the Marsh refinery, which seemed to be oddly free from the noise of industry. The building stood on the steep river bluff near a bridge and an open confluence of streets which I took to be the earliest civic center, displaced after the Revolution by the present Town Square.

Re-crossing the gorge on the Main Street bridge, I struck a region of utter desertion which somehow made me shudder. Collapsing huddles of gambrel roofs formed a jagged and fantastic skyline, above which rose the ghoulish, decapitated steeple of an ancient church. Some houses along Main Street were tenanted, but most were tightly boarded up. Down unpaved side streets I saw the black, gaping windows of deserted hovels, many of which leaned at perilous and incredible angles through the sinking of part of the foundations. Those windows stared so spectrally that it took courage to turn eastward toward the waterfront. Certainly, the terror of a deserted house swells in geometrical rather than arithmetical progression as houses multiply to form a city of stark desolation.

The sight of such endless avenues of fishy-eyed vacancy and death, and the thought of such linked infinities of black, brooding compartments given over to cobwebs and memories and the conqueror worm, start up vestigial fears and aversions that not even the stoutest philosophy can disperse.

Fish Street was as deserted as Main, though it differed in having many brick and stone warehouses still in excellent shape. Water Street was almost its duplicate, save that there were great seaward gaps where wharves had been. Not a living thing did I see except for the scattered fishermen on the distant break-water, and not a sound did I hear save the lapping of the harbour tides and the roar of the falls in the Manuxet. The town was getting more and more on my nerves, and I looked behind me furtively as I picked my way back over the tottering Water Street bridge. The Fish Street bridge, according to the sketch, was in ruins.

North of the river there were traces of squalid life – active fish-packing houses in Water Street, smoking chimneys and patched roofs here and there, occasional sounds from indeterminate sources, and infrequent shambling forms in the dismal streets and unpaved lanes – but I seemed to find this even more oppressive than the southerly desertion. For one thing, the people were more hideous and abnormal than those near the centre of the town; so that I was several times evilly reminded of something utterly fantastic which I could not quite place. Undoubtedly the alien strain in the Innsmouth folk was stronger here than farther inland – unless, indeed, the 'Innsmouth look' were a disease rather than a blood stain, in which case this district might be held to harbour the more advanced cases.

One detail that annoyed me was the distribution of the few faint sounds I heard. They ought naturally to have come wholly from the visibly inhabited houses, yet in reality were often strongest inside the most rigidly boarded-up facades. There were creakings, scurryings, and hoarse doubtful noises; and I thought uncomfortably about the hidden tunnels suggested by the grocery boy. Suddenly I found myself wondering what the voices of those denizens would be like. I had heard no speech so far in this quarter, and was unaccountably anxious not to do so.

Pausing only long enough to look at two fine but ruinous old churches at Main and Church Streets, I hastened out of that vile waterfront slum. My next logical goal was New Church Green, but somehow or other I could not bear to repass the church in whose basement I had glimpsed the inexplicably frightening form of that strangely diademmed priest or pastor. Besides, the grocery youth had told me that churches, as well as the Order of Dagon Hall, were not advisable neighbourhoods for strangers.

Accordingly I kept north along Main to Martin, then turning inland, crossing Federal Street safely north of the Green, and entering the decayed patrician neighbourhood of northern Broad, Washington, Lafayette, and Adams Streets. Though these stately old avenues were ill-surfaced and unkempt, their elm-shaded dignity had not entirely departed. Mansion after mansion claimed my gaze, most of them decrepit and boarded up amidst neglected grounds, but one or two in each street shewing signs of occupancy. In Washington Street there was a row of four or five in excellent repair and with finely-tended lawns and gardens. The most sumptuous of these – with wide terraced parterres extending back the whole way to Lafayette Street – I took to be the home of Old Man Marsh, the afflicted refinery owner.

In all these streets no living thing was visible, and I wondered at the complete absence of cats and dogs from Innsmouth. Another thing which puzzled and disturbed me, even in some of the best-preserved mansions, was the tightly shuttered condition of many third-story and attic windows. Furtiveness and secretiveness seemed universal in this hushed city of alienage and death, and I could not escape the sensation of being watched from ambush on every hand by sly, staring eyes that never shut.

I shivered as the cracked stroke of three sounded from a belfry on my left. Too well did I recall the squat church from which those notes came. Following Washington street toward the river, I now faced a new zone of former industry and commerce; noting the ruins of a factory ahead, and seeing others, with the traces of an old railway station and covered railway bridge beyond, up the gorge on my right.

The uncertain bridge now before me was posted with a warning sign, but I took the risk and crossed again to the south bank where traces of life reappeared. Furtive, shambling creatures stared cryptically in my direction, and more normal faces eyed me coldly and curiously. Innsmouth was rapidly becoming intolerable, and I turned down Paine Street toward the Square in the hope of getting some vehicle to take me to Arkham before the still-distant starting-time of that sinister bus.

It was then that I saw the tumbledown fire station on my left, and noticed the red faced, bushy-bearded, watery eyed old man in nondescript rags who sat on a bench in front of it talking with a pair of unkempt but not abnormal looking firemen. This, of course, must be Zadok Allen, the half-crazed, liquorish nonagenarian whose tales of old Innsmouth and its shadow were so hideous and incredible.

Chapter III

IT MUST HAVE BEEN some imp of the perverse – or some sardonic pull from dark, hidden sources – which made me change my plans as I did. I had long before resolved to limit my observations to architecture alone, and I was even then hurrying toward the Square in an effort to get quick transportation out of this festering city of death and decay; but the sight of old Zadok Allen set up new currents in my mind and made me slacken my pace uncertainly.

I had been assured that the old man could do nothing but hint at wild, disjointed, and incredible legends, and I had been warned that the natives made it unsafe to be seen talking with him; yet the thought of this aged witness to the town's decay, with memories going back to the early days of ships and factories, was a lure that no amount of reason could make me resist. After all, the strangest and maddest of myths are often merely symbols or allegories based upon truth – and old Zadok must have seen everything which went on around Innsmouth for the last ninety years. Curiosity flared up beyond sense and caution, and in my youthful egotism I fancied I might be able to sift a nucleus of real history from the confused, extravagant outpouring I would probably extract with the aid of raw whiskey.

I knew that I could not accost him then and there, for the firemen would surely notice and object. Instead, I reflected, I would prepare by getting some bootleg liquor at a place where the grocery boy had told me it was plentiful. Then I would loaf near the fire station in apparent casualness, and fall in with old Zadok after he had started on one of his frequent rambles. The youth had said that he was very restless, seldom sitting around the station for more than an hour or two at a time.

A quart bottle of whiskey was easily, though not cheaply, obtained in the rear of a dingy variety-store just off the Square in Eliot Street. The dirty-looking fellow who waited on me had a touch of the staring 'Innsmouth look', but was quite civil in his way; being perhaps used to the custom of such convivial strangers – truckmen, gold-buyers, and the like – as were occasionally in town.

Reentering the Square I saw that luck was with me; for – shuffling out of Paine street around the corner of the Gilman House – I glimpsed nothing less than the tall, lean, tattered form of old Zadok Allen himself. In accordance with my plan, I attracted his attention by brandishing my newly-purchased bottle: and soon realised that he had begun to shuffle wistfully after me as I turned into Waite Street on my way to the most deserted region I could think of.

I was steering my course by the map the grocery boy had prepared, and was aiming for the wholly abandoned stretch of southern waterfront which I had previously visited. The only people in sight there had been the fishermen on the distant breakwater; and by going a few squares south I could get beyond the range of these, finding a pair of seats on some abandoned wharf and being free to question old Zadok unobserved for an indefinite time. Before I reached Main Street I could hear a faint and wheezy "Hey, Mister!" behind me and I presently allowed the old man to catch up and take copious pulls from the quart bottle.

I began putting out feelers as we walked amidst the omnipresent desolation and crazily tilted ruins, but found that the aged tongue did not loosen as quickly as I had expected. At length I saw a grass-grown opening toward the sea between crumbling brick walls, with the weedy length of an earth-and-masonry wharf projecting beyond. Piles of moss-covered stones near the water promised tolerable seats, and the scene was sheltered from all possible view by a ruined warehouse on the north. Here, I thought was the ideal place for a long secret colloquy; so I guided my companion down the lane and picked out spots to sit in among the mossy stones. The air of death and desertion was ghoulish, and the smell of fish almost insufferable; but I was resolved to let nothing deter me.

About four hours remained for conversation if I were to catch the eight o'clock coach for Arkham, and I began to dole out more liquor to the ancient tippler; meanwhile eating my own frugal lunch. In my donations I was careful not to overshoot the mark, for I did not wish Zadok's vinous garrulousness to pass into a stupor. After an hour his furtive taciturnity shewed signs of disappearing, but much to my disappointment he still sidetracked my questions about Innsmouth and its shadow-haunted past. He would babble of current topics, revealing a wide acquaintance with newspapers and a great tendency to philosophise in a sententious village fashion.

Toward the end of the second hour I feared my quart of whiskey would not be enough to produce results, and was wondering whether I had better leave old Zadok and go back for more. Just then, however, chance made the opening which my questions had been unable to make; and the wheezing ancient's rambling took a turn that caused me to lean forward and listen alertly. My back was toward the fishy-smelling sea, but he was facing it and something or other had caused his wandering gaze to light on the low, distant line of Devil Reef, then showing plainly and almost fascinatingly above the waves. The sight seemed to displease him, for he began a series of weak curses which ended in a confidential whisper and a knowing leer. He bent toward me, took hold of my coat lapel, and hissed out some hints that could not be mistaken,

"Thar's whar it all begun – that cursed place of all wickedness whar the deep water starts. Gate o' hell – sheer drop daown to a bottom no saoundin'-line kin tech. Ol' Cap'n Obed done it – him that faound aout more'n was good fer him in the Saouth Sea islands.

"Everybody was in a bad way them days. Trade fallin' off, mills losin' business – even the new ones – an' the best of our menfolks kilt aprivateerin' in the War of 1812 or lost with the Elizy brig an' the Ranger scow – both on 'em Gilman venters. Obed Marsh he had three ships afloat – brigantine Columby, brig Hefty, an' barque Sumatry Queen. He was the only

THE SHADOW OVER INNSMOUTH

one as kep' on with the East-Injy an' Pacific trade, though Esdras Martin's barkentine Malay Bride made a venter as late as twenty-eight.

"Never was nobody like Cap'n Obed – old limb o' Satan! Heh, heh! I kin mind him a-tellin' abaout furren parts, an' callin' all the folks stupid for goin' to Christian meetin' an' bearin' their burdns meek an' lowly. Says they'd orter git better gods like some o' the folks in the Injies – gods as ud bring 'em good fishin' in return for their sacrifices, an' ud reely answer folks's prayers.

"Matt Eliot his fust mate, talked a lot too, only he was again' folks's doin' any heathen things. Told abaout an island east of Othaheite whar they was a lot o' stone ruins older'n anybody knew anying abaout, kind o' like them on Ponape, in the Carolines, but with carven's of faces that looked like the big statues on Easter Island. Thar was a little volcanic island near thar, too, whar they was other ruins with diff'rent carvin' – ruins all wore away like they'd ben under the sea onct, an' with picters of awful monsters all over 'em.

"Wal, Sir, Matt he says the natives araound thar had all the fish they cud ketch, an' sported bracelets an' armlets an' head rigs made aout o' a queer kind o' gold an' covered with picters o' monsters jest like the ones carved over the ruins on the little island – sorter fish-like frogs or froglike fishes that was drawed in all kinds o' positions likes they was human bein's. Nobody cud get aout o' them whar they got all the stuff, an' all the other natives wondered haow they managed to find fish in plenty even when the very next island had lean pickin's. Matt he got to wonderon' too an' so did Cap'n Obed. Obed he notices, besides, that lots of the hn'some young folks ud drop aout o' sight fer good from year to year, an' that they wan't many old folks araound. Also, he thinks some of the folks looked dinned queer even for Kanakys.

"It took Obed to git the truth aout o' them heathen. I dun't know haow he done it, but be begun by tradin' fer the gold-like things they wore. Ast 'em whar they come from, an' ef they cud git more, an' finally wormed the story aout o' the old chief – Walakea, they called him. Nobody but Obed ud ever a believed the old yeller devil, but the Cap'n cud read folks like they was books. Heh, heh! Nobody never believes me naow when I tell 'em, an' I dun't s'pose you will, young feller – though come to look at ye, ye hev kind o' got them sharp-readin' eyes like Obed had."

The old man's whisper grew fainter, and I found myself shuddering at the terrible and sincere portentousness of his intonation, even though I knew his tale could be nothing but drunken phantasy.

"Wal, Sir, Obed he 'lart that they's things on this arth as most folks never heerd about – an' wouldn't believe ef they did hear. It seems these Kanakys was sacrificin' heaps o' their young men an' maidens to some kind o' god-things that lived under the sea, an' gittin' all kinds o' favour in return. They met the things on the little islet with the queer ruins, an' it seems them awful picters o' frog-fish monsters was supposed to be picters o' these things. Mebbe they was the kind o' critters as got all the mermaid stories an' sech started.

"They had all kinds a' cities on the sea-bottom, an' this island was heaved up from thar. Seem they was some of the things alive in the stone buildin's when the island come up sudden to the surface. That's how the Kanakys got wind they was daown thar. Made sign-talk as soon as they got over bein' skeert, an' pieced up a bargain afore long.

"Them things liked human sacrifices. Had had 'em ages afore, but lost track o' the upper world after a time. What they done to the victims it ain't fer me to say, an' I guess Obed was'n't none too sharp abaout askin'. But it was all right with the heathens, because they'd ben havin' a hard time an' was desp'rate abaout everything. They give a sarten number o' young folks to the sea-things twice every year – May-Eve an' Hallowe'en – reg'lar as cud be. Also give some a' the carved knick-knacks they made. What the things agreed to give in return was plenty a' fish – they druv 'em in from all over the sea – an' a few gold like things naow an' then.

"Wal, as I says, the natives met the things on the little volcanic islet – goin' thar in canoes with the sacrifices et cet'ry, and bringin' back any of the gold-like jools as was comin' to 'em. At fust the things didn't never go onto the main island, but arter a time they come to want to. Seems they hankered arter mixin' with the folks, an' havin' j'int ceremonies on the big days – May-Eve an' Hallowe'en. Ye see, they was able to live both in ant aout o' water – what they call amphibians, I guess. The Kanakys told 'em as haow folks from the other islands might wanta wipe 'em out if they got wind o' their bein' thar, but they says they dun't keer much, because they cud wipe aout the hull brood o' humans ef they was willin' to bother – that is, any as didn't be, sarten signs sech as was used onct by the lost Old Ones, whoever they was. But not wantin' to bother, they'd lay low when anybody visited the island.

"When it come to matin' with them toad-lookin' fishes, the Kanakys kind o' balked, but finally they larnt something as put a new face on the matter. Seems that human folks has got a kind a' relation to sech water-beasts – that everything alive come aout o' the water onct an' only needs a little change to go back agin. Them things told the Kanakys that ef they mixed bloods there'd be children as ud look human at fust, but later turn more'n more like the things, till finally they'd take to the water an' jine the main lot o' things daown har. An' this is the important part, young feller – them as turned into fish things an' went into the water wouldn't never die. Them things never died excep' they was kilt violent.

"Wal, Sir, it seems by the time Obed knowed them islanders they was all full o' fish blood from them deep water things. When they got old an' begun to shew it, they was kep' hid until they felt like takin' to the water an' quittin' the place. Some was more teched than others, an' some never did change quite enough to take to the water; but mosily they turned out jest the way them things said. Them as was born more like the things changed arly, but them as was nearly human sometimes stayed on the island till they was past seventy, though they'd usually go daown under for trial trips afore that. Folks as had took to the water gen'rally come back a good deal to visit, so's a man ud often be a'talkin' to his own five-times-great-grandfather who'd left the dry land a couple o' hundred years or so afore.

"Everybody got aout o' the idee o' dyin' – excep' in canoe wars with the other islanders, or as sacrifices to the sea-gods daown below, or from snakebite or plague or sharp gallopin' ailments or somethin' afore they cud take to the water – but simply looked forrad to a kind o' change that wa'n't a bit horrible artet a while. They thought what they'd got was well wuth all they'd had to give up – an' I guess Obed kind o' come to think the same hisself when he'd chewed over old Walakea's story a bit. Walakea, though, was one of the few as hadn't got none of the fish blood – bein' of a royal line that intermarried with royal lines on other islands.

"Walakea he shewed Obed a lot o' rites an' incantations as had to do with the sea things, an' let him see some o' the folks in the village as had changed a lot from human shape. Somehaow or other, though, he never would let him see one of the reg'lar things from right aout o' the water. In the end he give him a funny kind o' thingumajig made aout o' lead or something, that he said ud bring up the fish things from any place in the water whar they might be a nest o' 'em. The idee was to drop it daown with the right kind o' prayers an' sech. Walakea allowed as the things was scattered all over the world, so's anybody that looked abaout cud find a nest an' bring 'em up ef they was wanted.

"Matt he didn't like this business at all, an' wanted Obed shud keep away from the island; but the Cap'n was sharp fer gain, an' faound he cud get them gold-like things so cheap it ud pay him to make a specialty of them. Things went on that way for years an' Obed got enough o' that gold-like stuff to make him start the refinery in Waite's old run-daown fullin' mill. He didn't dass sell the pieces like they was, for folks ud be all the time askin' questions. All the same his crews ud get a piece an' dispose of it naow and then, even though they was swore to keep quiet; an' he let his women-folks wear some o' the pieces as was more human-like than most.

"Well, come abaout thutty-eight – when I was seven year' old – Obed he faound the island people all wiped aout between v'yages. Seems the other islanders had got wind o' what was goin' on, and had took matters into their own hands. S'pose they must a had, after all, them old magic signs as the sea things says was the only things they was afeard of. No tellin' what any o' them Kanakys will chance to git a holt of when the sea-bottom throws up some island with ruins older'n the deluge. Pious cusses, these was – they didn't leave nothin' standin' on either the main island or the little volcanic islet excep' what parts of the ruins was too big to knock daown. In some places they was little stones strewed abaout – like charms – with somethin' on 'em like what ye call a swastika naowadays. Prob'ly them was the Old Ones' signs. Folks all wiped aout no trace o' no gold-like things an' none the nearby Kanakys ud breathe a word abaout the matter. Wouldn't even admit they'd ever ben any people on that island.

"That naturally hit Obed pretty hard, seein' as his normal trade was doin' very poor. It hit the whole of Innsmouth, too, because in seafarint days what profited the master of a ship gen'lly profited the crew proportionate. Most of the folks araound the taown took the hard times kind o' sheep-like an' resigned, but they was in bad shape because the fishin' was peterin' aout an' the mills wan't doin' none too well.

"Then's the time Obed he begun a-cursin' at the folks fer bein' dull sheep an' prayin' to a Christian heaven as didn't help 'em none. He told 'em he'd knowed o' folks as prayed to gods that give somethin' ye reely need, an' says ef a good bunch o' men ud stand by him, he cud mebbe get a holt o' sarten paowers as ud bring plenty o' fish an' quite a bit of gold. O' course them as sarved on the Sumatry Queen, an' seed the island knowed what he meant, an' wa'n't none too anxious to get clost to sea-things like they'd heard tell on, but them as didn't know what 'twas all abaout got kind o' swayed by what Obed had to say, and begun to ast him what he cud do to sit 'em on the way to the faith as ud bring 'em results."

Here the old man faltered, mumbled, and lapsed into a moody and apprehensive silence; glancing nervously over his shoulder and then turning back to stare fascinatedly at the distant black reef. When I spoke to him he did not answer, so I knew I would have to let him finish the bottle. The insane yarn I was hearing interested me profoundly, for I fancied there was contained within it a sort of crude allegory based upon the strangeness of Innsmouth and elaborated by an imagination at once creative and full of scraps of exotic legend. Not for a moment did I believe that the tale had any really substantial foundation; but none the less the account held a hint of genuine terror if only because it brought in references to strange jewels clearly akin to the malign tiara I had seen at Newburyport. Perhaps the ornaments had, after all, come from some strange island;

and possibly the wild stories were lies of the bygone Obed himself rather than of this antique toper.

I handed Zadok the bottle, and he drained it to the last drop. It was curious how he could stand so much whiskey, for not even a trace of thickness had come into his high, wheezy voice. He licked the nose of the bottle and slipped it into his pocket, then beginning to nod and whisper softly to himself. I bent close to catch any articulate words he might utter, and thought I saw a sardonic smile behind the stained bushy whiskers. Yes – he was really forming words, and I could grasp a fair proportion of them.

"Poor Matt – Matt he allus was agin it – tried to line up the folks on his side, an' had long talks with the preachers – no use – they run the Congregational parson aout o' taown, an' the Methodist feller quit – never did see Resolved Babcock, the Baptist parson, agin – Wrath o' Jehovy – I was a mightly little critter, but I heerd what I heerd an, seen what I seen – Dagon an' Ashtoreth – Belial an' Beelzebub – Golden Caff an' the idols o' Canaan an' the Philistines – Babylonish abominations – Mene, mene, tekel, upharsin –."

He stopped again, and from the look in his watery blue eyes I feared he was close to a stupor after all. But when I gently shook his shoulder he turned on me with astonishing alertness and snapped out some more obscure phrases.

"Dun't believe me, hey? Hey, heh, heh – then jest tell me, young feller, why Cap'n Obed an' twenty odd other folks used to row aout to Devil Reef in the dead o' night an' chant things so laoud ye cud hear 'em all over taown when the wind was right? Tell me that, hey? An' tell me why Obed was allus droppin' heavy things daown into the deep water t'other side o' the reef whar the bottom shoots daown like a cliff lower'n ye kin saound? Tell me what he done with that funny-shaped lead thingumajig as Walakea give him? Hey, boy? An' what did they all haowl on May-Eve, an, agin the next Hallowe'en? An' why'd the new church parsons – fellers as used to be sailors – wear them queer robes an' cover their-selves with them gold-like things Obed brung? Hey?"

The watery blue eyes were almost savage and maniacal now, and the dirty white beard bristled electrically. Old Zadok probably saw me shrink back, for he began to cackle evilly.

"Heh, heh, heh, heh! Beginni'n to see hey? Mebbe ye'd like to a ben me in them days, when I seed things at night aout to sea from the cupalo top o' my haouse. Oh, I kin tell ye' little pitchers hev big ears, an' I wa'n't missin' nothin' o' what was gossiped abaout Cap'n Obed an' the folks aout to the reef! Heh, heh, heh! Haow abaout the night I took my pa's ship's glass up to the cupalo an' seed the reef a-bristlin' thick with shapes that dove off quick soon's the moon riz?

"Obed an' the folks was in a dory, but them shapes dove off the far side into the deep water an' never come up....

"Haow'd ye like to be a little shaver alone up in a cupola a-watchin' shapes as wa'n't human shapes?... Heh?... Heh, heh, heh...."

The old man was getting hysterical, and I began to shiver with a nameless alarm. He laid a gnarled claw on my shoulder, and it seemed to me that its shaking was not altogether that of mirth.

"S'pose one night ye seed somethin' heavy heaved offen Obed's dory beyond the reef and then learned next day a young feller was missin' from home. Hey! Did anybody ever see hide or hair o' Hiram Gilman agin? Did they? An' Nick Pierce, an' Luelly Waite, an' Adoniram Saouthwick, an' Henry Garrison. Hey? Heh, heh, heh, heh ...Shapes talkin' sign language with their hands ...them as had reel hands ...

"Wal, Sir, that was the time Obed begun to git on his feet agin. Folks see his three darters a-wearin' gold-like things as nobody'd never see on 'em afore, an' smoke stared comin' aout o' the refin'ry chimbly. Other folks was prosp'rin, too – fish begun to swarm into the harbour fit to kill' an' heaven knows what sized cargoes we begun to ship aout to Newb'ryport, Arkham, an' Boston. T'was then Obed got the ol' branch railrud put through. Some Kingsport fishermen heerd abaout the ketch an' come up in sloops, but they was all lost. Nobody never see 'em agin. An' jest then our folk organised the Esoteric Order o' Dagon, an' bought Masonic Hall offen Calvary Commandery for it ...heh, heh, heh! Matt Eliot was a Mason an' agin the sellin', but he dropped aout o' sight jest then.

"Remember, I ain't sayin' Obed was set on hevin' things jest like they was on that Kanaky isle. I dun't think he aimed at fust to do no mixin', nor raise no younguns to take to the water an' turn into fishes with eternal life. He wanted them gold things, an' was willin' to pay heavy, an' I guess the others was satisfied fer a while....

"Come in' forty-six the taown done some lookin' an' thinkin' fer itself. Too many folks missin' – too much wild preachin' at meetin' of a Sunday – too much talk abaout that reef. I guess I done a bit by tellin' Selectman Mowry what I see from the cupalo. They was a party one night as follered Obed's craowd aout to the reef, an' I heerd shots betwixt the dories. Nex' day Obed and thutty-two others was in gaol, with everybody a-wonderin' jest what was afoot and jest what charge agin 'em cud he got to holt. God, ef anybody'd look'd ahead ...a couple o' weeks later, when nothin' had ben throwed into the sea fer thet long....

Zadok was shewing sings of fright and exhaustion, and I let him keep silence for a while, though glancing apprehensively at my watch. The tide had turned and was coming in now, and the sound of the waves seemed to arouse him. I was glad of that tide, for at high water the fishy smell might not be so bad. Again I strained to catch his whispers.

"That awful night ...I seed 'em. I was up in the cupalo ...hordes of 'em ...swarms of 'em ...all over the reef an' swimmin' up the harbour into the Manuxet ...God, what happened in the streets of Innsmouth that night ...they rattled our door, but pa wouldn't open ...then he clumb aout the kitchen winder with his musket to find Selecman Mowry an' see what he cud do ...Maounds o' the dead an' the dyin' ...shots and screams ...shaoutin' in Ol Squar an' Taown Squar an' New Church Green – gaol throwed open ...– proclamation ...treason ...called it the plague when folks come in an' faoud haff our people missin' ...nobody left but them as ud jine in with Obed an' them things or else keep quiet ...never heard o' my pa no more ..."

The old man was panting and perspiring profusely. His grip on my shoulder tightened.

"Everything cleaned up in the mornin' – but they was traces ...Obed he kinder takes charge an' says things is goin' to be changed ...others'll worship with us at meetin'-time, an' sarten haouses hez got to entertin guests ...they wanted to mix like they done with the Kanakys, an' he for one didn't feel baound to stop 'em. Far gone, was Obed ...jest like a crazy man on the subjeck. He says they brung us fish an' treasure, an' shud hev what they hankered after ..."

"Nothin' was to be diff'runt on the aoutsid; only we was to keep shy o' strangers ef we knowed what was good fer us.

"We all hed to take the Oath o' Dagon, an' later on they was secon' an' third oaths that some o' us took. Them as ud help special, ud git special rewards – gold an' sech – No use balkin', fer they was millions of 'em daown thar. They'd ruther not start risin' an' wipin' aout human-kind, but ef they was gave away an' forced to, they cud do a lot toward jest that. We didn't hev them old charms to cut 'em off like folks in the Saouth Sea did, an' them Kanakys wudu't never give away their secrets.

"Yield up enough sacrifices an' savage knick-knacks an' harbourage in the taown when they wanted it, an' they'd let well enough alone. Wudn't bother no strangers as might bear tales aoutside – that is, withaout they got pryin'. All in the band of the faithful – Order o' Dagon – an' the children shud never die, but go back to the Mother Hydra an' Father Dagon what we all come from onct …*Iä! Iä! Cthulhu fhtagn! Ph'nglui mglw'nafh Cthulhu R'lyeh wgah-nagl fhtagn –*"

Old Zadok was fast lapsing into stark raving, and I held my breath. Poor old soul – to what pitiful depths of hallucination had his liquor, plus his hatred of the decay, alienage, and disease around him, brought that fertile, imaginative brain? He began to moan now, and tears were coursing down his channelled cheeks into the depths of his beard.

"God, what I seen senct I was fifteen year' old – *Mene, mene, tekel, upharsin!* – the folks as was missin', and them as kilt theirselves – them as told things in Arkham or Ipswich or sech places was all called crazy, like you're callin' me right naow – but God, what I seen – they'd a kilt me long ago fer' what I know, only I'd took the fust an' secon' Oaths o' Dago offen Obed, so was pertected unlessen a jury of 'em proved I told things knowin' an' delib'rit …but I wudn't take the third Oath – I'd a died ruther'n take that – "It got wuss araound Civil War time, when children born senct 'forty-six begun to grow up – some 'em, that is. I was afeared – never did no pryin' arter that awful night, an' never see one o' – *them* – clost to in all my life. That is, never no full-blooded one. I went to the war, an' ef I'd a had any guts or sense I'd a never come back, but settled away from here. But folks wrote me things wa'n't so bad. That, I s'pose, was because gov'munt draft men was in taown arter 'sixty-three. Arter the war it was jest as bad agin. People begun to fall off – mills an' shops shet daown – shippin' stopped an' the harbour choked up – railrud give up – but they … they never stopped swimmin' in an' aout o' the river from that cursed reef o' Satan – an' more an' more attic winders got a-boarded up, an' more an' more noises was heerd in haouses as wa'n't s'posed to hev nobody in 'em …

"Folks aoutside hev their stories abaout us – s'pose you've heerd a plenty on 'em, seein' what questions ye ast – stories abaout things they've seed naow an' then, an' abaout that queer joolry as still comes in from somewhars an' ain't quite all melted up – but nothin' never gits def'nite. Nobody'll believe nothin'. They call them gold-like things pirate loot, an' allaow the Innsmouth folks hez furren blood or is dis-tempered or somethin'. Beside, them that lives here shoo off as many strangers as they kin, an' encourage the rest not to git very cur'ous, specially raound night time. Beasts balk at the critters – hosses wuss'n mules – but when they got autos that was all right.

"In forty-six Cap'n Obed took a second wife that nobody in the taown never see – some says he didn't want to, but was made to by them as he'd called in – had three children by her – two as disappeared young, but one gal as looked like anybody else an' was eddicated in Europe. Obed finally got her married off by a trick to an Arkham feller as didn't suspect nothin'. But nobody aoutside'll hav nothin' to do with Innsmouth folks naow. Barnabas Marsh that runs the refin'ry now is Obed's grandson by his fust wife – son of Onesiphorus, his eldest son, but his mother was another o' them as wa'n't never seen aoutdoors.

"Right naow Barnabas is abaout changed. Can't shet his eyes no more, an' is all aout o' shape. They say he still wears clothes, but he'll take to the water soon. Mebbe he's tried it already – they do sometimes go daown for little spells afore they go daown for good. Ain't ben seed abaout in public fer nigh on ten year'. Dun't know haow his poor wife kin feel – she come from Ipswich, an' they nigh lynched Barnabas when he courted her fifty odd year' ago.

Obed he died in 'seventy-eight an' all the next gen'ration is gone naow – the fust wife's children dead, and the rest …God knows…."

The sound of the incoming tide was now very insistent, and little by little it seemed to change the old man's mood from maudlin tearfulness to watchful fear. He would pause now and then to renew those nervous glances over his shoulder or out toward the reef, and despite the wild absurdity of his tale, I could not help beginning to share his apprehensiveness. Zadok now grew shriller, seemed to be trying to whip up his courage with louder speech.

"Hey, yew, why dun't ye say somethin'? Haow'd ye like to he livin' in a taown like this, with everything a-rottin' an' dyin', an' boarded-up monsters crawlin' an' bleatin' an' barkin' an' hoppin' araoun' black cellars an' attics every way ye turn? Hey? Haow'd ye like to hear the haowlin' night arter night from the churches an' Order o' Dagon Hall, an' know what's doin' part o' the haowlin'? Haow'd ye like to hear what comes from that awful reef every May-Eve an' Hallowmass? Hey? Think the old man's crazy, eh? Wal, Sir, let me tell ye that ain't the wust!"

Zadok was really screaming now, and the mad frenzy of his voice disturbed me more than I care to own.

"Curse ye, dun't set thar a'starin' at me with them eyes – I tell Obed Marsh he's in hell, an, hez got to stay thar! Heh, heh …in hell, I says! Can't git me – I hain't done nothin' nor told nobody nothin' –

"Oh, you, young feller? Wal, even ef I hain't told nobody nothin' yet, I'm a'goin' to naow! Yew jest set still an' listen to me, boy – this is what I ain't never told nobody …I says I didn't get to do pryin' arter that night – but I faound things about jest the same!"

"Yew want to know what the reel horror is, hey? Wal, it's this – it ain't what them fish devils hez done, but what they're a-goin' to do! They're a-bringin' things up aout o' whar they come from into the taown – been doin' it fer years, an' slackenin' up lately. Them haouses north o' the river betwixt Water an' Main Streets is full of 'em – them devils an' what they brung – an' when they git ready …I say, when they git …ever hear tell of a *shoggoth*?

"Hey, d'ye hear me? I tell ye I know what them things be – I seen 'em one night when … eh-ahhh-ah! E'yahhh…."

The hideous suddenness and inhuman frightfulness of the old man's shriek almost made me faint. His eyes, looking past me toward the malodorous sea, were positively starting from his head; while his face was a mask of fear worthy of Greek tragedy. His bony claw dug monstrously into my shoulder, and he made no motion as I turned my head to look at whatever he had glimpsed.

There was nothing that I could see. Only the incoming tide, with perhaps one set of ripples more local than the long-flung line of breakers. But now Zadok was shaking me, and I turned back to watch the melting of that fear-frozen face into a chaos of twitching eyelids and mumbling gums. Presently his voice came back – albeit as a trembling whisper.

"Git aout o' here! Get aout o' here! They seen us – git aout fer your life! Dun't wait fer nothin' – they know naow – Run fer it – quick – aout o' this taown –"

Another heavy wave dashed against the loosing masonry of the bygone wharf, and changed the mad ancient's whisper to another inhuman and blood-curdling scream. "E-yaahhhh! …Yheaaaaaa! …"

Before I could recover my scattered wits he had relaxed his clutch on my shoulder and dashed wildly inland toward the street, reeling northward around the ruined warehouse wall.

I glanced back at the sea, but there was nothing there. And when I reached Water Street and looked along it toward the north there was no remaining trace of Zadok Allen.

Chapter IV

I CAN HARDLY DESCRIBE the mood in which I was left by this harrowing episode – an episode at once mad and pitiful, grotesque and terrifying. The grocery boy had prepared me for it, yet the reality left me none the less bewildered and disturbed. Puerile though the story was, old Zadok's insane earnestness and horror had communicated to me a mounting unrest which joined with my earlier sense of loathing for the town and its blight of intangible shadow.

Later I might sift the tale and extract some nucleus of historic allegory; just now I wished to put it out of my head. The hour grown perilously late – my watch said 7:15, and the Arkham bus left Town Square at eight – so I tried to give my thoughts as neutral and practical a cast as possible, meanwhile walking rapidly through the deserted streets of gaping roofs and leaning houses toward the hotel where I had checked my valise and would find my bus.

Though the golden light of late afternoon gave the ancient roofs and decrepit chimneys an air of mystic loveliness and peace, I could not help glancing over my shoulder now and then. I would surely be very glad to get out of malodorous and fear-shadowed Innsmouth, and wished there were some other vehicle than the bus driven by that sinister-looking fellow Sargent. Yet I did not hurry too precipitately, for there were architectural details worth viewing at every silent corner; and I could easily, I calculated, cover the necessary distance in a half-hour.

Studying the grocery youth's map and seeking a route I had not traversed before, I chose Marsh Street instead of State for my approach to Town Square. Near the corner of Fall street I began to see scattered groups of furtive whisperers, and when I finally reached the Square I saw that almost all the loiterers were congregated around the door of the Gilman House. It seemed as if many bulging, watery, unwinking eyes looked oddly at me as I claimed my valise in the lobby, and I hoped that none of these unpleasant creatures would be my fellow-passengers on the coach.

The bus, rather early, rattled in with three passengers somewhat before eight, and an evil-looking fellow on the sidewalk muttered a few indistinguishable words to the driver. Sargent threw out a mail-bag and a roll of newspapers, and entered the hotel; while the passengers – the same men whom I had seen arriving in Newburyport that morning – shambled to the sidewalk and exchanged some faint guttural words with a loafer in a language I could have sworn was not English. I boarded the empty coach and took the seat I had taken before, but was hardly settled before Sargent re-appeared and began mumbling in a throaty voice of peculiar repulsiveness.

I was, it appeared, in very bad luck. There had been something wrong with the engine, despite the excellent time made from Newburyport, and the bus could not complete the journey to Arkham. No, it could not possibly be repaired that night, nor was there any other way of getting transportation out of Innsmouth either to Arkham or elsewhere. Sargent was sorry, but I would have to stop over at the Gilman. Probably the clerk would make the price easy for me, but there was nothing else to do. Almost dazed by this sudden obstacle, and violently dreading the fall of night in this decaying and half-unlighted town, I left the bus and reentered the hotel lobby; where the sullen queer-looking night clerk told me I could have Room 428 on next the top floor – large, but without running water – for a dollar.

Despite what I had heard of this hotel in Newburyport, I signed the register, paid my dollar, let the clerk take my valise, and followed that sour, solitary attendant up three creaking flights of stairs past dusty corridors which seemed wholly devoid of life. My room was a dismal rear one with two windows and bare, cheap furnishings, overlooked a dingy court-yard otherwise hemmed in by low, deserted brick blocks, and commanded a view of decrepit westward-stretching roofs with a marshy countryside beyond. At the end of the corridor was a bathroom – a discouraging relique with ancient marble bowl, tin tub, faint electric light, and musty wooded paneling around all the plumbing fixtures.

It being still daylight, I descended to the Square and looked around for a dinner of some sort; noticing as I did so the strange glances I received from the unwholesome loafers. Since the grocery was closed, I was forced to patronise the restaurant I had shunned before; a stooped, narrow-headed man with staring, unwinking eyes, and a flat-nosed wench with unbelievably thick, clumsy hands being in attendance. The service was all of the counter type, and it relieved me to find that much was evidently served from cans and packages. A bowl of vegetable soup with crackers was enough for me, and I soon headed back for my cheerless room at the Gilman; getting a evening paper and a fly-specked magazine from the evil-visaged clerk at the rickety stand beside his desk.

As twilight deepened I turned on the one feeble electric bulb over the cheap, iron-framed bed, and tried as best I could to continue the reading I had begun. I felt it advisable to keep my mind wholesomely occupied, for it would not do to brood over the abnormalities of this ancient, blight-shadowed town while I was still within its borders. The insane yarn I had heard from the aged drunkard did not promise very pleasant dreams, and I felt I must keep the image of his wild, watery eyes as far as possible from my imagination.

Also, I must not dwell on what that factory inspector had told the Newburyport ticket-agent about the Gilman House and the voices of its nocturnal tenants – not on that, nor on the face beneath the tiara in the black church doorway; the face for whose horror my conscious mind could not account. It would perhaps have been easier to keep my thoughts from disturbing topics had the room not been so gruesomely musty. As it was, the lethal mustiness blended hideously with the town's general fishy odour and persistently focussed one's fancy on death and decay.

Another thing that disturbed me was the absence of a bolt on the door of my room. One had been there, as marks clearly shewed, but there were signs of recent removal. No doubt it had been out of order, like so many other things in this decrepit edifice. In my nervousness I looked around and discovered a bolt on the clothes press which seemed to be of the same size, judging from the marks, as the one formerly on the door. To gain a partial relief from the general tension I busied myself by transferring this hardware to the vacant place with the aid of a handy three-in-one device including a screwdriver which I kept on my key-ring. The bolt fitted perfectly, and I was somewhat relieved when I knew that I could shoot it firmly upon retiring. Not that I had any real apprehension of its need, but that any symbol of security was welcome in an environment of this kind. There were adequate bolts on the two lateral doors to connecting rooms, and these I proceeded to fasten.

I did not undress, but decided to read till I was sleepy and then lie down with only my coat, collar, and shoes off. Taking a pocket flash light from my valise, I placed it in my trousers, so that I could read my watch if I woke up later in the dark. Drowsiness, however, did not come; and when I stopped to analyse my thoughts I found to my disquiet that I was really unconsciously listening for something – listening for something which I dreaded but could not name. That inspector's story must have worked on my imagination more deeply than I had suspected. Again I tried to read, but found that I made no progress.

After a time I seemed to hear the stairs and corridors creak at intervals as if with footsteps, and wondered if the other rooms were beginning to fill up. There were no voices, however, and it struck me that there was something subtly furtive about the creaking. I did not like it, and debated whether I had better try to sleep at all. This town had some queer people, and there had undoubtedly been several disappearances. Was this one of those inns where travelers were slain for their money? Surely I had no look of excessive prosperity. Or were the towns folk really so resentful about curious visitors? Had my obvious sightseeing, with its frequent map-consultations, aroused unfavorable notice? It occurred to me that I must be in a highly nervous state to let a few random creakings set me off speculating in this fashion – but I regretted none the less that I was unarmed.

At length, feeling a fatigue which had nothing of drowsiness in it, I bolted the newly outfitted hall door, turned off the light, and threw myself down on the hard, uneven bed – coat, collar, shoes, and all. In the darkness every faint noise of the night seemed magnified, and a flood of doubly unpleasant thoughts swept over me. I was sorry I had put out the light, yet was too tired to rise and turn it on again. Then, after a long, dreary interval, and prefaced by a fresh creaking of stairs and corridor, there came that soft, damnably unmistakable sound which seemed like a malign fulfillment of all my apprehensions. Without the least shadow of a doubt, the lock of my door was being tried – cautiously, furtively, tentatively – with a key.

My sensations upon recognising this sign of actual peril were perhaps less rather than more tumultuous because of my previous vague fears. I had been, albeit without definite reason, instinctively on my guard – and that was to my advantage in the new and real crisis, whatever it might turn out to be. Nevertheless the change in the menace from vague premonition to immediate reality was a profound shock, and fell upon me with the force of a genuine blow. It never once occurred to me that the fumbling might be a mere mistake. Malign purpose was all I could think of, and I kept deathly quiet, awaiting the would-be intruder's next move.

After a time the cautious rattling ceased, and I heard the room to the north entered with a pass key. Then the lock of the connecting door to my room was softly tried. The bolt held, of course, and I heard the floor creak as the prowler left the room. After a moment there came another soft rattling, and I knew that the room to the south of me was being entered. Again a furtive trying of a bolted connecting door, and again a receding creaking. This time the creaking went along the hall and down the stairs, so I knew that the prowler had realised the bolted condition of my doors and was giving up his attempt for a greater or lesser time, as the future would shew.

The readiness with which I fell into a plan of action proves that I must have been subconsciously fearing some menace and considering possible avenues of escape for hours. From the first I felt that the unseen fumbler meant a danger not to be met or dealt with, but only to be fled from as precipitately as possible. The one thing to do was to get out of that hotel alive as quickly as I could, and through some channel other than the front stairs and lobby.

Rising softly and throwing my flashlight on the switch, I sought to light the bulb over my bed in order to choose and pocket some belongings for a swift, valiseless flight. Nothing, however, happened; and I saw that the power had been cut off. Clearly, some cryptic, evil movement was afoot on a large scale – just what, I could not say. As I stood pondering with my hand on the now useless switch I heard a muffled creaking on the floor below, and thought I could barely distinguish voices in conversation. A moment later I felt less sure that the deeper sounds were voices, since the apparent hoarse barkings and loose-syllabled croakings bore so little resemblance to recognized human speech. Then I thought with renewed force of what the factory inspector had heard in the night in this mouldering and pestilential building.

Having filled my pockets with the flashlight's aid, I put on my hat and tiptoed to the windows to consider chances of descent. Despite the state's safety regulations there was no fire escape on this side of the hotel, and I saw that my windows commanded only a sheer three story drop to the cobbled courtyard. On the right and left, however, some ancient brick business blocks abutted on the hotel; their slant roofs coming up to a reasonable jumping distance from my fourth-story level. To reach either of these lines of buildings I would have to be in a room two from my own – in one case on the north and in the other case on the south – and my mind instantly set to work what chances I had of making the transfer.

I could not, I decided, risk an emergence into the corridor; where my footsteps would surely be heard, and where the difficulties of entering the desired room would be insuperable. My progress, if it was to be made at all, would have to be through the less solidly-built connecting doors of the rooms; the locks and bolts of which I would have to force violently, using my shoulder as a battering-ram whenever they were set against me. This, I thought, would be possible owing to the rickety nature of the house and its fixtures; but I realised I could not do it noiselessly. I would have to count on sheer speed, and the chance of getting to a window before any hostile forces became coordinated enough to open the right door toward me with a pass-key. My own outer door I reinforced by pushing the bureau against it – little by little, in order to make a minimum of sound.

I perceived that my chances were very slender, and was fully prepared for any calamity. Even getting to another roof would not solve the problem for there would then remain the task of reaching the ground and escaping from the town. One thing in my favour was the deserted and ruinous state of the abutting building and the number of skylights gaping blackly open in each row.

Gathering from the grocery boy's map that the best route out of town was southward, I glanced first at the connecting door on the south side of the room. It was designed to open in my direction, hence I saw – after drawing the bolt and finding other fastening in place – it was not a favorable one for forcing. Accordingly abandoning it as a route, I cautiously moved the bedstead against it to hamper any attack which might be made on it later from the next room. The door on the north was hung to open away from me, and this – though a test proved it to be locked or bolted from the other side – I knew must be my route. If I could gain the roofs of the buildings in Paine Street and descend successfully to the ground level, I might perhaps dart through the courtyard and the adjacent or opposite building to Washington or Bates – or else emerge in Paine and edge around southward into Washington. In any case, I would aim to strike Washington somehow and get quickly out of the Town Square region. My preference would be to avoid Paine, since the fire station there might be open all night.

As I thought of these things I looked out over the squalid sea of decaying roofs below me, now brightened by the beams of a moon not much past full. On the right the black gash of the river-gorge clove the panorama; abandoned factories and railway station clinging barnacle-like to its sides. Beyond it the rusted railway and the Rowley road led off through a flat marshy terrain dotted with islets of higher and dryer scrub-grown land. On the left the creek-threaded country-side was nearer, the narrow road to Ipswich gleaming white in the moonlight. I could not see from my side of the hotel the southward route toward Arkham which I had determined to take.

I was irresolutely speculating on when I had better attack the northward door, and on how I could least audibly manage it, when I noticed that the vague noises underfoot had given place to a fresh and heavier creaking of the stairs. A wavering flicker of light shewed through my transom, and the boards of the corridor began to groan with a ponderous load. Muffled sounds of possible vocal origin approached, and at length a firm knock came at my outer door.

For a moment I simply held my breath and waited. Eternities seemed to elapse, and the nauseous fishy odour of my environment seemed to mount suddenly and spectacularly. Then the knocking was repeated – continuously, and with growing insistence. I knew that the time for action had come, and forthwith drew the bolt of the northward connecting door, bracing myself for the task of battering it open. The knocking waxed louder, and I hoped that its volume would cover the sound of my efforts. At last beginning my attempt, I lunged again and again at the thin paneling with my left shoulder, heedless of shock or pain. The door resisted even more than I expected, but I did not give in. And all the while the clamour at the outer door increased.

Finally the connecting door gave, but with such a crash that I knew those outside must have heard. Instantly the outside knocking became a violent battering, while keys sounded ominously in the hall doors of the rooms on both sides of me. Rushing through the newly opened connexion, I succeeded in bolting the northerly hall door before the lock could he turned; but even as I did so I heard the hall door of the third room – the one from whose window I had hoped to reach the roof below – being tried with a pass key.

For an instant I felt absolute despair, since my trapping in a chamber with no window egress seemed complete. A wave of almost abnormal horror swept over me, and invested with a terrible but unexplainable singularity the flashlight-glimpsed dust prints made by the intruder who had lately tried my door from this room. Then, with a dazed automatism which persisted despite hopelessness, I made for the next connecting door and performed the blind motion of pushing at it in an effort to get through and – granting that fastenings might be as providentially intact as in this second room – bolt the hall door beyond before the lock could be turned from outside.

Sheer fortunate chance gave me my reprieve – for the connecting door before me was not only unlocked but actually ajar. In a second I was though, and had my right knee and shoulder against a hall door which was visibly opening inward. My pressure took the opener off guard, for the thing shut as I pushed, so that I could slip the well-conditioned bolt as I had done with the other door. As I gained this respite I heard the battering at the two other doors abate, while a confused clatter came from the connecting door I had shielded with the bedstead. Evidently the bulk of my assailants had entered the southerly room and were massing in a lateral attack. But at the same moment a pass key sounded in the next door to the north, and I knew that a nearer peril was at hand.

The northward connecting door was wide open, but there was no time to think about checking the already turning lock in the hall. All I could do was to shut and bolt the open connecting door, as well as its mate on the opposite side – pushing a bedstead against the one and a bureau against the other, and moving a washstand in front of the hall door.

I must, I saw, trust to such makeshift barriers to shield me till I could get out the window and on the roof of the Paine Street block. But even in this acute moment my chief horror was something apart from the immediate weakness of my defenses. I was shuddering because not one of my pursuers, despite some hideous panting, grunting, and subdued barkings at odd intervals, was uttering an unmuffled or intelligible vocal sound.

As I moved the furniture and rushed toward the windows I heard a frightful scurrying along the corridor toward the room north of me, and perceived that the southward battering had ceased. Plainly, most of my opponents were about to concentrate against the feeble connecting door which they knew must open directly on me. Outside, the moon played on the ridgepole of the block below, and I saw that the jump would be desperately hazardous because of the steep surface on which I must land.

Surveying the conditions, I chose the more southerly of the two windows as my avenue of escape; planning to land on the inner slope of the roof and make for the nearest sky-light. Once inside one of the decrepit brick structures I would have to reckon with pursuit; but I hoped to descend and dodge in and out of yawning doorways along the shadowed courtyard, eventually getting to Washington Street and slipping out of town toward the south.

The clatter at the northerly connecting door was now terrific, and I saw that the weak panelling was beginning to splinter. Obviously, the besiegers had brought some ponderous object into play as a battering-ram. The bedstead, however, still held firm; so that I had at least a faint chance of making good my escape. As I opened the window I noticed that it was flanked by heavy velour draperies suspended from a pole by brass rings, and also that there was a large projecting catch for the shutters on the exterior. Seeing a possible means of avoiding the dangerous jump, I yanked at the hangings and brought them down, pole and all; then quickly hooking two of the rings in the shutter catch and flinging the drapery outside. The heavy folds reached fully to the abutting roof, and I saw that the rings and catch would be likely to bear my weight. So, climbing out of the window and down the improvised rope ladder, I left behind me forever the morbid and horror-infested fabric of the Gilman House.

I landed safely on the loose slates of the steep roof, and succeeded in gaining the gaping black skylight without a slip. Glancing up at the window I had left, I observed it was still dark, though far across the crumbling chimneys to the north I could see lights ominously blazing in the Order of Dagon Hall, the Baptist church, and the Congregational church which I recalled so shiveringly. There had seemed to be no one in the courtyard below, and I hoped there would be a chance to get away before the spreading of a general alarm. Flashing my pocket lamp into the skylight, I saw that there were no steps down. The distance was slight, however, so I clambered over the brink and dropped; striking a dusty floor littered with crumbling boxes and barrels.

The place was ghoulish-looking, but I was past minding such impressions and made at once for the staircase revealed by my flashlight – after a hasty glance at my watch, which shewed the hour to be 2 a.m. The steps creaked, but seemed tolerably sound; and I raced down past a barnlike second storey to the ground floor. The desolation was complete, and only echoes answered my footfalls. At length I reached the lower hall at the end of which I saw a faint luminous rectangle marking the ruined Paine Street doorway. Heading the other way, I found the back door also open; and darted out and down five stone steps to the grass-grown cobblestones of the courtyard.

The moonbeams did not reach down here, but I could just see my way about without using the flashlight. Some of the windows on the Gilman House side were faintly glowing, and I thought I heard confused sounds within. Walking softly over to the Washington Street side I perceived several open doorways, and chose the nearest as my route out. The hallway inside was black, and when I reached the opposite end I saw that the street door was wedged immovably shut. Resolved to try another building, I groped my way back toward the courtyard, but stopped short when close to the doorway.

For out of an opened door in the Gilman House a large crowd of doubtful shapes was pouring – lanterns bobbing in the darkness, and horrible croaking voices exchanging low cries in what was certainly not English. The figures moved uncertainly, and I realized to my relief that they did not know where I had gone; but for all that they sent a shiver of horror through my frame. Their features were indistinguishable, but their crouching, shambling gait was abominably repellent. And worst of all, I perceived that one figure was strangely robed, and unmistakably surmounted by a tall tiara of a design altogether too familiar. As the figures spread throughout the courtyard, I felt my fears increase. Suppose I could find no egress from this building on the street side? The fishy odour was detestable, and I wondered I could stand it without fainting. Again groping toward the street, I opened a door off the hall and came upon an empty room with closely shuttered but sashless windows. Fumbling in the rays of my flashlight, I found I could open the shutters; and in another moment had climbed outside and was fully closing the aperture in its original manner.

I was now in Washington Street, and for the moment saw no living thing nor any light save that of the moon. From several directions in the distance, however, I could hear the sound of hoarse voices, of footsteps, and of a curious kind of pattering which did not sound quite like footsteps. Plainly I had no time to lose. The points of the compass were clear to me, and I was glad that all the street lights were turned off, as is often the custom on strongly moonlit nights in prosperous rural regions. Some of the sounds came from the south, yet I retained my design of escaping in that direction. There would, I knew, be plenty of deserted doorways to shelter me in case I met any person or group who looked like pursuers.

I walked rapidly, softly, and close to the ruined houses. While hatless and dishevelled after my arduous climb, I did not look especially noticeable; and stood a good chance of passing unheeded if forced to encounter any casual wayfarer.

At Bates Street I drew into a yawning vestibule while two shambling figures crossed in front of me, but was soon on my way again and approaching the open space where Eliot Street obliquely crosses Washington at the intersection of South. Though I had never seen this space, it had looked dangerous to me on the grocery youth's map; since the moonlight would have free play there. There was no use trying to evade it, for any alternative course would involve detours of possibly disastrous visibility and delaying effect. The only thing to do was to cross it boldly and openly; imitating the typical shamble of the Innsmouth folk as best I could, and trusting that no one – or at least no pursuer of mine – would be there.

Just how fully the pursuit was organised – and indeed, just what its purpose might be – I could form no idea. There seemed to be unusual activity in the town, but I judged that the news of my escape from the Gilman had not yet spread. I would, of course, soon have to shift from Washington to some other southward street; for that party from the hotel would doubtless be after me. I must have left dust prints in that last old building, revealing how I had gained the street.

The open space was, as I had expected, strongly moonlit; and I saw the remains of a parklike, iron-railed green in its center. Fortunately no one was about though a curious sort of buzz or roar seemed to be increasing in the direction of Town Square. South Street was very wide, leading directly down a slight declivity to the waterfront and commanding a long view out at sea; and I hoped that no one would be glancing up it from afar as I crossed in the bright moonlight.

My progress was unimpeded, and no fresh sound arose to hint that I had been spied. Glancing about me, I involuntarily let my pace slacken for a second to take in the sight of the sea, gorgeous in the burning moonlight at the street's end. Far out beyond the breakwater was the dim, dark line of Devil Reef, and as I glimpsed it I could not help thinking of all the hideous legends I had heard in the last twenty-four hours – legends which portrayed this ragged rock as a veritable gateway to realms of unfathomed horror and inconceivable abnormality.

Then, without warning, I saw the intermittent flashes of light on the distant reef. They were definite and unmistakable, and awaked in my mind a blind horror beyond all rational proportion. My muscles tightened for panic flight, held in only by a certain unconscious caution and half-hypnotic fascination. And to make matters worse, there now flashed forth from the lofty cupola of the Gilman House, which loomed up to the northeast behind me, a series of analogous though differently spaced gleams which could be nothing less than an answering signal.

Controlling my muscles, and realising afresh how plainly visible I was, I resumed my brisker and feignedly shambling pace; though keeping my eyes on that hellish and ominous reef as long as the opening of South Street gave me a seaward view. What the whole proceeding meant, I could not imagine; unless it involved some strange rite connected with Devil Reef, or unless some party had landed from a ship on that sinister rock. I now bent to the left around the ruinous green; still gazing toward the ocean as it blazed in the spectral summer moonlight, and watching the cryptical flashing of those nameless, unexplainable beacons.

It was then that the most horrible impression of all was borne in upon me – the impression which destroyed my last vestige of self-control and sent me running frantically southward past the yawning black doorways and fishily staring windows of that deserted nightmare street. For at a closer glance I saw that the moonlit waters between the reef and the shore were far from empty. They were alive with a teeming horde of shapes swimming inward toward the town; and even at my vast distance and in my single moment of perception I could tell that the bobbing heads and flailing arms were alien and aberrant in a way scarcely to be expressed or consciously formulated.

My frantic running ceased before I had covered a block, for at my left I began to hear something like the hue and cry of organised pursuit. There were footsteps and gutteral sounds, and a rattling motor wheezed south along Federal Street. In a second all my plans were utterly changed – for if the southward highway were blocked ahead of me, I must clearly find another egress from Innsmouth. I paused and drew into a gaping doorway, reflecting how lucky I was to have left the moonlit open space before these pursuers came down the parallel street.

A second reflection was less comforting. Since the pursuit was down another street, it was plain that the party was not following me directly. It had not seen me, but was simply obeying a general plan of cutting off my escape. This, however, implied that all roads leading out of Innsmouth were similarly patrolled; for the people could not have known what route I intended to take. If this were so, I would have to make my retreat across country away from any road; but how could I do that in view of the marshy and creek-riddled nature of all the surrounding region? For a moment my brain reeled – both from sheer hopelessness and from a rapid increase in the omnipresent fishy odour.

Then I thought of the abandoned railway to Rowley, whose solid line of ballasted, weed-grown earth still stretched off to the northwest from the crumbling station on the edge at the river-gorge. There was just a chance that the townsfolk would not think of that; since its briar-choked desertion made it half-impassable, and the unlikeliest of all avenues for a fugitive to choose. I had seen it clearly from my hotel window and knew about how it lay. Most of its earlier length was uncomfortably visible from the Rowley road, and from high places in the town itself; but one could perhaps crawl inconspicuously through the undergrowth. At any rate, it would form my only chance of deliverance, and there was nothing to do but try it.

Drawing inside the hall of my deserted shelter, I once more consulted the grocery boy's map with the aid of the flashlight. The immediate problem was how to reach the ancient railway; and I now saw that the safest course was ahead to Babson Street; then west to Lafayette – there edging around but not crossing an open space homologous to the one I had traversed – and subsequently back northward and westward in a zigzagging line through Lafayette, Bates, Adam, and Bank streets – the latter skirting the river gorge – to the abandoned and dilapidated station I had seen from my window. My reason for going ahead to Babson was that I wished neither to recross the earlier open space nor to begin my westward course along a cross street as broad as South.

Starting once more, I crossed the street to the right-hand side in order to edge around into Babson as inconspicuously as possible. Noises still continued in Federal Street, and as I glanced behind me I thought I saw a gleam of light near the building through which I had escaped. Anxious to leave Washington Street, I broke into a quiet dogtrot, trusting to luck not to encounter any observing eye. Next the corner of Babson Street I saw to my alarm that one of the houses was still inhabited, as attested by curtains at the window; but there were no lights within, and I passed it without disaster.

In Babson Street, which crossed Federal and might thus reveal me to the searchers, I clung as closely as possible to the sagging, uneven buildings; twice pausing in a doorway as the noises behind me momentarily increased. The open space ahead shone wide and desolate under the moon, but my route would not force me to cross it. During my second pause I began to detect a fresh distribution of vague sounds; and upon looking cautiously out from cover beheld a motor car darting across the open space, bound outward along Eliot Street, which there intersects both Babson and Lafayette.

As I watched – choked by a sudden rise in the fishy odour after a short abatement – I saw a band of uncouth, crouching shapes loping and shambling in the same direction; and knew that this must be the party guarding the Ipswich road, since that highway forms an extension of Eliot Street. Two of the figures I glimpsed were in voluminous robes, and one wore a peaked diadem which glistened whitely in the moonlight. The gait of this figure was so odd that it sent a chill through me – for it seemed to me the creature was almost hopping.

When the last of the band was out of sight I resumed my progress; darting around the corner into Lafayette Street, and crossing Eliot very hurriedly lest stragglers of the party be still advancing along that thoroughfare. I did hear some croaking and clattering sounds far off toward Town Square, but accomplished the passage without disaster. My greatest dread was in re-crossing broad and moonlit South Street – with its seaward view – and I had to nerve myself for the ordeal. Someone might easily be looking, and possible Eliot Street stragglers could not fail to glimpse me from either of two points. At the last moment I decided I had better slacken my trot and make the crossing as before in the shambling gait of an average Innsmouth native.

When the view of the water again opened out – this time on my right – I was half-determined not to look at it at all. I could not however, resist; but cast a sidelong glance as I carefully and imitatively shambled toward the protecting shadows ahead. There was no ship visible, as I had half-expected there would be. Instead, the first thing which caught my eye was a small rowboat pulling in toward the abandoned wharves and laden with some bulky, tarpaulin-covered object. Its rowers, though distantly and indistinctly seen, were of an especially repellent aspect. Several swimmers were still discernible; while on the far black reef I could see a faint, steady glow unlike the winking beacon visible before, and of a curious colour which I could not precisely identify. Above the slant roofs ahead and to the right there loomed the tall cupola of the Gilman House, but it was completely dark. The fishy odour, dispelled for a moment by some merciful breeze, now closed in again with maddening intensity.

I had not quite crossed the street when I heard a muttering band advancing along Washington from the north. As they reached the broad open space where I had had my first disquieting glimpse of the moonlit water I could see them plainly only a block away – and was horrified by the bestial abnormality of their faces and the doglike sub-humanness of their crouching gait. One man moved in a positively simian way, with long arms frequently touching the ground; while another figure – robed and tiaraed – seemed to progress in an almost hopping fashion. I judged this party to be the one I had seen in the Gilman's courtyard – the one, therefore, most closely on my trail. As some of the figures turned to look in my direction I was transfixed with fright, yet managed to preserve the casual, shambling gait I had assumed. To this day I do not know whether they saw me or not. If they did, my stratagem must have deceived them, for they passed on across the moonlit space without varying their course – meanwhile croaking and jabbering in some hateful guttural patois I could not identify.

Once more in shadow, I resumed my former dog-trot past the leaning and decrepit houses that stared blankly into the night. Having crossed to the western sidewalk I rounded the nearest corner into Bates Street where I kept close to the buildings on the southern side. I passed two houses shewing signs of habitation, one of which had faint lights in upper rooms, yet met with no obstacle. As I tuned into Adams Street I felt measurably safer, but received a shock when a man reeled out of a black doorway directly in front of me. He proved, however, too hopelessly drunk to be a menace; so that I reached the dismal ruins of the Bank Street warehouses in safety.

No one was stirring in that dead street beside the river-gorge, and the roar of the waterfalls quite drowned my foot steps. It was a long dog-trot to the ruined station, and the great brick warehouse walls around me seemed somehow more terrifying than the fronts of private houses. At last I saw the ancient arcaded station – or what was left of it – and made directly for the tracks that started from its farther end.

The rails were rusty but mainly intact, and not more than half the ties had rotted away. Walking or running on such a surface was very difficult; but I did my best, and on the whole made very fair time. For some distance the line kept on along the gorge's brink, but at length I reached the long covered bridge where it crossed the chasm at a dizzying height. The condition of this bridge would determine my next step. If humanly possible, I would use it; if not, I would have to risk more street wandering and take the nearest intact highway bridge.

The vast, barnlike length of the old bridge gleamed spectrally in the moonlight, and I saw that the ties were safe for at least a few feet within. Entering, I began to use my flashlight, and was almost knocked down by the cloud of bats that flapped past me. About half-way across there was a perilous gap in the ties which I feared for a moment would halt me; but in the end I risked a desperate jump which fortunately succeeded.

I was glad to see the moonlight again when I emerged from that macabre tunnel. The old tracks crossed River Street at grade, and at once veered off into a region increasingly rural and with less and less of Innsmouth's abhorrent fishy odour. Here the dense growth of weeds and briers hindered me and cruelly tore at my clothes, but I was none the less glad that they were there to give me concealment in case of peril. I knew that much of my route must be visible from the Rowley road.

The marshy region began very abruptly, with the single track on a low, grassy embankment where the weedy growth was somewhat thinner. Then came a sort of island of higher ground, where the line passed through a shallow open cut choked with bushes and brambles. I was very glad of this partial shelter, since at this point the Rowley road was uncomfortably near according to my window view. At the end of the cut it would cross the track and swerve off to a safer distance; but meanwhile I must be exceedingly careful. I was by this time thankfully certain that the railway itself was not patrolled.

Just before entering the cut I glanced behind me, but saw no pursuer. The ancient spires and roofs of decaying Innsmouth gleamed lovely and ethereal in the magic yellow moonlight, and I thought of how they must have looked in the old days before the shadow fell. Then, as my gaze circled inland from the town, something less tranquil arrested my notice and held me immobile for a second.

What I saw – or fancied I saw – was a disturbing suggestion of undulant motion far to the south; a suggestion which made me conclude that a very large horde must be pouring out of the city along the level Ipswich road. The distance was great and I could distinguish nothing in detail; but I did not at all like the look of that moving column. It undulated too much, and glistened too brightly in the rays of the now westering moon. There was a suggestion of sound, too, though the wind was blowing the other way – a suggestion of bestial scraping and bellowing even worse than the muttering of the parties I had lately overheard.

All sorts of unpleasant conjectures crossed my mind. I thought of those very extreme Innsmouth types said to be hidden in crumbling, centuried warrens near the waterfront; I thought, too, of those nameless swimmers I had seen. Counting the parties so far glimpsed, as well as those presumably covering other roads, the number of my pursuers must be strangely large for a town as depopulated as Innsmouth.

Whence could come the dense personnel of such a column as I now beheld? Did those ancient, unplumbed warrens teem with a twisted, uncatalogued, and unsuspected life? Or had some unseen ship indeed landed a legion of unknown outsiders on that hellish reef? Who were they? Why were they here? And if such a column of them was scouring the Ipswich road, would the patrols on the other roads be likewise augmented?

I had entered the brush-grown cut and was struggling along at a very slow pace when that damnable fishy odour again waxed dominant. Had the wind suddenly changed eastward, so that it blew in from the sea and over the town? It must have, I concluded, since I now began to hear shocking guttural murmurs from that hitherto silent direction. There was another sound, too – a kind of wholesale, colossal flopping or pattering which somehow called up images of the most detestable sort. It made me think illogically of that unpleasantly undulating column on the far-off Ipswich road.

And then both stench and sounds grew stronger, so that I paused shivering and grateful for the cut's protection. It was here, I recalled, that the Rowley road drew so close to the old railway before crossing westward and diverging. Something was coming along that road, and I must lie low till its passage and vanishment in the distance. Thank heaven these creatures employed no dogs for tracking – though perhaps that would have been impossible amidst the omnipresent regional odour. Crouched in the bushes of that sandy cleft I felt reasonably safe, even though I knew the searchers would have to cross the track in front of me not much more than a hundred yards away. I would be able to see them, but they could not, except by a malign miracle, see me.

All at once I began dreading to look at them as they passed. I saw the close moonlit space where they would surge by, and had curious thoughts about the irredeemable pollution of that space. They would perhaps be the worst of all Innsmouth types – something one would not care to remember.

The stench waxed overpowering, and the noises swelled to a bestial babel of croaking, baying and barking without the least suggestion of human speech. Were these indeed the voices of my pursuers? Did they have dogs after all? So far I had seen none of the lower animals in Innsmouth. That flopping or pattering was monstrous – I could not look upon the degenerate creatures responsible for it. I would keep my eyes shut till the sound receded toward the west. The horde was very close now – air foul with their hoarse snarlings, and the ground almost shaking with their alien-rhythmed footfalls. My breath nearly ceased to come, and I put every ounce of will-power into the task of holding my eyelids down.

I am not even yet willing to say whether what followed was a hideous actuality or only a nightmare hallucination. The later action of the government, after my frantic appeals, would tend to confirm it as a monstrous truth; but could not an hallucination have been repeated under the quasi-hypnotic spell of that ancient, haunted, and shadowed town? Such places have strange properties, and the legacy of insane legend might well have acted on more than one human imagination amidst those dead, stench-cursed streets and huddles of rotting roofs and crumbling steeples. Is it not possible that the germ of an actual contagious madness lurks in the depths of that shadow over Innsmouth? Who can be sure of reality after hearing things like the tale of old Zadok Allen? The government men never found poor Zadok, and have no conjectures to make as to what became of him. Where does madness leave off and reality begin? Is it possible that even my latest fear is sheer delusion?

But I must try to tell what I thought I saw that night under the mocking yellow moon – saw surging and hopping down the Rowley road in plain sight in front of me as I crouched among the wild brambles of that desolate railway cut. Of course my resolution to keep my eyes shut had failed. It was foredoomed to failure – for who could crouch blindly while a legion of croaking, baying entities of unknown source flopped noisomely past, scarcely more than a hundred yards away?

I thought I was prepared for the worst, and I really ought to have been prepared considering what I had seen before.

My other pursuers had been accursedly abnormal – so should I not have been ready to face a strengthening of the abnormal element; to look upon forms in which there was no mixture of the normal at all? I did not open my eyes until the raucous clamour came loudly from a point obviously straight ahead. Then I knew that a long section of them must be plainly in sight where the sides of the cut flattened out and the road crossed the track – and I could no longer keep myself from sampling whatever horror that leering yellow moon might have to shew.

It was the end, for whatever remains to me of life on the surface of this earth, of every vestige of mental peace and confidence in the integrity of nature and of the human mind.

Nothing that I could have imagined – nothing, even, that I could have gathered had I credited old Zadok's crazy tale in the most literal way – would be in any way comparable to the demoniac, blasphemous reality that I saw – or believe I saw. I have tried to hint what it was in order to postpone the horror of writing it down baldly. Can it be possible that this planet has actually spawned such things; that human eyes have truly seen, as objective flesh, what man has hitherto known only in febrile phantasy and tenuous legend?

And yet I saw them in a limitless stream – flopping, hopping, croaking, bleating – urging inhumanly through the spectral moonlight in a grotesque, malignant saraband of fantastic nightmare. And some of them had tall tiaras of that nameless whitish-gold metal …and some were strangely robed …and one, who led the way, was clad in a ghoulishly humped black coat and striped trousers, and had a man's felt hat perched on the shapeless thing that answered for a head.

I think their predominant colour was a greyish-green, though they had white bellies. They were mostly shiny and slippery, but the ridges of their backs were scaly. Their forms vaguely suggested the anthropoid, while their heads were the heads of fish, with prodigious bulging eyes that never closed. At the sides of their necks were palpitating gills, and their long paws were webbed. They hopped irregularly, sometimes on two legs and sometimes on four. I was somehow glad that they had no more than four limbs. Their croaking, baying voices, clearly used for articulate speech, held all the dark shades of expression which their staring faces lacked.

But for all of their monstrousness they were not unfamiliar to me. I knew too well what they must be – for was not the memory of the evil tiara at Newburyport still fresh? They were the blasphemous fish-frogs of the nameless design – living and horrible – and as I saw them I knew also of what that humped, tiaraed priest in the black church basement had fearsomely reminded me. Their number was past guessing. It seemed to me that there were limitless swarms of them and certainly my momentary glimpse could have shewn only the least fraction. In another instant everything was blotted out by a merciful fit of fainting; the first I had ever had.

Chapter V

IT WAS A GENTLE daylight rain that awaked me from my stupor in the brush-grown railway cut, and when I staggered out to the roadway ahead I saw no trace of any prints in the fresh mud. The fishy odour, too, was gone, Innsmouth's ruined roofs and toppling steeples loomed up greyly toward the southeast, but not a living creature did I spy in all the desolate salt marshes around. My watch was still going, and told me that the hour was past noon.

The reality of what I had been through was highly uncertain in my mind, but I felt that something hideous lay in the background. I must get away from evil-shadowed Innsmouth – and accordingly I began to test my cramped, wearied powers of locomotion. Despite weakness, hunger, horror, and bewilderment I found myself after a time able to walk; so started slowly along the muddy road to Rowley. Before evening I was in the village, getting a meal and providing myself with presentable clothes. I caught the night train to Arkham, and the next day talked long and earnestly with government officials there; a process I later repeated in Boston. With the main result of these colloquies the public is now familiar – and I wish, for normality's sake, there were nothing more to tell. Perhaps it is madness that is overtaking me – yet perhaps a greater horror – or a greater marvel – is reaching out.

As may well be imagined, I gave up most of the foreplanned features of the rest of my tour – the scenic, architectural, and antiquarian diversions on which I had counted so heavily. Nor did I dare look for that piece of strange jewelry said to be in the Miskatonic University Museum. I did, however, improve my stay in Arkham by collecting some genealogical notes I had long wished to possess; very rough and hasty data, it is true, but capable of good use later on when I might have time to collate and codify them. The curator of the historical society there – Mr. B. Lapham Peabody – was very courteous about assisting me, and expressed unusual interest when I told him I was a grandson of Eliza Orne of Arkham, who was born in 1867 and had married James Williamson of Ohio at the age of seventeen.

It seemed that a maternal uncle of mine had been there many years before on a quest much like my own; and that my grandmother's family was a topic of some local curiosity. There had, Mr. Peabody said, been considerable discussion about the marriage of her father, Benjamin Orne, just after the Civil War; since the ancestry of the bride was peculiarly puzzling. That bride was understood to have been an orphaned Marsh of New Hampshire – a cousin of the Essex County Marshes – but her education had been in France and she knew very little of her family. A guardian had deposited funds in a Boston bank to maintain her and her French governess; but that guardian's name was unfamiliar to Arkham people, and in time he dropped out of sight, so that the governess assumed the role by court appointment. The Frenchwoman – now long dead – was very taciturn, and there were those who said she would have told more than she did.

But the most baffling thing was the inability of anyone to place the recorded parents of the young woman – Enoch and Lydia (Meserve) Marsh – among the known families of New Hampshire. Possibly, many suggested, she was the natural daughter of some Marsh of prominence – she certainly had the true Marsh eyes. Most of the puzzling was done after her early death, which took place at the birth of my grandmother – her only child. Having formed some disagreeable impressions connected with the name of Marsh, I did not welcome the news that it belonged on my own ancestral tree; nor was I pleased by Mr. Peabody's suggestion that I had the true Marsh eyes myself. However, I was grateful for data which I knew would prove valuable; and took copious notes and lists of book references regarding the well-documented Orne family.

I went directly home to Toledo from Boston, and later spent a month at Maumee recuperating from my ordeal. In September I entered Oberlin for my final year, and from then till the next June was busy with studies and other wholesome activities – reminded of the bygone terror only by occasional official visits from government men in connexion with the campaign which my pleas and evidence had started. Around the middle of July – just a year after the Innsmouth experience – I spent a week with my late mother's family in Cleveland; checking some of my new genealogical data with the various notes, traditions, and bits of heirloom material in existence there, and seeing what kind of a connected chart I could construct.

I did not exactly relish this task, for the atmosphere of the Williamson home had always depressed me. There was a strain of morbidity there, and my mother had never encouraged my visiting her parents as a child, although she always welcomed her father when he came to Toledo. My Arkham-born grandmother had seemed strange and almost terrifying to me, and I do not think I grieved when she disappeared. I was eight years old then, and it was said that she had wandered off in grief after the suicide of my Uncle Douglas, her eldest son. He had shot himself after a trip to New England – the same trip, no doubt, which had caused him to be recalled at the Arkham Historical Society.

This uncle had resembled her, and I had never liked him either. Something about the staring, unwinking expression of both of them had given me a vague, unaccountable uneasiness. My mother and Uncle Walter had not looked like that. They were like their father, though poor little cousin Lawrence – Walter's son – had been an almost perfect duplicate of his grandmother before his condition took him to the permanent seclusion of a sanitarium at Canton. I had not seen him in four years, but my uncle once implied that his state, both mental and physical, was very bad. This worry had probably been a major cause of his mother's death two years before.

My grandfather and his widowed son Walter now comprised the Cleveland household, but the memory of older times hung thickly over it. I still disliked the place, and tried to get my researches done as quickly as possible. Williamson records and traditions were supplied in abundance by my grandfather; though for Orne material I had to depend on my uncle Walter, who put at my disposal the contents of all his files, including notes, letters, cuttings, heirlooms, photographs, and miniatures.

It was in going over the letters and pictures on the Orne side that I began to acquire a kind of terror of my own ancestry. As I have said, my grandmother and Uncle Douglas had always disturbed me. Now, years after their passing, I gazed at their pictured faces with a measurably heightened feeling of repulsion and alienation. I could not at first understand the change, but gradually a horrible sort of comparison began to obtrude itself on my unconscious mind despite the steady refusal of my consciousness to admit even the least suspicion of it. It was clear that the typical expression of these faces now suggested something it had not suggested before – something which would bring stark panic if too openly thought of.

But the worst shock came when my uncle shewed me the Orne jewelery in a downtown safe deposit vault. Some of the items were delicate and inspiring enough, but there was one box of strange old pieces descended from my mysterious great-grandmother which my uncle was almost reluctant to produce. They were, he said, of very grotesque and almost repulsive design, and had never to his knowledge been publicly worn; though my grandmother used to enjoy looking at them. Vague legends of bad luck clustered around them, and my great-grandmother's French governess had said they ought not to be worn in New England, though it would be quite safe to wear them in Europe.

As my uncle began slowly and grudgingly to unwrap the things he urged me not to be shocked by the strangeness and frequent hideousness of the designs. Artists and archaeologists who had seen them pronounced their workmanship superlatively and exotically exquisite, though no one seemed able to define their exact material or assign them to any specific art tradition. There were two armlets, a tiara, and a kind of pectoral; the latter having in high relief certain figures of almost unbearable extravagance.

During this description I had kept a tight rein on my emotions, but my face must have betrayed my mounting fears. My uncle looked concerned, and paused in his unwrapping to study my countenance. I motioned to him to continue, which he did with renewed signs of reluctance. He seemed to expect some demonstration when the first piece – the tiara – became visible, but I doubt if he expected quite what actually happened. I did not expect it, either, for I thought I was thoroughly forewarned regarding what the jewelery would turn out to be. What I did was to faint silently away, just as I had done in that brier choked railway cut a year before.

From that day on my life has been a nightmare of brooding and apprehension nor do I know how much is hideous truth and how much madness. My great-grandmother had been a Marsh of unknown source whose husband lived in Arkham – and did not old Zadok say that the daughter of Obed Marsh by a monstrous mother was married to an Arkham man through a trick? What was it the ancient toper had muttered about the line of my eyes to Captain Obed's? In Arkham, too, the curator had told me I had the true Marsh eyes. Was Obed Marsh my own great-great-grandfather? Who – or what – then, was my great-great-grandmother? But perhaps this was all madness. Those whitish-gold ornaments might easily have been bought from some Innsmouth sailor by the father of my great-grandmother, whoever he was. And that look in the staring-eyed faces of my grandmother and self-slain uncle might be sheer fancy on my part – sheer fancy, bolstered up by the Innsmouth shadow which had so darkly coloured my imagination. But why had my uncle killed himself after an ancestral quest in New England?

For more than two years I fought off these reflections with partial success. My father secured me a place in an insurance office, and I buried myself in routine as deeply as possible. In the winter of 1930–31, however, the dreams began. They were very sparse and insidious at first, but increased in frequency and vividness as the weeks went by. Great watery spaces opened out before me, and I seemed to wander through titanic sunken porticos and labyrinths of weedy cyclopean walls with grotesque fishes as my companions. Then the other shapes began to appear, filling me with nameless horror the moment I awoke. But during the dreams they did not horrify me at all – I was one with them; wearing their unhuman trappings, treading their aqueous ways, and praying monstrously at their evil sea-bottom temples.

There was much more than I could remember, but even what I did remember each morning would be enough to stamp me as a madman or a genius if ever I dared write it down. Some frightful influence, I felt, was seeking gradually to drag me out of the sane world of wholesome life into unnamable abysses of blackness and alienage; and the process told heavily on me. My health and appearance grew steadily worse, till finally I was forced to give up my position and adopt the static, secluded life of an invalid. Some odd nervous affliction had me in its grip, and I found myself at times almost unable to shut my eyes.

It was then that I began to study the mirror with mounting alarm. The slow ravages of disease are not pleasant to watch, but in my case there was something subtler and more puzzling in the background. My father seemed to notice it, too, for he began looking at me curiously and almost affrightedly. What was taking place in me? Could it be that I was coming to resemble my grandmother and uncle Douglas?

One night I had a frightful dream in which I met my grandmother under the sea. She lived in a phosphorescent palace of many terraces, with gardens of strange leprous corals and grotesque brachiate efflorescences, and welcomed me with a warmth that may have been sardonic. She had changed – as those who take to the water change – and told me she had never died. Instead, she had gone to a spot her dead son had learned about, and had leaped to a realm whose wonders – destined for him as well – he had spurned with a smoking pistol. This was to be my realm, too – I could not escape it. I would never die, but would live with those who had lived since before man ever walked the earth.

I met also that which had been her grandmother. For eighty thousand years Pth'thya-l'yi had lived in Y'ha-nthlei, and thither she had gone back after Obed Marsh was dead. Y'ha-nthlei was not destroyed when the upper-earth men shot death into the sea. It was hurt, but not destroyed. The Deep Ones could never be destroyed, even though the palaeogean magic of the forgotten Old Ones might sometimes check them. For the present they would rest; but some day, if they remembered, they would rise again for the tribute Great Cthulhu craved. It would be a city greater than Innsmouth next time. They had planned to spread, and had brought up that which would help them, but now they must wait once more. For bringing the upper-earth men's death I must do a penance, but that would not be heavy. This was the dream in which I saw a shoggoth for the first time, and the sight set me awake in a frenzy of screaming. That morning the mirror definitely told me I had acquired the Innsmouth look.

So far I have not shot myself as my uncle Douglas did. I bought an automatic and almost took the step, but certain dreams deterred me. The tense extremes of horror are lessening, and I feel queerly drawn toward the unknown sea-deeps instead of fearing them. I hear and do strange things in sleep, and awake with a kind of exaltation instead of terror. I do not believe I need to wait for the full change as most have waited. If I did, my father would probably shut me up in a sanitarium as my poor little cousin is shut up. Stupendous and unheard-of splendors await me below, and I shall seek them soon. *Iä-R'lyeh! Cthulhu fhtagn! Iä! Iä!* No, I shall not shoot myself – I cannot be made to shoot myself!

I shall plan my cousin's escape from that Canton mad-house, and together we shall go to marvel-shadowed Innsmouth. We shall swim out to that brooding reef in the sea and dive down through black abysses to Cyclopean and many-columned Y'ha-nthlei, and in that lair of the Deep Ones we shall dwell amidst wonder and glory for ever.

The Shadow out of Time

H.P. Lovecraft

Chapter I

AFTER TWENTY-TWO YEARS of nightmare and terror, saved only by a desperate conviction of the mythical source of certain impressions, I am unwilling to vouch for the truth of that which I think I found in Western Australia on the night of 17–18 July 1935. There is reason to hope that my experience was wholly or partly an hallucination – for which, indeed, abundant causes existed. And yet, its realism was so hideous that I sometimes find hope impossible.

If the thing did happen, then man must be prepared to accept notions of the cosmos, and of his own place in the seething vortex of time, whose merest mention is paralysing. He must, too, be placed on guard against a specific, lurking peril which, though it will never engulf the whole race, may impose monstrous and unguessable horrors upon certain venturesome members of it.

It is for this latter reason that I urge, with all the force of my being, final abandonment of all the attempts at unearthing those fragments of unknown, primordial masonry which my expedition set out to investigate.

Assuming that I was sane and awake, my experience on that night was such as has befallen no man before. It was, moreover, a frightful confirmation of all I had sought to dismiss as myth and dream. Mercifully there is no proof, for in my fright I lost the awesome object which would – if real and brought out of that noxious abyss – have formed irrefutable evidence.

When I came upon the horror I was alone – and I have up to now told no one about it. I could not stop the others from digging in its direction, but chance and the shifting sand have so far saved them from finding it. Now I must formulate some definite statement – not only for the sake of my own mental balance, but to warn such others as may read it seriously.

These pages – much in whose earlier parts will be familiar to close readers of the general and scientific press – are written in the cabin of the ship that is bringing me home. I shall give them to my son, Professor Wingate Peaslee of Miskatonic University – the only member of my family who stuck to me after my queer amnesia of long ago, and the man best informed on the inner facts of my case. Of all living persons, he is least likely to ridicule what I shall tell of that fateful night.

I did not enlighten him orally before sailing, because I think he had better have the revelation in written form. Reading and re-reading at leisure will leave with him a more convincing picture than my confused tongue could hope to convey.

He can do anything that he thinks best with this account – showing it, with suitable comment, in any quarters where it will be likely to accomplish good. It is for the sake of such readers as are unfamiliar with the earlier phases of my case that I am prefacing the revelation itself with a fairly ample summary of its background.

My name is Nathaniel Wingate Peaslee, and those who recall the newspaper tales of a generation back – or the letters and articles in psychological journals six or seven years ago – will know who and what I am. The press was filled with the details of my strange amnesia in 1908-13, and much was made of the traditions of horror, madness, and witchcraft which lurked behind the ancient Massachusetts town then and now forming my place of residence. Yet I would have it known that there is nothing whatever of the mad or sinister in my heredity and early life. This is a highly important fact in view of the shadow which fell so suddenly upon me from *outside* sources.

It may be that centuries of dark brooding had given to crumbling, whisper-haunted Arkham a peculiar vulnerability as regards such shadows – though even this seems doubtful in the light of those other cases which I later came to study. But the chief point is that my own ancestry and background are altogether normal. What came, came from *somewhere else* – where I even now hesitate to assert in plain words.

I am the son of Jonathan and Hannah (Wingate) Peaslee, both of wholesome old Haverhill stock. I was born and reared in Haverhill – at the old homestead in Boardman Street near Golden Hill – and did not go to Arkham till I entered Miskatonic University as instructor of political economy in 1895.

For thirteen years more my life ran smoothly and happily. I married Alice Keezar of Haverhill in 1896, and my three children, Robert, Wingate and Hannah were born in 1898, 1900, and 1903, respectively. In 1898 I became an associate professor, and in 1902 a full professor. At no time had I the least interest in either occultism or abnormal psychology.

It was on Thursday, 14 May 1908, that the queer amnesia came. The thing was quite sudden, though later I realized that certain brief, glimmering visions of several hours previous – chaotic visions which disturbed me greatly because they were so unprecedented – must have formed premonitory symptoms. My head was aching, and I had a singular feeling – altogether new to me – that some one else was trying to get possession of my thoughts.

The collapse occurred about 10.20 a.m., while I was conducting a class in Political Economy VI – history and present tendencies of economics – for juniors and a few sophomores. I began to see strange shapes before my eyes, and to feel that I was in a grotesque room other than the classroom.

My thoughts and speech wandered from my subject, and the students saw that something was gravely amiss. Then I slumped down, unconscious, in my chair, in a stupor from which no one could arouse me. Nor did my rightful faculties again look out upon the daylight of our normal world for five years, four months, and thirteen days.

It is, of course, from others that I have learned what followed. I showed no sign of consciousness for sixteen and a half hours though removed to my home at 27 Crane Street, and given the best of medical attention.

At 3 a.m. 15 May my eyes opened and I began to speak, but before long the doctor and my family were thoroughly frightened by the trend of my expression and language. It was clear that I had no remembrance of my identity and my past, though for some reason I seemed anxious to conceal this lack of knowledge. My eyes glazed strangely at the persons around me, and the flections of my facial muscles were altogether unfamiliar.

Even my speech seemed awkward and foreign. I used my vocal organs clumsily and gropingly, and my diction had a curiously stilted quality, as if I had laboriously learned the English language from books. The pronunciation was barbarously alien, whilst the idiom seemed to include both scraps of curious archaism and expressions of a wholly incomprehensible cast.

Of the latter, one in particular was very potently – even terrifiedly – recalled by the youngest of the physicians twenty years afterward. For at that late period such a phrase began to have an actual currency – first in England and then in the United States – and though of much complexity and indisputable newness, it reproduced in every least particular the mystifying words of the strange Arkham patient of 1908.

Physical strength returned at once, although I required an odd amount of re-education in the use of my hands, legs, and bodily apparatus in general. Because of this and other handicaps inherent in the mnemonic lapse, I was for some time kept under strict medical care.

When I saw that my attempts to conceal the lapse had failed, I admitted it openly, and became eager for information of all sorts. Indeed, it seemed to the doctors that I lost interest in my proper personality as soon as I found the case of amnesia accepted as a natural thing.

They noticed that my chief efforts were to master certain points in history, science, art, language, and folklore – some of them tremendously abstruse, and some childishly simple – which remained, very oddly in many cases, outside my consciousness.

At the same time they noticed that I had an inexplicable command of many almost unknown sorts of knowledge – a command which I seemed to wish to hide rather than display. I would inadvertently refer, with casual assurance, to specific events in dim ages outside of the range of accepted history – passing off such references as a jest when I saw the surprise they created. And I had a way of speaking of the future which two or three times caused actual fright.

These uncanny flashes soon ceased to appear, though some observers laid their vanishment more to a certain furtive caution on my part than to any waning of the strange knowledge behind them. Indeed, I seemed anomalously avid to absorb the speech, customs, and perspectives of the age around me; as if I were a studious traveller from a far, foreign land.

As soon as permitted, I haunted the college library at all hours; and shortly began to arrange for those odd travels, and special courses at American and European Universities, which evoked so much comment during the next few years.

I did not at any time suffer from a lack of learned contacts, for my case had a mild celebrity among the psychologists of the period. I was lectured upon as a typical example of secondary personality – even though I seemed to puzzle the lecturers now and then with some bizarre symptoms or some queer trace of carefully veiled mockery.

Of real friendliness, however, I encountered little. Something in my aspect and speech seemed to excite vague fears and aversions in every one I met, as if I were a being infinitely removed from all that is normal and healthful. This idea of a black, hidden horror connected with incalculable gulfs of some sort of *distance* was oddly widespread and persistent.

My own family formed no exception. From the moment of my strange waking my wife had regarded me with extreme horror and loathing, vowing that I was some utter alien usurping the body of her husband. In 1910 she obtained a legal divorce, nor would she ever consent to see me even after my return to normality in 1913. These feelings were shared by my elder son and my small daughter, neither of whom I have ever seen since.

Only my second son, Wingate, seemed able to conquer the terror and repulsion which my change aroused. He indeed felt that I was a stranger, but though only eight years old held fast to a faith that my proper self would return. When it did return he sought me out, and the courts gave me his custody. In succeeding years he helped me with the studies to which I was driven, and today, at thirty-five, he is a professor of psychology at Miskatonic.

But I do not wonder at the horror caused – for certainly, the mind, voice, and facial expression of the being that awakened on 15 May 1908, were not those of Nathaniel Wingate Peaslee.

I will not attempt to tell much of my life from 1908 to 1913, since readers may glean the outward essentials – as I largely had to do – from files of old newspapers and scientific journals.

I was given charge of my funds, and spent them slowly and on the whole wisely, in travel and in study at various centres of learning. My travels, however, were singular in the extreme, involving long visits to remote and desolate places.

In 1909 I spent a month in the Himalayas, and in 1911 roused much attention through a camel trip into the unknown deserts of Arabia. What happened on those journeys I have never been able to learn.

During the summer of 1912 I chartered a ship and sailed in the Arctic, north of Spitzbergen, afterward showing signs of disappointment.

Later in that year I spent weeks – alone beyond the limits of previous or subsequent exploration in the vast limestone cavern systems of western Virginia – black labyrinths so complex that no retracing of my steps could even be considered.

My sojourns at the universities were marked by abnormally rapid assimilation, as if the secondary personality had an intelligence enormously superior to my own. I have found, also, that my rate of reading and solitary study was phenomenal. I could master every detail of a book merely by glancing over it as fast as I could turn the leaves; while my skill at interpreting complex figures in an instant was veritably awesome.

At times there appeared almost ugly reports of my power to influence the thoughts and acts of others, though I seemed to have taken care to minimize displays of this faculty.

Other ugly reports concerned my intimacy with leaders of occultist groups, and scholars suspected of connection with nameless bands of abhorrent elder-world hierophants. These rumours, though never proved at the time, were doubtless stimulated by the known tenor of some of my reading – for the consultation of rare books at libraries cannot be effected secretly.

There is tangible proof – in the form of marginal notes – that I went minutely through such things as the Comte d'Erlette's *Cultes des Goules*, Ludvig Prinn's *De Vermis Mysteriis*, the *Unaussprechlichen Kulten* of von Junzt, the surviving fragments of the puzzling *Book of Eibon*, and the dreaded *Necronomicon* of the mad Arab Abdul Alhazred. Then, too, it is undeniable that a fresh and evil wave of underground cult activity set in about the time of my odd mutation.

In the summer of 1913 I began to display signs of ennui and flagging interest, and to hint to various associates that a change might soon be expected in me. I spoke of returning memories of my earlier life – though most auditors judged me insincere, since all the recollections I gave were casual, and such as might have been learned from my old private papers.

About the middle of August I returned to Arkham and re-opened my long-closed house in Crane Street. Here I installed a mechanism of the most curious aspect, constructed piecemeal by different makers of scientific apparatus in Europe and America, and guarded carefully from the sight of any one intelligent enough to analyse it.

Those who did see it – a workman, a servant, and the new housekeeper – say that it was a queer mixture of rods, wheels, and mirrors, though only about two feet tall, one foot wide, and one foot thick. The central mirror was circular and convex. All this is borne out by such makers of parts as can be located.

On the evening of Friday, 26 September, I dismissed the housekeeper and the maid until noon of the next day. Lights burned in the house till late, and a lean, dark, curiously foreign-looking man called in an automobile.

It was about one a.m. that the lights were last seen. At 2.15 a.m. a policeman observed the place in darkness, but the stranger's motor still at the curb. By 4 o'clock the motor was certainly gone.

It was at 6 o'clock that a hesitant, foreign voice on the telephone asked Dr. Wilson to call at my house and bring me out of a peculiar faint. This call – a long-distance one – was later traced to a public booth in the North Station in Boston, but no sign of the lean foreigner was ever unearthed.

When the doctor reached my house he found me unconscious in the sitting room – in an easy-chair with a table drawn up before it. On the polished top were scratches showing where some heavy object had rested. The queer machine was gone, nor was anything afterward heard of it. Undoubtedly the dark, lean foreigner had taken it away.

In the library grate were abundant ashes, evidently left from the burning of the every remaining scrap of paper on which I had written since the advent of the amnesia. Dr. Wilson found my breathing very peculiar, but after a hypodermic injection it became more regular.

At 11.15 a.m., 27 September, I stirred vigorously, and my hitherto masklike face began to show signs of expression. Dr. Wilson remarked that the expression was not that of my secondary personality, but seemed much like that of my normal self. About 11.30 I muttered some very curious syllables – syllables which seemed unrelated to any human speech. I appeared, too, to struggle against something. Then, just after noon – the housekeeper and the maid having meanwhile returned – I began to mutter in English:

"– of the orthodox economists of that period, Jevons typifies the prevailing trend toward scientific correlation. His attempt to link the commercial cycle of prosperity and depression with the physical cycle of the solar spots forms perhaps the apex of –"

Nathaniel Wingate Peaslee had come back – a spirit in whose time scale it was still Thursday morning in 1908, with the economics class gazing up at the battered desk on the platform.

Chapter II

MY REABSORPTION into normal life was a painful and difficult process. The loss of over five years creates more complications than can be imagined, and in my case there were countless matters to be adjusted.

What I heard of my actions since 1908 astonished and disturbed me, but I tried to view the matter as philosophically as I could. At last, regaining custody of my second son, Wingate, I settled down with him in the Crane Street house and endeavoured to resume my teaching – my old professorship having been kindly offered me by the college.

I began work with the February, 1914, term, and kept at it just a year. By that time I realized how badly my experience had shaken me. Though perfectly sane – I hoped – and with no flaw in my original personality, I had not the nervous energy of the old days. Vague dreams and queer ideas continually haunted me, and when the outbreak of the World War turned my mind to history I found myself thinking of periods and events in the oddest possible fashion.

My conception of time – my ability to distinguish between consecutiveness and simultaneousness – seemed subtly disordered so that I formed chimerical notions about living in one age and casting one's mind all over eternity for knowledge of past and future ages.

The war gave me strange impressions of remembering some of its far-off consequences – as if I knew how it was coming out and could look back upon it in the light of future information. All such quasi-memories were attended with much pain, and with a feeling that some artificial psychological barrier was set against them.

When I diffidently hinted to others about my impressions I met with varied responses. Some persons looked uncomfortably at me, but men in the mathematics department spoke of new developments in those theories of relativity – then discussed only in learned circles – which were later to become so famous. Dr. Albert Einstein, they said, was rapidly reducing time to the status of a mere dimension.

But the dreams and disturbed feelings gained on me, so that I had to drop my regular work in 1915. Certainly the impressions were taking an annoying shape – giving me the persistent notion that my amnesia had formed some unholy sort of exchange; that the secondary personality had indeed had suffered displacement.

Thus I was driven to vague and frightful speculations concerning the whereabouts of my true self during the years that another had held my body. The curious knowledge and strange conduct of my body's late tenant troubled me more and more as I learned further details from persons, papers, and magazines.

Queernesses that had baffled others seemed to harmonize terribly with some background of black knowledge which festered in the chasms of my subconscious. I began to search feverishly for every scrap of information bearing on the studies and travels of that other one during the dark years.

Not all of my troubles were as semi-abstract as this. There were the dreams – and these seemed to grow in vividness and concreteness. Knowing how most would regard them, I seldom mentioned them to anyone but my son or certain trusted psychologists, but eventually I commenced a scientific study of other cases in order to see how typical or nontypical such visions might be among amnesia victims.

My results, aided by psychologists, historians, anthropologists, and mental specialists of wide experience, and by a study that included all records of split personalities from the days of daemonic-possession legends to the medically realistic present, at first bothered me more than they consoled me.

I soon found that my dreams had, indeed, no counterpart in the overwhelming bulk of true amnesia cases. There remained, however, a tiny residue of accounts which for years baffled and shocked me with their parallelism to my own experience. Some of them were bits of ancient folklore; others were case histories in the annals of medicine; one or two were anecdotes obscurely buried in standard histories.

It thus appeared that, while my special kind of affliction was prodigiously rare, instances of it had occurred at long intervals ever since the beginning of men's annals. Some centuries might contain one, two, or three cases, others none – or at least none whose record survived.

The essence was always the same – a person of keen thoughtfulness seized a strange secondary life and leading for a greater or lesser period an utterly alien existence typified at first by vocal and bodily awkwardness, and later by a wholesale acquisition of scientific, historic, artistic, and anthropologic knowledge; an acquisition carried on with feverish zest and with a wholly abnormal absorptive power. Then a sudden return of rightful consciousness, intermittently plagued ever after with vague unplaceable dreams suggesting fragments of some hideous memory elaborately blotted out.

And the close resemblance of those nightmares to my own – even in some of the smallest particulars – left no doubt in my mind of their significantly typical nature. One or two of the cases had an added ring of faint, blasphemous familiarity, as if I had heard of them before through some cosmic channel too morbid and frightful to contemplate. In three instances there was specific mention of such an unknown machine as had been in my house before the second change.

Another thing that worried me during my investigation was the somewhat greater frequency of cases where a brief, elusive glimpse of the typical nightmares was afforded to persons not visited with well-defined amnesia.

These persons were largely of mediocre mind or less – some so primitive that they could scarcely be thought of as vehicles for abnormal scholarship and preternatural mental acquisitions. For a second they would be fired with alien force – then a backward lapse, and a thin, swift-fading memory of unhuman horrors.

There had been at least three such cases during the past half century – one only fifteen years before. Had something been groping blindly through time from some unsuspected abyss in Nature? Were these faint cases monstrous, sinister experiments of a kind and authorship utterly beyond sane belief?

Such were a few of the formless speculations of my weaker hours – fancies abetted by myths which my studies uncovered. For I could not doubt but that certain persistent legends of immemorial antiquity, apparently unknown to the victims and physicians connected with recent amnesia cases, formed a striking and awesome elaboration of memory lapses such as mine.

Of the nature of the dreams and impressions which were growing so clamorous I still almost fear to speak. They seemed to savor of madness, and at times I believed I was indeed going mad. Was there a special type of delusion afflicting those who had suffered lapses of memory? Conceivably, the efforts of the subconscious mind to fill up a perplexing blank with pseudo-memories might give rise to strange imaginative vagaries.

This indeed – though an alternative folklore theory finally seemed to me more plausible – was the belief of many of the alienists who helped me in my search for parallel cases, and who shared my puzzlement at the exact resemblances sometimes discovered.

They did not call the condition true insanity, but classed it rather among neurotic disorders. My course in trying to track down and analyze it, instead of vainly seeking to dismiss or forget it, they heartily endorsed as correct according to the best psychological principles. I especially valued the advice of such physicians as had studied me during my possession by the other personality.

My first disturbances were not visual at all, but concerned the more abstract matters which I have mentioned. There was, too, a feeling of profound and inexplicable horror concerning myself. I developed a queer fear of seeing my own form, as if my eyes would find it something utterly alien and inconceivably abhorrent.

When I did glance down and behold the familiar human shape in quiet grey or blue clothing, I always felt a curious relief, though in order to gain this relief I had to conquer an infinite dread. I shunned mirrors as much as possible, and was always shaved at the barber's.

It was a long time before I correlated any of these disappointed feelings with the fleeting, visual impressions which began to develop. The first such correlation had to do with the odd sensation of an external, artificial restraint on my memory.

I felt that the snatches of sight I experienced had a profound and terrible meaning, and a frightful connexion with myself, but that some purposeful influence held me from grasping that meaning and that connexion. Then came that queerness about the element of time, and with it desperate efforts to place the fragmentary dream-glimpses in the chronological and spatial pattern.

The glimpses themselves were at first merely strange rather than horrible. I would seem to be in an enormous vaulted chamber whose lofty stone groinings were well-nigh lost in the shadows overhead. In whatever time or place the scene might be, the principle of the arch was known as fully and used as extensively as by the Romans.

There were colossal, round windows and high, arched doors, and pedestals or tables each as tall as the height of an ordinary room. Vast shelves of dark wood lined the walls, holding what seemed to be volumes of immense size with strange hieroglyphs on their backs.

The exposed stonework held curious carvings, always in curvilinear mathematical designs, and there were chiselled inscriptions in the same characters that the huge books bore. The dark granite masonry was of a monstrous megalithic type, with lines of convex-topped blocks fitting the concave-bottomed courses which rested upon them.

There were no chairs, but the tops of the vast pedestals were littered with books, papers, and what seemed to be writing materials – oddly figured jars of a purplish metal, and rods with stained tips. Tall as the pedestals were, I seemed at times able to view them from above. On some of them were great globes of luminous crystal serving as lamps, and inexplicable machines formed of vitreous tubes and metal rods.

The windows were glazed, and latticed with stout-looking bars. Though I dared not approach and peer out them, I could see from where I was the waving tops of singular fern-like growths. The floor was of massive octagonal flagstones, while rugs and hangings were entirely lacking.

Later I had visions of sweeping through Cyclopean corridors of stone, and up and down gigantic inclined planes of the same monstrous masonry. There were no stairs anywhere, nor was any passageway less than thirty feet wide. Some of the structures through which I floated must have towered in the sky for thousands of feet.

There were multiple levels of black vaults below, and never-opened trap-doors, sealed down with metal bands and holding dim suggestions of some special peril.

I seemed to be a prisoner, and horror hung broodingly over everything I saw. I felt that the mocking curvilinear hieroglyphs on the walls would blast my soul with their message were I not guarded by a merciful ignorance.

Still later my dreams included vistas from the great round windows, and from the titanic flat roof, with its curious gardens, wide barren area, and high, scalloped parapet of stone, to which the topmost of the inclined planes led.

There were, almost endless leagues of giant buildings, each in its garden, and ranged along paved roads fully 200 feet wide. They differed greatly in aspect, but few were less than 500 feet square or a thousand feet high. Many seemed so limitless that they must have had a frontage of several thousand feet, while some shot up to mountainous altitudes in the grey, steamy heavens.

They seemed to be mainly of stone or concrete, and most of them embodied the oddly curvilinear type of masonry noticeable in the building that held me. Roofs were flat and garden-covered, and tended to have scalloped parapets. Sometimes there were terraces and higher levels, and wide, cleared spaces amidst the gardens. The great roads held hints of motion, but in the earlier visions I could not resolve this impression into details.

In certain places I beheld enormous dark cylindrical towers which climbed far above any of the other structures. These appeared to be of a totally unique nature and shewed signs of prodigious age and dilapidation. They were built of a bizarre type of square-cut basalt masonry, and tapered slightly toward their rounded tops. Nowhere in any of them could the least traces of windows or other apertures save huge doors be found. I noticed also some lower buildings – all crumbling with the weathering of aeons – which resembled these dark, cylindrical towers in basic architecture. Around all these aberrant piles of square-cut masonry there hovered an inexplicable aura of menace and concentrated fear, like that bred by the sealed trap-doors.

The omnipresent gardens were almost terrifying in their strangeness, with bizarre and unfamiliar forms of vegetation nodding over broad paths lined with curiously carven monoliths. Abnormally vast fern-like growths predominated – some green, and some of a ghastly, fungoid pallor.

Among them rose great spectral things resembling calamites, whose bamboo-like trunks towered to fabulous heights. Then there were tufted forms like fabulous cycads, and grotesque dark-green shrubs and trees of coniferous aspect.

Flowers were small, colourless, and unrecognizable, blooming in geometrical beds and at large among the greenery.

In a few of the terrace and roof-top gardens were larger and more blossoms of most offensive contours and seeming to suggest artificial breeding. Fungi of inconceivable size, outlines, and colours speckled the scene in patterns bespeaking some unknown but well-established horticultural tradition. In the larger gardens on the ground there seemed to be some attempt to preserve the irregularities of Nature, but on the roofs there was more selectiveness, and more evidences of the topiary art.

The skies were almost always moist and cloudy, and sometimes I would seem to witness tremendous rains. Once in a while, though, there would be glimpses of the sun – which looked abnormally large – and of the moon, whose markings held a touch of difference from the normal that I could never quite fathom. When – very rarely – the night sky was clear to any extent, I beheld constellations which were nearly beyond recognition. Known outlines were sometimes approximated, but seldom duplicated; and from the position of the few groups I could recognize, I felt I must be in the earth's southern hemisphere, near the Tropic of Capricorn.

The far horizon was always steamy and indistinct, but I could see that great jungles of unknown tree-ferns, calamites, lepidodendra, and sigillaria lay outside the city, their fantastic frondage waving mockingly in the shifting vapours. Now and then there would be suggestions of motion in the sky, but these my early visions never resolved.

By the autumn of 1914 I began to have infrequent dreams of strange floatings over the city and through the regions around it. I saw interminable roads through forests of fearsome growths with mottled, fluted, and banded trunks, and past other cities as strange as the one which persistently haunted me.

I saw monstrous constructions of black or iridescent tone in glades and clearings where perpetual twilight reigned, and traversed long causeways over swamps so dark that I could tell but little of their moist, towering vegetation.

Once I saw an area of countless miles strewn with age-blasted basaltic ruins whose architecture had been like that of the few windowless, round-topped towers in the haunting city.

And once I saw the sea – a boundless, steamy expanse beyond the colossal stone piers of an enormous town of domes and arches. Great shapeless suggestions of shadow moved over it, and here and there its surface was vexed with anomalous spoutings.

Chapter III

AS I HAVE SAID, it was not immediately that these wild visions began to hold their terrifying quality. Certainly, many persons have dreamed intrinsically stranger things – things compounded of unrelated scraps of daily life, pictures, and reading, and arranged in fantastically novel forms by the unchecked caprices of sleep.

For some time I accepted the visions as natural, even though I had never before been an extravagant dreamer. Many of the vague anomalies, I argued, must have come from trivial sources too numerous to track down; while others seemed to reflect a common text book knowledge of the plants and other conditions of the primitive world of a hundred and fifty million years ago – the world of the Permian or Triassic age.

In the course of some months, however, the element of terror did figure with accumulating force. This was when the dreams began so unfailingly to have the aspect of memories, and when my mind began to link them with my growing abstract disturbances – the feeling of mnemonic restraint, the curious impressions regarding time, and sense of a loathsome exchange with my secondary personality of 1908–13, and, considerably later, the inexplicable loathing of my own person.

As certain definite details began to enter the dreams, their horror increased a thousandfold – until by October, 1915, I felt I must do something. It was then that I began an intensive study of other cases of amnesia and visions, feeling that I might thereby objectivise my trouble and shake clear of its emotional grip.

However, as before mentioned, the result was at first almost exactly opposite. It disturbed me vastly to find that my dreams had been so closely duplicated; especially since some of the accounts were too early to admit of any geological knowledge – and therefore of any idea of primitive landscapes – on the subjects' part.

What is more, many of these accounts supplied very horrible details and explanations in connexion with the visions of great buildings and jungle gardens – and other things. The actual sights and vague impressions were bad enough, but what was hinted or asserted by some of the other dreamers savored of madness and blasphemy. Worst of all, my own pseudo-memory was aroused to wilder dreams and hints of coming revelations. And yet most doctors deemed my course, on the whole, an advisable one.

I studied psychology systematically, and under the prevailing stimulus my son Wingate did the same – his studies leading eventually to his present professorship. In 1917 and 1918 I took special courses at Miskatonic. Meanwhile, my examination of medical, historical, and anthropological records became indefatigable, involving travels to distant libraries, and finally including even a reading of the hideous books of forbidden elder lore in which my secondary personality had been so disturbingly interested.

Some of the latter were the actual copies I had consulted in my altered state, and I was greatly disturbed by certain marginal notations and ostensible corrections of the hideous text in a script and idiom which somehow seemed oddly unhuman.

These markings were mostly in the respective languages of the various books, all of which the writer seemed to know with equal, though obviously academic, facility. One note appended to von Junzt's *Unaussprechlichen Kulten*, however, was alarmingly otherwise. It consisted of certain curvilinear hieroglyphs in the same ink as that of the German corrections, but following no recognized human pattern. And these hieroglyphs were closely and unmistakably akin to the characters constantly met with in my dreams – characters whose meaning I would sometimes momentarily fancy I knew, or was just on the brink of recalling.

To complete my black confusion, my librarians assured me that, in view of previous examinations and records of consultation of the volumes in question, all of these notations must have been made by myself in my secondary state. This despite the fact that I was and still am ignorant of three of the languages involved.

Piecing together the scattered records, ancient and modern, anthropological and medical, I found a fairly consistent mixture of myth and hallucination whose scope and wildness left me utterly dazed. Only one thing consoled me, the fact that the myths were of such early existence. What lost knowledge could have brought pictures of the Palaeozoic or Mesozoic landscape into these primitive fables, I could not even guess; but the pictures had been there. Thus, a basis existed for the formation of a fixed type of delusion.

Cases of amnesia no doubt created the general myth pattern – but afterward the fanciful accretions of the myths must have reacted on amnesia sufferers and coloured their pseudo-memories. I myself had read and heard all the early tales during my memory lapse – my quest had amply proved that. Was it not natural, then, for my subsequent dreams and emotional impressions to become coloured and moulded by what my memory subtly held over from my secondary state?

A few of the myths had significant connexions with other cloudy legends of the pre-human world, especially those Hindu tales involving stupefying gulfs of time and forming part of the lore of modern theosophists.

Primal myth and modern delusion joined in their assumption that mankind is only one – perhaps the least – of the highly evolved and dominant races of this planet's long and largely unknown career. Things of inconceivable shape, they implied, had reared towers to the sky and delved into every secret of Nature before the first amphibian forbear of man had crawled out of the hot sea 300 million years ago.

Some had come down from the stars; a few were as old as the cosmos itself, others had arisen swiftly from terrene germs as far behind the first germs of our life-cycle as those germs are behind ourselves. Spans of thousands of millions of years, and linkages to other galaxies and universes, were freely spoken of. Indeed, there was no such thing as time in its humanly accepted sense.

But most of the tales and impressions concerned a relatively late race, of a queer and intricate shape, resembling no life-form known to science, which had lived till only fifty million years before the advent of man. This, they indicated, was the greatest race of all because it alone had conquered the secret of time.

It had learned all things that ever were known or ever would be known on the earth, through the power of its keener minds to project themselves into the past and future, even through gulfs of millions of years, and study the lore of every age. From the accomplishments of this race arose all legends of prophets, including those in human mythology.

In its vast libraries were volumes of texts and pictures holding the whole of earth's annals – histories and descriptions of every species that had ever been or that ever would be, with full records of their arts, their achievements, their languages, and their psychologies.

With this aeon-embracing knowledge, the Great Race chose from every era and life-form such thoughts, arts, and processes as might suit its own nature and situation.

Knowledge of the past, secured through a kind of mind-casting outside the recognized senses, was harder to glean than knowledge of the future.

In the latter case the course was easier and more material. With suitable mechanical aid a mind would project itself forward in time, feeling its dim, extra-sensory way till it approached the desired period. Then, after preliminary trials, it would seize on the best discoverable representative of the highest of that period's life-forms. It would enter the organism's brain and set up therein its own vibrations, while the displaced mind would strike back to the period of the displacer, remaining in the latter's body till a reverse process was set up.

The projected mind, in the body of the organism of the future, would then pose as a member of the race whose outward form it wore, learning as quickly as possible all that could be learned of the chosen age and its massed information and techniques.

Meanwhile the displaced mind, thrown back to the displacer's age and body, would be carefully guarded. It would be kept from harming the body it occupied, and would be drained of all its knowledge by trained questioners. Often it could be questioned in its own language, when previous quests into the future had brought back records of that language.

If the mind came from a body whose language the Great Race could not physically reproduce, clever machines would be made, on which the alien speech could be played as on a musical instrument.

The Great Race's members were immense rugose cones ten feet high, and with head and other organs attached to foot-thick, distensible limbs spreading from the apexes. They spoke by the clicking or scraping of huge paws or claws attached to the end of two of their four limbs, and walked by the expansion and contraction of a viscous layer attached to their vast, ten-foot bases.

When the captive mind's amazement and resentment had worn off, and when – assuming that it came from a body vastly different from the Great Race's – it had lost its horror at its unfamiliar temporary form, it was permitted to study its new environment and experience a wonder and wisdom approximating that of its displacer.

With suitable precautions, and in exchange for suitable services, it was allowed to rove all over the habitable world in titan airships or on the huge boatlike atomic-engined vehicles which traversed the great roads, and to delve freely into the libraries containing the records of the planet's past and future.

This reconciled many captive minds to their lot; since none were other than keen, and to such minds the unveiling of hidden mysteries of earth-closed chapters of inconceivable pasts and dizzying vortices of future time which include the years ahead of their own natural ages – forms always, despite the abysmal horrors often unveiled, the supreme experience of life.

Now and then certain captives were permitted to meet other captive minds seized from the future – to exchange thoughts with consciousnesses living a hundred or a thousand or a million years before or after their own ages. And all were urged to write copiously in their own languages of themselves and their respective periods; such documents to be filed in the great central archives.

It may be added that there was one special type of captive whose privileges were far greater than those of the majority. These were the dying permanent exiles, whose bodies in the future had been seized by keen-minded members of the Great Race who, faced with death, sought to escape mental extinction.

Such melancholy exiles were not as common as might be expected, since the longevity of the Great Race lessened its love of life – especially among those superior minds capable of projection. From cases of the permanent projection of elder minds arose many of those lasting changes of personality noticed in later history – including mankind's.

As for the ordinary cases of exploration – when the displacing mind had learned what it wished in the future, it would build an apparatus like that which had started its flight and reverse the process of projection. Once more it would be in its own body in its own age, while the lately captive mind would return to that body of the future to which it properly belonged.

Only when one or the other of the bodies had died during the exchange was this restoration impossible. In such cases, of course, the exploring mind had – like those of the death-escapers – to live out an alien-bodied life in the future; or else the captive mind – like the dying permanent exiles – had to end its days in the form and past age of the Great Race.

This fate was least horrible when the captive mind was also of the Great Race – a not infrequent occurrence, since in all its periods that race was intensely concerned with its own future. The number of dying permanent exiles of the Great Race was very slight – largely because of the tremendous penalties attached to displacements of future Great Race minds by the moribund.

Through projection, arrangements were made to inflict these penalties on the offending minds in their new future bodies – and sometimes forced re-exchanges were effected.

Complex cases of the displacement of exploring or already captive minds by minds in various regions of the past had been known and carefully rectified. In every age since the discovery of mind projection, a minute but well-recognised element of the population consisted of Great Race minds from past ages, sojourning for a longer or shorter while.

When a captive mind of alien origin was returned to its own body in the future, it was purged by an intricate mechanical hypnosis of all it had learned in the Great Race's age – this because of certain troublesome consequences inherent in the general carrying forward of knowledge in large quantities.

The few existing instances of clear transmission had caused, and would cause at known future times, great disasters. And it was largely in consequence of two cases of this kind – said the old myths – that mankind had learned what it had concerning the Great Race.

Of all things surviving physically and directly from that aeon-distant world, there remained only certain ruins of great stones in far places and under the sea, and parts of the text of the frightful *Pnakotic Manuscripts*.

Thus the returning mind reached its own age with only the faintest and most fragmentary visions of what it had undergone since its seizure. All memories that could be eradicated were eradicated, so that in most cases only a dream-shadowed blank stretched back to the time of the first exchange. Some minds recalled more than others, and the chance joining of memories had at rare times brought hints of the forbidden past to future ages.

There probably never was a time when groups or cults did not secretly cherish certain of these hints. In the *Necronomicon* the presence of such a cult among human beings was suggested – a cult that sometimes gave aid to minds voyaging down the aeons from the days of the Great Race.

And, meanwhile, the Great Race itself waxed well-nigh omniscient, and turned to the task of setting up exchanges with the minds of other planets, and of exploring their pasts and futures. It sought likewise to fathom the past years and origin of that black, aeon-dead orb in far space whence its own mental heritage had come – for the mind of the Great Race was older than its bodily form.

The beings of a dying elder world, wise with the ultimate secrets, had looked ahead for a new world and species wherein they might have long life; and had sent their minds en masse into that future race best adapted to house them – the cone-shaped beings that peopled our earth a billion years ago.

Thus the Great Race came to be, while the myriad minds sent backward were left to die in the horror of strange shapes. Later the race would again face death, yet would live through another forward migration of its best minds into the bodies of others who had a longer physical span ahead of them.

Such was the background of intertwined legend and hallucination. When, around 1920, I had my researches in coherent shape, I felt a slight lessening of the tension which their earlier stages had increased. After all, and in spite of the fancies prompted by blind emotions, were not most of my phenomena readily explainable? Any chance might have turned my mind to dark studies during the amnesia – and then I read the forbidden legends and met the members of ancient and ill-regarded cults. That, plainly, supplied the material for the dreams and disturbed feelings which came after the return of memory.

As for the marginal notes in dream-hieroglyphs and languages unknown to me, but laid at my door by librarians – I might easily have picked up a smattering of the tongues during my secondary state, while the hieroglyphs were doubtless coined by my fancy from descriptions in old legends, and afterward woven into my dreams. I tried to verify certain points through conversation with known cult leaders, but never succeeded in establishing the right connexions.

At times the parallelism of so many cases in so many distant ages continued to worry me as it had at first, but on the other hand I reflected that the excitant folklore was undoubtedly more universal in the past than in the present.

Probably all the other victims whose cases were like mine had had a long and familiar knowledge of the tales I had learned only when in my secondary state. When these victims had lost their memory, they had associated themselves with the creatures of their household myths – the fabulous invaders supposed to displace men's minds – and had thus embarked upon quests for knowledge which they thought they could take back to a fancied, non-human past.

Then, when their memory returned, they reversed the associative process and thought of themselves as the former captive minds instead of as the displacers. Hence the dreams and pseudo-memories following the conventional myth pattern.

Despite the seeming cumbrousness of these explanations, they came finally to supersede all others in my mind – largely because of the greater weakness of any rival theory. And a substantial number of eminent psychologists and anthropologists gradually agreed with me.

The more I reflected, the more convincing did my reasoning seem; till in the end I had a really effective bulwark against the visions and impressions which still assailed me. Suppose I did see strange things at night? These were only what I had heard and read of. Suppose I did have odd loathings and perspectives and pseudo-memories? These, too, were only echoes of myths absorbed in my secondary state. Nothing that I might dream, nothing that I might feel, could be of any actual significance.

Fortified by this philosophy, I greatly improved in nervous equilibrium, even though the visions – rather than the abstract impressions – steadily became more frequent and more disturbingly detailed. In 1922 I felt able to undertake regular work again, and put my newly gained knowledge to practical use by accepting an instructorship in psychology at the university.

My old chair of political economy had long been adequately filled – besides which, methods of teaching economics had changed greatly since my heyday. My son was at this time just entering on the post-graduate studies leading to his present professorship, and we worked together a great deal.

Chapter IV

I CONTINUED, however, to keep a careful record of the outré dreams which crowded upon me so thickly and vividly. Such a record, I argued, was of genuine value as a psychological document. The glimpses still seemed damnably like memories, though I fought off this impression with a goodly measure of success.

In writing, I treated the phantasmata as things seen; but at all other times I brushed them aside like any gossamer illusions of the night. I had never mentioned such matters in common conversation; though reports of them, filtering out as such things will, had aroused sundry rumors regarding my mental health. It is amusing to reflect that these rumors were confined wholly to laymen, without a single champion among physicians or psychologists.

Of my visions after 1914 I will here mention only a few, since fuller accounts and records are at the disposal of the serious student. It is evident that with time the curious inhibitions somewhat waned, for the scope of my visions vastly increased. They have never, though, become other than disjointed fragments seemingly without clear motivation.

Within the dreams I seemed gradually to acquire a greater and greater freedom of wandering. I floated through many strange buildings of stone, going from one to the other along mammoth underground passages which seemed to form the common avenues of transit. Sometimes I encountered those gigantic sealed trap-doors in the lowest level, around which such an aura of fear and forbiddenness clung.

I saw tremendously tessellated pools, and rooms of curious and inexplicable utensils of myriad sorts. Then there were colossal caverns of intricate machinery whose outlines and purpose were wholly strange to me, and whose sound manifested itself only after many years of dreaming. I may here remark that sight and sound are the only senses I have ever exercised in the visionary world.

The real horror began in May, 1915, when I first saw the living things. This was before my studies had taught me what, in view of the myths and case histories, to expect. As mental barriers wore down, I beheld great masses of thin vapour in various parts of the building and in the streets below.

These steadily grew more solid and distinct, till at last I could trace their monstrous outlines with uncomfortable ease. They seemed to be enormous, iridescent cones, about ten feet high and ten feet wide at the base, and made up of some ridgy, scaly, semi-elastic matter. From their apexes projected four flexible, cylindrical members, each a foot thick, and of a ridgy substance like that of the cones themselves.

These members were sometimes contracted almost to nothing, and sometimes extended to any distance up to about ten feet. Terminating two of them were enormous claws or nippers. At the end of a third were four red, trumpetlike appendages. The fourth terminated in an irregular yellowish globe some two feet in diameter and having three great dark eyes ranged along its central circumference.

Surmounting this head were four slender grey stalks bearing flower-like appendages, whilst from its nether side dangled eight greenish antennae or tentacles. The great base of the central cone was fringed with a rubbery, grey substance which moved the whole entity through expansion and contraction.

Their actions, though harmless, horrified me even more than their appearance – for it is not wholesome to watch monstrous objects doing what one had known only human beings to do. These objects moved intelligently about the great rooms, getting books from the shelves and taking them to the great tables, or vice versa, and sometimes writing diligently with a peculiar rod gripped in the greenish head tentacles. The huge nippers were used in carrying books and in conversation-speech consisting of a kind of clicking and scraping.

The objects had no clothing, but wore satchels or knapsacks suspended from the top of the conical trunk. They commonly carried their head and its supporting member at the level of the cone top, although it was frequently raised or lowered.

The other three great members tended to rest downward at the sides of the cone, contracted to about five feet each when not in use. From their rate of reading, writing, and operating their machines – those on the tables seemed somehow connected with thought – I concluded that their intelligence was enormously greater than man's.

Afterward I saw them everywhere; swarming in all the great chambers and corridors, tending monstrous machines in vaulted crypts, and racing along the vast roads in gigantic, boat-shaped cars. I ceased to be afraid of them, for they seemed to form supremely natural parts of their environment.

Individual differences amongst them began to be manifest, and a few appeared to be under some kind of restraint. These latter, though shewing no physical variation, had a diversity of gestures and habits which marked them off not only from the majority, but very largely from one another.

They wrote a great deal in what seemed to my cloudy vision a vast variety of characters – never the typical curvilinear hieroglyphs of the majority. A few, I fancied, used our own familiar alphabet. Most of them worked much more slowly than the general mass of the entities.

All this time my own part in the dreams seemed to be that of a disembodied consciousness with a range of vision wider than the normal, floating freely about, yet confined to the ordinary avenues and speeds of travel. Not until August, 1915, did any suggestions of bodily existence begin to harass me. I say harass, because the first phase was a purely abstract, though infinitely terrible, association of my previously noted body loathing with the scenes of my visions.

For a while my chief concern during dreams was to avoid looking down at myself, and I recall how grateful I was for the total absence of large mirrors in the strange rooms. I was mightily troubled by the fact that I always saw the great tables – whose height could not be under ten feet – from a level not below that of their surfaces.

And then the morbid temptation to look down at myself became greater and greater, till one night I could not resist it. At first my downward glance revealed nothing whatever. A moment later I perceived that this was because my head lay at the end of a flexible neck of enormous length. Retracting this neck and gazing down very sharply, I saw the scaly, rugose, iridescent bulk of a vast cone ten feet tall and ten feet wide at the base.

That was when I waked half of Arkham with my screaming as I plunged madly up from the abyss of sleep.

Only after weeks of hideous repetition did I grow half-reconciled to these visions of myself in monstrous form. In the dreams I now moved bodily among the other unknown entities, reading terrible books from the endless shelves and writing for hours at the great tables with a stylus managed by the green tentacles that hung down from my head.

Snatches of what I read and wrote would linger in my memory. There were horrible annals of other worlds and other universes, and of stirrings of formless life outside of all universes. There were records of strange orders of beings which had peopled the world in forgotten pasts, and frightful chronicles of grotesque-bodied intelligences which would people it millions of years after the death of the last human being.

I learned of chapters in human history whose existence no scholar of today has ever suspected. Most of these writings were in the language of the hieroglyphs; which I studied in a queer way with the aid of droning machines, and which was evidently an agglutinative speech with root systems utterly unlike any found in human languages.

Other volumes were in other unknown tongues learned in the same queer way. A very few were in languages I knew. Extremely clever pictures, both inserted in the records and forming separate collections, aided me immensely. And all the time I seemed to be setting down a history of my own age in English. On waking, I could recall only minute and meaningless scraps of the unknown tongues which my dream-self had mastered, though whole phrases of the history stayed with me.

I learned – even before my waking self had studied the parallel cases or the old myths from which the dreams doubtless sprang – that the entities around me were of the world's greatest race, which had conquered time and had sent exploring minds into every age. I knew, too, that I had been snatched from my age while another used my body in that age, and that a few of the other strange forms housed similarly captured minds. I seemed to talk, in some odd language of claw clickings, with exiled intellects from every corner of the solar system.

There was a mind from the planet we know as Venus, which would live incalculable epochs to come, and one from an outer moon of Jupiter six million years in the past. Of earthly minds there were some from the winged, star-headed, half-vegetable race of palaeogean Antarctica; one from the reptile people of fabled Valusia; three from the furry pre-human Hyperborean worshippers of Tsathoggua; one from the wholly abominable Tcho-Tchos; two from the arachnid denizens of earth's last age; five from the hardy coleopterous species immediately following mankind, to which the Great Race was some day to transfer its keenest minds en masse in the face of horrible peril; and several from different branches of humanity.

I talked with the mind of Yiang-Li, a philosopher from the cruel empire of Tsan-Chan, which is to come in 5,000 A.D.; with that of a general of the greatheaded brown people who held South Africa in 50,000 B.C.; with that of a twelfth-century Florentine monk named Bartolomeo Corsi; with that of a king of Lomar who had ruled that terrible polar land one hundred thousand years before the squat, yellow Inutos came from the west to engulf it.

I talked with the mind of Nug-Soth, a magician of the dark conquerors of 16,000 A.D.; with that of a Roman named Titus Sempronius Blaesus, who had been a quaestor in Sulla's time; with that of Khephnes, an Egyptian of the 14th Dynasty, who told me the hideous secret of Nyarlathotep; with that of a priest of Atlantis' middle kingdom; with that of a Suffolk gentleman of Cromwell's day, James Woodville; with that of a court astronomer of pre-Inca Peru; with that of the Australian physicist Nevil Kingston-Brown, who will die in 2,518 A.D.; with that of an archimage of vanished Yhe in the Pacific; with that of Theodotides, a Greco-Bactrian official of 200 B.C.; with that of an aged Frenchman of Louis XIII's time named Pierre-Louis Montagny; with that of Crom-Ya, a Cimmerian chieftain of 15,000 B.C.; and with so many others that my brain cannot hold the shocking secrets and dizzying marvels I learned from them.

I awaked each morning in a fever, sometimes frantically trying to verify or discredit such information as fell within the range of modern human knowledge. Traditional facts took on new and doubtful aspects, and I marvelled at the dream-fancy which could invent such surprising addenda to history and science.

I shivered at the mysteries the past may conceal, and trembled at the menaces the future may bring forth. What was hinted in the speech of post-human entities of the fate of mankind produced such an effect on me that I will not set it down here.

After man there would be the mighty beetle civilisation, the bodies of whose members the cream of the Great Race would seize when the monstrous doom overtook the elder world. Later, as the earth's span closed, the transferred minds would again migrate through time and space – to another stopping-place in the bodies of the bulbous vegetable entities of Mercury. But there would be races after them, clinging pathetically to the cold planet and burrowing to its horror-filled core, before the utter end.

Meanwhile, in my dreams, I wrote endlessly in that history of my own age which I was preparing – half voluntarily and half through promises of increased library and travel opportunities – for the Great Race's central archives. The archives were in a colossal subterranean structure near the city's center, which I came to know well through frequent labors and consultations. Meant to last as long as the race, and to withstand the fiercest of earth's convulsions, this titan repository surpassed all other buildings in the massive, mountain-like firmness of its construction.

The records, written or printed on great sheets of a curiously tenacious cellulose fabric were bound into books that opened from the top, and were kept in individual cases of a strange, extremely light, rustless metal of greyish hue, decorated with mathematical designs and bearing the title in the Great Race's curvilinear hieroglyphs.

These cases were stored in tiers of rectangular vaults – like closed, locked shelves – wrought of the same rustless metal and fastened by knobs with intricate turnings. My own history was assigned a specific place in the vaults of the lowest or vertebrate level – the section devoted to the culture of mankind and of the furry and reptilian races immediately preceding it in terrestrial dominance.

But none of the dreams ever gave me a full picture of daily life. All were the merest misty, disconnected fragments, and it is certain that these fragments were not unfolded in their rightful sequence. I have, for example, a very imperfect idea of my own living arrangements in the dream-world; though I seem to have possessed a great stone room of my own. My restrictions as a prisoner gradually disappeared, so that some of the visions included vivid travels over the mighty jungle roads, sojourns in strange cities, and explorations of some of the vast, dark, windowless ruins from which the Great Race shrank in curious fear. There were also long sea voyages in enormous, many-decked boats of incredible swiftness, and trips over wild regions in closed projectile-like airships lifted and moved by electrical repulsion.

Beyond the wide, warm ocean were other cities of the Great Race, and on one far continent I saw the crude villages of the black-snouted, winged creatures who would evolve as a dominant stock after the Great Race had sent its foremost minds into the future to escape the creeping horror. Flatness and exuberant green life were always the keynote of the scene. Hills were low and sparse, and usually displayed signs of volcanic forces.

Of the animals I saw, I could write volumes. All were wild; for the Great Race's mechanised culture had long since done away with domestic beasts, while food was wholly vegetable or synthetic. Clumsy reptiles of great bulk floundered in steaming morasses, fluttered in the heavy air, or spouted in the seas and lakes; and among these I fancied I could vaguely recognise lesser, archaic prototypes of many forms – dinosaurs, pterodactyls, ichthyosaurs, labyrinthodonts, plesiosaurs, and the like-made familiar through palaeontology. Of birds or mammals there were none that I could discover.

The ground and swamps were constantly alive with snakes, lizards, and crocodiles while insects buzzed incessantly among the lush vegetation. And far out at sea, unspied and unknown monsters spouted mountainous columns of foam into the vaporous sky. Once I was taken under the ocean in a gigantic submarine vessel with searchlights, and glimpsed some living horrors of awesome magnitude. I saw also the ruins of incredible sunken cities, and the wealth of crinoid, brachiopod, coral, and ichthyic life which everywhere abounded.

Of the physiology, psychology, folkways, and detailed history of the Great Race my visions preserved but little information, and many of the scattered points I here set down were gleaned from my study of old legends and other cases rather than from my own dreaming.

For in time, of course, my reading and research caught up with and passed the dreams in many phases, so that certain dream-fragments were explained in advance and formed verifications of what I had learned. This consolingly established my belief that similar reading and research, accomplished by my secondary self, had formed the source of the whole terrible fabric of pseudomemories.

The period of my dreams, apparently, was one somewhat less than 150,000,000 years ago, when the Palaeozoic age was giving place to the Mesozoic. The bodies occupied by the Great Race represented no surviving – or even scientifically known – line of terrestrial evolution, but were of a peculiar, closely homogeneous, and highly specialised organic type inclining as much as to the vegetable as to the animal state.

Cell action was of an unique sort almost precluding fatigue, and wholly eliminating the need of sleep. Nourishment, assimilated through the red trumpet-like appendages on one of the great flexible limbs, was always semi-fluid and in many aspects wholly unlike the food of existing animals.

The beings had but two of the senses which we recognise – sight and hearing, the latter accomplished through the flower-like appendages on the grey stalks above their heads. Of other and incomprehensible senses – not, however, well utilizable by alien captive minds inhabiting their bodies – they possessed many. Their three eyes were so situated as to give them a range of vision wider than the normal. Their blood was a sort of deep-greenish ichor of great thickness.

They had no sex, but reproduced through seeds or spores which clustered on their bases and could be developed only under water. Great, shallow tanks were used for the growth of their young – which were, however, reared only in small numbers on account of the longevity of individuals – four or five thousand years being the common life span.

Markedly defective individuals were quickly disposed of as soon as their defects were noticed. Disease and the approach of death were, in the absence of a sense of touch or of physical pain, recognised by purely visual symptoms.

The dead were incinerated with dignified ceremonies. Once in a while, as before mentioned, a keen mind would escape death by forward projection in time; but such cases were not numerous. When one did occur, the exiled mind from the future was treated with the utmost kindness till the dissolution of its unfamiliar tenement.

The Great Race seemed to form a single, loosely knit nation or league, with major institutions in common, though there were four definite divisions. The political and economic system of each unit was a sort of fascistic socialism, with major resources rationally distributed, and power delegated to a small governing board elected by the votes of all able to pass certain educational and psychological tests. Family organisation was not overstressed, though ties among persons of common descent were recognised, and the young were generally reared by their parents.

Resemblances to human attitudes and institutions were, of course, most marked in those fields where on the one hand highly abstract elements were concerned, or where on the other hand there was a dominance of the basic, unspecialised urges common to all organic life. A few added likenesses came through conscious adoption as the Great Race probed the future and copied what it liked.

Industry, highly mechanised, demanded but little time from each citizen; and the abundant leisure was filled with intellectual and aesthetic activities of various sorts.

The sciences were carried to an unbelievable height of development, and art was a vital part of life, though at the period of my dreams it had passed its crest and meridian. Technology was enormously stimulated through the constant struggle to survive, and to keep in existence the physical fabric of great cities, imposed by the prodigious geologic upheavals of those primal days.

Crime was surprisingly scant, and was dealt with through highly efficient policing. Punishments ranged from privilege deprivation and imprisonment to death or major emotion wrenching, and were never administered without a careful study of the criminal's motivations.

Warfare, largely civil for the last few millennia though sometimes waged against reptilian or octopodic invaders, or against the winged, star-headed Old Ones who centered in the antarctic, was infrequent though infinitely devastating. An enormous army, using camera-like weapons which produced tremendous electrical effects, was kept on hand for purposes seldom mentioned, but obviously connected with the ceaseless fear of the dark, windowless elder ruins and of the great sealed trap-doors in the lowest subterranean levels.

This fear of the basalt ruins and trap-doors was largely a matter of unspoken suggestion – or, at most, of furtive quasi-whispers. Everything specific which bore on it was significantly absent from such books as were on the common shelves. It was the one subject lying altogether under a taboo among the Great Race, and seemed to be connected alike with horrible bygone struggles, and with that future peril which would some day force the race to send its keener minds ahead en masse in time.

Imperfect and fragmentary as were the other things presented by dreams and legends, this matter was still more bafflingly shrouded. The vague old myths avoided it – or perhaps all allusions had for some reason been excised. And in the dreams of myself and others, the hints were peculiarly few. Members of the Great Race never intentionally referred to the matter, and what could be gleaned came only from some of the more sharply observant captive minds.

According to these scraps of information, the basis of the fear was a horrible elder race of half-polypous, utterly alien entities which had come through space from immeasurably distant universes and had dominated the earth and three other solar planets about 600 million years ago. They were only partly material – as we understand matter – and their type of consciousness and media of perception differed widely from those of terrestrial organisms. For example, their senses did not include that of sight; their mental world being a strange, non-visual pattern of impressions.

They were, however, sufficiently material to use implements of normal matter when in cosmic areas containing it; and they required housing – albeit of a peculiar kind. Though their senses could penetrate all material barriers, their substance could not; and certain forms of electrical energy could wholly destroy them. They had the power of aerial motion, despite the absence of wings or any other visible means of levitation. Their minds were of such texture that no exchange with them could be effected by the Great Race.

When these things had come to the earth they had built mighty basalt cities of windowless towers, and had preyed horribly upon the beings they found. Thus it was when the minds of the Great Race sped across the void from that obscure, trans-galactic world known in the disturbing and debatable Eltdown Shards as Yith.

The newcomers, with the instruments they created, had found it easy to subdue the predatory entities and drive them down to those caverns of inner earth which they had already joined to their abodes and begun to inhabit.

Then they had sealed the entrances and left them to their fate, afterward occupying most of their great cities and preserving certain important buildings for reasons connected more with superstition than with indifference, boldness, or scientific and historical zeal.

But as the aeons passed there came vague, evil signs that the elder things were growing strong and numerous in the inner world. There were sporadic irruptions of a particularly hideous character in certain small and remote cities of the Great Race, and in some of the deserted elder cities which the Great Race had not peopled – places where the paths to the gulfs below had not been properly sealed or guarded.

After that greater precautions were taken, and many of the paths were closed forever – though a few were left with sealed trap-doors for strategic use in fighting the elder things if ever they broke forth in unexpected places.

The irruptions of the elder things must have been shocking beyond all description, since they had permanently coloured the psychology of the Great Race. Such was the fixed mood of horror that the very aspect of the creatures was left unmentioned. At no time was I able to gain a clear hint of what they looked like.

There were veiled suggestions of a monstrous plasticity, and of temporary lapses of visibility, while other fragmentary whispers referred to their control and military use of great winds. Singular whistling noises, and colossal footprints made up of five circular toe marks, seemed also to be associated with them.

It was evident that the coming doom so desperately feared by the Great Race – the doom that was one day to send millions of keen minds across the chasm of time to strange bodies in the safer future – had to do with a final successful irruption of the elder beings.

Mental projections down the ages had clearly foretold such a horror, and the Great Race had resolved that none who could escape should face it. That the foray would be a matter of vengeance, rather than an attempt to reoccupy the outer world, they knew from the planet's later history – for their projections shewed the coming and going of subsequent races untroubled by the monstrous entities.

Perhaps these entities had come to prefer earth's inner abysses to the variable, storm-ravaged surface, since light meant nothing to them. Perhaps, too, they were slowly weakening with the aeons. Indeed, it was known that they would be quite dead in the time of the post-human beetle race which the fleeing minds would tenant.

Meanwhile, the Great Race maintained its cautious vigilance, with potent weapons ceaselessly ready despite the horrified banishing of the subject from common speech and visible records. And always the shadow of nameless fear hung about the sealed trap-doors and the dark, windowless elder towers.

Chapter V

THAT IS THE WORLD of which my dreams brought me dim, scattered echoes every night. I cannot hope to give any true idea of the horror and dread contained in such echoes, for it was upon a wholly intangible quality – the sharp sense of pseudo-memory – that such feelings mainly depended.

As I have said, my studies gradually gave me a defence against these feelings in the form of rational psychological explanations; and this saving influence was augmented by the subtle touch of accustomedness which comes with the passage of time. Yet in spite of everything the vague, creeping terror would return momentarily now and then. It did not, however, engulf me as it had before; and after 1922 I lived a very normal life of work and recreation.

In the course of years I began to feel that my experience – together with the kindred cases and the related folklore – ought to be definitely summarised and published for the benefit of serious students; hence I prepared a series of articles briefly covering the whole ground and illustrated with crude sketches of some of the shapes, scenes, decorative motifs, and hieroglyphs remembered from the dreams.

These appeared at various times during 1928 and 1929 in the *Journal of the American Psychological Society*, but did not attract much attention. Meanwhile I continued to record my dreams with the minutest care, even though the growing stack of reports attained troublesomely vast proportions. On July 10, 1934, there was forwarded to me by the Psychological Society the letter which opened the culminating and most horrible phase of the whole mad ordeal. It was postmarked Pilbarra, Western Australia, and bore the signature of one whom I found, upon inquiry, to be a mining engineer of considerable prominence. Enclosed were some very curious snapshots. I will reproduce the text in its entirety, and no reader can fail to understand how tremendous an effect it and the photographs had upon me.

I was, for a time, almost stunned and incredulous; for although I had often thought that some basis of fact must underlie certain phases of the legends which had coloured my dreams, I was none the less unprepared for anything like a tangible survival from a lost world remote beyond all imagination. Most devastating of all were the photographs – for here, in cold, incontrovertible realism, there stood out against a background of sand certain worn-down, water-ridged, storm-weathered blocks of stone whose slightly convex tops and slightly concave bottoms told their own story.

And when I studied them with a magnifying glass I could see all too plainly, amidst the batterings and pittings, the traces of those vast curvilinear designs and occasional hieroglyphs whose significance had become so hideous to me. But here is the letter, which speaks for itself.

49, Dampier St.,
Pilbarra, W. Australia,
May 18, 1934.

Prof. N. W Peaslee,
c/o Am. Psychological Society,
30 E. 41st St.,
New York City, U.S.A.

My Dear Sir –

*A recent conversation with Dr. E.M. Boyle of Perth, and some papers with
your articles which he has just sent me, make it advisable for me to tell you about
certain things I have seen in the Great Sandy Desert east of our gold field here. It
would seem, in view of the peculiar legends about old cities with huge stonework
and strange designs and hieroglyphs which you describe, that I have come upon
something very important.*

*The blackfellows have always been full of talk about 'great stones with marks
on them,' and seem to have a terrible fear of such things. They connect them in some
way with their common racial legends about Buddai, the gigantic old man who
lies asleep for ages underground with his head on his arm, and who will some day
awake and eat up the world.*

*There are some very old and half-forgotten tales of enormous underground
huts of great stones, where passages lead down and down, and where horrible
things have happened. The blackfellows claim that once some warriors, fleeing in
battle, went down into one and never came back, but that frightful winds began to
blow from the place soon after they went down. However, there usually isn't much
in what these natives say.*

*But what I have to tell is more than this. Two years ago, when I was prospecting
about 500 miles east in the desert, I came on a lot of queer pieces of dressed stone
perhaps 3 × 2 × 2 feet in size, and weathered and pitted to the very limit.*

*At first I couldn't find any of the marks the blackfellows told about, but
when I looked close enough I could make out some deeply carved lines in spite
of the weathering. There were peculiar curves, just like what the blackfellows
had tried to describe. I imagine there must have been thirty or forty blocks, some
nearly buried in the sand, and all within a circle perhaps a quarter of a mile
in diameter.*

*When I saw some, I looked around closely for more, and made a careful
reckoning of the place with my instruments. I also took pictures of ten or twelve of
the most typical blocks, and will enclose the prints for you to see.*

*I turned my information and pictures over to the government at Perth, but
they have done nothing about them.*

*Then I met Dr. Boyle, who had read your articles in the Journal of the
American Psychological Society, and, in time, happened to mention the stones.
He was enormously interested, and became quite excited when I shewed him
my snapshots, saying that the stones and the markings were just like those of the
masonry you had dreamed about and seen described in legends.*

*He meant to write you, but was delayed. Meanwhile, he sent me most of
the magazines with your articles, and I saw at once, from your drawings and*

descriptions, that my stones are certainly the kind you mean. You can appreciate this from the enclosed prints. Later on you will hear directly from Dr. Boyle.

Now I can understand how important all this will be to you. Without question we are faced with the remains of an unknown civilization older than any dreamed of before, and forming a basis for your legends.

As a mining engineer, I have some knowledge of geology, and can tell you that these blocks are so ancient they frighten me. They are mostly sandstone and granite, though one is almost certainly made of a queer sort of cement or concrete.

They bear evidence of water action, as if this part of the world had been submerged and come up again after long ages – all since those blocks were made and used. It is a matter of hundreds of thousands of years – or heaven knows how much more. I don't like to think about it.

In view of your previous diligent work in tracking down the legends and everything connected with them, I cannot doubt but that you will want to lead an expedition to the desert and make some archaeological excavations. Both Dr. Boyle and I are prepared to cooperate in such work if you – or organizations known to you – can furnish the funds.

I can get together a dozen miners for the heavy digging – the blackfellows would be of no use, for I've found that they have an almost maniacal fear of this particular spot. Boyle and I are saying nothing to others, for you very obviously ought to have precedence in any discoveries or credit.

The place can be reached from Pilbarra in about four days by motor tractor – which we'd need for our apparatus. It is somewhat west and south of Warburton's path of 1873, and 100 miles southeast of Joanna Spring. We could float things up the De Grey River instead of starting from Pilbarra – but all that can be talked over later.

Roughly the stones lie at a point about 22° 3' 14" South Latitude, 125° 0' 39" East Longitude. The climate is tropical, and the desert conditions are trying.

I shall welcome further correspondence upon this subject, and am keenly eager to assist in any plan you may devise. After studying your articles I am deeply impressed with the profound significance of the whole matter. Dr. Boyle will write later. When rapid communication is needed, a cable to Perth can be relayed by wireless.

Hoping profoundly for an early message,
Believe me,
Most faithfully yours,
Robert B.F. Mackenzie

Of the immediate aftermath of this letter, much can be learned from the press. My good fortune in securing the backing of Miskatonic University was great, and both Mr. Mackenzie and Dr. Boyle proved invaluable in arranging matters at the Australian end. We were not too specific with the public about our objects, since the whole matter would have lent itself unpleasantly to sensational and jocose treatment by the cheaper newspapers. As a result, printed reports were sparing; but enough appeared to tell of our quest for reported Australian ruins and to chronicle our various preparatory steps.

Professor William Dyer of the college's geology department – leader of the Miskatonic Antarctic Expedition Of 1930–31 – Ferdinand C. Ashley of the department of ancient history, and Tyler M. Freeborn of the department of anthropology – together with my son Wingate – accompanied me.

My correspondent, Mackenzie, came to Arkham early in 1935 and assisted in our final preparations. He proved to be a tremendously competent and affable man of about fifty, admirably well-read, and deeply familiar with all the conditions of Australian travel.

He had tractors waiting at Pilbarra, and we chartered a tramp steamer sufficiently small to get up the river to that point. We were prepared to excavate in the most careful and scientific fashion, sifting every particle of sand, and disturbing nothing which might seem to be in or near its original situation.

Sailing from Boston aboard the wheezy *Lexington* on March 28, 1935, we had a leisurely trip across the Atlantic and Mediterranean, through the Suez Canal, down the Red Sea, and across the Indian Ocean to our goal. I need not tell how the sight of the low, sandy West Australian coast depressed me, and how I detested the crude mining town and dreary gold fields where the tractors were given their last loads.

Dr. Boyle, who met us, proved to be elderly, pleasant, and intelligent – and his knowledge of psychology led him into many long discussions with my son and me.

Discomfort and expectancy were oddly mingled in most of us when at length our party of eighteen rattled forth over the arid leagues of sand and rock. On Friday, May 31st, we forded a branch of the De Grey and entered the realm of utter desolation. A certain positive terror grew on me as we advanced to this actual site of the elder world behind the legends – a terror, of course, abetted by the fact that my disturbing dreams and pseudo-memories still beset me with unabated force.

It was on Monday, June 3rd, that we saw the first of the half-buried blocks. I cannot describe the emotions with which I actually touched – in objective reality – a fragment of Cyclopean masonry in every respect like the blocks in the walls of my dream-buildings. There was a distinct trace of carving – and my hands trembled as I recognised part of a curvilinear decorative scheme made hellish to me through years of tormenting nightmare and baffling research.

A month of digging brought a total of some 1250 blocks in varying stages of wear and disintegration. Most of these were carven megaliths with curved tops and bottoms. A minority were smaller, flatter, plain-surfaced, and square or octagonally cut-like those of the floors and pavements in my dreams – while a few were singularly massive and curved or slanted in such a manner as to suggest use in vaulting or groining, or as parts of arches or round window casings.

The deeper – and the farther north and east – we dug, the more blocks we found; though we still failed to discover any trace of arrangement among them. Professor Dyer was appalled at the measureless age of the fragments, and Freeborn found traces of symbols which fitted darkly into certain Papuan and Polynesian legends of infinite antiquity. The condition and scattering of the blocks told mutely of vertiginous cycles of time and geologic upheavals of cosmic savagery.

We had an aeroplane with us, and my son Wingate would often go up to different heights and scan the sand-and-rock waste for signs of dim, large-scale outlines – either differences of level or trails of scattered blocks. His results were virtually negative; for whenever he would one day think he had glimpsed some significant trend, he would on his next trip find the impression replaced by another equally insubstantial – a result of the shifting, wind-blown sand.

One or two of these ephemeral suggestions, though, affected me queerly and disagreeably. They seemed, after a fashion, to dovetail horribly with something I had dreamed or read, but which I could no longer remember. There was a terrible familiarity about them – which somehow made me look furtively and apprehensively over the abominable, sterile terrain toward the north and northeast.

Around the first week in July I developed an unaccountable set of mixed emotions about that general northeasterly region. There was horror, and there was curiosity – but more than that, there was a persistent and perplexing illusion of memory.

I tried all sorts of psychological expedients to get these notions out of my head, but met with no success. Sleeplessness also gained upon me, but I almost welcomed this because of the resultant shortening of my dream-periods. I acquired the habit of taking long, lone walks in the desert late at night – usually to the north or northeast, whither the sum of my strange new impulses seemed subtly to pull me.

Sometimes, on these walks, I would stumble over nearly buried fragments of the ancient masonry. Though there were fewer visible blocks here than where we had started, I felt sure that there must be a vast abundance beneath the surface. The ground was less level than at our camp, and the prevailing high winds now and then piled the sand into fantastic temporary hillocks – exposing low traces of the elder stones while it covered other traces.

I was queerly anxious to have the excavations extend to this territory, yet at the same time dreaded what might be revealed. Obviously, I was getting into a rather bad state – all the worse because I could not account for it.

An indication of my poor nervous health can be gained from my response to an odd discovery which I made on one of my nocturnal rambles. It was on the evening of July 11th, when the moon flooded the mysterious hillocks with a curious pallor.

Wandering somewhat beyond my usual limits, I came upon a great stone which seemed to differ markedly from any we had yet encountered. It was almost wholly covered, but I stooped and cleared away the sand with my hands, later studying the object carefully and supplementing the moonlight with my electric torch.

Unlike the other very large rocks, this one was perfectly square-cut, with no convex or concave surface. It seemed, too, to be of a dark basaltic substance, wholly dissimilar to the granite and sandstone and occasional concrete of the now familiar fragments.

Suddenly I rose, turned, and ran for the camp at top speed. It was a wholly unconscious and irrational flight, and only when I was close to my tent did I fully realise why I had run. Then it came to me. The queer dark stone was something which I had dreamed and read about, and which was linked with the uttermost horrors of the aeon-old legendry.

It was one of the blocks of that basaltic elder masonry which the fabled Great Race held in such fear – the tall, windowless ruins left by those brooding, half-material, alien things that festered in earth's nether abysses and against whose wind-like, invisible forces the trap-doors were sealed and the sleepless sentinels posted.

I remained awake all night, but by dawn realised how silly I had been to let the shadow of a myth upset me. Instead of being frightened, I should have had a discoverer's enthusiasm.

The next forenoon I told the others about my find, and Dyer, Freeborn, Boyle, my son, and I set out to view the anomalous block. Failure, however, confronted us. I had formed no clear idea of the stone's location, and a late wind had wholly altered the hillocks of shifting sand.

Chapter VI

I COME NOW to the crucial and most difficult part of my narrative – all the more difficult because I cannot be quite certain of its reality. At times I feel uncomfortably sure that I was not dreaming or deluded; and it is this feeling in view of the stupendous implications which the objective truth of my experience would raise – which impels me to make this record.

My son – a trained psychologist with the fullest and most sympathetic knowledge of my whole case – shall be the primary judge of what I have to tell.

First let me outline the externals of the matter, as those at the camp know them. On the night of July 17–18, after a windy day, I retired early but could not sleep. Rising shortly before eleven, and afflicted as usual with that strange feeling regarding the northeastward terrain, I set out on one of my typical nocturnal walks; seeing and greeting only one person – an Australian miner named Tupper – as I left our precincts.

The moon, slightly past full, shone from a clear sky, and drenched the ancient sands with a white, leprous radiance which seemed to me somehow infinitely evil. There was no longer any wind, nor did any return for nearly five hours, as amply attested by Tupper and others who saw me walking rapidly across the pallid, secret-guarding hillocks toward the northeast.

About 3:30 a.m. a violent wind blew up, waking everyone in camp and felling three of the tents. The sky was unclouded, and the desert still blazed with that leprous moonlight. As the party saw to the tents my absence was noted, but in view of my previous walks this circumstance gave no one alarm. And yet, as many as three men – all Australians – seemed to feel something sinister in the air.

Mackenzie explained to Professor Freeborn that this was a fear picked up from blackfellow folklore – the natives having woven a curious fabric of malignant myth about the high winds which at long intervals sweep across the sands under a clear sky. Such winds, it is whispered, blow out of the great stone huts under the ground, where terrible things have happened – and are never felt except near places where the big marked stones are scattered. Close to four the gale subsided as suddenly as it had begun, leaving the sand hills in new and unfamiliar shapes.

It was just past five, with the bloated, fungoid moon sinking in the west, when I staggered into camp – hatless, tattered, features scratched and ensanguined, and without my electric torch. Most of the men had returned to bed, but Professor Dyer was smoking a pipe in front of his tent. Seeing my winded and almost frenzied state, he called Dr. Boyle, and the two of them got me on my cot and made me comfortable. My son, roused by the stir, soon joined them, and they all tried to force me to lie still and attempt sleep.

But there was no sleep for me. My psychological state was very extraordinary – different from anything I had previously suffered. After a time I insisted upon talking – nervously and elaborately explaining my condition. I told them I had become fatigued, and had lain down in the sand for a nap. There had, I said, been dreams even more frightful than usual – and when I was awaked by the sudden high wind my overwrought nerves had snapped. I had fled in panic, frequently falling over half-buried stones and thus gaining my tattered and bedraggled aspect. I must have slept long – hence the hours of my absence.

Of anything strange either seen or experienced I hinted absolutely nothing – exercising the greatest self-control in that respect. But I spoke of a change of mind regarding the whole work of the expedition, and urged a halt in all digging toward the northeast. My reasoning was patently weak – for I mentioned a dearth of blocks, a wish not to offend the superstitious miners, a possible shortage of funds from the college, and other things either untrue or irrelevant. Naturally, no one paid the least attention to my new wishes – not even my son, whose concern for my health was obvious.

The next day I was up and around the camp, but took no part in the excavations. Seeing that I could not stop the work, I decided to return home as soon as possible for the sake of my nerves, and made my son promise to fly me in the plane to Perth – a thousand miles to the southwest – as soon as he had surveyed the region I wished let alone.

If, I reflected, the thing I had seen was still visible, I might decide to attempt a specific warning even at the cost of ridicule. It was just conceivable that the miners who knew the local folklore might back me up. Humouring me, my son made the survey that very afternoon, flying over all the terrain my walk could possibly have covered. Yet nothing of what I had found remained in sight.

It was the case of the anomalous basalt block all over again – the shifting sand had wiped out every trace. For an instant I half regretted having lost a certain awesome object in my stark fright – but now I know that the loss was merciful. I can still believe my whole experience an illusion – especially if, as I devoutly hope, that hellish abyss is never found.

Wingate took me to Perth on July 20th, though declining to abandon the expedition and return home. He stayed with me until the 25th, when the steamer for Liverpool sailed. Now, in the cabin of the *Empress*, I am pondering long and frantically upon the entire matter, and have decided that my son at least must be informed. It shall rest with him whether to diffuse the matter more widely.

In order to meet any eventuality I have prepared this summary of my background – as already known in a scattered way to others – and will now tell as briefly as possible what seemed to happen during my absence from the camp that hideous night.

Nerves on edge, and whipped into a kind of perverse eagerness by that inexplicable, dread-mingled, mnemonic urge toward the northeast, I plodded on beneath the evil, burning moon. Here and there I saw, half shrouded by sand, those primal Cyclopean blocks left from nameless and forgotten aeons.

The incalculable age and brooding horror of this monstrous waste began to oppress me as never before, and I could not keep from thinking of my maddening dreams, of the frightful legends which lay behind them, and of the present fears of natives and miners concerning the desert and its carven stones.

And yet I plodded on as if to some eldritch rendezvous – more and more assailed by bewildering fancies, compulsions, and pseudo-memories. I thought of some of the possible contours of the lines of stones as seen by my son from the air, and wondered why they seemed at once so ominous and so familiar. Something was fumbling and rattling at the latch of my recollection, while another unknown force sought to keep the portal barred.

The night was windless, and the pallid sand curved upward and downward like frozen waves of the sea. I had no goal, but somehow ploughed along as if with fate-bound assurance. My dreams welled up into the waking world, so that each sand-embedded megalith seemed part of endless rooms and corridors of pre-human masonry, carved and hieroglyphed with symbols that I knew too well from years of custom as a captive mind of the Great Race.

At moments I fancied I saw those omniscient, conical horrors moving about at their accustomed tasks, and I feared to look down lest I find myself one with them in aspect. Yet all the while I saw the sand-covered blocks as well as the rooms and corridors; the evil, burning moon as well as the lamps of luminous crystal; the endless desert as well as the waving ferns beyond the windows. I was awake and dreaming at the same time.

I do not know how long or how far – or indeed, in just what direction – I had walked when I first spied the heap of blocks bared by the day's wind. It was the largest group in one place that I had seen so far, and so sharply did it impress me that the visions of fabulous aeons faded suddenly away.

Again there were only the desert and the evil moon and the shards of an unguessed past. I drew close and paused, and cast the added light of my electric torch over the tumbled pile. A hillock had blown away, leaving a low, irregularly round mass of megaliths and smaller fragments some forty feet across and from two to eight feet high.

From the very outset I realized that there was some utterly unprecedented quality about those stones. Not only was the mere number of them quite without parallel, but something in the sandworn traces of design arrested me as I scanned them under the mingled beams of the moon and my torch.

Not that any one differed essentially from the earlier specimens we had found. It was something subtler than that. The impression did not come when I looked at one block alone, but only when I ran my eye over several almost simultaneously.

Then, at last, the truth dawned upon me. The curvilinear patterns on many of those blocks were closely related – parts of one vast decorative conception. For the first time in this aeon-shaken waste I had come upon a mass of masonry in its old position – tumbled and fragmentary, it is true, but none the less existing in a very definite sense.

Mounting at a low place, I clambered laboriously over the heap; here and there clearing away the sand with my fingers, and constantly striving to interpret varieties of size, shape, and style, and relationships of design.

After a while I could vaguely guess at the nature of the bygone structure, and at the designs which had once stretched over the vast surfaces of the primal masonry. The perfect identity of the whole with some of my dream-glimpses appalled and unnerved me.

This was once a Cyclopean corridor thirty feet tall, paved with octagonal blocks and solidly vaulted overhead. There would have been rooms opening off on the right, and at the farther end one of those strange inclined planes would have wound down to still lower depths.

I started violently as these conceptions occurred to me, for there was more in them than the blocks themselves had supplied. How did I know that this level should have been far underground? How did I know that the plane leading upward should have been behind me? How did I know that the long subterrene passage to the Square of Pillars ought to lie on the left one level above me?

How did I know that the room of machines and the rightward-leading tunnel to the central archives ought to lie two levels below? How did I know that there would be one of those horrible, metal-banded trap-doors at the very bottom four levels down? Bewildered by this intrusion from the dream-world, I found myself shaking and bathed in a cold perspiration.

Then, as a last, intolerable touch, I felt that faint, insidious stream of cool air trickling upward from a depressed place near the center of the huge heap. Instantly, as once before, my visions faded, and I saw again only the evil moonlight, the brooding desert, and the spreading tumulus of palaeogean masonry. Something real and tangible, yet fraught with infinite suggestions of nighted mystery, now confronted me. For that stream of air could argue but one thing – a hidden gulf of great size beneath the disordered blocks on the surface.

My first thought was of the sinister blackfellow legends of vast underground huts among the megaliths where horrors happen and great winds are born. Then thoughts of my own dreams came back, and I felt dim pseudo-memories tugging at my mind. What manner of place lay below me? What primal, inconceivable source of age-old myth-cycles and haunting nightmares might I be on the brink of uncovering?

It was only for a moment that I hesitated, for more than curiosity and scientific zeal was driving me on and working against my growing fear.

I seemed to move almost automatically, as if in the clutch of some compelling fate. Pocketing my torch, and struggling with a strength that I had not thought I possessed, I wrenched aside first one titan fragment of stone and then another, till there welled up a strong draught whose dampness contrasted oddly with the desert's dry air. A black rift began to yawn, and at length – when I had pushed away every fragment small enough to budge – the leprous moonlight blazed on an aperture of ample width to admit me.

I drew out my torch and cast a brilliant beam into the opening. Below me was a chaos of tumbled masonry, sloping roughly down toward the north at an angle of about forty-five degrees, and evidently the result of some bygone collapse from above.

Between its surface and the ground level was a gulf of impenetrable blackness at whose upper edge were signs of gigantic, stress-heaved vaulting. At this point, it appeared, the desert's sands lay directly upon a floor of some titan structure of earth's youth – how preserved through aeons of geologic convulsion I could not then and cannot now even attempt to guess.

In retrospect, the barest idea of a sudden, lone descent into such a doubtful abyss – and at a time when one's whereabouts were unknown to any living soul – seems like the utter apex of insanity. Perhaps it was – yet that night I embarked without hesitancy upon such a descent.

Again there was manifest that lure and driving of fatality which had all along seemed to direct my course. With torch flashing intermittently to save the battery, I commenced a mad scramble down the sinister, Cyclopean incline below the opening – sometimes facing forward as I found good hand and foot holds, and at other times turning to face the heap of megaliths as I clung and fumbled more precariously.

In two directions beside me, distant walls of carven, crumbling masonry loomed dimly under the direct beams of my torch. Ahead, however, was only unbroken darkness.

I kept no track of time during my downward scramble. So seething with baffling hints and images was my mind that all objective matters seemed withdrawn into incalculable distances. Physical sensation was dead, and even fear remained as a wraith-like, inactive gargoyle leering impotently at me.

Eventually, I reached a level floor strewn with fallen blocks, shapeless fragments of stone, and sand and detritus of every kind. On either side – perhaps thirty feet apart – rose massive walls culminating in huge groinings. That they were carved I could just discern, but the nature of the carvings was beyond my perception.

What held me the most was the vaulting overhead. The beam from my torch could not reach the roof, but the lower parts of the monstrous arches stood out distinctly. And so perfect was their identity with what I had seen in countless dreams of the elder world, that I trembled actively for the first time.

Behind and high above, a faint luminous blur told of the distant moonlit world outside. Some vague shred of caution warned me that I should not let it out of my sight, lest I have no guide for my return.

I now advanced toward the wall at my left, where the traces of carving were plainest. The littered floor was nearly as hard to traverse as the downward heap had been, but I managed to pick my difficult way.

At one place I heaved aside some blocks and locked away the detritus to see what the pavement was like, and shuddered at the utter, fateful familiarity of the great octagonal stones whose buckled surface still held roughly together.

Reaching a convenient distance from the wall, I cast the searchlight slowly and carefully over its worn remnants of carving. Some bygone influx of water seemed to have acted on the sandstone surface, while there were curious incrustations which I could not explain.

In places the masonry was very loose and distorted, and I wondered how many aeons more this primal, hidden edifice could keep its remaining traces of form amidst earth's heavings.

But it was the carvings themselves that excited me most. Despite their time-crumbled state, they were relatively easy to trace at close range; and the complete, intimate familiarity of every detail almost stunned my imagination.

That the major attributes of this hoary masonry should be familiar, was not beyond normal credibility.

Powerfully impressing the weavers of certain myths, they had become embodied in a stream of cryptic lore which, somehow, coming to my notice during the amnesic period, had evoked vivid images in my subconscious mind.

But how could I explain the exact and minute fashion in which each line and spiral of these strange designs tallied with what I had dreamed for more than a score of years? What obscure, forgotten iconography could have reproduced each subtle shading and nuance which so persistently, exactly, and unvaryingly besieged my sleeping vision night after night?

For this was no chance or remote resemblance. Definitely and absolutely, the millennially ancient, aeon-hidden corridor in which I stood was the original of something I knew in sleep as intimately as I knew my own house in Crane Street, Arkham. True, my dreams shewed the place in its undecayed prime; but the identity was no less real on that account. I was wholly and horribly oriented.

The particular structure I was in was known to me. Known, too, was its place in that terrible elder city of dreams. That I could visit unerringly any point in that structure or in that city which had escaped the changes and devastations of uncounted ages, I realized with hideous and instinctive certainty. What in heaven's name could all this mean? How had I come to know what I knew? And what awful reality could lie behind those antique tales of the beings who had dwelt in this labyrinth of primordial stone?

Words can convey only fractionally the welter of dread and bewilderment which ate at my spirit. I knew this place. I knew what lay before me, and what had lain overhead before the myriad towering stories had fallen to dust and debris and the desert. No need now, I thought with a shudder, to keep that faint blur of moonlight in view.

I was torn betwixt a longing to flee and a feverish mixture of burning curiosity and driving fatality. What had happened to this monstrous megalopolis of old in the millions of years since the time of my dreams? Of the subterrene mazes which had underlain the city and linked all the titan towers, how much had still survived the writhings of earth's crust?

Had I come upon a whole buried world of unholy archaism? Could I still find the house of the writing master, and the tower where S'gg'ha, the captive mind from the star-headed vegetable carnivores of Antarctica, had chiselled certain pictures on the blank spaces of the walls?

Would the passage at the second level down, to the hall of the alien minds, be still unchoked and traversable? In that hall the captive mind of an incredible entity – a half-plastic denizen of the hollow interior of an unknown trans-Plutonian planet eighteen million years in the future – had kept a certain thing which it had modelled from clay.

I shut my eyes and put my hand to my head in a vain, pitiful effort to drive these insane dream-fragments from my consciousness. Then, for the first time, I felt acutely the coolness, motion, and dampness of the surrounding air. Shuddering, I realized that a vast chain of aeon-dead black gulfs must indeed be yawning somewhere beyond and below me.

I thought of the frightful chambers and corridors and inclines as I recalled them from my dreams. Would the way to the central archives still be open? Again that driving fatality tugged insistently at my brain as I recalled the awesome records that once lay cased in those rectangular vaults of rustless metal.

There, said the dreams and legends, had reposed the whole history, past and future, of the cosmic space-time continuum – written by captive minds from every orb and every age in the solar system. Madness, of course – but had I not now stumbled into a nighted world as mad as I?

I thought of the locked metal shelves, and of the curious knob twistings needed to open each one. My own came vividly into my consciousness. How often had I gone through that intricate routine of varied turns and pressures in the terrestrial vertebrate section on the lowest level! Every detail was fresh and familiar.

If there were such a vault as I had dreamed of, I could open it in a moment. It was then that madness took me utterly. An instant later, and I was leaping and stumbling over the rocky debris toward the well-remembered incline to the depths below.

Chapter VII

FROM THAT POINT forward my impressions are scarcely to be relied on – indeed, I still possess a final, desperate hope that they all form parts of some daemonic dream or illusion born of delirium. A fever raged in my brain, and everything came to me through a kind of haze – sometimes only intermittently.

The rays of my torch shot feebly into the engulfing blackness, bringing phantasmal flashes of hideously familiar walls and carvings, all blighted with the decay of ages. In one place a tremendous mass of vaulting had fallen, so that I had to clamber over a mighty mound of stones reaching almost to the ragged, grotesquely stalactited roof.

It was all the ultimate apex of nightmare, made worse by the blasphemous tug of pseudo-memory. One thing only was unfamiliar, and that was my own size in relation to the monstrous masonry. I felt oppressed by a sense of unwonted smallness, as if the sight of these towering walls from a mere human body was something wholly new and abnormal. Again and again I looked nervously down at myself, vaguely disturbed by the human form I possessed.

Onward through the blackness of the abyss I leaped, plunged, and staggered – often falling and bruising myself, and once nearly shattering my torch. Every stone and corner of that daemonic gulf was known to me, and at many points I stopped to cast beams of light through choked and crumbling, yet familiar, archways.

Some rooms had totally collapsed; others were bare, or debris-filled. In a few I saw masses of metal – some fairly intact, some broken, and some crushed or battered – which I recognised as the colossal pedestals or tables of my dreams. What they could in truth have been, I dared not guess.

I found the downward incline and began its descent – though after a time halted by a gaping, ragged chasm whose narrowest point could not be much less than four feet across. Here the stonework had fallen through, revealing incalculable inky depths beneath.

I knew there were two more cellar levels in this titan edifice, and trembled with fresh panic as I recalled the metal-clamped trap-door on the lowest one. There could be no guards now – for what had lurked beneath had long since done its hideous work and sunk into its long decline. By the time of the posthuman beetle race it would be quite dead. And yet, as I thought of the native legends, I trembled anew.

It cost me a terrible effort to vault that yawning chasm, since the littered floor prevented a running start – but madness drove me on. I chose a place close to the left-hand wall – where the rift was least wide and the landing-spot reasonably clear of dangerous debris – and after one frantic moment reached the other side in safety.

At last, gaining the lower level, I stumbled on past the archway of the room of machines, within which were fantastic ruins of metal, half buried beneath fallen vaulting. Everything was where I knew it would be, and I climbed confidently over the heaps which barred the entrance of a vast transverse corridor. This, I realised, would take me under the city to the central archives.

Endless ages seemed to unroll as I stumbled, leaped, and crawled along that debris-cluttered corridor. Now and then I could make out carvings on the ages-stained walls – some familiar, others seemingly added since the period of my dreams. Since this was a subterrene house-connecting highway, there were no archways save when the route led through the lower levels of various buildings.

At some of these intersections I turned aside long enough to look down well-remembered corridors and into well-remembered rooms. Twice only did I find any radical changes from what I had dreamed of – and in one of these cases I could trace the sealed-up outlines of the archway I remembered.

I shook violently, and felt a curious surge of retarding weakness, as I steered a hurried and reluctant course through the crypt of one of those great windowless, ruined towers whose alien, basalt masonry bespoke a whispered and horrible origin.

This primal vault was round and fully two hundred feet across, with nothing carved upon the dark-hued stonework. The floor was here free from anything save dust and sand, and I could see the apertures leading upward and downward. There were no stairs or inclines – indeed, my dreams had pictured those elder towers as wholly untouched by the fabulous Great Race. Those who had built them had not needed stairs or inclines.

In the dreams, the downward aperture had been tightly sealed and nervously guarded. Now it lay open – black and yawning, and giving forth a current of cool, damp air. Of what limitless caverns of eternal night might brood below, I would not permit myself to think.

Later, clawing my way along a badly heaped section of the corridor, I reached a place where the roof had wholly caved in. The debris rose like a mountain, and I climbed up over it, passing through a vast, empty space where my torchlight could reveal neither walls nor vaulting. This, I reflected, must be the cellar of the house of the metal-purveyors, fronting on the third square not far from the archives. What had happened to it I could not conjecture.

I found the corridor again beyond the mountain of detritus and stone, but after a short distance encountered a wholly choked place where the fallen vaulting almost touched the perilously sagging ceiling. How I managed to wrench and tear aside enough blocks to afford a passage, and how I dared disturb the tightly packed fragments when the least shift of equilibrium might have brought down all the tons of superincumbent masonry to crush me to nothingness, I do not know.

It was sheer madness that impelled and guided me – if, indeed, my whole underground adventure was not – as I hope – a hellish delusion or phase of dreaming. But I did make – or dream that I made – a passage that I could squirm through. As I wiggled over the mound of debris – my torch, switched continuously on, thrust deeply in my mouth – I felt myself torn by the fantastic stalactites of the jagged floor above me.

I was now close to the great underground archival structure which seemed to form my goal. Sliding and clambering down the farther side of the barrier, and picking my way along the remaining stretch of corridor with hand-held, intermittently flashing torch, I came at last to a low, circular crypt with arches – still in a marvelous state of preservation – opening off on every side.

The walls, or such parts of them as lay within reach of my torchlight, were densely hieroglyphed and chiselled with typical curvilinear symbols – some added since the period of my dreams.

This, I realised, was my fated destination, and I turned at once through a familiar archway on my left. That I could find a clear passage up and down the incline to all the surviving levels, I had, oddly, little doubt. This vast, earth-protected pile, housing the annals of all the solar system, had been built with supernal skill and strength to last as long as that system itself.

Blocks of stupendous size, poised with mathematical genius and bound with cements of incredible toughness, had combined to form a mass as firm as the planet's rocky core. Here, after ages more prodigious than I could sanely grasp, its buried bulk stood in all its essential contours, the vast, dust-drifted floors scarce sprinkled with the litter elsewhere so dominant.

The relatively easy walking from this point onward went curiously to my head. All the frantic eagerness hitherto frustrated by obstacles now took itself out in a kind of febrile speed, and I literally raced along the low-roofed, monstrously well-remembered aisles beyond the archway.

I was past being astonished by the familiarity of what I saw. On every hand the great hieroglyphed metal shelf-doors loomed monstrously; some yet in place, others sprung open, and still others bent and buckled under bygone geological stresses not quite strong enough to shatter the titan masonry.

Here and there a dust-covered heap beneath a gaping, empty shelf seemed to indicate where cases had been shaken down by earth tremors. On occasional pillars were great symbols or letters proclaiming classes and subclasses of volumes.

Once I paused before an open vault where I saw some of the accustomed metal cases still in position amidst the omnipresent gritty dust. Reaching up, I dislodged one of the thinner specimens with some difficulty, and rested it on the floor for inspection. It was titled in the prevailing curvilinear hieroglyphs, though something in the arrangement of the characters seemed subtly unusual.

The odd mechanism of the hooked fastener was perfectly well known to me, and I snapped up the still rustless and workable lid and drew out the book within. The latter, as expected, was some twenty by fifteen inches in area, and two inches thick; the thin metal covers opening at the top.

Its tough cellulose pages seemed unaffected by the myriad cycles of time they had lived through, and I studied the queerly pigmented, brush-drawn letters of the text-symbols unlike either the usual curved hieroglyphs or any alphabet known to human scholarship – with a haunting, half-aroused memory.

It came to me that this was the language used by a captive mind I had known slightly in my dreams – a mind from a large asteroid on which had survived much of the archaic life and lore of the primal planet whereof it formed a fragment. At the same time I recalled that this level of the archives was devoted to volumes dealing with the non-terrestrial planets.

As I ceased poring over this incredible document I saw that the light of my torch was beginning to fail, hence quickly inserted the extra battery I always had with me. Then, armed with the stronger radiance, I resumed my feverish racing through unending tangles of aisles and corridors – recognising now and then some familiar shelf, and vaguely annoyed by the acoustic conditions which made my footfalls echo incongruously in these catacombs.

The very prints of my shoes behind me in the millennially untrodden dust made me shudder. Never before, if my mad dreams held anything of truth, had human feet pressed upon those immemorial pavements.

Of the particular goal of my insane racing, my conscious mind held no hint. There was, however, some force of evil potency pulling at my dazed will and buried recollection, so that I vaguely felt I was not running at random.

I came to a downward incline and followed it to profounder depths. Floors flashed by me as I raced, but I did not pause to explore them. In my whirling brain there had begun to beat a certain rhythm which set my right hand twitching in unison. I wanted to unlock something, and felt that I knew all the intricate twists and pressures needed to do it. It would be like a modern safe with a combination lock.

Dream or not, I had once known and still knew. How any dream – or scrap of unconsciously absorbed legend – could have taught me a detail so minute, so intricate, and so complex, I did not attempt to explain to myself. I was beyond all coherent thought. For was not this whole experience – this shocking familiarity with a set of unknown ruins, and this monstrously exact identity of everything before me with what only dreams and scraps of myth could have suggested – a horror beyond all reason?

Probably it was my basic conviction then – as it is now during my saner moments – that I was not awake at all, and that the entire buried city was a fragment of febrile hallucination.

Eventually, I reached the lowest level and struck off to the right of the incline. For some shadowy reason I tried to soften my steps, even though I lost speed thereby. There was a space I was afraid to cross on this last, deeply buried floor.

As I drew near it I recalled what thing in that space I feared. It was merely one of the metal-barred and closely guarded trap-doors. There would be no guards now, and on that account I trembled and tiptoed as I had done in passing through that black basalt vault where a similar trap-door had yawned.

I felt a current of cool, damp air as I had felt there, and wished that my course led in another direction. Why I had to take the particular course I was taking, I did not know.

When I came to the space I saw that the trap-door yawned widely open. Ahead, the shelves began again, and I glimpsed on the floor before one of them a heap very thinly covered with dust, where a number of cases had recently fallen. At the same moment a fresh wave of panic clutched me, though for some time I could not discover why.

Heaps of fallen cases were not uncommon, for all through the aeons this lightless labyrinth had been racked by the heavings of earth and had echoed at intervals of the deafening clatter of toppling objects. It was only when I was nearly across the space that I realized why I shook so violently.

Not the heap, but something about the dust of the level floor was troubling me. In the light of my torch it seemed as if that dust were not as even as it ought to be – there were places where it looked thinner, as if it had been disturbed not many months before. I could not be sure, for even the apparently thinner places were dusty enough; yet a certain suspicion of regularity in the fancied unevenness was highly disquieting.

When I brought the torchlight close to one of the queer places I did not like what I saw – for the illusion of regularity became very great. It was as if there were regular lines of composite impressions – impressions that went in threes, each slightly over a foot square, and consisting of five nearly circular three-inch prints, one in advance of the other four.

These possible lines of foot-square impressions appeared to lead in two directions, as if something had gone somewhere and returned. They were, of course, very faint, and may have been illusions or accidents; but there was an element of dim, fumbling terror about the way I thought they ran. For at one end of them was the heap of cases which must have clattered down not long before, while at the other end was the ominous trap-door with the cool, damp wind, yawning unguarded down to abysses past imagination.

Chapter VIII

THAT MY STRANGE SENSE of compulsion was deep and overwhelming is shewn by its conquest of my fear. No rational motive could have drawn me on after that hideous suspicion of prints and the creeping dream-memories it excited. Yet my right hand, even as it shook with fright, still twitched rhythmically in its eagerness to turn a lock it hoped to find. Before I knew it I was past the heap of lately fallen cases and running on tiptoe through aisles of utterly unbroken dust toward a point which I seemed to know morbidly, horribly well.

My mind was asking itself questions whose origin and relevancy I was only beginning to guess. Would the shelf be reachable by a human body? Could my human hand master all the aeon-remembered motions of the lock? Would the lock be undamaged and workable? And what would I do – what dare I do with what – as I now commenced to realise – I both hoped and feared to find? Would it prove the awesome, brain-shattering truth of something past normal conception, or shew only that I was dreaming?

The next I knew I had ceased my tiptoed racing and was standing still, staring at a row of maddeningly familiar hieroglyphed shelves. They were in a state of almost perfect preservation, and only three of the doors in this vicinity had sprung open.

My feelings toward these shelves cannot be described – so utter and insistent was the sense of old acquaintance. I was looking high up at a row near the top and wholly out of my reach, and wondering how I could climb to best advantage. An open door four rows from the bottom would help, and the locks of the closed doors formed possible holds for hands and feet. I would grip the torch between my teeth, as I had in other places where both hands were needed. Above all I must make no noise.

How to get down what I wished to remove would be difficult, but I could probably hook its movable fastener in my coat collar and carry it like a knapsack. Again I wondered whether the lock would be undamaged. That I could repeat each familiar motion I had not the least doubt. But I hoped the thing would not scrape or creak – and that my hand could work it properly.

Even as I thought these things I had taken the torch in my mouth and begun to climb. The projecting locks were poor supports; but, as I had expected, the opened shelf helped greatly.

I used both the swinging door and the edge of the aperture itself in my ascent, and managed to avoid any loud creaking.

Balanced on the upper edge of the door, and leaning far to my right, I could just reach the lock I sought. My fingers, half numb from climbing, were very clumsy at first; but I soon saw that they were anatomically adequate. And the memory-rhythm was strong in them.

Out of unknown gulfs of time the intricate, secret motions had somehow reached my brain correctly in every detail – for after less than five minutes of trying there came a click whose familiarity was all the more startling because I had not consciously anticipated it. In another instant the metal door was slowly swinging open with only the faintest grating sound.

Dazedly I looked over the row of greyish case ends thus exposed, and felt a tremendous surge of some wholly inexplicable emotion. Just within reach of my right hand was a case whose curving hieroglyphs made me shake with a pang infinitely more complex than one of mere fright. Still shaking, I managed to dislodge it amidst a shower of gritty flakes, and ease it over toward myself without any violent noise.

Like the other case I had handled, it was slightly more than twenty by fifteen inches in size, with curved mathematical designs in low relief. In thickness it just exceeded three inches.

Crudely wedging it between myself and the surface I was climbing, I fumbled with the fastener and finally got the hook free. Lifting the cover, I shifted the heavy object to my back, and let the hook catch hold of my collar. Hands now free, I awkwardly clambered down to the dusty floor, and prepared to inspect my prize.

Kneeling in the gritty dust, I swung the case around and rested it in front of me. My hands shook, and I dreaded to draw out the book within almost as much as I longed – and felt compelled – to do so. It had very gradually become clear to me what I ought to find, and this realisation nearly paralysed my faculties.

If the thing were there – and if I were not dreaming – the implications would be quite beyond the power of the human spirit to bear. What tormented me most was my momentary inability to feel that my surroundings were a dream. The sense of reality was hideous – and again becomes so as I recall the scene.

At length I tremblingly pulled the book from its container and stared fascinatedly at the well-known hieroglyphs on the cover. It seemed to be in prime condition, and the curvilinear letters of the title held me in almost as hypnotised a state as if I could read them. Indeed, I cannot swear that I did not actually read them in some transient and terrible access of abnormal memory.

I do not know how long it was before I dared to lift that thin metal cover. I temporized and made excuses to myself. I took the torch from my mouth and shut it off to save the battery. Then, in the dark, I collected my courage finally lifting the cover without turning on the light. Last of all, I did indeed flash the torch upon the exposed page – steeling myself in advance to suppress any sound no matter what I should find.

I looked for an instant, then collapsed. Clenching my teeth, however, I kept silent. I sank wholly to the floor and put a hand to my forehead amidst the engulfing blackness. What I dreaded and expected was there. Either I was dreaming, or time and space had become a mockery.

I must be dreaming – but I would test the horror by carrying this thing back and shewing it to my son if it were indeed a reality. My head swam frightfully, even though there were no visible objects in the unbroken gloom to swirl about me. Ideas and images of the starkest terror – excited by vistas which my glimpse had opened up – began to throng in upon me and cloud my senses.

I thought of those possible prints in the dust, and trembled at the sound of my own breathing as I did so. Once again I flashed on the light and looked at the page as a serpent's victim may look at his destroyer's eyes and fangs.

Then, with clumsy fingers, in the dark, I closed the book, put it in its container, and snapped the lid and the curious, hooked fastener. This was what I must carry back to the outer world if it truly existed – if the whole abyss truly existed – if I, and the world itself, truly existed.

Just when I tottered to my feet and commenced my return I cannot be certain. It comes to me oddly – as a measure of my sense of separation from the normal world – that I did not even once look at my watch during those hideous hours underground.

Torch in hand, and with the ominous case under one arm, I eventually found myself tiptoeing in a kind of silent panic past the draught-giving abyss and those lurking suggestions of prints. I lessened my precautions as I climbed up the endless inclines, but could not shake off a shadow of apprehension which I had not felt on the downward journey.

I dreaded having to repass through the black basalt crypt that was older than the city itself, where cold draughts welled up from unguarded depths. I thought of that which the Great Race had feared, and of what might still be lurking – be it ever so weak and dying – down there. I thought of those five-circle prints and of what my dreams had told me of such prints – and of strange winds and whistling noises associated with them. And I thought of the tales of the modern blackfellows, wherein the horror of great winds and nameless subterrene ruins was dwelt upon.

I knew from a carven wall symbol the right floor to enter, and came at last – after passing that other book I had examined – to the great circular space with the branching archways. On my right, and at once recognisable, was the arch through which I had arrived. This I now entered, conscious that the rest of my course would be harder because of the tumbled state of the masonry outside the archive building. My new metal-cased burden weighed upon me, and I found it harder and harder to be quiet as I stumbled among debris and fragments of every sort.

Then I came to the ceiling-high mound of debris through which I had wrenched a scanty passage. My dread at wriggling through again was infinite, for my first passage had made some noise, and I now – after seeing those possible prints – dreaded sound above all things. The case, too, doubled the problem of traversing the narrow crevice.

But I clambered up the barrier as best I could, and pushed the case through the aperture ahead of me. Then, torch in mouth, I scrambled through myself – my back torn as before by stalactites.

As I tried to grasp the case again, it fell some distance ahead of me down the slope of the debris, making a disturbing clatter and arousing echoes which sent me into a cold perspiration. I lunged for it at once, and regained it without further noise – but a moment afterward the slipping of blocks under my feet raised a sudden and unprecedented din.

The din was my undoing. For, falsely or not, I thought I heard it answered in a terrible way from spaces far behind me. I thought I heard a shrill, whistling sound, like nothing else on earth, and beyond any adequate verbal description. If so, what followed has a grim irony – since, save for the panic of this thing, the second thing might never have happened.

As it was, my frenzy was absolute and unrelieved. Taking my torch in my hand and clutching feebly at the case, I leaped and bounded wildly ahead with no idea in my brain beyond a mad desire to race out of these nightmare ruins to the waking world of desert and moonlight which lay so far above.

I hardly knew it when I reached the mountain of debris which towered into the vast blackness beyond the caved-in roof, and bruised and cut myself repeatedly in scrambling up its steep slope of jagged blocks and fragments.

Then came the great disaster. Just as I blindly crossed the summit, unprepared for the sudden dip ahead, my feet slipped utterly and I found myself involved in a mangling avalanche of sliding masonry whose cannon-loud uproar split the black cavern air in a deafening series of earth-shaking reverberations.

I have no recollection of emerging from this chaos, but a momentary fragment of consciousness shows me as plunging and tripping and scrambling along the corridor amidst the clangour – case and torch still with me.

Then, just as I approached that primal basalt crypt I had so dreaded, utter madness came. For as the echoes of the avalanche died down, there became audible a repetition of that frightful alien whistling I thought I had heard before. This time there was no doubt about it – and what was worse, it came from a point not behind but ahead of me.

Probably I shrieked aloud then. I have a dim picture of myself as flying through the hellish basalt vault of the elder things, and hearing that damnable alien sound piping up from the open, unguarded door of limitless nether blacknesses. There was a wind, too – not merely a cool, damp draught, but a violent, purposeful blast belching savagely and frigidly from that abominable gulf whence the obscene whistling came.

There are memories of leaping and lurching over obstacles of every sort, with that torrent of wind and shrieking sound growing moment by moment, and seeming to curl and twist purposefully around me as it struck out wickedly from the spaces behind and beneath.

Though in my rear, that wind had the odd effect of hindering instead of aiding my progress; as if it acted like a noose or lasso thrown around me. Heedless of the noise I made, I clattered over a great barrier of blocks and was again in the structure that led to the surface.

I recall glimpsing the archway to the room of machines and almost crying out as I saw the incline leading down to where one of those blasphemous trap-doors must be yawning two levels below. But instead of crying out I muttered over and over to myself that this was all a dream from which I must soon awake. Perhaps I was in camp – perhaps I was at home in Arkham. As these hopes bolstered up my sanity I began to mount the incline to the higher level.

I knew, of course, that I had the four-foot cleft to re-cross, yet was too racked by other fears to realise the full horror until I came almost upon it. On my descent, the leap across had been easy – but could I clear the gap as readily when going uphill, and hampered by fright, exhaustion, the weight of the metal case, and the anomalous backward tug of that daemon wind? I thought of these things at the last moment, and thought also of the nameless entities which might be lurking in the black abysses below the chasm.

My wavering torch was growing feeble, but I could tell by some obscure memory when I neared the cleft. The chill blasts of wind and the nauseous whistling shrieks behind me were for the moment like a merciful opiate, dulling my imagination to the horror of the yawning gulf ahead. And then I became aware of the added blasts and whistling in front of me – tides of abomination surging up through the cleft itself from depths unimagined and unimaginable.

Now, indeed, the essence of pure nightmare was upon me. Sanity departed – and, ignoring everything except the animal impulse of flight, I merely struggled and plunged upward over the incline's debris as if no gulf had existed. Then I saw the chasm's edge, leaped frenziedly with every ounce of strength I possessed, and was instantly engulfed in a pandaemoniae vortex of loathsome sound and utter, materially tangible blackness.

This is the end of my experience, so far as I can recall. Any further impressions belong wholly to the domain of phantasmagoria delirium. Dream, madness, and memory merged wildly together in a series of fantastic, fragmentary delusions which can have no relation to anything real.

There was a hideous fall through incalculable leagues of viscous, sentient darkness, and a babel of noises utterly alien to all that we know of the earth and its organic life. Dormant, rudimentary senses seemed to start into vitality within me, telling of pits and voids peopled by floating horrors and leading to sunless crags and oceans and teeming cities of windowless, basalt towers upon which no light ever shone.

Secrets of the primal planet and its immemorial aeons flashed through my brain without the aid of sight or sound, and there were known to me things which not even the wildest of my former dreams had ever suggested. And all the while cold fingers of damp vapor clutched and picked at me, and that eldritch, damnable whistling shrieked fiendishly above all the alternations of babel and silence in the whirlpools of darkness around.

Afterward there were visions of the Cyclopean city of my dreams – not in ruins, but just as I had dreamed of it. I was in my conical, non-human body again, and mingled with crowds of the Great Race and the captive minds who carried books up and down the lofty corridors and vast inclines.

Then, superimposed upon these pictures, were frightful, momentary flashes of a non-vistial consciousness involving desperate struggles, a writhing free from clutching tentacles of whistling wind, an insane, bat-like flight through half-solid air, a feverish burrowing through the cyclone-whipped dark, and a wild stumbling and scrambling over fallen masonry.

Once there was a curious, intrusive flash of half sight – a faint, diffuse suspicion of bluish radiance far overhead. Then there came a dream of wind – pursued climbing and crawling – of wriggling into a blaze of sardonic moonlight through a jumble of debris which slid and collapsed after me amidst a morbid hurricane. It was the evil, monotonous beating of that maddening moonlight which at last told me of the return of what I had once known as the objective, waking world.

I was clawing prone through the sands of the Australian desert, and around me shrieked such a tumult of wind as I had never before known on our planet's surface. My clothing was in rags, and my whole body was a mass of bruises and scratches.

Full consciousness returned very slowly, and at no time could I tell just where delirious dream left off and true memory began. There had seemed to be a mound of titan blocks, an abyss beneath it, a monstrous revelation from the past, and a nightmare horror at the end – but how much of this was real?

My flashlight was gone, and likewise any metal case I may have discovered. Had there been such a case – or any abyss – or any mound? Raising my head, I looked behind me, and saw only the sterile, undulant sands of the desert.

The daemon wind died down, and the bloated, fungoid moon sank reddeningly in the west. I lurched to my feet and began to stagger southwestward toward the camp. What in truth had happened to me? Had I merely collapsed in the desert and dragged a dream-racked body over miles of sand and buried blocks? If not, how could I bear to live any longer?

For, in this new doubt, all my faith in the myth-born unreality of my visions dissolved once more into the hellish older doubting. If that abyss was real, then the Great Race was real – and its blasphemous reachings and seizures in the cosmos-wide vortex of time were no myths or nightmares, but a terrible, soul-shattering actuality.

Had I, in full, hideous fact, been drawn back to a pre-human world of a hundred and fifty million years ago in those dark, baffling days of the amnesia? Had my present body been the vehicle of a frightful alien consciousness from palaeogean gulfs of time?

Had I, as the captive mind of those shambling horrors, indeed known that accursed city of stone in its primordial heyday, and wriggled down those familiar corridors in the loathsome shape of my captor? Were those tormenting dreams of more than twenty years the offspring of stark, monstrous memories?

Had I once veritably talked with minds from reachless corners of time and space, learned the universe's secrets, past and to come, and written the annals of my own world for the metal cases of those titan archives? And were those others – those shocking elder things of the mad winds and daemon pipings – in truth a lingering, lurking menace, waiting and slowly weakening in black abysses while varied shapes of life drag out their multimillennial courses on the planet's age-racked surface?

I do not know. If that abyss and what I held were real, there is no hope. Then, all too truly, there lies upon this world of man a mocking and incredible shadow out of time. But, mercifully, there is no proof that these things are other than fresh phases of my myth-born dreams. I did not bring back the metal case that would have been a proof, and so far those subterrene corridors have not been found.

If the laws of the universe are kind, they will never be found. But I must tell my son what I saw or thought I saw, and let him use his judgment as a psychologist in gauging the reality of my experience, and communicating this account to others.

I have said that the awful truth behind my tortured years of dreaming hinges absolutely upon the actuality of what I thought I saw in those Cyclopean, buried ruins. It has been hard for me, literally, to set down that crucial revelation, though no reader can have failed to guess it. Of course, it lay in that book within the metal case – the case which I pried out of its lair amidst the dust of a million centuries.

No eye had seen, no hand had touched that book since the advent of man to this planet. And yet, when I flashed my torch upon it in that frightful abyss, I saw that the queerly pigmented letters on the brittle, aeon-browned cellulose pages were not indeed any nameless hieroglyphs of earth's youth. They were, instead, the letters of our familiar alphabet, spelling out the words of the English language in my own handwriting.

The Hunted

Angus McIntyre

THE WAR OFFICE had sent an escort for Rachel, a young army officer who met her at the Glasgow landing field and summoned a hansom cab to carry her and her trunk to the railway station. After the smoothness and silence of her flight from London, the lurching and jolting of the cab and the din of its wheels on the cobbles left her feeling battered.

"I don't suppose you can tell us where we're going," she said.

Her escort, whose name and rank she had already forgotten, shook his head.

"No, miss," he said. "Orders."

He looked very young, his khaki battledress crisp and neat. She thought he might be a lieutenant, or perhaps a sergeant. She tried to remember whether either of those ranks was higher than captain, the only other military rank she could remember.

She saw almost nothing of Glasgow, her eyes still dazzled by the miraculous visions she had seen from the window of the flying machine: houses and fields shrunk to the size of toys, ragged streamers of white cloud over the Midlands, sunlight glinting on the silver ribbon of a river. Amidst the beauty were uglier reminders of the recent fighting: the ragged black wasteland that had been Birmingham before the Martians burned it, clusters of shell craters marking the site of some futile battle, patches of lingering red weed like open wounds in the green landscape.

At the station, the soldier led her directly to the platform and the waiting train. She had hoped he might let slip the name of their destination when he bought tickets, but evidently he had the tickets or something like them already in his pocket. A board at the platform entrance had a list of stops written on it in precise chalked capitals, but she could only make out a handful of names – Dumbarton, Bridge of Orchy, Fort William – before he hurried her past. None of them meant anything to her.

The carriage was shabby and the seats bore a patina of grime. Too few people left to clean, she supposed. Even eight months on, Britain still seemed a land populated mostly by ghosts, the survivors too few to fill the nation's once-bustling cities. Each face she saw still bore the mark of those weeks of terror and the long months of privation that followed.

The train whistle sounded and she felt again that residual frisson of fear, hearing in the familiar sound an evil echo of the hooting of the Martian hunting machines. She saw her companion start in his seat and guessed that he heard it the same way. The train jolted into motion.

She had some papers with her, drafts of a monograph on ancient Akkadian that she had been writing before the invasion. It seemed absurd to be still working on it when so many of her colleagues had died, when the university itself was a blackened shell. It might be decades before anyone cared about logosyllabic cuneiform again. Yet she found that immersing herself in her studies calmed her. Besides, she suspected that their journey was going to be long and it would be good to have something to occupy her.

As they passed through Clydebank, the soldier touched her sleeve and pointed out the window. A trio of fighting machines had been pressed into service as cranes. She watched one step into the water with that spindly, menacing stride she remembered too well. A pallet laden with cargo dangled beneath it, destined for a schooner berthed at a nearby wharf.

It was only right, she thought, that the machines that had wrought so much devastation should be used to rebuild the world, alien swords beaten into plowshares. Yet she would have been happier not to see them at all.

The train picked up speed, the panting of the engine settling into a steady rhythm. The city dwindled and fell away behind.

"Now," said Rachel with a touch of acerbity. "Where are we going?"

The soldier glanced up and down the almost empty carriage as if to assure himself that the other passengers were too far away to hear him.

"Mallaig," he said.

"And what, pray, is at Mallaig?"

He leaned closer. "A cylinder," he whispered. "They found a cylinder."

* * *

Mallaig was not much more than a row of white houses facing a broad bay tucked into a curve of green hills. Late afternoon sunlight glinted on the gray sea and gilded the low islands offshore.

To the north of the harbor lay a military camp, with regular lines of long khaki tents drawn up between barbed wire fences. A pair of fighting machines towered over the camp, monstrous insects straddling the fence line.

"Those are ours," Rachel's escort said. He pointed to the Union Jacks dangling from flagstaffs attached to the hull of each machine. "See?"

Rachel liked the look of them no better for that. She suppressed a shudder at the sight of the black funnels hanging from the machines, the projectors of the terrible heat-ray. Domesticated they might be, but they were still killers.

At the edge of the camp stood a long building of new red brick, roofed with gleaming sheets of tin. It was built right on the shore with a ramp at one end sloping down to the water's edge. A tall chimney puffed smoke into the clear summer sky.

"That's the laboratory," the soldier told her, answering her unspoken question. "That's where they keep the creatures."

"Creatures," Rachel said. "Do you mean –"

"Yes," he said. "Martians. Three of them. Alive, alive-oh."

* * *

"I imagine you must be wondering what you're doing here, Miss Thompson," Colonel Porter said.

He was a stout man in his fifties with a florid complexion and a gray mustache. From the way the flesh sagged from his face and neck, Rachel guessed that he must have been a good deal stouter before the Martians landed and food ran scarce.

"I confess to a certain curiosity," she said, injecting as much ice into the words as possible.

On arrival, her escort had handed her over to a second officer and disappeared. Her new guardian had been even less forthcoming than his colleague, answering her questions only with the assurance that "the colonel will explain everything in the morning". He showed her to her lodgings, a small, very clean room in one of the houses overlooking the harbor, with a narrow bed and a basin and ewer for washing. Then he too vanished, leaving her to stew alone. Later, an old woman with a cast in one eye brought her food – floury bap rolls with luncheon meat for supper, a bowl of salted porridge and a mug of tea for breakfast. Aside from that, she saw no one and spoke to no one until nine the next morning when the officer came back to take her to the colonel.

"You were highly recommended," the colonel said. "As an expert in languages ancient and modern. I was told –"

"What is it you want from me?" Rachel cut in.

The colonel stiffened. She guessed that he was unaccustomed to being interrupted, especially by a woman.

"You have studied the Martian language," he said.

"I've looked at samples of their writing system. I suppose that makes me as much of an authority as anyone else."

"Could you speak to a Martian?"

She shook her head, frustrated. "Colonel, I –"

He held up his hand. "Let me put it another way. I need you to speak to a Martian for me."

She had suspected it, of course, even before the lieutenant had told her about the cylinder. But suspicion and confirmation were two different things.

"Six weeks ago, we discovered a cylinder that had landed in shallow water," the colonel continued. "The scientists tell me that the accident of its landing in water probably prevented the Martians inside from emerging and left them in the state of hibernation in which they made the crossing from Mars."

And you brought it ashore, Rachel thought. You should have dragged it into deeper water or blown it up, but instead you opened it up and let them out.

"We opened the cylinder yesterday morning. The Martians inside were overpowered before they could assemble their weapons. As far as we know, they are the last living Martians anywhere on Earth."

She thought of the two fighting machines that she had seen, their weapons trained on the laboratory building. There had been a battery of guns too, and grim-faced Tommies with rifles and bayonets patrolling the barbed wire fence surrounding the building. She wondered if it was enough.

"I need you to talk to them," the colonel said. "I don't know how long we can keep them alive. We may never have another chance."

* * *

The lieutenant had spoken of three Martians, but she saw only two.

"Taken for vivisection," the colonel explained when she asked about it. "We're keeping another alive to study. The third is yours."

She felt a dull unease at the idea. Whatever else they were, the Martians were living, intelligent creatures. She pictured gleaming knives slicing flesh and muscle, the trapped being writhing in pain as it was slowly butchered. Then she remembered London and burned corpses in the streets, the choking fog of the black smoke, the rumors about what the Martians did to their captives. Let the doctors do what they want, she thought. It's no more than those monsters deserve.

Seen through the broad window that looked onto the holding area, the Martians were gray-brown blobs, big as horses, sprawled on the white tiles of their pen like great leather sacks. They looked a little like the sketches she had seen, but no sketch could convey the sense of the living thing – the way the skin seemed to pulsate, the slow movements of the great black eyes, the febrile stirrings of the tentacles that fringed their triangular mouths. She felt a wave of revulsion.

She became aware that the colonel was watching her. "Well?"

She looked back at the Martians. One of them was watching her with eyes the size of footballs.

"I can try," she said.

* * *

Before they let her into the room with the Martians, they made her put on a kind of diving suit, a pleated, cumbersome affair of waxed canvas and rubber. A soldier showed her how to put it on, then went out so that she could change in privacy. Ten minutes of struggling with the heavy garment left her almost exhausted, but at last she got it on and duck-waddled to the door to be let out.

With the suit came a helmet and an air hose. She felt a moment's panic when they sealed the glass porthole in the front of the helmet. The clammy fabric of the suit seemed to tighten around her limbs and torso, the air inside growing thick and warm. Then the hose tautened and belched rubber-scented air into the interior and she could breathe again.

The antechamber to the Martians' prison was closed off at each end by a metal hatch. A suited soldier spun the hand wheel to seal the hatch, then sprayed her down with carbolic acid to kill any microbes that might be clinging to the outside of her suit. When he was done, he handed her the sprayer and motioned her to do the same for him.

The thought that the whole process was for the protection of the Martians calmed her slightly. They were the vulnerable ones, not her. All she needed to do was open the faceplate of her suit and exhale. They would die then, not immediately, but probably within weeks. It was ironic to think that she was more a threat to them than they were to her.

The soldier was waiting for her, one hand on the wheel that opened the inner hatch. Through his glass faceplate she saw him raise his eyebrows. She nodded, the heavy helmet swaying on her shoulders.

"I'm ready," she said.

* * *

At first, Rachel found the Martians less intimidating than she had expected. It was hard to be intimidated by something so plainly helpless, lying sluggish and bloated on the white tile, all but immobilized by Earth's gravity. Rounded stubs that she guessed to be vestigial limbs strained feebly against the floor, incapable of moving them more than a few inches at a time.

Then she caught sight of their eyes and the impression of harmlessness vanished. The great orbs glittered with a malign intelligence, following her as she moved. The tentacles that flanked the triangular mouths twitched, flexing and uncoiling like a nest of snakes. She took a step backward.

The soldier was watching her, one hand on the club at his belt. On the other hip he carried a long bayonet in a sheath. She marveled for a moment at the idea of creatures who could fly between worlds being subdued by men with sticks and knives. She wondered if the Martians saw the irony too.

The colonel had given her a metal tablet and a pack of chinagraph pencils. She took a pencil between gauntleted fingers and painstakingly drew out one of the Martian symbols that she remembered. She thought the symbol might mean Mars. It seemed like a good starting point. The Martian watched her, its eyes swiveling to follow the motion of the pencil.

She finished the complex shape and held up the tablet. The Martian studied it briefly and then its eyes shifted away as if it had lost interest. Something like a clear eyelid slid down over the globes of its eyes, dulling their shine.

She wiped away the first symbol she had drawn and scrawled another in its place, one that she thought meant 'machine'. She had given no real thought to the meaning of her first message. All she wanted was to establish some kind of communication, showing them that she could reproduce their writing. She held up the tablet again.

The Martian refused to look at it.

* * *

That night, Rachel walked on the beach, breathing down deep lungfuls of the cool, clean air. After a day in the suffocating confines of the suit, sucking oxygen through a rubber hose, the Scottish air was like an elixir.

Pebbles crunched behind her. She turned and recognized the young officer from the train.

He stopped a little distance from her. "How did it go?"

She shook her head. "I don't think they want to talk to me. I wrote out all the symbols I knew. After the first few, they stopped paying attention."

"Ah," he said.

"Maybe we're too far beneath them. As if we're no cleverer than cows or sheep. Not worthy of their time."

"If a sheep started writing out the alphabet, I'd certainly pay attention," the soldier said. She laughed.

They stood in silence, looking up at the stars. It was a clear night and the blue-black sky was dusted with a thousand tiny dots of light.

"I wonder which is Mars," she said. "Maybe that bright one?"

He followed her pointing finger.

"Too bright," he said. "I don't know what it is. Too high for Venus. Maybe Jupiter."

"Oh."

She wondered if the Martians were looking down on Earth and asking themselves why their plan had failed. Maybe they were already making new plans.

"Do you think they'll try again?" she asked.

"If they do, we'll be ready," he said. "We can fight them with their own weapons now. We'll track the cylinders and blow them up before the Martians inside can come out." He shook his head. "Funny. They tried to conquer us and ended up giving us all their science. Things we would have taken a hundred years to invent. Flying machines, tripods. Now the whole world is changing."

She yawned, suddenly exhausted.

"I should get some rest," she said.

He bowed. "Good night, Miss Thompson. Sleep well."

* * *

On the third day, the Martian responded.

Not knowing what else to do, she had kept on writing symbols. Certain combinations, she observed, seemed to arouse the Martian's interest. Others produced a reaction that she could only describe as contempt: a turning away, a weary closing of that membranous eyelid. She tried to keep notes on which symbols seemed to fit together.

As she sketched one of the more promising pairs for the fifth time, the tentacles around the Martian's mouth began to twitch in violent agitation. She stopped, startled.

"He wants you to give him the pencil," the soldier said, his voice echoing muffled from within his helmet. One of the Martian's tentacles coiled and uncoiled, beckoning.

Cautiously, she moved closer. She wiped the tablet clean and set it on the floor between them, then held out the pencil at arm's length. The Martian reached out and took it from her with surprising delicacy. Gripping the pencil in its tentacles, it inched forward a foot or two until it could reach the tablet, then began to write. When it was done, it set the pencil down and waited for her to take the tablet.

She picked it up. Half the surface was covered with tiny, precise glyphs.

The soldier peered over her shoulder. "What does it mean?"

"I have no idea," Rachel said.

* * *

"They say you're making progress," the lieutenant said when they met on the beach that night. She suspected that their meetings were never accidental, that the young officer was timing his patrols to coincide with her nightly walks. She didn't mind. He had never said or suggested anything improper and she found his attention flattering.

"Only a little," she said.

It was slow going. She had a working vocabulary of ten or fifteen symbols, and only the shakiest sense of how to fit them together. Her biggest breakthrough had been identifying the marker that seemed to turn a statement into a question. She still had no idea how to read the answers.

"Colonel Porter said the smaller one might be getting sick."

"Yes," Rachel said.

It was difficult to describe a creature that scarcely moved as listless, but the smaller of the two Martians definitely seemed more subdued. Its tentacles moved only fitfully, and its skin had acquired a greenish sheen, with tiny droplets of moisture accumulating in the folds of flesh. Sometimes it made a low hooting sound that she thought might indicate distress.

"I suppose it takes some courage," the soldier said. "To launch yourself out into space like that, not knowing how you'll end up."

Courage, Rachel thought. How like a man to see it that way. Men could never resist the appeal of the gallant enemy, even if the enemy in question was a bloated sack with tentacles for hands.

I do not care if they are brave, she thought. I do not care if they live or die. I only care whether they live long enough for me to learn to speak to them.

* * *

By the end of the week, both Martians were visibly sick.

MARS MAN DEATH, the large Martian printed on her tablet. The symbol for DEATH was one that it had taught her, miming collapse with movements of its tentacles. The glyph was annotated with a marker that she guessed indicated a future event.

Now that the end was inevitable, she no longer wore her suit. Unencumbered by the bulky gloves, she could write more quickly and precisely. She sat cross-legged on the floor, breathing in the rank, heavy scent of the Martian, feeling the febrile heat that radiated from its body.

I have so many questions, she thought. You cannot die until you have answered them.

She covered her tablet with lines of symbols, laboriously building sentences from the thirty or forty glyphs she had memorized, then adding a giant question marker to show they were all questions. The Martian shuffled forward to study what she had written. It took the sponge from her and wiped the tablet clean.

In place of her questions, it wrote a question of its own. Tentacles trembling, it sketched an asterisk, five intersecting lines that almost filled the tablet. Beside the star, it added the squiggle that signified a question.

Rachel stared at the tablet. She had no idea what it was asking.

It wiped the tablet clean. MARS MAN DEATH it wrote again.

* * *

"You'll be leaving now?" the lieutenant said.

She nodded. Her trunk was already packed. She would take the train in the morning. If she caught the flying machine at Glasgow, she could be home by evening.

There was nothing more for her to do. Both Martians were dead, their bodies already beginning to putrefy. The big one had left her one final message, a tablet covered with a forest of tiny glyphs. She supposed she might find answers to her questions on it, if only she could make sense of the mass of unfamiliar symbols. But that was work she could do from London. There was no reason to stay in Mallaig.

She looked up at the sky again. The bright star she had seen before was a whitish smudge, blurred by cloud.

The lieutenant held out his hand. "Goodbye then, Miss Thompson."

She took his hand and squeezed it gently. "Goodbye, lieutenant."

* * *

Rachel crossed Whitehall carefully, slowing to avoid a gleaming electric car that shot past her like a tiny meteor. On the pavement, a newspaper seller's placard declared in block letters 'PROFS SAY COMET NO THREAT.' She looked at it for a moment, shaking her head.

The committee room was dark and quiet, the wood-paneled walls decorated with plaques commemorating wars gone by. A whiskered general, shoulders heavy with gold braid, showed her to her seat.

"Perhaps you could summarize what you have learned for us, Miss Thompson." The speaker was a civilian with a lean, saturnine face, an under-secretary for something or other.

She spread out her papers in front of her.

"I don't have a complete transcription yet," she said. "But I understand enough."

The committee members were silent, waiting for her to continue.

"It wasn't bacteria that killed the Martians," she said.

The man opposite frowned. "I don't see how that's important."

"They died from radiation," she said. "From traveling in space. As they knew they would."

One or two of the army officers shook their heads. "But if they knew they would die, why invade?" one asked.

"Because conquering Earth was never their goal."

Someone made a snorting noise.

"Go on, Miss Thompson," the dark man said.

"The Martians aren't from Mars. Not originally. They came from another star." She paused, but no one said anything. "They were fugitives, fleeing from an enemy that wanted to destroy them."

"An enemy?"

"An enemy too powerful to fight. All they could do was hide. And the best way to hide their home on Mars was to build a decoy."

The generals were both frowning now. The civilian leaned forward, his eyes narrowed.

"They came here to build a civilization from nothing," Rachel continued. "To cover the planet with their machines. Make a target too tempting for the enemy to ignore, one that might trick them into overlooking their real target." She thought of flying machines circling the globe, the fighting machines turned builders raising new cities on the ruins of the old. The Martians had died too soon to finish their task, but humanity had seized on their technology.

"The Martian asked me only one question. I didn't understand it at the time." She drew out the paper copy she had made, the scribbled asterisk with its question marker. She pushed it forward so that they could all see it. "'Have you seen the star?' That was the question."

She turned her head and looked toward the window where the comet blazed, bright and malign in the heavens.

The Metal Monster
Prologue–Chapter IV

A. Merritt

Prologue

BEFORE THE NARRATIVE which follows was placed in my hands, I had never seen Dr. Walter T. Goodwin, its author.

When the manuscript revealing his adventures among the pre-historic ruins of the Nan-Matal in the Carolines (*The Moon Pool*) had been given me by the International Association of Science for editing and revision to meet the requirements of a popular presentation, Dr. Goodwin had left America. He had explained that he was still too shaken, too depressed, to be able to recall experiences that must inevitably carry with them freshened memories of those whom he loved so well and from whom, he felt, he was separated in all probability forever.

I had understood that he had gone to some remote part of Asia to pursue certain botanical studies, and it was therefore with the liveliest surprise and interest that I received a summons from the President of the Association to meet Dr. Goodwin at a designated place and hour.

Through my close study of the Moon Pool papers I had formed a mental image of their writer. I had read, too, those volumes of botanical research which have set him high above all other American scientists in this field, gleaning from their curious mingling of extremely technical observations and minutely accurate but extraordinarily poetic descriptions, hints to amplify my picture of him. It gratified me to find I had drawn a pretty good one.

The man to whom the President of the Association introduced me was sturdy, well-knit, a little under average height. He had a broad but rather low forehead that reminded me somewhat of the late electrical wizard Steinmetz. Under level black brows shone eyes of clear hazel, kindly, shrewd, a little wistful, lightly humorous; the eyes both of a doer and a dreamer.

Not more than forty I judged him to be. A close-trimmed, pointed beard did not hide the firm chin and the clean-cut mouth. His hair was thick and black and oddly sprinkled with white; small streaks and dots of gleaming silver that shone with a curiously metallic luster.

His right arm was closely bound to his breast. His manner as he greeted me was tinged with shyness. He extended his left hand in greeting, and as I clasped the fingers I was struck by their peculiar, pronounced, yet pleasant warmth; a sensation, indeed, curiously electric.

The Association's President forced him gently back into his chair.

"Dr. Goodwin," he said, turning to me, "is not entirely recovered as yet from certain consequences of his adventures. He will explain to you later what these are. In the meantime, Mr. Merritt, will you read this?"

I took the sheets he handed me, and as I read them felt the gaze of Dr. Goodwin full upon me, searching, weighing, estimating. When I raised my eyes from the letter I found in his a new expression. The shyness was gone; they were filled with complete friendliness. Evidently I had passed muster.

"You will accept, sir?" It was the president's gravely courteous tone.

"Accept!" I exclaimed. "Why, of course, I accept. It is not only one of the greatest honors, but to me one of the greatest delights to act as a collaborator with Dr. Goodwin."

The president smiled.

"In that case, sir, there is no need for me to remain longer," he said. "Dr. Goodwin has with him his manuscript as far as he has progressed with it. I will leave you two alone for your discussion."

He bowed to us and, picking up his old-fashioned bell-crowned silk hat and his quaint, heavy cane of ebony, withdrew. Dr. Goodwin turned to me.

"I will start," he said, after a little pause, "from when I met Richard Drake on the field of blue poppies that are like a great prayer-rug at the gray feet of the nameless mountain."

The sun sank, the shadows fell, the lights of the city sparkled out, for hours New York roared about me unheeded while I listened to the tale of that utterly weird, stupendous drama of an unknown life, of unknown creatures, unknown forces, and of unconquerable human heroism played among the hidden gorges of unknown Asia.

It was dawn when I left him for my own home. Nor was it for many hours after that I laid his then incomplete manuscript down and sought sleep – and found a troubled sleep.

A. Merritt

Chapter I
Valley of the Blue Poppies

IN THIS GREAT CRUCIBLE OF LIFE we call the world – in the vaster one we call the universe – the mysteries lie close packed, uncountable as grains of sand on ocean's shores. They thread gigantic, the star-flung spaces; they creep, atomic, beneath the microscope's peering eye. They walk beside us, unseen and unheard, calling out to us, asking why we are deaf to their crying, blind to their wonder.

Sometimes the veils drop from a man's eyes, and he sees – and speaks of his vision. Then those who have not seen pass him by with the lifted brows of disbelief, or they mock him, or if his vision has been great enough they fall upon and destroy him.

For the greater the mystery, the more bitterly is its verity assailed; upon what seem the lesser a man may give testimony and at least gain for himself a hearing.

There is reason for this. Life is a ferment, and upon and about it, shifting and changing, adding to or taking away, beat over legions of forces, seen and unseen, known and unknown. And man, an atom in the ferment, clings desperately to what to him seems stable; nor greets with joy him who hazards that what he grips may be but a broken staff, and, so saying, fails to hold forth a sturdier one.

Earth is a ship, plowing her way through uncharted oceans of space wherein are strange currents, hidden shoals and reefs, and where blow the unknown winds of Cosmos.

If to the voyagers, painfully plotting their course, comes one who cries that their charts must be remade, nor can tell *why* they must be – that man is not welcome – no!

Therefore it is that men have grown chary of giving testimony upon mysteries. Yet knowing each in his own heart the truth of that vision he has himself beheld, lo, it is that in whose reality he most believes.

The spot where I had encamped was of a singular beauty; so beautiful that it caught the throat and set an ache within the breast – until from it a tranquillity distilled that was like healing mist.

Since early March I had been wandering. It was now mid-July. And for the first time since my pilgrimage had begun I drank – not of forgetfulness, for that could never be – but of anodyne for a sorrow which had held fast upon me since my return from the Carolines a year before.

No need to dwell here upon that – it has been written. Nor shall I recite the reasons for my restlessness – for these are known to those who have read that history of mine. Nor is there cause to set forth at length the steps by which I had arrived at this vale of peace.

Sufficient is to tell that in New York one night, reading over what is perhaps the most sensational of my books – *The Poppies and Primulas of Southern Tibet*, the result of my travels of 1910–11, I determined to return to that quiet, forbidden land. There, if anywhere, might I find something akin to forgetting.

There was a certain flower which I long had wished to study in its mutations from the singular forms appearing on the southern slopes of the Elburz – Persia's mountainous chain that extends from Azerbaijan in the west to Khorasan in the east; from thence I would follow its modified types in the Hindu-Kush ranges and its migrations along the southern scarps of the Trans-Himalayas – the unexplored upheaval, higher than the Himalayas themselves, more deeply cut with precipice and gorge, which Sven Hedin had touched and named on his journey to Lhasa.

Having accomplished this, I planned to push across the passes to the Manasarowar Lakes, where, legend has it, the strange, luminous purple lotuses grow.

An ambitious project, undeniably fraught with danger; but it is written that desperate diseases require desperate remedies, and until inspiration or message how to rejoin those whom I had loved so dearly came to me, nothing less, I felt, could dull my heartache.

And, frankly, feeling that no such inspiration or message could come, I did not much care as to the end.

In Teheran I had picked up a most unusual servant; yes, more than this, a companion and counselor and interpreter as well.

He was a Chinese; his name Chiu-Ming. His first thirty years had been spent at the great Lamasery of Palkhor-Choinde at Gyantse, west of Lhasa. Why he had gone from there, how he had come to Teheran, I never asked. It was most fortunate that he had gone, and that I had found him. He recommended himself to me as the best cook within ten thousand miles of Pekin.

For almost three months we had journeyed; Chiu-Ming and I and the two ponies that carried my impedimenta.

We had traversed mountain roads which had echoed to the marching feet of the hosts of Darius, to the hordes of the Satraps. The highways of the Achaemenids – yes, and which before them had trembled to the tramplings of the myriads of the godlike Dravidian conquerors.

We had slipped over ancient Iranian trails; over paths which the warriors of conquering Alexander had traversed; dust of bones of Macedons, of Greeks, of Romans, beat about us; ashes of the flaming ambitions of the Sassanidae whimpered beneath our feet – the feet of an American botanist, a Chinaman, two Tibetan ponies. We had crept through clefts whose walls had sent back the howlings of the Ephthalites, the White Huns who had sapped the strength of these same proud Sassanids until at last both fell before the Turks.

Over the highways and byways of Persia's glory, Persia's shame and Persia's death we four – two men, two beasts – had passed. For a fortnight we had met no human soul, seen no sign of human habitation.

Game had been plentiful – green things Chiu-Ming might lack for his cooking, but meat never. About us was a welter of mighty summits. We were, I knew, somewhere within the blending of the Hindu-Kush with the Trans-Himalayas.

That morning we had come out of a ragged defile into this valley of enchantment, and here, though it had been so early, I had pitched my tent, determining to go no farther till the morrow.

It was a Phocean vale; a gigantic cup filled with tranquillity. A spirit brooded over it, serene, majestic, immutable – like the untroubled calm which rests, the Burmese believe, over every place which has guarded the Buddha, sleeping.

At its eastern end towered the colossal scarp of the unnamed peak through one of whose gorges we had crept. On his head was a cap of silver set with pale emeralds – the snow fields and glaciers that crowned him. Far to the west another gray and ochreous giant reared its bulk, closing the vale. North and south, the horizon was a chaotic sky land of pinnacles, spired and minareted, steepled and turreted and domed, each diademed with its green and argent of eternal ice and snow.

And all the valley was carpeted with the blue poppies in wide, unbroken fields, luminous as the morning skies of mid-June; they rippled mile after mile over the path we had followed, over the still untrodden path which we must take. They nodded, they leaned toward each other, they seemed to whisper – then to lift their heads and look up like crowding swarms of little azure fays, half impudently, wholly trustfully, into the faces of the jeweled giants standing guard over them. And when the little breeze walked upon them it was as though they bent beneath the soft tread and were brushed by the sweeping skirts of unseen, hastening Presences.

Like a vast prayer-rug, sapphire and silken, the poppies stretched to the gray feet of the mountain. Between their southern edge and the clustering summits a row of faded brown, low hills knelt – like brown-robed, withered and weary old men, backs bent, faces hidden between outstretched arms, palms to the earth and brows touching earth within them – in the East's immemorial attitude of worship.

I half expected them to rise – and as I watched a man appeared on one of the bowed, rocky shoulders, abruptly, with the ever-startling suddenness which in the strange light of these latitudes objects spring into vision. As he stood scanning my camp there arose beside him a laden pony, and at its head a Tibetan peasant. The first figure waved its hand; came striding down the hill.

As he approached I took stock of him. A young giant, three good inches over six feet, a vigorous head with unruly clustering black hair; a clean-cut, clean-shaven American face.

"I'm Dick Drake," he said, holding out his hand. "Richard Keen Drake, recently with Uncle's engineers in France."

"My name is Goodwin." I took his hand, shook it warmly. "Dr. Walter T. Goodwin."

"Goodwin the botanist? Then I know you!" he exclaimed. "Know all about you, that is. My father admired your work greatly. You knew him – Professor Alvin Drake."

I nodded. So he was Alvin Drake's son. Alvin, I knew, had died about a year before I had started on this journey. But what was his son doing in this wilderness?

"Wondering where I came from?" he answered my unspoken question. "Short story. War ended. Felt an irresistible desire for something different. Couldn't think of anything more different from Tibet – always wanted to go there anyway. Went. Decided to strike over toward Turkestan. And here I am."

I felt at once a strong liking for this young giant. No doubt, subconsciously, I had been feeling the need of companionship with my own kind. I even wondered, as I led the way into my little camp, whether he would care to join fortunes with me in my journeyings.

His father's work I knew well, and although this stalwart lad was unlike what one would have expected Alvin Drake – a trifle dried, precise, wholly abstracted with his experiments – to beget, still, I reflected, heredity like the Lord sometimes works in mysterious ways its wonders to perform.

It was almost with awe that he listened to me instruct Chiu-Ming as to just how I wanted supper prepared, and his gaze dwelt fondly upon the Chinese busy among his pots and pans.

We talked a little, desultorily, as the meal was prepared – fragments of traveler's news and gossip, as is the habit of journeyers who come upon each other in the silent places. Ever the speculation grew in his face as he made away with Chiu-Ming's artful concoctions.

Drake sighed, drawing out his pipe.

"A cook, a marvel of a cook. Where did you get him?"

Briefly I told him.

Then a silence fell upon us. Suddenly the sun dipped down behind the flank of the stone giant guarding the valley's western gate; the whole vale swiftly darkened – a flood of crystal-clear shadows poured within it. It was the prelude to that miracle of unearthly beauty seen nowhere else on this earth – the sunset of Tibet.

We turned expectant eyes to the west. A little, cool breeze raced down from the watching steeps like a messenger, whispered to the nodding poppies, sighed and was gone. The poppies were still. High overhead a homing kite whistled, mellowly.

As if it were a signal there sprang out in the pale azure of the western sky row upon row of cirrus cloudlets, rank upon rank of them, thrusting their heads into the path of the setting sun. They changed from mottled silver into faint rose, deepened to crimson.

"The dragons of the sky drink the blood of the sunset," said Chiu-Ming.

As though a gigantic globe of crystal had dropped upon the heavens, their blue turned swiftly to a clear and glowing amber – then as abruptly shifted to a luminous violet A soft green light pulsed through the valley.

Under it, like hills ensorcelled, the rocky walls about it seemed to flatten. They glowed and all at once pressed forward like gigantic slices of palest emerald jade, translucent, illumined, as though by a circlet of little suns shining behind them.

The light faded, robes of deepest amethyst dropped around the mountain's mighty shoulders. And then from every snow and glacier-crowned peak, from minaret and pinnacle and towering turret, leaped forth a confusion of soft peacock flames, a host of irised prismatic gleamings, an ordered chaos of rainbows.

Great and small, interlacing and shifting, they ringed the valley with an incredible glory – as if some god of light itself had touched the eternal rocks and bidden radiant souls stand forth.

Through the darkening sky swept a rosy pencil of living light; that utterly strange, pure beam whose coming never fails to clutch the throat of the beholder with the hand of ecstasy, the ray which the Tibetans name the Ting-Pa. For a moment this rosy finger pointed to the east, then arched itself, divided slowly into six shining, rosy bands; began to creep downward toward the eastern horizon where a nebulous, pulsing splendor arose to meet it.

And as we watched I heard a gasp from Drake. And it was echoed by my own.

For the six beams were swaying, moving with ever swifter motion from side to side in ever-widening sweep, as though the hidden orb from which they sprang were swaying like a pendulum.

Faster and faster the six high-flung beams swayed – and then broke – broke as though a gigantic, unseen hand had reached up and snapped them!

An instant the severed ends ribboned aimlessly, then bent, turned down and darted earthward into the welter of clustered summits at the north and swiftly were gone, while down upon the valley fell night.

"Good God!" whispered Drake. "It was as though something reached up, broke those rays and drew them down – like threads."

"I saw it." I struggled with bewilderment. "I saw it. But I never saw anything like it before," I ended, most inadequately.

"It was *purposeful*," he whispered. "It was *deliberate*. As though something reached up, juggled with the rays, broke them, and drew them down like willow withes."

"The devils that dwell here!" quavered Chiu-Ming.

"Some magnetic phenomenon." I was half angry at myself for my own touch of panic. "Light can be deflected by passage through a magnetic field. Of course that's it. Certainly."

"I don't know." Drake's tone was doubtful indeed. "It would take a whale of a magnetic field to have done *that* – it's inconceivable." He harked back to his first idea. "It was so – so *damned* deliberate," he repeated.

"Devils –" muttered the frightened Chinese.

"What's that?" Drake gripped my arm and pointed to the north. A deeper blackness had grown there while we had been talking, a pool of darkness against which the mountain summits stood out, blade-sharp edges faintly luminous.

A gigantic lance of misty green fire darted from the blackness and thrust its point into the heart of the zenith; following it, leaped into the sky a host of the sparkling spears of light, and now the blackness was like an ebon hand, brandishing a thousand javelins of tinseled flame.

"The aurora," I said.

"It ought to be a good one," mused Drake, gaze intent upon it. "Did you notice the big sun spot?"

I shook my head.

"The biggest I ever saw. Noticed it first at dawn this morning. Some little aurora lighter – that spot. I told you – look at that!" he cried.

The green lances had fallen back. The blackness gathered itself together – then from it began to pulse billows of radiance, spangled with infinite darting swarms of flashing corpuscles like uncounted hosts of dancing fireflies.

Higher the waves rolled – phosphorescent green and iridescent violet, weird copperous yellows and metallic saffrons and a shimmer of glittering ash of rose – then wavered, split and formed into gigantic, sparkling, marching curtains of splendor.

A vast circle of light sprang out upon the folds of the flickering, rushing curtains. Misty at first, its edges sharpened until they rested upon the blazing glory of the northern sky like a pale ring of cold flame. And about it the aurora began to churn, to heap itself, to revolve.

Toward the ring from every side raced the majestic folds, drew themselves together, circled, seethed around it like foam of fire about the lip of a cauldron, and poured through the shining circle as though it were the mouth of that fabled cavern where old Aeolus sits blowing forth and breathing back the winds that sweep the earth.

Yes – into the ring's mouth the aurora flew, cascading in a columned stream to earth. Then swiftly, a mist swept over all the heavens, veiled that incredible cataract.

"Magnetism?" muttered Drake. "I guess *not*!"

"It struck about where the Ting-Pa was broken and seemed drawn down like the rays," I said.

"Purposeful," Drake said. "And devilish. It hit on all my nerves like a – like a metal claw. Purposeful and deliberate. There was intelligence behind that."

"Intelligence? Drake – what intelligence could break the rays of the setting sun and suck down the aurora?"

"I don't know," he answered.

"Devils," croaked Chiu-Ming. "The devils that defied Buddha – and have grown strong –"

"Like a metal claw!" breathed Drake.

Far to the west a sound came to us; first a whisper, then a wild rushing, a prolonged wailing, a crackling. A great light flashed through the mist, glowed about us and faded. Again the wailing, the vast rushing, the retreating whisper.

Then silence and darkness dropped embraced upon the valley of the blue poppies.

Chapter II
The Sigil on the Rocks

DAWN CAME. Drake had slept well. But I, who had not his youthful resiliency, lay for long, awake and uneasy. I had hardly sunk into troubled slumber before dawn awakened me.

As we breakfasted, I approached directly that matter which my growing liking for him was turning into strong desire.

"Drake," I asked. "Where are you going?"

"With you," he laughed. "I'm foot loose and fancy free. And I think you ought to have somebody with you to help watch that cook. He might get away."

The idea seemed to appall him.

"Fine!" I exclaimed heartily, and thrust out my hand to him. "I'm thinking of striking over the range soon to the Manasarowar Lakes. There's a curious flora I'd like to study."

"Anywhere you say suits me," he answered.

We clasped hands on our partnership and soon we were on our way to the valley's western gate; our united caravans stringing along behind us. Mile after mile we trudged through the blue poppies, discussing the enigmas of the twilight and of the night.

In the light of day their breath of vague terror was dissipated. There was no place for mystery nor dread under this floor of brilliant sunshine. The smiling sapphire floor rolled ever on before us.

Whispering little playful breezes flew down the slopes to gossip for a moment with the nodding flowers. Flocks of rose finches raced chattering overhead to quarrel with the tiny willow warblers, the chi-u-teb-tok, holding fief of the drooping, graceful bowers bending down to the little laughing stream that for the past hour had chuckled and gurgled like a friendly water baby beside us.

I had proven, almost to my own satisfaction, that what we had beheld had been a creation of the extraordinary atmospheric attributes of these highlands, an atmosphere so unique as to make almost anything of the kind possible. But Drake was not convinced.

"I know," he said. "Of course I understand all that – superimposed layers of warmer air that might have bent the ray; vortices in the higher levels that might have produced just that effect of the captured aurora. I admit it's all possible. I'll even admit it's all probable, but damn me, Doc, if I *believe* it! I had too clearly the feeling of a *conscious* force, a something that *knew* exactly what it was doing – and had a *reason* for it."

It was mid-afternoon.

The spell of the valley upon us, we had gone leisurely. The western mount was close, the mouth of the gorge through which we must pass, now plain before us. It did not seem as though we could reach it before dusk, and Drake and I were reconciled to spending another night in the peaceful vale. Plodding along, deep in thought, I was startled by his exclamation.

He was staring at a point some hundred yards to his right. I followed his gaze.

The towering cliffs were a scant half mile away. At some distant time there had been an enormous fall of rock. This, disintegrating, had formed a gently-curving breast which sloped down to merge with the valley's floor. Willow and witch alder, stunted birch and poplar had found roothold, clothed it, until only their crowding outposts, thrusting forward in a wavering semicircle, held back seemingly by the blue hordes, showed where it melted into the meadows.

In the center of this breast, beginning half way up its slopes and stretching down into the flowered fields was a colossal imprint.

Gray and brown, it stood out against the green and blue of slope and level; a rectangle all of thirty feet wide, two hundred long, the heel faintly curved and from its hither end, like claws, four slender triangles radiating from it like twenty-four points of a ten-rayed star.

Irresistibly was it like a footprint – but what thing was there whose tread could leave such a print as this?

I ran up the slope – Drake already well in advance. I paused at the base of the triangles where, were this thing indeed a footprint, the spreading claws sprang from the flat of it.

The track was fresh. At its upper edges were clipped bushes and split trees, the white wood of the latter showing where they had been sliced as though by the stroke of a scimitar.

I stepped out upon the mark. It was as level as though planed; bent down and stared in utter disbelief of what my own eyes beheld. For stone and earth had been crushed, compressed, into a smooth, microscopically grained, adamantine complex, and in this matrix poppies still bearing traces of their coloring were imbedded like fossils. A cyclone can and does grip straws and thrust them unbroken through an inch board – but what force was there which could take the delicate petals of a flower and set them like inlay within the surface of a stone?

Into my mind came recollection of the wailings, the crashings in the night, of the weird glow that had flashed about us when the mist arose to hide the chained aurora.

"It was what we heard," I said. "The sounds – it was then that this was made."

"The foot of Shin-je!" Chiu-Ming's voice was tremulous. "The lord of Hell has trodden here!"

I translated for Drake's benefit.

"Has the lord of Hell but one foot?" asked Dick, politely.

"He bestrides the mountains," said Chiu-Ming. "On the far side is his other footprint. Shin-je it was who strode the mountains and set here his foot."

Again I interpreted.

Drake cast a calculating glance up to the cliff top.

"Two thousand feet, about," he mused. "Well, if Shin-je is built in our proportions that makes it about right. The length of this thing would give him just about a two thousand foot leg. Yes – he could just about straddle that hill."

"You're surely not serious?" I asked in consternation.

"What the hell!" he exclaimed, "Am I crazy? This is no foot mark. How could it be? Look at the mathematical nicety with which these edges are stamped out – as though by a die –

"That's what it reminds me of – a die. It's as if some impossible power had been used to press it down. Like – like a giant seal of metal in a mountain's hand. A sigil – a seal –"

"But why?" I asked. "What could be the purpose –"

"Better ask where the devil such a force could be gotten together and how it came here," he said. "Look – except for this one place there isn't a mark anywhere. All the bushes and the trees, all the poppies and the grass are just as they ought to be.

"How did whoever or whatever it was that made this, get here and get away without leaving any trace but this? Damned if I don't think Chiu-Ming's explanation puts less strain upon the credulity than any I could offer."

I peered about. It was so. Except for the mark, there was no slightest sign of the unusual, the abnormal.

But the mark was enough!

"I'm for pushing up a notch or two and getting into the gorge before dark," he was voicing my own thought. "I'm willing to face anything human – but I'm not keen to be pressed into a rock like a flower in a maiden's book of poems." Just at twilight we drew out of the valley into the pass. We traveled a full mile along it before darkness forced us to make camp. The gorge was narrow. The far walls but a hundred feet away; but we had no quarrel with them for their neighborliness, no! Their solidity, their immutability, breathed confidence back into us.

And after we had found a deep niche capable of holding the entire caravan we filed within, ponies and all, I for one perfectly willing thus to spend the night, let the air at dawn be what it would. We dined within on bread and tea, and then, tired to the bone, sought each his place upon the rocky floor. I slept well, waking only once or twice by Chiu-Ming's groanings; his dreams evidently were none of the pleasantest. If there was an aurora I neither knew nor cared. My slumber was dreamless.

Chapter III
Ruth Ventnor

THE DAWN, streaming into the niche, awakened us. A covey of partridges venturing too close yielded three to our guns. We breakfasted well, and a little later were pushing on down the cleft.

Its descent, though gradual, was continuous, and therefore I was not surprised when soon we began to come upon evidences of semi-tropical vegetation. Giant rhododendrons and tree ferns gave way to occasional clumps of stately kopek and clumps of the hardier bamboos. We added a few snow cocks to our larder – although they were out of their habitat, flying down into the gorge from their peaks and table-lands for some choice tidbit.

All that day we marched on, and when at night we made camp, sleep came to us quickly and overmastering. An hour after dawn we were on our way. A brief stop we made for lunch; pressed forward.

It was close to two when we caught the first sight of the ruins.

The soaring, verdure-clad walls of the canyon had long been steadily marching closer. Above, between their rims the wide ribbon of sky was like a fantastically shored river, shimmering, dazzling; every cove and headland edged with an opalescent glimmering as of shining pearly beaches.

And as though we were sinking in that sky stream's depths its light kept lessening, darkening imperceptibly with luminous shadows of ghostly beryl, drifting veils of pellucid aquamarine, limpid mists of glaucous chrysolite.

Fainter, more crepuscular became the light, yet never losing its crystalline quality. Now the high overhead river was but a brook; became a thread. Abruptly it vanished.

We passed into a tunnel, fern walled, fern roofed, garlanded with tawny orchids, gay with carmine fungus and golden moss. We stepped out into a blaze of sunlight.

Before us lay a wide green bowl held in the hands of the clustered hills; shallow, circular, as though, while plastic still, the thumb of God had run round its rim, shaping it. Around it the peaks crowded, craning their lofty heads to peer within.

It was about a mile in its diameter, this hollow, as my gaze then measured it. It had three openings – one that lay like a crack in the northeast slope; another, the tunnel mouth through which we had come. The third lifted itself out of the bowl, creeping up the precipitous bare scarp of the western barrier straight to the north, clinging to the ochreous rock up and up until it vanished around a far distant shoulder.

It was a wide and bulwarked road, a road that spoke as clearly as though it had tongue of human hands which had cut it there in the mountain's breast. An ancient road weary beyond belief beneath the tread of uncounted years.

From the hollow the blind soul of loneliness groped out to greet us!

Never had I felt such loneliness as that which lapped the lip of the verdant bowl. It was tangible – as though it had been poured from some reservoir of misery. A pool of despair –

Half the width of the valley away the ruins began. Weirdly were they its visible expression. They huddled in two bent rows to the bottom. They crouched in a wide cluster against the cliffs. From the cluster a curving row of them ran along the southern crest of the hollow.

A flight of shattered, cyclopean steps lifted to a ledge and here a crumbling fortress stood.

Irresistibly did the ruins seem a colossal hag, flung prone, lying listlessly, helplessly, against the barrier's base. The huddled lower ranks were the legs, the cluster the body, the upper row an outflung arm and above the neck of the stairway the ancient fortress, rounded and with two huge ragged apertures in its northern front was an aged, bleached and withered head staring, watching.

I looked at Drake – the spell of the bowl was heavy upon him, his face drawn. The Chinaman and Tibetan were murmuring, terror written large upon them.

"A hell of a joint!" Drake turned to me, a shadow of a grin lightening the distress on his face. "But I'd rather chance it than go back. What d'you say?"

I nodded, curiosity mastering my oppression. We stepped over the rim, rifles on the alert. Close behind us crowded the two servants and the ponies.

The vale was shallow, as I have said. We trod the fragments of an olden approach to the green tunnel so the descent was not difficult. Here and there beside the path upreared huge broken blocks. On them I thought I could see faint tracings as of carvings – now a suggestion of gaping, arrow-fanged dragon jaws, now the outline of a scaled body, a hint of enormous, batlike wings.

Now we had reached the first of the crumbling piles that stretched down into the valley's center.

Half fainting, I fell against Drake, clutching to him for support.

A stream of utter hopelessness was racing upon us, swirling and eddying around us, reaching to our hearts with ghostly fingers dripping with despair. From every shattered heap it seemed to pour, rushing down the road upon us like a torrent, engulfing us, submerging, drowning.

Unseen it was – yet tangible as water; it sapped the life from every nerve. Weariness filled me, a desire to drop upon the stones, to be rolled away. To die. I felt Drake's body quivering even as mine; knew that he was drawing upon every reserve of strength.

"Steady," he muttered. "Steady –"

The Tibetan shrieked and fled, the ponies scrambling after him. Dimly I remembered that mine carried precious specimens; a surge of anger passed, beating back the anguish. I heard a sob from Chiu-Ming, saw him drop.

Drake stopped, drew him to his feet. We placed him between us, thrust each an arm through his own. Then, like swimmers, heads bent, we pushed on, buffeting that inexplicable invisible flood.

As the path rose, its force lessened, my vitality grew, and the terrible desire to yield and be swept away waned. Now we had reached the foot of the cyclopean stairs, now we were half up them – and now as we struggled out upon the ledge on which the watching fortress stood, the clutching stream shoaled swiftly, the shoal became safe, dry land and the cheated, unseen maelstrom swirled harmlessly beneath us.

We stood erect, gasping for breath, again like swimmers who have fought their utmost and barely, so barely, won.

There was an almost imperceptible movement at the side of the ruined portal.

Out darted a girl. A rifle dropped from her hands. Straight she sped toward me.

And as she ran I recognized her.

Ruth Ventnor!

The flying figure reached me, threw soft arms around my neck, was weeping in relieved gladness on my shoulder.

"Ruth!" I cried. "What on earth are *you* doing here?"

"Walter!" she sobbed. "Walter Goodwin – Oh, thank God! Thank God!"

She drew herself from my arms, catching her breath; laughed shakily.

I took swift stock of her. Save for fear upon her, she was the same Ruth I had known three years before; wide, deep blue eyes that were now all seriousness, now sparkling wells of mischief; petite, rounded and tender; the fairest skin; an impudent little nose; shining clusters of intractable curls; all human, sparkling and sweet.

Drake coughed, insinuatingly. I introduced him.

"I – I watched you struggling through that dreadful pit." She shuddered. "I could not see who you were, did not know whether friend or enemy – but oh, my heart almost died in pity for you, Walter," she breathed. "What can it be – *there*?"

I shook my head.

"Martin could not see you," she went on. "He was watching the road that leads above. But I ran down – to help."

"Mart watching?" I asked. "Watching for what?"

"I —" she hesitated oddly. "I think I'd rather tell you before him. It's so strange – so incredible."

She led us through the broken portal and into the fortress. It was more gigantic even than I had thought. The floor of the vast chamber we had entered was strewn with fragments fallen from the crackling, stone-vaulted ceiling. Through the breaks light streamed from the level above us.

We picked our way among the debris to a wide crumbling stairway, crept up it, Ruth flitting ahead. We came out opposite one of the eye-like apertures. Black against it, perched high upon a pile of blocks, I recognized the long, lean outline of Ventnor, rifle in hand, gazing intently up the ancient road whose windings were plain through the opening. He had not heard us.

"Martin," called Ruth softly.

He turned. A shaft of light from a crevice in the gap's edge struck his face, flashing it out from the semidarkness of the corner in which he crouched. I looked into the quiet gray eyes, upon the keen face.

"Goodwin!" he shouted, tumbling down from his perch, shaking me by the shoulders. "If I had been in the way of praying – you're the man I'd have prayed for. How did you get here?"

"Just wandering, Mart," I answered. "But Lord! I'm sure *glad* to see you."

"Which way did you come?" he asked, keenly. I threw my hand toward the south.

"Not through that hollow?" he asked incredulously.

"And some hell of a place to get through," Drake broke in. "It cost us our ponies and all my ammunition."

"Richard Drake," I said. "Son of old Alvin – you knew him, Mart."

"Knew him well," cried Ventnor, seizing Dick's hand. "Wanted me to go to Kamchatka to get some confounded sort of stuff for one of his devilish experiments. Is he well?"

"He's dead," replied Dick soberly.

"Oh!" said Ventnor. "Oh – I'm sorry. He was a great man."

Briefly I acquainted him with my wanderings, my encounter with Drake.

"That place out there –" he considered us thoughtfully. "Damned if I know what it is. Thought maybe it's gas – of a sort. If it hadn't been for it we'd have been out of this hole two days ago. I'm pretty sure it must be gas. And it must be much less than it was this morning, for then we made an attempt to get through again – and couldn't."

I was hardly listening. Ventnor had certainly advanced a theory of our unusual symptoms that had not occurred to me. That hollow might indeed be a pocket into which a gas flowed; just as in the mines the deadly coal damp collects in pits, flows like a stream along the passages. It might be that – some odorless, colorless gas of unknown qualities; and yet –

"Did you try respirators?" asked Dick.

"Surely," said Ventnor. "First off the go. But they weren't of any use. The gas, if it is gas, seems to operate as well through the skin as through the nose and mouth. We just couldn't make it – and that's all there is to it. But if you made it – could we try it now, do you think?" he asked eagerly.

I felt myself go white.

"Not – not for a little while," I stammered.

He nodded, understandingly.

"I see," he said. "Well, we'll wait a bit, then."

"But why are you staying here? Why didn't you make for the road up the mountain? What are you watching for, anyway?" asked Drake.

"Go to it, Ruth," Ventnor grinned. "Tell 'em. After all – it was *your* party you know."

"Mart!" she cried, blushing.

"Well – it wasn't *me* they admired," he laughed.

"Martin!" she cried again, and stamped her foot.

"Shoot," he said. "I'm busy. I've got to watch."

"Well" – Ruth's voice was uncertain – "we'd been hunting up in Kashmir. Martin wanted to come over somewhere here. So we crossed the passes. That was about a month ago. The fourth day out we ran across what looked like a road running south.

"We thought we'd take it. It looked sort of old and lost – but it was going the way we wanted to go. It took us first into a country of little hills; then to the very base of the great range itself; finally into the mountains – and then it ran blank."

"Bing!" interjected Ventnor, looking around for a moment. "Bing – just like that. Slap dash against a prodigious fall of rock. We couldn't get over it."

"So we cast about to find another road," went on Ruth. "All we could strike were – just strikes."

"No fish on the end of 'em," said Ventnor. "God! But I'm glad to see you, Walter Goodwin. Believe me, I am. However – go on, Ruth."

"At the end of the second week," she said, "we knew we were lost. We were deep in the heart of the range. All around us was a forest of enormous, snow-topped peaks. The gorges, the canyons, the valleys that we tried led us east and west, north and south.

"It was a maze, and in it we seemed to be going ever deeper. There was not the *slightest* sign of human life. It was as though no human beings except ourselves had ever been there. Game was plentiful. We had no trouble in getting food. And sooner or later, of course, we were bound to find our way out. We didn't worry.

"It was five nights ago that we camped at the head of a lovely little valley. There was a mound that stood up like a tiny watch-tower, looking down it. The trees grew round like tall sentinels.

"We built our fire in that mound; and after we had eaten, Martin slept. I sat watching the beauty of the skies and of the shadowy vale. I heard no one approach – but something made me leap to my feet, look behind me.

"A man was standing just within the glow of firelight, watching me."

"A Tibetan?" I asked. She shook her head, trouble in her eyes.

"Not at all." Ventnor turned his head. "Ruth screamed and awakened me. I caught a glimpse of the fellow before he vanished.

"A short purple mantle hung from his shoulders. His chest was covered with fine chain mail. His legs were swathed and bound by the thongs of his high buskins. He carried a small, round, hide-covered shield and a short two-edged sword. His head was helmeted. He belonged, in fact – oh, at least twenty centuries back."

He laughed in plain enjoyment of our amazement.

"Go on, Ruth," he said, and took up his watch.

"But Martin did not see his face," she went on. "And oh, but I wish I could forget it. It was as white as mine, Walter, and cruel, so cruel; the eyes glowed and they looked upon me like a – like a slave dealer. They shamed me – I wanted to hide myself. "I cried out and Martin awakened. As he moved, the man stepped out of the light and was gone. I think he had not seen Martin; had believed that I was alone.

"We put out the fire, moved farther into the shadow of the trees. But I could not sleep – I sat hour after hour, my pistol in my hand," she patted the automatic in her belt, "my rifle close beside me.

"The hours went by – dreadfully. At last I dozed. When I awakened again it was dawn – and – and –" she covered her eyes, then: "*Two* men were looking down on me. One was he who had stood in the firelight."

"They were talking," interrupted Ventnor again, "in archaic Persian."

"Persian," I repeated blankly; "archaic Persian?"

"Very much so," he nodded. "I've a fair knowledge of the modern tongue, and a rather unusual command of Arabic. The modern Persian, as you know, comes straight through from the speech of Xerxes, of Cyrus, of Darius whom Alexander of Macedon conquered. It has been changed mainly by taking on a load of Arabic words. Well – there wasn't a trace of the Arabic in the tongue they were speaking.

"It sounded odd, of course – but I could understand quite easily. They were talking about Ruth. To be explicit, they were discussing her with exceeding frankness –"

"Martin!" she cried wrathfully.

"Well, all right," he went on, half repentantly. "As a matter of fact, I had seen the pair steal up. My rifle was under my hand. So I lay there quietly, listening.

"You can realize, Walter, that when I caught sight of those two, looking as though they had materialized from Darius's ghostly hordes, my scientific curiosity was aroused – prodigiously. So in my interest I passed over the matter of their speech; not alone because I thought Ruth asleep but also because I took into consideration that the mode of polite expression changes with the centuries – and these gentlemen clearly belonged at least twenty centuries back – the real truth is I was consumed with curiosity.

"They had got to a point where they were detailing with what pleasure a certain mysterious person whom they seemed to regard with much fear and respect would contemplate her. I was wondering how long my desire to observe – for to the anthropologist they were most fascinating – could hold my hand back from my rifle when Ruth awakened.

"She jumped up like a little fury. Fired a pistol point blank at them. Their amazement was – well – ludicrous. I know it seems incredible, but they seemed to know nothing of firearms – they certainly acted as though they didn't.

"They simply flew into the timber. I took a pistol shot at one but missed. Ruth hadn't though; she had winged her man; he left a red trail behind him.

"We didn't follow the trail. We made for the opposite direction – and as fast as possible.

"Nothing happened that day or night. Next morning, creeping up a slope, we caught sight of a suspicious glitter a mile or two away in the direction we were going. We sought shelter in a small ravine. In a little while, over the hill and half a mile away from us, came about two hundred of these fellows, marching along.

"And they were indeed Darius's men. Men of that Persia which had been dead for millenniums. There was no mistaking them, with their high, covering shields, their great bows, their javelins and armor.

"They passed; we doubled. We built no fires that night – and we ought to have turned the pony loose, but we didn't. It carried my instruments, and ammunition, and I felt we were going to need the latter.

"The next morning we caught sight of another band   or the same. We turned again. We stole through a tree-covered plain; we struck an ancient road. It led south, into the peaks again. We followed it. It brought us here.

"It isn't, as you observe, the most comfortable of places. We struck across the hollow to the crevice – we knew nothing of the entrance you came through. The hollow was not pleasant, either. But it was penetrable, then.

"We crossed. As we were about to enter the cleft there issued out of it a most unusual and disconcerting chorus of sounds – wailings, crashings, splinterings."

I started, shot a look at Dick; absorbed, he was drinking in Ventnor's every word.

"So unusual, so – well, disconcerting is the best word I can think of, that we were not encouraged to proceed. Also the peculiar unpleasantness of the hollow was increasing rapidly.

"We made the best time we could back to the fortress. And when next we tried to go through the hollow, to search for another outlet – we couldn't. You know why," he ended abruptly.

"But men in ancient armor. Men like those of Darius." Dick broke the silence that had followed this amazing recital. "It's incredible!"

"Yes," agreed Ventnor, "isn't it. But there they were. Of course, I don't maintain that they *were* relics of Darius's armies. They might have been of Xerxes before him – or of Artaxerxes after him. But there they certainly were, Drake, living, breathing replicas of exceedingly ancient Persians.

"Why, they might have been the wall carvings on the tomb of Khosroes come to life. I mention Darius because he fits in with the most plausible hypothesis. When Alexander the Great smashed his empire he did it rather thoroughly. There wasn't much sympathy for the vanquished in those days. And it's entirely conceivable that a city or two in Alexander's way might have gathered up a fleeting regiment or so for protection and have decided not to wait for him, but to hunt for cover.

"Naturally, they would have gone into the almost inaccessible heart of the high ranges. There is nothing impossible in the theory that they found shelter at last up here. As long as history runs this has been a well-nigh unknown land. Penetrating some mountain-guarded, easily defended valley they might have decided to settle down for a time, have rebuilt a city, raised a government; laying low, in a sentence, waiting for the storm to blow over.

"Why did they stay? Well, they might have found the new life more pleasant than the old. And they might have been locked in their valley by some accident – landslides, rockfalls sealing up the entrance. There are a dozen reasonable possibilities."

"But those who hunted you weren't locked in," objected Drake.

"No," Ventnor grinned ruefully. "No, they certainly weren't. Maybe we drifted into their preserves by a way they don't know. Maybe they've found another way out. I'm sure I don't know. But I *do* know what I saw."

"The noises, Martin," I said, for his description of these had been the description of those we had heard in the blue valley. "Have you heard them since?"

"Yes," he answered, hesitating oddly.

"And you think those – those soldiers you saw are still hunting for you?"

"Haven't a doubt of it," he replied more cheerfully. "They didn't look like chaps who would give up a hunt easily – at least not a hunt for such novel, interesting, and therefore desirable and delectable game as we must have appeared to them."

"Martin," I said decisively, "where's your pony? We'll try the hollow again, at once. There's Ruth – and we'd never be able to hold back such numbers as you've described."

"You feel strong enough to try it?"

Chapter IV
Metal with a Brain

THE EAGERNESS, the relief in his voice betrayed the tension, the anxiety which until now he had hidden so well; and hot shame burned me for my shrinking, my dread of again passing through that haunted vale.

"I certainly *do*." I was once more master of myself. "Drake – don't you agree?"

"Sure," he replied. "Sure. I'll look after Ruth – er – I mean Miss Ventnor."

The glint of amusement in Ventnor's eyes at this faded abruptly; his face grew somber.

"Wait," he said. "I carried away some – some exhibits from the crevice of the noises, Goodwin."

"What kind of exhibits?" I asked, eagerly.

"Put 'em where they'd be safe," he continued. "I've an idea they're far more curious than our armored men – and of far more importance. At any rate, we must take them with us.

"Go with Ruth, you and Drake, and look at them. And bring them back with the pony. Then we'll make a start. A few minutes more probably won't make much difference – but hurry."

He turned back to his watch. Ordering Chiu-Ming to stay with him I followed Ruth and Drake down the ruined stairway. At the bottom she came to me, laid little hands on my shoulders.

"Walter," she breathed, "I'm frightened. I'm so frightened I'm afraid to tell even Mart. He doesn't like them, either, these little things you're going to see. He likes them so little that he's afraid to let me know how little he does like them."

"But what are they? What's to fear about them?" asked Drake.

"See what you think!" She led us slowly, almost reluctantly toward the rear of the fortress. "They lay in a little heap at the mouth of the cleft where we heard the noises. Martin picked them up and dropped them in a sack before we ran through the hollow.

"They're grotesque and they're almost *cute*, and they make me feel as though they were the tiniest tippy-tip of the claw of some incredibly large cat just stealing around the corner, a terrible cat, a cat as big as a mountain," she ended breathlessly.

We climbed through the crumbling masonry into a central, open court. Here a clear spring bubbled up in a ruined and choked stone basin; close to the ancient well was their pony, contentedly browsing in the thick grass that grew around it. From one of its hampers Ruth took a large cloth bag.

"To carry them," she said, and trembled.

We passed through what had once been a great door into another chamber larger than that we had just left; and it was in better preservation, the ceiling unbroken, the light dim after the blazing sun of the court. Near its center she halted us.

Before me ran a two-feet-wide ragged crack, splitting the floor and dropping down into black depths. Beyond was an expanse of smooth flagging, almost clear of debris.

Drake gave a low whistle. I followed his pointing finger. In the wall at the end whirled two enormous dragon shapes, cut in low relief. Their gigantic wings, their monstrous coils, covered the nearly unbroken surface, and these *chimerae* were the shapes upon the upthrust blocks of the haunted roadway.

In Ruth's gaze I read a nameless fear, a half shuddering fascination.

But she was not looking at the cavern dragons.

Her gaze was fixed upon what at my first glance seemed to be a raised and patterned circle in the dust-covered floor. Not more than a foot in width, it shone wanly with a pale, metallic bluish luster, as though, I thought, it had been recently polished. Compared with the wall's tremendous winged figures this floor design was trivial, ludicrously insignificant. What could there be about it to stamp that dread upon Ruth's face?

I leaped the crevice; Dick joined me. Now I could see that the ring was not continuous. Its broken circle was made of sharply edged cubes about an inch in height, separated from each other with mathematical exactness by another inch of space. I counted them – there were nineteen.

Almost touching them with their bases were an equal number of pyramids, of tetrahedrons, as sharply angled and of similar length. They lay on their sides with tips pointing starlike to six spheres clustered like a conventionalized five petaled primrose in the exact center. Five of these spheres – the petals – were, I roughly calculated, about an inch and a half in diameter, the ball they enclosed larger by almost an inch.

So orderly was their arrangement, so much like a geometrical design nicely done by some clever child that I hesitated to disturb it. I bent, and stiffened, the first touch of dread upon me.

For within the ring, close to the clustering globes, was a miniature replica of the giant track in the poppied valley!

It stood out from the dust with the same hint of crushing force, the same die cut sharpness, the same *metallic* suggestion – and pointing toward the globes were the claw marks of the four spreading star points.

I reached down and picked up one of the pyramids. It seemed to cling to the rock; it was with effort that I wrenched it away. It gave to the touch a slight sensation of warmth – how can I describe it? – a warmth that was living.

I weighed it in my hand. It was oddly heavy, twice the weight, I should say, of platinum. I drew out a glass and examined it. Decidedly the pyramid was metallic, but of finest, almost silken texture – and I could not place it among any of the known metals. It certainly was none I had ever seen; yet it was as certainly metal. It was striated – slender filaments radiating from tiny, dully lustrous points within the polished surface.

And suddenly I had the weird feeling that each of these points was an eye, peering up at me, scrutinizing me. There came a startled cry from Dick.

"Look at the ring!"

The ring was in motion!

Faster the cubes moved; faster the circle revolved; the pyramids raised themselves, stood bolt upright on their square bases; the six rolling spheres touched them, joined the spinning, and with sleight-of-hand suddenness the ring drew together; its units coalesced, cubes and pyramids and globes threading with a curious suggestion of ferment.

With the same startling abruptness there stood erect, where but a moment before they had seethed, a little figure, grotesque; a weirdly humorous, a vaguely terrifying foot-high shape, squared and angled and pointed and *animate* – as though a child should build from nursery blocks a fantastic shape which abruptly is filled with throbbing life.

A troll from the kindergarten! A kobold of the toys!

Only for a second it stood, then began swiftly to change, melting with quicksilver quickness from one outline into another as square and triangle and spheres changed places. Their shiftings were like the transformations one sees within a kaleidoscope. And in each vanishing form was the suggestion of unfamiliar harmonies, of a subtle, a transcendental geometric art as though each swift shaping were a symbol, a *word* –

Euclid's problems given volition!

Geometry endowed with consciousness!

It ceased. Then the cubes drew one upon the other until they formed a pedestal nine inches high; up this pillar rolled the larger globe, balanced itself upon the top; the five spheres followed it, clustered like a ring just below it. The other cubes raced up, clicked two by two on the outer arc of each of the five balls; at the ends of these twin blocks a pyramid took its place, tipping each with a point.

The Lilliputian fantasy was now a pedestal of cubes surmounted by a ring of globes from which sprang a star of five arms.

The spheres began to revolve. Faster and faster they spun around the base of the crowning globe; the arms became a disc upon which tiny brilliant sparks appeared, clustered, vanished only to reappear in greater number.

The troll swept toward me. It *glided*. The finger of panic touched me. I sprang aside, and swift as light it followed, seemed to poise itself to leap.

"Drop it!" It was Ruth's cry.

But, before I could let fall the pyramid I had forgotten was in my hand, the little figure touched me and a paralyzing shock ran through me. My fingers clenched, locked. I stood, muscle and nerve bound, unable to move.

The little figure paused. Its whirling disc shifted from the horizontal plane on which it spun. It was as though it cocked its head to look up at me – and again I had the sense of innumerable eyes peering at me. It did not seem menacing – its attitude was inquisitive, waiting; almost as though it had asked for something and wondered why I did not let it have it. The shock still held me rigid, although a tingle in every nerve told me of returning force.

The disc tilted back to place, bent toward me again. I heard a shout; heard a bullet strike the pigmy that now clearly menaced; heard the bullet ricochet without the slightest effect upon it. Dick leaped beside me, raised a foot and kicked at the thing. There was a flash of light and upon the instant he crashed down as though struck by a giant hand, lay sprawling and inert upon the floor.

There was a scream from Ruth; there was softly sibilant rustling all about her. I saw her leap the crevice, drop on her knees beside Drake.

There was movement on the flagging where she stood. A score or more of faintly shining, bluish shapes were marching there – pyramids and cubes and spheres like those forming the shape that stood before me. There was a curious sharp tang of ozone in the air, a perceptible tightening as of electrical tension.

They swept to the edge of the fissure, swam together, and there, hanging half over the gap was a bridge, half spanning it, a weird and fairy arch made up of alternate cube and angle. The shape at my feet disintegrated; resolved itself into units that raced over to the beckoning span.

At the hither side of the crack they clicked into place, even as had the others. Before me now was a bridge complete except for the one arc near the middle where an angled gap marred it.

I felt the little object I held pulse within my hand, striving to escape. I dropped it. The tiny shape swept to the bridge, ascended it – dropped into the gap.

The arch was complete – hanging in one flying span over the depths!

Upon it, over it, as though they had but awaited this completion, rolled the six globes. And as they dropped to the farther side the end of the bridge nearest me raised itself in air, curved itself like a scorpion's tail, drew itself into a closer circled arc, and dropped upon the floor beyond.

Again the sibilant rustling – and cubes and pyramids and spheres were gone.

Nerves tingling slowly back to life, mazed in absolute bewilderment, my gaze sought Drake. He was sitting up, feebly, his head supported by Ruth's hands.

"Goodwin!" he whispered. "What – what were they?"

"Metal," I said – it was the only word to which my whirling mind could cling – "metal –"

"Metal!" he echoed. "These things metal? Metal – *alive and thinking!*"

Suddenly he was silent, his face a page on which, visibly, dread gathered slowly and ever deeper.

And as I looked at Ruth, white-faced, and at him, I knew that my own was as pallid, as terror-stricken as theirs.

"They were such *little things*," muttered Drake. "Such little things – bits of metal – little globes and pyramids and cubes – just little *things*."

"Babes! Only babes!" It was Ruth – "*Babes!*"

"Bits of metal" – Dick's gaze sought mine, held it – "and they looked for each other, they worked with each other – *thinkingly, consciously* – they were deliberate, purposeful – little things – and with the force of a score of dynamos – living, *thinking* –"

"Don't!" Ruth laid white hands over his eyes. "Don't – don't *you* be frightened!"

"Frightened?" he echoed. "*I'm* not afraid – yes, I *am* afraid –"

He arose, stiffly – and stumbled toward me.

Afraid? Drake afraid. Well – so was I. Bitterly, *terribly* afraid.

For what we had beheld in the dusk of that dragoned, ruined chamber was outside all experience, beyond all knowledge or dream of science. Not their shapes – that was nothing. Not even that, being metal, they had moved.

But that being metal, they had moved consciously, thoughtfully, deliberately.

They were metal things with – *minds*!

That – that was the incredible, the terrifying thing. That – and their power.

Thor compressed within Hop-o'-my-thumb – and thinking. The lightnings incarnate in metal minacules – and thinking.

The inert, the immobile, given volition, movement, cognoscence – thinking.

Metal with a brain!

The complete and unabridged text is available online, *from flametreepublishing.com/extras*

Last Breath Day

Stephen G. Parks

Day 263

EVERY DAY is the same: we get up, we work hard, one of us dies. We call it Last Breath Day. It hasn't been me yet, obviously, but our numbers are getting down. It'll be my turn soon enough.

Who are we? We're the human slaves, the last survivors of the Thrup's invasion of our solar system. Where are we now? I really don't know. The nearest star is a faint yellow orb. It might still be Sol. We traveled about three weeks to get here, but I don't know if we were traveling faster than light.

There were almost three hundred of us in the beginning, the remnants of the Mars colonies. We were given clear instructions: work to live.

* * *

Yesterday was a big assembly day. Whatever they've had us building, it's now in five large pieces – maybe twenty kilometers a side – with perhaps another twelve or fifteen small ones orbiting them. Two of the bigger pieces finally joined together.

Near the end of our workday, Kayla Wilkins came over and touched helmets with me, which should have given our conversation privacy.

"I can prove it. We're not in Sol anymore. That star," She pointed at the bright yellow-ish disc that was the largest object in our black night, "is Tau Ceti!"

"Kayla, you imbecile, your comm channel's open!" Jed Barkly's voice came through clearly. Leaving the comms open was a foolish mistake and everyone, and I mean everyone, figured she would have her air ration shortened for that.

Jed was just making sure that our ever-watchful overseers would know who to punish for the information spoken.

Kayla's about a decade older than me and was an astronomy post-doc before the invasion. We all figured she'd be useless at hard labour and face her last breath day early on, but here she is. Some still say she's useless, but I don't know. They keep letting her live. She must be doing something right.

Of course, they hadn't always been too discrete in who they killed.

Once it became obvious that they were going to kill each of us once they didn't need us, we tried collectively to slow down, to give ourselves a little hope at living longer. Three days in a row, they shorted air on five of us. By the second day we were back working at it, full force. They still killed five. And the third day, too. Lesson learned, we didn't try to slow down anymore.

We have an agreement of sorts: on your Last Breath Day, you turn off comms. There's no need to upset the others, and frankly there's more dignity in being remembered as a hardy co-worker than as a screaming freak begging uselessly for your life.

There were only thirty-eight of us left, the day Kayla misspoke. At dinner that night no one would sit with her but me. We know they monitor us. The Thrup are often very accurate at who they kill: organizers, rebels, troublemakers…

But somehow they missed Kayla. The next day, thirty-seven of us came home, including Kayla, but not Paula Glint. She'd died silently working on some task somewhere in our floating hell. Initially I thought the Thrup had made a mistake and would catch it. But when I was helping out of her suit, I noticed that Kayla's air tank had 'Glint' stenciled on it.

Later that night she confessed to me that she'd quietly switched air bottles with Paula that morning, then taking her ration card from her body later. As far as the Thrup were concerned, they had killed Kayla. This was Paula.

I didn't know what to do, what to say. Should I turn her in? But to who? Besides which, she was letting me sleep with her. I didn't want to lose that.

* * *

Day 274

It's a hard life, with few distractions. We try all kinds of little subversions, ways of secretly rebelling against them, but nothing that'd get us killed. Painting our helmets is one way. Kayla helped me decorate mine, a fancy dragonhead design on both sides. She has a simple design, just one stripe, no, she's added another one: two stripes on her helmet.

I'm sure that we all think we're fighting the good fight, the last remnants of humanity not going quietly into that cold, dark night.

* * *

Day 281

I owe Kayla my life. Two days ago, Kayla helped me finish a bunch of tasks. Each day we get our instructions through a task queuing system in our suit HUDs. You have a task and duration. Do the task within the duration, get assigned a new task. Fail to do the task…well…learn to breath very shallowly.

I'd gotten behind, couldn't get two pieces to fit, was sure I was going to die.

Barkly was cackling at me. He was shift boss and could see all the reds I was loading up.

"Faster boy," he'd shout into the comms, unnecessarily drawing attention to my failings. "Faster or get ready to die!" He almost sounded gleeful. "Don't forget to turn your comms off, boy! We don't want to hear you squirm."

Kayla had come over and taken on three of my tasks. I finally got the two pieces to align; it wasn't hard once Jed's pressure tactics faded. But I worried that Kayla would pull a last breath day – helping me had hurt her productivity.

But then, kind of shockingly, yesterday was Jed Barkly's Last Breath Day. He didn't turn his comms off, the bastard. His last words had been, "Kayla, damn you!"

That night, Kayla told me that Jed had been secretly nursing a dislocated shoulder. It had stopped him from being able to complete an assigned task. Kayla had had to crawl into that hole, brace herself and tighten down that joint. She had claimed the completion. Jed had failed to do his task.

* * *

Day 285

Everyone remembers where they were when the first rock hit Earth. I was on Mars, a seventeen year old, just qualified for local commercial flight – not passenger, just cargo. My biggest worry was that I wasn't life-support qualified yet.

Then it happened.

That first rock landed in the north Pacific, not far from Seattle. It wasn't the tsunami it unleashed that was so fatal, nor even the earthquakes when the fault lines gave. It was all the rain mixed with ash from suddenly active volcanoes. The northern hemisphere wouldn't see sunlight for at least two years, maybe three. That one rock was enough to finish life on Earth, and probably everywhere else, if you were patient.

But the Thrup weren't patient, and were keen to show that it wasn't a random event. At least four more rocks hit the planet, mostly in the north, but one in the southern Indian Ocean was big enough to ensure that eastern Africa, the Indian subcontinent, and western Australia were permanently depopulated.

Earth was made unlivable in less than a week.

The only survivors were those of us off-world at the time – in one of the orbital colonies or on the Moon or Mars. And most of us didn't live much longer.

Once their mammoth ships arrived, they tore apart the orbital colonies. It wasn't quick, and some of it seemed almost like they were playing games, trying to knock detritus into colonies. They gunned down the Moon colonies too, but never seemed to know about us on Mars.

We did what we could to hide our presence. All comms were already encrypted and limited to line of sight or hardwire-only traffic. We buried our colonies, hid the airlocks beneath deep awnings covered in dust and sand. Tracks and trails were erased. Blackout curtains and curfews were mandatory, the death the penalty for violating them.

They did a low fly-by of Mars. We had left out some rovers and automated equipment, hoping that was enough to fool them into thinking we were pre-colonial. They destroyed all of it, but never found any of our bases.

Mars was close to self-sustainable by that point. We probably could have waited them out, but for those damned Lunarians. At least one lunar colony, maybe more, had escaped notice – at first. But the Moon wasn't anywhere near self-sustainable, and Earth was no longer hospitable to the colonists. In the second year, they fled to Mars.

The Thrup took their own sweet time dealing with the fleeing Lunarians. Once the idiots thought they'd actually escaped, they tried to contact us on open frequencies, even after they landed. Of course we didn't reply, but then the Thrup knew enough to come looking for us.

I don't know why they didn't just kill us immediately too, but here we are, in deep space, slaves working for our air.

* * *

Day 288

And I remember seeing Kayla among the survivors when we first were captured, but we didn't talk or really pay any attention to each other. I was still processing the loss of my family; parents and brothers. I was seventeen, scared shitless, and alone. She'd apparently been widowed in the attack. It was only later that I ended up with her. Still not sure how that happened.

Kayla and I have got a unique problem developing, pardon the pun: Kayla's pregnant, probably the last human ever to be so. For the first few weeks, she did everything she could think of to terminate it – asking people to punch her in the stomach, injecting weird concoctions, fasting, doing crazy exercises…. Still, she's pregnant. Almost six months now. It's hard to hide. She can barely fit into her spacesuit.

Her productivity must be going way down. She can't bend as well, move as fast, or climb into tight spaces…hell, even her stamina is down.

One thing's for sure, the Thrup aren't going to allow humanity to grow in numbers, not even by one.

* * *

Day 293

Today's tasks seem to be about fitting smaller pieces to the new large assembly. We're working in small groups today. My assembly team is just me and Kayla. I'm really not happy. I don't want to have to compensate for her slowness, her immobility, but I don't want to appear to be missing my deadlines either. Ya gotta earn that air.

What the…? I'm getting a red light? Air is critically low and falling fast? That can't be right. Oh God! It's me…it's me…I'm the one they're shorting? No! It can't be…I've got a full task list today.

Maybe it's a micro-puncture? Where? Where?

"Kayla, come here! Is there a tear in my suit?" What's she doing? She's coming over too slowly, she's distracted. She's adding a third, no fourth, stripe to her helmet! "Hey, stop smiling…this is serious!"

We touch helmets.

"So loverboy, can I take your ration card now or do I have to come back when you finish squirming?" she says, smiling. What the…? I…I don't understand. "Don't worry, I'll still name the baby after you."

She pushes off. I can't hear her but I can see she's laughing. She twists away and I can see my name stenciled on her air tank.

"Damn you, Kayla! No, I won't turn off my comms channel, you little…."

The Merger

Sunil Patel

PARESH CAME ACROSS the alien while hurrying to catch the 7:45 bus. It was much quieter than the 8:15 bus, which always contained a group of rowdy teenage boys who asked him about his day at the Kwik-E-Mart, as if his fine button-down shirt and leather laptop bag weren't a clue that he had been a valued programmer at Oracle for five years, thank you very much. It looked like it would be the 8:15 bus tonight, however, because standing in the parking lot behind his office was a six-foot-tall gelatinous blob with horns.

"Congratulations on your exciting opportunity!" declared the blob in a voice that sounded like a mix between sandpaper and nails on a chalkboard. It appeared to be wholly ignorant of the way its voice sounded, its words infused with a joyful sincerity Paresh found unsettling.

"Excuse me?" asked Paresh, who had never encountered an alien before but decided that if the first thing they did when they invaded was congratulate you, they couldn't be all that bad.

"We have identified you as a potential host body. We find your body very desirable."

No one was allowed to find his body desirable but his wife, dammit. "Host body?"

"Our analysts have determined that your body's complexion, specific gravity, and the length of its extremities are optimal for our experience."

Sita had never commented on his specific gravity, but Paresh took it as a compliment. She *had* commented on the length of his extremity.

"We are prepared to offer substantial compensation equivalent to the value and potential value of your body. We understand that you may have had other offers but hope that you accept ours." The blob was glowing with excitement now. At least Paresh thought it was excitement. It could have been arousal.

"What if I don't want to be a host body?"

"We are prepared to offer substantial compensation equivalent to the value and potential value of your body."

Paresh repeated himself.

The blob repeated itself.

This wasn't getting him anywhere. "Look, thanks for the offer, but I have to catch the bus."

The blob looked at him quizzically. Paresh didn't understand how that was possible since he wasn't sure where its eyes were, but it managed.

"As our bylaws do not allow for hostile takeover, we must act in the best interests of the shareholders and prevent dilution of market share. Accordingly, please note that refusal of this offer may result in the destruction of your planet. As added incentive, we have increased our offer of compensation by 12.5%."

Paresh chose to ignore the phrase 'destruction of your planet' because it was absurd, even though his bar for absurd had recently risen. Instead, he focused on the 'exciting opportunity,' which included money. Sita *had* been wanting to remodel the kitchen (or as she called it, her cooking laboratory). And their car was old, an embarrassment among his colleagues. Paresh raised his eyebrow. "What kind of compensation are we talking here?"

The blob jumped up and down, making disgusting squishing noises with every impact on the sidewalk. "Are you willing to enter into negotiations with the BlarbTech/SnarbCo, Inc. Intraplanetary Conglomerate, hereinafter referred to as 'the Blarbsnarb'?"

He was definitely going to miss his bus. The 8:45 bus was pretty quiet, at least. "I am willing to hear you out."

"We believe this will be a beneficial arrangement for us both. Please allow me to contact our chairman and we will begin negotiations this very evening."

"This evening? Where do I go? I'll have to tell my wife where –"

"Agreement to begin negotiations constitutes acceptance of a non-disclosure agreement. Please do not speak of this impending transaction to any uninvolved parties as it is considered proprietary information and may result in serious legal consequences." The blob had stopped glowing. It was possibly angry. Possibly calm. Paresh couldn't tell. "The negotiations will begin this very evening at a location to be determined."

And then the blob disappeared. Paresh expected a spectacular buzz and light show, but it was just gone, like it had never been there at all. Apprehensive, Paresh searched the parking lot for any other aliens before rushing to the bus stop.

He watched the 8:15 bus leave with a sigh and sat on the bench, alone. The 8:45 bus arrived, and he got on.

"Hey, Apu!"

He wasn't the only one who had been delayed.

* * *

Paresh walked home from the bus stop, laptop bag in hand. He clutched the handle tightly, imagining using it as a weapon against those stupid kids with their stupid hats and their stupid skateboards. They didn't actually have skateboards, but he thought they should. Although if they had skateboards, they wouldn't be riding the bus. He *definitely* thought they should have skateboards.

Two blocks up and one block to the left. Three hundred feet and: "Your destination is on the right." No one ever heard him say it, but it made him feel at home.

Sita would wonder why he was late. The blob thing had warned him not to talk about the 'impending transaction,' but was he allowed to tell her that he'd met an alien? It had never specified. He could leave out the details.

"They kept you late?" said Sita, opening the door.

Or she could do that. Paresh nodded and kissed her, hating that he had lied to his wife but grateful not to have to see her look of disbelief when he told her the truth. When he learned more about the offer, he would come clean.

He took off his shoes, placed his laptop bag in the closet, and went straight to the kitchen. "Turkey chili pizza in the oven," Sita said, pointing.

"That's not a real thing."

"It is too a real thing, and you're going to eat it."

"I met an alien today," Paresh blurted out.

"Paresh, that's not polite, they're called immigrants," said Sita. "Your company change their hiring policy?"

"Yes," he said, flushing. He was the absolute worst at keeping secrets. At the department retreat, they'd had a baby picture guessing game and every time someone pointed to his picture, he'd giggled.

"Where were they from?"

"Ecuador," said Paresh, naming the first country that came to mind. Maybe he should go get the shovel in his garage if he was going to keep digging himself deeper into this hole.

"Very cool!" she said. "I've never been to Ecuador. You should find out how it is. We could take a vacation."

The oven dinged and saved Paresh from having to continue the conversation. He had already begun to make up fake facts about Ecuador (their main export is kumquats, the capital city of Ecuador City has the rarest Dalí in the world, everyone owns a pet capybara). Sita knew more than Paresh about most things, but she taught biology, not geography.

She set a plate in front of him. Already sliced, the turkey chili pizza resembled a pizza in the way a veggie dog resembled a hot dog. Paresh suspected Sita had applied the principles of aggressive mimicry to food. She had been gushing about the anglerfish a few nights ago.

Paresh took a bite and appreciated the smoky taste of chili but stopped chewing as he was assailed by an unexpected flavor. "Is that *mustard*?"

"Aioli garlic mustard sauce! Do you like it?"

There was no sense in starting to tell the truth now; he was on a roll. "It's great!" he said, swallowing, then almost choking as a face appeared on his pizza.

"Greetings, human!" the face said with a voice like nails on sandpaper. It was missing a part of its mouth, which Paresh had eaten. He looked up at Sita, who didn't react. "We are ready to begin the negotiation process!"

"*Not now*," he hissed.

"Not now what?" asked Sita.

"I was having this really great idea, and I wished it would come *later tonight, when I was alone.*"

Sita took a bite of her own pizza. "I know how that goes. I hate when I come up with a great lesson plan while I'm driving. I can't write it down!"

"Please confirm the rescheduling of the negotiations," Paresh's pizza said.

Paresh had never eaten a whole pizza so fast in his entire life.

* * *

Later that evening in his office, Paresh turned around and there was the horned blob thing. He assumed it was the same one, but he couldn't be sure. When it spoke, however, the voice was unmistakable.

"We apologize for the previous inconvenience," it said.

"You can't just talk to a man through his dinner," said Paresh. "It's rude and unprofessional." He ran his fingers through his hair in frustration. "*At* dinner, but not *through* dinner."

"May we begin the negotiations?" it said. Paresh checked that the door was closed. "Your partner will not hear our discussion. This enclosure has been soundlocked for confidentiality."

"Good. Now explain to me what it is you want from me, and what you are prepared to offer."

"The BlarbTech/SnarbCo, Inc. Intraplanetary Conglomerate, heretofore and hereinafter referred to as 'the Blarbsnarb,' would like to acquire your body."

"I'm using it at the moment."

"We believe that your body has a great deal of potential and is being undervalued in the market."

"Market? What market? Are there more of you?"

"That information is not relevant to this discussion."

"Fine," said Paresh. He had enough trouble with one alien; he didn't need to think about more. "If you acquire my body, when do I get it back?"

"Upon corporeal incorporation, your body would become a wholly owned subsidiary of the Blarbsnarb, with partial autonomy on weekends vesting over four solar years."

Some of that sounded good. Some of that sounded like gibberish. "And how much would you pay me?"

"The current offer is 0.0001 United States of American cents per cell."

A fraction of a penny? But Paresh figured he had a lot of cells in his body, maybe even ten million. Which would be one whole cent. "I'm afraid that's not enough," he said. "Speaking of *undervalued*." This was some kind of joke, surely. They didn't understand numbers or money or something.

The blob's horns began to glow, pulsating lightly. Then they stopped. "The Blarbsnarb Board of Directors has agreed to determine a higher, more suitable offer for you, Mr. Gupta. We will contact you when the new offer is ready."

"Can I discuss this with my wife? I don't feel comfortable" – he came this close to saying 'selling my body' before he caught himself – "accepting an offer without her input."

The blob's horns pulsated again. "As preliminary negotiations have concluded, you may consult your partner in this matter. We are aware that by law she owns half of your body and thus must approve any acquisition." Paresh was going to dispute its statement, but the blob continued. "Have a good evening, Mr. Gupta. We look forward to conducting a successful business transaction." Then it disappeared.

Paresh didn't bring the topic up in bed that night. He knew better than to disturb Sita's reading.

* * *

At breakfast, he asked her, "How many cells are in the human body?"

She swallowed her blueberry sweet potato waffle and said, "That depends on the body. And are we counting intestinal flora?"

Paresh wasn't sure what that was. "My body. All the cells in it. Including the intestinal things, I guess."

"Stand up," she said. She stood up herself.

Paresh stood and stepped away from the table. Sita looked him up and down, and Paresh felt self-conscious about the months he hadn't gone to the gym. "Now give me a spin," she said, twirling her finger in the air. Reluctantly, he turned around in a circle, still feeling her eyes on him. When he was done, she nodded at him to sit down and took her seat.

Sita cut another piece of waffle and ate it. She pulled out her phone and did some quick calculations. "I'd say you've got about ten trillion cells in your body."

Paresh almost choked on his waffle. "Did you say *trillion*?"

"Like a million billions," she said. "Or a billion millions."

He moved the decimal point in his head. They'd offered him *ten million dollars*.

And he'd asked for more.

"Sita, I have something to tell you."

He told her.

After a moment, she put her finger to her nose and pointed at him. "So when you said last night that you'd met an alien…?"

He nodded.

"Okay, first of all, here's a new lesson plan, hitting me at breakfast when I can't write it down, but I'll wing it. My kids won't mind if we talk about aliens instead of the Golgi apparatus today."

"No!" said Paresh. "You can't tell anyone!"

"Why, do they have ray guns?"

"I don't know what they have. They don't even have hands, so ray guns are out of the question. But the…alien thing –"

"The Blarbsnarb representative."

"The Blarbsnarb rep threatened to destroy the planet if I said no. They might do that if we talk about the deal."

Sita rolled her eyes. "That planet-destroying shit is absurd. It's got to be a bluff. They want your body like I do, and they're going to pay for –" She put her head in her hands. "That is not where I wanted that sentence to go."

Paresh chuckled. "Yes, I went down that road too."

She gestured at him with the piece of waffle on her fork, syrup dripping on the table. "You should find out the details of the deal, what happens to you and how you get the money. Don't sign anything until you read all the fine print."

Paresh promised not to sign anything until he read all the fine print.

At the time, he meant it.

* * *

The blob appeared that afternoon in the Oracle bathroom. Thankfully, Paresh had completed his business.

"This is highly inappropriate," he said.

"You did not leave appropriate hours and means by which to contact you," said the blob. Paresh had forgotten how discordant its voice was. Hoping no one had heard it, he went to lock the door only to realize that the door had no lock. The blob continued, "We have increased our offer by 10% and have prepared the paperwork."

"Let me see it," he said, and a tiny wormhole opened up between them. Out popped three stacks of paper, which hovered in the air. White, yellow, and pink.

"Please sign and return the white copy," said the blob. "The yellow copy is for you to keep."

"And the pink copy?"

"The pink copy belongs to your partner."

"Don't you think that's kind of sexist?"

The blob blinked. So that's where its eyes were. "You may take the pink copy if it is sexiest."

Paresh plucked the stack of white paper out of the air and began to look it over. He knew he ought to have a lawyer review it – at the very least someone like Carey in Contracts could take a look – but how could he even begin to explain what it was for? He didn't want people at work talking about him like he was crazy. He read quickly; someone could walk in on them any minute.

He had to give the Blarbsnarb credit: they were pretty fluent in legalese. Paresh, sadly, was not. Had the contract been written in Java, he would have stood a chance at comprehending what they intended to do to his body. As it was, he understood that there would be a transition period following the completion of the transaction in which the terms of the possession would be finalized.

Paresh thought of what he could do with eleven million dollars. Forget remodeling the kitchen, they could buy a new house, a bigger one where they could start a family. He could quit his job and be a stay-at-home dad (Sita would never quit her job; she loved it too much). It was such an obscene amount of money that he didn't know what he could do with it all, but he knew it would remove obstacles and pave the way for a brighter future. As long as they had a future. The phrase 'destruction of your planet' came back to him.

He signed the contract.

In several different places. They were really fluent in legalese.

* * *

When he handed Sita the pink copy, she said, "This is the pink copy."

"Yes?" he said, pretending not to know what she was getting at.

"Where's the white copy? The *real* copy?"

Paresh said nothing. He looked up at the ceiling.

Sita spoke calmly. "Do you remember this morning when you made what we humans like to call a 'promise'?"

Paresh recalled all of his rationalizations, and now they seemed insufficient. Sita loved their house. The kitchen counters were chipped, but she knew the layout by heart. Why would she want to sell a place she could navigate with her eyes closed? (Sometimes she did walk around the house with her eyes closed. Once she bumped into the living room sofa, and that was only because Paresh had moved it a few inches to retrieve the remote without setting it back.)

He hadn't done it for her. He had done it for him.

"I'm sorry, honey," he said. "I thought it was for the best, but I should have brought it home."

"Did you at least read the fine print?" she asked.

It had all been fine print. "I read...most of it." The ceiling became very interesting to him again. They could repaint the ceiling. That would be a good use of money.

"Most of it," she said.

"You know, by not refusing the deal, I kind of saved the world." He shot Sita a hopeful glance.

"You kind of did it without me." Sita chose not to stare at the ceiling, or even the floor. She looked right into Paresh's eyes. "I'm going to bed."

Paresh watched her leave. He waited, expecting the blob to appear, since this was an inconvenient time in his life. But he was left standing alone in the kitchen. He stood there for an hour before joining his wife.

* * *

The next morning, Paresh woke to find his wife sitting up with her arms crossed, glaring at him. "No more signing away your body without consulting me," she said. "Deal?"

"Deal," muttered Paresh.

"Did you find out how the process works? If you're a subsidiary, they should let you stay in there, and we can work out how to spend the money."

Paresh shrugged.

"Paresh, dear, I love you, but you have the business sense of a marmoset." Sita poked him. "We need to contact the Blarbsnarb. This is a huge transaction; they ought to be more transparent." Then she threw the covers off. "Wait, I've got a better idea."

Sita walked out of the bedroom and returned with the pink copy of the contract. She tossed it to Paresh. "Let's get some answers."

Paresh turned to the first page of the contract and began to read it aloud.

* * *

"That was incredibly thorough," said Sita.

"I did say they were fluent in legalese."

"You think they're a whole race of lawyers? Like maybe somewhere out there lawyers evolved into horned blobs bent on intergalactic domination?"

Paresh restrained himself from making a lawyer joke. Sita had set him up for so many responses, and he could see her trying to guess which one he would use. But it would have been so easy, like signing a contract without reading every word.

Sita's face fell. "Come on, not even 'You mean they haven't already?' It's the low-hanging fruit."

Paresh drew her close. "A lawyer might be our only way to understand this deal. I should treat them with respect. For now."

According to the contract, the next step in the process was to begin removing redundancies. Paresh had authorized the Blarbsnarb to make changes as they saw fit, evaluating his body for its capabilities in relation to human function versus its utility after the blob took possession. Even having read the fine print, he was unclear on his status after the process was complete. The word 'annihilated' appeared nowhere, which was promising.

"You've read me better stories in bed," said Sita. "But I love the main character in this one. I was very invested in his fate."

"Sorry for the spoilers," said Paresh.

"Seriously!" said Sita. "Now I'm going to be sitting here waiting to see how the Blarbsnarb eliminate redundancies."

Paresh's appendix burst and he screamed.

As she drove him to the hospital, she shook her head and repeated, "I'm not saying anything ever again. I'm not saying anything ever again."

The operation went smoothly, and Sita sat by his bed and held his hand. Her hand was the first thing he felt as he regained the ability to feel. He squeezed it.

"I forgot I still had that thing," he said weakly.

"Not anymore you don't," she said.

"They could have given me some sort of warning."

"They're not legally required to," she said. "California is an at-will state."

"That leaves the rest of my body in a very precarious position."

The blob appeared at the foot of the bed. Sita yanked Paresh's hand in surprise, Paresh yelped in pain, and the blob yodeled in glee. Or distress. "We are pleased to see that the termination of your appendix has been successful. We do wish it the best and thank it for its many years of service."

"The appendix doesn't do anything," said Sita, taking Paresh's hand again.

"We thank it for its many years of service," the blob repeated.

"That really hurt," said Paresh. "I would appreciate a heads up next time." He scanned the blob, not seeing any clear distinction between head and body. But if they knew what an appendix was, they knew what a head was.

"We apologize for the inconvenience. Per your request, I am informing you that we have identified a redundancy in your mitochondria. You will not require them."

"My midicholorians?"

"Mitochondria," said Sita. "How could you forget the powerhouses of the cell? They make all the energy in your body." She slapped his head lightly. "Paresh, *I have a poster of one in my classroom.*"

He looked away and smiled to himself. He remembered almost nothing of what Sita's classroom looked like because whenever he visited, he was so focused on how in her element she was when teaching. Poised and animated, she spoke about topics he knew nothing about with such passion that he wished he'd had her in high school instead of Mrs. Klages.

"Right," said Paresh. "How could I forget? Those things. Sounds like I need them, though."

The blob shook its head, which allowed Paresh to see the subtle distinction. "The Blarbsnarb equivalent are twenty times more efficient and powerful. They will now be replaced."

Paresh, who was still groggy to this point, jerked fully awake. "How now is now?"

"It is done," noted the blob with triumph. Or disinterest. It was so hard to tell with it.

Paresh tried to sit up, raise his head. Sita had said he had trillions of cells in his body. He must have had trillions of midichlo– mitochondria. And now they were gone, and he had alien substitutes in his body. Did that make him a hybrid? Was he even human anymore? He felt human. Sita stared at him like he might not be.

She turned to the blob. "Will there be any side effects? What if his body rejects the alien organelles?"

The blob scoffed, an expression represented by a shift in the density of blob in its upper half. "His body was deemed suitable for this procedure before it was conducted. He will experience no complications beyond enhanced productivity."

Paresh found it much easier to sit up now. His head felt clearer. He heard a faint hum emanating from his body, like white noise from his laptop.

"I appreciate these enhancements, but I don't know if I'm comfortable living the rest of my life with alien…stuff." Having an alien inside his body was one thing, but if his body was also part-alien, that was weird (his bar for weird had also risen recently).

"Per the contract, corporeal incorporation requires modification of the asset."

"His asset is just fine," said Sita.

"I don't like this," said Paresh. "It's creepy."

The blob hummed with excitement or disapproval. "By expressing concern regarding the original arrangement, you have authorized the alternative arrangement specified in Section XII, Clause 23."

Sita squeezed Paresh's hand. "What did he just authorize?"

The blob remained silent for a few seconds, as if the answer should have been obvious. "He will go into you." The sandpapery voice made the statement sound more ominous.

"Into me?" repeated Sita. "There's no room in here for him. Do you understand how humans work?"

"We have conducted an extensive study of human body-self conformational metaphysics, and we believe that one body can contain two selves, as outlined in the terms of the contract."

Paresh didn't know how he'd leapt past weird and into bizarre without even trying. Did the Blarbsnarb allow for takebacksies? He would ask for a second ruling, but he suspected that Carey in Contracts was not well versed in clauses this esoteric.

Sita, however, was a teacher, and she spoke with confidence about subjects she knew much about and even greater confidence about subjects she knew nothing about. "The original agreement was made between the Blarbsnarb and Paresh. As I am not a signatory on the contract, you have no authority to modify my body."

Paresh didn't know the word 'signatory' could sound so sexy.

The blob replied with exasperation, its rough voice somehow becoming high-pitched. "Section XII, Clause 23 clearly states that for the purposes of this arrangement the undersigned and spouse of undersigned, if one exists, are equal by law, dependent on tax filing status."

Paresh groaned. "We file...jointly."

Sita bit her lip. "I know the accountant said there were some minor disadvantages, but I don't think she meant this."

Then she held up a finger, smiling brightly. "I contest that Paresh's statement constituted an expression of concern." She punctuated this assertion with a triumphant, emphatic nod.

The blob sighed, or possibly farted. Paresh sniffed the air but still couldn't tell. Before he could ask for clarification, the blob spoke. "I must consult with the Board on this matter. You will hear from us shortly." The blob disappeared.

"If this works," said Paresh, "all it means is that I get to live with that thing inside me."

"Maybe if we confuse them enough, they'll leave us alone," said Sita.

* * *

On the drive home, Paresh spotted his least favorite kids at the bus stop and asked Sita to stop. They climbed out of the copper 1991 Sentra to sneers of "Hey, it's Apu and Mrs. Apu!" Paresh was disappointed they didn't know that Apu's wife was named Manjula.

"It's Jimbo!" bellowed Paresh, throwing his hands in the air. He jabbed a finger at each boy as he continued, "And Preston! And Clifford!"

The kids stopped their hollering, confused. Their apparent leader sputtered, "Whatever, man, my name –"

Paresh had alien midichlorians and no more fear. "The other day I met an alien blob I respect more than you because it respects me more than you do. And so I saved the world. All of it. Even you."

Sita looked at him like she didn't care whether he was human, that was the hottest he had been in all their years of marriage. She pulled him in for a deep, passionate kiss. Out of the corner of his eye, Paresh thought he saw her give the boys the finger. They weren't her students, but they did just get schooled.

Paresh and Sita returned to the car, leaving the boys standing with expressions almost as indecipherable as the blob's.

As they drove off, Paresh rolled down the window and yelled with a fist in the air, "And it said my complexion was optimal! *Optimal!*"

* * *

Sita experimented with barbecue chicken pasta for dinner, combining barbecue sauce and marinara sauce in what Paresh thought were haphazard amounts.

They ate in relative silence. This concoction tasted better than that mustard pizza from a couple nights ago – from the night his troubles began. What had possessed him to agree to this arrangement (ha, possessed)? Maybe he could blame it on the pizza.

Paresh tried to pick apart the mélange of flavors in his mouth. He didn't think a slight tinge of barbecue would be so pleasant in tomato sauce. He slurped up some of the remaining sauce in his plate.

"That was really good!" he said.

"So what the hell are we going to do?" she said.

"If they buy your legal argument, then at least I get to stay in my body. Maybe there's a loophole to get out of the thing entirely."

"We read through the whole contract. I didn't see anything."

Paresh shook his fork at her. Unfortunately, the fork still had sauce on it. Fortunately, the sauce didn't reach her. "We're not lawyers or aliens. We wouldn't."

Sita stood up and began clearing the table. "There is also the issue of money." She reached for Paresh's plate.

Paresh grabbed her wrist. "We don't need the money. We never had it anyway. I'd rather be myself than myself plus an alien plus money." He let her go.

Sita took his plate. "You'd rather be yourself plus money."

He looked her right in the eyes. "I'd rather be myself plus you."

* * *

That night while Paresh was being himself plus Sita, the blob appeared by the bed. Sita screamed – a different sort of scream than she'd been making a few seconds ago – and toppled off Paresh. Paresh let loose a stream of creative expletives.

Out of breath, Paresh said, "Has anyone told you guys you have the worst timing imaginable?"

The blob gazed upon their naked bodies and appeared to blush, a subtle red shimmer that coursed over its body for a second. "I apologize for interrupting your mating ritual. The Board has reviewed the statement and determined it to be legally binding. The alternative arrangement has been authorized."

Sita pulled the comforter over her. "So he'll go inside me?" She looked at Paresh, scanned down, and chuckled at her choice of words.

"His being will be temporarily relocated into your body until it can find a suitable home," said the blob, apparently still unclear on how humans worked. Sita had *said* there was no room for him, and he believed the woman with the graduate degree. For an intelligent alien species, they did not seem to have done all the necessary research.

"What if he says no?" asked Sita. She pulled Paresh close to her, away from the blob. "What if he backs out of the contract?"

The blob looked puzzled. "Why would he refuse to proceed with what has been agreed upon? We are offering appropriate compensation for the body."

Paresh put up a hand. "Your compensation is more than appropriate. Hell, it's inappropriate. But I've changed my mind. I like my body. I want to stay in it. Only me."

"And I love him, but I'd prefer he stay in his own body. I'm equal by law, right? Spouse of undersigned? What if I say no too?"

The blob's horns glowed. "This is highly unusual."

"You're highly unusual," muttered Sita.

Paresh knew Carey in Contracts had dealt with people like him before, assholes who reneged at the last minute. It happened. It was business. These aliens must have encountered it. "If there's an early cancellation fee or something, I'll pay it." He suspected it would be more than the $300 he paid for cancelling his cable deal, but they would find a way to make it work.

The blob hopped onto the bed. Paresh was relieved to see it didn't leave a trail of goo behind it; in fact, it left no residue at all. Yet he cringed to see its blobby blobness on his sheets. The blob spoke, its scratchy, sandpapery voice familiar to the both of them by now: "Declining to complete the transaction at this stage is equivalent to refusal before agreement and carries the same consequences."

Sita and Paresh looked at each other, silently having an entire conversation about the fact that they were going to be responsible for the destruction of Earth, well, mostly Paresh was, it's not like Sita hadn't told him to read before signing, can we not bring that up right now, but it's true, and also I love you.

Paresh took Sita's hand. Ignoring the fact that he was completely naked, he mustered up all the dignity and gravity he had, sat straight up and said, "I'll do it." Sita squeezed his hand and sat straight up with him. "We'll do it. For Earth."

"For Earth," repeated Sita, who could not ignore the fact that they were completely naked and burst out laughing and fell over. The blob surveyed them with bewilderment, waves undulating back and forth across what Paresh took to be its facial region.

It jumped up and down on the bed. "The completion of transaction will commence immediately."

Sita stopped laughing. "You're going to take him now?"

Paresh's heart broke to hear the fear in his wife's voice. He would be leaving her and joining her in the same instant.

He turned to face his wife. "Before it happens, I want you to hear it from me one last time: I love you."

Sita kissed him. "I love you, too."

"When they tied our clothes together at the wedding, that was supposed to be a *symbolic* union, right?"

"I knew I should have been paying more attention to the Sanskrit."

Paresh admired her smile with his own eyes while he still could. "Also, in case you can hear my thoughts when I'm in there, I didn't really like that turkey chili pizza."

"I knew it!" She kissed him again. "But I'm still going to make it for us to eat. It's delicious. And it's my body I'll be putting it into, even if you're in there too."

"It'll be one hundred percent yours except for whatever metaphysical confor-whatsit things happen with me."

Sita turned to the blob. "*Will* I be able to hear his thoughts? Will he be able to control me? He'd better not be able to control me. I read that clause again and that is *not* in there."

A tiny wormhole opened up and spat out a spiral-bound stack of papers thicker than any database user manual Paresh had ever seen. It plopped onto the bed in front of the blob. "The Blarbsnarb have helpfully provided this list of Frequently Asked Questions." When Sita reached for it, the blob hopped on top of it. "It is to be read after the completion of the transaction, which must commence before close of business."

Sita drew her hand away, slowly curling four of her fingers back.

"Wait!" said Paresh. "I don't want to be possessed with my pants off." He reached around for his clothes and hastily dressed. Sita took the opportunity to do the same. The process was made somewhat more difficult by the blob, who continued to jump up and down on the bed, making Sita's bra fall off onto the floor.

"Thank you for your patience," said Sita after they were both clothed. She turned to Paresh. "You ready?"

"No," he said.

"Neither am I," she said. "Let's do this." She reached for his hand, and the blob honked like an angry goose.

"Please refrain from all physical contact during the transaction," it said. Sita reluctantly kept her hand at her side.

Paresh closed his eyes.

He peeked a tiny bit out of one eye in time to see the blob disintegrate and congeal into a ball of light that had to be visible outside, even through the curtains. Before he had time to wonder what the neighbors thought, the light shot toward his barely open eye, and then it was in him, going everywhere inside him, even places he didn't know he had, and he wanted to scream but he no longer had control of his mouth, and for one terrible second – or was it an hour – the only thought in his head was *it didn't say it would hurt*.

And then he felt himself move to the right a couple feet. A warm, welcoming body. The strange sensation of having a part-alien body was gone, replaced by the strange sensation of having an all-woman body. He felt top-heavy.

"You in there?" said Sita.

"Yes," said the Paresh inside her and the Paresh outside her.

"The transaction is complete," the blob said in Paresh's voice, a vast improvement from its own. Was that how Paresh sounded? He had been told he had the faintest traces of an accent, but he'd never heard it until now. Inside Sita's head, Paresh sounded the way he was used to sounding.

"Good," said Sita. Not wanting to look at the alien wearing her husband's body, she got up and went to the bathroom, looking instead at her husband wearing her body. "You said you wanted to be yourself plus me," she said into the mirror. "Looks like it's going to be the other way around."

Paresh looked at himself. Herself? Themself? They shared a body but not a mind, as far he could tell before reading the FAQ. He had no motor control of Sita's body, and he knew she wouldn't relinquish it. He would never ask her to. Since the moment he signed the contract, he had resigned himself to this fate, riding along with either an alien or his wife. He preferred the alternative arrangement. Sita had always been his better half, and now they were a better whole.

He hadn't quit his job. He hoped the blob could code.

"The first thing that blob did was congratulate me," he said, his voice sounding hollow inside Sita. "Well, congratulations! We're millionaires!"

From the bedroom came a thud, like the sound of a man falling off a bed.
Sita sighed. She took one last look in the mirror.
"Let's go teach that thing how to use its legs."

Some Things I Probably Should Have Mentioned Earlier

Laura Pearlman

DEAR KEVIN,

I'm sorry I waited so long to tell you this, but I really hate your vacation cabin. Everything about it creeps me out. The sound of crickets at night makes my skin crawl. They sound like impending doom: like a critical piece of equipment being worn down by friction, or a thousand tiny voices, hoarse from screaming, reduced to a raspy warning chant in some ancient language.

The crickets aren't the only problem. The smell of so much wood in one place makes my eyes burn. And is it really necessary to throw pine cones into the fireplace? Are the burnt-wood fumes not overpowering enough? I used to lie awake at night fantasizing about finding whoever came up with that idea, grinding them up, feeding them to the crickets, and then gathering up the crickets, stuffing them into the fireplace, burning the cabin down, and watching from a safe distance. Upwind, of course.

Do crickets even eat meat? You probably know. You grew up with all this. That's why you're comfortable with it. I'm not; to me, it's alien and disturbing. I wish I'd told you this the first time you took me there, right after we started dating. But your friends were having such a good time. I wanted to be the fun girlfriend who liked what everyone else liked.

It must seem strange that I'm bringing this up now, when neither of us will ever go back there. I mention it because saying I loved your cabin set off the chain of events that led us to where we are today. It wasn't the first lie I'd told you, of course, but the others were just my cover story.

I wish I'd been honest with you then. I wish I'd had the courage to tell you who and what I am. I wish I'd shown you images of the different shapes I'd taken before committing myself to human form. I wish I'd been able to make you feel the joy and freedom that comes with flowing from one shape to another and the profound sense of loss I felt when I gave that up.

I wish I'd been able to share what life was like on the ship. It was a total immersive experience. We spoke human languages, ate human food, and molded ourselves into closer and closer approximations of human shapes, with human-form instructors as our guides. We read your literature, tapped into your networks, and watched your videos. We received our cover stories and fashioned our human personalities.

One of the hardest things to master was food preferences. They're just so arbitrary. Remember the time your sister came over for dinner, and we made chocolate fondue for dessert? We started with apple slices, orange sections, and strawberries. Then Janice wanted to try dipping something salty, so I brought out the saltiest fruit we had: a jar of olives. Oops.

I seem to mess up a lot during meals with your family. I'm sorry I laughed at your uncle at that first Thanksgiving dinner. I know you wanted me to ignore him, but nformation-gathering is my job. I just couldn't keep a straight face. If he only knew: my people are far more illegal and far more alien than anyone he was ranting about, and believe me, we're not here to steal anyone's jobs.

I won't go so far as to say I should have told you our plan. Not our complete plan. But the research phase is scheduled to continue for another seventy-three years – we're nothing if not methodical – and I could have just said we were here to learn more about you. I should have told you at least that much when I found out I was pregnant.

I honestly hadn't believed that was possible. And then I remembered something I'd read during the journey to this planet. The ship was stocked with most of your classic literature, including a story about a husband and wife who exchanged gifts. He sold his watch to buy her a hair accessory; she sold her hair to buy him a watch accessory. It was supposed to convey irony, I think. For a long time after I read it, I thought human hair stopped growing at adulthood. Otherwise, the story lacks symmetry. The husband is permanently deprived of his watch, but the wife's hair will grow back with no effort on her part.

I thought perhaps you and I were like the characters in that story. Maybe this wasn't an inter-species pregnancy after all. I'd spent the last four-and-a-half years deceiving my apparently human spouse into thinking I was human; maybe you'd been doing the same. The more I thought about it, the more certain I became that this was true.

I began to make preparations for the traditional Strellyrian pregnancy announcement ritual, pared down for just the two of us. I planned a feast of guinea pigs and salamanders, the closest things I could find to our traditional delicacies. I thought we'd break the rules just this once and gorge ourselves on live meat. At the same time – just as a formality, really – I collected hair and cell samples while you slept and took them in for analysis. I repeated the tests three times, and the results were devastating: you were totally and undeniably human. Dr. Tran says we were able to produce that tiny zygote because my human-cell mimicry was so accurate, and it was able to survive because human stem cells are almost as malleable as ours.

I should have told you all this gradually throughout the course of the pregnancy. I had so many opportunities to do so. When you asked me why I wouldn't even consider your sister's obstetrician, I could have told you everything and explained that Dr. Tran was the only Strellyrian physician in the area. But what if you didn't believe me? I convinced myself at the time that it would be better to wait for the ultrasound. We'd watch it together, and you'd see the baby stretch and contract and reshape itself.

As the day of the ultrasound approached, I became more and more preoccupied with my own fears. What if there was a human fetus inside me, with one of those enormous human baby heads? I've seen how you people give birth. I began having nightmares about one of those things bursting out of me. I was awash in a sea of fear and regret; that's why I 'forgot' to tell you I'd rescheduled the appointment. I can't begin to tell you how relieved I was to see the images of our perfect little angel flowing into an ovoid, an almost-cube, and an adorably lopsided dodecahedron before returning to her resting spherical form.

I'm sorry things were so tense when my relatives arrived right before my due date. They've never approved of this marriage. My parents hated the idea of a human raising their grandchild. Three of them wanted to kill you outright; the others just wanted me to leave you. The only thing they agreed about was how irresponsible I'd been: getting pregnant, getting married, even the way I'd made decisions back on the ship (to be fair, they were right about that last bit: "I don't know; you pick one for me" is probably the worst possible answer you can give when asked to pick a gender).

Eventually, they reached a compromise. They concocted an elaborate plan for me to fake my own death, leave the country, and raise our baby alone. They arranged everything – new passport, plane ticket, apartment, even a new wardrobe – and wrote a new cover story for me. I refused to go along with it. I was sure our love was strong enough to withstand this challenge. Half of all marriages end in divorce, and I was determined that ours wouldn't be one of them.

I should have planned a better distraction for you when I confronted my family. Leaving you alone with my parent-adjunct (sorry, I mean 'Uncle Roger') was a mistake. He's not as bad as your uncle, but he does love to talk, and he tends to forget some of your more nonsensical cultural taboos. I should have warned him not to tell his war stories, and especially not the parts about feasting on his fallen enemies. Seriously, what's wrong with that? It's not like they'd be any less dead if we left their bodies to rot. And as I tried to explain, we maintain proper hygiene, eating only healthy people we've slain in battle, not anyone who's died from disease.

Arguing with you about that was a mistake; that's valuable time I could have spent telling you about my background and what to expect with the baby. And then I went into labor, and it was too late to say much of anything at all. Still, I was sure you'd come around once our baby was born. A powerful love for our offspring is something our two species have in common.

I didn't expect you to freak out at the sight of a few baby teeth. Yes, they appear within minutes of birth instead of however long it takes for your kind, and yes, they're longer and pointier and more numerous than you're accustomed to, but that's a perfectly natural phase of infant development. For the next couple weeks, she'll be flopping around, all teeth and digestive tract, eating everything in sight to support her neonatal growth spurt. She's so adorable! And clever – it looks like she's developing venom sacs! Only about 15% of Strellyrian babies have that instinct. Her grandparents are very impressed.

Goodbye, Kevin. I can see now that you'll never be the kind of parent our child deserves. I'm putting this into a letter instead of speaking to you in person because I don't want to subject our baby – or, let's face it, myself – to the escalating anger and, frankly, xenophobia you've displayed ever since my parents showed up.

I'm sorry it's come to this. I'm sure you understand why we can't let you go. I know the basement can get a little chilly, but you shouldn't be there much longer. I hope you'll find some comfort in the knowledge that, although you won't be around to help raise our child, you won't have failed her completely. You won't nurture her, but you will nourish her. Tonight, when her teeth have completely hardened, you'll have the honor of being her first solid meal.

All (well, some) of my love,

LYSSA

Outvasion

Tim Pieraccini

"CHLOE."

There's a tone of voice Alice uses, discernible even in a single word, when she's about to introduce a subject she knows I won't want to discuss.

I don't answer at once. With my head nestled underneath her right breast and the rest of me stretched out the length of the bed, I can't easily turn and look at her, but I can see the top three-quarters of her face in the dresser mirror. Her eyes are down, fixed on the top of my head, and partly covered by stray wispy locks of blonde hair. This makes her expression difficult to read. I suspect she knows she's visible in the mirror, and *wants* her expression to be difficult to read.

I still haven't answered, and she fills the silence with an exhalation meant to convey how difficult this is for her. This is followed by a drawing-in of breath – but she still doesn't say anything.

The last hour has been spectacular, so I stop torturing her and lever myself upright, bending briefly to scoop my top from the floor. Pulling it over my head, I wriggle around to face her, tucking my legs beneath me. She crosses her arms in front of her as if ashamed of her own nakedness, and that's when I know I'm *really* not going to like what's coming. I even, suddenly, have an inkling what it will be.

But the last hour really *has* been something, so I'm feeling unusually secure about her feelings for me. So secure, I offer encouragement in the form of her shirt, retrieved by means of another stretching scoop and draped with a ceremonial flourish around her shoulders. This I follow by taking one of her hands in both of mine.

Then I give her the ultimate proof of my goodwill by saying the name myself. "Have you seen Serafina? Has she been in touch?"

She lets out the breath she's holding, relieved and grateful, although there's still a touch of wariness in her nod. Understandable. I'm lifting her hand to my lips – further reassurance – when it suddenly occurs to me that this news might have a lot to do with what went on in the sixty minutes just passed, and I unconsciously tighten my grip. I tighten it quite a lot. She flinches, and I let her go.

"I'm sorry…" I hold my hands up. She leans back against the headboard; I try to recapture her hand, ashamed of my own paranoia, but she refuses to co-operate. I let my hands drop and lean forward a little, keeping eye contact. "I'm sorry. Tell me. Tell me about Serafina."

Alice holds my gaze but still can't seem to speak. The expression on her face is difficult to describe; it's something I've never seen before. If I had to guess I'd say that talking to me about Serafina is not what's actually troubling her.

Seeing her continue to struggle, I try to help out, get her started. "Did you…bump into her at the library? Bound to happen…I mean, you'd both be heading for archaeology…"

She manages a shake of the head. "It wasn't..." She looks away, her lips pressed together and her eyes restless. It's unnerving, seeing her search for words like this. I make a determined effort and recapture a hand, pulling it up close to my face and trying to focus her attention. "Let it out, whatever it is."

She draws in a deep breath, holds it for a moment. "I saw her in the street. Talking to a couple of homeless – well, no, not talking...not just talking..." Her eyes fix on mine, finally. "She was...she seemed to be giving them food."

I understand the confusion I've been seeing, but not the trace of real alarm. "Hmm. Well. I grant you that's unusual behaviour, but maybe...maybe if she bought sandwiches she didn't have time to eat..."

"She was sitting with them. On the pavement. In her...in the...you know, the Gucci poppy print..."

"I actually don't know, but..." Finally I grasp the seriousness of this. "Are you...sure it was Serafina? Did you see her clearly...?"

Alice gives me a look, and I nod. "All right. Sorry. Well...it could be she's got..." I discard that notion as preposterous. A few moments' thought brings up only one other possibility. "There wasn't anyone with her? She wasn't trying to impress –"

Alice shakes her head. "No. Just her and these two..." She lets out a kind of helpless sigh. "I think she was giving them the entire contents of her shopping bag. So, not just a couple of sandwiches..."

Something else occurs to me. "Part of a project? Some kind of social experiment?"

Her eyes are wide. "She looked like she...like she wanted to be there, to be talking to them. I mean, everything – her body language, her gestures, her face..."

"Fuck." We are finally united in understanding. But immediately I see another shadow in Alice's eyes, and I suspect I know what it is. "Did you speak to her?"

She looks down for a moment. "I wasn't going to. You know what she was like, last time. I've kept out of her way ever since. But, you know...I was so gobsmacked by what I saw, I just stood there...and she saw me. She came over."

I try a wonky smile. "You could have legged it..." Then I shrug. "All right, I s'pose not." And despite everything, I am curious. "Did she...I mean, was there an explanation?"

Alice is having difficulty yet again, but she takes control of herself. "This is where it gets really weird." She brings her other hand forward, resting it on top of our tangled fingers, and for a moment I want to stop this conversation dead, throw myself at her and bury my face against her neck, because something about this is frightening me. The feeling is gone in a moment, but still I shiver as Alice speaks again. "She asked about you; how you were, how the exhibition went, what's coming up..."

My laugh is brittle. "Did she have a temperature?"

"She didn't look ill. She looked...wonderful." Alice's tone is apologetic. "Radiant. I kept listening for sarcasm, passive-aggressive digs, some hint of her agenda...I couldn't hear anything. She just looked and sounded...amazing." She sees my expression and squeezes my hands. "Don't worry. Don't worry. It's just...I've seen her drunk, and high, and completely relaxed after..." she catches herself and shoots me a look that is a plea for patience, "but I've never seen her like this. It wasn't...it wasn't that she wasn't herself, exactly, she was just...better than herself. Better than her best self. Odd moments that I've seen...hints and flashes...this was her...but it wasn't." She sighs. "I'm sorry, I don't know how to explain it."

"Well," I say, slowly, "it doesn't seem, based on what you've said, like the worst thing in the world…" I stop because of what I see in her eyes.

"I know," she says. "But it was so scary."

* * *

I walk around the block twice before I can bring myself to press the buzzer.

As I wait it dawns on me that I'm expecting the old Serafina, the familiar Serafina. I think about the stranger Alice described and I'm not sure which prospect is more unsettling.

But the face behind the slightly-opened door is completely unfamiliar, sporting heavy-rimmed glasses beneath cropped bright blue hair. It makes a noise which is not quite a word, which seems to be a reluctant invitation for me to speak.

"Serafina? Is she here?"

A squint, and the ghost of a scowl. The owner of the face thrusts it forward, stepping halfway over the threshold with one fist bunched. I shuffle back instinctively; she appraises me, but seems reassured. I've passed some kind of test. She nods slowly, unclenching her fist. "What do you want her for?"

A question to which I have not prepared an answer. "I…I'd heard…someone said she…"

"Haven't seen you before."

I take a breath. "Sorry. I'm Chloe. I'm…I'm with Alice…now."

Understanding appears in the magnified brown eyes. There is another unclassifiable murmur. Then: "She's out."

"Right. Do you know where she's gone?"

"Some kind of meeting. With them." She can see the obvious question on my face and offers a wriggle of her shoulders. "Her new friends."

"D'you know…where…?"

"No." She steps back over the threshold, half-hiding behind the door again. "Why d'you wanna see her? I wouldn't…"

"Why? What's the matter with her?" When this goes unanswered: "She spoke to Alice. It…worried her – Alice, I mean. And…and I want…"

I want what, precisely? To make sure that this seeming new leaf is not some sort of gambit to win back Alice? That's certainly part of it. But there's also a healthy dollop of pure curiosity; I don't know Serafina well, but to meet her even once is to be left with a pretty strong impression. I want to see this transformation for myself.

"I wouldn't," says the girl behind the door. "I wouldn't bother. And keep Alice away from her. Away from all of them." She shuts the door, not quite slamming it, before I have a chance to do the polite thing and ask her name.

* * *

I can't bring myself to simply surrender and crawl home. I head for the city centre – more precisely, for Depravity's Rainbow, reasoning that since Serafina has always been a leader of whatever group she's in, that much at least will not have changed.

I am not wrong; she's brought her new friends to her favourite haunt. My pleasure at guessing correctly is very quickly swept away, though – by bewilderment, as I look at the group surrounding Serafina. Whatever I was expecting, it was not this.

I've quite literally never seen such a motley assortment. A couple of them look too young to go to the bar; a couple of them look like they were around when the place was a stagecoach stopover. There are two men and one woman in suits, a homeless girl I recognise, a housewife-type and maybe two who fit the mould of Serafina's usual hangers-on.

The bar staff clearly don't know what to make of it, either; two of them are leaning at the far end of the bar, heads together and eyes on their surprise flood of customers. Mid-week afternoons are dead here.

Movement from the hub of Serafina's assembly – she's seen me. Now is the moment I realise I haven't worked out what I want to say. Paralysis takes hold of me as she picks her way over. Behind her, the group fall into conversation with one another; that's comforting because it means they won't be watching, but also…unusual. As if Serafina is not especially important. She doesn't throw a look behind her, either, which is practically a reflex for her in these situations.

"Chloe!" The tone is one I've never heard from her – and not just in speaking to me. If I had to describe it, I'd have to plump for 'undisguised warmth'.

She lays a hand on my sleeve, and I can't keep from flinching. I'm not sure I've ever been this close to her. I'd like to report the sighting of a million tiny flaws, but the truth is she's even more overwhelming from a foot away; eyes so deep brown they're almost black, and a great explosion of hair to match. The killer smile has always been faintly sarcastic or patronising when aimed at me, but today it's…different. Different how, I can't say.

"I was talking to Alice about you yesterday. You admired that Burberry I had. I wondered if you wanted it?"

I'm not sure what my face is showing, because I'm not sure what I'm feeling. I can't read her face, either; every line and feature is in the right place, but she's like a twin of herself. I can't read this face because it never shows me what I'm expecting. 'I've given away most of the rest,' the face says, 'but I kept that back, in case.'

'Given away…?' I thrash about mentally, trying to make sense of this. I look over her shoulder at the others, and return to the idea I dismissed earlier. "Is this…are you…is it some kind of religious group?"

I already know the answer, but her reaction still surprises me. She doesn't scowl; she doesn't laugh. "No. Come and talk, find out." Her brown hand brushes my pallid one, I yelp and jump back.

Did I feel a shock? An instant after it's happened, I'm already unsure. Serafina's looking at me – no impatience, no curiosity, just looking. She doesn't move or speak – or even smile, quite. She's just there. And I understand Alice. It's the most frightening thing I've ever seen Serafina do; nothing. She's either totally in your face or showing you her back. This isn't her. And yet, it is.

"N-no. Thank you." This is all I can manage, followed by a step back. "Don't…don't worry about the coat. I mean, thank you, but…it's ok."

"All right." She nods, her arms folded loosely, her head slightly on one side. She appears utterly relaxed, neither waiting for anything nor about to launch into a monologue. I can think of nothing to say, and after a couple of moments she gestures in the direction of her new friends. "Are you sure you don't want to talk…?"

"Not…at the moment." I move another two steps back. "Thanks. Another time, maybe…"

"There'll be another time. Soon." Her smile is gentleness itself, and it literally makes me shiver. "Say hi to Alice."

"I will." I'm already almost to the door, trying not to run.

* * *

Halfway up the block I already feel ridiculous. I'm also not exercising regularly, so I have two reasons to stop running. I sink down onto a bench and look towards the pub, wondering if I should try again. I can't find a sensible reason to go back, but lack of a sensible reason didn't stop me running away.

Someone approaches the bench from the other direction. I whip around to see Serafina's housemate. Or whatever she is. She looks at me with the wariness I remember from the beginning of our earlier encounter, stopping a few feet away. "You saw them?"

"Yes. Did you...follow me?"

My manner obviously reassures her and she sits down beside me. "When I saw you running I thought you were probably still ok – they don't seem to run – but you were in there a few minutes..."

I'm staring at her, and she seems to intuit at least part of the reason. "Sorry...I'm Di. Came after you because..." She makes a little noise. "Shouldn't have let you walk off, before. Knew you'd still look for her." She glances over at Depravity's Rainbow. "Got here too late to stop you going in."

"Thanks for trying." Without thinking I make to lay a hand on her arm, but she's not quite at that level of reassured; she comes to her feet.

"Sorry," I say. I lean back, making an effort to seem relaxed. "What happened to her – to them? Do you know? Is it a drug? I mean, they don't look..."

She's shaking her head. "Not a drug. Dunno." Her eyes unfocus for a moment; a memory? "Unless...no, I dunno."

"What? What did you...?"

She doesn't answer for a moment. Her eyes are on the pavement. "Two of her – Serafina's – friends came round yesterday. They were...as normal. Freaked out by her. She...they... they were talking in the kitchen. They were getting more and more wigged out, but she kept the same tone of voice, the same look on her face...and then she took hold of one of them, by the hand. That's all. And..." She looks up. "And that was it. That one calmed down, right off. The other one got out of there, pronto." She looks at her own hands. "Guess I'm lucky not liking to be touched."

I lift my own hand, remembering the shock I seemed to feel. "How did...I mean, how long were they touching? Did it...was the change immediate?"

Di shakes her head. "A few seconds...maybe ten...fifteen."

I exhale. "And you really think it was the touch that did it?"

"Stood there and watched it."

* * *

"Sorry, I have to go. She wouldn't call me unless she was in total panic." Alice is throwing clothes and books into a holdall.

"What did she say?"

"Dad's...I don't know...just kind of lost it. Wants to sell the car, keeps giving people things..."

"Like Serafina."

She barely glances up. "I can't think about her now. You shouldn't worry about that. I'm sure it's just…"

I step closer to her. Has she already forgotten, the way I was unsure about the jolt when our hands touched? Is this something else that happens, this amnesia? "I mean, it sounds like the same thing. The exact same thing. Don't you think –"

"What?" Now she does pause. "No, I don't see…I mean, they're two hundred miles… unless some new cult's sprung up overnight, all over the place…" She sees my face. "I mean, come on. How is it possible? There can't be any…"

"I don't know." We're really close now, face to face, and yet I'm afraid to touch her. "I don't think you should go."

"What??" She tosses her head in dismissal. "I have to; you know I do. Can you remember the last Mum asked me for help…?" She zips up the bag, takes a moment. She turns to me and opens her arms.

I hesitate, but then step into the embrace, wrapping my arms tight about her, leaning my head against hers.

"Christ you're tense." She pulls her head back and looks into my eyes. "Take it easy. It'll be a couple of days. They've got Skype now – we can have a filthy midnight session once Mum and Dad have gone to bed."

"Don't go."

* * *

I saw her onto the train, and then bought a few bits of food so I wouldn't have to leave the house for a couple of days. I was on edge the whole time I was out; someone held a door open for me and I gave them such a look, they must have thought I was on something. I walked right at the edge of the pavement to avoid passing close to anyone. I turned into side streets to avoid two people I know.

Now I'm home, and I think about it, and at odd moments I'm convinced I must be losing my grip. What have I seen? What have I *actually* seen? Some people being perfectly pleasant. That's literally all. Maybe I should go out again, see a film, lose myself in something for a couple of hours. I'd come out and the world would be back to normal.

But what *has* happened to Serafina? What happened to the ego, the game-playing, the needling? Serafina used to live her life like a performance, but the woman I saw in the pub was completely open, completely without masks. Something in her was utterly transformed. Di saw it. Alice saw it, before she was distracted by this family crisis.

I'm searching online. There's nothing in the news outlets – how could there be? What would they report? But on social media, it's starting to filter through. A few statuses, a few conversations. Most people doubting their own perception, like me.

I want – I desperately want – to talk to Alice, but apart from a text when she arrived, I've heard nothing. She didn't answer when I called mid-evening, so I'll have to wait for the promised Skype session. I'm not much in the mood, I admit.

* * *

She doesn't Skype. She doesn't pick up. I get nice, perfectly bland texts saying she'll be back soon.

* * *

When she comes through the front door it's a kind of shock – something normal, something that feels like the life before. The life of two days before.

But it isn't like before, because there's something in her face that I've seen in other faces. In Serafina's, in the newsreader who went off script, in the politician shaking hands at that premiere. In the videos now being posted on social media.

"Chloe."

There's a tone of voice she uses, like nothing I've ever heard from her before. Warm and friendly, open and positive – but completely lacking in any kind of passion, any undertone of what we are to each other. Any sense of what links us – and separates us from the rest of the world.

She steps toward me and I grab up a knife from one of the plates lying around. "Keep back."

She doesn't seem alarmed, or surprised. "We should talk," she says gently.

"What about? What happened? What is happening?" I am babbling, holding up a blunt knife stained with baked bean sauce.

"Nothing's happening." She looks around, taking in the mess. "Do you want me to tidy up?"

"What is happening to people? What happened to your dad? What happened to you?"

"I'm fine." She spreads her hands. "I'm wonderful."

Tell me what happened.

"Chloe, perhaps you should have a lie down – maybe a shower." She steps over a couple of plates, slipping her bag off her shoulder and onto the end of the sofa, and extending a hand. "Let me –"

I scramble away from her. "Don't touch me!"

She doesn't react to my screech, simply looks at me for a second. "I'll tidy up."

"Where does it come from?"

She looks up from gathering the plates and cutlery. "Where does what come from?"

"This – you know. This whatever-it-is. What's changed you. Is it some kind of virus...?" I'm still looking for something in her eyes, some trace of the old Alice. "Something... something from a lab? Or even...something from space...a meteor landed, or...I don't know."

She stands up, holding the plates, the cutlery on the top one. She holds out a hand for the knife I'm still brandishing. "Not from outside. Inside."

"What?"

There's a faint smile on her face. "They come, originally, from right next to us." She withdraws her hand. "Right next to us, and a universe away."

"What? I don't..."

"Have a shower. You'll feel better." She turns away. Not even a glance back as she leaves the room.

While I sob, I'm peripherally aware that she is filling the sink; there is the clatter of plates. I think about the online attempts I saw to understand what this is. Another dimension, they were talking about. Just speculation, but something that seeped through, or came through, and...it's all ridiculous. Nobody knows anything. And there's hardly anyone left who cares to ask the questions.

I look at the knife in my hand. How much would it hurt? A hell of a lot, I suspect. So many people decided it was the only way out, decided *so quickly*…but what do we know about what it's like on…the other side? They're not unhappy, they're not upset by anything, they work together to make life better – materially better – for everyone. What's so wrong with that? Why is it so frightening?

I think about Di. I barely know her, but she's the person I feel closest to in this moment. I wonder if she's still herself.

My fist is closed tight around the knife.

Alice appears in the doorway. "You really need to relax. Never mind the shower; I'll run you a bath." Without the slightest change in her tone, she says: "Would you like me to wash you?"

The Germ Growers
Preliminary–Chapter II

Robert Potter

Preliminary

WHEN I FIRST HEARD the name of Kimberley [a region in North-west Australia] it did not remind me of the strange things which I have here to record, and which I had witnessed somewhere in its neighbourhood years before. But one day, in the end of last summer, I overheard a conversation about its geography which led me to recognise it as a place that I had formerly visited under very extraordinary circumstances. The recognition was in this wise. Jack Wilbraham and I were spending a little while at a hotel in Gippsland, partly on a tour of pleasure and partly, so at least we persuaded ourselves, on business. The fact was, however, that for some days past, the business had quite retreated into the background, or, to speak more correctly, we had left it behind at Bairnsdale, and had come in search of pleasure a little farther south.

It was delicious weather, warm enough for light silk coats in the daytime, and cold enough for two pairs of blankets at night. We had riding and sea-bathing to our hearts' content, and even a rough kind of yachting and fishing. The ocean was before us – we heard its thunder night and day; and the lakes were behind us, stretching away to the promontory which the Mitchell cuts in two, and thence to the mouth of the Latrobe, which is the highway to Sale. Three times a week a coach passed our door, bound for the Snowy River and the more savage regions beyond. Any day for a few shillings we could be driven to Lake Tyers, to spend a day amidst scenery almost comparable with the incomparable Hawkesbury. Last of all, if we grew tired of the bell-birds and the gum-trees and the roar of the ocean, we were within a day's journey of Melbourne by lake and river and rail.

It was our custom to be out all day, but home early and early to bed. We used to take our meals in a low long room which was well aired but poorly lighted, whether by day or night. And here, when tea was over and the womenkind had retired, we smoked, whenever, as often happened, the evening was cold enough to make a shelter desirable; smoked and chatted. There was light enough to see the smoke of your pipe and the faces of those near you; but if you were listening to the chatter of a group in the other end of the room the faces of the speakers were so indistinct as often to give a startling challenge to your imagination if you had one, and if it was accustomed to take the bit in its teeth. I sometimes caught myself partly listening to a story-teller in the other end of the room and partly fashioning a face out of his dimly seen features, which quite belied the honest fellow's real countenance when the flash of a pipelight or a shifted lamp revealed it more fully.

Jack and I were more of listeners than talkers, and we were usually amongst the earliest who retired. But one evening there was a good deal of talk about the new gold-field in the north-west, and a keen-looking bushman who seemed to have just returned from the place began to describe its whereabouts. Then I listened attentively, and at one point in his talk, I started and looked over at Jack, and I saw that he was already looking at me. I got up and left the room without a sign to him, but I knew that he would follow me, and he did. It was bright moonlight, and when we met outside we strolled down to the beach together. It was a wide, long, and lonely beach, lonely to the very last degree, and it was divided from the house by a belt of scrub near a mile wide. We said not a word to one another till we got quite near the sea. Then I turned round and looked Jack in the face and said, "Why, man, it must have been quite near the place."

"No," said he, "it may have been fifty miles or more away, their knowledge is loose, and their description looser, but it must be somewhere in the neighbourhood, and I suppose they are sure to find it."

"I do not know," said I; and after a pause I added, "Jack, it seems to me they might pass all over the place and see nothing of what we saw."

"God knows," he muttered, and then he sat down on a hummock of sand and I beside him. Then he said, "Why have you never told the story, Bob?"

"Don't you know why, Jack?" I answered. "They would lock me up in a madhouse; there would be no one to corroborate me but you, and if you did so you would be locked up along with me."

"That might be," said he, "if they believed you; but they would not believe you, they would think you were simply romancing."

"What would be the good of speaking then?" said I.

"Don't speak," he repeated, "but write, litera scripta manet, you will be believed sometime. But meanwhile you can take as your motto that verse in Virgil about the gate of ivory, and that will save you from being thought mad. You have a knack of the pen, Bob, you ought to try it."

"Well," said I, "let it be a joint concern between you and me, and I'll do my best."

Then we lit our pipes and walked home, and settled the matter in a very few words on the way. I was to write, but all I should write was to be read over to Jack, who should correct and supplement it from his own memory. And no account of anything which was witnessed by both of us was to stand finally unless it was fully vouched for by the memory of both. Thus for any part of the narrative which would concern one of us only that one should be alone responsible, but for all of it in which we were both concerned there should be a joint responsibility.

Out of this agreement comes the following history, and thus it happens that it is told in the first person singular, although there are two names on the title-page.

Chapter I
Disappearances

BEFORE I BEGIN MY STORY I must give you some account of certain passages in my early life, which seem to have some connection with the extraordinary facts that I am about to put on record.

To speak more precisely, of the connection of one of them with those facts there can be no doubt at all, and of the connection of the other with them I at least have none.

When I was quite a boy, scarce yet fifteen years old, I happened to be living in a parish on the Welsh coast, which I will here call Penruddock. There were some bold hills inland

and some very wild and rugged cliffs along the coast. But there was also a well-sheltered beach and a little pier where some small fishing vessels often lay. Penruddock was not yet reached by rail, but forty miles of a splendid road, through very fine scenery, took you to a railway station. And this journey was made by a well-appointed coach on five days of every week.

The people of Penruddock were very full of a queer kind of gossip, and were very superstitious. And I took the greatest interest in their stories. I cannot say that I really believed them, or that they affected me with any real fear. But I was not without that mingled thrill of doubt and wonder which helps one to enjoy such things. I had a double advantage in this way, for I could understand the Welsh language, although I spoke it but little and with difficulty, and I often found a startling family likeness between the stories which I heard in the cottages of the peasantry three or four miles out of town and those which circulated among the English-speaking people in whose village I lived.

There was one such story which was constantly reproduced under various forms. Sometimes it was said to have happened in the last generation; sometimes as far back as the civil wars, of which, strange to say, a lively traditional recollection still remained in the neighbourhood; and sometimes it seemed to have been handed down from prehistoric times, and was associated with tales of enchantment and fairyland. In such stories the central event was always the unaccountable disappearance of some person, and the character of the person disappearing always presented certain unvarying features. He was always bold and fascinating, and yet in some way or other very repulsive. And when you tried to find out why, some sort of inhumanity was always indicated, some unconscious lack of sympathy which was revolting in a high degree or even monstrous. The stories had one other feature in common, of which I will tell you presently.

I seldom had any companions of my own age, and I was in consequence more given to dreaming than was good for me. And I used to marshal the heroes of these queer stories in my day-dreams and trace their likeness one to another. They were often so very unlike in other points, and yet so strangely like in that one point. I remember very well the first day that I thought I detected in a living man a resemblance to those dreadful heroes of my Welsh friend's folk-lore. There was a young fellow whom I knew, about five or six years my senior, and so just growing into manhood. His name, let us say, was James Redpath. He was well built, of middle height, and, as I thought, at first at least, quite beautiful to look upon. And, indeed, why I did not continue to think so is more than I can exactly say. For he possessed very fine and striking features, and although not very tall his presence was imposing. But nobody liked him. The girls especially, although he was so good-looking, almost uniformly shrank from him. But I must confess that he did not seem to care much for their society.

I went about with him a good deal at one time on fishing and shooting excursions and made myself useful to him, and except that he was rather cruel to dogs and cats, and had a nasty habit of frightening children, I do not know that I noticed anything particular about him. Not, at least, until one day of which I am going to tell you. James Redpath and I were coming back together to Penruddock, and we called at a cottage about two miles from the village. Here we found a little boy of about four years old, who had been visiting at the cottage and whom they wanted to send home. They asked us to take charge of him and we did so. On the way home the little boy's shoe was found to have a nail or a peg in it that hurt his foot, and we were quite unable to get it out. It was nothing, however, to James Redpath to carry him, and so he took him in his arms.

The little boy shrank and whimpered as he did so. James had under his arm some parts of a fishing-rod and one of these came in contact with the little boy's leg and scratched it rather severely so as to make him cry. I took it away and we went on. I was walking a little behind Redpath, and as I walked I saw him deliberately take another joint of the rod, put it in the same place and then watch the little boy's face as it came in contact with the wire, and as the child cried out I saw quite a malignant expression of pleasure pass over James's face. The thing was done in a moment and it was over in a moment; but I felt as if I should like to have killed him if I dared. I always dreaded and shunned him, more or less, afterwards, and I began from that date to associate him with the inhuman heroes of my Welsh stories.

I don't think that I should ever have got over the dislike of him which I then conceived, but I saw the last of him, at least Penruddock saw the last of him, about three months later. I had been sitting looking over the sea between the pier and the cliffs and trying to catch a glimpse of the Wicklow Mountains which were sometimes to be seen from that point. Just then James Redpath came up from the beach beyond the pier, and passing me with a brief "good morning," went away inland, leaving the cliffs behind him. I don't know how long I lay there, it might be two hours or more, and I think I slept a little. But I suddenly started up to find it high day and past noon, and I began to think of looking for some shelter. There was not a cloud visible, but nevertheless two shadows like, or something like, the shadows of clouds lay near me on the ground. What they were the shadows of I could not tell, and I was about to get up to see, for there was nothing to cast such a shadow within the range of my sight as I lay. Just then one of the shadows came down over me and seemed to stand for a moment between me and the sun. It had a well-defined shape, much too well defined for a cloud. I thought as I looked that it was just such a shadow as might be cast by a yawl-built boat lying on the body of a large wheelbarrow. Then the two shadows seemed to move together and to move very quickly. I had just noticed that they were exactly like one another when the next moment they passed out of my sight.

I started to my feet with a bound, my heart beating furiously. But there was nothing more to alarm the weakest. It was broad day. Houses and gardens were to be seen close at hand and in every direction but one, and in that direction there were three or four fishermen drawing their nets. But as I looked away to the part of the sky where the strange cloudlike shadows had just vanished, I remembered with a shudder that other feature in common of the strange stories of which I told you just now. It was a feature that forcibly reminded me of what I had just witnessed. Sometimes in the later stories you would be told of a cloud coming and going in an otherwise cloudless sky. And sometimes in the elder stories you would be told of an invisible car, invisible but not shadowless. I used always to identify the shadow of the invisible car in the elder stories with the cloud in the later stories, the cloud that unaccountably came and went.

As I thought it all over and tried to persuade myself that I had been dreaming I suddenly remembered that James Redpath had passed by a few hours before, and as suddenly I came to the conclusion that I should never see him again. And certainly he never was again seen, dead or alive, anywhere in Wales or England. His father, and his uncle, and their families, continued to live about Penruddock, but Penruddock never knew James Redpath any more. Whether I myself saw him again or not is more than I can say with absolute certainty. You shall know as much as I know about it if you hear my story to the end.

Chapter II
The Red Sickness

OF COURSE James Redpath's disappearance attracted much attention, and was the talk not only of the village, but of the whole country-side. It was the general opinion that he must have been drowned by falling over the cliffs, and that his body had been washed out to sea. I proved, however, to have been the very last person to see him, and my testimony, as far as it went, was against that opinion. For I certainly had seen him walking straight inland. Of course he might have returned to the coast afterwards, but at least nobody had seen him return. I gave a full account of place and time as far as I could fix them, and I mentioned the queer-looking clouds and even described their shape. This I remember, was considered to have some value as fixing my memory of the matter, but no further notice was taken of it. And I myself did not venture to suggest any connection between it and Redpath's disappearance, because I did not see how I could reasonably do so. I had, nevertheless, a firm conviction that there was such a connection, but I knew very well that to declare it would only bring a storm of ridicule upon me.

But a public calamity just then befell Penruddock which made men forget James Redpath's disappearance. A pestilence broke out in the place of which nobody knew either the nature or the source. It seemed to spring up in the place. At least, all efforts to trace it were unsuccessful. The first two or three cases were attributed to some inflammatory cold, but it soon became clear that there were specific features about it, that they were quite unfamiliar, that the disease was extremely dangerous to life and highly infectious.

Then a panic set in, and I believe that the disease would soon have been propagated all over England and farther, if it had not been for the zeal and ability of two young physicians who happened very fortunately to be living in the village just then. Their names were Leopold and Furniss. I forget if I ever knew their Christian names. We used to call them Doctor Leopold and Doctor Furniss. They had finished their studies for some little time, but they found it advisable on the score of health to take a longish holiday before commencing practice, and they were spending part of their holiday at Penruddock. They were just about to leave us when the disease I am telling you of broke out.

The first case occurred in a valley about two miles from the village. In this valley there were several cottages inhabited mostly by farm labourers and artisans. These cottages lay one after another in the direction of the rising ground which separated the valley from Penruddock. Then there were no houses for a considerable space. Then, just over the hill, there was another and yet another. The disease had made its way gradually up the hill from one cottage to another, day after day a fresh case appearing. Then there had been no new cases for four days, but on the fifth day a new case appeared in the cottage just over the brow of the hill. And when this became known, also that every case (there had now been eleven) had hitherto been fatal, serious alarm arose. Then, too, the disease became known as the "red sickness." This name was due to a discoloration which set in on the shoulders, neck, and forehead very shortly after seizure.

How the two doctors, as we called them, became armed with the needful powers I do not know. They certainly contrived to obtain some sort of legal authority, but I think that they acted in great measure on their own responsibility.

By the time they commenced operations there were three or four more cases in the valley, and one more in the second cottage on the Penruddock side. There was a large stone house, partly ruinous, in the valley, near the sea, and hither they brought every one of the sick. Plenty of help was given them in the way of beds, bedding, and all sorts of material, but such was the height which the panic had now attained that no one from the village would go near any of the sick folk, nor even enter the valley. The physicians themselves and their two men servants, who seemed to be as fearless and brave as they, did all the work. Fortunately, the two infected cottages on the Penruddock side were each tenanted only by the person who had fallen ill, and the tenant in each case was a labourer whose work lay in the valley. The physicians burnt down these cottages and everything that was in them. Then they established a strict quarantine between the village and the valley. There was a light fence running from the sea for about a mile inland, along the brow of the rising ground on the Penruddock side. This they never passed nor suffered any one to pass, during the prevalence of the sickness. Butchers and bakers and other tradesmen left their wares at a given point at a given time, and the people from the valley came and fetched them.

The excitement and terror in Penruddock were very great. All but the most necessary business was suspended, and of social intercourse during the panic there was next to none. Ten cases in all were treated by the physicians, and four of these recovered. The last two cases were three or four days apart, but they were no less malignant in character: the very last case was one of the fatal ones. I learned nothing of the treatment; but the means used to prevent the disease spreading, besides the strict quarantine, were chiefly fire and lime. Everything about the sick was passed through the fire, and of these everything that the fire would destroy was destroyed. Lime, which abounded in the valley, was largely used.

A month after the last case the two physicians declared the quarantine at an end, and a month later all fear of the disease had ceased. And then the people of the village began to think of consoling themselves for the dull and uncomfortable time they had had, and of doing some honour to the two visitors who had served the village so well. With this double purpose in view a picnic on a large scale was organized, and there was plenty of eating and drinking and speech-making and dancing, all of which I pass over. But at that picnic I heard a conversation which made a very powerful impression on me then, and which often has seemed to provide a bond which binds together all the strange things of which I had experience at the time and afterwards.

In the heat of the afternoon I had happened to be with Mr. Leopold and Mr. Furniss helping them in some arrangements which they were making for the amusement of the children who took part in the picnic. After these were finished they two strolled away together to the side of a brook which ran through the park where we were gathered. I followed them, attracted mainly by Mr. Furniss's dog, but encouraged also by an occasional word from the young men. At the brook Mr. Furniss sat upon a log, and leaned his back against a rustic fence. The dog sat by him; a very beautiful dog he was, black and white, with great intelligent eyes, and an uncommonly large and well-shaped head. He would sometimes stretch himself at length, and then again he would put his paw upon his master's shoulder and watch Mr. Leopold and me.

Mr. Leopold stood with his back to an oak-tree, and I leant against the fence beside him listening to him. He was a tall, dark man, with a keen, thoughtful, and benevolent expression. He was quite strong and healthy-looking, and there was a squareness about his features that I think one does not often see in dark people. Mr. Furniss was of lighter complexion and hardly as tall; there was quite as much intelligence and benevolence in his face, but not so much of what I have called thoughtfulness as distinguished from intelligence, and there was a humorous glint in his eye which the other lacked. They began to talk about the disease which had been so successfully dealt with, and this was what they said:

Leopold. Well, Furniss, an enemy hath done this.

Furniss. Done what? The picnic or the red sickness?

Leopold. The red sickness, of course. Can't you see what I mean?

Furniss. No, I can't. You're too much of a mystic for me, Leopold; but I'll tell you what, England owes a debt to you and me, my boy, for it was near enough to being a new edition of the black death or the plague.

Leopold. Only the black death and the plague were imported, and this was indigenous. It sprung up under our noses in a healthy place. It came from nowhere, and, thank God, it is gone nowhither.

Furniss. But surely the black death and the plague must have begun somewhere, and they too seem to have gone nowhither.

Leopold. You're right this far that they all must have had the same sort of beginning. Only it is given to very few to see the beginning, as you and I have seen it, or so near the beginning.

Furniss. Now, Leopold, I hardly see what you are driving at. I am not much on religion, as they say in America, but I believe there is a Power above all. Call that power God, and let us say that God does as He pleases, and on the whole that it is best that He should. I don't see that you can get much further than that.

Leopold. I don't believe that God ever made the plague, or the black death, or the red sickness.

Furniss. Oh, don't you? Then you are, I suppose, what the churchmen call a Manichee – you believe in the two powers of light and darkness, good and evil. Well, it is not a bad solution of the question as far as it goes, but I can hardly accept it.

Leopold. No, I don't believe in any gods but the One. But let me explain. That is a nice dog of yours, Furniss. You told me one day something about his breeding, and you promised to tell me more.

Furniss. Yes, it is quite a problem in natural history. Do you know, Tommy's ancestors have been in our family for four or five generations of men, and, I suppose, that is twenty generations of dogs.

Leopold. You told me something of it. You improved the breed greatly, I believe?

Furniss. Yes; but I have some distant cousins, and they have the same breed and yet not the same, for they have cultivated it in quite another direction.

Leopold. What are the differences?

Furniss. Our dogs are all more or less like Tommy here, gentle and faithful, very intelligent, and by no means deficient in pluck. My cousin's dogs are fierce and quarrelsome, so much so that they have not been suffered for generations to associate with children. And so they have lost intelligence and are become ill-conditioned and low-lived brutes.

Leopold. But I think I understood you to say that the change in the breed did not come about in the ordinary course of nature.

Furniss. I believe not. I heard my grandfather say that his father had told him that when he was a young man he had set about improving the breed. He had marked out the most intelligent and best tempered pups, and he had bred from them only and had given away or destroyed the others.

Leopold. And about your cousin's dogs?

Furniss. Just let me finish. It seems that while one brother began to cultivate the breed upward, so to speak, another brother was living in a part of the country where thieves were numerous and daring, and there were smugglers and gipsies, and what not, about. And so he began to improve the breed in quite another direction. He selected the fierce and snappish pups and bred exclusively from them.

Leopold. And so from one ancestral pair of, say, a hundred or a hundred and fifty years ago, you have Tommy there, with his wonderful mixture of gentleness and pluck, and his intelligence all but human, and your cousin has a kennel of unintelligent and bloodthirsty brutes, that have to be caged and chained as if they were wild beasts.

Furniss. Just so, but I don't quite see what you are driving at.

Leopold. Wait a minute. Do you suppose the germs of cow-pox and small-pox to be of the same breed?

Furniss. Well, yes; you know that I hold them to be specifically identical. I see what you are at now.

Leopold. But one of them fulfils some obscure function in the physique of the cow, some function certainly harmless and probably beneficent, and the other is the malignant small-pox of the London hospitals.

Furniss. So you mean to infer that in the latter case the germ has been cultivated downwards by intelligent purpose.

Leopold. What if I do?

Furniss. You think, then, that there is a secret guild of malignant men of medicine sworn to wage war against their fellow-men, that they are spread over all the world and have existed since before the dawn of history. I don't believe that there are any men as bad as that, and if there were, I should call them devils and hunt them down like mad dogs.

Leopold. I don't wish to use misleading words, but I will say that I believe there are intelligences, not human, who have access to realms of nature that we are but just beginning to explore; and I believe that some of them are enemies to humanity, and that they use their knowledge to breed such things as malignant small-pox or the red sickness out of germs which were originally of a harmless or even of a beneficent nature.

Furniss. Just as my cousins have bred those wild beasts of theirs out of such harmless creatures as poor Tommy's ancestors.

Leopold. Just so.

Furniss. And you think that we can contend successfully against such enemies.

Leopold. Why not? They can only have nature to work upon. And very likely their only advantage over us is that they know more of nature than we do. They cannot go beyond the limits of nature to do less or more. As long as we sought after spells and enchantments and that sort of nonsense we were very much at their mercy. But we are now learning to fight them with their own weapons, which consist of the knowledge of nature. Witness vaccination, and witness also our little victory over the red sickness.

Furniss. You're a queer mixture, Leopold, but we must get back to the picnic people.

And so they got up and went back together to the dancers, nodding to me as they went. I sat there for awhile, going over and over the conversation in my mind and putting together my own thoughts and Mr. Leopold's.

Then I joined the company and was merry as the merriest for the remainder of the day. But that night I dreamt of strange-looking clouds and of the shadows of invisible cars, and of demons riding in the cars and sowing the seeds of pestilence on the earth and catching away such evil specimens of humanity as James Redpath to reinforce the ranks of their own malignant order.

The complete and unabridged text is available online, *from flametreepublishing.com/extras*

Lovers at Dawn

Eric Reitan

HE'S ON THE BALCONY, the small of his back pressed so hard into the rusty metal railing that it digs into his flesh. He faces his lover. She's always been too beautiful to think about with anything but an ache, but now he's learned disgust.

She stands inside the bedroom, half in shadow, the other half limned in yellow light from the hall. He thinks about the Phantom of the Opera, about the deformities hidden by the half-mask.

It would be hypocrisy not to kill her.

"Leave," he rasps.

She shakes her head. "I won't make it that easy for you."

He heaves a sigh and turns away, toward the reddening sky. Her name sits in his mouth like something overripe, something he should spit over the railing. And yet it still has sweetness.

He isn't surprised when he feels her hand on his back. She slips into place beside him, careless of her nakedness.

"Yours is a beautiful world," she says.

* * *

On the very day of the Intrusion, David Conlan's wife slipped on wet leaves crossing Maple Road, and she fell backwards into the path of a silver Volvo. She died before the ambulance arrived.

David was at work when it happened. As the ambulance was skidding through the rainy streets, he was flirting with the new receptionist. Her name was Sarah, and he was saying it aloud, the name like silk, while the paramedics worked to keep his wife alive. He was brazen and Sarah was blushing, and he saw the affair unfolding before him like something inevitable, as if it weren't his doing at all.

He was on the phone, laying a variant of the same seducer's charm on one of his corporate clients, when they came to tell him. They spoke in low voices as if that would make it easier to bear. At first he didn't react. When they were gone he stood behind his desk, straightening papers and staring at the institutional painting on the far wall, the kind he sold to lawyers and doctors and modelling agencies. When he walked out, Sarah stared just past him in mortified silence. She would've slept with him if he'd been happily married. But not now.

It wasn't until he was in his car, driving towards the hospital, that his knuckles began to whiten. He had to pull over. He sat for a long while, clinging to the wheel. The sounds he made were the kind no one but his wife had ever heard. Which meant that there was not a single person, no living person on Earth, who'd ever heard his heaving sobs.

That night, when the rest of the world gathered in wonder and fear to watch or listen to reports of the Intrusion, David Conlan sat alone in darkness, holding his wedding album on his lap. Because that was the pathetically clichéd choice, the only option for someone like him, someone who had clichéd office affairs in a business that sold clichéd office décor.

The news cameras were fixed on the crystalline ships, the reporters' voices trembling with fear and excitement and uncertainty, but as David stared at the screen he was thinking about the first time he'd made love to her, in a sleeping bag at Kathy Jensen's cottage. That's when they'd become lovers, and lovers is what they'd stayed until the word 'wife' pushed its way into things and did its domesticating work.

But in the wedding photos he saw the Jensen cottage girl, the girl who smelled like campfire smoke and tasted like s'mores. And he was weeping and clawing at his face, digging his nails into his cheeks as if that could tear away all the wasted years.

When he rose and went to bed, he saw the dent in her pillow, the tangible evidence of nearness in space and time. In the night, when he reached for her and his fingers settled on an empty blanket, he woke in surprise.

* * *

"Don't touch me," he says, and when she pulls her hand away he feels the cold place it leaves behind. He remembers her touch. He remembers last night's kisses, his impassioned proposal, and the long, hot silence before her words: "There's something you need to know."

A part of him still wants to reach out, to fight his own gag reflex for another moment of contact. He's disgusting. He disgusts himself.

"I never lied to you," she says, but her voice is uncertain. "I would have told you sooner, if –"

"Leave," he says.

"You don't want me to leave, David."

He spins towards her, a scathing curse ready on his lips; but her face is beautiful in the crimson light, and her eyes are deep. The first time he saw her, on a park bench feeding squirrels, the sun made copper highlights in her hair. Now the dawn light casts shadows laced with richer reds.

He looks away, silenced.

"I haven't changed, David. I'm still the woman you fell in love with."

"Woman?" He tries to laugh, but the sound withers in his mouth.

"I'm a woman now."

"No!" The pain in her voice somehow revives his anger. He wants to hurt her, to hear her pain again. "You're a…a cheap imitation. We saw what you look like. We know what you are."

She sucks in ragged breath. The tears are spilling free. "I'm *human*!" Her tiny fist smashes his chest, hurting more than it should.

* * *

David Conlan did not pay much attention to the news in the days that followed his wife's death. But even he couldn't help but share the dread anticipation when the ships, at last, began to open. Along with all the rest he sat that night before his television. He imagined his wife beside him. He imagined holding her hand, squeezing it, feeling for the pounding pulse.

The news reporter tried, helplessly, to voice the currents of their collective emotions. "What do they want from us? What will they look like?" And all the while, the great crystal doors cracking open onto darkness.

Then, at last, movement. The world, even David Conlan, held its breath. A floodlight blazed onto the opening.

And then the screams, the nausea, the gunshots as the soldiers' fingers convulsed on their triggers. And one by one, the aliens poured or dripped or sloshed into the world. All across the planet, from a hundred different ships, they made their oozing entrance.

Those who'd gathered near the ships fled in horror. The soldiers continued to spray bullets into the putrescence until their guns were empty. The aliens, if that was the proper name for moving gore, seeped forward undaunted. The soldiers fled in advance of the bombers.

At one point David vomited onto the floor. "Look," he said to no one, pointing at his own puke. "It's an alien." He laughed at his own joke, a manic kind of laugh. He was laughing still as the explosives vaporized the dirt around the ships. The crystal was made of stronger stuff, and so the ships – sealed up again – remained untouched by the bombs.

For a time, at least, the world hoped that the monsters were gone.

* * *

He seizes her wrists to stop her pounding rage. "I saw," he hisses. "I saw."

She presses forward, mashing her face against the clenched tangle of their hands. "You know me, David. I *am* human. I am *human*."

David shoves her away.

She stumbles on the threshold, falling gracelessly. "Please," she sobs.

He pushes past her into the house. He pours himself the dregs of last night's wine. He's already swigging it down when the scent of Syrah fills his sinuses, redolent with the memory of last night's passion. Her mouth had been flavored by this, sips and splashes between each liquid kiss.

He's seeing again the oozing gore, and he runs into the bathroom. When he's finished retching he stands at the mirror, staring at his pasty features and the dark bags under his eyes, every pore somehow more hideous than it has ever been. He scrubs his face furiously, hopelessly.

She's so much like his wife, the way she used to be when he couldn't get enough of her, before matrimony tamed what was best left wild. The same cheekbones. The same full breasts. The same dimples at the crown of her ass.

When he comes out of the bathroom he sees her, still sitting where she'd fallen on the balcony threshold, the morning sunlight yellowing her naked skin. He sinks onto the edge of the bed and drags a hand through his hair. She stands and returns to the railing, her hair splashing her back. A passing car honks madly. Cat calls are whisked away by speed.

He imagines her melting under him as he makes love to her. For some reason, he imagines that the gore is sticky.

* * *

It was too much to hope that bombs could vaporize the horror. There were countless stories of contact. One woman told of how she'd turned on her shower and it had come pouring out onto her before she could escape, entering her nostrils and ears. She woke an hour later, terrified it was still inside her.

A man David knew said he'd seen one rise from a sewer grate to consume a child, only to spit the boy out again, unconscious, a moment later. Stories like this were frequent enough to have the ring of truth: the creatures were *making contact*: enveloping, intruding, and then slipping back into hiding, their victims shaken but intact.

As the months went by, the tales became less frequent but more sensational – stories of abduction, of blobs of prehensile slime committing acts of brutal sexual violation. The reputable newspapers stopped printing them, and eventually they became once again just a subject for the tabloids. But then a different kind of story began to emerge. The aliens were masquerading as human. They were hiding among us. There were even a few who claimed to have witnessed the ooze coalesce into human forms.

For a long time David didn't pay much attention. While the thought of aliens in human form made him shift uneasily, he was too absorbed in his own misery to contemplate the implications of the Intrusion. He called in sick too often to keep his job, and spent his days sitting in his house drinking beer and watching soap operas, carefully avoiding the shows he knew his wife had enjoyed. At night he'd take long walks around the neighborhood, remembering the walks he'd taken with his wife. He'd stop by the thick-boled oak on the corner of Chestnut Lane, remembering when they'd climbed it together to get a better view of a lunar eclipse. One of those few, last untamed moments after their wedding day.

He'd pause at the stucco house she used to admire and imagine them living there together, lighting fires in the fireplace, raising children, fighting over which shows to watch and whose turn it was to do the laundry.

The idea that somehow the aliens had stolen her from him, that her death was part of their plot, a scheme to borrow her form and live among the humans in some cheap copy of her body – that idea, incoherent as it was, didn't occur to him until later.

* * *

When she finally comes off the balcony, her despair has been replaced by anger. "Don't you see? David, look at me! Look at my face!" Because he's thrown on a t-shirt by now she has something to grab onto, and she does, seizing the collar. She brings her face close to his, her features fierce. But her voice has become quiet. "When we changed we *became* human, David. I have human blood, human skin, human eyes. I have human DNA. My needs are human needs. My desires…David, they're human desires."

"No." He shakes his head.

"Do you know the most ironic thing, David? Do you? I am so human that the thought of what I used to be…it disgusts me! That's how human I've become."

"I made love to you, dammit!"

"Yes! To me. To a human woman. It doesn't matter where I came from."

"It does!"

"Have you ever looked at a fetus, David? Slimy. Translucent skin. Huge head and a tiny body. If you ask me, it looks more alien than…than a pile of goo! But then it becomes a person. Does it matter that your wife was once one of those things?"

"Don't talk to me about my wife!"

"*Does it matter?*"

"It's different!"
"How?"
"It just is!"

* * *

The problem was the regret. He'd always believed he'd be a good husband: faithful, sensitive. But when the problems started he stewed about them silently, never saying a word, never complaining, but growing angrier and angrier inside until he started imagining with something like anticipation that she'd die and he'd be free of her.

Her relentless complaining was at the heart of it. Once, he fantasized about tape-recording her morning monologues and playing them back to her: "Shit! I broke a nail.... This toothpaste tastes awful.... David, can't you ever hang the toilet paper right?... Oh God, I don't want to go to work today.... There's nothing to wear. I hate my wardrobe.... Shit! I've got a run in my stockings.... Where the hell are those keys?... Your beard looks all scraggly, David; you need to trim that.... You're not really going to wear that awful tie again, are you?... Oh, I hate this weather.... David, can you for *once* remember to pick up those prints from the frame shop?"

How he'd wanted to scream at her when she was alive: "It's no wonder you're so miserable! You focus every ounce of your attention on every little thing that's wrong and never notice any of the good things!" He wanted to tell her to grow up, to stop being a whining cry-baby, to count her blessings rather than giving voice to every little irritant. But he never had the guts. He started thinking of her as an emotional black hole that could suck all good cheer out of any room she entered.

And then through work he'd meet some vibrant, laughing saleswoman who knew that closing a deal called for a habit of yeses, that every *no* demanded a redirect or rebuttal, that life was about seizing the prize...and even though she was less beautiful, less brilliant than his wife, a few drinks in the hotel bar were enough to turn the swimming euphoria of affirmations into something else: a groping search for meaning in a few minutes of undomesticated sex.

And now his wife was dead, and he remembered the delicacy of her features, and the way she'd looked at their wedding with the head-dress sitting slightly askew and an eyelash on her cheek. He recalled the time she'd read him German poetry while he languished with the swine flu; and the time he tried to cross-country ski at the golf course while she laughed at his clumsiness. And there was nothing he could do now to fix things, no way to take back his infidelities or even apologize for them. He paced through the new place, the one he'd moved into to escape the memories, and he ached to have her back. Just to tell her, one last time, that he loved her. Another damned cliché.

At some point he began to pay attention to the stories of the aliens, and he began to care. Steeped in an atmosphere of grief and global paranoia, the wild theory that they'd killed her, that her death was part of their infiltration of the human world, became irresistible. It was such a pleasure to loathe them, to wish them dead the way he'd once wished his wife were dead. He listened with growing fervor to the conspiracy stories and the speculations: they were taking over the planet by slowly replacing people with duplicates; they were breeding with humans to create some kind of hybrid species; they were stealing the water, or the air; they were turning human beings into livestock. All the clichéd stories, gleefully retold in the tabloids and just as gleefully consumed by David – lost in his empty apartment, lost in grief and guilt and flailing loneliness.

He read it all, and when his new neighbor sensed a kindred hate and told him about the Hunters, David went to a meeting.

At first it was just talk. The government was doing nothing. The threat was real and nobody in a position of authority seemed to care. Maybe they'd been compromised. The shapeshifters could be anywhere, anyone. It was up to the Hunters to be vigilant, to find them if they could, to protect the world from this new and unprecedented threat.

The Hunters gave him purpose. He was energized again, focused again. He found that he could sleep at night, and in the mornings he had reason to rise from bed. By the time the aliens made their announcement, he was too deeply entrenched in the Hunter ideology to take it seriously.

"We are no longer alien," the message said, resounding from each of the crystalline ships at once, clear and unmistakable and heard around the world in every language. "Our world was destroyed. We are refugees, but we do not desire to disrupt your lives or your ways of life in any way. To that end, we have made ourselves one with you. We have *become* human. We learned your ways – your languages and cultures and beliefs – long before we came. We needed only to touch you to take the final step. Now we are human. You need do nothing to accommodate us. We will make all the changes. We have changed our very being to suit you, and we will live by your laws and your values. Our children will be human children. There is nothing to fear from us. Nothing at all."

The announcement went on, but for the Hunters the only message that mattered was the confirmation of their fears: the aliens were still alive; they'd taken on human form. And the worst part, the most intolerable part, the part that negated all their assurances: *Our children will be human children.*

They were plotting to mate with humanity, to infect the human bloodline with their sick, alien substance.

Eventually, talk gave way to action. There were demonstrations in the streets, public demands for new policies to identify and quarantine the Intruders. And when the government was slow to respond, the Hunters went to work themselves. Targets were identified. Those who were new to town and couldn't account for their histories. Those who were strange, who seemed a little off. The Hunters became what their names proclaimed them to be. They researched their targets and studied them for signs of inhumanity. And when they were sure, they did what needed to be done.

* * *

"I'm a Hunter," he says.

She gapes, taking a horrified step back. She tries to say something. She swallows. "My God," she breathes.

"Your people have a god?"

She glowers at him, but her body language is that of a trembling fawn. "When?" she croaks.

"Since before I met you. It's where I go on Thursday nights. We meet at Michael Jameson's house. There are seven of us in my chapter."

She shakes her head. "Why? You...do you wear one of those hoods? Do you...have you been on a raid?"

He shrugs and looks away.

* * *

David met her in the park. The first thing he noticed was how closely she resembled his wife: dark hair laced with copper, fragile features. But she also had a brightness to her, a cheerfulness that his wife never had: the quirky smile, the flash of humor in the eyes. She was throwing seeds to the ducks, who were largely ignoring her in favor of a boy throwing bits of bread.

"It's terrible," she said as he came up beside her. "Bread is terrible for them. Swells in their bellies." She looked up at him and smiled. "Could even kill them. But everybody keeps throwing them bread, and when I give them a healthy alternative, they don't want it."

"Like people and fried food," David said.

"Yeah. You like French fries?"

David laughed. "Love 'em. With vinegar."

"I've never had them with vinegar."

"Tell you what," he said, his salesman's instincts coming alive. "I'll go to the supermarket and get some vinegar, you go to McDonald's and get the fries. We'll meet back here in half an hour."

Her eyes gleamed. "It's a deal."

They became lovers that night. She moved in with him two weeks later. Their lovemaking was fierce, feral. For David it was laced through with the urgency to reclaim his humanity from the ruins of his past. She seemed happy to lose herself in his mad desire, and for a month they lived half-drunk on wine and fully drunk on each other. A sweat-soaked surrogate for happiness.

* * *

She sits in silence next to him on the bed, trembling. She's fragile; he can probably kill her with his hands.

Her. An Intruder. A horror. A violation. Her existence defiles him and all humanity. The words of the Hunters ring in his head, and he remembers the one time his local chapter was part of a raid. Two women living together, both in their middle years. They were black, probably lesbians. They'd moved to town only a month after the Intrusion. One worked as a short-order cook at a diner, the other cleaned houses – the kinds of menial jobs that didn't require any history. There was no indication that either one had a family.

The Hunters spent a month watching them, digging through their trash, quietly learning what they could from neighbors and co-workers. They debated their options.

"What if we're wrong?" someone said.

"We're not wrong," said the leader.

"We need to," David said. He was usually silent, but he felt a flare of urgency, as if this were the moment that decided whether his lifeline out of despair was just a rope leading nowhere. "We need to do this."

"Exactly," said the leader, clenching his fists. "Humanity's at stake!"

No, thought David. That's not it at all.

The Hunters broke into the house wearing black masks and carrying ropes. The women were in bed together. The Hunters dragged them naked into the yard and hung them from an old oak. David stood watch near the street. He had no part in the killing. When it was over they dangled from the tree like sacks.

What if we're wrong?

We're not wrong.

A week later he met her in the park.

And now.

He looks at her tapering thigh and remembers touching it. The sun is shining on her goose-bumped arms, her breasts, her hair, blazing in the wetness of her eyes.

A violation, and her hands are soft.

"Will you kill me?" she asks.

His hand goes to her neck. It is downy at the nape. He runs a thumb along the rippling hardness of her trachea. His other hand goes to her hip by habit.

She looks into his eyes. "I love you," she whispers.

His thumb slips down to the hollow of her throat. He remembers the women hanging from the tree. "My wife," he begins, but falls silent because he can't remember what he meant to say. He shakes his head. He doesn't want to kill her. He wants to kiss her and touch her and lose himself inside her, like he has a hundred times before.

"How can you be human?"

She reaches up to touch the hand against her throat. She strokes the fingers, then lifts the hand and brings it to her lips.

"I'm so human," she says.

Edison's Conquest of Mars
Chapters I–IV
Garrett P. Serviss

[Publisher's Note: This story was written as a sequel to Fighters on Mars, *an unauthorized, altered version of H.G. Wells's* The War of the Worlds.*]*

Chapter I

IT IS IMPOSSIBLE that the stupendous events which followed the disastrous invasion of the earth by the Martians should go without record, and circumstances having placed the facts at my disposal, I deem it a duty, both to posterity and to those who were witnesses of and participants in the avenging counterstroke that the earth dealt back at its ruthless enemy in the heavens, to write down the story in a connected form.

The Martians had nearly all perished, not through our puny efforts, but in consequence of disease, and the few survivors fled in one of their projectile cars, inflicting their cruellest blow in the act of departure.

They possessed a mysterious explosive, of unimaginable puissance, with whose aid they set their car in motion for Mars from a point in Bergen County, N.J., just back of the Palisades.

The force of the explosion may be imagined when it is recollected that they had to give the car a velocity of more than seven miles per second in order to overcome the attraction of the earth and the resistance of the atmosphere.

The shock destroyed all of New York that had not already fallen a prey, and all the buildings yet standing in the surrounding towns and cities fell in one far-circling ruin.

The Palisades tumbled in vast sheets, starting a tidal wave in the Hudson that drowned the opposite shore.

The victims of this ferocious explosion were numbered by tens of thousands, and the shock, transmitted through the rocky frame of the globe, was recorded by seismographic pendulums in England and on the Continent of Europe.

The terrible results achieved by the invaders had produced everywhere a mingled feeling of consternation and hopelessness. The devastation was widespread. The death-dealing engines which the Martians had brought with them had proved irresistible and the inhabitants of the earth possessed nothing capable of contending against them. There had been no protection for the great cities; no protection even for the open country. Everything had gone down before the savage onslaught of those merciless invaders from space. Savage ruins covered the sites of many formerly flourishing towns and villages, and the broken walls of great cities stared at the heavens like the exhumed skeletons of Pompeii. The awful agencies had extirpated pastures and meadows and dried up the very springs of fertility in the earth where they had touched it. In some parts of the devastated lands pestilence broke out; elsewhere there was famine. Despondency black as night brooded over some of the fairest portions of the globe.

Yet all had not been destroyed, because all had not been reached by the withering hand of the destroyer. The Martians had not had time to complete their work before they themselves fell a prey to the diseases that carried them off at the very culmination of their triumph.

From those lands which had, fortunately, escaped invasion, relief was sent to the sufferers. The outburst of pity and of charity exceeded anything that the world had known. Differences of race and religion were swallowed up in the universal sympathy which was felt for those who had suffered so terribly from an evil that was as unexpected as it was unimaginable in its enormity.

But the worst was not yet. More dreadful than the actual suffering and the scenes of death and devastation which overspread the afflicted lands was the profound mental and moral depression that followed. This was shared even by those who had not seen the Martians and had not witnessed the destructive effects of the frightful engines of war that they had imported for the conquest of the earth. All mankind was sunk deep in this universal despair, and it became tenfold blacker when the astronomers announced from their observatories that strange lights were visible, moving and flashing upon the red surface of the Planet of War. These mysterious appearances could only be interpreted in the light of past experience to mean that the Martians were preparing for another invasion of the earth, and who could doubt that with the invincible powers of destruction at their command they would this time make their work complete and final?

This startling announcement was the more pitiable in its effects because it served to unnerve and discourage those few of stouter hearts and more hopeful temperaments who had already begun the labor of restoration and reconstruction amid the embers of their desolated homes. In New York this feeling of hope and confidence, this determination to rise against disaster and to wipe out the evidences of its dreadful presence as quickly as possible, had especially manifested itself. Already a company had been formed and a large amount of capital subscribed for the reconstruction of the destroyed bridges over the East River. Already architects were busily at work planning new twenty-story hotels and apartment houses; new churches and new cathedrals on a grander scale than before.

Amid this stir of renewed life came the fatal news that Mars was undoubtedly preparing to deal us a death blow. The sudden revulsion of feeling flitted like the shadow of an eclipse over the earth. The scenes that followed were indescribable. Men lost their reason. The faint-hearted ended the suspense with self-destruction, the stout-hearted remained steadfast, but without hope and knowing not what to do.

But there was a gleam of hope of which the general public as yet knew nothing. It was due to a few dauntless men of science, conspicuous among whom were Lord Kelvin, the great English savant; Herr Roentgen, the discoverer of the famous X ray, and especially Thomas A. Edison, the American genius of science. These men and a few others had examined with the utmost care the engines of war, the flying machines, the generators of mysterious destructive forces that the Martians had produced, with the object of discovering, if possible, the sources of their power.

Suddenly from Mr. Edison's laboratory at Orange flashed the startling intelligence that he had not only discovered the manner in which the invaders had been able to produce the mighty energies which they employed with such terrible effect, but that, going further, he had found a way to overcome them.

The glad news was quickly circulated throughout the civilized world. Luckily the Atlantic cables had not been destroyed by the Martians, so that communication between the Eastern and Western continents was uninterrupted. It was a proud day for America. Even while the Martians had been upon the earth, carrying everything before them, demonstrating to the confusion of the most optimistic that there was no possibility of standing against them, a feeling – a confidence had manifested itself in France, to a minor extent in England, and particularly in Russia, that the Americans might discover means to meet and master the invaders.

Now, it seemed, this hope and expectation were to be realized. Too late, it is true, in a certain sense, but not too late to meet the new invasion which the astronomers had announced was impending. The effect was as wonderful and indescribable as that of the despondency which but a little while before had overspread the world. One could almost hear the universal sigh of relief which went up from humanity. To relief succeeded confidence – so quickly does the human spirit recover like an elastic spring, when pressure is released.

"Let them come," was the almost joyous cry. "We shall be ready for them now. The Americans have solved the problem. Edison has placed the means of victory within our power."

Looking back upon that time now, I recall, with a thrill, the pride that stirred me at the thought that, after all, the inhabitants of the Earth were a match for those terrible men from Mars, despite all the advantage which they had gained from their millions of years of prior civilization and science.

As good fortunes, like bad, never come singly, the news of Mr. Edison's discovery was quickly followed by additional glad tidings from that laboratory of marvels in the lap of the Orange mountains. During their career of conquest the Martians had astonished the inhabitants of the earth no less with their flying machines – which navigated our atmosphere as easily as they had that of their native planet – than with their more destructive inventions. These flying machines in themselves had given them an enormous advantage in the contest. High above the desolation that they had caused to reign on the surface of the earth, and, out of the range of our guns, they had hung safe in the upper air. From the clouds they had dropped death upon the earth.

Now, rumor declared that Mr. Edison had invented and perfected a flying machine much more complete and manageable than those of the Martians had been. Wonderful stories quickly found their way into the newspapers concerning what Mr. Edison had already accomplished with the aid of his model electrical balloon. His laboratory was carefully guarded against the invasion of the curious, because he rightly felt that a premature announcement, which should promise more than could be actually fulfilled, would, at this critical juncture, plunge mankind back again into the gulf of despair, out of which it had just begun to emerge.

Nevertheless, inklings of the truth leaked out. The flying machine had been seen by many persons hovering by night high above the Orange hills and disappearing in the faint starlight as if it had gone away into the depths of space, out of which it would re-emerge before the morning light had streaked the east, and be seen settling down again within the walls that surrounded the laboratory of the great inventor. At length the rumor, gradually deepening into a conviction, spread that Edison himself, accompanied by a few scientific friends, had made an experimental trip to the moon. At a time when the spirit of mankind was less profoundly stirred, such a story would have been received with complete incredulity, but now, rising on the wings of the new hope that was buoying up the earth, this extraordinary rumor became a day star of truth to the nations.

And it was true. I had myself been one of the occupants of the car of the flying Ship of Space on that night when it silently left the earth, and rising out of the great shadow of the globe, sped on to the moon. We had landed upon the scarred and desolate face of the earth's satellite, and but that there are greater and more interesting events, the telling of which must not be delayed, I should undertake to describe the particulars of this first visit of men to another world.

But, as I have already intimated, this was only an experimental trip. By visiting this little nearby island in the ocean of space, Mr. Edison simply wished to demonstrate the practicability of his invention, and to convince, first of all, himself and his scientific friends that it was possible for men – mortal men – to quit and to revisit the earth at their will. That aim this experimental trip triumphantly attained.

It would carry me into technical details that would hardly interest the reader to describe the mechanism of Mr. Edison's flying machine. Let it suffice to say that it depended upon the principal of electrical attraction and repulsion. By means of a most ingenious and complicated construction he had mastered the problem of how to produce, in a limited space, electricity of any desired potential and of any polarity, and that without danger to the experimenter or to the material experimented upon. It is gravitation, as everybody knows, that makes man a prisoner on the earth. If he could overcome, or neutralize, gravitation he could float away a free creature of interstellar space. Mr. Edison in his invention had pitted electricity against gravitation. Nature, in fact, had done the same thing long before. Every astronomer knew it, but none had been able to imitate or to reproduce this miracle of nature. When a comet approaches the sun, the orbit in which it travels indicates that it is moving under the impulse of the sun's gravitation. It is in reality falling in a great parabolic or elliptical curve through space. But, while a comet approaches the sun it begins to display – stretching out for millions, and sometimes hundreds of millions of miles on the side away from the sun – an immense luminous train called its tail. This train extends back into that part of space from which the comet is moving. Thus the sun at one and the same time is drawing the comet toward itself and driving off from the comet in an opposite direction minute particles or atoms which, instead of obeying the gravitational force, are plainly compelled to disobey it. That this energy, which the sun exercises against its own gravitation, is electrical in its nature, hardly anybody will doubt. The head of the comet being comparatively heavy and massive, falls on toward the sun, despite the electrical repulsion. But the atoms which form the tail, being almost without weight, yield to the electrical rather than to the gravitational influence, and so fly away from the sun.

Now, what Mr. Edison had done was, in effect, to create an electrified particle which might be compared to one of the atoms composing the tail of a comet, although in reality it was a kind of car, of metal, weighing some hundreds of pounds and capable of bearing some thousands of pounds with it in its flight. By producing, with the aid of the electrical generator contained in this car, an enormous charge of electricity, Mr. Edison was able to counterbalance, and a trifle more than counterbalance, the attraction of the earth, and thus cause the car to fly off from the earth as an electrified pithball flies from the prime conductor.

As we sat in the brilliantly lighted chamber that formed the interior of the car, and where stores of compressed air had been provided together with chemical apparatus, by means of which fresh supplies of oxygen and nitrogen might be obtained for our consumption during the flight through space, Mr. Edison touched a polished button, thus causing the generation of the required electrical charge on the exterior of the car, and immediately we began to rise.

The moment and direction of our flight had been so timed and prearranged, that the original impulse would carry us straight toward the moon.

When we fell within the sphere of attraction of that orb it only became necessary to so manipulate the electrical charge upon our car as nearly, but not quite, to counterbalance the effect of the moon's attraction in order that we might gradually approach it and with an easy motion, settle, without shock, upon its surface.

We did not remain to examine the wonders of the moon, although we could not fail to observe many curious things therein. Having demonstrated the fact that we could not only leave the earth, but could journey through space and safely land upon the surface of another planet, Mr. Edison's immediate purpose was fulfilled, and we hastened back to the earth, employing in leaving the moon and landing again upon our own planet the same means of control over the electrical attraction and repulsion between the respective planets and our car which I have already described.

When actual experiment had thus demonstrated the practicability of the invention, Mr. Edison no longer withheld the news of what he had been doing from the world. The telegraph lines and the ocean cables labored with the messages that in endless succession, and burdened with an infinity of detail, were sent all over the earth. Everywhere the utmost enthusiasm was aroused.

"Let the Martians come," was the cry. "If necessary, we can quit the earth as the Athenians fled from Athens before the advancing host of Xerxes, and like them, take refuge upon our ships – these new ships of space, with which American inventiveness has furnished us."

And then, like a flash, some genius struck out an idea that fired the world.

"Why should we wait? Why should we run the risk of having our cities destroyed and our lands desolated a second time? Let us go to Mars. We have the means. Let us beard the lion in his den. Let us ourselves turn conquerors and take possession of that detestable planet, and if necessary, destroy it in order to relieve the earth of this perpetual threat which now hangs over us like the sword of Damocles."

Chapter II

THIS ENTHUSIASM would have had but little justification had Mr. Edison done nothing more than invent a machine which could navigate the atmosphere and the regions of interplanetary space.

He had, however, and this fact was generally known, although the details had not yet leaked out – invented also machines of war intended to meet the utmost that the Martians could do for either offence or defence in the struggle which was now about to ensue.

Acting upon the hint which had been conveyed from various investigations in the domain of physics, and concentrating upon the problem all those unmatched powers of intellect which distinguished him, the great inventor had succeeded in producing a little implement which one could carry in his hand, but which was more powerful than any battleship that ever floated. The details of its mechanism could not be easily explained, without the use of tedious technicalities and the employment of terms, diagrams and mathematical statements, all of which would lie outside the scope of this narrative. But the principle of the thing was simple enough. It was upon the great scientific doctrine, which we have since seen so completely and brilliantly developed, of the law of harmonic vibrations, extending from atoms and molecules at one end of the series up to worlds and suns at the other end, that Mr. Edison based his invention.

Every kind of substance has its own vibratory rhythm. That of iron differs from that of pine wood. The atoms of gold do not vibrate in the same time or through the same range as those of lead, and so on for all known substances, and all the chemical elements. So, on a larger scale, every massive body has its period of vibration. A great suspension bridge vibrates, under the impulse of forces that are applied to it, in long periods. No company of soldiers ever crosses such a bridge without breaking step. If they tramped together, and were followed by other companies keeping the same time with their feet, after a while the vibrations of the bridge would become so great and destructive that it would fall in pieces. So any structure, if its vibration rate is known, could easily be destroyed by a force applied to it in such a way that it should simply increase the swing of those vibrations up to the point of destruction.

Now Mr. Edison had been able to ascertain the vibratory swing of many well-known substances, and to produce, by means of the instrument which he had contrived, pulsations in the ether which were completely under his control, and which could be made long or short, quick or slow, at his will. He could run through the whole gamut from the slow vibrations of sound in air up to the four hundred and twenty-five millions of millions of vibrations per second of the ultra red rays.

Having obtained an instrument of such power, it only remained to concentrate its energy upon a given object in order that the atoms composing that object should be set into violent undulation, sufficient to burst it asunder and to scatter its molecules broadcast. This the inventor effected by the simplest means in the world – simply a parabolic reflector by which the destructive waves could be sent like a beam of light, but invisible, in any direction and focused upon any desired point.

I had the good fortune to be present when this powerful engine of destruction was submitted to its first test. We had gone upon the roof of Mr. Edison's laboratory and the inventor held the little instrument, with its attached mirror, in his hand. We looked about for some object on which to try its powers. On a bare limb of a tree not far away, for it was late in the Fall, sat a disconsolate crow.

"Good," said Mr. Edison, "that will do." He touched a button at the side of the instrument and a soft, whirring noise was heard.

"Feathers," said Mr. Edison, "have a vibration period of three hundred and eighty-six million per second."

He adjusted the index as he spoke. Then, through a sighting tube, he aimed at the bird.

"Now watch," he said.

Another soft whir in the instrument, a momentary flash of light close around it, and, behold, the crow had turned from black to white!

"Its feathers are gone," said the inventor; "they have been dissipated into their constituent atoms. Now, we will finish the crow."

Instantly there was another adjustment of the index, another outshooting of vibratory force, a rapid up and down motion of the index to include a certain range of vibrations, and the crow itself was gone – vanished in empty space! There was the bare twig on which a moment before it had stood. Behind, in the sky, was the white cloud against which its black form had been sharply outlined, but there was no more crow.

"That looks bad for the Martians, doesn't it?" said the Wizard. "I have ascertained the vibration rate of all the materials of which their war engines whose remains we have collected together are composed. They can be shattered into nothingness in the fraction of a second. Even if the vibration period were not known, it could quickly be hit upon by simply running through the gamut."

"Hurrah!" cried one of the onlookers. "We have met the Martians and they are ours."

Such in brief was the first of the contrivances which Mr. Edison invented for the approaching war with Mars.

And these facts had become widely known. Additional experiments had completed the demonstration of the inventor's ability, with the aid of his wonderful instrument, to destroy any given object, or any part of an object, provided that that part differed in its atomic constitution, and consequently in its vibratory period, from the other parts.

A most impressive public exhibition of the powers of the little disintegrator was given amid the ruins of New York. On lower Broadway a part of the walls of one of the gigantic buildings, which had been destroyed by the Martians, impended in such a manner that it threatened at any moment to fall upon the heads of the passers-by. The Fire Department did not dare touch it. To blow it up seemed a dangerous expedient, because already new buildings had been erected in its neighborhood, and their safety would be imperiled by the flying fragments. The fact happened to come to my knowledge.

"Here is an opportunity," I said to Mr. Edison, "to try the powers of your machine on a large scale."

"Capital!" he instantly replied. "I shall go at once."

For the work now in hand it was necessary to employ a battery of disintegrators, since the field of destruction covered by each was comparatively limited. All of the impending portions of the wall must be destroyed at once and together, for otherwise the danger would rather be accentuated than annihilated. The disintegrators were placed upon the roof of a neighboring building, so adjusted that their fields of destruction overlapped one another upon the wall. Their indexes were all set to correspond with the vibration period of the peculiar kind of brick of which the wall consisted. Then the energy was turned on, and a shout of wonder arose from the multitudes which had assembled at a safe distance to witness the experiment.

The wall did not fall; it did not break asunder; no fragments shot this way and that and high in the air; there was no explosion; no shock or noise disturbed the still atmosphere – only a soft whirr, that seemed to pervade everything and to tingle in the nerves of the spectators; and – what had been was not! The wall was gone! But high above and all around the place where it had hung over the street with its threat of death there appeared, swiftly billowing outward in every direction, a faint, bluish cloud. It was the scattered atoms of the destroyed wall.

And now the cry "On to Mars!" was heard on all sides. But for such an enterprise funds were needed – millions upon millions. Yet some of the fairest and richest portions of the earth had been impoverished by the frightful ravages of those enemies who had dropped down upon them from the skies. Still, the money must be had. The salvation of the planet, as everybody was now convinced, depended upon the successful negotiation of a gigantic war fund, in comparison with which all the expenditures in all of the wars that had been waged by the nations for 2,000 years would be insignificant. The electrical ships and the vibration engines must be constructed by scores and thousands. Only Mr. Edison's immense resources and unrivaled equipment had enabled him to make the models whose powers had been so satisfactorily shown. But to multiply these upon a war scale was not only beyond the resources of any individual – hardly a nation on the globe in the period of its greatest prosperity could have undertaken such a work. All the nations, then, must now conjoin. They must unite their resources, and, if necessary, exhaust all their hoards, in order to raise the needed sum.

Negotiations were at once begun. The United States naturally took the lead, and their leadership was never for a moment questioned abroad.

Washington was selected as the place of meeting for a great congress of the nations. Washington, luckily, had been one of the places which had not been touched by the Martians. But if Washington had been a city composed of hotels alone, and every hotel so great as to be a little city in itself, it would have been utterly insufficient for the accommodation of the innumerable throngs which now flocked to the banks of the Potomac. But when was American enterprise unequal to a crisis? The necessary hotels, lodging houses and restaurants were constructed with astounding rapidity. One could see the city growing and expanding day by day and week after week. It flowed over Georgetown Heights; it leaped the Potomac; it spread east and west, south and north; square mile after square mile of territory was buried under the advancing buildings, until the gigantic city, which had thus grown up like a mushroom in a night, was fully capable of accommodating all its expected guests.

At first it had been intended that the heads of the various governments should in person attend this universal congress, but as the enterprise went on, as the enthusiasm spread, as the necessity for haste became more apparent through the warning notes which were constantly sounded from the observatories where the astronomers were nightly beholding new evidences of threatening preparations in Mars, the kings and queens of the old world felt that they could not remain at home; that their proper place was at the new focus and centre of the whole world – the city of Washington. Without concerted action, without interchange of suggestion, this impulse seemed to seize all the old world monarchs at once. Suddenly cablegrams flashed to the Government at Washington, announcing that Queen Victoria, the Emperor William, the Czar Nicholas, Alphonso of Spain, with his mother, Maria Christina; the old Emperor Francis Joseph and the Empress Elizabeth, of Austria; King Oscar and Queen Sophia, of Sweden and Norway; King Humbert and Queen Margherita, of Italy; King George and Queen Olga, of Greece; Abdul Hamid, of Turkey; Tsait'ien, Emperor of China; Mutsuhito, the Japanese Mikado, with his beautiful Princess Haruko; the President of France, the President of Switzerland, the First Syndic of the little republic of Andorra, perched on the crest of the Pyrenees, and the heads of all the Central and South American republics, were coming to Washington to take part in the deliberations, which, it was felt, were to settle the fate of earth and Mars.

One day, after this announcement had been received, and the additional news had come that nearly all the visiting monarchs had set out, attended by brilliant suites and convoyed by fleets of warships, for their destination, some coming across the Atlantic to the port of New York, others across the Pacific to San Francisco, Mr. Edison said to me:

"This will be a fine spectacle. Would you like to watch it?"

"Certainly," I replied.

The Ship of Space was immediately at our disposal. I think I have not yet mentioned the fact that the inventor's control over the electrical generator carried in the car was so perfect that by varying the potential or changing the polarity he could cause it slowly or swiftly, as might be desired, to approach or recede from any object. The only practical difficulty was presented when the polarity of the electrical charge upon an object in the neighborhood of the car was unknown to those in the car, and happened to be opposite to that of the charge which the car, at that particular moment, was bearing. In such a case, of course, the car would fly toward the object, whatever it might be, like a pith ball or a feather, attracted to the knob of an electrical machine. In this way, considerable danger was occasionally encountered, and a few accidents could not be avoided. Fortunately, however, such cases were rare. It was only now and then that, owing to some local cause, electrical polarities unknown to or unexpected by the navigators, endangered the safety of the car. As I shall have occasion to relate, however, in the course of the narrative, this danger became more acute and assumed at times a most formidable phase, when we had ventured outside the sphere of the earth and were moving through the unexplored regions beyond.

On this occasion, having embarked, we rose rapidly to a height of some thousands of feet and directed our course over the Atlantic. When half way to Ireland, we beheld, in the distance, steaming westward, the smoke of several fleets. As we drew nearer a marvellous spectacle unfolded itself to our eyes. From the northeast, their great guns flashing in the sunlight and their huge funnels belching black volumes that rested like thunder clouds upon the sea, came the mighty warships of England, with her meteor flag streaming red in the breeze, while the royal insignia, indicating the presence of the ruler of the British Empire, was conspicuously displayed upon the flagship of the squadron.

Following a course more directly westward appeared, under another black cloud of smoke, the hulls and guns and burgeons of another great fleet, carrying the tri-color of France, and bearing in its midst the head of the magnificent republic of western Europe.

Further south, beating up against the northerly winds, came a third fleet with the gold and red of Spain fluttering from its masthead. This, too, was carrying its King westward, where now, indeed, the star of empire had taken its way.

Rising a little higher, so as to extend our horizon, we saw coming down the English channel, behind the British fleet, the black ships of Russia. Side by side, or following one another's lead, these war fleets were on a peaceful voyage that belied their threatening appearance. There had been no thought of danger to or from the forts and ports of rival nations which they had passed. There was no enmity, and no fear between them when the throats of their ponderous guns yawned at one another across the waves. They were now, in spirit, all one fleet, having one object, bearing against one enemy, ready to defend but one country, and that country was the entire earth.

It was some time before we caught sight of the Emperor William's fleet. It seems that the Kaiser, although at first consenting to the arrangement by which Washington had been selected as the assembling place for the nations, afterwards objected to it.

"I ought to do this thing myself," he had said. "My glorious ancestors would never have consented to allow these upstart Republicans to lead in a warlike enterprise of this kind.

What would my grandfather have said to it? I suspect that it is some scheme aimed at the divine right of kings."

But the good sense of the German people would not suffer their ruler to place them in a position so false and so untenable. And swept along by their enthusiasm the Kaiser had at last consented to embark on his flagship at Kiel, and now he was following the other fleets on their great mission to the Western Continent.

Why did they bring their warships when their intentions were peaceable, do you ask? Well, it was partly the effect of ancient habit, and partly due to the fact that such multitudes of officials and members of ruling families wished to embark for Washington that the ordinary means of ocean communications would have been utterly inadequate to convey them.

After we had feasted our eyes on this strange sight, Mr. Edison suddenly exclaimed: "Now let us see the fellows from the rising sun."

The car was immediately directed toward the west. We rapidly approached the American coast, and as we sailed over the Alleghany Mountains and the broad plains of the Ohio and the Mississippi, we saw crawling beneath us from west, south and north, an endless succession of railway trains bearing their multitudes on to Washington. With marvellous speed we rushed westward, rising high to skim over the snow-topped peaks of the Rocky Mountains and then the glittering rim of the Pacific was before us. Half way between the American coast and Hawaii we met the fleets coming from China and Japan. Side by side they were ploughing the main, having forgotten, or laid aside, all the animosities of their former wars.

I well remember how my heart was stirred at this impressive exhibition of the boundless influence which my country had come to exercise over all the people of the world, and I turned to look at the man to whose genius this uprising of the earth was due. But Mr. Edison, after his wont, appeared totally unconscious of the fact that he was personally responsible for what was going on. His mind, seemingly, was entirely absorbed in considering problems, the solution of which might be essential to our success in the terrific struggle which was soon to begin.

"Well, have you seen enough?" he asked. "Then let us go back to Washington."

As we speeded back across the continent we beheld beneath us again the burdened express trains rushing toward the Atlantic, and hundreds of thousands of upturned eyes watched our swift progress, and volleys of cheers reached our ears, for every one knew that this was Edison's electrical warship, on which the hope of the nation, and the hopes of all the nations, depended. These scenes were repeated again and again until the car hovered over the still expanding capital on the Potomac, where the unceasing ring of hammers rose to the clouds.

Chapter III

THE DAY APPOINTED for the assembling of the nations in Washington opened bright and beautiful. Arrangements had been made for the reception of the distinguished guests at the Capitol. No time was to be wasted, and, having assembled in the Senate Chamber, the business that had called them together was to be immediately begun. The scene in Pennsylvania avenue, when the procession of dignitaries and royalties passed up toward the Capitol, was one never to be forgotten. Bands were playing, magnificent equipages flashed in the morning sunlight, the flags of every nation on the earth fluttered in the breeze.

Queen Victoria, with the Prince of Wales escorting her, and riding in an open carriage, was greeted with roars of cheers; the Emperor William, following in another carriage with Empress Victoria at his side, condescended to bow and smile in response to the greetings of a free people. Each of the other monarchs was received in a similar manner. The Czar of Russia proved to be an especial favorite with the multitude on account of the ancient friendship of his house for America. But the greatest applause of all came when the President of France, followed by the President of Switzerland and the First Syndic of the little Republic of Andorra, made their appearance. Equally warm were the greetings extended to the representatives of Mexico and the South American States.

The crowd apparently hardly knew at first how to receive the Sultan of Turkey, but the universal good feeling was in his favor, and finally rounds of hand clapping and cheers greeted his progress along the splendid avenue.

A happy idea had apparently occurred to the Emperor of China and the Mikado of Japan, for, attended by their intermingled suites, they rode together in a single carriage. This object lesson in the unity of international feeling immensely pleased the spectators.

The scene in the Senate Chamber stirred every one profoundly. That it was brilliant and magnificent goes without saying, but there was a seriousness, an intense feeling of expectancy, pervading both those who looked on and those who were to do the work for which these magnates of the earth had assembled, which produced an ineradicable impression. The President of the United States, of course, presided. Representatives of the greater powers occupied the front seats, and some of them were honored with special chairs near the President.

No time was wasted in preliminaries. The President made a brief speech.

"We have come together," he said, "to consider a question that equally interests the whole earth. I need not remind you that unexpectedly and without provocation on our part the people – the monsters, I should rather say – of Mars, recently came down upon the earth, attacked us in our homes and spread desolation around them. Having the advantage of ages of evolution, which for us are yet in the future, they brought with them engines of death and of destruction against which we found it impossible to contend. It is within the memory of every one in reach of my voice that it was through the entirely unexpected succor which Providence sent us that we were suddenly and effectually freed from the invaders. By our own efforts we could have done nothing."

"But, as you all know, the first feeling of relief which followed the death of our foes was quickly succeeded by the fearful news which came to us from the observatories, that the Martians were undoubtedly preparing for a second invasion of our planet. Against this we should have had no recourse and no hope but for the genius of one of my countrymen, who, as you are all aware, has perfected means which may enable us not only to withstand the attack of those awful enemies, but to meet them, and, let us hope, to conquer them on their own ground."

"Mr. Edison is here to explain to you what those means are. But we have also another object. Whether we send a fleet of interplanetary ships to invade Mars or whether we simply confine our attention to works of defence, in either case it will be necessary to raise a very large sum of money. None of us has yet recovered from the effects of the recent invasion. The earth is poor today compared to its position a few years ago; yet we cannot allow our poverty to stand in the way. The money, the means, must be had. It will be part of our business here to raise a gigantic war fund by the aid of which we can construct the equipment and machinery that we shall require. This, I think, is all I need to say. Let us proceed to business."

"Where is Mr. Edison?" cried a voice.

"Will Mr. Edison please step forward?" said the President.

There was a stir in the assembly, and the iron-gray head of the great inventor was seen moving through the crowd. In his hand he carried one of his marvellous disintegrators. He was requested to explain and illustrate its operation. Mr. Edison smiled.

"Will Mr. Edison please step forward?" said the President. There was a stir in the assembly, and the iron gray head of the great inventor was seen moving through the crowd. In his hand he carried one of his marvellous disintegrators.

"I can explain its details," he said, "to Lord Kelvin, for instance, but if Their Majesties will excuse me, I doubt whether I can make it plain to the crowned heads."

The Emperor William smiled superciliously. Apparently he thought that another assault had been committed upon the divine right of kings. But the Czar Nicholas appeared to be amused, and the Emperor of China, who had been studying English, laughed in his sleeve, as if he suspected that a joke had been perpetrated.

"I think," said one of the deputies, "that a simple exhibition of the powers of the instrument, without a technical explanation of its method of working, will suffice for our purpose."

This suggestion was immediately approved. In response to it, Mr. Edison, by a few simple experiments, showed how he could quickly and certainly shatter into its constituent atoms any object upon which the vibratory force of the disintegrator should be directed. In this manner he caused an inkstand to disappear under the very nose of the Emperor William without a spot of ink being scattered upon his sacred person, but evidently the odor of the disunited atoms was not agreeable to the nostrils of the Kaiser.

Mr. Edison also explained in general terms the principle on which the instrument worked. He was greeted with round after round of applause, and the spirit of the assembly rose high.

Next the workings of the electrical ship were explained, and it was announced that after the meeting had adjourned an exhibition of the flying powers of the ship would be given in the open air.

These experiments, together with the accompanying explanations, added to what had already been disseminated through the public press, were quite sufficient to convince all the representatives who had assembled in Washington that the problem of how to conquer the Martians had been solved. The means were plainly at hand. It only remained to apply them. For this purpose, as the President had pointed out, it would be necessary to raise a very large sum of money.

"How much will be needed?" asked one of the English representatives.

"At least ten thousand millions of dollars," replied the President.

"It would be safer," said a Senator from the Pacific Coast, "to make it twenty-five thousand millions."

"I suggest," said the King of Italy, "that the nations be called in alphabetical order, and that the representatives of each name a sum which it is ready and able to contribute."

"We want the cash or its equivalent," shouted the Pacific Coast Senator.

"I shall not follow the alphabet strictly," said the President, "but shall begin with the larger nations first. Perhaps, under the circumstances, it is proper that the United States should lead the way. Mr. Secretary," he continued, turning to the Secretary of the Treasury, "how much can we stand?"

"At least a thousand millions," replied the Secretary of the Treasury.

A roar of applause that shook the room burst from the assembly. Even some of the monarchs threw up their hats. The Emperor Tsait'ten smiled from ear to ear. One of the Roko Tuis, or native chiefs, from Fiji, sprang up and brandished a war club.

The President then proceeded to call the other nations, beginning with Austria-Hungary and ending with Zanzibar, whose Sultan, Hamoud bin Mahomed, had come to the congress in the escort of Queen Victoria. Each contributed liberally.

Germany coming in alphabetical order just before Great Britain, had named, through its Chancellor, the sum of $500,000,000, but when the First Lord of the British Treasury, not wishing to be behind the United States, named double that sum as the contribution of the British Empire, the Emperor William looked displeased. He spoke a word in the ear of the Chancellor, who immediately raised his hand.

"We will give a thousand million dollars," said the Chancellor.

Queen Victoria seemed surprised, though not displeased. The First Lord of the Treasury met her eye, and then, rising in his place, said:

"Make it fifteen hundred million for Great Britain."

Emperor William consulted again with his Chancellor, but evidently concluded not to increase his bid.

But, at any rate, the fund had benefited to the amount of a thousand millions by this little outburst of imperial rivalry.

The greatest surprise of all, however, came when the King of Siam was called upon for his contribution. He had not been given a foremost place in the Congress, but when the name of his country was pronounced he rose by his chair, dressed in a gorgeous specimen of the peculiar attire of his country, then slowly pushed his way to the front, stepped up to the President's desk and deposited upon it a small box.

"This is our contribution," he said, in broken English.

The cover was lifted, and there darted, shimmering in the half gloom of the Chamber, a burst of iridescence from the box.

"My friends of the Western world," continued the King of Siam, "will be interested in seeing this gem. Only once before has the eye of a European been blessed with the sight of it. Your books will tell you that in the seventeenth century a traveler, Tavernier, saw in India an unmatched diamond which afterward disappeared like a meteor, and was thought to have been lost from the earth. You all know the name of that diamond and its history. It is the Great Mogul, and it lies before you. How it came into my possession I shall not explain. At any rate, it is honestly mine, and I freely contribute it here to aid in protecting my native planet against those enemies who appear determined to destroy it."

When the excitement which the appearance of this long lost treasure, that had been the subject of so many romances and of such long and fruitless search, had subsided, the President continued calling the list, until he had completed it.

Upon taking the sum of the contributions (the Great Mogul was reckoned at three millions) it was found to be still one thousand millions short of the required amount.

The Secretary of the Treasury was instantly on his feet.

"Mr. President," he said, "I think we can stand that addition. Let it be added to the contribution of the United States of America."

When the cheers that greeted the conclusion of the business were over, the President announced that the next affair of the Congress was to select a director who should have entire charge of the preparations for the war. It was the universal sentiment that no man could be so well suited for this post as Mr. Edison himself. He was accordingly selected by the unanimous and enthusiastic choice of the great assembly.

"How long a time do you require to put everything in readiness?" asked the President.

"Give me carte blanche," replied Mr. Edison, "and I believe I can have a hundred electric ships and three thousand disintegrators ready within six months."

A tremendous cheer greeted this announcement.

"Your powers are unlimited," said the President, "draw on the fund for as much money as you need," whereupon the Treasurer of the United States was made the disbursing officer of the fund, and the meeting adjourned.

Not less than 5,000,000 people had assembled at Washington from all parts of the world. Every one of this immense multitude had been able to listen to the speeches and the cheers in the Senate chamber, although not personally present there. Wires had been run all over the city, and hundreds of improved telephonic receivers provided, so that every one could hear. Even those who were unable to visit Washington, people living in Baltimore, New York, Boston, and as far away as New Orleans, St. Louis and Chicago, had also listened to the proceedings with the aid of these receivers. Upon the whole, probably not less than 50,000,000 people had heard the deliberations of the great congress of the nations.

The telegraph and the cable had sent the news across the oceans to all the capitols of the earth. The exultation was so great that the people seemed mad with joy.

The promised exhibition of the electrical ship took place the next day. Enormous multitudes witnessed the experiment, and there was a struggle for places in the car. Even Queen Victoria, accompanied by the Prince of Wales, ventured to take a ride in it, and they enjoyed it so much that Mr. Edison prolonged the journey as far as Boston and the Bunker Hill monument.

Most of the other monarchs also took a high ride, but when the turn of the Emperor of China came he repeated a fable which he said had come down from the time of Confucius:

"Once upon a time there was a Chinaman living in the valley of the Hoang-Ho River, who was accustomed frequently to lie on his back, gazing at, and envying, the birds that he saw flying away in the sky. One day he saw a black speck which rapidly grew larger and larger, until as it got near he perceived that it was an enormous bird, which overshadowed the earth with its wings. It was the elephant of birds, the roc. 'Come with me,' said the roc, 'and I will show you the wonders of the kingdom of the birds.' The man caught hold of its claw and nestled among its feathers, and they rapidly rose high in the air, and sailed away to the Kuen-Lun Mountains.

Here, as they passed near the top of the peaks, another roc made its appearance. The wings of the two great birds brushed together, and immediately they fell to fighting. In the midst of the melee the man lost his hold and tumbled into the top of a tree, where his pigtail caught on a branch, and he remained suspended. There the unfortunate man hung helpless, until a rat, which had its home in the rocks at the foot of the tree, took compassion upon him, and, climbing up, gnawed off the branch. As the man slowly and painfully wended his weary way homeward, he said: 'This teaches me that creatures to whom nature has given neither feathers nor wings should leave the kingdom of the birds to those who are fitted to inhabit it.'"

Having told this story, Tsait'ien turned his back on the electrical ship.

After the exhibition was finished, and amid the fresh outburst of enthusiasm that followed, it was suggested that a proper way to wind up the Congress and give suitable expression to the festive mood which now possessed mankind would be to have a grand ball. This suggestion met with immediate and universal approval.

But for so gigantic an affair it was, of course, necessary to make special preparations. A convenient place was selected on the Virginia side of the Potomac; a space of ten acres was carefully levelled and covered with a polished floor, rows of columns one hundred feet apart were run across it in every direction, and these were decorated with electric lights, displaying every color of the spectrum.

Above this immense space, rising in the centre to a height of more than a thousand feet, was anchored a vast number of balloons, all aglow with lights, and forming a tremendous dome, in which brilliant lamps were arranged in such a manner as to exhibit, in an endless succession of combinations, all the national colors, ensigns and insignia of the various countries represented at the Congress. Blazing eagles, lions, unicorns, dragons and other imaginary creatures that the different nations had chosen for their symbols appeared to hover high above the dancers, shedding a brilliant light upon the scene.

Circles of magnificent thrones were placed upon the floor in convenient locations for seeing. A thousand bands of music played, and tens of thousands of couples, gayly dressed and flashing with gems, whirled together upon the polished floor.

The Queen of England led the dance, on the arm of the President of the United States.

The Prince of Wales led forth the fair daughter of the President, universally admired as the most beautiful woman upon the great ballroom floor.

The Emperor William, in his military dress, danced with the beauteous Princess Masaco, the daughter of the Mikado, who wore for the occasion the ancient costume of the women of her country, sparkling with jewels, and glowing with quaint combinations of color like a gorgeous butterfly.

The Chinese Emperor, with his pigtail flying high as he spun, danced with the Empress of Russia.

The King of Siam essayed a waltz with the Queen Ranavalona, of Madagascar, while the Sultan of Turkey basked in the smiles of a Chicago heiress to a hundred millions.

The Czar choose for his partner a dark-eyed beauty from Peru, but King Malietoa, of Samoa, was suspicious of civilized charmers and, avoiding all of their allurements, expressed his joy and gave vent to his enthusiasm in a pas seul. In this he was quickly joined by a band of Sioux Indian chiefs, whose whoops and yells so startled the leader of a German band on their part of the floor that he dropped his baton and, followed by the musicians, took to his heels.

This incident amused the good-natured Emperor of China more than anything else that had occurred.

"Make muchee noisee," he said, indicating the fleeing musicians with his thumb. "Allee same muchee flaid noisee," and then his round face dimpled into another laugh.

The scene from the outside was even more imposing than that which greeted the eye within the brilliantly lighted enclosure. Far away in the night, rising high among the stars, the vast dome of illuminated balloons seemed like some supernatural creation, too grand and glorious to have been constructed by the inhabitants of the earth.

All around it, and from some of the balloons themselves, rose jets and fountains of fire, ceaselessly playing, and blotting out the constellations of the heavens by their splendor.

The dance was followed by a grand banquet, at which the Prince of Wales proposed a toast to Mr. Edison:

"It gives me much pleasure," he said, "to offer, in the name of the nations of the Old World, this tribute of our admiration for, and our confidence in, the genius of the New World. Perhaps on such an occasion as this, when all racial differences and prejudices ought to be, and are, buried and forgotten, I should not recall anything that might revive them; yet I cannot refrain from expressing my happiness in knowing that the champion who is to achieve the salvation of the earth has come forth from the bosom of the Anglo-Saxon race."

Several of the great potentates looked grave upon hearing the Prince of Wales's words, and the Czar and the Kaiser exchanged glances; but there was no interruption to the cheers that followed. Mr. Edison, whose modesty and dislike to display and to speechmaking were well known, simply said:

"I think we have got the machine that can whip them. But we ought not to be wasting any time. Probably they are not dancing on Mars, but are getting ready to make us dance."

These words instantly turned the current of feeling in the vast assembly. There was no longer any disposition to expend time in vain boastings and rejoicings. Everywhere the cry now became, "Let us make haste! Let us get ready at once! Who knows but the Martians have already embarked, and are now on their way to destroy us?"

Under the impulse of this new feeling, which, it must be admitted, was very largely inspired by terror, the vast ballroom was quickly deserted. The lights were suddenly put out in the great dome of balloons, for someone had whispered:

"Suppose they should see that from Mars? Would they not guess what we were about, and redouble their preparations to finish us?"

Upon the suggestion of the President of the United States, an executive committee, representing all the principal nations, was appointed, and without delay a meeting of this committee was assembled at the White House. Mr. Edison was summoned before it, and asked to sketch briefly the plan upon which he proposed to work.

I need not enter into the details of what was done at this meeting. Let it suffice to say that when it broke up, in the small hours of the morning, it had been unanimously resolved that as many thousands of men as Mr. Edison might require should be immediately placed at his disposal; that as far as possible all the great manufacturing establishments of the country should be instantly transformed into factories where electrical ships and disintegrators could be built, and upon the suggestion of Professor Sylvanus P. Thompson, the celebrated English electrical expert, seconded by Lord Kelvin, it was resolved that all the leading men of science in the world should place their services at the disposal of Mr. Edison in any capacity in which, in his judgment, they might be useful to him.

The members of this committee were disposed to congratulate one another on the good work which they had so promptly accomplished, when at the moment of their adjournment, a telegraphic dispatch was handed to the President from Professor George E. Hale, the director of the great Yerkes Observatory, in Wisconsin. The telegram read:

Professor Barnard, watching Mars tonight with the forty-inch telescope, saw a sudden outburst of reddish light, which we think indicates that something has been shot from the planet. Spectroscopic observations of this moving light indicated that it was coming earthward, while visible, at the rate of not less than one hundred miles a second.

Hardly had the excitement caused by the reading of this dispatch subsided, when others of a similar import came from the Lick Observatory, in California; from the branch of the Harvard Observatory at Arequipa, in Peru, and from the Royal Observatory, at Potsdam.

When the telegram from this last-named place was read the Emperor William turned to his Chancellor and said:

"I want to go home. If I am to die I prefer to leave my bones among those of my Imperial ancestors, and not in this vulgar country, where no king has ever ruled. I don't like this atmosphere. It makes me feel limp."

And now, whipped on by the lash of alternate hope and fear, the earth sprang to its work of preparation.

Chapter IV

IT IS NOT NECESSARY for me to describe the manner in which Mr. Edison performed his tremendous task. He was as good as his word, and within six months from the first stroke of the hammer, a hundred electrical ships, each provided with a full battery of disintegrators, were floating in the air above the harbor and the partially rebuilt city of New York.

It was a wonderful scene. The polished sides of the huge floating cars sparkled in the sunlight, and, as they slowly rose and fell, and swung this way and that, upon the tides of the air, as if held by invisible cables, the brilliant pennons streaming from their peaks waved up and down like the wings of an assemblage of gigantic humming birds.

Not knowing whether the atmosphere of Mars would prove suitable to be breathed by inhabitants of the earth, Mr. Edison had made provision, by means of an abundance of glass-protected openings, to permit the inmates of the electrical ships to survey their surroundings without quitting the interior. It was possible by properly selecting the rate of undulation, to pass the vibratory impulse from the disintegrators through the glass windows of a car, without damage to the glass itself. The windows were so arranged that the disintegrators could sweep around the car on all sides, and could also be directed above or below, as necessity might dictate.

To overcome the destructive forces employed by the Martians no satisfactory plan had yet been devised, because there was no means to experiment with them. The production of those forces was still the secret of our enemies. But Mr. Edison had no doubt that if we could not resist their effects we might at least be able to avoid them by the rapidity of our motions. As he pointed out, the war machines which the Martians had employed in their invasion of the earth, were really very awkward and unmanageable affairs. Mr. Edison's electrical ships, on the other hand, were marvels of speed and of manageability. They could dart about, turn, reverse their course, rise, fall, with the quickness and ease of a fish in the water. Mr. Edison calculated that even if mysterious bolts should fall upon our ships we could diminish their power to cause injury by our rapid evolutions.

We might be deceived in our expectations, and might have overestimated our powers, but at any rate we must take our chances and try.

A multitude, exceeding even that which had assembled during the great congress at Washington, now thronged New York and its neighborhood to witness the mustering and the departure of the ships bound for Mars. Nothing further had been heard of the mysterious phenomenon reported from the observatories six months before, and which at the time was believed to indicate the departure of another expedition from Mars for the invasion of the earth. If the Martians had set out to attack us they had evidently gone astray; or, perhaps, it was some other world that they were aiming at this time.

The expedition had, of course, profoundly stirred the interest of the scientific world, and representatives of every branch of science, from all the civilized nations, urged their claims to places in the ships. Mr. Edison was compelled, from lack of room, to refuse transportation to more than one in a thousand of those who now, on the plea that they might be able to bring back something of advantage to science, wished to embark for Mars.

On the model of the celebrated corps of literary and scientific men which Napoleon carried with him in his invasion of Egypt, Mr. Edison selected a company of the foremost astronomers, archaeologists, anthropologists, botanists, bacteriologists, chemists, physicists, mathematicians, mechanicians, meteorologists and experts in mining, metallurgy and every other branch of practical science, as well as artists and photographers. It was but reasonable to believe that in another world, and a world so much older than the earth as Mars was, these men would be able to gather materials in comparison with which the discoveries made among the ruins of ancient empires in Egypt and Babylonia would be insignificant indeed.

It was a wonderful undertaking and a strange spectacle. There was a feeling of uncertainty which awed the vast multitude whose eyes were upturned to the ships. The expedition was not large, considering the gigantic character of the undertaking. Each of the electrical ships carried about twenty men, together with an abundant supply of compressed provisions, compressed air, scientific apparatus and so on. In all, there were about 2,000 men, who were going to conquer, if they could, another world!

But though few in numbers, they represented the flower of the earth, the culmination of the genius of the planet. The greatest leaders in science, both theoretical and practical, were there. It was the evolution of the earth against the evolution of Mars. It was a planet in the heyday of its strength matched against an aged and decrepit world which, nevertheless, in consequence of its long ages of existence, had acquired an experience which made it a most dangerous foe. On both sides there was desperation. The earth was desperate because it foresaw destruction unless it could first destroy its enemy. Mars was desperate because nature was gradually depriving it of the means of supporting life, and its teeming population was compelled to swarm like the inmates of an overcrowded hive of bees, and find new homes elsewhere. In this respect the situation on Mars, as we were well aware, resembled what had already been known upon the earth, where the older nations overflowing with population had sought new lands in which to settle, and for that purpose had driven out the native inhabitants, whenever those natives had proven unable to resist the invasion.

No man could foresee the issue of what we were about to undertake, but the tremendous powers which the disintegrators had exhibited and the marvellous efficiency of the electrical ships bred almost universal confidence that we should be successful.

The car in which Mr. Edison travelled was, of course, the flagship of the squadron, and I had the good fortune to be included among its inmates. Here, besides several leading men of science from our own country, were Lord Kelvin, Lord Rayleigh, Professor Roentgen, Dr. Moissan – the man who first made artificial diamonds – and several others whose fame had encircled the world. Each of these men cherished hopes of wonderful discoveries, along his line of investigation, to be made in Mars.

An elaborate system of signals had, of course, to be devised for the control of the squadron. These signals consisted of brilliant electric lights displayed at night and so controlled that by their means long sentences and directions could be easily and quickly transmitted.

The day signals consisted partly of brightly colored pennons and flags, which were to serve only when, shadowed by clouds or other obstructions, the full sunlight should not fall upon the ships. This could naturally only occur near the surface of the earth or of another planet.

Once out of the shadow of the earth we should have no more clouds and no more night until we arrived at Mars. In open space the sun would be continually shining. It would be perpetual day for us, except as, by artificial means, we furnished ourselves with darkness for the purpose of promoting sleep. In this region of perpetual day, then, the signals were also to be transmitted by flashes of light from mirrors reflecting the rays of the sun.

Yet this perpetual day would be also, in one sense, a perpetual night. There would be no more blue sky for us, because without an atmosphere the sunlight could not be diffused. Objects would be illuminated only on the side toward the sun. Anything that screened off the direct rays of sunlight would produce absolute darkness behind it. There would be no graduation of shadow. The sky would be as black as ink on all sides.

While it was the intention to remain as much as possible within the cars, yet since it was probable that necessity would arise for occasionally quitting the interior of the electrical ships, Mr. Edison had provided for this emergency by inventing an air-tight dress constructed somewhat after the manner of a diver's suit, but of much lighter material. Each ship was provided with several of these suits, by wearing which one could venture outside the car even when it was beyond the atmosphere of the earth.

Provision had been made to meet the terrific cold which we knew would be encountered the moment we had passed beyond the atmosphere – that awful absolute zero which men had measured by anticipation, but never yet experienced – by a simple system of producing within the air-tight suits a temperature sufficiently elevated to counteract the effects of the frigidity without. By means of long, flexible tubes, air could be continually supplied to the wearers of the suits, and by an ingenious contrivance a store of compressed air sufficient to last for several hours was provided for each suit, so that in case of necessity the wearer could throw off the tubes connecting him with the air tanks in the car. Another object which had been kept in view in the preparation of these suits was the possible exploration of an airless planet, such as the moon.

The necessity of some contrivance by means of which we should be enabled to converse with one another when on the outside of the cars in open space, or when in an airless world, like the moon, where there would be no medium by which the waves of sound could be conveyed as they are in the atmosphere of the earth, had been foreseen by our great inventor, and he had not found it difficult to contrive suitable devices for meeting the emergency.

Inside the headpiece of each of the electrical suits was the mouthpiece of a telephone. This was connected with a wire which, when not in use, could be conveniently coiled upon the arm of the wearer. Near the ears, similarly connected with wires, were telephonic receivers.

When two persons wearing the air-tight dresses wished to converse with one another it was only necessary for them to connect themselves by the wires, and conversation could then be easily carried on.

Careful calculations of the precise distance of Mars from the earth at the time when the expedition was to start had been made by a large number of experts in mathematical astronomy. But it was not Mr. Edison's intention to go direct to Mars. With the exception of the first electrical ship, which he had completed, none had yet been tried in a long voyage. It was desirable that the qualities of each of the ships should first be carefully tested, and for this reason the leader of the expedition determined that the moon should be the first port of space at which the squadron would call.

It chanced that the moon was so situated at this time as to be nearly in a line between the earth and Mars, which latter was in opposition to the sun, and consequently as favorably situated as possible for the purposes of the voyage. What would be, then, for 99 out of the 100 ships of the squadron, a trial trip would at the same time be a step of a quarter of a million of miles gained in the direction of our journey, and so no time would be wasted.

The departure from the earth was arranged to occur precisely at midnight. The moon near the full was hanging high over head, and a marvellous spectacle was presented to the eyes of those below as the great squadron of floating ships, with their signal lights ablaze, cast loose and began slowly to move away on their adventurous and unprecedented expedition into the great unknown. A tremendous cheer, billowing up from the throats of millions of excited men and women, seemed to rend the curtain of the night, and made the airships tremble with the atmospheric vibrations that were set in motion.

Instantly magnificent fireworks were displayed in honor of our departure. Rockets by hundreds of thousands shot heaven-ward, and then burst in constellations of fiery drops. The sudden illumination thus produced, overspreading hundreds of square miles of the surface of the earth with a light almost like that of day, must certainly have been visible to the inhabitants of Mars, if they were watching us at the time. They might, or might not, correctly interpret its significance; but, at any rate, we did not care. We were off, and were confident that we could meet our enemy on his own ground before he could attack us again.

And now, as we slowly rose higher, a marvellous scene was disclosed. At first the earth beneath us, buried as it was in night, resembled the hollow of a vast cup of ebony blackness, in the centre of which, like the molten lava run together at the bottom of a volcanic crater, shone the light of the illuminations around New York. But when we got beyond the atmosphere, and the earth still continued to recede below us, its aspect changed. The cup-shaped appearance was gone, and it began to round out beneath our eyes in the form of a vast globe – an enormous ball mysteriously suspended under us, glimmering over most of its surface, with the faint illumination of the moon, and showing toward its eastern edge the oncoming light of the rising sun.

When we were still further away, having slightly varied our course so that the sun was once more entirely hidden behind the centre of the earth, we saw its atmosphere completely illuminated, all around it, with prismatic lights, like a gigantic rainbow in the form of a ring.

Another shift in our course rapidly carried us out of the shadow of the earth and into the all pervading sunshine. Then the great planet beneath us hung unspeakable in its beauty. The outlines of several of the continents were clearly discernible on its surface, streaked and spotted with delicate shades of varying color, and the sunlight flashed and glowed in long lanes across the convex surface of the oceans. Parallel with the Equator and along the regions of the ever blowing trade winds, were vast belts of clouds, gorgeous with crimson and purple as the sunlight fell upon them. Immense expanses of snow and ice lay like a glittering garment upon both land and sea around the North Pole.

As we gazed upon this magnificent spectacle, our hearts bounded within us. This was our earth – this was the planet we were going to defend – our home in the trackless wilderness of space. And it seemed to us indeed a home for which we might gladly expend our last breath. A new determination to conquer or die sprung up in our hearts, and I saw Lord Kelvin, after gazing at the beauteous scene which the earth presented through his eyeglass, turn about and peer in the direction in which we knew that Mars lay, with a sudden frown that caused the glass to lose its grip and fall dangling from its string upon his breast. Even Mr. Edison seemed moved.

"I am glad I thought of the disintegrator," he said. "I shouldn't like to see that world down there laid waste again."

"And it won't be," said Professor Sylvanus P. Thompson, gripping the handle of an electric machine, "not if we can help it."

The complete and unabridged text is available online, *from flametreepublishing.com/extras*

Gulliver's Travels
Part III, Chapters I–III
Jonathan Swift

[Publisher's Note: Gulliver's Travels follows the adventures of Lemuel Gulliver as he encounters strange lands and their inhabitants. Before this point in the story he has met such people as the Liliputians – a race of tiny people; and the giants of Brobdingnag. At the end of Part II he returns to England, but as Part III begins, he soon finds himself setting out on a new voyage.]

Part III – A Voyage to Laputa

Chapter I

I HAD NOT been at home above ten days, when Captain William Robinson, a Cornish man, commander of the Hopewell, a stout ship of three hundred tons, came to my house. I had formerly been surgeon of another ship where he was master, and a fourth part owner, in a voyage to the Levant. He had always treated me more like a brother, than an inferior officer; and, hearing of my arrival, made me a visit, as I apprehended only out of friendship, for nothing passed more than what is usual after long absences. But repeating his visits often, expressing his joy to find I me in good health, asking, "whether I were now settled for life?" adding, "that he intended a voyage to the East Indies in two months," at last he plainly invited me, though with some apologies, to be surgeon of the ship; "that I should have another surgeon under me, beside our two mates; that my salary should be double to the usual pay; and that having experienced my knowledge in sea-affairs to be at least equal to his, he would enter into any engagement to follow my advice, as much as if I had shared in the command."

He said so many other obliging things, and I knew him to be so honest a man, that I could not reject this proposal; the thirst I had of seeing the world, notwithstanding my past misfortunes, continuing as violent as ever. The only difficulty that remained, was to persuade my wife, whose consent however I at last obtained, by the prospect of advantage she proposed to her children.

We set out the 5th day of August, 1706, and arrived at Fort St. George the 11th of April, 1707. We staid there three weeks to refresh our crew, many of whom were sick. From thence we went to Tonquin, where the captain resolved to continue some time, because many of the goods he intended to buy were not ready, nor could he expect to be dispatched in several months. Therefore, in hopes to defray some of the charges he must be at, he bought a sloop, loaded it with several sorts of goods, wherewith the Tonquinese usually trade to the neighbouring islands, and putting fourteen men on board, whereof three were of the country, he appointed me master of the sloop, and gave me power to traffic, while he transacted his affairs at Tonquin.

We had not sailed above three days, when a great storm arising, we were driven five days to the north-north-east, and then to the east: after which we had fair weather, but still with a pretty strong gale from the west. Upon the tenth day we were chased by two pirates, who soon overtook us; for my sloop was so deep laden, that she sailed very slow, neither were we in a condition to defend ourselves.

We were boarded about the same time by both the pirates, who entered furiously at the head of their men; but finding us all prostrate upon our faces (for so I gave order), they pinioned us with strong ropes, and setting guard upon us, went to search the sloop.

I observed among them a Dutchman, who seemed to be of some authority, though he was not commander of either ship. He knew us by our countenances to be Englishmen, and jabbering to us in his own language, swore we should be tied back to back and thrown into the sea. I spoken Dutch tolerably well; I told him who we were, and begged him, in consideration of our being Christians and Protestants, of neighbouring countries in strict alliance, that he would move the captains to take some pity on us. This inflamed his rage; he repeated his threatenings, and turning to his companions, spoke with great vehemence in the Japanese language, as I suppose, often using the word *Christianos*.

The largest of the two pirate ships was commanded by a Japanese captain, who spoke a little Dutch, but very imperfectly. He came up to me, and after several questions, which I answered in great humility, he said, "we should not die." I made the captain a very low bow, and then, turning to the Dutchman, said, "I was sorry to find more mercy in a heathen, than in a brother christian." But I had soon reason to repent those foolish words: for that malicious reprobate, having often endeavoured in vain to persuade both the captains that I might be thrown into the sea (which they would not yield to, after the promise made me that I should not die), however, prevailed so far, as to have a punishment inflicted on me, worse, in all human appearance, than death itself. My men were sent by an equal division into both the pirate ships, and my sloop new manned. As to myself, it was determined that I should be set adrift in a small canoe, with paddles and a sail, and four days' provisions; which last, the Japanese captain was so kind to double out of his own stores, and would permit no man to search me. I got down into the canoe, while the Dutchman, standing upon the deck, loaded me with all the curses and injurious terms his language could afford.

About an hour before we saw the pirates I had taken an observation, and found we were in the latitude of 46 N. and longitude of 183. When I was at some distance from the pirates, I discovered, by my pocket-glass, several islands to the south-east. I set up my sail, the wind being fair, with a design to reach the nearest of those islands, which I made a shift to do, in about three hours. It was all rocky: however I got many birds' eggs; and, striking fire, I kindled some heath and dry sea-weed, by which I roasted my eggs. I ate no other supper, being resolved to spare my provisions as much as I could. I passed the night under the shelter of a rock, strewing some heath under me, and slept pretty well.

The next day I sailed to another island, and thence to a third and fourth, sometimes using my sail, and sometimes my paddles. But, not to trouble the reader with a particular account of my distresses, let it suffice, that on the fifth day I arrived at the last island in my sight, which lay south-south-east to the former.

This island was at a greater distance than I expected, and I did not reach it in less than five hours. I encompassed it almost round, before I could find a convenient place to land in; which was a small creek, about three times the wideness of my canoe. I found the island to be all rocky, only a little intermingled with tufts of grass, and sweet-smelling herbs. I took out my small provisions and after having refreshed myself, I secured the remainder in a cave, whereof there were great numbers; I gathered plenty of eggs upon the rocks, and got a quantity of dry sea-weed, and parched grass, which I designed to kindle the next day, and roast my eggs as well as I could, for I had about me my flint, steel, match, and burning-glass. I lay all night in the cave where I had lodged my provisions. My bed was the same dry grass and sea-weed which I intended for fuel. I slept very little, for the disquiets of my mind prevailed over my weariness, and kept me awake. I considered how impossible it was to preserve my life in so desolate a place, and how miserable my end must be: yet found myself so listless and desponding, that I had not the heart to rise; and before I could get spirits enough to creep out of my cave, the day was far advanced. I walked awhile among the rocks: the sky was perfectly clear, and the sun so hot, that I was forced to turn my face from it: when all on a sudden it became obscure, as I thought, in a manner very different from what happens by the interposition of a cloud. I turned back, and perceived a vast opaque body between me and the sun moving forwards towards the island: it seemed to be about two miles high, and hid the sun six or seven minutes; but I did not observe the air to be much colder, or the sky more darkened, than if I had stood under the shade of a mountain. As it approached nearer over the place where I was, it appeared to be a firm substance, the bottom flat, smooth, and shining very bright, from the reflection of the sea below. I stood upon a height about two hundred yards from the shore, and saw this vast body descending almost to a parallel with me, at less than an English mile distance. I took out my pocket perspective, and could plainly discover numbers of people moving up and down the sides of it, which appeared to be sloping; but what those people where doing I was not able to distinguish.

The natural love of life gave me some inward motion of joy, and I was ready to entertain a hope that this adventure might, some way or other, help to deliver me from the desolate place and condition I was in. But at the same time the reader can hardly conceive my astonishment, to behold an island in the air, inhabited by men, who were able (as it should seem) to raise or sink, or put it into progressive motion, as they pleased. But not being at that time in a disposition to philosophise upon this phenomenon, I rather chose to observe what course the island would take, because it seemed for awhile to stand still. Yet soon after, it advanced nearer, and I could see the sides of it encompassed with several gradations of galleries, and stairs, at certain intervals, to descend from one to the other. In the lowest gallery, I beheld some people fishing with long angling rods, and others looking on. I waved my cap (for my hat was long since worn out) and my handkerchief toward the island; and upon its nearer approach, I called and shouted with the utmost strength of my voice; and then looking circumspectly, I beheld a crowd gather to that side which was most in my view. I found by their pointing towards me and to each other, that they plainly discovered me, although they made no return to my shouting. But I could see four or five men running in great haste, up the stairs, to the top of the island, who then disappeared. I happened rightly to conjecture, that these were sent for orders to some person in authority upon this occasion.

The number of people increased, and, in less than half all hour, the island was moved and raised in such a manner, that the lowest gallery appeared in a parallel of less then a hundred yards distance from the height where I stood. I then put myself in the most supplicating posture, and spoke in the humblest accent, but received no answer.

Those who stood nearest over against me, seemed to be persons of distinction, as I supposed by their habit. They conferred earnestly with each other, looking often upon me. At length one of them called out in a clear, polite, smooth dialect, not unlike in sound to the Italian: and therefore I returned an answer in that language, hoping at least that the cadence might be more agreeable to his ears. Although neither of us understood the other, yet my meaning was easily known, for the people saw the distress I was in.

They made signs for me to come down from the rock, and go towards the shore, which I accordingly did; and the flying island being raised to a convenient height, the verge directly over me, a chain was let down from the lowest gallery, with a seat fastened to the bottom, to which I fixed myself, and was drawn up by pulleys.

Chapter II

AT MY ALIGHTING, I was surrounded with a crowd of people, but those who stood nearest seemed to be of better quality. They beheld me with all the marks and circumstances of wonder; neither indeed was I much in their debt, having never till then seen a race of mortals so singular in their shapes, habits, and countenances. Their heads were all reclined, either to the right, or the left; one of their eyes turned inward, and the other directly up to the zenith. Their outward garments were adorned with the figures of suns, moons, and stars; interwoven with those of fiddles, flutes, harps, trumpets, guitars, harpsichords, and many other instruments of music, unknown to us in Europe. I observed, here and there, many in the habit of servants, with a blown bladder, fastened like a flail to the end of a stick, which they carried in their hands. In each bladder was a small quantity of dried peas, or little pebbles, as I was afterwards informed. With these bladders, they now and then flapped the mouths and ears of those who stood near them, of which practice I could not then conceive the meaning. It seems the minds of these people are so taken up with intense speculations, that they neither can speak, nor attend to the discourses of others, without being roused by some external taction upon the organs of speech and hearing; for which reason, those persons who are able to afford it always keep a flapper (the original is *climenole*) in their family, as one of their domestics; nor ever walk abroad, or make visits, without him. And the business of this officer is, when two, three, or more persons are in company, gently to strike with his bladder the mouth of him who is to speak, and the right ear of him or them to whom the speaker addresses himself. This flapper is likewise employed diligently to attend his master in his walks, and upon occasion to give him a soft flap on his eyes; because he is always so wrapped up in cogitation, that he is in manifest danger of falling down every precipice, and bouncing his head against every post; and in the streets, of justling others, or being justled himself into the kennel.

It was necessary to give the reader this information, without which he would be at the same loss with me to understand the proceedings of these people, as they conducted me up the stairs to the top of the island, and from thence to the royal palace. While we were ascending, they forgot several times what they were about, and left me to myself, till their memories were again roused by their flappers; for they appeared altogether unmoved by the sight of my foreign habit and countenance, and by the shouts of the vulgar, whose thoughts and minds were more disengaged.

At last we entered the palace, and proceeded into the chamber of presence, where I saw the king seated on his throne, attended on each side by persons of prime quality. Before the throne, was a large table filled with globes and spheres, and mathematical instruments of all kinds. His majesty took not the least notice of us, although our entrance was not without sufficient noise, by the concourse of all persons belonging to the court. But he was then deep in a problem; and we attended at least an hour, before he could solve it. There stood by him, on each side, a young page with flaps in their hands, and when they saw he was at leisure, one of them gently struck his mouth, and the other his right ear; at which he startled like one awaked on the sudden, and looking towards me and the company I was in, recollected the occasion of our coming, whereof he had been informed before. He spoke some words, whereupon immediately a young man with a flap came up to my side, and flapped me gently on the right ear; but I made signs, as well as I could, that I had no occasion for such an instrument; which, as I afterwards found, gave his majesty, and the whole court, a very mean opinion of my understanding. The king, as far as I could conjecture, asked me several questions, and I addressed myself to him in all the languages I had. When it was found I could neither understand nor be understood, I was conducted by his order to an apartment in his palace (this prince being distinguished above all his predecessors for his hospitality to strangers), where two servants were appointed to attend me. My dinner was brought, and four persons of quality, whom I remembered to have seen very near the king's person, did me the honour to dine with me. We had two courses, of three dishes each. In the first course, there was a shoulder of mutton cut into an equilateral triangle, a piece of beef into a rhomboides, and a pudding into a cycloid. The second course was two ducks trussed up in the form of fiddles; sausages and puddings resembling flutes and hautboys, and a breast of veal in the shape of a harp. The servants cut our bread into cones, cylinders, parallelograms, and several other mathematical figures.

While we were at dinner, I made bold to ask the names of several things in their language, and those noble persons, by the assistance of their flappers, delighted to give me answers, hoping to raise my admiration of their great abilities if I could be brought to converse with them. I was soon able to call for bread and drink, or whatever else I wanted.

After dinner my company withdrew, and a person was sent to me by the king's order, attended by a flapper. He brought with him pen, ink, and paper, and three or four books, giving me to understand by signs, that he was sent to teach me the language. We sat together four hours, in which time I wrote down a great number of words in columns, with the translations over against them; I likewise made a shift to learn several short sentences; for my tutor would order one of my servants to fetch something, to turn about, to make a bow, to sit, or to stand, or walk, and the like. Then I took down the sentence in writing. He showed me also, in one of his books, the figures of the sun, moon, and stars, the zodiac, the tropics, and polar circles, together with the denominations of many plains and solids. He gave me the names and descriptions of all the musical instruments, and the general terms of art in playing on each of them. After he had left me, I placed all my words, with their interpretations, in alphabetical order. And thus, in a few days, by the help of a very faithful memory, I got some insight into their language. The word, which I interpret the flying or floating island, is in the original *Laputa*, whereof I could never learn the true etymology. *Lap*, in the old obsolete language, signifies high; and *untuh*, a governor; from which they say, by corruption, was derived *Laputa*, from *Lapuntuh*. But I do not approve of this derivation, which seems to be a little strained. I ventured to offer to the learned among them a conjecture of my own, that Laputa was *quasi lap outed*; *lap*, signifying properly, the dancing of the sunbeams in the sea, and *outed*, a wing; which, however, I shall not obtrude, but submit to the judicious reader.

Those to whom the king had entrusted me, observing how ill I was clad, ordered a tailor to come next morning, and take measure for a suit of clothes. This operator did his office after a different manner from those of his trade in Europe. He first took my altitude by a quadrant, and then, with a rule and compasses, described the dimensions and outlines of my whole body, all which he entered upon paper; and in six days brought my clothes very ill made, and quite out of shape, by happening to mistake a figure in the calculation. But my comfort was, that I observed such accidents very frequent, and little regarded.

During my confinement for want of clothes, and by an indisposition that held me some days longer, I much enlarged my dictionary; and when I went next to court, was able to understand many things the king spoke, and to return him some kind of answers. His majesty had given orders, that the island should move north-east and by east, to the vertical point over Lagado, the metropolis of the whole kingdom below, upon the firm earth. It was about ninety leagues distant, and our voyage lasted four days and a half. I was not in the least sensible of the progressive motion made in the air by the island. On the second morning, about eleven o'clock, the king himself in person, attended by his nobility, courtiers, and officers, having prepared all their musical instruments, played on them for three hours without intermission, so that I was quite stunned with the noise; neither could I possibly guess the meaning, till my tutor informed me. He said that, the people of their island had their ears adapted to hear "the music of the spheres, which always played at certain periods, and the court was now prepared to bear their part, in whatever instrument they most excelled."

In our journey towards Lagado, the capital city, his majesty ordered that the island should stop over certain towns and villages, from whence he might receive the petitions of his subjects. And to this purpose, several packthreads were let down, with small weights at the bottom. On these packthreads the people strung their petitions, which mounted up directly, like the scraps of paper fastened by school boys at the end of the string that holds their kite. Sometimes we received wine and victuals from below, which were drawn up by pulleys.

The knowledge I had in mathematics, gave me great assistance in acquiring their phraseology, which depended much upon that science, and music; and in the latter I was not unskilled. Their ideas are perpetually conversant in lines and figures. If they would, for example, praise the beauty of a woman, or any other animal, they describe it by rhombs, circles, parallelograms, ellipses, and other geometrical terms, or by words of art drawn from music, needless here to repeat. I observed in the king's kitchen all sorts of mathematical and musical instruments, after the figures of which they cut up the joints that were served to his majesty's table.

Their houses are very ill built, the walls bevil, without one right angle in any apartment; and this defect arises from the contempt they bear to practical geometry, which they despise as vulgar and mechanic; those instructions they give being too refined for the intellects of their workmen, which occasions perpetual mistakes. And although they are dexterous enough upon a piece of paper, in the management of the rule, the pencil, and the divider, yet in the common actions and behaviour of life, I have not seen a more clumsy, awkward, and unhandy people, nor so slow and perplexed in their conceptions upon all other subjects, except those of mathematics and music. They are very bad reasoners, and vehemently given to opposition, unless when they happen to be of the right opinion, which is seldom their case. Imagination, fancy, and invention, they are wholly strangers to, nor have any words in their language, by which those ideas can be expressed; the whole compass of their thoughts and mind being shut up within the two forementioned sciences.

Most of them, and especially those who deal in the astronomical part, have great faith in judicial astrology, although they are ashamed to own it publicly. But what I chiefly admired, and thought altogether unaccountable, was the strong disposition I observed in them towards news and politics, perpetually inquiring into public affairs, giving their judgments in matters of state, and passionately disputing every inch of a party opinion. I have indeed observed the same disposition among most of the mathematicians I have known in Europe, although I could never discover the least analogy between the two sciences; unless those people suppose, that because the smallest circle has as many degrees as the largest, therefore the regulation and management of the world require no more abilities than the handling and turning of a globe; but I rather take this quality to spring from a very common infirmity of human nature, inclining us to be most curious and conceited in matters where we have least concern, and for which we are least adapted by study or nature.

These people are under continual disquietudes, never enjoying a minutes peace of mind; and their disturbances proceed from causes which very little affect the rest of mortals. Their apprehensions arise from several changes they dread in the celestial bodies: for instance, that the earth, by the continual approaches of the sun towards it, must, in course of time, be absorbed, or swallowed up; that the face of the sun, will, by degrees, be encrusted with its own effluvia, and give no more light to the world; that the earth very narrowly escaped a brush from the tail of the last comet, which would have infallibly reduced it to ashes; and that the next, which they have calculated for one-and-thirty years hence, will probably destroy us. For if, in its perihelion, it should approach within a certain degree of the sun (as by their calculations they have reason to dread) it will receive a degree of heat ten thousand times more intense than that of red hot glowing iron, and in its absence from the sun, carry a blazing tail ten hundred thousand and fourteen miles long, through which, if the earth should pass at the distance of one hundred thousand miles from the nucleus, or main body of the comet, it must in its passage be set on fire, and reduced to ashes: that the sun, daily spending its rays without any nutriment to supply them, will at last be wholly consumed and annihilated; which must be attended with the destruction of this earth, and of all the planets that receive their light from it.

They are so perpetually alarmed with the apprehensions of these, and the like impending dangers, that they can neither sleep quietly in their beds, nor have any relish for the common pleasures and amusements of life. When they meet an acquaintance in the morning, the first question is about the sun's health, how he looked at his setting and rising, and what hopes they have to avoid the stroke of the approaching comet. This conversation they are apt to run into with the same temper that boys discover in delighting to hear terrible stories of spirits and hobgoblins, which they greedily listen to, and dare not go to bed for fear.

The women of the island have abundance of vivacity: they, contemn their husbands, and are exceedingly fond of strangers, whereof there is always a considerable number from the continent below, attending at court, either upon affairs of the several towns and corporations, or their own particular occasions, but are much despised, because they want the same endowments. Among these the ladies choose their gallants: but the vexation is, that they act with too much ease and security; for the husband is always so rapt in speculation, that the mistress and lover may proceed to the greatest familiarities before his face, if he be but provided with paper and implements, and without his flapper at his side.

The wives and daughters lament their confinement to the island, although I think it the most delicious spot of ground in the world; and although they live here in the greatest plenty and magnificence, and are allowed to do whatever they please, they long to see the world, and take the diversions of the metropolis, which they are not allowed to do without a particular license from the king; and this is not easy to be obtained, because the people of quality have found, by frequent experience, how hard it is to persuade their women to return from below. I was told that a great court lady, who had several children – is married to the prime minister, the richest subject in the kingdom, a very graceful person, extremely fond of her, and lives in the finest palace of the island – went down to Lagado on the pretence of health, there hid herself for several months, till the king sent a warrant to search for her; and she was found in an obscure eating-house all in rags, having pawned her clothes to maintain an old deformed footman, who beat her every day, and in whose company she was taken, much against her will. And although her husband received her with all possible kindness, and without the least reproach, she soon after contrived to steal down again, with all her jewels, to the same gallant, and has not been heard of since.

This may perhaps pass with the reader rather for an European or English story, than for one of a country so remote. But he may please to consider, that the caprices of womankind are not limited by any climate or nation, and that they are much more uniform, than can be easily imagined.

In about a month's time, I had made a tolerable proficiency in their language, and was able to answer most of the king's questions, when I had the honour to attend him. His majesty discovered not the least curiosity to inquire into the laws, government, history, religion, or manners of the countries where I had been; but confined his questions to the state of mathematics, and received the account I gave him with great contempt and indifference, though often roused by his flapper on each side.

Chapter III

I DESIRED LEAVE of this prince to see the curiosities of the island, which he was graciously pleased to grant, and ordered my tutor to attend me. I chiefly wanted to know, to what cause, in art or in nature, it owed its several motions, whereof I will now give a philosophical account to the reader.

The flying or floating island is exactly circular, its diameter 7837 yards, or about four miles and a half, and consequently contains ten thousand acres. It is three hundred yards thick. The bottom, or under surface, which appears to those who view it below, is one even regular plate of adamant, shooting up to the height of about two hundred yards. Above it lie the several minerals in their usual order, and over all is a coat of rich mould, ten or twelve feet deep. The declivity of the upper surface, from the circumference to the centre, is the natural cause why all the dews and rains, which fall upon the island, are conveyed in small rivulets toward the middle, where they are emptied into four large basins, each of about half a mile in circuit, and two hundred yards distant from the centre. From these basins the water is continually exhaled by the sun in the daytime, which effectually prevents their overflowing. Besides, as it is in the power of the monarch to raise the island above the region of clouds and vapours, he can prevent the falling of dews and rain whenever he pleases. For the highest clouds cannot rise above two miles, as naturalists agree, at least they were never known to do so in that country.

At the centre of the island there is a chasm about fifty yards in diameter, whence the astronomers descend into a large dome, which is therefore called *flandona gagnole*, or the astronomer's cave, situated at the depth of a hundred yards beneath the upper surface of the adamant. In this cave are twenty lamps continually burning, which, from the reflection of the adamant, cast a strong light into every part. The place is stored with great variety of sextants, quadrants, telescopes, astrolabes, and other astronomical instruments. But the greatest curiosity, upon which the fate of the island depends, is a loadstone of a prodigious size, in shape resembling a weaver's shuttle. It is in length six yards, and in the thickest part at least three yards over. This magnet is sustained by a very strong axle of adamant passing through its middle, upon which it plays, and is poised so exactly that the weakest hand can turn it. It is hooped round with a hollow cylinder of adamant, four feet yards in diameter, placed horizontally, and supported by eight adamantine feet, each six yards high. In the middle of the concave side, there is a groove twelve inches deep, in which the extremities of the axle are lodged, and turned round as there is occasion.

The stone cannot be removed from its place by any force, because the hoop and its feet are one continued piece with that body of adamant which constitutes the bottom of the island.

By means of this loadstone, the island is made to rise and fall, and move from one place to another. For, with respect to that part of the earth over which the monarch presides, the stone is endued at one of its sides with an attractive power, and at the other with a repulsive. Upon placing the magnet erect, with its attracting end towards the earth, the island descends; but when the repelling extremity points downwards, the island mounts directly upwards. When the position of the stone is oblique, the motion of the island is so too: for in this magnet, the forces always act in lines parallel to its direction.

By this oblique motion, the island is conveyed to different parts of the monarch's dominions. To explain the manner of its progress, let *A B* represent a line drawn across the dominions of Balnibarbi, let the line *c d* represent the loadstone, of which let *d* be the repelling end, and *c* the attracting end, the island being over *C*: let the stone be placed in position *c d*, with its repelling end downwards; then the island will be driven upwards obliquely towards *D*. When it is arrived at *D*, let the stone be turned upon its axle, till its attracting end points towards *E*, and then the island will be carried obliquely towards *E*; where, if the stone be again turned upon its axle till it stands in the position *E F*, with its repelling point downwards, the island will rise obliquely towards *F*, where, by directing the attracting end towards *G*, the island may be carried to *G*, and from *G* to *H*, by turning the stone, so as to make its repelling extremity to point directly downward. And thus, by changing the situation of the stone, as often as there is occasion, the island is made to rise and fall by turns in an oblique direction, and by those alternate risings and fallings (the obliquity being not considerable) is conveyed from one part of the dominions to the other.

But it must be observed, that this island cannot move beyond the extent of the dominions below, nor can it rise above the height of four miles. For which the astronomers (who have written large systems concerning the stone) assign the following reason: that the magnetic virtue does not extend beyond the distance of four miles, and that the mineral, which acts upon the stone in the bowels of the earth, and in the sea about six leagues distant from the shore, is not diffused through the whole globe, but terminated with the limits of the king's dominions; and it was easy, from the great advantage of such a superior situation, for a prince to bring under his obedience whatever country lay within the attraction of that magnet.

When the stone is put parallel to the plane of the horizon, the island stands still; for in that case the extremities of it, being at equal distance from the earth, act with equal force, the one in drawing downwards, the other in pushing upwards, and consequently no motion can ensue.

This loadstone is under the care of certain astronomers, who, from time to time, give it such positions as the monarch directs. They spend the greatest part of their lives in observing the celestial bodies, which they do by the assistance of glasses, far excelling ours in goodness. For, although their largest telescopes do not exceed three feet, they magnify much more than those of a hundred with us, and show the stars with greater clearness. This advantage has enabled them to extend their discoveries much further than our astronomers in Europe; for they have made a catalogue of ten thousand fixed stars, whereas the largest of ours do not contain above one third part of that number. They have likewise discovered two lesser stars, or satellites, which revolve about Mars; whereof the innermost is distant from the centre of the primary planet exactly three of his diameters, and the outermost, five; the former revolves in the space of ten hours, and the latter in twenty-one and a half; so that the squares of their periodical times are very near in the same proportion with the cubes of their distance from the centre of Mars; which evidently shows them to be governed by the same law of gravitation that influences the other heavenly bodies.

They have observed ninety-three different comets, and settled their periods with great exactness. If this be true (and they affirm it with great confidence) it is much to be wished, that their observations were made public, whereby the theory of comets, which at present is very lame and defective, might be brought to the same perfection with other arts of astronomy.

The king would be the most absolute prince in the universe, if he could but prevail on a ministry to join with him; but these having their estates below on the continent, and considering that the office of a favourite has a very uncertain tenure, would never consent to the enslaving of their country.

If any town should engage in rebellion or mutiny, fall into violent factions, or refuse to pay the usual tribute, the king has two methods of reducing them to obedience. The first and the mildest course is, by keeping the island hovering over such a town, and the lands about it, whereby he can deprive them of the benefit of the sun and the rain, and consequently afflict the inhabitants with dearth and diseases: and if the crime deserve it, they are at the same time pelted from above with great stones, against which they have no defence but by creeping into cellars or caves, while the roofs of their houses are beaten to pieces. But if they still continue obstinate, or offer to raise insurrections, he proceeds to the last remedy, by letting the island drop directly upon their heads, which makes a universal destruction both of houses and men. However, this is an extremity to which the prince is seldom driven, neither indeed is he willing to put it in execution; nor dare his ministers advise him to an action, which, as it would render them odious to the people, so it would be a great damage to their own estates, which all lie below; for the island is the king's demesne.

But there is still indeed a more weighty reason, why the kings of this country have been always averse from executing so terrible an action, unless upon the utmost necessity. For, if the town intended to be destroyed should have in it any tall rocks, as it generally falls out in the larger cities, a situation probably chosen at first with a view to prevent such a catastrophe; or if it abound in high spires, or pillars of stone, a sudden fall might endanger the bottom or under surface of the island, which, although it consist, as I have said, of one entire adamant, two hundred yards thick, might happen to crack by too great a shock, or burst by approaching too near the fires from the houses below, as the backs, both of iron and stone, will often do in our chimneys. Of all this the people are well apprised, and understand how far to carry their obstinacy, where their liberty or property is concerned. And the king, when he is highest provoked, and most determined to press a city to rubbish, orders the island to descend with great gentleness, out of a pretence of tenderness to his people, but, indeed, for fear of breaking the adamantine bottom; in which case, it is the opinion of all their philosophers, that the loadstone could no longer hold it up, and the whole mass would fall to the ground.

By a fundamental law of this realm, neither the king, nor either of his two eldest sons, are permitted to leave the island; nor the queen, till she is past child-bearing.

The complete and unabridged text is available online, *from flametreepublishing.com/extras*

Micromégas

Voltaire

Chapter I
Voyage of an Inhabitant of the Sirius Star to the Planet Saturn

ON ONE OF THE PLANETS that orbits the star named Sirius there lived a spirited young man, who I had the honour of meeting on the last voyage he made to our little ant hill. He was called Micromégas, a fitting name for anyone so great. He was eight leagues tall, or 24,000 geometric paces of five feet each.

Certain geometers, always of use to the public, will immediately take up their pens, and will find that since Mr. Micromégas, inhabitant of the country of Sirius, is 24,000 paces tall, which is equivalent to 20,000 feet, and since we citizens of the earth are hardly five feet tall, and our sphere 9,000 leagues around; they will find, I say, that it is absolutely necessary that the sphere that produced him was 21,600,000 times greater in circumference than our little Earth. Nothing in nature is simpler or more orderly. The sovereign states of Germany or Italy, which one can traverse in a half hour, compared to the empires of Turkey, Moscow, or China, are only feeble reflections of the prodigious differences that nature has placed in all beings.

His excellency's size being as great as I have said, all our sculptors and all our painters will agree without protest that his belt would have been 50,000 feet around, which gives him very good proportions. His nose taking up one third of his attractive face, and his attractive face taking up one seventh of his attractive body, it must be admitted that the nose of the Sirian is 6,333 feet plus a fraction; which is manifest.

As for his mind, it is one of the most cultivated that we have. He knows many things. He invented some of them. He was not even 250 years old when he studied, as is customary, at the most celebrated colleges of his planet, where he managed to figure out by pure willpower more than 50 of Euclid's propositions. That makes 18 more than Blaise Pascal, who, after having figured out 32 while screwing around, according to his sister's reports, later became a fairly mediocre geometer and a very bad metaphysician.

Towards his 450th year, near the end of his infancy, he dissected many small insects no more than 100 feet in diameter, which would evade ordinary microscopes. He wrote a very curious book about this, and it gave him some income. The mufti of his country, an extremely ignorant worrywart, found some suspicious, rash, disagreeable, and heretical propositions in the book, smelled heresy, and pursued it vigorously; it was a matter of finding out whether the substantial form of the fleas of Sirius were of the same nature as those of the snails. Micromégas gave a spirited defence; he brought in some women to testify in his favour; the trial lasted 220 years. Finally the mufti had the book condemned by jurisconsults who had not read it, and the author was ordered not to appear in court for 800 years.

He was thereby dealt the minor affliction of being banished from a court that consisted of nothing but harassment and pettiness. He wrote an amusing song at the expense of the mufti, which the latter hardly noticed; and he took to voyaging from planet to planet in order to develop his heart and mind, as the saying goes. Those that travel only by stage coach or sedan will probably be surprised learn of the carriage of this vessel; for we, on our little pile of mud, can only conceive of that to which we are accustomed. Our voyager was very familiar with the laws of gravity and with all the other attractive and repulsive forces. He utilized them so well that, whether with the help of a ray of sunlight or some comet, he jumped from globe to globe like a bird vaulting itself from branch to branch. He quickly spanned the Milky Way, and I am obliged to report that he never saw, throughout the stars it is made up of, the beautiful empyrean sky that the vicar Derham boasts of having seen at the other end of his telescope. I do not claim that Mr. Derham has poor eyesight, God forbid! But Micromégas was on site, which makes him a reliable witness, and I do not want to contradict anyone.

Micromégas, after having toured around, arrived at the planet Saturn. As accustomed as he was to seeing new things, he could not, upon seeing the smallness of the planet and its inhabitants, stop himself from smiling with the superiority that occasionally escapes the wisest of us. For in the end Saturn is hardly nine times bigger than Earth, and the citizens of this country are dwarfs, no more than a thousand fathoms tall, or somewhere around there. He and his men poked fun at them at first, like Italian musicians laughing at the music of Lully when he comes to France. But, as the Sirian had a good heart, he understood very quickly that a thinking being is not necessarily ridiculous just because he is only 6,000 feet tall. He got to know the Saturnians after their shock wore off. He built a strong friendship with the secretary of the academy of Saturn, a spirited man who had not invented anything, to tell the truth, but who understood the inventions of others very well, and who wrote some passable verses and carried out some complicated calculations. I will report here, for the reader's satisfaction, a singular conversation that Micromégas had with the secretary one day.

Chapter II
Conversation between the Inhabitant of Sirius Bnd that of Saturn

AFTER HIS EXCELLENCY laid himself down to rest the secretary approached him.

"You have to admit," said Micromégas, "that nature is extremely varied."

"Yes," said the Saturnian, "nature is like a flower bed wherein the flowers –"

"Ugh!" said the other, "Leave off with flower beds."

The secretary began again. "Nature is like an assembly of blonde and brown-haired girls whose jewels –"

"What am I supposed to do with your brown-haired girls?" said the other.

"Then she is like a gallery of paintings whose features –"

"Certainly not!" said the voyager. "I say again that nature is like nature. Why bother looking for comparisons?"

"To please you," replied the Secretary.

"I do not want to be pleased," answered the voyager. "I want to be taught. Tell me how many senses the men of your planet have."

"We only have 72," said the academic, "and we always complain about it. Our imagination surpasses our needs. We find that with our 72 senses, our ring, our five moons, we are too restricted; and in spite of all our curiosity and the fairly large number of passions that result from our 72 senses, we have plenty of time to get bored."

"I believe it," said Micromégas, "for on our planet we have almost 1,000 senses; and yet we still have a kind of vague feeling, a sort of worry, that warns us that there are even more perfect beings. I have travelled a bit; and I have seen mortals that surpass us, some far superior. But I have not seen any that desire only what they truly need, and who need only what they indulge in. Maybe someday I will happen upon a country that lacks nothing; but so far no one has given me any word of a place like that."

The Saturnian and the Sirian proceeded to wear themselves out in speculating; but after a lot of very ingenious and very dubious reasoning, it was necessary to return to the facts.

"How long do you live?" said the Sirian.

"Oh! For a very short time," replied the small man from Saturn.

"Same with us," said the Sirian. "we always complain about it. It must be a universal law of nature."

"Alas! We only live through 500 revolutions around the sun," said the Saturnian. (This translates to about 15,000 years, by our standards.) "You can see yourself that this is to die almost at the moment one is born; our existence is a point, our lifespan an instant, our planet an atom. Hardly do we begin to learn a little when death arrives, before we get any experience. As for me, I do not dare make any plans. I see myself as a drop of water in an immense ocean. I am ashamed, most of all before you, of how ridiculously I figure in this world."

Micromégas replied, "If you were not a philosopher, I would fear burdening you by telling you that our lifespan is 700 times longer than yours; but you know very well when it is necessary to return your body to the elements, and reanimate nature in another form, which we call death. When this moment of metamorphosis comes, to have lived an eternity or to have lived a day amounts to precisely the same thing. I have been to countries where they live a thousand times longer than we do, and they also die. But people everywhere have the good sense to know their role and to thank the Author of nature. He has scattered across this universe a profusion of varieties with a kind of admirable uniformity. For example, all the thinking beings are different, and all resemble one another in the gift of thought and desire. Matter is extended everywhere, but has different properties on each planet. How many diverse properties do you count in yours?"

"If you mean those properties," said the Saturnian, "without which we believe that the planet could not subsist as it is, we count 300 of them, like extension, impenetrability, mobility, gravity, divisibility, and the rest."

"Apparently," replied the voyager, "this small number suffices for what the Creator had in store for your dwelling. I admire his wisdom in everything; I see differences everywhere, but also proportion. Your planet is small, your inhabitants are as well. You have few sensations; your matter has few properties; all this is the work of Providence. What colour is your sun upon examination?"

"A very yellowish white," said the Saturnian. "And when we divide one of its rays, we find that it contains seven colours."

"Our sun strains at red," said the Sirian, "and we have 39 primary colours. There is no one sun, among those that I have gotten close to that resembles it, just as there is no one face among you that is identical to the others."

After numerous questions of this nature, he learned how many essentially different substances are found on Saturn. He learned that there were only about thirty, like God, space, matter, the beings with extension that sense, the beings with extension that sense and think, the thinking beings that have no extension; those that are penetrable, those that are not, and the rest. The Sirian, whose home contained 300 and who had discovered 3,000 of them in his voyages, prodigiously surprised the philosopher of Saturn. Finally, after having told each other a little of what they knew and a lot of what they did not know, after having reasoned over the course of a revolution around the sun, they resolved to go on a small philosophical voyage together.

Chapter III
Voyage of the Two Inhabitants of Sirius and Saturn

OUR TWO PHILOSOPHERS were just ready to take off into Saturn's atmosphere with a very nice provision of mathematical instrument when the ruler of Saturn, who had heard news of the departure, came in tears to remonstrate. She was a pretty, petite brunette who was only 660 fathoms tall, but who compensated for this small size with many other charms.

"Cruelty!" she cried, "After resisting you for 1,500 years, just when I was beginning to come around, when I'd spent hardly a hundred years in your arms, you leave me to go on a voyage with a giant from another world; go, you're only curious, you've never been in love: if you were a true Saturnian, you would be faithful. Where are you running off to? What do you want? Our five moons are less errant than you, our ring less inconsistent. It's over, I will never love anyone ever again."

The philosopher embraced her, cried with her, philosopher that he was; and the woman, after swooning, went off to console herself with the help of one of the dandies of the country.

Our two explorers left all the same; they alighted first on the ring, which they found to be fairly flat, as conjectured by an illustrious inhabitant of our little sphere; from there they went easily from moon to moon. A comet passed by the last; they flew onto it with their servants and their instruments. When they had travelled about one hundred fifty million leagues, they met with the satellites of Jupiter. They stopped at Jupiter and stayed for a week, during which time they learned some very wonderful secrets that would have been forthcoming in print if not for the inquisition, which found some of the propositions to be a little harsh. But I have read the manuscript in the library of the illustrious archbishop of –, who with a generosity and goodness that is impossible to praise allowed me to see his books. I promised him a long article in the first edition of Moréri, and I will not forget his children, who give such a great hope of perpetuating the race of their illustrious father.

But let us now return to our travellers. Upon leaving Jupiter they traversed a space of around one hundred million leagues and approached the planet Mars, which, as we know, is five times smaller than our own; they swung by two moons that cater to this planet but have escaped the notice of our astronomers. I know very well that Father Castel will write, perhaps even agreeably enough, against the existence of these two moons; but I rely on those who reason by analogy. These good philosophers know how unlikely it would be for Mars, so far from the sun, to have gotten by with less than two moons. Whatever the case may be, our explorers found it so small that they feared not being able to land on it, and they passed it by like two travellers disdainful of a bad village cabaret, pressing on towards a neighbouring city. But the Sirian and his companion soon regretted it. They travelled a long time without finding anything. Finally they perceived a small candle, it was earth; this was a pitiful sight to those who had just left Jupiter. Nevertheless, from fear of further regret, they resolved to touch down. Carried by the tail of a comet, and finding an aurora borealis at the ready, they started towards it, and arrived at Earth on the northern coast of the Baltic sea, July 5, 1737, new style.

Chapter IV
What Happened on Planet Earth

AFTER RESTING FOR SOME TIME they ate two mountains for lunch, which their crew fixed up pretty nicely. Then they decided to get to know the small country they were in. They went first from north to south. The usual stride of the Sirian and his crew was around 30,000 feet. The dwarf from Saturn, who clocked in at no more than a thousand fathoms, trailed behind, breathing heavily. He had to make twelve steps each time the other took a stride; imagine (if it is alright to make such a comparison) a very small lapdog following a captain of the guards of the Prussian king.

Since our strangers moved fairly rapidly, they circumnavigated the globe in 36 hours. The sun, in truth, or rather the Earth, makes a similar voyage in a day; but you have to imagine that the going is much easier when one turns on one's axis instead of walking on one's feet. So there they were, back where they started, after having seen the nearly imperceptible pond we call *the Mediterranean*, and the other little pool that, under the name *Ocean*, encircles the molehill. The dwarf never got in over his knees, and the other hardly wet his heels. On their way they did all they could to see whether the planet was inhabited or not. They crouched, laid down, felt around everywhere; but their eyes and their hands were not proportionate to the little beings that crawl here, they could not feel in the least any sensation that might lead them to suspect that we and our associates, the other inhabitants of this planet, have the honour of existing.

The dwarf, who was a bit hasty sometimes, decided straightaway that the planet was uninhabited. His first reason was that he had not seen anyone. Micromégas politely indicated that this logic was rather flawed: "For," said he, "you do not see with your little eyes certain stars of the 50th magnitude that I can perceive very distinctly. Do you conclude that these stars do not exist?"

"But," said the dwarf, "I felt around a lot."

"But," answered the other, "you have pretty weak senses."

"But," replied the dwarf, "this planet is poorly constructed. It is so irregular and has such a ridiculous shape! Everything here seems to be in chaos: you see these little rivulets, none of which run in a straight line, these pools of water that are neither round, nor square, nor oval, nor regular by any measure; all these little pointy specks scattered across the earth that grate on my feet? (This was in reference to mountains.) Look at its shape again, how it is flat at the poles, how it clumsily revolves around the sun in a way that necessarily eliminates the climates of the poles? To tell the truth, what really makes me think it is uninhabited is that it seems that no one of good sense would want to stay."

"Well," said Micromégas, "maybe the inhabitants of this planet are not of good sense! But in the end it looks like this may be for a reason. Everything appears irregular to you here, you say, because everything on Saturn and Jupiter is drawn in straight lines. This might be the reason that you are a bit puzzled here. Have I not told you that I have continually noticed variety in my travels?"

The Saturnian responded to all these points. The dispute might never have finished if it were not for Micromégas who, getting worked up, had the good luck to break the thread of his diamond necklace. The diamonds fell; they were pretty little carats of fairly irregular size, of which the largest weighed four hundred pounds and the smallest fifty. The dwarf recaptured some of them; bending down for a better look, he perceived that these diamonds were cut with the help of an excellent microscope. So he took out a small microscope of 160 feet in diameter and put it up to his eye; and Micromégas took up one of 2,005 feet in diameter. They were excellent; but neither one of them could see anything right away and had to adjust them. Finally the Saturnian saw something elusive that moved in the shallow waters of the Baltic sea; it was a whale. He carefully picked it up with his little finger and, resting it on the nail of his thumb, showed it to the Sirian, who began laughing for a second time at the ludicrously small scale of the things on our planet. The Saturnian, persuaded that our world was inhabited, figured very quickly that it was inhabited only by whales; and as he was very good at reasoning, he was determined to infer the origin and evolution of such a small atom; whether it had ideas, a will, liberty. Micromégas was confused. He examined the animal very patiently and found no reason to believe that a soul was lodged in it. The two voyagers were therefore inclined to believe that there is no spirit in our home, when with the help of the microscope they perceived something as large as a whale floating on the Baltic Sea. We know that a flock of philosophers was at this time returning from the Arctic Circle, where they had made some observations, which no one had dared make up to then. The gazettes claimed that their vessel ran aground on the coast of Bothnia, and that they were having a lot of difficulty setting things straight; but the world never shows its cards. I am going to tell how it really happened, artlessly and without bias; which is no small thing for an historian.

Chapter V
Experiments and Reasonings of the Two Voyagers

MICROMÉGAS SLOWLY REACHED his hand towards the place where the object had appeared, extended two fingers, and withdrew them for fear of being mistaken, then opened and closed them, and skillfully seized the vessel that carried these fellows, putting it on his fingernail without pressing it too hard for fear of crushing it.

"Here is a very different animal from the first," said the dwarf from Saturn.

The Sirian put the so-called animal in the palm of his hand. The passengers and the crew, who believed themselves to have been lifted up by a hurricane, and who thought they were on some sort of boulder, scurried around; the sailors took the barrels of wine, threw them overboard onto Micromégas hand, and followed after. The geometers took their quadrants, their sextants, two Lappland girls, and descended onto the Sirian's fingers. They made so much fuss that he finally felt something move, tickling his fingers. It was a steel-tipped baton being pressed into his index finger. He judged, by this tickling, that it had been ejected from some small animal that he was holding; but he did not suspect anything else at first. The microscope, which could barely distinguish a whale from a boat, could not capture anything as elusive as a man. I do not claim to outrage anyone's vanity, but I am obliged to ask that important men make an observation here. Taking the size of a man to be about five feet, the figure we strike on Earth is like that struck by an animal of about six hundred thousandths the height of a flea on a ball five feet around. Imagine something that can hold the Earth in its hands, and which has organs in proportion to ours

– and it may very well be that there are such things – conceive, I beg of you, what these things would think of the battles that allow a vanquisher to take a village only to lose it later.

I do not doubt that if ever some captain of some troop of imposing grenadiers reads this work he will increase the size of the hats of his troops by at least two imposing feet. But I warn him that it will have been done in vain; that he and his will never grow any larger than infinitely small.

What marvellous skill it must have taken for our philosopher from Sirius to perceive the atoms I have just spoken of. When Leuwenhoek and Hartsoeker tinkered with the first or thought they saw the grains that make us up, they did not by any means make such an astonishing discovery. What pleasure Micromégas felt at seeing these little machines move, at examining all their scurrying, at following them in their enterprises! How he cried out! With what joy he placed one of his microscopes in the hands of his traveling companion!

"I see them," they said at the same time, "look how they are carrying loads, stooping, getting up again." They spoke like that, hands trembling from the pleasure of seeing such new objects, and from fear of losing them. The Saturnian, passing from an excess of incredulity to an excess of credulity, thought he saw them mating.

"Ah!" he said. "I have caught nature in the act". But he was fooled by appearances, which happens only too often, whether one is using a microscope or not.

Chapter VI
What Happened to them Among Men

MICROMÉGAS, a much better observer than his dwarf, clearly saw that the atoms were speaking to each other, and pointed this out to his companion, who, ashamed of being mistaken about them reproducing, did not want to believe that such a species could communicate. He had the gift of language as well as the Sirian. He could not hear the atoms talk, and he supposed that they did not speak. Moreover, how could these impossibly small beings have vocal organs, and what would they have to say? To speak, one must think, more or less; but if they think, they must therefore have the equivalent of a soul. But to attribute the equivalent of a soul to this species seemed absurd to him.

"But," said the Sirian, "you believed right away that they made love. Do you believe that one can make love without thinking and without uttering one word, or at least without making oneself heard? Do you suppose as well that it is more difficult to produce an argument than an infant? Both appear to be great mysteries to me."

"I do not dare believe or deny it," said the dwarf. "I have no more opinions. We must try to examine these insects and reason after."

"That is very well said," echoed Micromégas, and he briskly took out a pair of scissors with which he cut his fingernails, and from the parings of his thumbnail he improvised a kind of speaking-trumpet, like a vast funnel, and put the end up to his ear. The circumference of the funnel enveloped the vessel and the entire crew. The weakest voice entered into the circular fibres of the nails in such a way that, thanks to his industriousness, the philosopher above could hear the drone of our insects below perfectly. In a small number of hours he was able to distinguish words, and finally to understand French. The dwarf managed to do the same, though with more difficulty. The voyagers' surprise redoubled each second. They heard the mites speak fairly intelligently. This performance of nature's seemed inexplicable to them. You may well believe that the Sirian and the dwarf burned with impatience to converse with the atoms. The dwarf feared that his thunderous voice, and assuredly Micromégas, would deafen the mites without being understood. They had to diminish its force. They placed toothpicks in their mouths, whose tapered ends fell around the ship. The Sirian put the dwarf on his knees and the ship with its crew on a fingernail. He lowered his head and spoke softly. Finally, relying on these precautions and many others, he began his speech like so:

"Invisible insects, that the hand of the Creator has caused to spring up in the abyss of the infinitely small, I thank him for allowing me to uncover these seemingly impenetrable secrets. Perhaps those at my court would not deign to give you audience, but I mistrust no one, and I offer you my protection."

If anyone has ever been surprised, it was the people who heard these words. They could not figure out where they were coming from. The chaplain of the vessel recited the exorcism prayers, the sailors swore, and the philosophers of the vessel constructed systems; but no matter what systems they came up with, they could not figure out who was talking. The dwarf from Saturn, who had a softer voice than Micromégas, told them in a few words what species they were dealing with. He told them about the voyage from Saturn, brought them up to speed on what Mr. Micromégas was, and after lamenting how small they were, asked them if they had always been in this miserable state so near nothingness, what they were doing on a globe that appeared to belong to whales, whether they were happy, if they reproduced, if they had a soul, and a hundred other questions of this nature.

A reasoner among the troop, more daring than the others, and shocked that someone might doubt his soul, observed the interlocutor with sight-vanes pointed at a quarter circle from two different stations, and at the third spoke thusly: "You believe then, Sir, that because you are a thousand fathoms tall from head to toe, that you are a –"

"A thousand fathoms!" cried the dwarf. "Good heavens! How could he know my height? A thousand fathoms! You cannot mistake him for a flea. This atom just measured me! He is a surveyor, he knows my size; and I, who can only see him through a microscope, I still do not know his!"

"Yes, I measured you," said the physician, "and I will measure your large companion as well." The proposition was accepted, his excellency laid down flat; for were he to stay upright his head would have been among the clouds. Our philosophers planted a great shaft on him, in a place that doctor Swift would have named, but that I will restrain myself from calling by its name, out of respect for the ladies. Next, by a series of triangles linked together, they concluded that what they saw was in effect a young man of 120,000 feet.

So Micromégas delivered these words: "I see more than ever that one must not judge anything by its apparent size. Oh God! you who have given intelligence to substance that appears contemptible. The infinitely small costs you as little as the infinitely large; and if it is possible that there are such small beings as these, there may just as well be a spirit bigger than those of the superb animals that I have seen in the heavens, whose feet alone would cover this planet."

One of the philosophers responded that he could certainly imagine that there are intelligent beings much smaller than man. He recounted, not every fabulous thing Virgil says about bees, but what Swammerdam discovered, and what Réaumur has anatomized. He explained finally that there are animals that are to bees what bees are to man, what the Sirian himself was for the vast animals he had spoken of, and what these large animals are to other substances before which they looked like atoms. Little by little the conversation became interesting, and Micromégas spoke thusly:

Chapter VII
Conversation with the Men

"OH INTELLIGENT ATOMS, in which the Eternal Being desired to make manifest his skill and his power, you must, no doubt, taste pure joys on your planet; for having so little matter, and appearing to be entirely spirit, you must live out your life thinking and loving, the veritable life of the mind. Nowhere have I seen true bliss, but it is here, without a doubt."

At this all the philosophers shook their heads, and one of them, more frank than the others, avowed that if one excepts a small number of inhabitants held in poor regard, all the rest are an assembly of mad, vicious, and wretched people. "We have more substance than is necessary," he said, "to do evil, if evil comes from substance; and too much spirit, if evil comes from spirit. Did you know, for example, that as I am speaking with you, there are 100,000 madmen of our species wearing hats, killing 100,000 other animals wearing turbans, or being massacred by them, and that we have used almost surface of the Earth for this purpose since time immemorial?"

The Sirian shuddered, and asked the reason for these horrible quarrels between such puny animals.

"It is a matter," said the philosopher, "of some piles of mud as big as your heel. It is not that any of these millions of men that slit each other's throats care about this pile of mud. It is only a matter of determining if it should belong to a certain man who we call 'Sultan,' or to another who we call, for whatever reason, 'Czar.' Neither one has ever seen nor will ever see the little piece of Earth, and almost none of these animals that mutually kill themselves have ever seen the animal for which they kill."

"Oh! Cruel fate!" cried the Sirian with indignation, "Who could conceive of this excess of maniacal rage! It makes me want to take three steps and crush this whole anthill of ridiculous assassins."

"Do not waste your time," someone responded, "they are working towards ruin quickly enough. Know that after ten years only one hundredth of these scoundrels will be here. Know that even if they have not drawn swords, hunger, fatigue, or intemperance will overtake them. Furthermore, it is not they that should be punished, it is those sedentary barbarians who from the depths of their offices order, while they are digesting their last meal, the massacre of a million men, and who subsequently give solemn thanks to God."

The voyager was moved with pity for the small human race, where he was discovering such surprising contrasts.

"Since you are amongst the small number of wise men," he told these sirs, "and since apparently you do not kill anyone for money, tell me, I beg of you, what occupies your time."

"We dissect flies," said the philosopher, "we measure lines, we gather figures; we agree with each other on two or three points that we do not understand."

It suddenly took the Sirian and the Saturnian's fancy to question these thinking atoms, to learn what it was they agreed on.

"What do you measure," said the Saturnian, "from the Dog Star to the great star of the Gemini?"

They responded all at once, "thirty-two and a half degrees."

"What do you measure from here to the moon?"

"60 radii of the Earth even."

"How much does your air weigh?"

He thought he had caught them, but they all told him that air weighed around 900 times less than an identical volume of the purest water, and 19,000 times less than a gold ducat. The little dwarf from Saturn, surprised at their responses, was tempted to accuse of witchcraft the same people he had refused a soul fifteen minutes earlier.

Finally Micromégas said to them, "Since you know what is exterior to you so well, you must know what is interior even better. Tell me what your soul is, and how you form ideas." The philosophers spoke all at once as before, but they were of different views. The oldest cited Aristotle, another pronounced the name of Descartes; this one here, Malebranche; another Leibnitz; another Locke. An old peripatetic spoke up with confidence: "The soul is an entelechy, and a reason gives it the power to be what it is." This is what Aristotle expressly declares, page 633 of the Louvre edition. He cited the passage.

Entele'xeia' tis esi kai' lo'gos toû dy'namin e'xontos toude' ei'nai. B.

"I do not understand Greek very well," said the giant.

"Neither do I," said the philosophical mite.

"Why then," the Sirian retorted, "are you citing some man named Aristotle in the Greek?"

"Because," replied the savant, "one should always cite what one does not understand at all in the language one understands the least."

The Cartesian took the floor and said: "The soul is a pure spirit that has received in the belly of its mother all metaphysical ideas, and which, leaving that place, is obliged to go to school, and to learn all over again what it already knew, and will not know again."

"It is not worth the trouble," responded the animal with the height of eight leagues, "for your soul to be so knowledgeable in its mother's stomach, only to be so ignorant when you have hair on your chin. But what do you understand by the mind?"

"You are asking me?" said the reasoner. "I have no idea. We say that it is not matter –"

"But do you at least know what matter is?"

"Certainly," replied the man. "For example this stone is grey, has such and such a form, has three dimensions, is heavy and divisible."

"Well!" said the Sirian, "this thing that appears to you to be divisible, heavy, and grey, will you tell me what it is? You see some attributes, but behind those, are you familiar with that?"

"No," said the other.

"– So you do not know what matter is."

So Micromégas, addressing another sage that he held on a thumb, asked what his soul was, and what it did.

"Nothing at all," said the Malebranchist philosopher. "God does everything for me. I see everything in him, I do everything in him; it is he who does everything that I get mixed up in."

"It would be just as well not to exist," retorted the sage of Sirius. "And you, my friend," he said to a Leibnitzian who was there, "what is your soul?"

"It is," answered the Leibnitzian, "the hand of a clock that tells the time while my body rings out. Or, if you like, it is my soul that rings out while my body tells the time, or my soul is the mirror of the universe, and my body is the border of the mirror. All that is clear."

A small partisan of Locke was nearby, and when he was finally given the floor: "I do not know," said he, "how I think, but I know that I have only ever thought through my senses. That there are immaterial and intelligent substances I do not doubt, but that it is impossible for God to communicate thought to matter I doubt very much. I revere the eternal power. It is not my place to limit it. I affirm nothing, and content myself with believing that many more things are possible than one would think."

The animal from Sirius smiled. He did not find this the least bit sage, while the dwarf from Saturn would have kissed the sectarian of Locke were it not for the extreme disproportion. But there was, unfortunately, a little animalcule in a square hat who interrupted all the other animalcule philosophers. He said that he knew the secret: that everything would be found in the *Summa* of Saint Thomas. He looked the two celestial inhabitants up and down. He argued that their people, their worlds, their suns, their stars, had all been made uniquely for mankind. At this speech, our two voyagers nearly fell over with that inextinguishable laughter which, according to Homer, is shared with the gods. Their shoulders and their stomachs heaved up and down, and in these convulsions the vessel that the Sirian had on his nail fell into one of the Saturnian's trouser pockets. These two good men searched for it a long time, found it finally, and tidied it up neatly. The Sirian resumed his discussion with the little mites. He spoke to them with great kindness, although in the depths of his heart he was a little angry that the infinitely small had an almost infinitely great pride. He promised to make them a beautiful philosophical book, written very small for their usage, and said that in this book they would see the point of everything. Indeed, he gave them this book before leaving. It was taken to the academy of science in Paris, but when the ancient secretary opened it, he saw nothing but blank pages. "Ah!" he said, "I suspected as much."

Dark Mirrors

John Walters

HER FACE AND ARMS bore the yellow marks of old bruises and the purple marks of new ones; her left forefinger and middle finger were in rough splints of cardboard and tape; the half-a-centimeter-thick bright red scar of a recently-healed cut ran from her right temple to the top of her nose near the corner of her left eye. Add to all this her hard, determined expression that suggested she wouldn't take shit from anyone, and she looked like a fighter, a brawler, a troublemaker.

But Margaret Keller knew she was anything but that.

The loose gray prison coveralls made her appear diminutive, like a little girl. She *was* very thin, abnormally so. Her scalp could be seen through her light brown hair; obviously much of the hair had fallen out. The hard work, scanty food, derision and beatings were obviously telling on her. But she held her head defiantly high; she had obviously kept herself together through it all.

Margaret, despite herself, was impressed. However, she assumed a calm, cold, professional air as she said, "Bethany Williamson?" and when the woman nodded, "Sit down."

They were in the mess hall, a small table with obscenities carved into its gray Formica surface between them. Prisoners shuffled to and fro, with wide frightened eyes glancing around as if already in the line of fire. The guards watching them were whispering intently together in a corner. They too would be called up, as soon as the last prisoner had left.

"Do you want my decision now?" asked Bethany. "I thought I had another day."

"Your decision?"

Bethany smiled ironically. "Service or dismemberment: aren't those the options?"

Momentarily taken aback, Margaret quickly recovered her poise. "Those are your choices, yes. Do you need another day to decide?"

Bethany slowly shook her head.

"How long have you been here?" Margaret asked.

Bethany smiled again, though her eyes narrowed and her jaw tightened. "I'm sure you in your fancy uniform, all clean and polished and obviously more than well-fed, have access to my file. You don't need to be asking me any questions like that."

"Don't you dare get insubordinate with me…"

"Or else what? I have been here for a year, three months, and seventeen days, and I have been beaten and abused on almost every one of those days. I was ripped away from my parents, my school, and everything else from my former life. I am about to be cut up and used as spare parts for wounded soldiers. There's nothing you can threaten me with that can make any difference to me." The hard look remained, but a teardrop formed in the corner of her right eye, though it did not trickle down.

Margaret forced the twinge of sympathy out of her conscious mind as if it were an enemy, but then adopted a more solicitous tone. "All right, all right. It seems we got off on the wrong foot."

"Is there a right foot? I don't think so. I'm a condemned woman." Bethany stood up. "Please sit down."

"No."

They stared at each other for a long time, as if in mental combat. Finally Margaret nodded at a guard, who led Bethany away.

* * *

For her next interview with Bethany Margaret went down to her cell.

The section guard was a short stocky woman with a clean-shaven head, thick lower lip, and a pasty complexion. "That's murderer's row. It's been almost cleaned out," the guard said. "There're just a few prisoners left. Some are unaccounted for, though. They're trying to hide to avoid service. It could be dangerous if they find you. I can come with you if you want."

"I'll be all right." To emphasize the point Margaret pulled out her pistol, checked that it was loaded, and put it away again. "By the way, what is she doing down there with murderers?"

The guard shrugged. "They don't like her kind much. Maybe the warden thought it would break her. Anyway, there are maps on the guard post walls in case you get lost. There're a lot of corridors."

Margaret descended a flight of stairs and turned left into a wide but low-ceilinged hallway. The cells on either side were vacant; her footsteps echoed loudly in the empty spaces. Since the facility was being shut down regular cleaning had stopped. Humidity beaded on the graffiti-covered walls and then trickled down in rivulets to form puddles on the muddy floor. Black specks of mold had begun to grow in the corners of the ceiling. Cockroaches were everywhere; Margaret saw an occasional rat as well. The air smelled musty from the damp, rotting mattresses.

After having navigated the maze of corridors for a quarter of an hour Margaret became convinced she was lost, and was just about to try to find her way back when she spotted Bethany alone in her cell, sitting on the edge of the lower bunk reading a book.

Once again a burst of sympathy erupted from somewhere within; once again Margaret stifled it and sent it back where it came from. She reminded herself that she despised Bethany and everything she stood for, and she resented the circumstance that forced her into this hellhole to deal with her. She had turned her back on her people; she *deserved* the dismemberment. At least then she could be of some use.

But even as she thought these things, Margaret wondered whether these were her own thoughts or others had implanted them in her. Things had taken such a crazy turn that she didn't know what to believe anymore. But whenever she became confused she thought of her husband and son, both early casualties of the war. Her husband she remembered as he had looked the day he left for the last time: balding with gray hair at the temples, but sharp and strong and determined in his uniform. Her son, however, she could never picture as an adult. She saw him as a toddler, running into her arms with a big smile to be scooped up and hugged, or grade school age either in bed with one of his myriad childhood illnesses, or pale and thin playing basketball at a nearby park with his friends. Though he had never been very healthy, when the conflict began he had wanted to enlist right away; he was rejected at first though, and was only allowed to join up after several defeats had been suffered and the medical checkup consisted of feeling you to see if you were still warm. He had been thrilled to be a part of it all, but he hadn't lasted a week once he was out on the field.

A part of her desperately wanted to consider it Bethany's fault that they were dead, but another part of her knew that it was not true, that what she had done had made no difference one way or the other.

Margaret remembered Bethany's photograph from her file: long thick straight shining hair, round almost chubby face, big smile, large light brown eyes full of trust and confidence. She had looked like a completely different person. She had been a seventeen-year-old university student majoring in pharmacology when the draft law had been amended to make the minimum age fifteen instead of eighteen and to include women as well as men. She had right away filed for conscientious objector status, on secular moral grounds rather than theological. In her statement she had quoted Jesus, Buddha, Gandhi, Thoreau, and others, but by then it hadn't mattered what personal convictions she'd held: conscientious objection had been officially abolished. The choices had been military service or prison.

Bethany heard Margaret's footsteps and looked up. Without enthusiasm she said, "Well, look who's here. What brings you to my humble home?"

Margaret stood on the other side of the bars. "We're alone. We can talk."

Bethany threw the book on the bed. "Twenty-year-old almanac. Not much in the prison library. I have nothing to say to you."

Margaret wanted to shout, to order her, to force her somehow to listen, but she knew it wouldn't work. "Just give me a few minutes, please."

"I suppose I can spare a few minutes. Don't threaten me."

"I won't." Margaret slipped the key-card into the slot and went inside; when she swung the door behind her she left it open a few centimeters.

"Aren't you afraid I'm going to try to run?"

"No." Margaret sat down on the lone stool. The strong smell of the mattress combined with the stench of the filthy open toilet in the corner almost made her gag, but she managed to control the impulse. "Have you heard much recent news, Bethany?"

She chuckled humorlessly. "Just rumors. I'm denied newspapers, magazines, and TV. Does the war go on?"

Margaret nodded.

"And how goes it for our side?"

"Please don't be sarcastic with me. If you know nothing else you know it goes poorly. Otherwise why would we be conscripting prisoners into military service?"

"Or butchering them if they refuse."

"That's just supposed to be a threat to scare you into fighting."

"It's real enough to me, isn't it? And I'm still not fighting."

"Why are you so stubborn?"

"Why should I explain myself again? What's the point?"

"Sorry. Sorry." This was not how Margaret wanted things to go. "Let me give you a brief summary of what's been happening out there."

Bethany cautiously nodded. "All right."

"Around the time of your incarceration, after the fiasco with the tactical nukes, more ships landed and we planned another major offensive."

"Now that the depleted ranks were swelled with female cannon fodder."

Margaret ignored the comment and continued. "We had been developing a new type of weapon, a hand-held laser. We thought it would turn the tide. But as soon as we attacked, they retaliated with lasers that were more powerful than ours. It was another route. We lost a lot of troops. A lot."

"I'm sorry for them."

"Are you? You're certainly safer inside than out there."

"That's not why I'm here."

Margaret sighed. "All right. Well, we had still never actually *seen* them, they still used those robotic dolls that were obviously imitations of *us*, but the assumption was that somewhere in those ships there must be something of flesh and blood – or some kind of biological life, anyway, and so somebody proposed that we try to hit them with bacteriological warfare – try to burn them out from the inside. We tried it. We threw everything we could think of at them. Only it didn't work. And when we were done, they unleashed a plague that destroyed about half the world's remaining population."

"So everything you hit them with, they send back at you, only more so."

"That's the way it's been so far. As a matter of fact, a group of mathematicians put all the data into a computer, and as close as they can figure it whatever we do to them, they do exactly double back to us."

"Did they *ever* initiate an attack?"

"At first we were convinced that they had started it all, back when they were just circling the Earth and the missiles began to fly. But upon further analysis we think maybe our automatic orbiting defense system may have fired the first shot."

"So they have only been countering your moves."

"It seems so. I got up close to one of their ships once. It was many-sided, like a cut diamond or something, and it was dark. But the strangest thing was how reflective it was. I could see myself and everything else around as if in a huge mirror. And that's like what they seem to be doing in the war: they reflect and magnify everything we do."

"You should have done nothing."

"It's too late for that now."

"Too late for you. Not for me."

"You still have no compassion for your fellow humans? Remember, these are not people we're fighting, but something else, something – alien."

"What's the difference? Obviously they're intelligent. And anyway, is it doing any good to fight them?"

"Look, I know how you feel. You're right: I've read your file, I've read transcripts of interviews, I've traced your family history as far back as I could."

Bethany smiled, still without warmth. "Why would you be so interested in one little Conscientious Objector? No one has cared until now. I've been thrown in with these crazy-ass wackos and forgotten."

Margaret raised her hands in a gesture of futility. "We're bolstering armies with prisoners, old folks, pre-teens, the insane – anyone we can grab. But we know it won't do any good. Face-to-face, or I guess I should say face to no-face, we know we're no match for them. So we've been brainstorming, trying to come up with something unusual, unconventional, something wild and unexpected we could try. And that's when we thought of you."

"Me?" For the first time since Margaret had met her an unguarded emotion crossed Bethany's face: surprise.

"Well, not just you. People like you."

"I was led to believe I was unique. An anomaly, an abnormality."

"No. There are quite a few others, both men and women."

"And they are all willing, like me, to be dismembered rather than fight?"

"Yes."

"If that doesn't beat everything. You isolated us from each other to break down our wills, to make us think that we were all alone. Unity would only strengthen our convictions, right?"

"That's right. Only now... Only now..."

Comprehension lit up Bethany's face. "You want to send us to them. You're hoping they'll mirror the way *we* feel. If they do they'll stop fighting. They might even pack up and go home."

Margaret nodded. "We want to surrender, to plead for mercy, but there's no one to surrender to. We figure if we send you to them, they might pick up our intentions."

For a moment Bethany was incredulous, then she started to cry. "You bastards! You bastards! After all I've been through – after all *we've* been through – you ask us to walk right out to the enemy and try to save the world!"

"I'm sorry," Margaret said. "I..."

Wiping her tear-stained face, with a chuckle that sounded like a sob, Bethany said, "This must have killed you. This must have just killed an old military warhorse like you to come here and tell me this."

In her confusion of emotions Margaret was finding it hard to keep her composure. "It... It's a last resort."

"Meaning that if you had your way you'd blow them to hell first, right?"

"We've been trying to defend our country, our world."

"But it hasn't worked." Bethany grabbed some toilet paper and wiped her eyes, blew her nose. "Have you talked to the others? What do they say?"

"What do *you* say?"

"I say why should I? You say either I do this or I'll be torn to pieces. Forget it. You're not worth saving. Let *them* have this messed-up world. Maybe they'll do better with it than we have."

"It's not like that."

"What do you mean?"

"I mean the dismemberment. It was just a threat. We never intended to do it."

"What?"

"We had to know who was sincere and who was just a coward."

Bethany shook her head in disbelief. "You still don't understand, do you? Maybe you never will."

"I'm trying to."

"And if you're not going to cut us up if we refuse to help, what *are* you going to do with us?"

"Nothing."

"Nothing?"

"We realized for this to have any chance to work it must be sincere – completely voluntary. As of this moment you are a free woman, whether you choose to help us or not."

"You're kidding. Do you mean I can just walk out that cell door and out of this prison and never look back?"

"Yes. Well, you'd have to come with me to the warden's office first to sign some forms."

Bethany sat motionless, still as a statue, her jaws set in a frown of concentration, rivulets of tears gleaming on her cheeks. Finally she spoke in a low voice. "If we did this, there would be no tricks, right? No hidden bombs or bugs on us, no backstabbing them if they drop their weapons."

"No."

"You powers-that-be are behind it? You're willing to back it for the long term?"

"Yes."

"What's your name? You never told me your name."

"Margaret Keller."

"Are you, Margaret, personally, willing to unequivocally turn your sword into a plowshare? Figuratively speaking, of course."

Margaret hesitated before saying, "Yes."

"I see. You'll do it, but reluctantly. I guess that's the best that can be expected at this stage. How soon are you planning to try it?"

"As soon as possible. As soon as we assemble the team. Volunteers are being sought out around the world, everywhere where ships have landed. When everyone is ready we'll synchronize the advance."

Bethany thought again for a time and then said, "I miss my mother. I want to go home."

"That's understandable."

"Can we leave now?"

"All right."

Margaret swung the door open, and Bethany stepped gingerly through, as if unsure whether she really had permission to do so or not. She waited for Margaret to come alongside her before she went farther.

Margaret hesitated. "Uh... I seem to have lost my sense of direction. Which way?"

"This way. Come on." They turned right towards an intersection of corridors. Some of the ceiling fixtures ahead had been smashed, so that part of the hall was in shadow, and part washed in pale yellow light.

They had gone but a few steps when five women in gray prison coveralls appeared from around a corner and blocked their way. Two were black, one looked Hispanic, and two were white. They all brandished makeshift weapons: steel pipes from bunk frames, and metal scraps shaped like knives, taped at one end for a handle and sharpened at the other.

A tall heavy-set black woman tapped her pipe rhythmically on the palm of her hand. "Where you goin', Bethy?" she said. "We haven't said goodbye yet."

"Back off," Margaret said. "My business is only with Bethany. Stay out of it."

The woman continued the thump of pipe on palm. "Well, our business is with Bethany too. And if you don't want some of it yourself, *you'd* better back off. Don't you know what she is? She's a coward."

"No, Emma," said Bethany. "I'm not a coward. I'm willing to be dismembered. You're the ones who ran away."

Emma gripped her pipe with both hands and raised it over her head. "Why, you bitch!"

Bethany began to slowly walk towards the prisoners. "It's natural to be scared, Emma. Everyone's scared. Even those who pretend they're not."

Emma half-lowered the pipe and said, "Don't be callin' *me* a coward."

"All right. I'm sorry. Please let us pass."

For a moment Margaret was mesmerized. She had considered Bethany a coward, nothing more, yet here she was advancing on women who had already announced their intention of thrashing or possibly even killing her. And the women, spellbound by her boldness, were slowly stepping back, and even lowering their weapons. It looked like they would make it past the prisoners unscathed.

But then Margaret's training reasserted itself. Bethany was a part of the larger plan now, and too valuable to take a chance with. She drew her pistol, held it at arm's length, and shouted, "I said back off! Do it now!"

The Hispanic woman shouted, "She's got a gun!" They all raised their weapons again, as if they were going to charge Margaret.

Five deafening shots boomed through the corridor.

For a timeless moment Margaret became disoriented, and imagined herself on a battlefield, with bombs exploding, bullets flying, smoke filling the air, and all around the stench of burning flesh.

Then there was a long silence.

When her vision cleared Margaret saw that four of the women lay still on the floor, shots to the head having killed them instantly. Emma, however, was bleeding from the chest, and more blood gathered between her lips and flowed down her cheek; Bethany sat in the mud and blood cradling Emma's head in her lap, looking into Emma's frightened eyes.

Margaret's arm fell to her side; the pistol dropped to the floor with a loud clatter. Then the only sound was Emma's quiet bubbling cough.

From a distant corridor came shouts and footfalls.

Bethany raised her head and looked at Margaret. "You don't deserve it," she said. "You don't deserve to be saved."

* * *

For months the enemy had been dormant.

The time had come.

The plain was littered with the debris of old battles: crumpled and rusting vehicles, shattered weapons, bits and shreds of materials and components of the robotic soldiers the enemy used to fight for them. In the distance, at the edge of the sere hills, sat three of the enemy's dark multifaceted ships.

Some people were milling about, some standing still; some were talking, some silent. They were men and women, young and old, black, brown, and white, tall and short, fat and thin, some bald and some with hair down to their waists, some with tattoos, some with bangles and beads and necklaces and bracelets and earrings and nose rings and rings in their lips; some were formally dressed and some casually, some sported clothes with wild flamboyant colors and some were scarcely dressed at all.

It was almost time to start. Margaret hurried through the crowd, searching.

Then she saw her, standing by herself gazing at the dark ships. She wore brown leather sandals, blue jeans, and a pink blouse. The scar and bruise-marks were still on her face, but she looked healthier, more robust, like she'd been eating well and had filled out.

"Bethany."

Margaret had expected bitterness and animosity, but Bethany merely smiled. "Oh. Hello."

"What made you change your mind?"

"Well, it's true what I said, that you don't deserve to be saved. But then, none of us do."

"You must hate me."

"No. How could I walk out now with these others if I did?"

"I came to say…" Margaret's voice broke; she hesitated and tried again. "I came to say I'm sorry."

"There were times at the prison, after they had worked me over, that I wanted to kill them too."

"But I…"

"It's all right." Bethany hugged her, and kissed her cheek. "Come. Walk with me."

Margaret shook her head. "I can't."

"Why?"

"I have responsibilities. No, that's not the reason. I guess I'm not ready." Margaret felt the urge to cover up her confusion, so she turned and left the crowd. A three-story-high platform had been erected from which military personnel could view the outcome of the event; she rode the lift to the top.

She spotted Bethany's pink blouse; she was still standing where Margaret had left her.

The signal was given. The people below began to move slowly forward, some walking hand-in-hand, some alone, and some in groups.

Beyond, the dark ships waited.

The War of the Worlds

H.G. Wells

But who shall dwell in these worlds if they be inhabited?... Are we or they Lords of the World? ... And how are all things made for man?
Kepler (quoted in *The Anatomy of Melancholy*)

Book I – The Coming of the Martians

Chapter I
The Eve of the War

NO ONE WOULD HAVE BELIEVED in the last years of the nineteenth century that this world was being watched keenly and closely by intelligences greater than man's and yet as mortal as his own; that as men busied themselves about their various concerns they were scrutinised and studied, perhaps almost as narrowly as a man with a microscope might scrutinise the transient creatures that swarm and multiply in a drop of water. With infinite complacency men went to and fro over this globe about their little affairs, serene in their assurance of their empire over matter. It is possible that the infusoria under the microscope do the same. No one gave a thought to the older worlds of space as sources of human danger, or thought of them only to dismiss the idea of life upon them as impossible or improbable. It is curious to recall some of the mental habits of those departed days. At most terrestrial men fancied there might be other men upon Mars, perhaps inferior to themselves and ready to welcome a missionary enterprise. Yet across the gulf of space, minds that are to our minds as ours are to those of the beasts that perish, intellects vast and cool and unsympathetic, regarded this earth with envious eyes, and slowly and surely drew their plans against us. And early in the twentieth century came the great disillusionment.

The planet Mars, I scarcely need remind the reader, revolves about the sun at a mean distance of 140,000,000 miles, and the light and heat it receives from the sun is barely half of that received by this world. It must be, if the nebular hypothesis has any truth, older than our world; and long before this earth ceased to be molten, life upon its surface must have begun its course. The fact that it is scarcely one seventh of the volume of the earth must have accelerated its cooling to the temperature at which life could begin. It has air and water and all that is necessary for the support of animated existence.

Yet so vain is man, and so blinded by his vanity, that no writer, up to the very end of the nineteenth century, expressed any idea that intelligent life might have developed there far, or indeed at all, beyond its earthly level. Nor was it generally understood that since Mars is older than our earth, with scarcely a quarter of the superficial area and remoter from the sun, it necessarily follows that it is not only more distant from time's beginning but nearer its end.

The secular cooling that must someday overtake our planet has already gone far indeed with our neighbour. Its physical condition is still largely a mystery, but we know now that even in its equatorial region the midday temperature barely approaches that of our coldest winter. Its air is much more attenuated than ours, its oceans have shrunk until they cover but a third of its surface, and as its slow seasons change huge snowcaps gather and melt about either pole and periodically inundate its temperate zones. That last stage of exhaustion, which to us is still incredibly remote, has become a present-day problem for the inhabitants of Mars. The immediate pressure of necessity has brightened their intellects, enlarged their powers, and hardened their hearts. And looking across space with instruments, and intelligences such as we have scarcely dreamed of, they see, at its nearest distance only 35,000,000 of miles sunward of them, a morning star of hope, our own warmer planet, green with vegetation and grey with water, with a cloudy atmosphere eloquent of fertility, with glimpses through its drifting cloud wisps of broad stretches of populous country and narrow, navy-crowded seas.

And we men, the creatures who inhabit this earth, must be to them at least as alien and lowly as are the monkeys and lemurs to us. The intellectual side of man already admits that life is an incessant struggle for existence, and it would seem that this too is the belief of the minds upon Mars. Their world is far gone in its cooling and this world is still crowded with life, but crowded only with what they regard as inferior animals. To carry warfare sunward is, indeed, their only escape from the destruction that, generation after generation, creeps upon them.

And before we judge of them too harshly we must remember what ruthless and utter destruction our own species has wrought, not only upon animals, such as the vanished bison and the dodo, but upon its inferior races. The Tasmanians, in spite of their human likeness, were entirely swept out of existence in a war of extermination waged by European immigrants, in the space of fifty years. Are we such apostles of mercy as to complain if the Martians warred in the same spirit?

The Martians seem to have calculated their descent with amazing subtlety – their mathematical learning is evidently far in excess of ours – and to have carried out their preparations with a well-nigh perfect unanimity. Had our instruments permitted it, we might have seen the gathering trouble far back in the nineteenth century. Men like Schiaparelli watched the red planet – it is odd, by-the-bye, that for countless centuries Mars has been the star of war – but failed to interpret the fluctuating appearances of the markings they mapped so well. All that time the Martians must have been getting ready.

During the opposition of 1894 a great light was seen on the illuminated part of the disk, first at the Lick Observatory, then by Perrotin of Nice, and then by other observers. English readers heard of it first in the issue of *Nature* dated August 2. I am inclined to think that this blaze may have been the casting of the huge gun, in the vast pit sunk into their planet, from which their shots were fired at us. Peculiar markings, as yet unexplained, were seen near the site of that outbreak during the next two oppositions.

The storm burst upon us six years ago now. As Mars approached opposition, Lavelle of Java set the wires of the astronomical exchange palpitating with the amazing intelligence of a huge outbreak of incandescent gas upon the planet. It had occurred towards midnight of the twelfth; and the spectroscope, to which he had at once resorted, indicated a mass of flaming gas, chiefly hydrogen, moving with an enormous velocity towards this earth. This jet of fire had become invisible about a quarter past twelve. He compared it to a colossal puff of flame suddenly and violently squirted out of the planet, 'as flaming gases rushed out of a gun.'

A singularly appropriate phrase it proved. Yet the next day there was nothing of this in the papers except a little note in the *Daily Telegraph*, and the world went in ignorance of one of the gravest dangers that ever threatened the human race. I might not have heard of the eruption at all had I not met Ogilvy, the well-known astronomer, at Ottershaw. He was immensely excited at the news, and in the excess of his feelings invited me up to take a turn with him that night in a scrutiny of the red planet.

In spite of all that has happened since, I still remember that vigil very distinctly: the black and silent observatory, the shadowed lantern throwing a feeble glow upon the floor in the corner, the steady ticking of the clockwork of the telescope, the little slit in the roof – an oblong profundity with the stardust streaked across it. Ogilvy moved about, invisible but audible. Looking through the telescope, one saw a circle of deep blue and the little round planet swimming in the field. It seemed such a little thing, so bright and small and still, faintly marked with transverse stripes, and slightly flattened from the perfect round. But so little it was, so silvery warm – a pin's-head of light! It was as if it quivered, but really this was the telescope vibrating with the activity of the clockwork that kept the planet in view.

As I watched, the planet seemed to grow larger and smaller and to advance and recede, but that was simply that my eye was tired. Forty millions of miles it was from us – more than forty millions of miles of void. Few people realise the immensity of vacancy in which the dust of the material universe swims.

Near it in the field, I remember, were three faint points of light, three telescopic stars infinitely remote, and all around it was the unfathomable darkness of empty space. You know how that blackness looks on a frosty starlight night. In a telescope it seems far profounder. And invisible to me because it was so remote and small, flying swiftly and steadily towards me across that incredible distance, drawing nearer every minute by so many thousands of miles, came the Thing they were sending us, the Thing that was to bring so much struggle and calamity and death to the earth. I never dreamed of it then as I watched; no one on earth dreamed of that unerring missile.

That night, too, there was another jetting out of gas from the distant planet. I saw it. A reddish flash at the edge, the slightest projection of the outline just as the chronometer struck midnight; and at that I told Ogilvy and he took my place. The night was warm and I was thirsty, and I went stretching my legs clumsily and feeling my way in the darkness, to the little table where the siphon stood, while Ogilvy exclaimed at the streamer of gas that came out towards us.

That night another invisible missile started on its way to the earth from Mars, just a second or so under twenty-four hours after the first one. I remember how I sat on the table there in the blackness, with patches of green and crimson swimming before my eyes. I wished I had a light to smoke by, little suspecting the meaning of the minute gleam I had seen and all that it would presently bring me. Ogilvy watched till one, and then gave it up; and we lit the lantern and walked over to his house. Down below in the darkness were Ottershaw and Chertsey and all their hundreds of people, sleeping in peace.

He was full of speculation that night about the condition of Mars, and scoffed at the vulgar idea of its having inhabitants who were signalling us. His idea was that meteorites might be falling in a heavy shower upon the planet, or that a huge volcanic explosion was in progress. He pointed out to me how unlikely it was that organic evolution had taken the same direction in the two adjacent planets.

"The chances against anything manlike on Mars are a million to one," he said.

Hundreds of observers saw the flame that night and the night after about midnight, and again the night after; and so for ten nights, a flame each night. Why the shots ceased after the tenth no one on earth has attempted to explain. It may be the gases of the firing caused the Martians inconvenience. Dense clouds of smoke or dust, visible through a powerful telescope on earth as little grey, fluctuating patches, spread through the clearness of the planet's atmosphere and obscured its more familiar features.

Even the daily papers woke up to the disturbances at last, and popular notes appeared here, there, and everywhere concerning the volcanoes upon Mars. The seriocomic periodical *Punch*, I remember, made a happy use of it in the political cartoon. And, all unsuspected, those missiles the Martians had fired at us drew earthward, rushing now at a pace of many miles a second through the empty gulf of space, hour by hour and day by day, nearer and nearer. It seems to me now almost incredibly wonderful that, with that swift fate hanging over us, men could go about their petty concerns as they did. I remember how jubilant Markham was at securing a new photograph of the planet for the illustrated paper he edited in those days. People in these latter times scarcely realise the abundance and enterprise of our nineteenth-century papers. For my own part, I was much occupied in learning to ride the bicycle, and busy upon a series of papers discussing the probable developments of moral ideas as civilisation progressed.

One night (the first missile then could scarcely have been 10,000,000 miles away) I went for a walk with my wife. It was starlight and I explained the Signs of the Zodiac to her, and pointed out Mars, a bright dot of light creeping zenithward, towards which so many telescopes were pointed. It was a warm night. Coming home, a party of excursionists from Chertsey or Isleworth passed us singing and playing music. There were lights in the upper windows of the houses as the people went to bed. From the railway station in the distance came the sound of shunting trains, ringing and rumbling, softened almost into melody by the distance. My wife pointed out to me the brightness of the red, green, and yellow signal lights hanging in a framework against the sky. It seemed so safe and tranquil.

Chapter II
The Falling Star

THEN CAME THE NIGHT of the first falling star. It was seen early in the morning, rushing over Winchester eastward, a line of flame high in the atmosphere. Hundreds must have seen it, and taken it for an ordinary falling star. Albin described it as leaving a greenish streak behind it that glowed for some seconds. Denning, our greatest authority on meteorites, stated that the height of its first appearance was about ninety or one hundred miles. It seemed to him that it fell to earth about one hundred miles east of him.

I was at home at that hour and writing in my study; and although my French windows face towards Ottershaw and the blind was up (for I loved in those days to look up at the night sky), I saw nothing of it. Yet this strangest of all things that ever came to earth from outer space must have fallen while I was sitting there, visible to me had I only looked up as it passed. Some of those who saw its flight say it travelled with a hissing sound. I myself heard nothing of that. Many people in Berkshire, Surrey, and Middlesex must have seen the fall of it, and, at most, have thought that another meteorite had descended. No one seems to have troubled to look for the fallen mass that night.

But very early in the morning poor Ogilvy, who had seen the shooting star and who was persuaded that a meteorite lay somewhere on the common between Horsell, Ottershaw, and Woking, rose early with the idea of finding it. Find it he did, soon after dawn, and not far from the sand pits. An enormous hole had been made by the impact of the projectile, and the sand and gravel had been flung violently in every direction over the heath, forming heaps visible a mile and a half away. The heather was on fire eastward, and a thin blue smoke rose against the dawn.

The Thing itself lay almost entirely buried in sand, amidst the scattered splinters of a fir tree it had shivered to fragments in its descent. The uncovered part had the appearance of a huge cylinder, caked over and its outline softened by a thick scaly dun-coloured incrustation. It had a diameter of about thirty yards. He approached the mass, surprised at the size and more so at the shape, since most meteorites are rounded more or less completely. It was, however, still so hot from its flight through the air as to forbid his near approach. A stirring noise within its cylinder he ascribed to the unequal cooling of its surface; for at that time it had not occurred to him that it might be hollow.

He remained standing at the edge of the pit that the Thing had made for itself, staring at its strange appearance, astonished chiefly at its unusual shape and colour, and dimly perceiving even then some evidence of design in its arrival. The early morning was wonderfully still, and the sun, just clearing the pine trees towards Weybridge, was already warm. He did not remember hearing any birds that morning, there was certainly no breeze stirring, and the only sounds were the faint movements from within the cindery cylinder. He was all alone on the common.

Then suddenly he noticed with a start that some of the grey clinker, the ashy incrustation that covered the meteorite, was falling off the circular edge of the end. It was dropping off in flakes and raining down upon the sand. A large piece suddenly came off and fell with a sharp noise that brought his heart into his mouth.

For a minute he scarcely realised what this meant, and, although the heat was excessive, he clambered down into the pit close to the bulk to see the Thing more clearly. He fancied even then that the cooling of the body might account for this, but what disturbed that idea was the fact that the ash was falling only from the end of the cylinder.

And then he perceived that, very slowly, the circular top of the cylinder was rotating on its body. It was such a gradual movement that he discovered it only through noticing that a black mark that had been near him five minutes ago was now at the other side of the circumference. Even then he scarcely understood what this indicated, until he heard a muffled grating sound and saw the black mark jerk forward an inch or so. Then the thing came upon him in a flash. The cylinder was artificial – hollow – with an end that screwed out! Something within the cylinder was unscrewing the top!

"Good heavens!" said Ogilvy. "There's a man in it – men in it! Half roasted to death! Trying to escape!"

At once, with a quick mental leap, he linked the Thing with the flash upon Mars.

The thought of the confined creature was so dreadful to him that he forgot the heat and went forward to the cylinder to help turn. But luckily the dull radiation arrested him before he could burn his hands on the still-glowing metal. At that he stood irresolute for a moment, then turned, scrambled out of the pit, and set off running wildly into Woking. The time then must have been somewhere about six o'clock. He met a waggoner and tried to make him understand, but the tale he told and his appearance were so wild – his hat had fallen off in the pit – that the man simply drove on. He was equally unsuccessful with the potman who was just unlocking the doors of the public-house by Horsell Bridge. The fellow thought he was a lunatic at large and made an unsuccessful attempt to shut him into the taproom. That sobered him a little; and when he saw Henderson, the London journalist, in his garden, he called over the palings and made himself understood.

"Henderson," he called, "you saw that shooting star last night?"

"Well?" said Henderson.

"It's out on Horsell Common now."

"Good Lord!" said Henderson. "Fallen meteorite! That's good."

"But it's something more than a meteorite. It's a cylinder – an artificial cylinder, man! And there's something inside."

Henderson stood up with his spade in his hand.

"What's that?" he said. He was deaf in one ear.

Ogilvy told him all that he had seen. Henderson was a minute or so taking it in. Then he dropped his spade, snatched up his jacket, and came out into the road. The two men hurried back at once to the common, and found the cylinder still lying in the same position. But now the sounds inside had ceased, and a thin circle of bright metal showed between the top and the body of the cylinder. Air was either entering or escaping at the rim with a thin, sizzling sound.

They listened, rapped on the scaly burnt metal with a stick, and, meeting with no response, they both concluded the man or men inside must be insensible or dead.

Of course the two were quite unable to do anything. They shouted consolation and promises, and went off back to the town again to get help. One can imagine them, covered with sand, excited and disordered, running up the little street in the bright sunlight just as the shop folks were taking down their shutters and people were opening their bedroom windows. Henderson went into the railway station at once, in order to telegraph the news to London. The newspaper articles had prepared men's minds for the reception of the idea.

By eight o'clock a number of boys and unemployed men had already started for the common to see the "dead men from Mars." That was the form the story took. I heard of it first from my newspaper boy about a quarter to nine when I went out to get my *Daily Chronicle*. I was naturally startled, and lost no time in going out and across the Ottershaw bridge to the sand pits.

Chapter III
On Horsell Common

I FOUND A LITTLE CROWD of perhaps twenty people surrounding the huge hole in which the cylinder lay. I have already described the appearance of that colossal bulk, embedded in the ground. The turf and gravel about it seemed charred as if by a sudden explosion. No doubt its impact had caused a flash of fire. Henderson and Ogilvy were not there. I think they perceived that nothing was to be done for the present, and had gone away to breakfast at Henderson's house.

There were four or five boys sitting on the edge of the Pit, with their feet dangling, and amusing themselves – until I stopped them – by throwing stones at the giant mass. After I had spoken to them about it, they began playing at 'touch' in and out of the group of bystanders.

Among these were a couple of cyclists, a jobbing gardener I employed sometimes, a girl carrying a baby, Gregg the butcher and his little boy, and two or three loafers and golf caddies who were accustomed to hang about the railway station. There was very little talking. Few of the common people in England had anything but the vaguest astronomical ideas in those days. Most of them were staring quietly at the big table like end of the cylinder, which was still as Ogilvy and Henderson had left it. I fancy the popular expectation of a heap of charred corpses was disappointed at this inanimate bulk. Some went away while I was there, and other people came. I clambered into the pit and fancied I heard a faint movement under my feet. The top had certainly ceased to rotate.

It was only when I got thus close to it that the strangeness of this object was at all evident to me. At the first glance it was really no more exciting than an overturned carriage or a tree blown across the road. Not so much so, indeed. It looked like a rusty gas float. It required a certain amount of scientific education to perceive that the grey scale of the Thing was no common oxide, that the yellowish-white metal that gleamed in the crack between the lid and the cylinder had an unfamiliar hue. 'Extra-terrestrial' had no meaning for most of the onlookers.

At that time it was quite clear in my own mind that the Thing had come from the planet Mars, but I judged it improbable that it contained any living creature. I thought the unscrewing might be automatic. In spite of Ogilvy, I still believed that there were men in Mars. My mind ran fancifully on the possibilities of its containing manuscript, on the difficulties in translation that might arise, whether we should find coins and models in it, and so forth. Yet it was a little too large for assurance on this idea. I felt an impatience to see it opened. About eleven, as nothing seemed happening, I walked back, full of such thought, to my home in Maybury. But I found it difficult to get to work upon my abstract investigations.

In the afternoon the appearance of the common had altered very much. The early editions of the evening papers had startled London with enormous headlines:

A MESSAGE RECEIVED FROM MARS

REMARKABLE STORY FROM WOKING

and so forth. In addition, Ogilvy's wire to the Astronomical Exchange had roused every observatory in the three kingdoms.

There were half a dozen flies or more from the Woking station standing in the road by the sand pits, a basket-chaise from Chobham, and a rather lordly carriage. Besides that, there was quite a heap of bicycles. In addition, a large number of people must have walked, in spite of the heat of the day, from Woking and Chertsey, so that there was altogether quite a considerable crowd – one or two gaily dressed ladies among the others.

It was glaringly hot, not a cloud in the sky nor a breath of wind, and the only shadow was that of the few scattered pine trees. The burning heather had been extinguished, but the level ground towards Ottershaw was blackened as far as one could see, and still giving off vertical streamers of smoke. An enterprising sweet-stuff dealer in the Chobham Road had sent up his son with a barrow-load of green apples and ginger beer.

Going to the edge of the pit, I found it occupied by a group of about half a dozen men – Henderson, Ogilvy, and a tall, fair-haired man that I afterwards learned was Stent, the Astronomer Royal, with several workmen wielding spades and pickaxes. Stent was giving directions in a clear, high-pitched voice. He was standing on the cylinder, which was now evidently much cooler; his face was crimson and streaming with perspiration, and something seemed to have irritated him.

A large portion of the cylinder had been uncovered, though its lower end was still embedded. As soon as Ogilvy saw me among the staring crowd on the edge of the pit he called to me to come down, and asked me if I would mind going over to see Lord Hilton, the lord of the manor.

The growing crowd, he said, was becoming a serious impediment to their excavations, especially the boys. They wanted a light railing put up, and help to keep the people back. He told me that a faint stirring was occasionally still audible within the case, but that the workmen had failed to unscrew the top, as it afforded no grip to them. The case appeared to be enormously thick, and it was possible that the faint sounds we heard represented a noisy tumult in the interior.

I was very glad to do as he asked, and so become one of the privileged spectators within the contemplated enclosure. I failed to find Lord Hilton at his house, but I was told he was expected from London by the six o'clock train from Waterloo; and as it was then about a quarter past five, I went home, had some tea, and walked up to the station to waylay him.

Chapter IV
The Cylinder Opens

WHEN I RETURNED to the common the sun was setting. Scattered groups were hurrying from the direction of Woking, and one or two persons were returning. The crowd about the pit had increased, and stood out black against the lemon yellow of the sky – a couple of hundred people, perhaps. There were raised voices, and some sort of struggle appeared to be going on about the pit. Strange imaginings passed through my mind. As I drew nearer I heard Stent's voice:

"Keep back! Keep back!"

A boy came running towards me.

"It's a-movin'," he said to me as he passed; "a-screwin' and a-screwin' out. I don't like it. I'm a-goin' 'ome, I am."

I went on to the crowd. There were really, I should think, two or three hundred people elbowing and jostling one another, the one or two ladies there being by no means the least active.

"He's fallen in the pit!" cried some one.

"Keep back!" said several.

The crowd swayed a little, and I elbowed my way through. Every one seemed greatly excited. I heard a peculiar humming sound from the pit.

"I say!" said Ogilvy; "help keep these idiots back. We don't know what's in the confounded thing, you know!"

I saw a young man, a shop assistant in Woking I believe he was, standing on the cylinder and trying to scramble out of the hole again. The crowd had pushed him in.

The end of the cylinder was being screwed out from within. Nearly two feet of shining screw projected. Somebody blundered against me, and I narrowly missed being pitched onto the top of the screw. I turned, and as I did so the screw must have come out, for the lid of the cylinder fell upon the gravel with a ringing concussion. I stuck my elbow into the person behind me, and turned my head towards the Thing again. For a moment that circular cavity seemed perfectly black. I had the sunset in my eyes.

I think everyone expected to see a man emerge – possibly something a little unlike us terrestrial men, but in all essentials a man. I know I did. But, looking, I presently saw something stirring within the shadow: greyish billowy movements, one above another, and then two luminous disks – like eyes. Then something resembling a little grey snake, about the thickness of a walking stick, coiled up out of the writhing middle, and wriggled in the air towards me – and then another.

A sudden chill came over me. There was a loud shriek from a woman behind. I half turned, keeping my eyes fixed upon the cylinder still, from which other tentacles were now projecting, and began pushing my way back from the edge of the pit. I saw astonishment giving place to horror on the faces of the people about me. I heard inarticulate exclamations on all sides. There was a general movement backwards. I saw the shopman struggling still on the edge of the pit. I found myself alone, and saw the people on the other side of the pit running off, Stent among them. I looked again at the cylinder, and ungovernable terror gripped me. I stood petrified and staring.

A big greyish rounded bulk, the size, perhaps, of a bear, was rising slowly and painfully out of the cylinder. As it bulged up and caught the light, it glistened like wet leather.

Two large dark-coloured eyes were regarding me steadfastly. The mass that framed them, the head of the thing, was rounded, and had, one might say, a face. There was a mouth under the eyes, the lipless brim of which quivered and panted, and dropped saliva. The whole creature heaved and pulsated convulsively. A lank tentacular appendage gripped the edge of the cylinder, another swayed in the air.

Those who have never seen a living Martian can scarcely imagine the strange horror of its appearance. The peculiar V-shaped mouth with its pointed upper lip, the absence of brow ridges, the absence of a chin beneath the wedgelike lower lip, the incessant quivering of this mouth, the Gorgon groups of tentacles, the tumultuous breathing of the lungs in a strange atmosphere, the evident heaviness and painfulness of movement due to the greater gravitational energy of the earth – above all, the extraordinary intensity of the immense eyes – were at once vital, intense, inhuman, crippled and monstrous. There was something fungoid in the oily brown skin, something in the clumsy deliberation of the tedious movements unspeakably nasty. Even at this first encounter, this first glimpse, I was overcome with disgust and dread.

Suddenly the monster vanished. It had toppled over the brim of the cylinder and fallen into the pit, with a thud like the fall of a great mass of leather. I heard it give a peculiar thick cry, and forthwith another of these creatures appeared darkly in the deep shadow of the aperture.

I turned and, running madly, made for the first group of trees, perhaps a hundred yards away; but I ran slantingly and stumbling, for I could not avert my face from these things.

There, among some young pine trees and furze bushes, I stopped, panting, and waited further developments. The common round the sand pits was dotted with people, standing like myself in a half-fascinated terror, staring at these creatures, or rather at the heaped gravel at the edge of the pit in which they lay. And then, with a renewed horror, I saw a round, black object bobbing up and down on the edge of the pit. It was the head of the shopman who had fallen in, but showing as a little black object against the hot western sun. Now he got his shoulder and knee up, and again he seemed to slip back until only his head was visible. Suddenly he vanished, and I could have fancied a faint shriek had reached me. I had a momentary impulse to go back and help him that my fears overruled.

Everything was then quite invisible, hidden by the deep pit and the heap of sand that the fall of the cylinder had made. Anyone coming along the road from Chobham or Woking would have been amazed at the sight – a dwindling multitude of perhaps a hundred people or more standing in a great irregular circle, in ditches, behind bushes, behind gates and hedges, saying little to one another and that in short, excited shouts, and staring, staring hard at a few heaps of sand. The barrow of ginger beer stood, a queer derelict, black against the burning sky, and in the sand pits was a row of deserted vehicles with their horses feeding out of nosebags or pawing the ground.

Chapter V
The Heat-Ray

AFTER THE GLIMPSE I had had of the Martians emerging from the cylinder in which they had come to the earth from their planet, a kind of fascination paralysed my actions. I remained standing knee-deep in the heather, staring at the mound that hid them. I was a battleground of fear and curiosity.

I did not dare to go back towards the pit, but I felt a passionate longing to peer into it. I began walking, therefore, in a big curve, seeking some point of vantage and continually looking at the sand heaps that hid these new-comers to our earth. Once a leash of thin black whips, like the arms of an octopus, flashed across the sunset and was immediately withdrawn, and afterwards a thin rod rose up, joint by joint, bearing at its apex a circular disk that spun with a wobbling motion. What could be going on there?

Most of the spectators had gathered in one or two groups – one a little crowd towards Woking, the other a knot of people in the direction of Chobham. Evidently they shared my mental conflict. There were few near me. One man I approached – he was, I perceived, a neighbour of mine, though I did not know his name – and accosted. But it was scarcely a time for articulate conversation.

"What ugly brutes!" he said. "Good God! What ugly brutes!" He repeated this over and over again.

"Did you see a man in the pit?" I said; but he made no answer to that. We became silent, and stood watching for a time side by side, deriving, I fancy, a certain comfort in one another's company. Then I shifted my position to a little knoll that gave me the advantage of a yard or more of elevation and when I looked for him presently he was walking towards Woking.

The sunset faded to twilight before anything further happened. The crowd far away on the left, towards Woking, seemed to grow, and I heard now a faint murmur from it. The little knot of people towards Chobham dispersed. There was scarcely an intimation of movement from the pit.

It was this, as much as anything, that gave people courage, and I suppose the new arrivals from Woking also helped to restore confidence. At any rate, as the dusk came on a slow, intermittent movement upon the sand pits began, a movement that seemed to gather force as the stillness of the evening about the cylinder remained unbroken. Vertical black figures in twos and threes would advance, stop, watch, and advance again, spreading out as they did so in a thin irregular crescent that promised to enclose the pit in its attenuated horns. I, too, on my side began to move towards the pit.

Then I saw some cabmen and others had walked boldly into the sand pits, and heard the clatter of hoofs and the gride of wheels. I saw a lad trundling off the barrow of apples. And then, within thirty yards of the pit, advancing from the direction of Horsell, I noted a little black knot of men, the foremost of whom was waving a white flag.

This was the Deputation. There had been a hasty consultation, and since the Martians were evidently, in spite of their repulsive forms, intelligent creatures, it had been resolved to show them, by approaching them with signals, that we too were intelligent.

Flutter, flutter, went the flag, first to the right, then to the left. It was too far for me to recognise anyone there, but afterwards I learned that Ogilvy, Stent, and Henderson were with others in this attempt at communication. This little group had in its advance dragged inward, so to speak, the circumference of the now almost complete circle of people, and a number of dim black figures followed it at discreet distances.

Suddenly there was a flash of light, and a quantity of luminous greenish smoke came out of the pit in three distinct puffs, which drove up, one after the other, straight into the still air.

This smoke (or flame, perhaps, would be the better word for it) was so bright that the deep blue sky overhead and the hazy stretches of brown common towards Chertsey, set with black pine trees, seemed to darken abruptly as these puffs arose, and to remain the darker after their dispersal. At the same time a faint hissing sound became audible.

Beyond the pit stood the little wedge of people with the white flag at its apex, arrested by these phenomena, a little knot of small vertical black shapes upon the black ground. As the green smoke arose, their faces flashed out pallid green, and faded again as it vanished. Then slowly the hissing passed into a humming, into a long, loud, droning noise. Slowly a humped shape rose out of the pit, and the ghost of a beam of light seemed to flicker out from it.

Forthwith flashes of actual flame, a bright glare leaping from one to another, sprang from the scattered group of men. It was as if some invisible jet impinged upon them and flashed into white flame. It was as if each man were suddenly and momentarily turned to fire.

Then, by the light of their own destruction, I saw them staggering and falling, and their supporters turning to run.

I stood staring, not as yet realising that this was death leaping from man to man in that little distant crowd. All I felt was that it was something very strange. An almost noiseless and blinding flash of light, and a man fell headlong and lay still; and as the unseen shaft of heat passed over them, pine trees burst into fire, and every dry furze bush became with one dull thud a mass of flames. And far away towards Knaphill I saw the flashes of trees and hedges and wooden buildings suddenly set alight.

It was sweeping round swiftly and steadily, this flaming death, this invisible, inevitable sword of heat. I perceived it coming towards me by the flashing bushes it touched, and was too astounded and stupefied to stir. I heard the crackle of fire in the sand pits and the sudden squeal of a horse that was as suddenly stilled. Then it was as if an invisible yet intensely heated finger were drawn through the heather between me and the Martians, and all along a curving line beyond the sand pits the dark ground smoked and crackled. Something fell with a crash far away to the left where the road from Woking station opens out on the common. Forth-with the hissing and humming ceased, and the black, dome-like object sank slowly out of sight into the pit.

All this had happened with such swiftness that I had stood motionless, dumbfounded and dazzled by the flashes of light. Had that death swept through a full circle, it must inevitably have slain me in my surprise. But it passed and spared me, and left the night about me suddenly dark and unfamiliar.

The undulating common seemed now dark almost to blackness, except where its roadways lay grey and pale under the deep blue sky of the early night. It was dark, and suddenly void of men. Overhead the stars were mustering, and in the west the sky was still a pale, bright, almost greenish blue. The tops of the pine trees and the roofs of Horsell came out sharp and black against the western afterglow. The Martians and their appliances were altogether invisible, save for that thin mast upon which their restless mirror wobbled. Patches of bush and isolated trees here and there smoked and glowed still, and the houses towards Woking station were sending up spires of flame into the stillness of the evening air.

Nothing was changed save for that and a terrible astonishment. The little group of black specks with the flag of white had been swept out of existence, and the stillness of the evening, so it seemed to me, had scarcely been broken.

It came to me that I was upon this dark common, helpless, unprotected, and alone. Suddenly, like a thing falling upon me from without, came – fear.

With an effort I turned and began a stumbling run through the heather.

The fear I felt was no rational fear, but a panic terror not only of the Martians, but of the dusk and stillness all about me. Such an extraordinary effect in unmanning me it had that I ran weeping silently as a child might do. Once I had turned, I did not dare to look back.

I remember I felt an extraordinary persuasion that I was being played with, that presently, when I was upon the very verge of safety, this mysterious death – as swift as the passage of light – would leap after me from the pit about the cylinder and strike me down.

Chapter VI
The Heat-Ray in the Chobham Road

IT IS STILL A MATTER of wonder how the Martians are able to slay men so swiftly and so silently. Many think that in some way they are able to generate an intense heat in a chamber of practically absolute non-conductivity. This intense heat they project in a parallel beam against any object they choose, by means of a polished parabolic mirror of unknown composition, much as the parabolic mirror of a lighthouse projects a beam of light. But no one has absolutely proved these details. However it is done, it is certain that a beam of heat is the essence of the matter. Heat, and invisible, instead of visible, light. Whatever is combustible flashes into flame at its touch, lead runs like water, it softens iron, cracks and melts glass, and when it falls upon water, incontinently that explodes into steam.

That night nearly forty people lay under the starlight about the pit, charred and distorted beyond recognition, and all night long the common from Horsell to Maybury was deserted and brightly ablaze.

The news of the massacre probably reached Chobham, Woking, and Ottershaw about the same time. In Woking the shops had closed when the tragedy happened, and a number of people, shop people and so forth, attracted by the stories they had heard, were walking over the Horsell Bridge and along the road between the hedges that runs out at last upon the common. You may imagine the young people brushed up after the labours of the day, and making this novelty, as they would make any novelty, the excuse for walking together and enjoying a trivial flirtation. You may figure to yourself the hum of voices along the road in the gloaming....

As yet, of course, few people in Woking even knew that the cylinder had opened, though poor Henderson had sent a messenger on a bicycle to the post office with a special wire to an evening paper.

As these folks came out by twos and threes upon the open, they found little knots of people talking excitedly and peering at the spinning mirror over the sand pits, and the newcomers were, no doubt, soon infected by the excitement of the occasion.

By half past eight, when the Deputation was destroyed, there may have been a crowd of three hundred people or more at this place, besides those who had left the road to approach the Martians nearer. There were three policemen too, one of whom was mounted, doing their best, under instructions from Stent, to keep the people back and deter them from approaching the cylinder. There was some booing from those more thoughtless and excitable souls to whom a crowd is always an occasion for noise and horse-play.

Stent and Ogilvy, anticipating some possibilities of a collision, had telegraphed from Horsell to the barracks as soon as the Martians emerged, for the help of a company of soldiers to protect these strange creatures from violence. After that they returned to lead that ill-fated advance. The description of their death, as it was seen by the crowd, tallies very closely with my own impressions: the three puffs of green smoke, the deep humming note, and the flashes of flame.

But that crowd of people had a far narrower escape than mine. Only the fact that a hummock of heathery sand intercepted the lower part of the Heat-Ray saved them. Had the elevation of the parabolic mirror been a few yards higher, none could have lived to tell the tale. They saw the flashes and the men falling and an invisible hand, as it were, lit the bushes as it hurried towards them through the twilight. Then, with a whistling note that rose above the droning of the pit, the beam swung close over their heads, lighting the tops of the beech trees that line the road, and splitting the bricks, smashing the windows, firing the window frames, and bringing down in crumbling ruin a portion of the gable of the house nearest the corner.

In the sudden thud, hiss, and glare of the igniting trees, the panic-stricken crowd seems to have swayed hesitatingly for some moments. Sparks and burning twigs began to fall into the road, and single leaves like puffs of flame. Hats and dresses caught fire. Then came a crying from the common. There were shrieks and shouts, and suddenly a mounted policeman came galloping through the confusion with his hands clasped over his head, screaming.

"They're coming!" a woman shrieked, and incontinently everyone was turning and pushing at those behind, in order to clear their way to Woking again. They must have bolted as blindly as a flock of sheep. Where the road grows narrow and black between the high banks the crowd jammed, and a desperate struggle occurred. All that crowd did not escape; three persons at least, two women and a little boy, were crushed and trampled there, and left to die amid the terror and the darkness.

Chapter VII
How I Reached Home

FOR MY OWN PART, I remember nothing of my flight except the stress of blundering against trees and stumbling through the heather. All about me gathered the invisible terrors of the Martians; that pitiless sword of heat seemed whirling to and fro, flourishing overhead before it descended and smote me out of life. I came into the road between the crossroads and Horsell, and ran along this to the crossroads.

At last I could go no further; I was exhausted with the violence of my emotion and of my flight, and I staggered and fell by the wayside. That was near the bridge that crosses the canal by the gasworks. I fell and lay still.

I must have remained there some time.

I sat up, strangely perplexed. For a moment, perhaps, I could not clearly understand how I came there. My terror had fallen from me like a garment. My hat had gone, and my collar had burst away from its fastener. A few minutes before, there had only been three real things before me – the immensity of the night and space and nature, my own feebleness and anguish, and the near approach of death. Now it was as if something turned over, and the point of view altered abruptly. There was no sensible transition from one state of mind to the other. I was immediately the self of every day again – a decent, ordinary citizen. The silent common, the impulse of my flight, the starting flames, were as if they had been in a dream. I asked myself had these latter things indeed happened? I could not credit it.

I rose and walked unsteadily up the steep incline of the bridge. My mind was blank wonder. My muscles and nerves seemed drained of their strength. I dare say I staggered drunkenly. A head rose over the arch, and the figure of a workman carrying a basket appeared. Beside him ran a little boy. He passed me, wishing me good night. I was minded to speak to him, but did not. I answered his greeting with a meaningless mumble and went on over the bridge.

Over the Maybury arch a train, a billowing tumult of white, firelit smoke, and a long caterpillar of lighted windows, went flying south – clatter, clatter, clap, rap, and it had gone. A dim group of people talked in the gate of one of the houses in the pretty little row of gables that was called Oriental Terrace. It was all so real and so familiar. And that behind me! It was frantic, fantastic! Such things, I told myself, could not be.

Perhaps I am a man of exceptional moods. I do not know how far my experience is common. At times I suffer from the strangest sense of detachment from myself and the world about me; I seem to watch it all from the outside, from somewhere inconceivably remote, out of time, out of space, out of the stress and tragedy of it all. This feeling was very strong upon me that night. Here was another side to my dream.

But the trouble was the blank incongruity of this serenity and the swift death flying yonder, not two miles away. There was a noise of business from the gasworks, and the electric lamps were all alight. I stopped at the group of people.

"What news from the common?" said I.

There were two men and a woman at the gate.

"Eh?" said one of the men, turning.

"What news from the common?" I said.

"'Ain't yer just *been* there?" asked the men.

"People seem fair silly about the common," said the woman over the gate. "What's it all abart?"

"Haven't you heard of the men from Mars?" said I; "The creatures from Mars?"

"Quite enough," said the woman over the gate. "Thenks"; and all three of them laughed. I felt foolish and angry. I tried and found I could not tell them what I had seen. They laughed again at my broken sentences.

"You'll hear more yet," I said, and went on to my home.

I startled my wife at the doorway, so haggard was I. I went into the dining room, sat down, drank some wine, and so soon as I could collect myself sufficiently I told her the things I had seen. The dinner, which was a cold one, had already been served, and remained neglected on the table while I told my story.

"There is one thing," I said, to allay the fears I had aroused; "they are the most sluggish things I ever saw crawl. They may keep the pit and kill people who come near them, but they cannot get out of it.... But the horror of them!"

"Don't, dear!" said my wife, knitting her brows and putting her hand on mine.

"Poor Ogilvy!" I said. "To think he may be lying dead there!"

My wife at least did not find my experience incredible. When I saw how deadly white her face was, I ceased abruptly.

"They may come here," she said again and again.

I pressed her to take wine, and tried to reassure her.

"They can scarcely move," I said.

I began to comfort her and myself by repeating all that Ogilvy had told me of the impossibility of the Martians establishing themselves on the earth. In particular I laid stress on the gravitational difficulty. On the surface of the earth the force of gravity is three times what it is on the surface of Mars. A Martian, therefore, would weigh three times more than on Mars, albeit his muscular strength would be the same. His own body would be a cope of lead to him. That, indeed, was the general opinion. Both *The Times* and the *Daily Telegraph*, for instance, insisted on it the next morning, and both overlooked, just as I did, two obvious modifying influences.

The atmosphere of the earth, we now know, contains far more oxygen or far less argon (whichever way one likes to put it) than does Mars. The invigorating influences of this excess of oxygen upon the Martians indisputably did much to counterbalance the increased weight of their bodies. And, in the second place, we all overlooked the fact that such mechanical intelligence as the Martian possessed was quite able to dispense with muscular exertion at a pinch.

But I did not consider these points at the time, and so my reasoning was dead against the chances of the invaders. With wine and food, the confidence of my own table, and the necessity of reassuring my wife, I grew by insensible degrees courageous and secure.

"They have done a foolish thing," said I, fingering my wineglass. "They are dangerous because, no doubt, they are mad with terror. Perhaps they expected to find no living things – certainly no intelligent living things."

"A shell in the pit" said I, "if the worst comes to the worst will kill them all."

The intense excitement of the events had no doubt left my perceptive powers in a state of erethism. I remember that dinner table with extraordinary vividness even now. My dear wife's sweet anxious face peering at me from under the pink lamp shade, the white cloth with its silver and glass table furniture – for in those days even philosophical writers had many little luxuries – the crimson-purple wine in my glass, are photographically distinct. At the end of it I sat, tempering nuts with a cigarette, regretting Ogilvy's rashness, and denouncing the shortsighted timidity of the Martians.

So some respectable dodo in the Mauritius might have lorded it in his nest, and discussed the arrival of that shipful of pitiless sailors in want of animal food. "We will peck them to death tomorrow, my dear."

I did not know it, but that was the last civilised dinner I was to eat for very many strange and terrible days.

Chapter VIII
Friday Night

THE MOST EXTRAORDINARY THING to my mind, of all the strange and wonderful things that happened upon that Friday, was the dovetailing of the commonplace habits of our social order with the first beginnings of the series of events that was to topple that social order headlong. If on Friday night you had taken a pair of compasses and drawn a circle with a radius of five miles round the Woking sand pits, I doubt if you would have had one human being outside it, unless it were some relation of Stent or of the three or four cyclists or London people lying dead on the common, whose emotions or habits were at all affected by the new-comers. Many people had heard of the cylinder, of course, and talked about it in their leisure, but it certainly did not make the sensation that an ultimatum to Germany would have done.

In London that night poor Henderson's telegram describing the gradual unscrewing of the shot was judged to be a canard, and his evening paper, after wiring for authentication from him and receiving no reply – the man was killed – decided not to print a special edition.

Even within the five-mile circle the great majority of people were inert. I have already described the behaviour of the men and women to whom I spoke. All over the district people were dining and supping; working men were gardening after the labours of the day, children were being put to bed, young people were wandering through the lanes love-making, students sat over their books.

Maybe there was a murmur in the village streets, a novel and dominant topic in the public-houses, and here and there a messenger, or even an eye-witness of the later occurrences, caused a whirl of excitement, a shouting, and a running to and fro; but for the most part the daily routine of working, eating, drinking, sleeping, went on as it had done for countless years – as though no planet Mars existed in the sky. Even at Woking station and Horsell and Chobham that was the case.

In Woking junction, until a late hour, trains were stopping and going on, others were shunting on the sidings, passengers were alighting and waiting, and everything was proceeding in the most ordinary way. A boy from the town, trenching on Smith's monopoly, was selling papers with the afternoon's news. The ringing impact of trucks, the sharp whistle of the engines from the junction, mingled with their shouts of "Men from Mars!" Excited men came into the station about nine o'clock with incredible tidings, and caused no more disturbance than drunkards might have done. People rattling Londonwards peered into the darkness outside the carriage windows, and saw only a rare, flickering, vanishing spark dance up from the direction of Horsell, a red glow and a thin veil of smoke driving across the stars, and thought that nothing more serious than a heath fire was happening. It was only round the edge of the common that any disturbance was perceptible. There were half a dozen villas burning on the Woking border. There were lights in all the houses on the common side of the three villages, and the people there kept awake till dawn.

A curious crowd lingered restlessly, people coming and going but the crowd remaining, both on the Chobham and Horsell bridges. One or two adventurous souls, it was afterwards found, went into the darkness and crawled quite near the Martians; but they never returned, for now and again a light-ray, like the beam of a warship's searchlight swept the common, and the Heat-Ray was ready to follow. Save for such, that big area of common was silent and desolate, and the charred bodies lay about on it all night under the stars, and all the next day. A noise of hammering from the pit was heard by many people.

So you have the state of things on Friday night. In the centre, sticking into the skin of our old planet Earth like a poisoned dart, was this cylinder. But the poison was scarcely working yet. Around it was a patch of silent common, smouldering in places, and with a few dark, dimly seen objects lying in contorted attitudes here and there. Here and there was a burning bush or tree. Beyond was a fringe of excitement, and farther than that fringe the inflammation had not crept as yet. In the rest of the world the stream of life still flowed as it had flowed for immemorial years. The fever of war that would presently clog vein and artery, deaden nerve and destroy brain, had still to develop.

All night long the Martians were hammering and stirring, sleepless, indefatigable, at work upon the machines they were making ready, and ever and again a puff of greenish-white smoke whirled up to the starlit sky.

About eleven a company of soldiers came through Horsell, and deployed along the edge of the common to form a cordon. Later a second company marched through Chobham to deploy on the north side of the common. Several officers from the Inkerman barracks had been on the common earlier in the day, and one, Major Eden, was reported to be missing. The colonel of the regiment came to the Chobham bridge and was busy questioning the crowd at midnight. The military authorities were certainly alive to the seriousness of the business. About eleven, the next morning's papers were able to say, a squadron of hussars, two Maxims, and about four hundred men of the Cardigan regiment started from Aldershot.

A few seconds after midnight the crowd in the Chertsey road, Woking, saw a star fall from heaven into the pine woods to the northwest. It had a greenish colour, and caused a silent brightness like summer lightning. This was the second cylinder.

Chapter IX
The Fighting Begins

SATURDAY LIVES IN MY MEMORY as a day of suspense. It was a day of lassitude too, hot and close, with, I am told, a rapidly fluctuating barometer. I had slept but little, though my wife had succeeded in sleeping, and I rose early. I went into my garden before breakfast and stood listening, but towards the common there was nothing stirring but a lark.

The milkman came as usual. I heard the rattle of his chariot and I went round to the side gate to ask the latest news. He told me that during the night the Martians had been surrounded by troops, and that guns were expected. Then – a familiar, reassuring note – I heard a train running towards Woking.

"They aren't to be killed," said the milkman, "if that can possibly be avoided."

I saw my neighbour gardening, chatted with him for a time, and then strolled in to breakfast. It was a most unexceptional morning. My neighbour was of opinion that the troops would be able to capture or to destroy the Martians during the day.

"It's a pity they make themselves so unapproachable," he said. "It would be curious to know how they live on another planet; we might learn a thing or two."

He came up to the fence and extended a handful of strawberries, for his gardening was as generous as it was enthusiastic. At the same time he told me of the burning of the pine woods about the Byfleet Golf Links.

"They say," said he, "that there's another of those blessed things fallen there – number two. But one's enough, surely. This lot'll cost the insurance people a pretty penny before everything's settled." He laughed with an air of the greatest good humour as he said this. The woods, he said, were still burning, and pointed out a haze of smoke to me. "They will be hot under foot for days, on account of the thick soil of pine needles and turf," he said, and then grew serious over "poor Ogilvy."

After breakfast, instead of working, I decided to walk down towards the common. Under the railway bridge I found a group of soldiers – sappers, I think, men in small round caps, dirty red jackets unbuttoned, and showing their blue shirts, dark trousers, and boots coming to the calf. They told me no one was allowed over the canal, and, looking along the road towards the bridge, I saw one of the Cardigan men standing sentinel there. I talked with these soldiers for a time; I told them of my sight of the Martians on the previous evening. None of them had seen the Martians, and they had but the vaguest ideas of them, so that they plied me with questions. They said that they did not know who had authorised the movements of the troops; their idea was that a dispute had arisen at the Horse Guards. The ordinary sapper is a great deal better educated than the common soldier, and they discussed the peculiar conditions of the possible fight with some acuteness. I described the Heat-Ray to them, and they began to argue among themselves.

"Crawl up under cover and rush 'em, say I," said one.

"Get aht!," said another. "What's cover against this 'ere 'eat? Sticks to cook yer! What we got to do is to go as near as the ground'll let us, and then drive a trench."

"Blow yer trenches! You always want trenches; you ought to ha' been born a rabbit Snippy."

"Ain't they got any necks, then?" said a third, abruptly – a little, contemplative, dark man, smoking a pipe.

I repeated my description.

"Octopuses," said he, "that's what I calls 'em. Talk about fishers of men – fighters of fish it is this time!"

"It ain't no murder killing beasts like that," said the first speaker.

"Why not shell the darned things strite off and finish 'em?" said the little dark man. "You carn tell what they might do."

"Where's your shells?" said the first speaker. "There ain't no time. Do it in a rush, that's my tip, and do it at once."

So they discussed it. After a while I left them, and went on to the railway station to get as many morning papers as I could.

But I will not weary the reader with a description of that long morning and of the longer afternoon. I did not succeed in getting a glimpse of the common, for even Horsell and Chobham church towers were in the hands of the military authorities. The soldiers I addressed didn't know anything; the officers were mysterious as well as busy. I found people in the town quite secure again in the presence of the military, and I heard for the first time from Marshall, the tobacconist, that his son was among the dead on the common. The soldiers had made the people on the outskirts of Horsell lock up and leave their houses.

I got back to lunch about two, very tired for, as I have said, the day was extremely hot and dull; and in order to refresh myself I took a cold bath in the afternoon. About half past four I went up to the railway station to get an evening paper, for the morning papers had contained only a very inaccurate description of the killing of Stent, Henderson, Ogilvy, and the others. But there was little I didn't know. The Martians did not show an inch of themselves. They seemed busy in their pit, and there was a sound of hammering and an almost continuous streamer of smoke. Apparently they were busy getting ready for a struggle. "Fresh attempts have been made to signal, but without success," was the stereotyped formula of the papers. A sapper told me it was done by a man in a ditch with a flag on a long pole. The Martians took as much notice of such advances as we should of the lowing of a cow.

I must confess the sight of all this armament, all this preparation, greatly excited me. My imagination became belligerent, and defeated the invaders in a dozen striking ways; something of my schoolboy dreams of battle and heroism came back. It hardly seemed a fair fight to me at that time. They seemed very helpless in that pit of theirs.

About three o'clock there began the thud of a gun at measured intervals from Chertsey or Addlestone. I learned that the smouldering pine wood into which the second cylinder had fallen was being shelled, in the hope of destroying that object before it opened. It was only about five, however, that a field gun reached Chobham for use against the first body of Martians.

About six in the evening, as I sat at tea with my wife in the summerhouse talking vigorously about the battle that was lowering upon us, I heard a muffled detonation from the common, and immediately after a gust of firing. Close on the heels of that came a violent rattling crash, quite close to us, that shook the ground; and, starting out upon the lawn, I saw the tops of the trees about the Oriental College burst into smoky red flame, and the tower of the little church beside it slide down into ruin. The pinnacle of the mosque had vanished, and the roof line of the college itself looked as if a hundred-ton gun had been at work upon it. One of our chimneys cracked as if a shot had hit it, flew, and a piece of it came clattering down the tiles and made a heap of broken red fragments upon the flower bed by my study window.

I and my wife stood amazed. Then I realised that the crest of Maybury Hill must be within range of the Martians' Heat-Ray now that the college was cleared out of the way.

At that I gripped my wife's arm, and without ceremony ran her out into the road. Then I fetched out the servant, telling her I would go upstairs myself for the box she was clamouring for.

"We can't possibly stay here," I said; and as I spoke the firing reopened for a moment upon the common.

"But where are we to go?" said my wife in terror.

I thought perplexed. Then I remembered her cousins at Leatherhead.

"Leatherhead!" I shouted above the sudden noise.

She looked away from me downhill. The people were coming out of their houses, astonished.

"How are we to get to Leatherhead?" she said.

Down the hill I saw a bevy of hussars ride under the railway bridge; three galloped through the open gates of the Oriental College; two others dismounted, and began running from house to house. The sun, shining through the smoke that drove up from the tops of the trees, seemed blood red, and threw an unfamiliar lurid light upon everything.

"Stop here," said I; "you are safe here"; and I started off at once for the Spotted Dog, for I knew the landlord had a horse and dog cart. I ran, for I perceived that in a moment everyone upon this side of the hill would be moving. I found him in his bar, quite unaware of what was going on behind his house. A man stood with his back to me, talking to him.

"I must have a pound," said the landlord, "and I've no one to drive it."

"I'll give you two," said I, over the stranger's shoulder.

"What for?"

"And I'll bring it back by midnight," I said.

"Lord!" said the landlord; "what's the hurry? I'm selling my bit of a pig. Two pounds, and you bring it back? What's going on now?"

I explained hastily that I had to leave my home, and so secured the dog cart. At the time it did not seem to me nearly so urgent that the landlord should leave his. I took care to have the cart there and then, drove it off down the road, and, leaving it in charge of my wife and servant, rushed into my house and packed a few valuables, such plate as we had, and so forth. The beech trees below the house were burning while I did this, and the palings up the road glowed red. While I was occupied in this way, one of the dismounted hussars came running up. He was going from house to house, warning people to leave. He was going on as I came out of my front door, lugging my treasures, done up in a tablecloth. I shouted after him:

"What news?"

He turned, stared, bawled something about "crawling out in a thing like a dish cover," and ran on to the gate of the house at the crest. A sudden whirl of black smoke driving across the road hid him for a moment. I ran to my neighbour's door and rapped to satisfy myself of what I already knew, that his wife had gone to London with him and had locked up their house. I went in again, according to my promise, to get my servant's box, lugged it out, clapped it beside her on the tail of the dog cart, and then caught the reins and jumped up into the driver's seat beside my wife. In another moment we were clear of the smoke and noise, and spanking down the opposite slope of Maybury Hill towards Old Woking.

In front was a quiet sunny landscape, a wheat field ahead on either side of the road, and the Maybury Inn with its swinging sign. I saw the doctor's cart ahead of me. At the bottom of the hill I turned my head to look at the hillside I was leaving. Thick streamers of black smoke shot with threads of red fire were driving up into the still air, and throwing dark shadows upon the green treetops eastward. The smoke already extended far away to the east and west – to the Byfleet pine woods eastward, and to Woking on the west. The road was dotted with people running towards us. And very faint now, but very distinct through the hot, quiet air, one heard the whirr of a machine-gun that was presently stilled, and an intermittent cracking of rifles. Apparently the Martians were setting fire to everything within range of their Heat-Ray.

I am not an expert driver, and I had immediately to turn my attention to the horse. When I looked back again the second hill had hidden the black smoke. I slashed the horse with the whip, and gave him a loose rein until Woking and Send lay between us and that quivering tumult. I overtook and passed the doctor between Woking and Send.

Chapter X
In the Storm

LEATHERHEAD IS ABOUT twelve miles from Maybury Hill. The scent of hay was in the air through the lush meadows beyond Pyrford, and the hedges on either side were sweet and gay with multitudes of dog-roses. The heavy firing that had broken out while we were driving down Maybury Hill ceased as abruptly as it began, leaving the evening very peaceful and still. We got to Leatherhead without misadventure about nine o'clock, and the horse had an hour's rest while I took supper with my cousins and commended my wife to their care.

My wife was curiously silent throughout the drive, and seemed oppressed with forebodings of evil. I talked to her reassuringly, pointing out that the Martians were tied to the Pit by sheer heaviness, and at the utmost could but crawl a little out of it; but she answered only in monosyllables. Had it not been for my promise to the innkeeper, she would, I think, have urged me to stay in Leatherhead that night. Would that I had! Her face, I remember, was very white as we parted.

For my own part, I had been feverishly excited all day. Something very like the war fever that occasionally runs through a civilised community had got into my blood, and in my heart I was not so very sorry that I had to return to Maybury that night. I was even afraid that that last fusillade I had heard might mean the extermination of our invaders from Mars. I can best express my state of mind by saying that I wanted to be in at the death.

It was nearly eleven when I started to return. The night was unexpectedly dark; to me, walking out of the lighted passage of my cousins' house, it seemed indeed black, and it was as hot and close as the day. Overhead the clouds were driving fast, albeit not a breath stirred the shrubs about us. My cousins' man lit both lamps. Happily, I knew the road intimately. My wife stood in the light of the doorway, and watched me until I jumped up into the dog cart. Then abruptly she turned and went in, leaving my cousins side by side wishing me good hap.

I was a little depressed at first with the contagion of my wife's fears, but very soon my thoughts reverted to the Martians. At that time I was absolutely in the dark as to the course of the evening's fighting. I did not know even the circumstances that had precipitated the conflict. As I came through Ockham (for that was the way I returned, and not through Send and Old Woking) I saw along the western horizon a blood-red glow, which as I drew nearer, crept slowly up the sky. The driving clouds of the gathering thunderstorm mingled there with masses of black and red smoke.

Ripley Street was deserted, and except for a lighted window or so the village showed not a sign of life; but I narrowly escaped an accident at the corner of the road to Pyrford, where a knot of people stood with their backs to me. They said nothing to me as I passed. I do not know what they knew of the things happening beyond the hill, nor do I know if the silent houses I passed on my way were sleeping securely, or deserted and empty, or harassed and watching against the terror of the night.

From Ripley until I came through Pyrford I was in the valley of the Wey, and the red glare was hidden from me. As I ascended the little hill beyond Pyrford Church the glare came into view again, and the trees about me shivered with the first intimation of the storm that was upon me. Then I heard midnight pealing out from Pyrford Church behind me, and then came the silhouette of Maybury Hill, with its tree-tops and roofs black and sharp against the red.

Even as I beheld this a lurid green glare lit the road about me and showed the distant woods towards Addlestone. I felt a tug at the reins. I saw that the driving clouds had been pierced as it were by a thread of green fire, suddenly lighting their confusion and falling into the field to my left. It was the third falling star!

Close on its apparition, and blindingly violet by contrast, danced out the first lightning of the gathering storm, and the thunder burst like a rocket overhead. The horse took the bit between his teeth and bolted.

A moderate incline runs towards the foot of Maybury Hill, and down this we clattered. Once the lightning had begun, it went on in as rapid a succession of flashes as I have ever seen. The thunderclaps, treading one on the heels of another and with a strange crackling accompaniment, sounded more like the working of a gigantic electric machine than the usual detonating reverberations. The flickering light was blinding and confusing, and a thin hail smote gustily at my face as I drove down the slope.

At first I regarded little but the road before me, and then abruptly my attention was arrested by something that was moving rapidly down the opposite slope of Maybury Hill. At first I took it for the wet roof of a house, but one flash following another showed it to be in swift rolling movement. It was an elusive vision – a moment of bewildering darkness, and then, in a flash like daylight, the red masses of the Orphanage near the crest of the hill, the green tops of the pine trees, and this problematical object came out clear and sharp and bright.

And this Thing I saw! How can I describe it? A monstrous tripod, higher than many houses, striding over the young pine trees, and smashing them aside in its career; a walking engine of glittering metal, striding now across the heather; articulate ropes of steel dangling from it, and the clattering tumult of its passage mingling with the riot of the thunder. A flash, and it came out vividly, heeling over one way with two feet in the air, to vanish and reappear almost instantly as it seemed, with the next flash, a hundred yards nearer. Can you imagine a milking stool tilted and bowled violently along the ground? That was the impression those instant flashes gave. But instead of a milking stool imagine it a great body of machinery on a tripod stand.

Then suddenly the trees in the pine wood ahead of me were parted, as brittle reeds are parted by a man thrusting through them; they were snapped off and driven headlong, and a second huge tripod appeared, rushing, as it seemed, headlong towards me. And I was galloping hard to meet it! At the sight of the second monster my nerve went altogether. Not stopping to look again, I wrenched the horse's head hard round to the right and in another moment the dog cart had heeled over upon the horse; the shafts smashed noisily, and I was flung sideways and fell heavily into a shallow pool of water.

I crawled out almost immediately, and crouched, my feet still in the water, under a clump of furze. The horse lay motionless (his neck was broken, poor brute!) and by the lightning flashes I saw the black bulk of the overturned dog cart and the silhouette of the wheel still spinning slowly. In another moment the colossal mechanism went striding by me, and passed uphill towards Pyrford.

Seen nearer, the Thing was incredibly strange, for it was no mere insensate machine driving on its way. Machine it was, with a ringing metallic pace, and long, flexible, glittering tentacles (one of which gripped a young pine tree) swinging and rattling about its strange body. It picked its road as it went striding along, and the brazen hood that surmounted it moved to and fro with the inevitable suggestion of a head looking about. Behind the main body was a huge mass of white metal like a gigantic fisherman's basket, and puffs of green smoke squirted out from the joints of the limbs as the monster swept by me. And in an instant it was gone.

So much I saw then, all vaguely for the flickering of the lightning, in blinding highlights and dense black shadows.

As it passed it set up an exultant deafening howl that drowned the thunder – "Aloo! Aloo!" – and in another minute it was with its companion, half a mile away, stooping over something in the field. I have no doubt this Thing in the field was the third of the ten cylinders they had fired at us from Mars.

For some minutes I lay there in the rain and darkness watching, by the intermittent light, these monstrous beings of metal moving about in the distance over the hedge tops. A thin hail was now beginning, and as it came and went their figures grew misty and then flashed into clearness again. Now and then came a gap in the lightning, and the night swallowed them up.

I was soaked with hail above and puddle water below. It was some time before my blank astonishment would let me struggle up the bank to a drier position, or think at all of my imminent peril.

Not far from me was a little one-roomed squatter's hut of wood, surrounded by a patch of potato garden. I struggled to my feet at last, and, crouching and making use of every chance of cover, I made a run for this. I hammered at the door, but I could not make the people hear (if there were any people inside), and after a time I desisted, and, availing myself of a ditch for the greater part of the way, succeeded in crawling, unobserved by these monstrous machines, into the pine woods towards Maybury.

Under cover of this I pushed on, wet and shivering now, towards my own house. I walked among the trees trying to find the footpath. It was very dark indeed in the wood, for the lightning was now becoming infrequent, and the hail, which was pouring down in a torrent, fell in columns through the gaps in the heavy foliage.

If I had fully realised the meaning of all the things I had seen I should have immediately worked my way round through Byfleet to Street Cobham, and so gone back to rejoin my wife at Leatherhead. But that night the strangeness of things about me, and my physical wretchedness, prevented me, for I was bruised, weary, wet to the skin, deafened and blinded by the storm.

I had a vague idea of going on to my own house, and that was as much motive as I had. I staggered through the trees, fell into a ditch and bruised my knees against a plank, and finally splashed out into the lane that ran down from the College Arms. I say splashed, for the storm water was sweeping the sand down the hill in a muddy torrent. There in the darkness a man blundered into me and sent me reeling back.

He gave a cry of terror, sprang sideways, and rushed on before I could gather my wits sufficiently to speak to him. So heavy was the stress of the storm just at this place that I had the hardest task to win my way up the hill. I went close up to the fence on the left and worked my way along its palings.

Near the top I stumbled upon something soft, and, by a flash of lightning, saw between my feet a heap of black broadcloth and a pair of boots. Before I could distinguish clearly how the man lay, the flicker of light had passed. I stood over him waiting for the next flash. When it came, I saw that he was a sturdy man, cheaply but not shabbily dressed; his head was bent under his body, and he lay crumpled up close to the fence, as though he had been flung violently against it.

Overcoming the repugnance natural to one who had never before touched a dead body, I stooped and turned him over to feel for his heart. He was quite dead. Apparently his neck had been broken. The lightning flashed for a third time, and his face leaped upon me. I sprang to my feet. It was the landlord of the Spotted Dog, whose conveyance I had taken.

I stepped over him gingerly and pushed on up the hill. I made my way by the police station and the College Arms towards my own house. Nothing was burning on the hillside, though from the common there still came a red glare and a rolling tumult of ruddy smoke beating up against the drenching hail. So far as I could see by the flashes, the houses about me were mostly uninjured. By the College Arms a dark heap lay in the road.

Down the road towards Maybury Bridge there were voices and the sound of feet, but I had not the courage to shout or to go to them. I let myself in with my latchkey, closed, locked and bolted the door, staggered to the foot of the staircase, and sat down.

My imagination was full of those striding metallic monsters, and of the dead body smashed against the fence.

I crouched at the foot of the staircase with my back to the wall, shivering violently.

Chapter XI
At the Window

I HAVE ALREADY SAID that my storms of emotion have a trick of exhausting themselves. After a time I discovered that I was cold and wet, and with little pools of water about me on the stair carpet. I got up almost mechanically, went into the dining room and drank some whiskey, and then I was moved to change my clothes.

After I had done that I went upstairs to my study, but why I did so I do not know. The window of my study looks over the trees and the railway towards Horsell Common. In the hurry of our departure this window had been left open. The passage was dark, and, by contrast with the picture the window frame enclosed, the side of the room seemed impenetrably dark. I stopped short in the doorway.

The thunderstorm had passed. The towers of the Oriental College and the pine trees about it had gone, and very far away, lit by a vivid red glare, the common about the sand pits was visible. Across the light huge black shapes, grotesque and strange, moved busily to and fro.

It seemed indeed as if the whole country in that direction was on fire – a broad hillside set with minute tongues of flame, swaying and writhing with the gusts of the dying storm, and throwing a red reflection upon the cloud scud above. Every now and then a haze of smoke from some nearer conflagration drove across the window and hid the Martian shapes. I could not see what they were doing, nor the clear form of them, nor recognise the black objects they were busied upon. Neither could I see the nearer fire, though the reflections of it danced on the wall and ceiling of the study. A sharp, resinous tang of burning was in the air.

I closed the door noiselessly and crept towards the window. As I did so, the view opened out until, on the one hand, it reached to the houses about Woking station, and on the other to the charred and blackened pine woods of Byfleet. There was a light down below the hill, on the railway, near the arch, and several of the houses along the Maybury road and the streets near the station were glowing ruins. The light upon the railway puzzled me at first, there were a black heap and a vivid glare, and to the right of that a row of yellow oblongs. Then I perceived this was a wrecked train, the fore part smashed and on fire, the hinder carriages still upon the rails.

Between these three main centres of light – the houses, the train, and the burning county towards Chobham – stretched irregular patches of dark country, broken here and there by intervals of dimly glowing and smoking ground. It was the strangest spectacle, that black expanse set with fire. It reminded me, more than anything else, of the Potteries at night. At first I could distinguish no people at all, though I peered intently for them. Later I saw against the light of Woking station a number of black figures hurrying one after the other across the line.

And this was the little world in which I had been living securely for years, this fiery chaos! What had happened in the last seven hours I still did not know; nor did I know, though I was beginning to guess, the relation between these mechanical colossi and the sluggish lumps I had seen disgorged from the cylinder. With a queer feeling of impersonal interest

I turned my desk chair to the window, sat down, and stared at the blackened country, and particularly at the three gigantic black things that were going to and fro in the glare about the sand pits.

They seemed amazingly busy. I began to ask myself what they could be. Were they intelligent mechanisms? Such a thing I felt was impossible. Or did a Martian sit within each, ruling, directing, using, much as a man's brain sits and rules in his body? I began to compare the things to human machines, to ask myself for the first time in my life how an ironclad or a steam engine would seem to an intelligent lower animal.

The storm had left the sky clear, and over the smoke of the burning land the little fading pinpoint of Mars was dropping into the west, when a soldier came into my garden. I heard a slight scraping at the fence, and rousing myself from the lethargy that had fallen upon me, I looked down and saw him dimly, clambering over the palings. At the sight of another human being my torpor passed, and I leaned out of the window eagerly.

"Hist!" said I, in a whisper.

He stopped astride of the fence in doubt. Then he came over and across the lawn to the corner of the house. He bent down and stepped softly.

"Who's there?" he said, also whispering, standing under the window and peering up.

"Where are you going?" I asked.

"God knows."

"Are you trying to hide?"

"That's it."

"Come into the house," I said.

I went down, unfastened the door, and let him in, and locked the door again. I could not see his face. He was hatless, and his coat was unbuttoned.

"My God!" he said, as I drew him in.

"What has happened?" I asked.

"What hasn't?" In the obscurity I could see he made a gesture of despair. "They wiped us out – simply wiped us out," he repeated again and again.

He followed me, almost mechanically, into the dining room.

"Take some whiskey," I said, pouring out a stiff dose.

He drank it. Then abruptly he sat down before the table, put his head on his arms, and began to sob and weep like a little boy, in a perfect passion of emotion, while I, with a curious forgetfulness of my own recent despair, stood beside him, wondering.

It was a long time before he could steady his nerves to answer my questions, and then he answered perplexingly and brokenly. He was a driver in the artillery, and had only come into action about seven. At that time firing was going on across the common, and it was said the first party of Martians were crawling slowly towards their second cylinder under cover of a metal shield.

Later this shield staggered up on tripod legs and became the first of the fighting-machines I had seen. The gun he drove had been unlimbered near Horsell, in order to command the sand pits, and its arrival it was that had precipitated the action. As the limber gunners went to the rear, his horse trod in a rabbit hole and came down, throwing him into a depression of the ground. At the same moment the gun exploded behind him, the ammunition blew up, there was fire all about him, and he found himself lying under a heap of charred dead men and dead horses.

"I lay still," he said, "scared out of my wits, with the fore quarter of a horse atop of me. We'd been wiped out. And the smell – good God! Like burnt meat! I was hurt across the back by the fall of the horse, and there I had to lie until I felt better. Just like parade it had been a minute before – then stumble, bang, swish!"

"Wiped out!" he said.

He had hid under the dead horse for a long time, peeping out furtively across the common. The Cardigan men had tried a rush, in skirmishing order, at the pit, simply to be swept out of existence. Then the monster had risen to its feet and had begun to walk leisurely to and fro across the common among the few fugitives, with its headlike hood turning about exactly like the head of a cowled human being. A kind of arm carried a complicated metallic case, about which green flashes scintillated, and out of the funnel of this there smoked the Heat-Ray.

In a few minutes there was, so far as the soldier could see, not a living thing left upon the common, and every bush and tree upon it that was not already a blackened skeleton was burning. The hussars had been on the road beyond the curvature of the ground, and he saw nothing of them. He heard the Martians rattle for a time and then become still. The giant saved Woking station and its cluster of houses until the last; then in a moment the Heat-Ray was brought to bear, and the town became a heap of fiery ruins. Then the Thing shut off the Heat-Ray, and turning its back upon the artilleryman, began to waddle away towards the smouldering pine woods that sheltered the second cylinder. As it did so a second glittering Titan built itself up out of the pit.

The second monster followed the first, and at that the artilleryman began to crawl very cautiously across the hot heather ash towards Horsell. He managed to get alive into the ditch by the side of the road, and so escaped to Woking. There his story became ejaculatory. The place was impassable. It seems there were a few people alive there, frantic for the most part and many burned and scalded. He was turned aside by the fire, and hid among some almost scorching heaps of broken wall as one of the Martian giants returned. He saw this one pursue a man, catch him up in one of its steely tentacles, and knock his head against the trunk of a pine tree. At last, after nightfall, the artilleryman made a rush for it and got over the railway embankment.

Since then he had been skulking along towards Maybury, in the hope of getting out of danger Londonward. People were hiding in trenches and cellars, and many of the survivors had made off towards Woking village and Send. He had been consumed with thirst until he found one of the water mains near the railway arch smashed, and the water bubbling out like a spring upon the road.

That was the story I got from him, bit by bit. He grew calmer telling me and trying to make me see the things he had seen. He had eaten no food since midday, he told me early in his narrative, and I found some mutton and bread in the pantry and brought it into the room. We lit no lamp for fear of attracting the Martians, and ever and again our hands would touch upon bread or meat. As he talked, things about us came darkly out of the darkness, and the trampled bushes and broken rose trees outside the window grew distinct. It would seem that a number of men or animals had rushed across the lawn. I began to see his face, blackened and haggard, as no doubt mine was also.

When we had finished eating we went softly upstairs to my study, and I looked again out of the open window. In one night the valley had become a valley of ashes. The fires had dwindled now. Where flames had been there were now streamers of smoke; but the countless ruins of shattered and gutted houses and blasted and blackened trees that the night had hidden stood out now gaunt and terrible in the pitiless light of dawn. Yet here and there some object had had the luck to escape – a white railway signal here, the end of a greenhouse there, white and fresh amid the wreckage. Never before in the history of warfare had destruction been so indiscriminate and so universal. And shining with the growing light of the east, three of the metallic giants stood about the pit, their cowls rotating as though they were surveying the desolation they had made.

It seemed to me that the pit had been enlarged, and ever and again puffs of vivid green vapour streamed up and out of it towards the brightening dawn – streamed up, whirled, broke, and vanished.

Beyond were the pillars of fire about Chobham. They became pillars of bloodshot smoke at the first touch of day.

Chapter XII
What I Saw of the Destruction of Weybridge and Shepperton

AS THE DAWN grew brighter we withdrew from the window from which we had watched the Martians, and went very quietly downstairs.

The artilleryman agreed with me that the house was no place to stay in. He proposed, he said, to make his way Londonward, and thence rejoin his battery – No. 12, of the Horse Artillery. My plan was to return at once to Leatherhead; and so greatly had the strength of the Martians impressed me that I had determined to take my wife to Newhaven, and go with her out of the country forthwith. For I already perceived clearly that the country about London must inevitably be the scene of a disastrous struggle before such creatures as these could be destroyed.

Between us and Leatherhead, however, lay the third cylinder, with its guarding giants. Had I been alone, I think I should have taken my chance and struck across country. But the artilleryman dissuaded me: "It's no kindness to the right sort of wife," he said, "to make her a widow"; and in the end I agreed to go with him, under cover of the woods, northward as far as Street Cobham before I parted with him. Thence I would make a big detour by Epsom to reach Leatherhead.

I should have started at once, but my companion had been in active service and he knew better than that. He made me ransack the house for a flask, which he filled with whiskey; and we lined every available pocket with packets of biscuits and slices of meat. Then we crept out of the house, and ran as quickly as we could down the ill-made road by which I had come overnight. The houses seemed deserted. In the road lay a group of three charred bodies close together, struck dead by the Heat-Ray; and here and there were things that people had dropped – a clock, a slipper, a silver spoon, and the like poor valuables. At the corner turning up towards the post office a little cart, filled with boxes and furniture, and horseless, heeled over on a broken wheel. A cash box had been hastily smashed open and thrown under the debris.

Except the lodge at the Orphanage, which was still on fire, none of the houses had suffered very greatly here. The Heat-Ray had shaved the chimney tops and passed. Yet, save ourselves, there did not seem to be a living soul on Maybury Hill. The majority of the inhabitants had escaped, I suppose, by way of the Old Woking road – the road I had taken when I drove to Leatherhead – or they had hidden.

We went down the lane, by the body of the man in black, sodden now from the overnight hail, and broke into the woods at the foot of the hill. We pushed through these towards the railway without meeting a soul. The woods across the line were but the scarred and blackened ruins of woods; for the most part the trees had fallen, but a certain proportion still stood, dismal grey stems, with dark brown foliage instead of green.

On our side the fire had done no more than scorch the nearer trees; it had failed to secure its footing. In one place the woodmen had been at work on Saturday; trees, felled and freshly trimmed, lay in a clearing, with heaps of sawdust by the sawing-machine and its engine. Hard by was a temporary hut, deserted. There was not a breath of wind this morning, and everything was strangely still. Even the birds were hushed, and as we hurried along I and the artilleryman talked in whispers and looked now and again over our shoulders. Once or twice we stopped to listen.

After a time we drew near the road, and as we did so we heard the clatter of hoofs and saw through the tree stems three cavalry soldiers riding slowly towards Woking. We hailed them, and they halted while we hurried towards them. It was a lieutenant and a couple of privates of the 8th Hussars, with a stand like a theodolite, which the artilleryman told me was a heliograph.

"You are the first men I've seen coming this way this morning," said the lieutenant. "What's brewing?"

His voice and face were eager. The men behind him stared curiously. The artilleryman jumped down the bank into the road and saluted.

"Gun destroyed last night, sir. Have been hiding. Trying to rejoin battery, sir. You'll come in sight of the Martians, I expect, about half a mile along this road."

"What the dickens are they like?" asked the lieutenant.

"Giants in armour, sir. Hundred feet high. Three legs and a body like 'luminium, with a mighty great head in a hood, sir."

"Get out!" said the lieutenant. "What confounded nonsense!"

"You'll see, sir. They carry a kind of box, sir, that shoots fire and strikes you dead."

"What d'ye mean – a gun?"

"No, sir," and the artilleryman began a vivid account of the Heat-Ray. Halfway through, the lieutenant interrupted him and looked up at me. I was still standing on the bank by the side of the road.

"It's perfectly true," I said.

"Well," said the lieutenant, "I suppose it's my business to see it too. Look here" – to the artilleryman – "we're detailed here clearing people out of their houses. You'd better go along and report yourself to Brigadier-General Marvin, and tell him all you know. He's at Weybridge. Know the way?"

"I do," I said; and he turned his horse southward again.

"Half a mile, you say?" said he.

"At most," I answered, and pointed over the treetops southward. He thanked me and rode on, and we saw them no more.

Farther along we came upon a group of three women and two children in the road, busy clearing out a labourer's cottage. They had got hold of a little hand truck, and were piling it up with unclean-looking bundles and shabby furniture. They were all too assiduously engaged to talk to us as we passed.

By Byfleet station we emerged from the pine trees, and found the country calm and peaceful under the morning sunlight. We were far beyond the range of the Heat-Ray there, and had it not been for the silent desertion of some of the houses, the stirring movement of packing in others, and the knot of soldiers standing on the bridge over the railway and staring down the line towards Woking, the day would have seemed very like any other Sunday.

Several farm waggons and carts were moving creakily along the road to Addlestone, and suddenly through the gate of a field we saw, across a stretch of flat meadow, six twelve-pounders standing neatly at equal distances pointing towards Woking. The gunners stood by the guns waiting, and the ammunition waggons were at a business-like distance. The men stood almost as if under inspection.

"That's good!" said I. "They will get one fair shot, at any rate."

The artilleryman hesitated at the gate.

"I shall go on," he said.

Farther on towards Weybridge, just over the bridge, there were a number of men in white fatigue jackets throwing up a long rampart, and more guns behind.

"It's bows and arrows against the lightning, anyhow," said the artilleryman. "They 'aven't seen that fire-beam yet."

The officers who were not actively engaged stood and stared over the treetops southwestward, and the men digging would stop every now and again to stare in the same direction.

Byfleet was in a tumult; people packing, and a score of hussars, some of them dismounted, some on horseback, were hunting them about. Three or four black government waggons, with crosses in white circles, and an old omnibus, among other vehicles, were being loaded in the village street. There were scores of people, most of them sufficiently sabbatical to have assumed their best clothes. The soldiers were having the greatest difficulty in making them realise the gravity of their position. We saw one shrivelled old fellow with a huge box and a score or more of flower pots containing orchids, angrily expostulating with the corporal who would leave them behind. I stopped and gripped his arm.

"Do you know what's over there?" I said, pointing at the pine tops that hid the Martians.

"Eh?" said he, turning. "I was explainin' these is vallyble."

"Death!" I shouted. "Death is coming! Death!" and leaving him to digest that if he could, I hurried on after the artillery-man. At the corner I looked back. The soldier had left him, and he was still standing by his box, with the pots of orchids on the lid of it, and staring vaguely over the trees.

No one in Weybridge could tell us where the headquarters were established; the whole place was in such confusion as I had never seen in any town before. Carts, carriages everywhere, the most astonishing miscellany of conveyances and horseflesh. The respectable inhabitants of the place, men in golf and boating costumes, wives prettily dressed, were packing, river-side loafers energetically helping, children excited, and, for the most part, highly delighted at this astonishing variation of their Sunday experiences. In the midst of it all the worthy vicar was very pluckily holding an early celebration, and his bell was jangling out above the excitement.

I and the artilleryman, seated on the step of the drinking fountain, made a very passable meal upon what we had brought with us. Patrols of soldiers – here no longer hussars, but grenadiers in white – were warning people to move now or to take refuge in their cellars as soon as the firing began. We saw as we crossed the railway bridge that a growing crowd of people had assembled in and about the railway station, and the swarming platform was piled with boxes and packages. The ordinary traffic had been stopped, I believe, in order to allow of the passage of troops and guns to Chertsey, and I have heard since that a savage struggle occurred for places in the special trains that were put on at a later hour.

We remained at Weybridge until midday, and at that hour we found ourselves at the place near Shepperton Lock where the Wey and Thames join. Part of the time we spent helping two old women to pack a little cart. The Wey has a treble mouth, and at this point boats are to be hired, and there was a ferry across the river. On the Shepperton side was an inn with a lawn, and beyond that the tower of Shepperton Church – it has been replaced by a spire – rose above the trees.

Here we found an excited and noisy crowd of fugitives. As yet the flight had not grown to a panic, but there were already far more people than all the boats going to and fro could enable to cross. People came panting along under heavy burdens; one husband and wife were even carrying a small outhouse door between them, with some of their household goods piled thereon. One man told us he meant to try to get away from Shepperton station.

There was a lot of shouting, and one man was even jesting. The idea people seemed to have here was that the Martians were simply formidable human beings, who might attack and sack the town, to be certainly destroyed in the end. Every now and then people would glance nervously across the Wey, at the meadows towards Chertsey, but everything over there was still.

Across the Thames, except just where the boats landed, everything was quiet, in vivid contrast with the Surrey side. The people who landed there from the boats went tramping off down the lane. The big ferryboat had just made a journey. Three or four soldiers stood on the lawn of the inn, staring and jesting at the fugitives, without offering to help. The inn was closed, as it was now within prohibited hours.

"What's that?" cried a boatman, and "Shut up, you fool!" said a man near me to a yelping dog. Then the sound came again, this time from the direction of Chertsey, a muffled thud – the sound of a gun.

The fighting was beginning. Almost immediately unseen batteries across the river to our right, unseen because of the trees, took up the chorus, firing heavily one after the other. A woman screamed. Everyone stood arrested by the sudden stir of battle, near us and yet invisible to us. Nothing was to be seen save flat meadows, cows feeding unconcernedly for the most part, and silvery pollard willows motionless in the warm sunlight.

"The sojers'll stop 'em," said a woman beside me, doubtfully. A haziness rose over the treetops.

Then suddenly we saw a rush of smoke far away up the river, a puff of smoke that jerked up into the air and hung; and forthwith the ground heaved under foot and a heavy explosion shook the air, smashing two or three windows in the houses near, and leaving us astonished.

"Here they are!" shouted a man in a blue jersey. "Yonder! D'yer see them? Yonder!"

Quickly, one after the other, one, two, three, four of the armoured Martians appeared, far away over the little trees, across the flat meadows that stretched towards Chertsey, and striding hurriedly towards the river. Little cowled figures they seemed at first, going with a rolling motion and as fast as flying birds.

Then, advancing obliquely towards us, came a fifth. Their armoured bodies glittered in the sun as they swept swiftly forward upon the guns, growing rapidly larger as they drew nearer. One on the extreme left, the remotest that is, flourished a huge case high in the air, and the ghostly, terrible Heat-Ray I had already seen on Friday night smote towards Chertsey, and struck the town.

At sight of these strange, swift, and terrible creatures the crowd near the water's edge seemed to me to be for a moment horror-struck. There was no screaming or shouting, but a silence. Then a hoarse murmur and a movement of feet – a splashing from the water. A man, too frightened to drop the portmanteau he carried on his shoulder, swung round and sent me staggering with a blow from the corner of his burden. A woman thrust at me with her hand and rushed past me. I turned with the rush of the people, but I was not too terrified for thought. The terrible Heat-Ray was in my mind. To get under water! That was it!

"Get under water!" I shouted, unheeded.

I faced about again, and rushed towards the approaching Martian, rushed right down the gravelly beach and headlong into the water. Others did the same. A boatload of people putting back came leaping out as I rushed past. The stones under my feet were muddy and slippery, and the river was so low that I ran perhaps twenty feet scarcely waist-deep. Then, as the Martian towered overhead scarcely a couple of hundred yards away, I flung myself forward under the surface. The splashes of the people in the boats leaping into the river sounded like thunderclaps in my ears. People were landing hastily on both sides of the river. But the Martian machine took no more notice for the moment of the people running this way and that than a man would of the confusion of ants in a nest against which his foot has kicked. When, half suffocated, I raised my head above water, the Martian's hood pointed at the batteries that were still firing across the river, and as it advanced it swung loose what must have been the generator of the Heat-Ray.

In another moment it was on the bank, and in a stride wading halfway across. The knees of its foremost legs bent at the farther bank, and in another moment it had raised itself to its full height again, close to the village of Shepperton. Forthwith the six guns which, unknown to anyone on the right bank, had been hidden behind the outskirts of that village, fired simultaneously. The sudden near concussion, the last close upon the first, made my heart jump. The monster was already raising the case generating the Heat-Ray as the first shell burst six yards above the hood.

I gave a cry of astonishment. I saw and thought nothing of the other four Martian monsters; my attention was riveted upon the nearer incident. Simultaneously two other shells burst in the air near the body as the hood twisted round in time to receive, but not in time to dodge, the fourth shell.

The shell burst clean in the face of the Thing. The hood bulged, flashed, was whirled off in a dozen tattered fragments of red flesh and glittering metal.

"Hit!" shouted I, with something between a scream and a cheer.

I heard answering shouts from the people in the water about me. I could have leaped out of the water with that momentary exultation.

The decapitated colossus reeled like a drunken giant; but it did not fall over. It recovered its balance by a miracle, and, no longer heeding its steps and with the camera that fired the Heat-Ray now rigidly upheld, it reeled swiftly upon Shepperton. The living intelligence, the Martian within the hood, was slain and splashed to the four winds of heaven, and the Thing was now but a mere intricate device of metal whirling to destruction. It drove along in a straight line, incapable of guidance. It struck the tower of Shepperton Church, smashing it down as the impact of a battering ram might have done, swerved aside, blundered on and collapsed with tremendous force into the river out of my sight.

A violent explosion shook the air, and a spout of water, steam, mud, and shattered metal shot far up into the sky. As the camera of the Heat-Ray hit the water, the latter had immediately flashed into steam. In another moment a huge wave, like a muddy tidal bore but almost scaldingly hot, came sweeping round the bend upstream. I saw people struggling shorewards, and heard their screaming and shouting faintly above the seething and roar of the Martian's collapse.

For a moment I heeded nothing of the heat, forgot the patent need of self-preservation. I splashed through the tumultuous water, pushing aside a man in black to do so, until I could see round the bend. Half a dozen deserted boats pitched aimlessly upon the confusion of the waves. The fallen Martian came into sight downstream, lying across the river, and for the most part submerged.

Thick clouds of steam were pouring off the wreckage, and through the tumultuously whirling wisps I could see, intermittently and vaguely, the gigantic limbs churning the water and flinging a splash and spray of mud and froth into the air. The tentacles swayed and struck like living arms, and, save for the helpless purposelessness of these movements, it was as if some wounded thing were struggling for its life amid the waves. Enormous quantities of a ruddy-brown fluid were spurting up in noisy jets out of the machine.

My attention was diverted from this death flurry by a furious yelling, like that of the thing called a siren in our manufacturing towns. A man, knee-deep near the towing path, shouted inaudibly to me and pointed. Looking back, I saw the other Martians advancing with gigantic strides down the riverbank from the direction of Chertsey. The Shepperton guns spoke this time unavailingly.

At that I ducked at once under water, and, holding my breath until movement was an agony, blundered painfully ahead under the surface as long as I could. The water was in a tumult about me, and rapidly growing hotter.

When for a moment I raised my head to take breath and throw the hair and water from my eyes, the steam was rising in a whirling white fog that at first hid the Martians altogether. The noise was deafening. Then I saw them dimly, colossal figures of grey, magnified by the mist. They had passed by me, and two were stooping over the frothing, tumultuous ruins of their comrade.

The third and fourth stood beside him in the water, one perhaps two hundred yards from me, the other towards Laleham. The generators of the Heat-Rays waved high, and the hissing beams smote down this way and that.

The air was full of sound, a deafening and confusing conflict of noises – the clangorous din of the Martians, the crash of falling houses, the thud of trees, fences, sheds flashing into flame, and the crackling and roaring of fire. Dense black smoke was leaping up to mingle with the steam from the river, and as the Heat-Ray went to and fro over Weybridge its impact was marked by flashes of incandescent white, that gave place at once to a smoky dance of lurid flames. The nearer houses still stood intact, awaiting their fate, shadowy, faint and pallid in the steam, with the fire behind them going to and fro.

For a moment perhaps I stood there, breast-high in the almost boiling water, dumbfounded at my position, hopeless of escape. Through the reek I could see the people who had been with me in the river scrambling out of the water through the reeds, like little frogs hurrying through grass from the advance of a man, or running to and fro in utter dismay on the towing path.

Then suddenly the white flashes of the Heat-Ray came leaping towards me. The houses caved in as they dissolved at its touch, and darted out flames; the trees changed to fire with a roar. The Ray flickered up and down the towing path, licking off the people who ran this way and that, and came down to the water's edge not fifty yards from where I stood. It swept across the river to Shepperton, and the water in its track rose in a boiling weal crested with steam. I turned shoreward.

In another moment the huge wave, well-nigh at the boiling-point had rushed upon me. I screamed aloud, and scalded, half blinded, agonised, I staggered through the leaping, hissing water towards the shore. Had my foot stumbled, it would have been the end. I fell helplessly, in full sight of the Martians, upon the broad, bare gravelly spit that runs down to mark the angle of the Wey and Thames. I expected nothing but death.

I have a dim memory of the foot of a Martian coming down within a score of yards of my head, driving straight into the loose gravel, whirling it this way and that and lifting again; of a long suspense, and then of the four carrying the debris of their comrade between them, now clear and then presently faint through a veil of smoke, receding interminably, as it seemed to me, across a vast space of river and meadow. And then, very slowly, I realised that by a miracle I had escaped.

Chapter XIII
How I Fell in with the Curate

AFTER GETTING THIS sudden lesson in the power of terrestrial weapons, the Martians retreated to their original position upon Horsell Common; and in their haste, and encumbered with the debris of their smashed companion, they no doubt overlooked many such a stray and negligible victim as myself. Had they left their comrade and pushed on forthwith, there was nothing at that time between them and London but batteries of twelve-pounder guns, and they would certainly have reached the capital in advance of the tidings of their approach; as sudden, dreadful, and destructive their advent would have been as the earthquake that destroyed Lisbon a century ago.

But they were in no hurry. Cylinder followed cylinder on its interplanetary flight; every twenty-four hours brought them reinforcement. And meanwhile the military and naval authorities, now fully alive to the tremendous power of their antagonists, worked with furious energy. Every minute a fresh gun came into position until, before twilight, every copse, every row of suburban villas on the hilly slopes about Kingston and Richmond, masked an expectant black muzzle. And through the charred and desolated area – perhaps twenty square miles altogether – that encircled the Martian encampment on Horsell Common, through charred and ruined villages among the green trees, through the blackened and smoking arcades that had been but a day ago pine spinneys, crawled the devoted scouts with the heliographs that were presently to warn the gunners of the Martian approach. But the Martians now understood our command of artillery and the danger of human proximity, and not a man ventured within a mile of either cylinder, save at the price of his life.

It would seem that these giants spent the earlier part of the afternoon in going to and fro, transferring everything from the second and third cylinders – the second in Addlestone Golf Links and the third at Pyrford – to their original pit on Horsell Common. Over that, above the blackened heather and ruined buildings that stretched far and wide, stood one as sentinel, while the rest abandoned their vast fighting-machines and descended into the pit. They were hard at work there far into the night, and the towering pillar of dense green smoke that rose therefrom could be seen from the hills about Merrow, and even, it is said, from Banstead and Epsom Downs.

And while the Martians behind me were thus preparing for their next sally, and in front of me Humanity gathered for the battle, I made my way with infinite pains and labour from the fire and smoke of burning Weybridge towards London.

I saw an abandoned boat, very small and remote, drifting down-stream; and throwing off the most of my sodden clothes, I went after it, gained it, and so escaped out of that destruction. There were no oars in the boat, but I contrived to paddle, as well as my parboiled hands would allow, down the river towards Halliford and Walton, going very tediously and continually looking behind me, as you may well understand. I followed the river, because I considered that the water gave me my best chance of escape should these giants return.

The hot water from the Martian's overthrow drifted downstream with me, so that for the best part of a mile I could see little of either bank. Once, however, I made out a string of black figures hurrying across the meadows from the direction of Weybridge. Halliford, it seemed, was deserted, and several of the houses facing the river were on fire. It was strange to see the place quite tranquil, quite desolate under the hot blue sky, with the smoke and little threads of flame going straight up into the heat of the afternoon. Never before had I seen houses burning without the accompaniment of an obstructive crowd. A little farther on the dry reeds up the bank were smoking and glowing, and a line of fire inland was marching steadily across a late field of hay.

For a long time I drifted, so painful and weary was I after the violence I had been through, and so intense the heat upon the water. Then my fears got the better of me again, and I resumed my paddling. The sun scorched my bare back. At last, as the bridge at Walton was coming into sight round the bend, my fever and faintness overcame my fears, and I landed on the Middlesex bank and lay down, deadly sick, amid the long grass. I suppose the time was then about four or five o'clock. I got up presently, walked perhaps half a mile without meeting a soul, and then lay down again in the shadow of a hedge. I seem to remember talking, wanderingly, to myself during that last spurt. I was also very thirsty, and bitterly regretful I had drunk no more water. It is a curious thing that I felt angry with my wife; I cannot account for it, but my impotent desire to reach Leatherhead worried me excessively.

I do not clearly remember the arrival of the curate, so that probably I dozed. I became aware of him as a seated figure in soot-smudged shirt sleeves, and with his upturned, clean-shaven face staring at a faint flickering that danced over the sky. The sky was what is called a mackerel sky – rows and rows of faint down-plumes of cloud, just tinted with the midsummer sunset.

I sat up, and at the rustle of my motion he looked at me quickly.

"Have you any water?" I asked abruptly.

He shook his head.

"You have been asking for water for the last hour," he said.

For a moment we were silent, taking stock of each other. I dare say he found me a strange enough figure, naked, save for my water-soaked trousers and socks, scalded, and my face and shoulders blackened by the smoke. His face was a fair weakness, his chin retreated, and his hair lay in crisp, almost flaxen curls on his low forehead; his eyes were rather large, pale blue, and blankly staring. He spoke abruptly, looking vacantly away from me.

"What does it mean?" he said. "What do these things mean?"

I stared at him and made no answer.

He extended a thin white hand and spoke in almost a complaining tone.

"Why are these things permitted? What sins have we done? The morning service was over, I was walking through the roads to clear my brain for the afternoon, and then – fire, earthquake, death! As if it were Sodom and Gomorrah! All our work undone, all the work – What are these Martians?"

"What are we?" I answered, clearing my throat.

He gripped his knees and turned to look at me again. For half a minute, perhaps, he stared silently.

"I was walking through the roads to clear my brain," he said. "And suddenly – fire, earthquake, death!"

He relapsed into silence, with his chin now sunken almost to his knees.

Presently he began waving his hand.

"All the work – all the Sunday schools – What have we done – what has Weybridge done? Everything gone – everything destroyed. The church! We rebuilt it only three years ago. Gone! Swept out of existence! Why?"

Another pause, and he broke out again like one demented.

"The smoke of her burning goeth up for ever and ever!" he shouted.

His eyes flamed, and he pointed a lean finger in the direction of Weybridge.

By this time I was beginning to take his measure. The tremendous tragedy in which he had been involved – it was evident he was a fugitive from Weybridge – had driven him to the very verge of his reason.

"Are we far from Sunbury?" I said, in a matter-of-fact tone.

"What are we to do?" he asked. "Are these creatures everywhere? Has the earth been given over to them?"

"Are we far from Sunbury?"

"Only this morning I officiated at early celebration –"

"Things have changed," I said, quietly. "You must keep your head. There is still hope."

"Hope!"

"Yes. Plentiful hope – for all this destruction!"

I began to explain my view of our position. He listened at first, but as I went on the interest dawning in his eyes gave place to their former stare, and his regard wandered from me.

"This must be the beginning of the end," he said, interrupting me. "The end! The great and terrible day of the Lord! When men shall call upon the mountains and the rocks to fall upon them and hide them – hide them from the face of Him that sitteth upon the throne!"

I began to understand the position. I ceased my laboured reasoning, struggled to my feet, and, standing over him, laid my hand on his shoulder.

"Be a man!" said I. "You are scared out of your wits! What good is religion if it collapses under calamity? Think of what earthquakes and floods, wars and volcanoes, have done before to men! Did you think God had exempted Weybridge? He is not an insurance agent."

For a time he sat in blank silence.

"But how can we escape?" he asked, suddenly. "They are invulnerable, they are pitiless."

"Neither the one nor, perhaps, the other," I answered. "And the mightier they are the more sane and wary should we be. One of them was killed yonder not three hours ago."

"Killed!" he said, staring about him. "How can God's ministers be killed?"

"I saw it happen." I proceeded to tell him. "We have chanced to come in for the thick of it," said I, "and that is all."

"What is that flicker in the sky?" he asked abruptly.

I told him it was the heliograph signalling – that it was the sign of human help and effort in the sky.

"We are in the midst of it," I said, "quiet as it is. That flicker in the sky tells of the gathering storm. Yonder, I take it are the Martians, and Londonward, where those hills rise about Richmond and Kingston and the trees give cover, earthworks are being thrown up and guns are being placed. Presently the Martians will be coming this way again."

And even as I spoke he sprang to his feet and stopped me by a gesture.

"Listen!" he said.

From beyond the low hills across the water came the dull resonance of distant guns and a remote weird crying. Then everything was still. A cockchafer came droning over the hedge and past us. High in the west the crescent moon hung faint and pale above the smoke of Weybridge and Shepperton and the hot, still splendour of the sunset.

"We had better follow this path," I said, "northward."

Chapter XIV
In London

MY YOUNGER BROTHER was in London when the Martians fell at Woking. He was a medical student working for an imminent examination, and he heard nothing of the arrival until Saturday morning. The morning papers on Saturday contained, in addition to lengthy special articles on the planet Mars, on life in the planets, and so forth, a brief and vaguely worded telegram, all the more striking for its brevity.

The Martians, alarmed by the approach of a crowd, had killed a number of people with a quick-firing gun, so the story ran. The telegram concluded with the words: "Formidable as they seem to be, the Martians have not moved from the pit into which they have fallen, and, indeed, seem incapable of doing so. Probably this is due to the relative strength of the earth's gravitational energy." On that last text their leader-writer expanded very comfortingly.

Of course all the students in the crammer's biology class, to which my brother went that day, were intensely interested, but there were no signs of any unusual excitement in the streets. The afternoon papers puffed scraps of news under big headlines. They had nothing to tell beyond the movements of troops about the common, and the burning of the pine woods between Woking and Weybridge, until eight. Then the *St. James's Gazette*, in an extra-special edition, announced the bare fact of the interruption of telegraphic communication. This was thought to be due to the falling of burning pine trees across the line. Nothing more of the fighting was known that night, the night of my drive to Leatherhead and back.

My brother felt no anxiety about us, as he knew from the description in the papers that the cylinder was a good two miles from my house. He made up his mind to run down that night to me, in order, as he says, to see the Things before they were killed. He dispatched a telegram, which never reached me, about four o'clock, and spent the evening at a music hall.

In London, also, on Saturday night there was a thunderstorm, and my brother reached Waterloo in a cab. On the platform from which the midnight train usually starts he learned, after some waiting, that an accident prevented trains from reaching Woking that night. The nature of the accident he could not ascertain; indeed, the railway authorities did not clearly know at that time. There was very little excitement in the station, as the officials, failing to realise that anything further than a breakdown between Byfleet and

Woking junction had occurred, were running the theatre trains which usually passed through Woking round by Virginia Water or Guildford. They were busy making the necessary arrangements to alter the route of the Southampton and Portsmouth Sunday League excursions. A nocturnal newspaper reporter, mistaking my brother for the traffic manager, to whom he bears a slight resemblance, waylaid and tried to interview him. Few people, excepting the railway officials, connected the breakdown with the Martians.

I have read, in another account of these events, that on Sunday morning 'all London was electrified by the news from Woking.' As a matter of fact, there was nothing to justify that very extravagant phrase. Plenty of Londoners did not hear of the Martians until the panic of Monday morning. Those who did took some time to realise all that the hastily worded telegrams in the Sunday papers conveyed. The majority of people in London do not read Sunday papers.

The habit of personal security, moreover, is so deeply fixed in the Londoner's mind, and startling intelligence so much a matter of course in the papers, that they could read without any personal tremors:

> About seven o'clock last night the Martians came out of the cylinder, and, moving about under an armour of metallic shields, have completely wrecked Woking station with the adjacent houses, and massacred an entire battalion of the Cardigan Regiment. No details are known. Maxims have been absolutely useless against their armour; the field guns have been disabled by them. Flying hussars have been galloping into Chertsey. The Martians appear to be moving slowly towards Chertsey or Windsor. Great anxiety prevails in West Surrey, and earthworks are being thrown up to check the advance Londonward.

That was how the Sunday *Sun* put it, and a clever and remarkably prompt 'handbook' article in the *Referee* compared the affair to a menagerie suddenly let loose in a village.

No one in London knew positively of the nature of the armoured Martians, and there was still a fixed idea that these monsters must be sluggish: 'crawling,' 'creeping painfully' – such expressions occurred in almost all the earlier reports. None of the telegrams could have been written by an eyewitness of their advance. The Sunday papers printed separate editions as further news came to hand, some even in default of it. But there was practically nothing more to tell people until late in the afternoon, when the authorities gave the press agencies the news in their possession. It was stated that the people of Walton and Weybridge, and all the district were pouring along the roads Londonward, and that was all.

My brother went to church at the Foundling Hospital in the morning, still in ignorance of what had happened on the previous night. There he heard allusions made to the invasion, and a special prayer for peace. Coming out, he bought a *Referee*. He became alarmed at the news in this, and went again to Waterloo station to find out if communication were restored. The omnibuses, carriages, cyclists, and innumerable people walking in their best clothes seemed scarcely affected by the strange intelligence that the news venders were disseminating. People were interested, or, if alarmed, alarmed only on account of the local residents. At the station he heard for the first time that the Windsor and Chertsey lines were now interrupted. The porters told him that several remarkable telegrams had been received in the morning from Byfleet and Chertsey stations, but that these had abruptly ceased. My brother could get very little precise detail out of them.

'There's fighting going on about Weybridge' was the extent of their information.

The train service was now very much disorganised. Quite a number of people who had been expecting friends from places on the South-Western network were standing about the station. One grey-headed old gentleman came and abused the South-Western Company bitterly to my brother. "It wants showing up," he said.

One or two trains came in from Richmond, Putney, and Kingston, containing people who had gone out for a day's boating and found the locks closed and a feeling of panic in the air. A man in a blue and white blazer addressed my brother, full of strange tidings.

"There's hosts of people driving into Kingston in traps and carts and things, with boxes of valuables and all that," he said. "They come from Molesey and Weybridge and Walton, and they say there's been guns heard at Chertsey, heavy firing, and that mounted soldiers have told them to get off at once because the Martians are coming. We heard guns firing at Hampton Court station, but we thought it was thunder. What the dickens does it all mean? The Martians can't get out of their pit, can they?"

My brother could not tell him.

Afterwards he found that the vague feeling of alarm had spread to the clients of the underground railway, and that the Sunday excursionists began to return from all over the South-Western 'lung' – Barnes, Wimbledon, Richmond Park, Kew, and so forth – at unnaturally early hours; but not a soul had anything more than vague hearsay to tell of. Everyone connected with the terminus seemed ill-tempered.

About five o'clock the gathering crowd in the station was immensely excited by the opening of the line of communication, which is almost invariably closed, between the South-Eastern and the South-Western stations, and the passage of carriage trucks bearing huge guns and carriages crammed with soldiers. These were the guns that were brought up from Woolwich and Chatham to cover Kingston. There was an exchange of pleasantries: "You'll get eaten!" "We're the beast-tamers!" and so forth. A little while after that a squad of police came into the station and began to clear the public off the platforms, and my brother went out into the street again.

The church bells were ringing for evensong, and a squad of Salvation Army lassies came singing down Waterloo Road. On the bridge a number of loafers were watching a curious brown scum that came drifting down the stream in patches. The sun was just setting, and the Clock Tower and the Houses of Parliament rose against one of the most peaceful skies it is possible to imagine, a sky of gold, barred with long transverse stripes of reddish-purple cloud. There was talk of a floating body. One of the men there, a reservist he said he was, told my brother he had seen the heliograph flickering in the west.

In Wellington Street my brother met a couple of sturdy roughs who had just been rushed out of Fleet Street with still-wet newspapers and staring placards. "Dreadful catastrophe!" they bawled one to the other down Wellington Street. "Fighting at Weybridge! Full description! Repulse of the Martians! London in Danger!" He had to give threepence for a copy of that paper.

Then it was, and then only, that he realised something of the full power and terror of these monsters. He learned that they were not merely a handful of small sluggish creatures, but that they were minds swaying vast mechanical bodies; and that they could move swiftly and smite with such power that even the mightiest guns could not stand against them.

They were described as 'vast spiderlike machines, nearly a hundred feet high, capable of the speed of an express train, and able to shoot out a beam of intense heat.' Masked batteries, chiefly of field guns, had been planted in the country about Horsell Common, and especially between the Woking district and London. Five of the machines had been seen moving towards the Thames, and one, by a happy chance, had been destroyed. In the other cases the shells had missed, and the batteries had been at once annihilated by the Heat-Rays. Heavy losses of soldiers were mentioned, but the tone of the dispatch was optimistic.

The Martians had been repulsed; they were not invulnerable. They had retreated to their triangle of cylinders again, in the circle about Woking. Signallers with heliographs were pushing forward upon them from all sides. Guns were in rapid transit from Windsor, Portsmouth, Aldershot, Woolwich – even from the north; among others, long wire-guns of ninety-five tons from Woolwich. Altogether one hundred and sixteen were in position or being hastily placed, chiefly covering London. Never before in England had there been such a vast or rapid concentration of military material.

Any further cylinders that fell, it was hoped, could be destroyed at once by high explosives, which were being rapidly manufactured and distributed. No doubt, ran the report, the situation was of the strangest and gravest description, but the public was exhorted to avoid and discourage panic. No doubt the Martians were strange and terrible in the extreme, but at the outside there could not be more than twenty of them against our millions.

The authorities had reason to suppose, from the size of the cylinders, that at the outside there could not be more than five in each cylinder – fifteen altogether. And one at least was disposed of – perhaps more. The public would be fairly warned of the approach of danger, and elaborate measures were being taken for the protection of the people in the threatened southwestern suburbs. And so, with reiterated assurances of the safety of London and the ability of the authorities to cope with the difficulty, this quasi-proclamation closed.

This was printed in enormous type on paper so fresh that it was still wet, and there had been no time to add a word of comment. It was curious, my brother said, to see how ruthlessly the usual contents of the paper had been hacked and taken out to give this place.

All down Wellington Street people could be seen fluttering out the pink sheets and reading, and the Strand was suddenly noisy with the voices of an army of hawkers following these pioneers. Men came scrambling off buses to secure copies. Certainly this news excited people intensely, whatever their previous apathy. The shutters of a map shop in the Strand were being taken down, my brother said, and a man in his Sunday raiment, lemon-yellow gloves even, was visible inside the window hastily fastening maps of Surrey to the glass.

Going on along the Strand to Trafalgar Square, the paper in his hand, my brother saw some of the fugitives from West Surrey. There was a man with his wife and two boys and some articles of furniture in a cart such as greengrocers use. He was driving from the direction of Westminster Bridge; and close behind him came a hay waggon with five or six respectable-looking people in it, and some boxes and bundles. The faces of these people were haggard, and their entire appearance contrasted conspicuously with the Sabbath-best appearance of the people on the omnibuses. People in fashionable clothing peeped at them out of cabs. They stopped at the Square as if undecided which way to take, and finally turned eastward along the Strand. Some way behind these came a man in workday clothes, riding one of those old-fashioned tricycles with a small front wheel. He was dirty and white in the face.

My brother turned down towards Victoria, and met a number of such people. He had a vague idea that he might see something of me. He noticed an unusual number of police regulating the traffic. Some of the refugees were exchanging news with the people on the omnibuses. One was professing to have seen the Martians. "Boilers on stilts, I tell you, striding along like men." Most of them were excited and animated by their strange experience.

Beyond Victoria the public-houses were doing a lively trade with these arrivals. At all the street corners groups of people were reading papers, talking excitedly, or staring at these unusual Sunday visitors. They seemed to increase as night drew on, until at last the roads, my brother said, were like Epsom High Street on a Derby Day. My brother addressed several of these fugitives and got unsatisfactory answers from most.

None of them could tell him any news of Woking except one man, who assured him that Woking had been entirely destroyed on the previous night.

"I come from Byfleet," he said; "man on a bicycle came through the place in the early morning, and ran from door to door warning us to come away. Then came soldiers. We went out to look, and there were clouds of smoke to the south – nothing but smoke, and not a soul coming that way. Then we heard the guns at Chertsey, and folks coming from Weybridge. So I've locked up my house and come on."

At the time there was a strong feeling in the streets that the authorities were to blame for their incapacity to dispose of the invaders without all this inconvenience.

About eight o'clock a noise of heavy firing was distinctly audible all over the south of London. My brother could not hear it for the traffic in the main thoroughfares, but by striking through the quiet back streets to the river he was able to distinguish it quite plainly.

He walked from Westminster to his apartments near Regent's Park, about two. He was now very anxious on my account, and disturbed at the evident magnitude of the trouble. His mind was inclined to run, even as mine had run on Saturday, on military details. He thought of all those silent, expectant guns, of the suddenly nomadic countryside; he tried to imagine 'boilers on stilts' a hundred feet high.

There were one or two cartloads of refugees passing along Oxford Street, and several in the Marylebone Road, but so slowly was the news spreading that Regent Street and Portland Place were full of their usual Sunday-night promenaders, albeit they talked in groups, and along the edge of Regent's Park there were as many silent couples 'walking out' together under the scattered gas lamps as ever there had been. The night was warm and still, and a little oppressive; the sound of guns continued intermittently, and after midnight there seemed to be sheet lightning in the south.

He read and re-read the paper, fearing the worst had happened to me. He was restless, and after supper prowled out again aimlessly. He returned and tried in vain to divert his attention to his examination notes. He went to bed a little after midnight, and was awakened from lurid dreams in the small hours of Monday by the sound of door knockers, feet running in the street, distant drumming, and a clamour of bells. Red reflections danced on the ceiling. For a moment he lay astonished, wondering whether day had come or the world gone mad. Then he jumped out of bed and ran to the window.

His room was an attic and as he thrust his head out, up and down the street there were a dozen echoes to the noise of his window sash, and heads in every kind of night disarray appeared. Enquiries were being shouted. "They are coming!" bawled a policeman, hammering at the door; "the Martians are coming!" and hurried to the next door.

The sound of drumming and trumpeting came from the Albany Street Barracks, and every church within earshot was hard at work killing sleep with a vehement disorderly tocsin. There was a noise of doors opening, and window after window in the houses opposite flashed from darkness into yellow illumination.

Up the street came galloping a closed carriage, bursting abruptly into noise at the corner, rising to a clattering climax under the window, and dying away slowly in the distance. Close on the rear of this came a couple of cabs, the forerunners of a long procession of flying vehicles, going for the most part to Chalk Farm station, where the North-Western special trains were loading up, instead of coming down the gradient into Euston.

For a long time my brother stared out of the window in blank astonishment, watching the policemen hammering at door after door, and delivering their incomprehensible message. Then the door behind him opened, and the man who lodged across the landing came in, dressed only in shirt, trousers, and slippers, his braces loose about his waist, his hair disordered from his pillow.

"What the devil is it?" he asked. "A fire? What a devil of a row!"

They both craned their heads out of the window, straining to hear what the policemen were shouting. People were coming out of the side streets, and standing in groups at the corners talking.

"What the devil is it all about?" said my brother's fellow lodger.

My brother answered him vaguely and began to dress, running with each garment to the window in order to miss nothing of the growing excitement. And presently men selling unnaturally early newspapers came bawling into the street:

"London in danger of suffocation! The Kingston and Richmond defences forced! Fearful massacres in the Thames Valley!"

And all about him – in the rooms below, in the houses on each side and across the road, and behind in the Park Terraces and in the hundred other streets of that part of Marylebone, and the Westbourne Park district and St. Pancras, and westward and northward in Kilburn and St. John's Wood and Hampstead, and eastward in Shoreditch and Highbury and Haggerston and Hoxton, and, indeed, through all the vastness of London from Ealing to East Ham – people were rubbing their eyes, and opening windows to stare out and ask aimless questions, dressing hastily as the first breath of the coming storm of Fear blew through the streets. It was the dawn of the great panic. London, which had gone to bed on Sunday night oblivious and inert, was awakened, in the small hours of Monday morning, to a vivid sense of danger.

Unable from his window to learn what was happening, my brother went down and out into the street, just as the sky between the parapets of the houses grew pink with the early dawn. The flying people on foot and in vehicles grew more numerous every moment. "Black Smoke!" he heard people crying, and again "Black Smoke!" The contagion of such a unanimous fear was inevitable. As my brother hesitated on the door-step, he saw another news vender approaching, and got a paper forthwith. The man was running away with the rest, and selling his papers for a shilling each as he ran – a grotesque mingling of profit and panic.

And from this paper my brother read that catastrophic dispatch of the Commander-in-Chief:

"The Martians are able to discharge enormous clouds of a black and poisonous vapour by means of rockets. They have smothered our batteries, destroyed Richmond, Kingston, and Wimbledon, and are advancing slowly towards London, destroying everything on the way. It is impossible to stop them. There is no safety from the Black Smoke but in instant flight."

That was all, but it was enough. The whole population of the great six-million city was stirring, slipping, running; presently it would be pouring *en masse* northward.

"Black Smoke!" the voices cried. "Fire!"

The bells of the neighbouring church made a jangling tumult, a cart carelessly driven smashed, amid shrieks and curses, against the water trough up the street. Sickly yellow lights went to and fro in the houses, and some of the passing cabs flaunted unextinguished lamps. And overhead the dawn was growing brighter, clear and steady and calm.

He heard footsteps running to and fro in the rooms, and up and down stairs behind him. His landlady came to the door, loosely wrapped in dressing gown and shawl; her husband followed ejaculating.

As my brother began to realise the import of all these things, he turned hastily to his own room, put all his available money – some ten pounds altogether – into his pockets, and went out again into the streets.

Chapter XV
What Had Happened in Surrey

IT WAS WHILE the curate had sat and talked so wildly to me under the hedge in the flat meadows near Halliford, and while my brother was watching the fugitives stream over Westminster Bridge, that the Martians had resumed the offensive. So far as one can ascertain from the conflicting accounts that have been put forth, the majority of them remained busied with preparations in the Horsell pit until nine that night, hurrying on some operation that disengaged huge volumes of green smoke.

But three certainly came out about eight o'clock and, advancing slowly and cautiously, made their way through Byfleet and Pyrford towards Ripley and Weybridge, and so came in sight of the expectant batteries against the setting sun. These Martians did not advance in a body, but in a line, each perhaps a mile and a half from his nearest fellow. They communicated with one another by means of sirenlike howls, running up and down the scale from one note to another.

It was this howling and firing of the guns at Ripley and St. George's Hill that we had heard at Upper Halliford. The Ripley gunners, unseasoned artillery volunteers who ought never to have been placed in such a position, fired one wild, premature, ineffectual volley, and bolted on horse and foot through the deserted village, while the Martian, without using his Heat-Ray, walked serenely over their guns, stepped gingerly among them, passed in front of them, and so came unexpectedly upon the guns in Painshill Park, which he destroyed.

The St. George's Hill men, however, were better led or of a better mettle. Hidden by a pine wood as they were, they seem to have been quite unsuspected by the Martian nearest to them. They laid their guns as deliberately as if they had been on parade, and fired at about a thousand yards' range.

The shells flashed all round him, and he was seen to advance a few paces, stagger, and go down. Everybody yelled together, and the guns were reloaded in frantic haste. The overthrown Martian set up a prolonged ululation, and immediately a second glittering giant, answering him, appeared over the trees to the south. It would seem that a leg of the tripod had been smashed by one of the shells. The whole of the second volley flew wide of the Martian on the ground, and, simultaneously, both his companions brought their Heat-Rays to bear on the battery. The ammunition blew up, the pine trees all about the guns flashed into fire, and only one or two of the men who were already running over the crest of the hill escaped.

After this it would seem that the three took counsel together and halted, and the scouts who were watching them report that they remained absolutely stationary for the next half hour. The Martian who had been overthrown crawled tediously out of his hood, a small brown figure, oddly suggestive from that distance of a speck of blight, and apparently engaged in the repair of his support. About nine he had finished, for his cowl was then seen above the trees again.

It was a few minutes past nine that night when these three sentinels were joined by four other Martians, each carrying a thick black tube. A similar tube was handed to each of the three, and the seven proceeded to distribute themselves at equal distances along a curved line between St. George's Hill, Weybridge, and the village of Send, southwest of Ripley.

A dozen rockets sprang out of the hills before them so soon as they began to move, and warned the waiting batteries about Ditton and Esher. At the same time four of their fighting machines, similarly armed with tubes, crossed the river, and two of them, black against the western sky, came into sight of myself and the curate as we hurried wearily and painfully along the road that runs northward out of Halliford. They moved, as it seemed to us, upon a cloud, for a milky mist covered the fields and rose to a third of their height.

At this sight the curate cried faintly in his throat, and began running; but I knew it was no good running from a Martian, and I turned aside and crawled through dewy nettles and brambles into the broad ditch by the side of the road. He looked back, saw what I was doing, and turned to join me.

The two halted, the nearer to us standing and facing Sunbury, the remoter being a grey indistinctness towards the evening star, away towards Staines.

The occasional howling of the Martians had ceased; they took up their positions in the huge crescent about their cylinders in absolute silence. It was a crescent with twelve miles between its horns. Never since the devising of gunpowder was the beginning of a battle so still. To us and to an observer about Ripley it would have had precisely the same effect – the Martians seemed in solitary possession of the darkling night, lit only as it was by the slender moon, the stars, the afterglow of the daylight, and the ruddy glare from St. George's Hill and the woods of Painshill.

But facing that crescent everywhere – at Staines, Hounslow, Ditton, Esher, Ockham, behind hills and woods south of the river, and across the flat grass meadows to the north of it, wherever a cluster of trees or village houses gave sufficient cover – the guns were waiting. The signal rockets burst and rained their sparks through the night and vanished, and the spirit of all those watching batteries rose to a tense expectation. The Martians had but to advance into the line of fire, and instantly those motionless black forms of men, those guns glittering so darkly in the early night, would explode into a thunderous fury of battle.

No doubt the thought that was uppermost in a thousand of those vigilant minds, even as it was uppermost in mine, was the riddle – how much they understood of us. Did they grasp that we in our millions were organized, disciplined, working together? Or did they interpret our spurts of fire, the sudden stinging of our shells, our steady investment of their encampment, as we should the furious unanimity of onslaught in a disturbed hive of bees? Did they dream they might exterminate us? (At that time no one knew what food they needed.) A hundred such questions struggled together in my mind as I watched that vast sentinel shape. And in the back of my mind was the sense of all the huge unknown and hidden forces Londonward. Had they prepared pitfalls? Were the powder mills at Hounslow ready as a snare? Would the Londoners have the heart and courage to make a greater Moscow of their mighty province of houses?

Then, after an interminable time, as it seemed to us, crouching and peering through the hedge, came a sound like the distant concussion of a gun. Another nearer, and then another. And then the Martian beside us raised his tube on high and discharged it, gunwise, with a heavy report that made the ground heave. The one towards Staines answered him. There was no flash, no smoke, simply that loaded detonation.

I was so excited by these heavy minute-guns following one another that I so far forgot my personal safety and my scalded hands as to clamber up into the hedge and stare towards Sunbury. As I did so a second report followed, and a big projectile hurtled overhead towards Hounslow. I expected at least to see smoke or fire, or some such evidence of its work. But all I saw was the deep blue sky above, with one solitary star, and the white mist spreading wide and low beneath. And there had been no crash, no answering explosion. The silence was restored; the minute lengthened to three.

"What has happened?" said the curate, standing up beside me.

"Heaven knows!" said I.

A bat flickered by and vanished. A distant tumult of shouting began and ceased. I looked again at the Martian, and saw he was now moving eastward along the riverbank, with a swift, rolling motion,

Every moment I expected the fire of some hidden battery to spring upon him; but the evening calm was unbroken. The figure of the Martian grew smaller as he receded, and presently the mist and the gathering night had swallowed him up. By a common impulse we clambered higher. Towards Sunbury was a dark appearance, as though a conical hill had suddenly come into being there, hiding our view of the farther country; and then, remoter across the river, over Walton, we saw another such summit. These hill-like forms grew lower and broader even as we stared.

Moved by a sudden thought, I looked northward, and there I perceived a third of these cloudy black kopjes had risen.

Everything had suddenly become very still. Far away to the southeast, marking the quiet, we heard the Martians hooting to one another, and then the air quivered again with the distant thud of their guns. But the earthly artillery made no reply.

Now at the time we could not understand these things, but later I was to learn the meaning of these ominous kopjes that gathered in the twilight. Each of the Martians, standing in the great crescent I have described, had discharged, by means of the gunlike tube he carried, a huge canister over whatever hill, copse, cluster of houses, or other possible cover for guns, chanced to be in front of him. Some fired only one of these, some two – as in the case of the one we had seen; the one at Ripley is said to have discharged no fewer than five at that time. These canisters smashed on striking the ground – they did not explode – and incontinently disengaged an enormous volume of heavy, inky vapour, coiling and pouring upward in a huge and ebony cumulus cloud, a gaseous hill that sank and spread itself slowly over the surrounding country. And the touch of that vapour, the inhaling of its pungent wisps, was death to all that breathes.

It was heavy, this vapour, heavier than the densest smoke, so that, after the first tumultuous uprush and outflow of its impact, it sank down through the air and poured over the ground in a manner rather liquid than gaseous, abandoning the hills, and streaming into the valleys and ditches and watercourses even as I have heard the carbonic-acid gas that pours from volcanic clefts is wont to do. And where it came upon water some chemical action occurred, and the surface would be instantly covered with a powdery scum that sank slowly and made way for more. The scum was absolutely insoluble, and it is a strange thing, seeing the instant effect of the gas, that one could drink without hurt the water from which it had been strained. The vapour did not diffuse as a true gas would do. It hung together in banks, flowing sluggishly down the slope of the land and driving reluctantly before the wind, and very slowly it combined with the mist and moisture of the air, and sank to the earth in the form of dust. Save that an unknown element giving a group of four lines in the blue of the spectrum is concerned, we are still entirely ignorant of the nature of this substance.

Once the tumultuous upheaval of its dispersion was over, the black smoke clung so closely to the ground, even before its precipitation, that fifty feet up in the air, on the roofs and upper stories of high houses and on great trees, there was a chance of escaping its poison altogether, as was proved even that night at Street Cobham and Ditton.

The man who escaped at the former place tells a wonderful story of the strangeness of its coiling flow, and how he looked down from the church spire and saw the houses of the village rising like ghosts out of its inky nothingness. For a day and a half he remained there, weary, starving and sun-scorched, the earth under the blue sky and against the prospect of the distant hills a velvet-black expanse, with red roofs, green trees, and, later, black-veiled shrubs and gates, barns, outhouses, and walls, rising here and there into the sunlight.

But that was at Street Cobham, where the black vapour was allowed to remain until it sank of its own accord into the ground. As a rule the Martians, when it had served its purpose, cleared the air of it again by wading into it and directing a jet of steam upon it.

This they did with the vapour banks near us, as we saw in the starlight from the window of a deserted house at Upper Halliford, whither we had returned. From there we could see the searchlights on Richmond Hill and Kingston Hill going to and fro, and about eleven the windows rattled, and we heard the sound of the huge siege guns that had been put in position there. These continued intermittently for the space of a quarter of an hour, sending chance shots at the invisible Martians at Hampton and Ditton, and then the pale beams of the electric light vanished, and were replaced by a bright red glow.

Then the fourth cylinder fell – a brilliant green meteor – as I learned afterwards, in Bushey Park. Before the guns on the Richmond and Kingston line of hills began, there was a fitful cannonade far away in the southwest, due, I believe, to guns being fired haphazard before the black vapour could overwhelm the gunners.

So, setting about it as methodically as men might smoke out a wasps' nest, the Martians spread this strange stifling vapour over the Londonward country. The horns of the crescent slowly moved apart, until at last they formed a line from Hanwell to Coombe and Malden. All night through their destructive tubes advanced. Never once, after the Martian at St. George's Hill was brought down, did they give the artillery the ghost of a chance against them. Wherever there was a possibility of guns being laid for them unseen, a fresh canister of the black vapour was discharged, and where the guns were openly displayed the Heat-Ray was brought to bear.

By midnight the blazing trees along the slopes of Richmond Park and the glare of Kingston Hill threw their light upon a network of black smoke, blotting out the whole valley of the Thames and extending as far as the eye could reach. And through this two Martians slowly waded, and turned their hissing steam jets this way and that.

They were sparing of the Heat-Ray that night, either because they had but a limited supply of material for its production or because they did not wish to destroy the country but only to crush and overawe the opposition they had aroused. In the latter aim they certainly succeeded. Sunday night was the end of the organised opposition to their movements. After that no body of men would stand against them, so hopeless was the enterprise. Even the crews of the torpedo-boats and destroyers that had brought their quick-firers up the Thames refused to stop, mutinied, and went down again. The only offensive operation men ventured upon after that night was the preparation of mines and pitfalls, and even in that their energies were frantic and spasmodic.

One has to imagine, as well as one may, the fate of those batteries towards Esher, waiting so tensely in the twilight. Survivors there were none. One may picture the orderly expectation, the officers alert and watchful, the gunners ready, the ammunition piled to hand, the limber gunners with their horses and waggons, the groups of civilian spectators standing as near as they were permitted, the evening stillness, the ambulances and hospital tents with the burned and wounded from Weybridge; then the dull resonance of the shots the Martians fired, and the clumsy projectile whirling over the trees and houses and smashing amid the neighbouring fields.

One may picture, too, the sudden shifting of the attention, the swiftly spreading coils and bellyings of that blackness advancing headlong, towering heavenward, turning the twilight to a palpable darkness, a strange and horrible antagonist of vapour striding upon its victims, men and horses near it seen dimly, running, shrieking, falling headlong, shouts of dismay, the guns suddenly abandoned, men choking and writhing on the ground, and the swift broadening-out of the opaque cone of smoke. And then night and extinction – nothing but a silent mass of impenetrable vapour hiding its dead.

Before dawn the black vapour was pouring through the streets of Richmond, and the disintegrating organism of government was, with a last expiring effort, rousing the population of London to the necessity of flight.

Chapter XVI
The Exodus from London

SO YOU UNDERSTAND the roaring wave of fear that swept through the greatest city in the world just as Monday was dawning – the stream of flight rising swiftly to a torrent, lashing in a foaming tumult round the railway stations, banked up into a horrible struggle about the shipping in the Thames, and hurrying by every available channel northward and eastward. By ten o'clock the police organisation, and by midday even the railway organisations, were losing coherency, losing shape and efficiency, guttering, softening, running at last in that swift liquefaction of the social body.

All the railway lines north of the Thames and the South-Eastern people at Cannon Street had been warned by midnight on Sunday, and trains were being filled. People were fighting savagely for standing-room in the carriages even at two o'clock. By three, people were being trampled and crushed even in Bishopsgate Street, a couple of hundred yards or more from Liverpool Street station; revolvers were fired, people stabbed, and the policemen who had been sent to direct the traffic, exhausted and infuriated, were breaking the heads of the people they were called out to protect.

And as the day advanced and the engine drivers and stokers refused to return to London, the pressure of the flight drove the people in an ever-thickening multitude away from the stations and along the northward-running roads. By midday a Martian had been seen at Barnes, and a cloud of slowly sinking black vapour drove along the Thames and across the flats of Lambeth, cutting off all escape over the bridges in its sluggish advance. Another bank drove over Ealing, and surrounded a little island of survivors on Castle Hill, alive, but unable to escape.

After a fruitless struggle to get aboard a North-Western train at Chalk Farm – the engines of the trains that had loaded in the goods yard there *ploughed* through shrieking people, and a dozen stalwart men fought to keep the crowd from crushing the driver against his furnace – my brother emerged upon the Chalk Farm road, dodged across through a hurrying swarm of vehicles, and had the luck to be foremost in the sack of a cycle shop. The front tire of the machine he got was punctured in dragging it through the window, but he got up and off, notwithstanding, with no further injury than a cut wrist. The steep foot of Haverstock Hill was impassable owing to several overturned horses, and my brother struck into Belsize Road.

So he got out of the fury of the panic, and, skirting the Edgware Road, reached Edgware about seven, fasting and wearied, but well ahead of the crowd. Along the road people were standing in the roadway, curious, wondering. He was passed by a number of cyclists, some horsemen, and two motor cars. A mile from Edgware the rim of the wheel broke, and the machine became unrideable. He left it by the roadside and trudged through the village. There were shops half opened in the main street of the place, and people crowded on the pavement and in the doorways and windows, staring astonished at this extraordinary procession of fugitives that was beginning. He succeeded in getting some food at an inn.

For a time he remained in Edgware not knowing what next to do. The flying people increased in number. Many of them, like my brother, seemed inclined to loiter in the place. There was no fresh news of the invaders from Mars.

At that time the road was crowded, but as yet far from congested. Most of the fugitives at that hour were mounted on cycles, but there were soon motor cars, hansom cabs, and carriages hurrying along, and the dust hung in heavy clouds along the road to St. Albans.

It was perhaps a vague idea of making his way to Chelmsford, where some friends of his lived, that at last induced my brother to strike into a quiet lane running eastward. Presently he came upon a stile, and, crossing it, followed a footpath northeastward. He passed near several farmhouses and some little places whose names he did not learn. He saw few fugitives until, in a grass lane towards High Barnet, he happened upon two ladies who became his fellow travellers. He came upon them just in time to save them.

He heard their screams, and, hurrying round the corner, saw a couple of men struggling to drag them out of the little pony-chaise in which they had been driving, while a third with difficulty held the frightened pony's head. One of the ladies, a short woman dressed in white, was simply screaming; the other, a dark, slender figure, slashed at the man who gripped her arm with a whip she held in her disengaged hand.

My brother immediately grasped the situation, shouted, and hurried towards the struggle. One of the men desisted and turned towards him, and my brother, realising from his antagonist's face that a fight was unavoidable, and being an expert boxer, went into him forthwith and sent him down against the wheel of the chaise.

It was no time for pugilistic chivalry and my brother laid him quiet with a kick, and gripped the collar of the man who pulled at the slender lady's arm. He heard the clatter of hoofs, the whip stung across his face, a third antagonist struck him between the eyes, and the man he held wrenched himself free and made off down the lane in the direction from which he had come.

Partly stunned, he found himself facing the man who had held the horse's head, and became aware of the chaise receding from him down the lane, swaying from side to side, and with the women in it looking back. The man before him, a burly rough, tried to close, and he stopped him with a blow in the face. Then, realising that he was deserted, he dodged round and made off down the lane after the chaise, with the sturdy man close behind him, and the fugitive, who had turned now, following remotely.

Suddenly he stumbled and fell; his immediate pursuer went headlong, and he rose to his feet to find himself with a couple of antagonists again. He would have had little chance against them had not the slender lady very pluckily pulled up and returned to his help. It seems she had had a revolver all this time, but it had been under the seat when she and her companion were attacked. She fired at six yards' distance, narrowly missing my brother. The less courageous of the robbers made off, and his companion followed him, cursing his cowardice. They both stopped in sight down the lane, where the third man lay insensible.

"Take this!" said the slender lady, and she gave my brother her revolver.

"Go back to the chaise," said my brother, wiping the blood from his split lip.

She turned without a word – they were both panting – and they went back to where the lady in white struggled to hold back the frightened pony.

The robbers had evidently had enough of it. When my brother looked again they were retreating.

"I'll sit here," said my brother, "if I may"; and he got upon the empty front seat. The lady looked over her shoulder.

"Give me the reins," she said, and laid the whip along the pony's side. In another moment a bend in the road hid the three men from my brother's eyes.

So, quite unexpectedly, my brother found himself, panting, with a cut mouth, a bruised jaw, and bloodstained knuckles, driving along an unknown lane with these two women.

He learned they were the wife and the younger sister of a surgeon living at Stanmore, who had come in the small hours from a dangerous case at Pinner, and heard at some railway station on his way of the Martian advance. He had hurried home, roused the women – their servant had left them two days before – packed some provisions, put his revolver under the seat – luckily for my brother – and told them to drive on to Edgware, with the idea of getting a train there. He stopped behind to tell the neighbours. He would overtake them, he said, at about half past four in the morning, and now it was nearly nine and they had seen nothing of him. They could not stop in Edgware because of the growing traffic through the place, and so they had come into this side lane.

That was the story they told my brother in fragments when presently they stopped again, nearer to New Barnet. He promised to stay with them, at least until they could determine what to do, or until the missing man arrived, and professed to be an expert shot with the revolver – a weapon strange to him – in order to give them confidence.

They made a sort of encampment by the wayside, and the pony became happy in the hedge. He told them of his own escape out of London, and all that he knew of these Martians and their ways. The sun crept higher in the sky, and after a time their talk died out and gave place to an uneasy state of anticipation. Several wayfarers came along the lane, and of these my brother gathered such news as he could. Every broken answer he had deepened his impression of the great disaster that had come on humanity, deepened his persuasion of the immediate necessity for prosecuting this flight. He urged the matter upon them.

"We have money," said the slender woman, and hesitated.

Her eyes met my brother's, and her hesitation ended.

"So have I," said my brother.

She explained that they had as much as thirty pounds in gold, besides a five-pound note, and suggested that with that they might get upon a train at St. Albans or New Barnet. My brother thought that was hopeless, seeing the fury of the Londoners to crowd upon the trains, and broached his own idea of striking across Essex towards Harwich and thence escaping from the country altogether.

Mrs. Elphinstone – that was the name of the woman in white – would listen to no reasoning, and kept calling upon "George"; but her sister-in-law was astonishingly quiet and deliberate, and at last agreed to my brother's suggestion. So, designing to cross the Great North Road, they went on towards Barnet, my brother leading the pony to save it as much as possible. As the sun crept up the sky the day became excessively hot, and under foot a thick, whitish sand grew burning and blinding, so that they travelled only very slowly. The hedges were grey with dust. And as they advanced towards Barnet a tumultuous murmuring grew stronger.

They began to meet more people. For the most part these were staring before them, murmuring indistinct questions, jaded, haggard, unclean. One man in evening dress passed them on foot, his eyes on the ground. They heard his voice, and, looking back at him, saw one hand clutched in his hair and the other beating invisible things. His paroxysm of rage over, he went on his way without once looking back.

As my brother's party went on towards the crossroads to the south of Barnet they saw a woman approaching the road across some fields on their left, carrying a child and with two other children; and then passed a man in dirty black, with a thick stick in one hand and a small portmanteau in the other. Then round the corner of the lane, from between the villas that guarded it at its confluence with the high road, came a little cart drawn by a sweating black pony and driven by a sallow youth in a bowler hat, grey with dust. There were three girls, East End factory girls, and a couple of little children crowded in the cart.

"This'll tike us rahnd Edgware?" asked the driver, wild-eyed, white-faced; and when my brother told him it would if he turned to the left, he whipped up at once without the formality of thanks.

My brother noticed a pale grey smoke or haze rising among the houses in front of them, and veiling the white facade of a terrace beyond the road that appeared between the backs of the villas. Mrs. Elphinstone suddenly cried out at a number of tongues of smoky red flame leaping up above the houses in front of them against the hot, blue sky. The tumultuous noise resolved itself now into the disorderly mingling of many voices, the gride of many wheels, the creaking of waggons, and the staccato of hoofs. The lane came round sharply not fifty yards from the crossroads.

"Good heavens!" cried Mrs. Elphinstone. "What is this you are driving us into?"

My brother stopped.

For the main road was a boiling stream of people, a torrent of human beings rushing northward, one pressing on another. A great bank of dust, white and luminous in the blaze of the sun, made everything within twenty feet of the ground grey and indistinct and was perpetually renewed by the hurrying feet of a dense crowd of horses and of men and women on foot, and by the wheels of vehicles of every description.

"Way!" my brother heard voices crying. "Make way!"

It was like riding into the smoke of a fire to approach the meeting point of the lane and road; the crowd roared like a fire, and the dust was hot and pungent. And, indeed, a little way up the road a villa was burning and sending rolling masses of black smoke across the road to add to the confusion.

Two men came past them. Then a dirty woman, carrying a heavy bundle and weeping. A lost retriever dog, with hanging tongue, circled dubiously round them, scared and wretched, and fled at my brother's threat.

So much as they could see of the road Londonward between the houses to the right was a tumultuous stream of dirty, hurrying people, pent in between the villas on either side; the black heads, the crowded forms, grew into distinctness as they rushed towards the corner, hurried past, and merged their individuality again in a receding multitude that was swallowed up at last in a cloud of dust.

"Go on! Go on!" cried the voices. "Way! Way!"

One man's hands pressed on the back of another. My brother stood at the pony's head. Irresistibly attracted, he advanced slowly, pace by pace, down the lane.

Edgware had been a scene of confusion, Chalk Farm a riotous tumult, but this was a whole population in movement. It is hard to imagine that host. It had no character of its own. The figures poured out past the corner, and receded with their backs to the group in the lane. Along the margin came those who were on foot threatened by the wheels, stumbling in the ditches, blundering into one another.

The carts and carriages crowded close upon one another, making little way for those swifter and more impatient vehicles that darted forward every now and then when an opportunity showed itself of doing so, sending the people scattering against the fences and gates of the villas.

"Push on!" was the cry. "Push on! They are coming!"

In one cart stood a blind man in the uniform of the Salvation Army, gesticulating with his crooked fingers and bawling, "Eternity! Eternity!" His voice was hoarse and very loud so that my brother could hear him long after he was lost to sight in the dust. Some of the people who crowded in the carts whipped stupidly at their horses and quarrelled with other drivers; some sat motionless, staring at nothing with miserable eyes; some gnawed their hands with thirst, or lay prostrate in the bottoms of their conveyances. The horses' bits were covered with foam, their eyes bloodshot.

There were cabs, carriages, shop cars, waggons, beyond counting; a mail cart, a road-cleaner's cart marked 'Vestry of St. Pancras,' a huge timber waggon crowded with roughs. A brewer's dray rumbled by with its two near wheels splashed with fresh blood.

"Clear the way!" cried the voices. "Clear the way!"

"Eter-nity! Eter-nity!" came echoing down the road.

There were sad, haggard women tramping by, well dressed, with children that cried and stumbled, their dainty clothes smothered in dust, their weary faces smeared with tears. With many of these came men, sometimes helpful, sometimes lowering and savage. Fighting side by side with them pushed some weary street outcast in faded black rags, wide-eyed, loud-voiced, and foul-mouthed. There were sturdy workmen thrusting their way along, wretched, unkempt men, clothed like clerks or shopmen, struggling spasmodically; a wounded soldier my brother noticed, men dressed in the clothes of railway porters, one wretched creature in a nightshirt with a coat thrown over it.

But varied as its composition was, certain things all that host had in common. There were fear and pain on their faces, and fear behind them. A tumult up the road, a quarrel for a place in a waggon, sent the whole host of them quickening their pace; even a man so scared and broken that his knees bent under him was galvanised for a moment into renewed activity. The heat and dust had already been at work upon this multitude. Their skins were dry, their lips black and cracked. They were all thirsty, weary, and footsore. And amid the various cries one heard disputes, reproaches, groans of weariness and fatigue; the voices of most of them were hoarse and weak. Through it all ran a refrain:

"Way! Way! The Martians are coming!"

Few stopped and came aside from that flood. The lane opened slantingly into the main road with a narrow opening, and had a delusive appearance of coming from the direction of London. Yet a kind of eddy of people drove into its mouth; weaklings elbowed out of the stream, who for the most part rested but a moment before plunging into it again. A little way down the lane, with two friends bending over him, lay a man with a bare leg, wrapped about with bloody rags. He was a lucky man to have friends.

A little old man, with a grey military moustache and a filthy black frock coat, limped out and sat down beside the trap, removed his boot – his sock was blood-stained – shook out a pebble, and hobbled on again; and then a little girl of eight or nine, all alone, threw herself under the hedge close by my brother, weeping.

"I can't go on! I can't go on!"

My brother woke from his torpor of astonishment and lifted her up, speaking gently to her, and carried her to Miss Elphinstone. So soon as my brother touched her she became quite still, as if frightened.

"Ellen!" shrieked a woman in the crowd, with tears in her voice – "Ellen!" And the child suddenly darted away from my brother, crying "Mother!"

"They are coming," said a man on horseback, riding past along the lane.

"Out of the way, there!" bawled a coachman, towering high; and my brother saw a closed carriage turning into the lane.

The people crushed back on one another to avoid the horse. My brother pushed the pony and chaise back into the hedge, and the man drove by and stopped at the turn of the way. It was a carriage, with a pole for a pair of horses, but only one was in the traces. My brother saw dimly through the dust that two men lifted out something on a white stretcher and put it gently on the grass beneath the privet hedge.

One of the men came running to my brother.

"Where is there any water?" he said. "He is dying fast, and very thirsty. It is Lord Garrick."

"Lord Garrick!" said my brother; "The Chief Justice?"

"The water?" he said.

"There may be a tap," said my brother, "in some of the houses. We have no water. I dare not leave my people."

The man pushed against the crowd towards the gate of the corner house.

"Go on!" said the people, thrusting at him. "They are coming! Go on!"

Then my brother's attention was distracted by a bearded, eagle-faced man lugging a small handbag, which split even as my brother's eyes rested on it and disgorged a mass of sovereigns that seemed to break up into separate coins as it struck the ground. They rolled hither and thither among the struggling feet of men and horses. The man stopped and looked stupidly at the heap, and the shaft of a cab struck his shoulder and sent him reeling. He gave a shriek and dodged back, and a cartwheel shaved him narrowly.

"Way!" cried the men all about him. "Make way!"

So soon as the cab had passed, he flung himself, with both hands open, upon the heap of coins, and began thrusting handfuls in his pocket. A horse rose close upon him, and in another moment, half rising, he had been borne down under the horse's hoofs.

"Stop!" screamed my brother, and pushing a woman out of his way, tried to clutch the bit of the horse.

Before he could get to it, he heard a scream under the wheels, and saw through the dust the rim passing over the poor wretch's back. The driver of the cart slashed his whip at my brother, who ran round behind the cart. The multitudinous shouting confused his ears.

The man was writhing in the dust among his scattered money, unable to rise, for the wheel had broken his back, and his lower limbs lay limp and dead. My brother stood up and yelled at the next driver, and a man on a black horse came to his assistance.

"Get him out of the road," said he; and, clutching the man's collar with his free hand, my brother lugged him sideways. But he still clutched after his money, and regarded my brother fiercely, hammering at his arm with a handful of gold. "Go on! Go on!" shouted angry voices behind.

"Way! Way!"

There was a smash as the pole of a carriage crashed into the cart that the man on horseback stopped. My brother looked up, and the man with the gold twisted his head round and bit the wrist that held his collar. There was a concussion, and the black horse came staggering sideways, and the carthorse pushed beside it. A hoof missed my brother's foot by a hair's breadth. He released his grip on the fallen man and jumped back. He saw anger change to terror on the face of the poor wretch on the ground, and in a moment he was hidden and my brother was borne backward and carried past the entrance of the lane, and had to fight hard in the torrent to recover it.

He saw Miss Elphinstone covering her eyes, and a little child, with all a child's want of sympathetic imagination, staring with dilated eyes at a dusty something that lay black and still, ground and crushed under the rolling wheels. "Let us go back!" he shouted, and began turning the pony round. "We cannot cross this – hell," he said and they went back a hundred yards the way they had come, until the fighting crowd was hidden. As they passed the bend in the lane my brother saw the face of the dying man in the ditch under the privet, deadly white and drawn, and shining with perspiration. The two women sat silent, crouching in their seat and shivering.

Then beyond the bend my brother stopped again. Miss Elphinstone was white and pale, and her sister-in-law sat weeping, too wretched even to call upon "George." My brother was horrified and perplexed. So soon as they had retreated he realised how urgent and unavoidable it was to attempt this crossing. He turned to Miss Elphinstone, suddenly resolute.

"We must go that way," he said, and led the pony round again.

For the second time that day this girl proved her quality. To force their way into the torrent of people, my brother plunged into the traffic and held back a cab horse, while she drove the pony across its head. A waggon locked wheels for a moment and ripped a long splinter from the chaise. In another moment they were caught and swept forward by the stream. My brother, with the cabman's whip marks red across his face and hands, scrambled into the chaise and took the reins from her.

"Point the revolver at the man behind," he said, giving it to her, "if he presses us too hard. No! – Point it at his horse."

Then he began to look out for a chance of edging to the right across the road. But once in the stream he seemed to lose volition, to become a part of that dusty rout. They swept through Chipping Barnet with the torrent; they were nearly a mile beyond the centre of the town before they had fought across to the opposite side of the way. It was din and confusion indescribable; but in and beyond the town the road forks repeatedly, and this to some extent relieved the stress.

They struck eastward through Hadley, and there on either side of the road, and at another place farther on they came upon a great multitude of people drinking at the stream, some fighting to come at the water. And farther on, from a lull near East Barnet, they saw two trains running slowly one after the other without signal or order – trains swarming with people, with men even among the coals behind the engines – going northward along the Great Northern Railway. My brother supposes they must have filled outside London, for at that time the furious terror of the people had rendered the central termini impossible.

Near this place they halted for the rest of the afternoon, for the violence of the day had already utterly exhausted all three of them. They began to suffer the beginnings of hunger; the night was cold, and none of them dared to sleep. And in the evening many people came hurrying along the road nearby their stopping place, fleeing from unknown dangers before them, and going in the direction from which my brother had come.

Chapter XVII
The Thunder Child

HAD THE MARTIANS aimed only at destruction, they might on Monday have annihilated the entire population of London, as it spread itself slowly through the home counties. Not only along the road through Barnet, but also through Edgware and Waltham Abbey, and along the roads eastward to Southend and Shoeburyness, and south of the Thames to Deal and Broadstairs, poured the same frantic rout. If one could have hung that June morning in a balloon in the blazing blue above London every northward and eastward road running out of the tangled maze of streets would have seemed stippled black with the streaming fugitives, each dot a human agony of terror and physical distress. I have set forth at length in the last chapter my brother's account of the road through Chipping Barnet, in order that my readers may realise how that swarming of black dots appeared to one of those concerned. Never before in the history of the world had such a mass of human beings moved and suffered together. The legendary hosts of Goths and Huns, the hugest armies Asia has ever seen, would have been but a drop in that current. And this was no disciplined march; it was a stampede – a stampede gigantic and terrible – without order and without a goal, six million people unarmed and unprovisioned, driving headlong. It was the beginning of the rout of civilisation, of the massacre of mankind.

Directly below him the balloonist would have seen the network of streets far and wide, houses, churches, squares, crescents, gardens – already derelict – spread out like a huge map, and in the southward *blotted*. Over Ealing, Richmond, Wimbledon, it would have seemed as if some monstrous pen had flung ink upon the chart. Steadily, incessantly, each black splash grew and spread, shooting out ramifications this way and that, now banking itself against rising ground, now pouring swiftly over a crest into a new-found valley, exactly as a gout of ink would spread itself upon blotting paper.

And beyond, over the blue hills that rise southward of the river, the glittering Martians went to and fro, calmly and methodically spreading their poison cloud over this patch of country and then over that, laying it again with their steam jets when it had served its purpose, and taking possession of the conquered country. They do not seem to have aimed at extermination so much as at complete demoralisation and the destruction of any opposition. They exploded any stores of powder they came upon, cut every telegraph, and wrecked the railways here and there. They were hamstringing mankind. They seemed in no hurry to extend the field of their operations, and did not come beyond the central part of London all that day. It is possible that a very considerable number of people in London stuck to their houses through Monday morning. Certain it is that many died at home suffocated by the Black Smoke.

Until about midday the Pool of London was an astonishing scene. Steamboats and shipping of all sorts lay there, tempted by the enormous sums of money offered by fugitives, and it is said that many who swam out to these vessels were thrust off with boathooks and drowned. About one o'clock in the afternoon the thinning remnant of a cloud of the black vapour appeared between the arches of Blackfriars Bridge. At that the Pool became a scene of mad confusion, fighting, and collision, and for some time a multitude of boats and barges jammed in the northern arch of the Tower Bridge, and the sailors and lightermen had to fight savagely against the people who swarmed upon them from the riverfront. People were actually clambering down the piers of the bridge from above.

When, an hour later, a Martian appeared beyond the Clock Tower and waded down the river, nothing but wreckage floated above Limehouse.

Of the falling of the fifth cylinder I have presently to tell. The sixth star fell at Wimbledon. My brother, keeping watch beside the women in the chaise in a meadow, saw the green flash of it far beyond the hills. On Tuesday the little party, still set upon getting across the sea, made its way through the swarming country towards Colchester. The news that the Martians were now in possession of the whole of London was confirmed. They had been seen at Highgate, and even, it was said, at Neasden. But they did not come into my brother's view until the morrow.

That day the scattered multitudes began to realise the urgent need of provisions. As they grew hungry the rights of property ceased to be regarded. Farmers were out to defend their cattle-sheds, granaries, and ripening root crops with arms in their hands. A number of people now, like my brother, had their faces eastward, and there were some desperate souls even going back towards London to get food. These were chiefly people from the northern suburbs, whose knowledge of the Black Smoke came by hearsay. He heard that about half the members of the government had gathered at Birmingham, and that enormous quantities of high explosives were being prepared to be used in automatic mines across the Midland counties.

He was also told that the Midland Railway Company had replaced the desertions of the first day's panic, had resumed traffic, and was running northward trains from St. Albans to relieve the congestion of the home counties. There was also a placard in Chipping Ongar announcing that large stores of flour were available in the northern towns and that within twenty-four hours bread would be distributed among the starving people in the neighbourhood. But this intelligence did not deter him from the plan of escape he had formed, and the three pressed eastward all day, and heard no more of the bread distribution than this promise. Nor, as a matter of fact, did anyone else hear more of it. That night fell the seventh star, falling upon Primrose Hill. It fell while Miss Elphinstone was watching, for she took that duty alternately with my brother. She saw it.

On Wednesday the three fugitives – they had passed the night in a field of unripe wheat – reached Chelmsford, and there a body of the inhabitants, calling itself the Committee of Public Supply, seized the pony as provisions, and would give nothing in exchange for it but the promise of a share in it the next day. Here there were rumours of Martians at Epping, and news of the destruction of Waltham Abbey Powder Mills in a vain attempt to blow up one of the invaders.

People were watching for Martians here from the church towers. My brother, very luckily for him as it chanced, preferred to push on at once to the coast rather than wait for food, although all three of them were very hungry. By midday they passed through Tillingham, which, strangely enough, seemed to be quite silent and deserted, save for a few furtive plunderers hunting for food. Near Tillingham they suddenly came in sight of the sea, and the most amazing crowd of shipping of all sorts that it is possible to imagine.

For after the sailors could no longer come up the Thames, they came on to the Essex coast, to Harwich and Walton and Clacton, and afterwards to Foulness and Shoebury, to bring off the people. They lay in a huge sickle-shaped curve that vanished into mist at last towards the Naze. Close inshore was a multitude of fishing smacks – English, Scotch, French, Dutch, and Swedish; steam launches from the Thames, yachts, electric boats; and beyond were ships of large burden, a multitude of filthy colliers, trim merchantmen, cattle ships, passenger boats, petroleum tanks, ocean tramps, an old white transport even, neat white and grey liners from Southampton and Hamburg; and along the blue coast across the Blackwater my brother could make out dimly a dense swarm of boats chaffering with the people on the beach, a swarm which also extended up the Blackwater almost to Maldon.

About a couple of miles out lay an ironclad, very low in the water, almost, to my brother's perception, like a water-logged ship. This was the ram *Thunder Child*. It was the only warship in sight, but far away to the right over the smooth surface of the sea – for that day there was a dead calm – lay a serpent of black smoke to mark the next ironclads of the Channel Fleet, which hovered in an extended line, steam up and ready for action, across the Thames estuary during the course of the Martian conquest, vigilant and yet powerless to prevent it.

At the sight of the sea, Mrs. Elphinstone, in spite of the assurances of her sister-in-law, gave way to panic. She had never been out of England before, she would rather die than trust herself friendless in a foreign country, and so forth. She seemed, poor woman, to imagine that the French and the Martians might prove very similar. She had been growing increasingly hysterical, fearful, and depressed during the two days' journeyings. Her great idea was to return to Stanmore. Things had been always well and safe at Stanmore. They would find George at Stanmore.

It was with the greatest difficulty they could get her down to the beach, where presently my brother succeeded in attracting the attention of some men on a paddle steamer from the Thames. They sent a boat and drove a bargain for thirty-six pounds for the three. The steamer was going, these men said, to Ostend.

It was about two o'clock when my brother, having paid their fares at the gangway, found himself safely aboard the steamboat with his charges. There was food aboard, albeit at exorbitant prices, and the three of them contrived to eat a meal on one of the seats forward.

There were already a couple of score of passengers aboard, some of whom had expended their last money in securing a passage, but the captain lay off the Blackwater until five in the afternoon, picking up passengers until the seated decks were even dangerously crowded. He would probably have remained longer had it not been for the sound of guns that began about that hour in the south. As if in answer, the ironclad seaward fired a small gun and hoisted a string of flags. A jet of smoke sprang out of her funnels.

Some of the passengers were of opinion that this firing came from Shoeburyness, until it was noticed that it was growing louder. At the same time, far away in the southeast the masts and upperworks of three ironclads rose one after the other out of the sea, beneath clouds of black smoke. But my brother's attention speedily reverted to the distant firing in the south. He fancied he saw a column of smoke rising out of the distant grey haze.

The little steamer was already flapping her way eastward of the big crescent of shipping, and the low Essex coast was growing blue and hazy, when a Martian appeared, small and faint in the remote distance, advancing along the muddy coast from the direction of Foulness. At that the captain on the bridge swore at the top of his voice with fear and anger at his own delay, and the paddles seemed infected with his terror. Every soul aboard stood at the bulwarks or on the seats of the steamer and stared at that distant shape, higher than the trees or church towers inland, and advancing with a leisurely parody of a human stride.

It was the first Martian my brother had seen, and he stood, more amazed than terrified, watching this Titan advancing deliberately towards the shipping, wading farther and farther into the water as the coast fell away. Then, far away beyond the Crouch, came another, striding over some stunted trees, and then yet another, still farther off, wading deeply through a shiny mudflat that seemed to hang halfway up between sea and sky. They were all stalking seaward, as if to intercept the escape of the multitudinous vessels that were crowded between Foulness and the Naze. In spite of the throbbing exertions of the engines of the little paddle-boat, and the pouring foam that her wheels flung behind her, she receded with terrifying slowness from this ominous advance.

Glancing northwestward, my brother saw the large crescent of shipping already writhing with the approaching terror; one ship passing behind another, another coming round from broadside to end on, steamships whistling and giving off volumes of steam, sails being let out, launches rushing hither and thither. He was so fascinated by this and by the creeping danger away to the left that he had no eyes for anything seaward. And then a swift movement of the steamboat (she had suddenly come round to avoid being run down) flung him headlong from the seat upon which he was standing. There was a shouting all about him, a trampling of feet, and a cheer that seemed to be answered faintly. The steamboat lurched and rolled him over upon his hands.

He sprang to his feet and saw to starboard, and not a hundred yards from their heeling, pitching boat, a vast iron bulk like the blade of a plough tearing through the water, tossing it on either side in huge waves of foam that leaped towards the steamer, flinging her paddles helplessly in the air, and then sucking her deck down almost to the waterline.

A douche of spray blinded my brother for a moment. When his eyes were clear again he saw the monster had passed and was rushing landward. Big iron upperworks rose out of this headlong structure, and from that twin funnels projected and spat a smoking blast shot with fire. It was the torpedo ram, *Thunder Child*, steaming headlong, coming to the rescue of the threatened shipping.

Keeping his footing on the heaving deck by clutching the bulwarks, my brother looked past this charging leviathan at the Martians again, and he saw the three of them now close together, and standing so far out to sea that their tripod supports were almost entirely submerged. Thus sunken, and seen in remote perspective, they appeared far less formidable than the huge iron bulk in whose wake the steamer was pitching so helplessly. It would seem they were regarding this new antagonist with astonishment. To their intelligence, it may be, the giant was even such another as themselves. The *Thunder Child* fired no gun, but simply drove full speed towards them. It was probably her not firing that enabled her to get so near the enemy as she did. They did not know what to make of her. One shell, and they would have sent her to the bottom forthwith with the Heat-Ray.

She was steaming at such a pace that in a minute she seemed halfway between the steamboat and the Martians – a diminishing black bulk against the receding horizontal expanse of the Essex coast.

Suddenly the foremost Martian lowered his tube and discharged a canister of the black gas at the ironclad. It hit her larboard side and glanced off in an inky jet that rolled away to seaward, an unfolding torrent of Black Smoke, from which the ironclad drove clear. To the watchers from the steamer, low in the water and with the sun in their eyes, it seemed as though she were already among the Martians.

They saw the gaunt figures separating and rising out of the water as they retreated shoreward, and one of them raised the camera-like generator of the Heat-Ray. He held it pointing obliquely downward, and a bank of steam sprang from the water at its touch. It must have driven through the iron of the ship's side like a white-hot iron rod through paper.

A flicker of flame went up through the rising steam, and then the Martian reeled and staggered. In another moment he was cut down, and a great body of water and steam shot high in the air. The guns of the *Thunder Child* sounded through the reek, going off one after the other, and one shot splashed the water high close by the steamer, ricocheted towards the other flying ships to the north, and smashed a smack to matchwood.

But no one heeded that very much. At the sight of the Martian's collapse the captain on the bridge yelled inarticulately, and all the crowding passengers on the steamer's stern shouted together. And then they yelled again. For, surging out beyond the white tumult, drove something long and black, the flames streaming from its middle parts, its ventilators and funnels spouting fire.

She was alive still; the steering gear, it seems, was intact and her engines working. She headed straight for a second Martian, and was within a hundred yards of him when the Heat-Ray came to bear. Then with a violent thud, a blinding flash, her decks, her funnels, leaped upward. The Martian staggered with the violence of her explosion, and in another moment the flaming wreckage, still driving forward with the impetus of its pace, had struck him and crumpled him up like a thing of cardboard. My brother shouted involuntarily. A boiling tumult of steam hid everything again.

"Two!," yelled the captain.

Everyone was shouting. The whole steamer from end to end rang with frantic cheering that was taken up first by one and then by all in the crowding multitude of ships and boats that was driving out to sea.

The steam hung upon the water for many minutes, hiding the third Martian and the coast altogether. And all this time the boat was paddling steadily out to sea and away from the fight; and when at last the confusion cleared, the drifting bank of black vapour intervened, and nothing of the *Thunder Child* could be made out, nor could the third Martian be seen. But the ironclads to seaward were now quite close and standing in towards shore past the steamboat.

The little vessel continued to beat its way seaward, and the ironclads receded slowly towards the coast, which was hidden still by a marbled bank of vapour, part steam, part black gas, eddying and combining in the strangest way. The fleet of refugees was scattering to the northeast; several smacks were sailing between the ironclads and the steamboat. After a time, and before they reached the sinking cloud bank, the warships turned northward, and then abruptly went about and passed into the thickening haze of evening southward. The coast grew faint, and at last indistinguishable amid the low banks of clouds that were gathering about the sinking sun.

Then suddenly out of the golden haze of the sunset came the vibration of guns, and a form of black shadows moving. Everyone struggled to the rail of the steamer and peered into the blinding furnace of the west, but nothing was to be distinguished clearly. A mass of smoke rose slanting and barred the face of the sun. The steamboat throbbed on its way through an interminable suspense.

The sun sank into grey clouds, the sky flushed and darkened, the evening star trembled into sight. It was deep twilight when the captain cried out and pointed. My brother strained his eyes. Something rushed up into the sky out of the greyness – rushed slantingly upward and very swiftly into the luminous clearness above the clouds in the western sky; something flat and broad, and very large, that swept round in a vast curve, grew smaller, sank slowly, and vanished again into the grey mystery of the night. And as it flew it rained down darkness upon the land.

Book II – The Earth Under the Martians

Chapter I
Under Foot

IN THE FIRST BOOK I have wandered so much from my own adventures to tell of the experiences of my brother that all through the last two chapters I and the curate have been lurking in the empty house at Halliford whither we fled to escape the Black Smoke. There I will resume. We stopped there all Sunday night and all the next day – the day of the panic – in a little island of daylight, cut off by the Black Smoke from the rest of the world. We could do nothing but wait in aching inactivity during those two weary days.

My mind was occupied by anxiety for my wife. I figured her at Leatherhead, terrified, in danger, mourning me already as a dead man. I paced the rooms and cried aloud when I thought of how I was cut off from her, of all that might happen to her in my absence. My cousin I knew was brave enough for any emergency, but he was not the sort of man to realise danger quickly, to rise promptly. What was needed now was not bravery, but circumspection. My only consolation was to believe that the Martians were moving London-ward and away from her. Such vague anxieties keep the mind sensitive and painful. I grew very weary and irritable with the curate's perpetual ejaculations; I tired of the sight of his selfish despair. After some ineffectual remonstrance I kept away from him, staying in a room – evidently a children's schoolroom – containing globes, forms, and copybooks. When he followed me thither, I went to a box room at the top of the house and, in order to be alone with my aching miseries, locked myself in.

We were hopelessly hemmed in by the Black Smoke all that day and the morning of the next. There were signs of people in the next house on Sunday evening – a face at a window and moving lights, and later the slamming of a door. But I do not know who these people were, nor what became of them. We saw nothing of them next day. The Black Smoke drifted slowly riverward all through Monday morning, creeping nearer and nearer to us, driving at last along the roadway outside the house that hid us.

A Martian came across the fields about midday, laying the stuff with a jet of superheated steam that hissed against the walls, smashed all the windows it touched, and scalded the curate's hand as he fled out of the front room. When at last we crept across the sodden rooms and looked out again, the country northward was as though a black snowstorm had passed over it. Looking towards the river, we were astonished to see an unaccountable redness mingling with the black of the scorched meadows.

For a time we did not see how this change affected our position, save that we were relieved of our fear of the Black Smoke. But later I perceived that we were no longer hemmed in, that now we might get away. So soon as I realised that the way of escape was open, my dream of action returned. But the curate was lethargic, unreasonable.

"We are safe here," he repeated; "safe here."

I resolved to leave him – would that I had! Wiser now for the artilleryman's teaching, I sought out food and drink. I had found oil and rags for my burns, and I also took a hat and a flannel shirt that I found in one of the bedrooms. When it was clear to him that I meant to go alone – had reconciled myself to going alone – he suddenly roused himself to come.

And all being quiet throughout the afternoon, we started about five o'clock, as I should judge, along the blackened road to Sunbury.

In Sunbury, and at intervals along the road, were dead bodies lying in contorted attitudes, horses as well as men, overturned carts and luggage, all covered thickly with black dust. That pall of cindery powder made me think of what I had read of the destruction of Pompeii. We got to Hampton Court without misadventure, our minds full of strange and unfamiliar appearances, and at Hampton Court our eyes were relieved to find a patch of green that had escaped the suffocating drift. We went through Bushey Park, with its deer going to and fro under the chestnuts, and some men and women hurrying in the distance towards Hampton, and so we came to Twickenham. These were the first people we saw.

Away across the road the woods beyond Ham and Petersham were still afire. Twickenham was uninjured by either Heat-Ray or Black Smoke, and there were more people about here, though none could give us news. For the most part they were like ourselves, taking advantage of a lull to shift their quarters. I have an impression that many of the houses here were still occupied by scared inhabitants, too frightened even for flight. Here too the evidence of a hasty rout was abundant along the road. I remember most vividly three smashed bicycles in a heap, pounded into the road by the wheels of subsequent carts. We crossed Richmond Bridge about half past eight. We hurried across the exposed bridge, of course, but I noticed floating down the stream a number of red masses, some many feet across. I did not know what these were – there was no time for scrutiny – and I put a more horrible interpretation on them than they deserved. Here again on the Surrey side were black dust that had once been smoke, and dead bodies – a heap near the approach to the station; but we had no glimpse of the Martians until we were some way towards Barnes.

We saw in the blackened distance a group of three people running down a side street towards the river, but otherwise it seemed deserted. Up the hill Richmond town was burning briskly; outside the town of Richmond there was no trace of the Black Smoke.

Then suddenly, as we approached Kew, came a number of people running, and the upperworks of a Martian fighting-machine loomed in sight over the housetops, not a hundred yards away from us. We stood aghast at our danger, and had the Martian looked down we must immediately have perished. We were so terrified that we dared not go on, but turned aside and hid in a shed in a garden. There the curate crouched, weeping silently, and refusing to stir again.

But my fixed idea of reaching Leatherhead would not let me rest, and in the twilight I ventured out again. I went through a shrubbery, and along a passage beside a big house standing in its own grounds, and so emerged upon the road towards Kew. The curate I left in the shed, but he came hurrying after me.

That second start was the most foolhardy thing I ever did. For it was manifest the Martians were about us. No sooner had the curate overtaken me than we saw either the fighting-machine we had seen before or another, far away across the meadows in the direction of Kew Lodge. Four or five little black figures hurried before it across the green-grey of the field, and in a moment it was evident this Martian pursued them. In three strides he was among them, and they ran radiating from his feet in all directions. He used no Heat-Ray to destroy them, but picked them up one by one. Apparently he tossed them into the great metallic carrier which projected behind him, much as a workman's basket hangs over his shoulder.

It was the first time I realised that the Martians might have any other purpose than destruction with defeated humanity. We stood for a moment petrified, then turned and fled through a gate behind us into a walled garden, fell into, rather than found, a fortunate ditch, and lay there, scarce daring to whisper to each other until the stars were out.

I suppose it was nearly eleven o'clock before we gathered courage to start again, no longer venturing into the road, but sneaking along hedgerows and through plantations, and watching keenly through the darkness, he on the right and I on the left, for the Martians, who seemed to be all about us. In one place we blundered upon a scorched and blackened area, now cooling and ashen, and a number of scattered dead bodies of men, burned horribly about the heads and trunks but with their legs and boots mostly intact; and of dead horses, fifty feet, perhaps, behind a line of four ripped guns and smashed gun carriages.

Sheen, it seemed, had escaped destruction, but the place was silent and deserted. Here we happened on no dead, though the night was too dark for us to see into the side roads of the place. In Sheen my companion suddenly complained of faintness and thirst, and we decided to try one of the houses.

The first house we entered, after a little difficulty with the window, was a small semi-detached villa, and I found nothing eatable left in the place but some mouldy cheese. There was, however, water to drink; and I took a hatchet, which promised to be useful in our next house-breaking.

We then crossed to a place where the road turns towards Mortlake. Here there stood a white house within a walled garden, and in the pantry of this domicile we found a store of food – two loaves of bread in a pan, an uncooked steak, and the half of a ham. I give this catalogue so precisely because, as it happened, we were destined to subsist upon this store for the next fortnight. Bottled beer stood under a shelf, and there were two bags of haricot beans and some limp lettuces. This pantry opened into a kind of wash-up kitchen, and in this was firewood; there was also a cupboard, in which we found nearly a dozen of burgundy, tinned soups and salmon, and two tins of biscuits.

We sat in the adjacent kitchen in the dark – for we dared not strike a light – and ate bread and ham, and drank beer out of the same bottle. The curate, who was still timorous and restless, was now, oddly enough, for pushing on, and I was urging him to keep up his strength by eating when the thing happened that was to imprison us.

"It can't be midnight yet," I said, and then came a blinding glare of vivid green light. Everything in the kitchen leaped out, clearly visible in green and black, and vanished again. And then followed such a concussion as I have never heard before or since. So close on the heels of this as to seem instantaneous came a thud behind me, a clash of glass, a crash and rattle of falling masonry all about us, and the plaster of the ceiling came down upon us, smashing into a multitude of fragments upon our heads. I was knocked headlong across the floor against the oven handle and stunned. I was insensible for a long time, the curate told me, and when I came to we were in darkness again, and he, with a face wet, as I found afterwards, with blood from a cut forehead, was dabbing water over me.

For some time I could not recollect what had happened. Then things came to me slowly. A bruise on my temple asserted itself.

"Are you better?" asked the curate in a whisper.

At last I answered him. I sat up.

"Don't move," he said. "The floor is covered with smashed crockery from the dresser. You can't possibly move without making a noise, and I fancy *they* are outside."

We both sat quite silent, so that we could scarcely hear each other breathing. Everything seemed deadly still, but once something near us, some plaster or broken brickwork, slid down with a rumbling sound. Outside and very near was an intermittent, metallic rattle.

"That!" said the curate, when presently it happened again.

"Yes," I said. "But what is it?"

"A Martian!" said the curate.

I listened again.

"It was not like the Heat-Ray," I said, and for a time I was inclined to think one of the great fighting-machines had stumbled against the house, as I had seen one stumble against the tower of Shepperton Church.

Our situation was so strange and incomprehensible that for three or four hours, until the dawn came, we scarcely moved. And then the light filtered in, not through the window, which remained black, but through a triangular aperture between a beam and a heap of broken bricks in the wall behind us. The interior of the kitchen we now saw greyly for the first time.

The window had been burst in by a mass of garden mould, which flowed over the table upon which we had been sitting and lay about our feet. Outside, the soil was banked high against the house. At the top of the window frame we could see an uprooted drainpipe. The floor was littered with smashed hardware; the end of the kitchen towards the house was broken into, and since the daylight shone in there, it was evident the greater part of the house had collapsed. Contrasting vividly with this ruin was the neat dresser, stained in the fashion, pale green, and with a number of copper and tin vessels below it, the wallpaper imitating blue and white tiles, and a couple of coloured supplements fluttering from the walls above the kitchen range.

As the dawn grew clearer, we saw through the gap in the wall the body of a Martian, standing sentinel, I suppose, over the still glowing cylinder. At the sight of that we crawled as circumspectly as possible out of the twilight of the kitchen into the darkness of the scullery.

Abruptly the right interpretation dawned upon my mind.

"The fifth cylinder," I whispered, "the fifth shot from Mars, has struck this house and buried us under the ruins!"

For a time the curate was silent, and then he whispered:

"God have mercy upon us!"

I heard him presently whimpering to himself.

Save for that sound we lay quite still in the scullery; I for my part scarce dared breathe, and sat with my eyes fixed on the faint light of the kitchen door. I could just see the curate's face, a dim, oval shape, and his collar and cuffs. Outside there began a metallic hammering, then a violent hooting, and then again, after a quiet interval, a hissing like the hissing of an engine. These noises, for the most part problematical, continued intermittently, and seemed if anything to increase in number as time wore on. Presently a measured thudding and a vibration that made everything about us quiver and the vessels in the pantry ring and shift, began and continued. Once the light was eclipsed, and the ghostly kitchen doorway became absolutely dark. For many hours we must have crouched there, silent and shivering, until our tired attention failed....

At last I found myself awake and very hungry. I am inclined to believe we must have spent the greater portion of a day before that awakening. My hunger was at a stride so insistent that it moved me to action. I told the curate I was going to seek food, and felt my way towards the pantry. He made me no answer, but so soon as I began eating the faint noise I made stirred him up and I heard him crawling after me.

Chapter II
What We Saw from the Ruined House

AFTER EATING we crept back to the scullery, and there I must have dozed again, for when presently I looked round I was alone. The thudding vibration continued with wearisome persistence. I whispered for the curate several times, and at last felt my way to the door of the kitchen. It was still daylight, and I perceived him across the room, lying against the triangular hole that looked out upon the Martians. His shoulders were hunched, so that his head was hidden from me.

I could hear a number of noises almost like those in an engine shed; and the place rocked with that beating thud. Through the aperture in the wall I could see the top of a tree touched with gold and the warm blue of a tranquil evening sky. For a minute or so I remained watching the curate, and then I advanced, crouching and stepping with extreme care amid the broken crockery that littered the floor.

I touched the curate's leg, and he started so violently that a mass of plaster went sliding down outside and fell with a loud impact. I gripped his arm, fearing he might cry out, and for a long time we crouched motionless. Then I turned to see how much of our rampart remained. The detachment of the plaster had left a vertical slit open in the debris, and by raising myself cautiously across a beam I was able to see out of this gap into what had been overnight a quiet suburban roadway. Vast, indeed, was the change that we beheld.

The fifth cylinder must have fallen right into the midst of the house we had first visited. The building had vanished, completely smashed, pulverised, and dispersed by the blow. The cylinder lay now far beneath the original foundations – deep in a hole, already vastly larger than the pit I had looked into at Woking. The earth all round it had splashed under that tremendous impact – 'splashed' is the only word – and lay in heaped piles that hid the masses of the adjacent houses. It had behaved exactly like mud under the violent blow of a hammer. Our house had collapsed backward; the front portion, even on the ground floor, had been destroyed completely; by a chance the kitchen and scullery had escaped, and stood buried now under soil and ruins, closed in by tons of earth on every side save towards the cylinder. Over that aspect we hung now on the very edge of the great circular pit the Martians were engaged in making. The heavy beating sound was evidently just behind us, and ever and again a bright green vapour drove up like a veil across our peephole.

The cylinder was already opened in the centre of the pit, and on the farther edge of the pit, amid the smashed and gravel-heaped shrubbery, one of the great fighting-machines, deserted by its occupant, stood stiff and tall against the evening sky. At first I scarcely noticed the pit and the cylinder, although it has been convenient to describe them first, on account of the extraordinary glittering mechanism I saw busy in the excavation, and on account of the strange creatures that were crawling slowly and painfully across the heaped mould near it.

The mechanism it certainly was that held my attention first. It was one of those complicated fabrics that have since been called handling-machines, and the study of which has already given such an enormous impetus to terrestrial invention. As it dawned upon me first, it presented a sort of metallic spider with five jointed, agile legs, and with an extraordinary number of jointed levers, bars, and reaching and clutching tentacles about its body. Most of its arms were retracted, but with three long tentacles it was fishing out a number of rods, plates, and bars which lined the covering and apparently strengthened the walls of the cylinder. These, as it extracted them, were lifted out and deposited upon a level surface of earth behind it.

Its motion was so swift, complex, and perfect that at first I did not see it as a machine, in spite of its metallic glitter. The fighting-machines were coordinated and animated to an extraordinary pitch, but nothing to compare with this. People who have never seen these structures, and have only the ill-imagined efforts of artists or the imperfect descriptions of such eye-witnesses as myself to go upon, scarcely realise that living quality.

I recall particularly the illustration of one of the first pamphlets to give a consecutive account of the war. The artist had evidently made a hasty study of one of the fighting-machines, and there his knowledge ended. He presented them as tilted, stiff tripods, without either flexibility or subtlety, and with an altogether misleading monotony of effect. The pamphlet containing these renderings had a considerable vogue, and I mention them here simply to warn the reader against the impression they may have created. They were no more like the Martians I saw in action than a Dutch doll is like a human being. To my mind, the pamphlet would have been much better without them.

At first, I say, the handling-machine did not impress me as a machine, but as a crablike creature with a glittering integument, the controlling Martian whose delicate tentacles actuated its movements seeming to be simply the equivalent of the crab's cerebral portion. But then I perceived the resemblance of its grey-brown, shiny, leathery integument to that of the other sprawling bodies beyond, and the true nature of this dexterous workman dawned upon me. With that realisation my interest shifted to those other creatures, the real Martians. Already I had had a transient impression of these, and the first nausea no longer obscured my observation. Moreover, I was concealed and motionless, and under no urgency of action.

They were, I now saw, the most unearthly creatures it is possible to conceive. They were huge round bodies – or, rather, heads – about four feet in diameter, each body having in front of it a face. This face had no nostrils – indeed, the Martians do not seem to have had any sense of smell, but it had a pair of very large dark-coloured eyes, and just beneath this a kind of fleshy beak. In the back of this head or body – I scarcely know how to speak of it – was the single tight tympanic surface, since known to be anatomically an ear, though it must have been almost useless in our dense air. In a group round the mouth were sixteen slender, almost whiplike tentacles, arranged in two bunches of eight each. These bunches have since been named rather aptly, by that distinguished anatomist, Professor Howes, the *hands*. Even as I saw these Martians for the first time they seemed to be endeavouring to raise themselves on these hands, but of course, with the increased weight of terrestrial conditions, this was impossible. There is reason to suppose that on Mars they may have progressed upon them with some facility.

The internal anatomy, I may remark here, as dissection has since shown, was almost equally simple. The greater part of the structure was the brain, sending enormous nerves to the eyes, ear, and tactile tentacles. Besides this were the bulky lungs, into which the mouth opened, and the heart and its vessels. The pulmonary distress caused by the denser atmosphere and greater gravitational attraction was only too evident in the convulsive movements of the outer skin.

And this was the sum of the Martian organs. Strange as it may seem to a human being, all the complex apparatus of digestion, which makes up the bulk of our bodies, did not exist in the Martians. They were heads – merely heads. Entrails they had none. They did not eat, much less digest. Instead, they took the fresh, living blood of other creatures, and *injected* it into their own veins. I have myself seen this being done, as I shall mention in its place. But, squeamish as I may seem, I cannot bring myself to describe what I could not endure even to continue watching. Let it suffice to say, blood obtained from a still living animal, in most cases from a human being, was run directly by means of a little pipette into the recipient canal....

The bare idea of this is no doubt horribly repulsive to us, but at the same time I think that we should remember how repulsive our carnivorous habits would seem to an intelligent rabbit.

The physiological advantages of the practice of injection are undeniable, if one thinks of the tremendous waste of human time and energy occasioned by eating and the digestive process. Our bodies are half made up of glands and tubes and organs, occupied in turning heterogeneous food into blood. The digestive processes and their reaction upon the nervous system sap our strength and colour our minds. Men go happy or miserable as they have healthy or unhealthy livers, or sound gastric glands. But the Martians were lifted above all these organic fluctuations of mood and emotion.

Their undeniable preference for men as their source of nourishment is partly explained by the nature of the remains of the victims they had brought with them as provisions from Mars. These creatures, to judge from the shrivelled remains that have fallen into human hands, were bipeds with flimsy, silicious skeletons (almost like those of the silicious sponges) and feeble musculature, standing about six feet high and having round, erect heads, and large eyes in flinty sockets. Two or three of these seem to have been brought in each cylinder, and all were killed before earth was reached. It was just as well for them, for the mere attempt to stand upright upon our planet would have broken every bone in their bodies.

And while I am engaged in this description, I may add in this place certain further details which, although they were not all evident to us at the time, will enable the reader who is unacquainted with them to form a clearer picture of these offensive creatures.

In three other points their physiology differed strangely from ours. Their organisms did not sleep, any more than the heart of man sleeps. Since they had no extensive muscular mechanism to recuperate, that periodical extinction was unknown to them. They had little or no sense of fatigue, it would seem. On earth they could never have moved without effort, yet even to the last they kept in action. In twenty-four hours they did twenty-four hours of work, as even on earth is perhaps the case with the ants.

In the next place, wonderful as it seems in a sexual world, the Martians were absolutely without sex, and therefore without any of the tumultuous emotions that arise from that difference among men. A young Martian, there can now be no dispute, was really born upon earth during the war, and it was found attached to its parent, partially *budded* off, just as young lily-bulbs bud off, or like the young animals in the fresh-water polyp.

In man, in all the higher terrestrial animals, such a method of increase has disappeared; but even on this earth it was certainly the primitive method. Among the lower animals, up even to those first cousins of the vertebrated animals, the Tunicates, the two processes occur side by side, but finally the sexual method superseded its competitor altogether. On Mars, however, just the reverse has apparently been the case.

It is worthy of remark that a certain speculative writer of quasi-scientific repute, writing long before the Martian invasion, did forecast for man a final structure not unlike the actual Martian condition. His prophecy, I remember, appeared in November or December, 1893, in a long-defunct publication, the *Pall Mall Budget*, and I recall a caricature of it in a pre-Martian periodical called *Punch*. He pointed out – writing in a foolish, facetious tone – that the perfection of mechanical appliances must ultimately supersede limbs; the perfection of chemical devices, digestion; that such organs as hair, external nose, teeth, ears, and chin were no longer essential parts of the human being, and that the tendency of natural selection would lie in the direction of their steady diminution through the coming ages. The brain alone remained a cardinal necessity. Only one other part of the body had a strong case for survival, and that was the hand, 'teacher and agent of the brain.' While the rest of the body dwindled, the hands would grow larger.

There is many a true word written in jest, and here in the Martians we have beyond dispute the actual accomplishment of such a suppression of the animal side of the organism by the intelligence. To me it is quite credible that the Martians may be descended from beings not unlike ourselves, by a gradual development of brain and hands (the latter giving rise to the two bunches of delicate tentacles at last) at the expense of the rest of the body. Without the body the brain would, of course, become a mere selfish intelligence, without any of the emotional substratum of the human being.

The last salient point in which the systems of these creatures differed from ours was in what one might have thought a very trivial particular. Micro-organisms, which cause so much disease and pain on earth, have either never appeared upon Mars or Martian sanitary science eliminated them ages ago. A hundred diseases, all the fevers and contagions of human life, consumption, cancers, tumours and such morbidities, never enter the scheme of their life. And speaking of the differences between the life on Mars and terrestrial life, I may allude here to the curious suggestions of the red weed.

Apparently the vegetable kingdom in Mars, instead of having green for a dominant colour, is of a vivid blood-red tint. At any rate, the seeds which the Martians (intentionally or accidentally) brought with them gave rise in all cases to red-coloured growths. Only that known popularly as the red weed, however, gained any footing in competition with terrestrial forms. The red creeper was quite a transitory growth, and few people have seen it growing. For a time, however, the red weed grew with astonishing vigour and luxuriance. It spread up the sides of the pit by the third or fourth day of our imprisonment, and its cactus-like branches formed a carmine fringe to the edges of our triangular window. And afterwards I found it broadcast throughout the country, and especially wherever there was a stream of water.

The Martians had what appears to have been an auditory organ, a single round drum at the back of the head-body, and eyes with a visual range not very different from ours except that, according to Philips, blue and violet were as black to them. It is commonly supposed that they communicated by sounds and tentacular gesticulations; this is asserted, for instance, in the able but hastily compiled pamphlet (written evidently by someone not an eye-witness of Martian actions) to which I have already alluded, and which, so far, has been the chief source of information concerning them. Now no surviving human being saw so much of the Martians in action as I did. I take no credit to myself for an accident, but the fact is so. And I assert that I watched them closely time after time, and that I have seen four, five, and (once) six of them sluggishly performing the most elaborately complicated operations together without either sound or gesture. Their peculiar hooting invariably preceded feeding; it had no modulation, and was, I believe, in no sense a signal, but merely the expiration of air preparatory to the suctional operation. I have a certain claim to at least an elementary knowledge of psychology, and in this matter I am convinced – as firmly as I am convinced of anything – that the Martians interchanged thoughts without any physical intermediation. And I have been convinced of this in spite of strong preconceptions. Before the Martian invasion, as an occasional reader here or there may remember, I had written with some little vehemence against the telepathic theory.

The Martians wore no clothing. Their conceptions of ornament and decorum were necessarily different from ours; and not only were they evidently much less sensible of changes of temperature than we are, but changes of pressure do not seem to have affected their health at all seriously. Yet though they wore no clothing, it was in the other artificial additions to their bodily resources that their great superiority over man lay. We men, with our bicycles and road-skates, our Lilienthal soaring-machines, our guns and sticks and so forth, are just in the beginning of the evolution that the Martians have worked out. They have become practically mere brains, wearing different bodies according to their needs just as men wear suits of clothes and take a bicycle in a hurry or an umbrella in the wet. And of their appliances, perhaps nothing is more wonderful to a man than the curious fact that what is the dominant feature of almost all human devices in mechanism is absent – the *wheel* is absent; among all the things they brought to earth there is no trace or suggestion of their use of wheels. One would have at least expected it in locomotion. And in this connection it is curious to remark that even on this earth Nature has never hit upon the wheel, or has preferred other expedients to its development. And not only did the Martians either not know of (which is incredible), or abstain from, the wheel, but in their apparatus singularly little use is made of the fixed pivot or relatively fixed pivot, with circular motions thereabout confined to one plane. Almost all the joints of the machinery present a complicated system of sliding parts moving over small but beautifully curved friction bearings. And while upon this matter of detail, it is remarkable that the long leverages of their machines are in most cases actuated by a sort of sham musculature of the disks in an elastic sheath; these disks become polarised and drawn closely and powerfully together when traversed by a current of electricity. In this way the curious parallelism to animal motions, which was so striking and disturbing to the human beholder, was attained. Such quasi-muscles abounded in the crablike handling-machine which, on my first peeping out of the slit, I watched unpacking the cylinder. It seemed infinitely more alive than the actual Martians lying beyond it in the sunset light, panting, stirring ineffectual tentacles, and moving feebly after their vast journey across space.

While I was still watching their sluggish motions in the sunlight, and noting each strange detail of their form, the curate reminded me of his presence by pulling violently at my arm. I turned to a scowling face, and silent, eloquent lips. He wanted the slit, which permitted only one of us to peep through; and so I had to forego watching them for a time while he enjoyed that privilege.

When I looked again, the busy handling-machine had already put together several of the pieces of apparatus it had taken out of the cylinder into a shape having an unmistakable likeness to its own; and down on the left a busy little digging mechanism had come into view, emitting jets of green vapour and working its way round the pit, excavating and embanking in a methodical and discriminating manner. This it was which had caused the regular beating noise, and the rhythmic shocks that had kept our ruinous refuge quivering. It piped and whistled as it worked. So far as I could see, the thing was without a directing Martian at all.

Chapter III
The Days of Imprisonment

THE ARRIVAL OF a second fighting-machine drove us from our peephole into the scullery, for we feared that from his elevation the Martian might see down upon us behind our barrier. At a later date we began to feel less in danger of their eyes, for to an eye in the dazzle of the sunlight outside our refuge must have been blank blackness, but at first the slightest suggestion of approach drove us into the scullery in heart-throbbing retreat. Yet terrible as was the danger we incurred, the attraction of peeping was for both of us irresistible. And I recall now with a sort of wonder that, in spite of the infinite danger in which we were between starvation and a still more terrible death, we could yet struggle bitterly for that horrible privilege of sight. We would race across the kitchen in a grotesque way between eagerness and the dread of making a noise, and strike each other, and thrust add kick, within a few inches of exposure.

The fact is that we had absolutely incompatible dispositions and habits of thought and action, and our danger and isolation only accentuated the incompatibility. At Halliford I had already come to hate the curate's trick of helpless exclamation, his stupid rigidity of mind. His endless muttering monologue vitiated every effort I made to think out a line of action, and drove me at times, thus pent up and intensified, almost to the verge of craziness. He was as lacking in restraint as a silly woman. He would weep for hours together, and I verily believe that to the very end this spoiled child of life thought his weak tears in some way efficacious. And I would sit in the darkness unable to keep my mind off him by reason of his importunities. He ate more than I did, and it was in vain I pointed out that our only chance of life was to stop in the house until the Martians had done with their pit, that in that long patience a time might presently come when we should need food. He ate and drank impulsively in heavy meals at long intervals. He slept little.

As the days wore on, his utter carelessness of any consideration so intensified our distress and danger that I had, much as I loathed doing it, to resort to threats, and at last to blows. That brought him to reason for a time. But he was one of those weak creatures, void of pride, timorous, anaemic, hateful souls, full of shifty cunning, who face neither God nor man, who face not even themselves.

It is disagreeable for me to recall and write these things, but I set them down that my story may lack nothing. Those who have escaped the dark and terrible aspects of life will find my brutality, my flash of rage in our final tragedy, easy enough to blame; for they know what is wrong as well as any, but not what is possible to tortured men. But those who have been under the shadow, who have gone down at last to elemental things, will have a wider charity.

And while within we fought out our dark, dim contest of whispers, snatched food and drink, and gripping hands and blows, without, in the pitiless sunlight of that terrible June, was the strange wonder, the unfamiliar routine of the Martians in the pit. Let me return to those first new experiences of mine. After a long time I ventured back to the peephole, to find that the new-comers had been reinforced by the occupants of no fewer than three of the fighting-machines. These last had brought with them certain fresh appliances that stood in an orderly manner about the cylinder. The second handling-machine was now completed, and was busied in serving one of the novel contrivances the big machine had brought. This was a body resembling a milk can in its general form, above which oscillated a pear-shaped receptacle, and from which a stream of white powder flowed into a circular basin below.

The oscillatory motion was imparted to this by one tentacle of the handling-machine. With two spatulate hands the handling-machine was digging out and flinging masses of clay into the pear-shaped receptacle above, while with another arm it periodically opened a door and removed rusty and blackened clinkers from the middle part of the machine. Another steely tentacle directed the powder from the basin along a ribbed channel towards some receiver that was hidden from me by the mound of bluish dust. From this unseen receiver a little thread of green smoke rose vertically into the quiet air. As I looked, the handling-machine, with a faint and musical clinking, extended, telescopic fashion, a tentacle that had been a moment before a mere blunt projection, until its end was hidden behind the mound of clay. In another second it had lifted a bar of white aluminium into sight, untarnished as yet, and shining dazzlingly, and deposited it in a growing stack of bars that stood at the side of the pit. Between sunset and starlight this dexterous machine must have made more than a hundred such bars out of the crude clay, and the mound of bluish dust rose steadily until it topped the side of the pit.

The contrast between the swift and complex movements of these contrivances and the inert panting clumsiness of their masters was acute, and for days I had to tell myself repeatedly that these latter were indeed the living of the two things.

The curate had possession of the slit when the first men were brought to the pit. I was sitting below, huddled up, listening with all my ears. He made a sudden movement backward, and I, fearful that we were observed, crouched in a spasm of terror. He came sliding down the rubbish and crept beside me in the darkness, inarticulate, gesticulating, and for a moment I shared his panic. His gesture suggested a resignation of the slit, and after a little while my curiosity gave me courage, and I rose up, stepped across him, and clambered up to it. At first I could see no reason for his frantic behaviour. The twilight had now come, the stars were little and faint, but the pit was illuminated by the flickering green fire that came from the aluminium-making. The whole picture was a flickering scheme of green gleams and shifting rusty black shadows, strangely trying to the eyes. Over and through it all went the bats, heeding it not at all. The sprawling Martians were no longer to be seen, the mound of blue-green powder had risen to cover them from sight, and a fighting-machine, with its legs contracted, crumpled, and abbreviated, stood across the corner of the pit. And then, amid the clangour of the machinery, came a drifting suspicion of human voices, that I entertained at first only to dismiss.

I crouched, watching this fighting-machine closely, satisfying myself now for the first time that the hood did indeed contain a Martian. As the green flames lifted I could see the oily gleam of his integument and the brightness of his eyes. And suddenly I heard a yell, and saw a long tentacle reaching over the shoulder of the machine to the little cage that hunched upon its back. Then something – something struggling violently – was lifted high against the sky, a black, vague enigma against the starlight; and as this black object came down again, I saw by the green brightness that it was a man. For an instant he was clearly visible. He was a stout, ruddy, middle-aged man, well dressed; three days before, he must have been walking the world, a man of considerable consequence. I could see his staring eyes and gleams of light on his studs and watch chain. He vanished behind the mound, and for a moment there was silence. And then began a shrieking and a sustained and cheerful hooting from the Martians.

I slid down the rubbish, struggled to my feet, clapped my hands over my ears, and bolted into the scullery. The curate, who had been crouching silently with his arms over his head, looked up as I passed, cried out quite loudly at my desertion of him, and came running after me.

That night, as we lurked in the scullery, balanced between our horror and the terrible fascination this peeping had, although I felt an urgent need of action I tried in vain to conceive some plan of escape; but afterwards, during the second day, I was able to consider our position with great clearness. The curate, I found, was quite incapable of discussion; this new and culminating atrocity had robbed him of all vestiges of reason or forethought. Practically he had already sunk to the level of an animal. But as the saying goes, I gripped myself with both hands. It grew upon my mind, once I could face the facts, that terrible as our position was, there was as yet no justification for absolute despair. Our chief chance lay in the possibility of the Martians making the pit nothing more than a temporary encampment. Or even if they kept it permanently, they might not consider it necessary to guard it, and a chance of escape might be afforded us. I also weighed very carefully the possibility of our digging a way out in a direction away from the pit, but the chances of our emerging within sight of some sentinel fighting-machine seemed at first too great. And I should have had to do all the digging myself. The curate would certainly have failed me.

It was on the third day, if my memory serves me right, that I saw the lad killed. It was the only occasion on which I actually saw the Martians feed. After that experience I avoided the hole in the wall for the better part of a day. I went into the scullery, removed the door, and spent some hours digging with my hatchet as silently as possible; but when I had made a hole about a couple of feet deep the loose earth collapsed noisily, and I did not dare continue. I lost heart, and lay down on the scullery floor for a long time, having no spirit even to move. And after that I abandoned altogether the idea of escaping by excavation.

It says much for the impression the Martians had made upon me that at first I entertained little or no hope of our escape being brought about by their overthrow through any human effort. But on the fourth or fifth night I heard a sound like heavy guns.

It was very late in the night, and the moon was shining brightly. The Martians had taken away the excavating-machine, and, save for a fighting-machine that stood in the remoter bank of the pit and a handling-machine that was buried out of my sight in a corner of the pit immediately beneath my peephole, the place was deserted by them. Except for the pale glow from the handling-machine and the bars and patches of white moonlight the pit was in darkness, and, except for the clinking of the handling-machine, quite still. That night was a beautiful serenity; save for one planet, the moon seemed to have the sky to herself. I heard a dog howling, and that familiar sound it was that made me listen. Then I heard quite distinctly a booming exactly like the sound of great guns. Six distinct reports I counted, and after a long interval six again. And that was all.

Chapter IV
The Death of the Curate

IT WAS ON THE SIXTH DAY of our imprisonment that I peeped for the last time, and presently found myself alone. Instead of keeping close to me and trying to oust me from the slit, the curate had gone back into the scullery. I was struck by a sudden thought. I went back quickly and quietly into the scullery. In the darkness I heard the curate drinking. I snatched in the darkness, and my fingers caught a bottle of burgundy.

For a few minutes there was a tussle. The bottle struck the floor and broke, and I desisted and rose. We stood panting and threatening each other. In the end I planted myself between him and the food, and told him of my determination to begin a discipline. I divided the food in the pantry, into rations to last us ten days. I would not let him eat any more that day. In the afternoon he made a feeble effort to get at the food. I had been dozing, but in an instant I was awake. All day and all night we sat face to face, I weary but resolute, and he weeping and complaining of his immediate hunger. It was, I know, a night and a day, but to me it seemed – it seems now – an inter – minable length of time.

And so our widened incompatibility ended at last in open conflict. For two vast days we struggled in undertones and wrestling contests. There were times when I beat and kicked him madly, times when I cajoled and persuaded him, and once I tried to bribe him with the last bottle of burgundy, for there was a rain-water pump from which I could get water. But neither force nor kindness availed; he was indeed beyond reason. He would neither desist from his attacks on the food nor from his noisy babbling to himself. The rudimentary precautions to keep our imprisonment endurable he would not observe. Slowly I began to realise the complete overthrow of his intelligence, to perceive that my sole companion in this close and sickly darkness was a man insane.

From certain vague memories I am inclined to think my own mind wandered at times. I had strange and hideous dreams whenever I slept. It sounds paradoxical, but I am inclined to think that the weakness and insanity of the curate warned me, braced me, and kept me a sane man.

On the eighth day he began to talk aloud instead of whispering, and nothing I could do would moderate his speech.

"It is just, O God!" he would say, over and over again. "It is just. On me and mine be the punishment laid. We have sinned, we have fallen short. There was poverty, sorrow; the poor were trodden in the dust, and I held my peace. I preached acceptable folly – my God, what folly! – when I should have stood up, though I died for it, and called upon them to repent-repent!... Oppressors of the poor and needy...! The wine press of God!"

Then he would suddenly revert to the matter of the food I withheld from him, praying, begging, weeping, at last threatening. He began to raise his voice – I prayed him not to. He perceived a hold on me – he threatened he would shout and bring the Martians upon us. For a time that scared me; but any concession would have shortened our chance of escape beyond estimating. I defied him, although I felt no assurance that he might not do this thing. But that day, at any rate, he did not. He talked with his voice rising slowly, through the greater part of the eighth and ninth days – threats, entreaties, mingled with a torrent of half-sane and always frothy repentance for his vacant sham of God's service, such as made me pity him. Then he slept awhile, and began again with renewed strength, so loudly that I must needs make him desist.

"Be still!" I implored.

He rose to his knees, for he had been sitting in the darkness near the copper.

"I have been still too long," he said, in a tone that must have reached the pit, "and now I must bear my witness. Woe unto this unfaithful city! Woe! Woe! Woe! Woe! Woe! To the inhabitants of the earth by reason of the other voices of the trumpet –"

"Shut up!" I said, rising to my feet, and in a terror lest the Martians should hear us. "For God's sake –"

"Nay," shouted the curate, at the top of his voice, standing likewise and extending his arms. "Speak! The word of the Lord is upon me!"

In three strides he was at the door leading into the kitchen.

"I must bear my witness! I go! It has already been too long delayed."

I put out my hand and felt the meat chopper hanging to the wall. In a flash I was after him. I was fierce with fear. Before he was halfway across the kitchen I had overtaken him. With one last touch of humanity I turned the blade back and struck him with the butt. He went headlong forward and lay stretched on the ground. I stumbled over him and stood panting. He lay still.

Suddenly I heard a noise without, the run and smash of slipping plaster, and the triangular aperture in the wall was darkened. I looked up and saw the lower surface of a handling-machine coming slowly across the hole. One of its gripping limbs curled amid the debris; another limb appeared, feeling its way over the fallen beams. I stood petrified, staring. Then I saw through a sort of glass plate near the edge of the body the face, as we may call it, and the large dark eyes of a Martian, peering, and then a long metallic snake of tentacle came feeling slowly through the hole.

I turned by an effort, stumbled over the curate, and stopped at the scullery door. The tentacle was now some way, two yards or more, in the room, and twisting and turning, with queer sudden movements, this way and that. For a while I stood fascinated by that slow, fitful advance. Then, with a faint, hoarse cry, I forced myself across the scullery. I trembled violently; I could scarcely stand upright. I opened the door of the coal cellar, and stood there in the darkness staring at the faintly lit doorway into the kitchen, and listening. Had the Martian seen me? What was it doing now?

Something was moving to and fro there, very quietly; every now and then it tapped against the wall, or started on its movements with a faint metallic ringing, like the movements of keys on a split-ring. Then a heavy body – I knew too well what – was dragged across the floor of the kitchen towards the opening. Irresistibly attracted, I crept to the door and peeped into the kitchen. In the triangle of bright outer sunlight I saw the Martian, in its Briareus of a handling-machine, scrutinizing the curate's head. I thought at once that it would infer my presence from the mark of the blow I had given him.

I crept back to the coal cellar, shut the door, and began to cover myself up as much as I could, and as noiselessly as possible in the darkness, among the firewood and coal therein. Every now and then I paused, rigid, to hear if the Martian had thrust its tentacles through the opening again.

Then the faint metallic jingle returned. I traced it slowly feeling over the kitchen. Presently I heard it nearer – in the scullery, as I judged. I thought that its length might be insufficient to reach me. I prayed copiously. It passed, scraping faintly across the cellar door. An age of almost intolerable suspense intervened; then I heard it fumbling at the latch! It had found the door! The Martians understood doors!

It worried at the catch for a minute, perhaps, and then the door opened.

In the darkness I could just see the thing – like an elephant's trunk more than anything else – waving towards me and touching and examining the wall, coals, wood and ceiling. It was like a black worm swaying its blind head to and fro.

Once, even, it touched the heel of my boot. I was on the verge of screaming; I bit my hand. For a time the tentacle was silent. I could have fancied it had been withdrawn.

Presently, with an abrupt click, it gripped something – I thought it had me! – and seemed to go out of the cellar again. For a minute I was not sure. Apparently it had taken a lump of coal to examine.

I seized the opportunity of slightly shifting my position, which had become cramped, and then listened. I whispered passionate prayers for safety.

Then I heard the slow, deliberate sound creeping towards me again. Slowly, slowly it drew near, scratching against the walls and tapping the furniture.

While I was still doubtful, it rapped smartly against the cellar door and closed it. I heard it go into the pantry, and the biscuit-tins rattled and a bottle smashed, and then came a heavy bump against the cellar door. Then silence that passed into an infinity of suspense.

Had it gone?

At last I decided that it had.

It came into the scullery no more; but I lay all the tenth day in the close darkness, buried among coals and firewood, not daring even to crawl out for the drink for which I craved. It was the eleventh day before I ventured so far from my security.

Chapter V
The Stillness

MY FIRST ACT before I went into the pantry was to fasten the door between the kitchen and the scullery. But the pantry was empty; every scrap of food had gone. Apparently, the Martian had taken it all on the previous day. At that discovery I despaired for the first time. I took no food, or no drink either, on the eleventh or the twelfth day.

At first my mouth and throat were parched, and my strength ebbed sensibly. I sat about in the darkness of the scullery, in a state of despondent wretchedness. My mind ran on eating. I thought I had become deaf, for the noises of movement I had been accustomed to hear from the pit had ceased absolutely. I did not feel strong enough to crawl noiselessly to the peephole, or I would have gone there.

On the twelfth day my throat was so painful that, taking the chance of alarming the Martians, I attacked the creaking rain-water pump that stood by the sink, and got a couple of glassfuls of blackened and tainted rain water. I was greatly refreshed by this, and emboldened by the fact that no enquiring tentacle followed the noise of my pumping.

During these days, in a rambling, inconclusive way, I thought much of the curate and of the manner of his death.

On the thirteenth day I drank some more water, and dozed and thought disjointedly of eating and of vague impossible plans of escape. Whenever I dozed I dreamt of horrible phantasms, of the death of the curate, or of sumptuous dinners; but, asleep or awake, I felt a keen pain that urged me to drink again and again. The light that came into the scullery was no longer grey, but red. To my disordered imagination it seemed the colour of blood.

On the fourteenth day I went into the kitchen, and I was surprised to find that the fronds of the red weed had grown right across the hole in the wall, turning the half-light of the place into a crimson-coloured obscurity.

It was early on the fifteenth day that I heard a curious, familiar sequence of sounds in the kitchen, and, listening, identified it as the snuffing and scratching of a dog. Going into the kitchen, I saw a dog's nose peering in through a break among the ruddy fronds. This greatly surprised me. At the scent of me he barked shortly.

I thought if I could induce him to come into the place quietly I should be able, perhaps, to kill and eat him; and in any case, it would be advisable to kill him, lest his actions attracted the attention of the Martians.

I crept forward, saying "Good dog!" very softly; but he suddenly withdrew his head and disappeared.

I listened – I was not deaf – but certainly the pit was still. I heard a sound like the flutter of a bird's wings, and a hoarse croaking, but that was all.

For a long while I lay close to the peephole, but not daring to move aside the red plants that obscured it. Once or twice I heard a faint pitter-patter like the feet of the dog going hither and thither on the sand far below me, and there were more birdlike sounds, but that was all. At length, encouraged by the silence, I looked out.

Except in the corner, where a multitude of crows hopped and fought over the skeletons of the dead the Martians had consumed, there was not a living thing in the pit.

I stared about me, scarcely believing my eyes. All the machinery had gone. Save for the big mound of greyish-blue powder in one corner, certain bars of aluminium in another, the black birds, and the skeletons of the killed, the place was merely an empty circular pit in the sand.

Slowly I thrust myself out through the red weed, and stood upon the mound of rubble. I could see in any direction save behind me, to the north, and neither Martians nor sign of Martians were to be seen. The pit dropped sheerly from my feet, but a little way along the rubbish afforded a practicable slope to the summit of the ruins. My chance of escape had come. I began to tremble.

I hesitated for some time, and then, in a gust of desperate resolution, and with a heart that throbbed violently, I scrambled to the top of the mound in which I had been buried so long.

I looked about again. To the northward, too, no Martian was visible.

When I had last seen this part of Sheen in the daylight it had been a straggling street of comfortable white and red houses, interspersed with abundant shady trees. Now I stood on a mound of smashed brickwork, clay, and gravel, over which spread a multitude of red cactus-shaped plants, knee-high, without a solitary terrestrial growth to dispute their footing. The trees near me were dead and brown, but further a network of red thread scaled the still living stems.

The neighbouring houses had all been wrecked, but none had been burned; their walls stood, sometimes to the second story, with smashed windows and shattered doors. The red weed grew tumultuously in their roofless rooms. Below me was the great pit, with the crows struggling for its refuse. A number of other birds hopped about among the ruins. Far away I saw a gaunt cat slink crouchingly along a wall, but traces of men there were none.

The day seemed, by contrast with my recent confinement, dazzlingly bright, the sky a glowing blue. A gentle breeze kept the red weed that covered every scrap of unoccupied ground gently swaying. And oh! the sweetness of the air!

Chapter VI
The Work of Fifteen Days

FOR SOME TIME I stood tottering on the mound regardless of my safety. Within that noisome den from which I had emerged I had thought with a narrow intensity only of our immediate security. I had not realised what had been happening to the world, had not anticipated this startling vision of unfamiliar things. I had expected to see Sheen in ruins – I found about me the landscape, weird and lurid, of another planet.

For that moment I touched an emotion beyond the common range of men, yet one that the poor brutes we dominate know only too well. I felt as a rabbit might feel returning to his burrow and suddenly confronted by the work of a dozen busy navvies digging the foundations of a house. I felt the first inkling of a thing that presently grew quite clear in my mind, that oppressed me for many days, a sense of dethronement, a persuasion that I was no longer a master, but an animal among the animals, under the Martian heel. With us it would be as with them, to lurk and watch, to run and hide; the fear and empire of man had passed away.

But so soon as this strangeness had been realised it passed, and my dominant motive became the hunger of my long and dismal fast. In the direction away from the pit I saw, beyond a red-covered wall, a patch of garden ground unburied. This gave me a hint, and I went knee-deep, and sometimes neck-deep, in the red weed. The density of the weed gave me a reassuring sense of hiding. The wall was some six feet high, and when I attempted to clamber it I found I could not lift my feet to the crest. So I went along by the side of it, and came to a corner and a rockwork that enabled me to get to the top, and tumble into the garden I coveted. Here I found some young onions, a couple of gladiolus bulbs, and a quantity of immature carrots, all of which I secured, and, scrambling over a ruined wall, went on my way through scarlet and crimson trees towards Kew – it was like walking through an avenue of gigantic blood drops – possessed with two ideas: to get more food, and to limp, as soon and as far as my strength permitted, out of this accursed unearthly region of the pit.

Some way farther, in a grassy place, was a group of mushrooms which also I devoured, and then I came upon a brown sheet of flowing shallow water, where meadows used to be. These fragments of nourishment served only to whet my hunger. At first I was surprised at this flood in a hot, dry summer, but afterwards I discovered that it was caused by the tropical exuberance of the red weed. Directly this extraordinary growth encountered water it straightway became gigantic and of unparalleled fecundity. Its seeds were simply poured down into the water of the Wey and Thames, and its swiftly growing and Titanic water fronds speedily choked both those rivers.

At Putney, as I afterwards saw, the bridge was almost lost in a tangle of this weed, and at Richmond, too, the Thames water poured in a broad and shallow stream across the meadows of Hampton and Twickenham. As the water spread the weed followed them, until the ruined villas of the Thames valley were for a time lost in this red swamp, whose margin I explored, and much of the desolation the Martians had caused was concealed.

In the end the red weed succumbed almost as quickly as it had spread. A cankering disease, due, it is believed, to the action of certain bacteria, presently seized upon it. Now by the action of natural selection, all terrestrial plants have acquired a resisting power against bacterial diseases – they never succumb without a severe struggle, but the red weed rotted like a thing already dead. The fronds became bleached, and then shrivelled and brittle. They broke off at the least touch, and the waters that had stimulated their early growth carried their last vestiges out to sea.

My first act on coming to this water was, of course, to slake my thirst. I drank a great deal of it and, moved by an impulse, gnawed some fronds of red weed; but they were watery, and had a sickly, metallic taste. I found the water was sufficiently shallow for me to wade securely, although the red weed impeded my feet a little; but the flood evidently got deeper towards the river, and I turned back to Mortlake. I managed to make out the road by means of occasional ruins of its villas and fences and lamps, and so presently I got out of this spate and made my way to the hill going up towards Roehampton and came out on Putney Common.

Here the scenery changed from the strange and unfamiliar to the wreckage of the familiar: patches of ground exhibited the devastation of a cyclone, and in a few score yards I would come upon perfectly undisturbed spaces, houses with their blinds trimly drawn and doors closed, as if they had been left for a day by the owners, or as if their inhabitants slept within. The red weed was less abundant; the tall trees along the lane were free from the red creeper. I hunted for food among the trees, finding nothing, and I also raided a couple of silent houses, but they had already been broken into and ransacked. I rested for the remainder of the daylight in a shrubbery, being, in my enfeebled condition, too fatigued to push on.

All this time I saw no human beings, and no signs of the Martians. I encountered a couple of hungry-looking dogs, but both hurried circuitously away from the advances I made them. Near Roehampton I had seen two human skeletons – not bodies, but skeletons, picked clean – and in the wood by me I found the crushed and scattered bones of several cats and rabbits and the skull of a sheep. But though I gnawed parts of these in my mouth, there was nothing to be got from them.

After sunset I struggled on along the road towards Putney, where I think the Heat-Ray must have been used for some reason. And in the garden beyond Roehampton I got a quantity of immature potatoes, sufficient to stay my hunger. From this garden one looked down upon Putney and the river. The aspect of the place in the dusk was singularly desolate: blackened trees, blackened, desolate ruins, and down the hill the sheets of the flooded river, red-tinged with the weed. And over all – silence. It filled me with indescribable terror to think how swiftly that desolating change had come.

For a time I believed that mankind had been swept out of existence, and that I stood there alone, the last man left alive. Hard by the top of Putney Hill I came upon another skeleton, with the arms dislocated and removed several yards from the rest of the body. As I proceeded I became more and more convinced that the extermination of mankind was, save for such stragglers as myself, already accomplished in this part of the world. The Martians, I thought, had gone on and left the country desolated, seeking food elsewhere. Perhaps even now they were destroying Berlin or Paris, or it might be they had gone northward.

Chapter VII
The Man on Putney Hill

I SPENT THAT NIGHT in the inn that stands at the top of Putney Hill, sleeping in a made bed for the first time since my flight to Leatherhead. I will not tell the needless trouble I had breaking into that house – afterwards I found the front door was on the latch – nor how I ransacked every room for food, until just on the verge of despair, in what seemed to me to be a servant's bedroom, I found a rat-gnawed crust and two tins of pineapple. The place had been already searched and emptied. In the bar I afterwards found some biscuits and sandwiches that had been overlooked. The latter I could not eat, they were too rotten, but the former not only stayed my hunger, but filled my pockets. I lit no lamps, fearing some Martian might come beating that part of London for food in the night. Before I went to bed I had an interval of restlessness, and prowled from window to window, peering out for some sign of these monsters. I slept little. As I lay in bed I found myself thinking consecutively – a thing I do not remember to have done since my last argument with the curate. During all the intervening time my mental condition had been a hurrying succession of vague emotional states or a sort of stupid receptivity. But in the night my brain, reinforced, I suppose, by the food I had eaten, grew clear again, and I thought.

Three things struggled for possession of my mind: the killing of the curate, the whereabouts of the Martians, and the possible fate of my wife. The former gave me no sensation of horror or remorse to recall; I saw it simply as a thing done, a memory infinitely disagreeable but quite without the quality of remorse. I saw myself then as I see myself now, driven step by step towards that hasty blow, the creature of a sequence of accidents leading inevitably to that. I felt no condemnation; yet the memory, static, unprogressive, haunted me. In the silence of the night, with that sense of the nearness of God that sometimes comes into the stillness and the darkness, I stood my trial, my only trial, for that moment of wrath and fear. I retraced every step of our conversation from the moment when I had found him crouching beside me, heedless of my thirst, and pointing to the fire and smoke that streamed up from the ruins of Weybridge. We had been incapable of co-operation – grim chance had taken no heed of that. Had I foreseen, I should have left him at Halliford. But I did not foresee; and crime is to foresee and do. And I set this down as I have set all this story down, as it was. There were no witnesses – all these things I might have concealed. But I set it down, and the reader must form his judgment as he will.

And when, by an effort, I had set aside that picture of a prostrate body, I faced the problem of the Martians and the fate of my wife. For the former I had no data; I could imagine a hundred things, and so, unhappily, I could for the latter. And suddenly that night became terrible. I found myself sitting up in bed, staring at the dark. I found myself praying that the Heat-Ray might have suddenly and painlessly struck her out of being. Since the night of my return from Leatherhead I had not prayed. I had uttered prayers, fetish prayers, had prayed as heathens mutter charms when I was in extremity; but now I prayed indeed, pleading steadfastly and sanely, face to face with the darkness of God. Strange night! Strangest in this, that so soon as dawn had come, I, who had talked with God, crept out of the house like a rat leaving its hiding place – a creature scarcely larger, an inferior animal, a thing that for any passing whim of our masters might be hunted and killed. Perhaps they also prayed confidently to God. Surely, if we have learned nothing else, this war has taught us pity – pity for those witless souls that suffer our dominion.

The morning was bright and fine, and the eastern sky glowed pink, and was fretted with little golden clouds. In the road that runs from the top of Putney Hill to Wimbledon was a number of poor vestiges of the panic torrent that must have poured Londonward on the Sunday night after the fighting began. There was a little two-wheeled cart inscribed with the name of Thomas Lobb, Greengrocer, New Malden, with a smashed wheel and an abandoned tin trunk; there was a straw hat trampled into the now hardened mud, and at the top of West Hill a lot of blood-stained glass about the overturned water trough. My movements were languid, my plans of the vaguest. I had an idea of going to Leatherhead, though I knew that there I had the poorest chance of finding my wife. Certainly, unless death had overtaken them suddenly, my cousins and she would have fled thence; but it seemed to me I might find or learn there whither the Surrey people had fled. I knew I wanted to find my wife, that my heart ached for her and the world of men, but I had no clear idea how the finding might be done. I was also sharply aware now of my intense loneliness. From the corner I went, under cover of a thicket of trees and bushes, to the edge of Wimbledon Common, stretching wide and far.

That dark expanse was lit in patches by yellow gorse and broom; there was no red weed to be seen, and as I prowled, hesitating, on the verge of the open, the sun rose, flooding it all with light and vitality. I came upon a busy swarm of little frogs in a swampy place among the trees. I stopped to look at them, drawing a lesson from their stout resolve to live. And presently, turning suddenly, with an odd feeling of being watched, I beheld something crouching amid a clump of bushes. I stood regarding this. I made a step towards it, and it rose up and became a man armed with a cutlass. I approached him slowly. He stood silent and motionless, regarding me.

As I drew nearer I perceived he was dressed in clothes as dusty and filthy as my own; he looked, indeed, as though he had been dragged through a culvert. Nearer, I distinguished the green slime of ditches mixing with the pale drab of dried clay and shiny, coaly patches. His black hair fell over his eyes, and his face was dark and dirty and sunken, so that at first I did not recognise him. There was a red cut across the lower part of his face.

"Stop!" he cried, when I was within ten yards of him, and I stopped. His voice was hoarse. "Where do you come from?" he said.

I thought, surveying him.

"I come from Mortlake," I said. "I was buried near the pit the Martians made about their cylinder. I have worked my way out and escaped."

"There is no food about here," he said. "This is my country. All this hill down to the river, and back to Clapham, and up to the edge of the common. There is only food for one. Which way are you going?"

I answered slowly.

"I don't know," I said. "I have been buried in the ruins of a house thirteen or fourteen days. I don't know what has happened."

He looked at me doubtfully, then started, and looked with a changed expression.

"I've no wish to stop about here," said I. "I think I shall go to Leatherhead, for my wife was there."

He shot out a pointing finger.

"It is you," said he; "the man from Woking. And you weren't killed at Weybridge?"

I recognised him at the same moment.

"You are the artilleryman who came into my garden."

"Good luck!" he said. "We are lucky ones! Fancy *you*!" He put out a hand, and I took it. "I crawled up a drain," he said. "But they didn't kill everyone. And after they went away I got off towards Walton across the fields. But – It's not sixteen days altogether – and your hair is grey." He looked over his shoulder suddenly. "Only a rook," he said. "One gets to know that birds have shadows these days. This is a bit open. Let us crawl under those bushes and talk."

"Have you seen any Martians?" I said. "Since I crawled out –"

"They've gone away across London," he said. "I guess they've got a bigger camp there. Of a night, all over there, Hampstead way, the sky is alive with their lights. It's like a great city, and in the glare you can just see them moving. By daylight you can't. But nearer – I haven't seen them –" (he counted on his fingers) "five days. Then I saw a couple across Hammersmith way carrying something big. And the night before last" – he stopped and spoke impressively – "it was just a matter of lights, but it was something up in the air. I believe they've built a flying-machine, and are learning to fly."

I stopped, on hands and knees, for we had come to the bushes.

"Fly!"

"Yes," he said, "fly."

I went on into a little bower, and sat down.

"It is all over with humanity," I said. "If they can do that they will simply go round the world."

He nodded.

"They will. But – It will relieve things over here a bit. And besides – " He looked at me. "Aren't you satisfied it *is* up with humanity? I am. We're down; we're beat."

I stared. Strange as it may seem, I had not arrived at this fact – a fact perfectly obvious so soon as he spoke. I had still held a vague hope; rather, I had kept a lifelong habit of mind. He repeated his words, "We're beat." They carried absolute conviction.

"It's all over," he said. "They've lost *one* – just ONE. And they've made their footing good and crippled the greatest power in the world. They've walked over us. The death of that one at Weybridge was an accident. And these are only pioneers. They kept on coming. These green stars – I've seen none these five or six days, but I've no doubt they're falling somewhere every night. Nothing's to be done. We're under! We're beat!"

I made him no answer. I sat staring before me, trying in vain to devise some countervailing thought.

"This isn't a war," said the artilleryman. "It never was a war, any more than there's war between man and ants."

Suddenly I recalled the night in the observatory.

"After the tenth shot they fired no more – at least, until the first cylinder came."

"How do you know?" said the artilleryman. I explained. He thought. "Something wrong with the gun," he said. "But what if there is? They'll get it right again. And even if there's a delay, how can it alter the end? It's just men and ants. There's the ants builds their cities, live their lives, have wars, revolutions, until the men want them out of the way, and then they go out of the way. That's what we are now – just ants. Only –"

"Yes," I said.

"We're eatable ants."

We sat looking at each other.

"And what will they do with us?" I said.

"That's what I've been thinking," he said; "that's what I've been thinking. After Weybridge I went south – thinking. I saw what was up. Most of the people were hard at it squealing and exciting themselves. But I'm not so fond of squealing. I've been in sight of death once or twice; I'm not an ornamental soldier, and at the best and worst, death – it's just death. And it's the man that keeps on thinking comes through. I saw everyone tracking away south. Says I, "Food won't last this way," and I turned right back. I went for the Martians like a sparrow goes for man. All round" – he waved a hand to the horizon – "they're starving in heaps, bolting, treading on each other...."

He saw my face, and halted awkwardly.

"No doubt lots who had money have gone away to France," he said. He seemed to hesitate whether to apologise, met my eyes, and went on: "There's food all about here. Canned things in shops; wines, spirits, mineral waters; and the water mains and drains are empty. Well, I was telling you what I was thinking. "Here's intelligent things," I said, "and it seems they want us for food. First, they'll smash us up – ships, machines, guns, cities, all the order and organisation. All that will go. If we were the size of ants we might pull through. But we're not. It's all too bulky to stop. That's the first certainty." Eh?"

I assented.

"It is; I've thought it out. Very well, then – next; at present we're caught as we're wanted. A Martian has only to go a few miles to get a crowd on the run. And I saw one, one day, out by Wandsworth, picking houses to pieces and routing among the wreckage. But they won't keep on doing that. So soon as they've settled all our guns and ships, and smashed our railways, and done all the things they are doing over there, they will begin catching us systematic, picking the best and storing us in cages and things. That's what they will start doing in a bit. Lord! They haven't begun on us yet. Don't you see that?"

"Not begun!" I exclaimed.

"Not begun. All that's happened so far is through our not having the sense to keep quiet – worrying them with guns and such foolery. And losing our heads, and rushing off in crowds to where there wasn't any more safety than where we were. They don't want to bother us yet. They're making their things – making all the things they couldn't bring with them, getting things ready for the rest of their people. Very likely that's why the cylinders have stopped for a bit, for fear of hitting those who are here. And instead of our rushing about blind, on the howl, or getting dynamite on the chance of busting them up, we've got to fix ourselves up according to the new state of affairs. That's how I figure it out. It isn't quite according to what a man wants for his species, but it's about what the facts point to. And that's the principle I acted upon. Cities, nations, civilisation, progress – it's all over. That game's up. We're beat."

"But if that is so, what is there to live for?"

The artilleryman looked at me for a moment.

"There won't be any more blessed concerts for a million years or so; there won't be any Royal Academy of Arts, and no nice little feeds at restaurants. If it's amusement you're after, I reckon the game is up. If you've got any drawing-room manners or a dislike to eating peas with a knife or dropping aitches, you'd better chuck 'em away. They ain't no further use."

"You mean –"

"I mean that men like me are going on living – for the sake of the breed. I tell you, I'm grim set on living. And if I'm not mistaken, you'll show what insides *you've* got, too, before long. We aren't going to be exterminated. And I don't mean to be caught either, and tamed and fattened and bred like a thundering ox. Ugh! Fancy those brown creepers!"

"You don't mean to say –"

"I do. I'm going on, under their feet. I've got it planned; I've thought it out. We men are beat. We don't know enough. We've got to learn before we've got a chance. And we've got to live and keep independent while we learn. See! That's what has to be done."

I stared, astonished, and stirred profoundly by the man's resolution.

"Great God!," cried I. "But you are a man indeed!" And suddenly I gripped his hand.

"Eh!" he said, with his eyes shining. "I've thought it out, eh?"

"Go on," I said.

"Well, those who mean to escape their catching must get ready. I'm getting ready. Mind you, it isn't all of us that are made for wild beasts; and that's what it's got to be. That's why I watched you. I had my doubts. You're slender. I didn't know that it was you, you see, or just how you'd been buried. All these – the sort of people that lived in these houses, and all those damn little clerks that used to live down that way – they'd be no good. They haven't any spirit in them – no proud dreams and no proud lusts; and a man who hasn't one or the other – Lord! What is he but funk and precautions? They just used to skedaddle off to work – I've seen hundreds of 'em, bit of breakfast in hand, running wild and shining to catch their little season-ticket train, for fear they'd get dismissed if they didn't; working at businesses they were afraid to take the trouble to understand; skedaddling back for fear they wouldn't be in time for dinner; keeping indoors after dinner for fear of the back streets, and sleeping with the wives they married, not because they wanted them, but because they had a bit of money that would make for safety in their one little miserable skedaddle through the world. Lives insured and a bit invested for fear of accidents. And on Sundays – fear of the hereafter. As if hell was built for rabbits! Well, the Martians will just be a godsend to these. Nice roomy cages, fattening food, careful breeding, no worry. After a week or so chasing about the fields and lands on empty stomachs, they'll come and be caught cheerful. They'll be quite glad after a bit. They'll wonder what people did before there were Martians to take care of them. And the bar loafers, and mashers, and singers – I can imagine them. I can imagine them," he said, with a sort of sombre gratification. "There'll be any amount of sentiment and religion loose among them. There's hundreds of things I saw with my eyes that I've only begun to see clearly these last few days. There's lots will take things as they are – fat and stupid; and lots will be worried by a sort of feeling that it's all wrong, and that they ought to be doing something. Now whenever things are so that a lot of people feel they ought to be doing something, the weak, and those who go weak with a lot of complicated thinking, always make for a sort of do-nothing religion, very pious and superior, and submit to persecution and the will of the Lord. Very likely you've seen the same thing. It's energy in a gale of funk, and turned clean inside out. These cages will be full of psalms and hymns and piety. And those of a less simple sort will work in a bit of – what is it? – eroticism."

He paused.

"Very likely these Martians will make pets of some of them; train them to do tricks – who knows? – get sentimental over the pet boy who grew up and had to be killed. And some, maybe, they will train to hunt us."

"No," I cried, "that's impossible! No human being –"

"What's the good of going on with such lies?" said the artilleryman. "There's men who'd do it cheerful. What nonsense to pretend there isn't!"

And I succumbed to his conviction.

"If they come after me," he said; "Lord, if they come after me!" and subsided into a grim meditation.

I sat contemplating these things. I could find nothing to bring against this man's reasoning. In the days before the invasion no one would have questioned my intellectual superiority to his – I, a professed and recognised writer on philosophical themes, and he, a common soldier; and yet he had already formulated a situation that I had scarcely realised.

"What are you doing?" I said presently. "What plans have you made?"

He hesitated.

"Well, it's like this," he said. "What have we to do? We have to invent a sort of life where men can live and breed, and be sufficiently secure to bring the children up. Yes – wait a bit, and I'll make it clearer what I think ought to be done. The tame ones will go like all tame beasts; in a few generations they'll be big, beautiful, rich-blooded, stupid – rubbish! The risk is that we who keep wild will go savage – degenerate into a sort of big, savage rat....

You see, how I mean to live is underground. I've been thinking about the drains. Of course those who don't know drains think horrible things; but under this London are miles and miles – hundreds of miles – and a few days rain and London empty will leave them sweet and clean. The main drains are big enough and airy enough for anyone. Then there's cellars, vaults, stores, from which bolting passages may be made to the drains. And the railway tunnels and subways. Eh? You begin to see? And we form a band – able-bodied, clean-minded men. We're not going to pick up any rubbish that drifts in. Weaklings go out again."

"As you meant me to go?"

"Well – I parleyed, didn't I?"

"We won't quarrel about that. Go on."

"Those who stop obey orders. Able-bodied, clean-minded women we want also – mothers and teachers. No lackadaisical ladies – no blasted rolling eyes. We can't have any weak or silly. Life is real again, and the useless and cumbersome and mischievous have to die. They ought to die. They ought to be willing to die. It's a sort of disloyalty, after all, to live and taint the race. And they can't be happy. Moreover, dying's none so dreadful; it's the funking makes it bad. And in all those places we shall gather. Our district will be London. And we may even be able to keep a watch, and run about in the open when the Martians keep away. Play cricket, perhaps. That's how we shall save the race. Eh? It's a possible thing? But saving the race is nothing in itself. As I say, that's only being rats. It's saving our knowledge and adding to it is the thing. There men like you come in. There's books, there's models. We must make great safe places down deep, and get all the books we can; not novels and poetry swipes, but ideas, science books. That's where men like you come in. We must go to the British Museum and pick all those books through. Especially we must keep up our science – learn more. We must watch these Martians. Some of us must go as spies. When it's all working, perhaps I will. Get caught, I mean. And the great thing is, we must leave the Martians alone. We mustn't even steal. If we get in their way, we clear out. We must show them we mean no harm. Yes, I know. But they're intelligent things, and they won't hunt us down if they have all they want, and think we're just harmless vermin."

The artilleryman paused and laid a brown hand upon my arm.

"After all, it may not be so much we may have to learn before – Just imagine this: four or five of their fighting machines suddenly starting off – Heat-Rays right and left, and not a Martian in 'em. Not a Martian in 'em, but men – men who have learned the way how. It may be in my time, even – those men. Fancy having one of them lovely things, with its Heat-Ray wide and free! Fancy having it in control! What would it matter if you smashed to smithereens at the end of the run, after a bust like that? I reckon the Martians'll open their beautiful eyes! Can't you see them, man? Can't you see them hurrying, hurrying – puffing and blowing and hooting to their other mechanical affairs? Something out of gear in every case. And swish, bang, rattle, swish! Just as they are fumbling over it, *swish* comes the Heat-Ray, and, behold! man has come back to his own."

For a while the imaginative daring of the artilleryman, and the tone of assurance and courage he assumed, completely dominated my mind. I believed unhesitatingly both in his forecast of human destiny and in the practicability of his astonishing scheme, and the reader who thinks me susceptible and foolish must contrast his position, reading steadily with all his thoughts about his subject, and mine, crouching fearfully in the bushes and listening, distracted by apprehension. We talked in this manner through the early morning time, and later crept out of the bushes, and, after scanning the sky for Martians, hurried precipitately to the house on Putney Hill where he had made his lair. It was the coal cellar of the place, and when I saw the work he had spent a week upon – it was a burrow scarcely ten yards long, which he designed to reach to the main drain on Putney Hill – I had my first inkling of the gulf between his dreams and his powers. Such a hole I could have dug in a day. But I believed in him sufficiently to work with him all that morning until past midday at his digging. We had a garden barrow and shot the earth we removed against the kitchen range. We refreshed ourselves with a tin of mock-turtle soup and wine from the neighbouring pantry. I found a curious relief from the aching strangeness of the world in this steady labour. As we worked, I turned his project over in my mind, and presently objections and doubts began to arise; but I worked there all the morning, so glad was I to find myself with a purpose again. After working an hour I began to speculate on the distance one had to go before the cloaca was reached, the chances we had of missing it altogether. My immediate trouble was why we should dig this long tunnel, when it was possible to get into the drain at once down one of the manholes, and work back to the house. It seemed to me, too, that the house was inconveniently chosen, and required a needless length of tunnel. And just as I was beginning to face these things, the artilleryman stopped digging, and looked at me.

"We're working well," he said. He put down his spade. "Let us knock off a bit" he said. "I think it's time we reconnoitred from the roof of the house."

I was for going on, and after a little hesitation he resumed his spade; and then suddenly I was struck by a thought. I stopped, and so did he at once.

"Why were you walking about the common," I said, "instead of being here?"

"Taking the air," he said. "I was coming back. It's safer by night."

"But the work?"

"Oh, one can't always work," he said, and in a flash I saw the man plain. He hesitated, holding his spade. "We ought to reconnoitre now," he said, "because if any come near they may hear the spades and drop upon us unawares."

I was no longer disposed to object. We went together to the roof and stood on a ladder peeping out of the roof door. No Martians were to be seen, and we ventured out on the tiles, and slipped down under shelter of the parapet.

From this position a shrubbery hid the greater portion of Putney, but we could see the river below, a bubbly mass of red weed, and the low parts of Lambeth flooded and red. The red creeper swarmed up the trees about the old palace, and their branches stretched gaunt and dead, and set with shrivelled leaves, from amid its clusters. It was strange how entirely dependent both these things were upon flowing water for their propagation. About us neither had gained a footing; laburnums, pink mays, snowballs, and trees of arbor-vitae, rose out of laurels and hydrangeas, green and brilliant into the sunlight. Beyond Kensington dense smoke was rising, and that and a blue haze hid the northward hills.

The artilleryman began to tell me of the sort of people who still remained in London.

"One night last week," he said, "some fools got the electric light in order, and there was all Regent Street and the Circus ablaze, crowded with painted and ragged drunkards, men and women, dancing and shouting till dawn. A man who was there told me. And as the day came they became aware of a fighting-machine standing near by the Langham and looking down at them. Heaven knows how long he had been there. It must have given some of them a nasty turn. He came down the road towards them, and picked up nearly a hundred too drunk or frightened to run away."

Grotesque gleam of a time no history will ever fully describe!

From that, in answer to my questions, he came round to his grandiose plans again. He grew enthusiastic. He talked so eloquently of the possibility of capturing a fighting-machine that I more than half believed in him again. But now that I was beginning to understand something of his quality, I could divine the stress he laid on doing nothing precipitately. And I noted that now there was no question that he personally was to capture and fight the great machine.

After a time we went down to the cellar. Neither of us seemed disposed to resume digging, and when he suggested a meal, I was nothing loath. He became suddenly very generous, and when we had eaten he went away and returned with some excellent cigars. We lit these, and his optimism glowed. He was inclined to regard my coming as a great occasion.

"There's some champagne in the cellar," he said.

"We can dig better on this Thames-side burgundy," said I.

"No," said he; "I am host today. Champagne! Great God! We've a heavy enough task before us! Let us take a rest and gather strength while we may. Look at these blistered hands!"

And pursuant to this idea of a holiday, he insisted upon playing cards after we had eaten. He taught me euchre, and after dividing London between us, I taking the northern side and he the southern, we played for parish points. Grotesque and foolish as this will seem to the sober reader, it is absolutely true, and what is more remarkable, I found the card game and several others we played extremely interesting.

Strange mind of man! that, with our species upon the edge of extermination or appalling degradation, with no clear prospect before us but the chance of a horrible death, we could sit following the chance of this painted pasteboard, and playing the 'joker' with vivid delight. Afterwards he taught me poker, and I beat him at three tough chess games. When dark came we decided to take the risk, and lit a lamp.

After an interminable string of games, we supped, and the artilleryman finished the champagne. We went on smoking the cigars. He was no longer the energetic regenerator of his species I had encountered in the morning. He was still optimistic, but it was a less kinetic, a more thoughtful optimism. I remember he wound up with my health, proposed in a speech of small variety and considerable intermittence. I took a cigar, and went upstairs to look at the lights of which he had spoken that blazed so greenly along the Highgate hills.

At first I stared unintelligently across the London valley. The northern hills were shrouded in darkness; the fires near Kensington glowed redly, and now and then an orange-red tongue of flame flashed up and vanished in the deep blue night. All the rest of London was black. Then, nearer, I perceived a strange light, a pale, violet-purple fluorescent glow, quivering under the night breeze. For a space I could not understand it, and then I knew that it must be the red weed from which this faint irradiation proceeded. With that realisation my dormant sense of wonder, my sense of the proportion of things, awoke again. I glanced from that to Mars, red and clear, glowing high in the west, and then gazed long and earnestly at the darkness of Hampstead and Highgate.

I remained a very long time upon the roof, wondering at the grotesque changes of the day. I recalled my mental states from the midnight prayer to the foolish card-playing. I had a violent revulsion of feeling. I remember I flung away the cigar with a certain wasteful symbolism. My folly came to me with glaring exaggeration. I seemed a traitor to my wife and to my kind; I was filled with remorse. I resolved to leave this strange undisciplined dreamer of great things to his drink and gluttony, and to go on into London. There, it seemed to me, I had the best chance of learning what the Martians and my fellowmen were doing. I was still upon the roof when the late moon rose.

Chapter VIII
Dead London

AFTER I HAD PARTED from the artilleryman, I went down the hill, and by the High Street across the bridge to Fulham. The red weed was tumultuous at that time, and nearly choked the bridge roadway; but its fronds were already whitened in patches by the spreading disease that presently removed it so swiftly.

At the corner of the lane that runs to Putney Bridge station I found a man lying. He was as black as a sweep with the black dust, alive, but helplessly and speechlessly drunk. I could get nothing from him but curses and furious lunges at my head. I think I should have stayed by him but for the brutal expression of his face.

There was black dust along the roadway from the bridge onwards, and it grew thicker in Fulham. The streets were horribly quiet. I got food – sour, hard, and mouldy, but quite eatable – in a baker's shop here. Some way towards Walham Green the streets became clear of powder, and I passed a white terrace of houses on fire; the noise of the burning was an absolute relief. Going on towards Brompton, the streets were quiet again.

Here I came once more upon the black powder in the streets and upon dead bodies. I saw altogether about a dozen in the length of the Fulham Road. They had been dead many days, so that I hurried quickly past them. The black powder covered them over, and softened their outlines. One or two had been disturbed by dogs.

Where there was no black powder, it was curiously like a Sunday in the City, with the closed shops, the houses locked up and the blinds drawn, the desertion, and the stillness. In some places plunderers had been at work, but rarely at other than the provision and wine shops. A jeweller's window had been broken open in one place, but apparently the thief had been disturbed, and a number of gold chains and a watch lay scattered on the pavement. I did not trouble to touch them. Farther on was a tattered woman in a heap on a doorstep; the hand that hung over her knee was gashed and bled down her rusty brown dress, and a smashed magnum of champagne formed a pool across the pavement. She seemed asleep, but she was dead.

The farther I penetrated into London, the profounder grew the stillness. But it was not so much the stillness of death – it was the stillness of suspense, of expectation. At any time the destruction that had already singed the northwestern borders of the metropolis, and had annihilated Ealing and Kilburn, might strike among these houses and leave them smoking ruins. It was a city condemned and derelict....

In South Kensington the streets were clear of dead and of black powder. It was near South Kensington that I first heard the howling. It crept almost imperceptibly upon my senses. It was a sobbing alternation of two notes, "Ulla, ulla, ulla, ulla," keeping on perpetually. When I passed streets that ran northward it grew in volume, and houses and buildings seemed to deaden and cut it off again. It came in a full tide down Exhibition Road. I stopped, staring towards Kensington Gardens, wondering at this strange, remote wailing. It was as if that mighty desert of houses had found a voice for its fear and solitude.

"Ulla, ulla, ulla, ulla," wailed that superhuman note – great waves of sound sweeping down the broad, sunlit roadway, between the tall buildings on each side. I turned northwards, marvelling, towards the iron gates of Hyde Park. I had half a mind to break into the Natural History Museum and find my way up to the summits of the towers, in order to see across the park. But I decided to keep to the ground, where quick hiding was possible, and so went on up the Exhibition Road. All the large mansions on each side of the road were empty and still, and my footsteps echoed against the sides of the houses. At the top, near the park gate, I came upon a strange sight – a bus overturned, and the skeleton of a horse picked clean. I puzzled over this for a time, and then went on to the bridge over the Serpentine. The voice grew stronger and stronger, though I could see nothing above the housetops on the north side of the park, save a haze of smoke to the northwest.

"Ulla, ulla, ulla, ulla," cried the voice, coming, as it seemed to me, from the district about Regent's Park. The desolating cry worked upon my mind. The mood that had sustained me passed. The wailing took possession of me. I found I was intensely weary, footsore, and now again hungry and thirsty.

It was already past noon. Why was I wandering alone in this city of the dead? Why was I alone when all London was lying in state, and in its black shroud? I felt intolerably lonely. My mind ran on old friends that I had forgotten for years. I thought of the poisons in the chemists' shops, of the liquors the wine merchants stored; I recalled the two sodden creatures of despair, who so far as I knew, shared the city with myself….

I came into Oxford Street by the Marble Arch, and here again were black powder and several bodies, and an evil, ominous smell from the gratings of the cellars of some of the houses. I grew very thirsty after the heat of my long walk. With infinite trouble I managed to break into a public-house and get food and drink. I was weary after eating, and went into the parlour behind the bar, and slept on a black horsehair sofa I found there.

I awoke to find that dismal howling still in my ears, "Ulla, ulla, ulla, ulla." It was now dusk, and after I had routed out some biscuits and a cheese in the bar – there was a meat safe, but it contained nothing but maggots – I wandered on through the silent residential squares to Baker Street – Portman Square is the only one I can name – and so came out at last upon Regent's Park. And as I emerged from the top of Baker Street, I saw far away over the trees in the clearness of the sunset the hood of the Martian giant from which this howling proceeded. I was not terrified. I came upon him as if it were a matter of course. I watched him for some time, but he did not move. He appeared to be standing and yelling, for no reason that I could discover.

I tried to formulate a plan of action. That perpetual sound of "Ulla, ulla, ulla, ulla," confused my mind. Perhaps I was too tired to be very fearful. Certainly I was more curious to know the reason of this monotonous crying than afraid. I turned back away from the park and struck into Park Road, intending to skirt the park, went along under the shelter of the terraces, and got a view of this stationary, howling Martian from the direction of St. John's Wood. A couple of hundred yards out of Baker Street I heard a yelping chorus, and saw, first a dog with a piece of putrescent red meat in his jaws coming headlong towards me, and then a pack of starving mongrels in pursuit of him. He made a wide curve to avoid me, as though he feared I might prove a fresh competitor. As the yelping died away down the silent road, the wailing sound of "Ulla, ulla, ulla, ulla," reasserted itself.

I came upon the wrecked handling-machine halfway to St. John's Wood station. At first I thought a house had fallen across the road. It was only as I clambered among the ruins that I saw, with a start, this mechanical Samson lying, with its tentacles bent and smashed and twisted, among the ruins it had made. The forepart was shattered. It seemed as if it had driven blindly straight at the house, and had been overwhelmed in its overthrow. It seemed to me then that this might have happened by a handling-machine escaping from the guidance of its Martian. I could not clamber among the ruins to see it, and the twilight was now so far advanced that the blood with which its seat was smeared, and the gnawed gristle of the Martian that the dogs had left, were invisible to me.

Wondering still more at all that I had seen, I pushed on towards Primrose Hill. Far away, through a gap in the trees, I saw a second Martian, as motionless as the first, standing in the park towards the Zoological Gardens, and silent. A little beyond the ruins about the smashed handling-machine I came upon the red weed again, and found the Regent's Canal, a spongy mass of dark-red vegetation.

As I crossed the bridge, the sound of "Ulla, ulla, ulla, ulla," ceased. It was, as it were, cut off. The silence came like a thunderclap.

The dusky houses about me stood faint and tall and dim; the trees towards the park were growing black. All about me the red weed clambered among the ruins, writhing to get above me in the dimness. Night, the mother of fear and mystery, was coming upon me. But while that voice sounded the solitude, the desolation, had been endurable; by virtue of it London had still seemed alive, and the sense of life about me had upheld me. Then suddenly a change, the passing of something – I knew not what – and then a stillness that could be felt. Nothing but this gaunt quiet.

London about me gazed at me spectrally. The windows in the white houses were like the eye sockets of skulls. About me my imagination found a thousand noiseless enemies moving. Terror seized me, a horror of my temerity. In front of me the road became pitchy black as though it was tarred, and I saw a contorted shape lying across the pathway. I could not bring myself to go on. I turned down St. John's Wood Road, and ran headlong from this unendurable stillness towards Kilburn. I hid from the night and the silence, until long after midnight, in a cabmen's shelter in Harrow Road. But before the dawn my courage returned, and while the stars were still in the sky I turned once more towards Regent's Park. I missed my way among the streets, and presently saw down a long avenue, in the half-light of the early dawn, the curve of Primrose Hill. On the summit, towering up to the fading stars, was a third Martian, erect and motionless like the others.

An insane resolve possessed me. I would die and end it. And I would save myself even the trouble of killing myself. I marched on recklessly towards this Titan, and then, as I drew nearer and the light grew, I saw that a multitude of black birds was circling and clustering about the hood. At that my heart gave a bound, and I began running along the road.

I hurried through the red weed that choked St. Edmund's Terrace (I waded breast-high across a torrent of water that was rushing down from the waterworks towards the Albert Road), and emerged upon the grass before the rising of the sun. Great mounds had been heaped about the crest of the hill, making a huge redoubt of it – it was the final and largest place the Martians had made – and from behind these heaps there rose a thin smoke against the sky. Against the sky line an eager dog ran and disappeared. The thought that had flashed into my mind grew real, grew credible. I felt no fear, only a wild, trembling exultation, as I ran up the hill towards the motionless monster. Out of the hood hung lank shreds of brown, at which the hungry birds pecked and tore.

In another moment I had scrambled up the earthen rampart and stood upon its crest, and the interior of the redoubt was below me. A mighty space it was, with gigantic machines here and there within it, huge mounds of material and strange shelter places. And scattered about it, some in their overturned war-machines, some in the now rigid handling-machines, and a dozen of them stark and silent and laid in a row, were the Martians – *dead*! – slain by the putrefactive and disease bacteria against which their systems were unprepared; slain as the red weed was being slain; slain, after all man's devices had failed, by the humblest things that God, in his wisdom, has put upon this earth.

For so it had come about, as indeed I and many men might have foreseen had not terror and disaster blinded our minds. These germs of disease have taken toll of humanity since the beginning of things – taken toll of our prehuman ancestors since life began here. But by virtue of this natural selection of our kind we have developed resisting power; to no germs do we succumb without a struggle, and to many – those that cause putrefaction in dead matter, for instance – our living frames are altogether immune. But there are no bacteria in Mars, and directly these invaders arrived, directly they drank and fed, our microscopic allies began to work their overthrow. Already when I watched them they were irrevocably doomed, dying and rotting even as they went to and fro. It was inevitable. By the toll of a billion deaths man has bought his birthright of the earth, and it is his against all comers; it would still be his were the Martians ten times as mighty as they are. For neither do men live nor die in vain.

Here and there they were scattered, nearly fifty altogether, in that great gulf they had made, overtaken by a death that must have seemed to them as incomprehensible as any death could be. To me also at that time this death was incomprehensible. All I knew was that these things that had been alive and so terrible to men were dead. For a moment I believed that the destruction of Sennacherib had been repeated, that God had repented, that the Angel of Death had slain them in the night.

I stood staring into the pit, and my heart lightened gloriously, even as the rising sun struck the world to fire about me with his rays. The pit was still in darkness; the mighty engines, so great and wonderful in their power and complexity, so unearthly in their tortuous forms, rose weird and vague and strange out of the shadows towards the light. A multitude of dogs, I could hear, fought over the bodies that lay darkly in the depth of the pit, far below me. Across the pit on its farther lip, flat and vast and strange, lay the great flying-machine with which they had been experimenting upon our denser atmosphere when decay and death arrested them. Death had come not a day too soon. At the sound of a cawing overhead I looked up at the huge fighting-machine that would fight no more for ever, at the tattered red shreds of flesh that dripped down upon the overturned seats on the summit of Primrose Hill.

I turned and looked down the slope of the hill to where, enhaloed now in birds, stood those other two Martians that I had seen overnight, just as death had overtaken them. The one had died, even as it had been crying to its companions; perhaps it was the last to die, and its voice had gone on perpetually until the force of its machinery was exhausted. They glittered now, harmless tripod towers of shining metal, in the brightness of the rising sun.

All about the pit, and saved as by a miracle from everlasting destruction, stretched the great Mother of Cities. Those who have only seen London veiled in her sombre robes of smoke can scarcely imagine the naked clearness and beauty of the silent wilderness of houses.

Eastward, over the blackened ruins of the Albert Terrace and the splintered spire of the church, the sun blazed dazzling in a clear sky, and here and there some facet in the great wilderness of roofs caught the light and glared with a white intensity.

Northward were Kilburn and Hampsted, blue and crowded with houses; westward the great city was dimmed; and southward, beyond the Martians, the green waves of Regent's Park, the Langham Hotel, the dome of the Albert Hall, the Imperial Institute, and the giant mansions of the Brompton Road came out clear and little in the sunrise, the jagged ruins of Westminster rising hazily beyond. Far away and blue were the Surrey hills, and the towers of the Crystal Palace glittered like two silver rods. The dome of St. Paul's was dark against the sunrise, and injured, I saw for the first time, by a huge gaping cavity on its western side.

And as I looked at this wide expanse of houses and factories and churches, silent and abandoned; as I thought of the multitudinous hopes and efforts, the innumerable hosts of lives that had gone to build this human reef, and of the swift and ruthless destruction that had hung over it all; when I realised that the shadow had been rolled back, and that men might still live in the streets, and this dear vast dead city of mine be once more alive and powerful, I felt a wave of emotion that was near akin to tears.

The torment was over. Even that day the healing would begin. The survivors of the people scattered over the country – leaderless, lawless, foodless, like sheep without a shepherd – the thousands who had fled by sea, would begin to return; the pulse of life, growing stronger and stronger, would beat again in the empty streets and pour across the vacant squares. Whatever destruction was done, the hand of the destroyer was stayed. All the gaunt wrecks, the blackened skeletons of houses that stared so dismally at the sunlit grass of the hill, would presently be echoing with the hammers of the restorers and ringing with the tapping of their trowels. At the thought I extended my hands towards the sky and began thanking God. In a year, thought I– in a year…

With overwhelming force came the thought of myself, of my wife, and the old life of hope and tender helpfulness that had ceased for ever.

Chapter IX
Wreckage

AND NOW COMES the strangest thing in my story. Yet, perhaps, it is not altogether strange. I remember, clearly and coldly and vividly, all that I did that day until the time that I stood weeping and praising God upon the summit of Primrose Hill. And then I forget.

Of the next three days I know nothing. I have learned since that, so far from my being the first discoverer of the Martian overthrow, several such wanderers as myself had already discovered this on the previous night. One man – the first – had gone to St. Martin's-le-Grand, and, while I sheltered in the cabmen's hut, had contrived to telegraph to Paris. Thence the joyful news had flashed all over the world; a thousand cities, chilled by ghastly apprehensions, suddenly flashed into frantic illuminations; they knew of it in Dublin, Edinburgh, Manchester, Birmingham, at the time when I stood upon the verge of the pit. Already men, weeping with joy, as I have heard, shouting and staying their work to shake hands and shout, were making up trains, even as near as Crewe, to descend upon London. The church bells that had ceased a fortnight since suddenly caught the news, until all England was bell-ringing. Men on cycles, lean-faced, unkempt, scorched along every country lane shouting of unhoped deliverance, shouting to gaunt, staring figures of despair. And for the food! Across the Channel, across the Irish Sea, across the Atlantic, corn, bread, and meat were tearing to our relief. All the shipping in the world seemed going Londonward in those days. But of all this I have no memory. I drifted – a demented man. I found myself in a house of kindly people, who had found me on the third day wandering, weeping, and raving through the streets of St. John's Wood. They have told me since that I was singing some insane doggerel about "The Last Man Left Alive! Hurrah! The Last Man Left Alive!" Troubled as they were with their own affairs, these people, whose name, much as I would like to express my gratitude to them, I may not even give here, nevertheless cumbered themselves with me, sheltered me, and protected me from myself. Apparently they had learned something of my story from me during the days of my lapse.

Very gently, when my mind was assured again, did they break to me what they had learned of the fate of Leatherhead. Two days after I was imprisoned it had been destroyed, with every soul in it, by a Martian. He had swept it out of existence, as it seemed, without any provocation, as a boy might crush an ant hill, in the mere wantonness of power.

I was a lonely man, and they were very kind to me. I was a lonely man and a sad one, and they bore with me. I remained with them four days after my recovery. All that time I felt a vague, a growing craving to look once more on whatever remained of the little life that seemed so happy and bright in my past. It was a mere hopeless desire to feast upon my misery. They dissuaded me. They did all they could to divert me from this morbidity. But at last I could resist the impulse no longer, and, promising faithfully to return to them, and parting, as I will confess, from these four-day friends with tears, I went out again into the streets that had lately been so dark and strange and empty.

Already they were busy with returning people; in places even there were shops open, and I saw a drinking fountain running water.

I remember how mockingly bright the day seemed as I went back on my melancholy pilgrimage to the little house at Woking, how busy the streets and vivid the moving life about me. So many people were abroad everywhere, busied in a thousand activities, that it seemed incredible that any great proportion of the population could have been slain. But then I noticed how yellow were the skins of the people I met, how shaggy the hair of the men, how large and bright their eyes, and that every other man still wore his dirty rags. Their faces seemed all with one of two expressions – a leaping exultation and energy or a grim resolution. Save for the expression of the faces, London seemed a city of tramps. The vestries were indiscriminately distributing bread sent us by the French government. The ribs of the few horses showed dismally. Haggard special constables with white badges stood at the corners of every street. I saw little of the mischief wrought by the Martians until I reached Wellington Street, and there I saw the red weed clambering over the buttresses of Waterloo Bridge.

At the corner of the bridge, too, I saw one of the common contrasts of that grotesque time – a sheet of paper flaunting against a thicket of the red weed, transfixed by a stick that kept it in place. It was the placard of the first newspaper to resume publication – the *Daily Mail*. I bought a copy for a blackened shilling I found in my pocket. Most of it was in blank, but the solitary compositor who did the thing had amused himself by making a grotesque scheme of advertisement stereo on the back page. The matter he printed was emotional; the news organisation had not as yet found its way back. I learned nothing fresh except that already in one week the examination of the Martian mechanisms had yielded astonishing results. Among other things, the article assured me what I did not believe at the time, that the 'Secret of Flying,' was discovered. At Waterloo I found the free trains that were taking people to their homes. The first rush was already over. There were few people in the train, and I was in no mood for casual conversation. I got a compartment to myself, and sat with folded arms, looking greyly at the sunlit devastation that flowed past the windows. And just outside the terminus the train jolted over temporary rails, and on either side of the railway the houses were blackened ruins. To Clapham Junction the face of London was grimy with powder of the Black Smoke, in spite of two days of thunderstorms and rain, and at Clapham Junction the line had been wrecked again; there were hundreds of out-of-work clerks and shopmen working side by side with the customary navvies, and we were jolted over a hasty relaying.

All down the line from there the aspect of the country was gaunt and unfamiliar; Wimbledon particularly had suffered. Walton, by virtue of its unburned pine woods, seemed the least hurt of any place along the line. The Wandle, the Mole, every little stream, was a heaped mass of red weed, in appearance between butcher's meat and pickled cabbage. The Surrey pine woods were too dry, however, for the festoons of the red climber. Beyond Wimbledon, within sight of the line, in certain nursery grounds, were the heaped masses of earth about the sixth cylinder. A number of people were standing about it, and some sappers were busy in the midst of it. Over it flaunted a Union Jack, flapping cheerfully in the morning breeze. The nursery grounds were everywhere crimson with the weed, a wide expanse of livid colour cut with purple shadows, and very painful to the eye. One's gaze went with infinite relief from the scorched greys and sullen reds of the foreground to the blue-green softness of the eastward hills.

The line on the London side of Woking station was still undergoing repair, so I descended at Byfleet station and took the road to Maybury, past the place where I and the artilleryman had talked to the hussars, and on by the spot where the Martian had appeared to me in the thunderstorm. Here, moved by curiosity, I turned aside to find, among a tangle of red fronds, the warped and broken dog cart with the whitened bones of the horse scattered and gnawed. For a time I stood regarding these vestiges....

Then I returned through the pine wood, neck-high with red weed here and there, to find the landlord of the Spotted Dog had already found burial, and so came home past the College Arms. A man standing at an open cottage door greeted me by name as I passed.

I looked at my house with a quick flash of hope that faded immediately. The door had been forced; it was unfast and was opening slowly as I approached.

It slammed again. The curtains of my study fluttered out of the open window from which I and the artilleryman had watched the dawn. No one had closed it since. The smashed bushes were just as I had left them nearly four weeks ago. I stumbled into the hall, and the house felt empty. The stair carpet was ruffled and discoloured where I had crouched, soaked to the skin from the thunderstorm the night of the catastrophe. Our muddy footsteps I saw still went up the stairs.

I followed them to my study, and found lying on my writing-table still, with the selenite paper weight upon it, the sheet of work I had left on the afternoon of the opening of the cylinder. For a space I stood reading over my abandoned arguments. It was a paper on the probable development of Moral Ideas with the development of the civilising process; and the last sentence was the opening of a prophecy: 'In about two hundred years,' I had written, 'we may expect –' The sentence ended abruptly. I remembered my inability to fix my mind that morning, scarcely a month gone by, and how I had broken off to get my *Daily Chronicle* from the newsboy. I remembered how I went down to the garden gate as he came along, and how I had listened to his odd story of 'Men from Mars.'

I came down and went into the dining room. There were the mutton and the bread, both far gone now in decay, and a beer bottle overturned, just as I and the artilleryman had left them. My home was desolate. I perceived the folly of the faint hope I had cherished so long. And then a strange thing occurred. "It is no use," said a voice. "The house is deserted.

No one has been here these ten days. Do not stay here to torment yourself. No one escaped but you."

I was startled. Had I spoken my thought aloud? I turned, and the French window was open behind me. I made a step to it, and stood looking out.

And there, amazed and afraid, even as I stood amazed and afraid, were my cousin and my wife – my wife white and tearless. She gave a faint cry.

"I came," she said. "I knew – knew –"

She put her hand to her throat – swayed. I made a step forward, and caught her in my arms.

Chapter X
The Epilogue

I CANNOT BUT REGRET, now that I am concluding my story, how little I am able to contribute to the discussion of the many debatable questions which are still unsettled. In one respect I shall certainly provoke criticism. My particular province is speculative philosophy. My knowledge of comparative physiology is confined to a book or two, but it seems to me that Carver's suggestions as to the reason of the rapid death of the Martians is so probable as to be regarded almost as a proven conclusion. I have assumed that in the body of my narrative.

At any rate, in all the bodies of the Martians that were examined after the war, no bacteria except those already known as terrestrial species were found. That they did not bury any of their dead, and the reckless slaughter they perpetrated, point also to an entire ignorance of the putrefactive process. But probable as this seems, it is by no means a proven conclusion.

Neither is the composition of the Black Smoke known, which the Martians used with such deadly effect, and the generator of the Heat-Rays remains a puzzle. The terrible disasters at the Ealing and South Kensington laboratories have disinclined analysts for further investigations upon the latter. Spectrum analysis of the black powder points unmistakably to the presence of an unknown element with a brilliant group of three lines in the green, and it is possible that it combines with argon to form a compound which acts at once with deadly effect upon some constituent in the blood. But such unproven speculations will scarcely be of interest to the general reader, to whom this story is addressed. None of the brown scum that drifted down the Thames after the destruction of Shepperton was examined at the time, and now none is forthcoming.

The results of an anatomical examination of the Martians, so far as the prowling dogs had left such an examination possible, I have already given. But everyone is familiar with the magnificent and almost complete specimen in spirits at the Natural History Museum, and the countless drawings that have been made from it; and beyond that the interest of their physiology and structure is purely scientific.

A question of graver and universal interest is the possibility of another attack from the Martians. I do not think that nearly enough attention is being given to this aspect of the matter. At present the planet Mars is in conjunction, but with every return to opposition I, for one, anticipate a renewal of their adventure. In any case, we should be prepared. It seems to me that it should be possible to define the position of the gun from which the shots are discharged, to keep a sustained watch upon this part of the planet, and to anticipate the arrival of the next attack.

In that case the cylinder might be destroyed with dynamite or artillery before it was sufficiently cool for the Martians to emerge, or they might be butchered by means of guns so soon as the screw opened. It seems to me that they have lost a vast advantage in the failure of their first surprise. Possibly they see it in the same light.

Lessing has advanced excellent reasons for supposing that the Martians have actually succeeded in effecting a landing on the planet Venus. Seven months ago now, Venus and Mars were in alignment with the sun; that is to say, Mars was in opposition from the point of view of an observer on Venus. Subsequently a peculiar luminous and sinuous marking appeared on the unillumined half of the inner planet, and almost simultaneously a faint dark mark of a similar sinuous character was detected upon a photograph of the Martian disk. One needs to see the drawings of these appearances in order to appreciate fully their remarkable resemblance in character.

At any rate, whether we expect another invasion or not, our views of the human future must be greatly modified by these events. We have learned now that we cannot regard this planet as being fenced in and a secure abiding place for Man; we can never anticipate the unseen good or evil that may come upon us suddenly out of space. It may be that in the larger design of the universe this invasion from Mars is not without its ultimate benefit for men; it has robbed us of that serene confidence in the future which is the most fruitful source of decadence, the gifts to human science it has brought are enormous, and it has done much to promote the conception of the commonweal of mankind. It may be that across the immensity of space the Martians have watched the fate of these pioneers of theirs and learned their lesson, and that on the planet Venus they have found a securer settlement. Be that as it may, for many years yet there will certainly be no relaxation of the eager scrutiny of the Martian disk, and those fiery darts of the sky, the shooting stars, will bring with them as they fall an unavoidable apprehension to all the sons of men.

The broadening of men's views that has resulted can scarcely be exaggerated. Before the cylinder fell there was a general persuasion that through all the deep of space no life existed beyond the petty surface of our minute sphere. Now we see further. If the Martians can reach Venus, there is no reason to suppose that the thing is impossible for men, and when the slow cooling of the sun makes this earth uninhabitable, as at last it must do, it may be that the thread of life that has begun here will have streamed out and caught our sister planet within its toils.

Dim and wonderful is the vision I have conjured up in my mind of life spreading slowly from this little seed bed of the solar system throughout the inanimate vastness of sidereal space. But that is a remote dream. It may be, on the other hand, that the destruction of the Martians is only a reprieve. To them, and not to us, perhaps, is the future ordained.

I must confess the stress and danger of the time have left an abiding sense of doubt and insecurity in my mind. I sit in my study writing by lamplight, and suddenly I see again the healing valley below set with writhing flames, and feel the house behind and about me empty and desolate. I go out into the Byfleet Road, and vehicles pass me, a butcher boy in a cart, a cabful of visitors, a workman on a bicycle, children going to school, and suddenly they become vague and unreal, and I hurry again with the artilleryman through the hot, brooding silence. Of a night I see the black powder darkening the silent streets, and the contorted bodies shrouded in that layer; they rise upon me tattered and dog-bitten. They gibber and grow fiercer, paler, uglier, mad distortions of humanity at last, and I wake, cold and wretched, in the darkness of the night.

I go to London and see the busy multitudes in Fleet Street and the Strand, and it comes across my mind that they are but the ghosts of the past, haunting the streets that I have seen silent and wretched, going to and fro, phantasms in a dead city, the mockery of life in a galvanised body. And strange, too, it is to stand on Primrose Hill, as I did but a day before writing this last chapter, to see the great province of houses, dim and blue through the haze of the smoke and mist, vanishing at last into the vague lower sky, to see the people walking to and fro among the flower beds on the hill, to see the sight-seers about the Martian machine that stands there still, to hear the tumult of playing children, and to recall the time when I saw it all bright and clear-cut, hard and silent, under the dawn of that last great day....

And strangest of all is it to hold my wife's hand again, and to think that I have counted her, and that she has counted me, among the dead.

What Survives of Us

S.A. Westerley

I WAS THERE the day we picked the last of them up. I'm not going to lie, it was pretty rough. No. Rough doesn't cover it. I don't know what word would but it was bad. Anyone who was there would be able to tell you how bad it was but none of them will really be able to describe it. Sure, the Retrieval is ancient history now but at the time….it was…so…vivid? No. Immediate? Real? Huge? See I don't have the words. None of us did really. At best we laughed it off. No, honestly. We made up jokes.

That day has entered popular idiom, at least the part of it I remember the most has. You won't know it, but you'll know the phrase for sure. I guess it's gallows humour but it was a phrase we all picked up on, all the pilots and security and…we weren't laughing at what we'd seen, what we'd been through, what we'd heard…we just…we knew how we meant it anyway.

'Oh come on man, don't leave the speakers up', you'll have heard the phrase, it's what you tell some asshole whose telling you his life story, half cut and without any due encouragement. We use that phrase all the time, it's too useful not to.

'Woah, woah, come on! Speakers up man!', it's what everyone says, anyone my age or younger, whenever somebody you know is getting a bit too frank or open with you, or when you're seeing something you'd sooner avoid, your pal admitting he's got a thing for your Mom or your roomie coming out of the bathroom without a towel wrapped round all the parts that ought to be hidden.

I guess people don't know what the original reference point is when they're saying it. And why the hell would they? To them it must just be another reference to some dirty joke they never actually heard or some foul and depraved act they don't really understand. To them all it means is 'I don't want to hear it', 'I don't want to know'. That's enough. I guess I wouldn't want them to know any more than that. My speakers are down. Unless you're really curious.

Ok, so…yeah, I was there. I was just a junior shuttle pilot, I'd never even been to Earth, little colonial kid that I was. Point of fact, it was more or less my first trip out of orbit. But they needed all the ships and pilots they could get. Anything that could fly they flew out there. It still never could have been close to enough.

The fact we were heading to Earth, like actual Earth, system centre, was pretty overwhelming to a lot of the younger pilots like me, despite all that had changed. Earth was a big deal to us, even then. Point of fact, even now we still speak of Earth. It's been so much a part of our lives, of our history, that it's difficult to process that it's gone. Or that there's no one left there to speak of it first hand.

Just like the open speakers it survives in idiom…'The good solid Earth', 'Give me one Earthly reason', 'What on Earth?', 'Why on Earth should that be?' as if there were only one world, as if that first world our ancestors knew was all there is. Nothing's there now. Nothing and no one. Nothing's been there for a long time.

It was a long slow apocalypse. Slow enough for folks to deny it, to kid themselves it wouldn't arrive, or that they'd be gone before it did.

The Earthers saw the last days coming but what could really be done, in the circumstances? Where else was there to go but the one world they had ever known? Those that could afford it arranged passage, tried to make lives for themselves elsewhere in the solar system, what might once have been their great wealth as privileged Earthers becoming suddenly worthless in the face of the new reality. My parents used to talk of Earth as this mythical place, something to be aspired to, someplace I was pretty sure I could never afford to live. But things turned round pretty quick. At first we were excited by the refugees, sophisticated Earthers bringing their fashions and wealth out to the colonies. My parents offered to let a room just in the hopes of getting a refugee in to tell them stories of what they still called 'back home'. But that was no kind of a solution. Not to a global problem. It was obvious that pretty soon they'd all have to leave. Every last Earther. Out to the already crowded colonies. No one had thought how we'd make room for them all. The colonies were a lot smaller then. There was a lot of opposition too. There were colonists who'd left Earth for hard ethical reasons and didn't want its soft, decadent ways following them out here.

But we couldn't just leave them, could we? We had to do something.

When I was in that fleet…I mean, man, I've never seen anything like it, before or since. Swear on my life, every part of everywhere you could look was ships and ships and then more ships. Every size, every shape and purpose; commercial, medical, heavy haulage, maintenance, pleasure cruisers, police, warships. It felt good to be human, for a brief glimmer, before you realized the scale of the job, the size of the Earth, the billions of people waiting, desperate, hopeless and helplessly alone.

The sea of people I saw as we came into land, that first overwhelming image, will never leave my mind. I guess I couldn't have seen individual faces but it still feels as if I did, each and every one of them staring into me, asking, imploring me that they should be the one to get out.

Some of the older guys in my crew seemed pretty relaxed. They read or they dozed as the refugees were allocated ships. It was a long process and it paid to have something to distract you. If I looked at the screen all I could see was bodies. But in that human sea where you'd think you couldn't make out any individual detail at all, that was all I could make out. A woman clutching a spare dress, so she could look her best when she arrived. A child fighting to hold a glass case steady, constantly buffeted by the contact of older, taller people who threatened to overturn it, an overturning that would have cast out the pet lizard basking oblivious at the heart of it onto the cold hard ground. Someone had brought a pile of books. They would have taken up a whole passenger's worth of space. There was no way those books could ever have been taken. Any fool could see that. And all the data contained in them could have been, probably would have been, stored some other way. But it was clung to doggedly just the same. It was one more thing the Earthers had to at least try to save.

Coordinators clung to the outer doors of each of the shuttle crafts, pointing and waving and gesturing, fighting to be heard over the sonic soup of shouts and tears and pleading. Just behind them security complements would mirror the gestures, emphasising them with guns and stun rods in their outstretched arms. I wish we hadn't needed them. But we did.

* * *

The shuttles had external microphones fitted so the co-ordinators could let us know when to ready the engines or how close we were to full, that kind of thing, or so we could hear for ourselves if they'd been overwhelmed and that great surge of humanity needed our electronic doors shutting fast on it. We tried to co-ordinate our take offs. We had been warned that the minute one shuttle went the crowds would just surge to the others. There was too much risk to human life, the officials had said, as if that made a difference by then, and too much of a risk that one or more shuttles, swamped by the press of bodies, mightn't have been able to take off, dooming the handful of lucky passengers and crew alike. We hadn't come here to make more corpses. So we kept them waiting. Ships that had been full for hours kept the queues in front of them patiently hanging on, clinging to their bundled clothing and parcels and pets and what little hope they had left when all the shuttle crews knew what we were shortly going to be doing to them. We didn't have a choice.

Inside the cab that soup of noise was most all I could hear, even with my 'phones clamped on my ears. The instruments beeped and chattered but it was their lights I registered, the hiss and crackle of radio static was all but inaudible over the sound of the desperate sea of humanity outside. I kept itching to dial the volume of it down, but I needed to hear our coordinator, to know when he was ready for us to leave.

Eventually we stared to hear the last of the ships declaring themselves full. Over our speaker system we heard our co-ordinator tell us the same. We got ready to start the engines. Security teams sat ready to force the refugees back.

In some places they promised the Earthers another convoy, another fleet of shuttles within hours or days, just to keep them passive, just to keep them from surging forward in a panic and overwhelming us as we took off. But the Earthers knew, most of them anyway. They must have.

So the screams, when we heard them, we knew must be as genuine as any death scream anyone ever heard. The engines couldn't drown them out. The onboard chatter, the crying and the shouting of the refugees that filled every spare foot of our ship, none of them could drown it out.

We just hadn't thought to take down the microphones, still in place on the outside of the ship. It seems such a stupid oversight, a joke almost. It would have been too much of a warning to the refugees, I guess, but still, it never even crossed the minds of our crew. It was a common mistake, crews from most of the sites did exactly the same thing. Common enough that it's become an idiom.

I can't describe the screams and I hope you couldn't imagine them if you tried. Tens or maybe hundreds of thousands of human beings who have lived their lives, worked at their jobs, studied and learned and loved and grown and raised their children for something, for some good reason, they were all of them sure of it, for every moment that they had lived out those dead end lives full of ambition and hope, watching the last justification for their lives disappear into space.

There would be no consolation for them. Not that the end would be quick, not that hope still remained for rescue, not that their children would survive them, maybe not even that later generations would remember them.

They survive as idiom, that's all. Their dying screams have been all but forgotten except for this one oblique reference to them, a glib phrase for 'I don't want to hear it'. 'Speakers down, buddy, huh? Speakers down.'

Which only leaves one question; on every shuttle from every site that made the same idiot mistake of leaving the external microphones attached, it only took the shifting of a single dial to turn that sound off, just one simple movement to be free of the memory of that sound, to remove the frozen look of guilt that followed every survivor for life, to not have to think about the hope we had just torn from the last Earthers there would ever be. So then why did I, why did every damn pilot I've ever spoken to, on every ship, from every site, all over that dying planet, leave that dial be, stay their hand and leave those speakers up?

Jars for Their Eyes

William R.D. Wood

"DADDY, my tummy hurts."

Lucas slid quickly from the dining room chair and knelt at little Zoe's side. He slipped an arm around her shoulder. Hopefully Emma hadn't overheard from the kitchen.

"Tummies do that sometimes," he said to the girl, pulling her close. The room was dark. The frequent power grid brownouts had finally stopped teasing them a few days ago leaving the house electricity-free and oddly quiet for a family of five.

No. Not five. Just three.

The house popped and creaked, settling in. The nights grew colder day by day. Summer had been hard on them. Maybe autumn would be gentler.

"Daddy?"

Keep the tremble out of your voice, Lucas "It'll be fine."

A hollow crack came from the kitchen followed by glass scraping across the countertop, the clank of a pan. Emma was getting some of their canned vegetables ready for tomorrow. She hadn't heard Zoe, otherwise she'd have come in by now. The only time she paid any mind to their daughter anymore was when the poor little thing was in pain.

He stroked the side of her head. A stomach ache was a symptom, sure, but could just as easily come from eating too many stewed potatoes. *Think positive. You're the parent here. That's your only job now.*

He swept a wayward strand behind Zoe's ear. She was adorable, inheriting Emma's jet black hair and his naturally tanned skin. She had Emma's cheekbones and chin but she'd gotten his nose. He'd always thought his nose was his worst feature but on his little angel, it was perfect. Her most striking features, though, were her sapphire green eyes. Where they'd come from in the family tree was anyone's guess.

Lucas took Zoe's chin in his hand, but didn't lift it, scared her eyes might have taken on a darker shade.

He choked up but quickly covered with a small cough. He had to be strong for Zoe. Emma was busy in the kitchen, not listening, so hopefully she wouldn't be freaking out tonight. And the dark things that had claimed the rest of the world were not coming for him or what remained of his family. For whatever reason, the three of them had been spared so far. Everything was fine. Everything was going to stay that way.

"Does your head hurt too, honey?" He wanted to smack himself. Concern had shoved the question out before fear could stop it.

"Uh-uh. Just my tummy."

That was something at least. Kids had growing pains all the time, apocalypse or not. Pulling her head against his chest, he kissed the top of her head. A few months ago, it would have been Emma who calmed their little girl with a kiss. He'd have looked on pretending not to be jealous.

You never knew how good you had it when you were in the moment. And now, even if *they* disappeared, there were so few people left, what kind of life could they hope to build?

Emma had been an accountant for God's sake. And who would want a graphic designer when everyone was already blaming that damned artist in Zurich for the end of days? Everyone who was still around, anyway.

Maybe Emma would become the sweet, loving mother and wife she had been before? So much had been lost. He thought of the twins' room, now empty.

No. He had to focus on Zoe. "Okay, that's good, then," he said keeping his voice low, hoping she'd continue to do the same.

"It's all cold and rumbly," whispered Zoe. She pushed her plate away. "I don't wanna eat any more."

"That's fine, that's fine. Here, Daddy will eat the rest all up." He scooped the few remaining potatoes into his mouth and swallowed without really chewing making the growling and grumbling noises that always made her smile. He wiped a drop of sauce from the corner of his mouth with his thumb and licked it off. "But don't tell Mommy, okay?"

Zoe was almost four now and loved secrets, her favorite being the hidden fortress under the pile of leaves in the yard. The stronghold was nothing more than the cardboard box from the refrigerator he and Emma had bought for one another for their anniversary last year.

The trees had shed their leaves all at once two weeks back instead of their usual seasonal decline. Zoe had helped him rake the leaves up the sides of the box. The top was only sparsely covered, the stained cardboard peeking through. As far as Zoe was concerned, it was invisible to all but her own gaze. And those select few with whom she'd entrusted with its secret location.

While he and Zoe had worked in the yard, Emma had sat on the edge of the porch smoking, watching the two of them as they giggled and shoved armfuls of leaves along the ground. At one point Lucas thought Emma was about to join them, but the hint of a smile had only crept out a millimeter from the corners of her mouth before returning.

"Sleepy, Daddy." Zoe nestled into him.

Kids picked up bugs all the time. Sniffles and stomach aches. Not a big deal. Besides, he'd scavenged plenty of medicine. "It's getting late. Let's get you ready for bed, big girl. I'll get a flashlight and read *Wonderstruck* to you again. How does that sound?"

Leaves rustled along the ground outside in the breeze, their sound like crackling flames. Through the window, Lucas glimpsed a child-sized figure ambling down the road. Probably Ms. Levesque's son from over on Charter. Almost had to be considering how damned few families stayed behind after the evacuation. The higher population densities in the refugee areas had only resulted in a proportionate increase in those claimed. That had been when they were still taking adults.

The boy in the street stopped. Lucas couldn't see his eyes in the gloom but you didn't really need to see them to know.

"The whole thing?" asked Zoe pushing away, suddenly more alert.

"What?"

"*Wonderstruck*. The whole thing?"

"The whole darned thing."

Zoe squirmed and he could tell she was grinning up at him, despite the shadows.

* * *

Lucas left Zoe's bedroom door open and moved quietly through the house, passed the locked door of the twins' room and down the stairs. Darkness had fallen completely outside. Moonlight seeped through thin, drab curtains. Cans and boxes lined the hallway to the kitchen. Zoe was fast asleep but he didn't want to disturb Emma. Maybe she'd gone to *couch* already. She never joined him in bed anymore. Hell, she wouldn't even sleep with Zoe in her room back when the girl still bothered to beg. Kids learned. Emma's refusals had never been angry, or impatient, or even irritated. Just quiet, empty *nos*.

It was like she'd said her goodbyes, made her peace, and Zoe was already wandering the streets with the Levesque boy.

Zoe had lasted only a quarter of the way through *Wonderstruck*. Lucas was thankful for that. Tomorrow, when the sun came up, dingy as it had become, he'd take a good look at her eyes.

Just a quick round through the house and he'd go back and bed down in the floor beside Zoe. The kitchen was dark, the tile cold through his threadbare socks and he slid his feet along surface to avoid the possibility of broken glass. Emma sometimes dropped jars. She seldom cleaned them up anymore.

Emma had proven invaluable in the early weeks, she'd been all over the internet learning all she could about frontier living and survival. The countertop brimmed with canned vegetables, the stockpile of supplies from neighboring houses and the mended clothes were a testament to her grit and tenacity. She'd changed as the months passed following the twins, though. As if her body was a fragile vessel, dropped and now riddled with tiny imperfections, fissures that had allowed her to leak away.

A tiny red light flared in the darkness.

Lucas jumped. "You scared me, babe."

A year ago, his Emma would have laughed at catching him unawares. Lucas heard her sharp intake of breath followed an instant later by the smell of her cigarette. She'd quit smoking when she'd gotten pregnant with Zoe but had started back the day they'd locked up the twins' room. "She asleep?"

"Out like a light. We played pretty hard outside this afternoon." Lucas moved to the sink and looked out the window. The world was shadows, dark and darker. Without the streetlights, the moon was barely enough to see by. Funny how a few tiny light bulbs had been so comforting before.

"In the fort," said Emma.

"She loves that thing," said Lucas, unable to keep the smile from his voice. "I'm so glad we kept that box. You should go out and play with her in it tomorrow. The days are getting colder and it'll give me a chance to drive into town. Ms. Levesque said there was another FEMA drop and we could use some more water."

Emma didn't answer.

"Zoe would love it. She misses you, babe. She doesn't understand all this. Just that her mommy isn't playing with her anymore."

"It doesn't matter, Lucas."

"Of course, it matters. She's our daughter."

"So, what then? It's our job? Is that it?"

He'd said that a few too many times and now she wasted no opportunity to use it against him. He refused the bait.

The tip of Emma's cigarette grew brighter. Long seconds later, it did so again.

The silence made the darkness heavy and the wall between them as impenetrable as the locked doorway down the hall. In the basin, a single jar lay on its side. Moonlight glinted in the crack. The tang of preserved tomatoes mixed with cigarette smoke.

"I heard her," said Emma.

Lucas sighed. "She felt fine as soon as I got her to bed. A little distraction was all she needed."

She slid something heavy across the kitchen table toward him.

"Kids get little aches and pains all the time," said Lucas.

"Look around, Lucas." Her voice was quiet, emotionless. "It's all theirs now. The whole fucking planet. And, one way or the other, we're all just waiting to be taken too."

He couldn't look at her, keeping his gaze fixed on the jar. Moonlight squirmed in the crack. Emma was always worse at night. "You shouldn't say stuff like that. They could leave any moment."

The tip of her cigarette glowed. "And we go back to our happy little lives?"

The base of his skull tingled as the moonlight in the jar vanished. The boy stood outside the window.

The object on the table scraped against the surface. The metallic snap of the slide being pulled back filled the room. In the dark, he couldn't tell if Emma were offering him the pistol or pointing it at him.

"We don't need that," he said. "I'll lead him away."

He crossed to the door, stopping to fumble in their clutter drawer. The muscles between his shoulder blades cramped where her gaze, or that of the gun, stared at him. He pointed an LED flashlight at the floor and clicked it on and off to make sure the batteries were good.

"You'd be doing *his* mother a favor," she said.

"He'll follow me. It'll be okay." Lucas opened the door. A gust of chilled autumn air entered. Leaves skittered in, crossing the floor like tiny clawed feet. "Get some sleep. It'll make a world of difference."

"Why, that's genius, Lucas. Thanks."

Lucas slipped outside. The steps were clear and the yard flat. Most of the leaves were mounded at the refrigerator box but each footfall crinkled and crackled. Lucas tightened the flashlight beam and played it across the boy's back where he still stood peering in the window.

Ms. Levesque had lost her husband early on. Did she even know her son wasn't in bed right now? That he'd been claimed?

The thin sweat pants and t-shirt the kid wore were woefully inadequate against the cold, but he didn't so much as shiver. They just didn't seem to care what happened to the bodies they took. Given long enough, their victims simply starved or died of dehydration.

Lucas ran the beam back and forth across the boy's back to get his attention. The logo of two children chasing a checkered ball on his shirt confirmed his identity. What was the kid's name?

The boy turned. The flashlight's wide-beam mode was enough to illuminate a good portion of the wall behind the boy. Even so, his head remained in shadow. As Lucas panned toward his face, the light tightened and bent, sucked into the darkness where the boy's eyes had been.

Lucas wavered, knees weak, his head throbbing. Madness tickled the corners of his mind the way it had before he and Emma had locked the hallway door. Resisting the urge to walk toward the boy was easier than he expected. Still he had to jerk his head to one side to avert his gaze, wincing at the shifting pressure behind his own eyes. This close you couldn't just casually glance away from their faces. An act of will was needed and that had never been his strength.

Maybe Emma was right. Maybe he should go back for the gun. He couldn't save the boy. No one had ever been able to do that. Taken was taken. And as far as anyone knew the things looking out through their eyes were unaffected by what happened to the bodies they took. They could not be banished, but the windows to this world could be closed.

Windows and doors. Lucas thought of the locked bedroom door in the house. And Zoe's own door, open and left wide so even the slightest whimper could be heard.

Swinging the light from the boy's face, heat flared in the back of Lucas' skull. The beam twitched, seeking to hold the boy's eyes until Lucas had swung it well away. The back of Lucas' head itched and burned. When guesses and gasps had still cluttered the air waves, scientists had blamed the visual cortex. Something in humanity's most rudimentary programming resisted processing what lay behind those cold empty voids.

Lucas just needed this boy as far away from Zoe as possible.

"Come on." Bile mixed with the taste of potato in his mouth. He spat into the dead grass and began a slow trek across the yard. A hint of cigarette smoke reached him but he didn't bother looking for Emma. "This way. Follow the light."

When Lucas reached the curb and stepped on the pavement, he paused until he made out the boy's slow, steady progress through the leaves.

He could lead the boy back to his home, his mother.

No. The thing staring out of him right now had never lived in there. It had never been on the soccer team. Never called the Levesques Mommy and Daddy.

Lucas regretted leaving the gun, but the choice had been made and he didn't want to extend his evening stroll any longer than absolutely necessary. A few more streets ahead and he'd switch off the light and take a winding jog back, giving the thing a wide berth. Tomorrow he'd visit Ms. Levesque.

Make sure she knew.

The peak of the art center loomed through the trees. Occasionally the taken would climb stairs to larger buildings, no one knew why. Then they would stop and stare at the structure, or outward, or at the sky.

Lucas was plenty far away from Zoe and Emma now. Solar-charged safety lighting glowed dimly through gaps in the boards nailed over the plate glass entrance. Something small lay unmoving on the stoop, pink and yellow in a print that might have been happy jungle animals.

A child's abandoned doll, he allowed himself.

The light coming through the door should be enough to catch the boy's attention so he would not attempt to follow Lucas back home.

Lucas glanced back just to make sure the boy was with him. Switching off the flashlight, Lucas cut left, running as far as he dared until his eyes adjusted.

The boy continued his casual course toward the art center. The throbbing in Lucas' skull abating as he got farther away, though the pressure behind his eyes remained constant. Seasonal allergies. Nothing to worry about.

He was halfway home before he considered turning on the flashlight again. He didn't really need it. The abandoned streets weren't scary anymore.

The moon and stars were bright enough and the way was clear. It had been a quiet apocalypse. A quick decline in population as people were claimed and the seasons moved from spring to summer to autumn.

Zoe was going to be fine.

And Emma? Well, Emma would work through this.

She had to.

Lucas slowed his pace and looked up at the smudge of the Milky Way, somewhat robbed of its glory by the moon this evening. Once upon a time he'd laid beneath the stars with Emma. She'd cuddled into him and he'd named off the stars and constellations. Now though, the night didn't seem so much about those ancient pinpricks of light as it was the emptiness between.

Thunder exploded and Lucas was in motion before it echoed from the side of a single house. His mind reeled, a muddle of white noise. Denials and promises.

She hadn't done it, he told himself. She wouldn't have. Zoe was okay. She was asleep in bed. Her tummy was better. In the morning, they'd crack open a new jar. Peaches. Yeah, they'd have peaches for breakfast. Emma would play with them both in the yard.

Lucas bolted across his front lawn, leaves swirling in his wake as he shoved through the kitchen door. He wanted to yell out their names but was afraid they wouldn't answer. He switched on the flashlight, blinding himself before clicking the switch down to minimum. The kitchen was empty.

His forward momentum turned inward like a punch to the gut as his footfalls slowed but his heart continued to pound. Emma lay on the couch in the living room, her eyes open, squinting into the flashlight beam.

"Turn that off," she muttered.

"Did you?"

"I heard it too. Woke me up. Figured you'd come to your senses." She sat up and reached for her cigarettes.

"It wasn't me. Where's the gun?"

"Still on the table, I guess."

And it was. Right where she'd left it. Right where he'd left it. He slipped it into his pocket. Leaving it behind for Emma was a mistake he wouldn't repeat.

"You should've done it, Lucas," mumbled Emma from the living room. He could picture the cigarette bobbing in her lips as she spoke. "His mother would've thanked you."

Gently, he touched the metal to make sure it was cold despite Emma's assurance. He walked by the locked room to stand in Zoe's doorway. The pressure behind his eyes had gotten a little better. A sliver of moonlight fell across his little angel, her chest rising and falling ever so slowly, the covers tucked up under her chin.

Lucas wiped the corners of his eyes and settled to the floor at her side.

* * *

"Daddy, don't go."

Lucas knelt and gave her a hug. The overcast morning made the green of her eyes dingy. The whites were muddy too. Poor baby was still exhausted.

Hell. Probably his own vision going. He was forty, after all.

At least she felt fine. Between the two of them, they'd polished off an entire jar of peaches. A gust of wind sent leaves whipping about. Zoe was bundled against the chill and took no notice of the temperature in perfect child-like fashion. Emma watched them both from the door.

Pulling away from Zoe's grip, he had to smile. With very little work, that pout was going to make her demands utterly irresistible by the time she was driving age. His smile faltered inwardly, but he was pretty sure he'd managed to keep it intact outwardly for Zoe.

"I'll be back in a little while. I'm just going to visit with one of the neighbors for a few minutes and when I get back we'll have some fun, okay?"

"Puzzles?"

Lucas nodded. "You betcha. While I'm gone you and Mommy can play in the fort. That is, if you're willing to tell her where it is."

Zoe's tiny brow scrunched, considering the ramifications.

He nodded reassuringly to the girl and stole a glance back at Emma. She scowled but gave a curt nod which prompted a rush of giggles from Zoe. "Be back in no time."

Before he turned the corner, he glanced back. Zoe had taken Emma's hand and was leading her toward the mound of leaves. Lucas thought he might have seen Zoe wince and rub her stomach but his own stomach was feeling rough. A whole jar of peaches had not been the best plan. His headache wasn't helping matters.

He should make a run down to Weaver's too. It was a small private pharmacy at the back edge of the subdivision. Maybe no one had thought to raid it. He could look for some vitamin C and cold medicine. Maybe their cache of antibiotics. He'd risk the noise and take the car so he could stock up. They couldn't afford to catch the flu.

The mystery of the gunshot from the night before was gone as soon as he approached the Levesque house. It's wrap-around porch made it odd in a neighborhood of condos. Probably the original house on this tract of land. The house's newest feature – the one he had to force himself to acknowledge – was the splash of red against the wall to the right of the door. A rocking chair lay on its side. A woman's body sprawled against the wall behind it as if the chair had been a jug and she'd spilled out when it tipped.

Lucas didn't need to look closer. In the early days, he would have buried her or covered her body.

At first, they had claimed folks randomly. Militaries and police forces around the world had treated their arrival as an invasion. An attack, mankind could resist. Once people realized there was no return for their loved ones, their bodies had been terminated with impunity. The visitors didn't run or hide, though. They didn't fight back. And they didn't stop coming.

The only indication they were reacting to the slaughter was the day they stopped taking adults. Most people would kill their doctor, their mechanic or even an old uncle if they were suddenly a monster, even a nonviolent one. But precious few would shoot a child.

Now there were probably more of *them* than people.

A car started, the noise bouncing around between the houses and Lucas couldn't be sure where it was coming from. The rattle of the engine he recognized.

He got home in time to see Emma backing out of the driveway. Zoe's booster seat was empty and he didn't see her small head poking up in the front seat the way he'd let her ride lately.

Emma came to a stop beside him but kept her gaze straight ahead. "Do her a favor, Lucas. And yourself."

"What are you talking about? Where are you going?" He leaned down and looked in the seats and floorboards. No bags or supplies of any kind. She wasn't going far at least. Unless she'd packed the trunk. "Where's Zoe?"

Emma didn't answer.

The back of his head throbbed, and his eyes ached. "Is she okay?"

"She's in the damned fort." Her voice was choked and when he leaned in he could see her eyes were sunken and red. She eased the car forward forcing him to withdraw. Before he knew it, she'd pulled away.

Dead leaves, brown and red and yellow, crawled along the surface of the mound in the yard. With each step, the tingle in the back of his skull grew hotter and the space behind his eyes more painful. Kneeling at the opening of the refrigerator box he couldn't see inside. He opened his mouth to speak but couldn't find the sound of a single word.

"Daddy?"

"Y-yes, honey." Tears ran down his cheeks. "Come on out, baby. Come on out."

"It's dark in here, Daddy," she said, her voice slow and sleepy. And far away. Much farther away than he could rationally account for given the size of the box.

"It's okay. Come on out. Let's go find a good puzzle."

A slow deliberate scuffle and scraping came from inside the box as she crawled out feet first. She was wearing her neon green boots and a purple jacket. The one they'd bought last year knowing she would grow into it.

She stood with her back to him as he reached out for her. He imagined he could hear the car engine over the rustling leaves and the black noise in his ears. That he and Emma could stretch out beneath the stars again. That the twins still cried in their cribs, just needing a feeding. Maybe clean diapers. That the screaming in the back of his skull and the pounding behind his face would quiet, if only for a second. That the gun was not so cold in his hand.

Zoe turned slowly as if far beneath the sea or deeper still within a dream. Her gaze bottomless and dark.

* * *

"Here, honey," said Lucas. "Open up for Daddy."

Lucas nudged the spoon between her lips. Some of the potato broth spilled and he wiped it from her cheek with his thumb. At least it was warm and that was good on a cold winter evening. She walked slowly beside him never looking up, never speaking.

She swallowed and he quickly spooned in another bite.

The pain behind his eyes had eased with the season but the pressure in the back of his skull had not. The throbbing screwed with his visual cortex most of the time these days. Sometimes he saw other worlds, especially on the nights when he set up a row of flashlights for her to stare at while he caught a few minutes of sleep.

Not tonight though. When the sun set today they would walk side by side while the million nameless stars blazed overhead. If he could find the strength, and the pain in his skull eased just a little, he would look into her eyes.

And they could look back into his.

Biographies & Sources

The Taking of Ireland
Retold Tales from The Book of Invasions
(Modern retelling of tales from *Lebor Gabála Érenn*, 11th century)
Lebor Gabála Érenn, or *The Book of Invasions* as it is also sometimes known in English,
dates back to the eleventh century. Written by an anonymous author, it is made up of 12
manuscripts consisting of five different versions of the story. Though up until the seventeenth
century the original manuscript was considered an authoritative historical source, it is now
believed to consist mainly of myths. Its plot closely echoes the Old Testament, starting
with the creation of the world and telling the history of Ireland until the Middle Ages.
It combines Biblical stories with pre-Christian history of the Celts and their pagan myths.
These are modern retellings taken from Flame Tree's *Celtic Myths and Tales* book; written,
compiled and edited by a team of experts and enthusiasts on mythological traditions.

Bo Balder
A House of Her Own
(Originally Published in *F&SF*, 2015)
Bo Balder is the first Dutch author to have been published in *F&SF* and *Clarkesworld*.
Her short fiction has also appeared in *Escape Pod* and other places. Her SF novel *The Wan*,
by Pink Narcissus Press, was published in 2016. She is a member of SFWA, Codex Writers
and a graduate of Viable Paradise. Bo has always wanted to be an SFF writer. For that
reason, she practised a series of pointless professions like dishwasher, rowing coach,
computer programmer, model and management consultant. When she isn't writing, you
can find her madly designing knitwear, painting or reading Ursula K. Le Guin, Iain M. Banks
or Jared Diamond. Visit her website at: www.boukjebalder.nl.

Jennifer Rachel Baumer
Sin Nombre
(First Publication)
Jennifer Rachel Baumer lives, writes, runs, bakes and procrastinates with her husband and
cats in the Sierra Nevada foothills. Her work can be found in publications from *Cosmos*
to *On Spec*, *Lady Churchill's Rosebud Wristlet*, *Penumbra*, and many genre anthologies.
She's fascinated by viruses and hemorrhagic fevers, and by the animals that carry them.
The first time she ever heard of a veterinary virologist was when one tried to take her to
emergency because of an infected cat scratch. Jennifer resisted, but added virologists to
the list of things that fascinate her.

George Chesney
The Battle of Dorking
(Originally Published in *Blackwood's Magazine*, May 1871)
George Tomkyns Chesney (1830–95) was a British Army general and the founder and first
president of the Royal Indian Civil Engineering College. He entered the army as second
lieutenant in 1848 and spent most of his military career in India. Upon his return to Britain
in 1892 he was elected the Oxford Conservative representative in the British Parliament.

While Chesney wrote several novels and contributed stories to magazines, he is best known for the highly influential *The Battle of Dorking*, originally published anonymously. The novella initiated the genre of invasion stories that became popular in Britain in the light of threatening German victory in the Franco Prussian War in 1871. The warning about the possibility of abrupt invasion was translated into several languages and published overseas. It became a popular read in the years preceding the First World War.

George Allan England
The Thing from – 'Outside'
(Originally Published in *Science and Invention*, April 1923)
George Allan England (1877–1936) was an American writer and explorer, best known for his speculative science fiction inspired by authors such as H.G. Wells and Jack London. After a period of translating fiction he published his first story in 1905, leading to over 330 pieces now accounted for. England attended Harvard University and later in life ran for Governor of Maine. Though unsuccessful in that endeavour, he transferred his interest in politics into his writing where themes of socialist utopia often appear. England died in a hospital in New Hampshire, though there is a legend claiming he disappeared on a treasure hunt.

Austin Hall
The Man Who Saved the Earth
(Originally Published in *All-Story*, December 1919)
Austin Hall (*c.* 1885–1933) was an American short story writer and novelist who claimed to have written over 600 stories. He was also a farmer and worked on a ranch. Though the majority of his works were westerns, Hall began writing science fiction and fantasy and in 1916 his story 'Almost Immortal' was published. Together with 'The Rebel Soul' and its sequel 'Into the Infinite', 'Almost Immortal' delves into the exploration of human personality while infusing it with the theme of vampirism and immortality. Along with George Allan England's 'The Thing from – "Outside"', 'The Man who Saved the Earth' was reprinted in the very first edition of the pulp magazine *Amazing Stories* (April, 1926).

Maria Haskins
Long as I Can See the Light
(Originally Published in *People Are Strange*, 2016)
Maria Haskins is a Swedish-Canadian writer and translator. She writes speculative fiction and poetry, and debuted as a writer in Sweden in the 1980s. Currently, she lives just outside Vancouver with a husband, two kids, and a very large black dog. She fell in love with fantasy and science fiction as a child while reading the works of Ursula K. Le Guin, Ray Bradbury, and J.R.R. Tolkien, and has no plans on ever falling out of love with these genres. Her work has appeared in several anthologies – *Flash Fiction Online*, *Shimmer*, *Gamut*, and elsewhere.

Suo Hefu (索何夫)
Blind Jump
Translated from the Chinese by Cai Yingqian (蔡盈倩) and Collin Kong (孔令武)
(Originally Published in *SFWorld*, China's largest circulation science fiction magazine, 2015)
Suo Hefu (索何夫) is a Chinese science fiction writer. Born in 1991 in Sichuan Province, he began writing in 2014 and has achieved greater notice since he won the Best New SF Writer

Galaxy Award and Chinese Nebula Award. He is studying History at Xinjiang University. He tends to write technically realistic stories with vivid details, and has written numerous short stories such as 'Exobabel', 'God's Servant', 'Blind Jump', '1871', 'Tinder' and 'Spartacus'; now he is working on his first novel. Cai Yingqian (蔡盈倩) and Collin Kong (孔令武) are both Masters Graduates of the School of Translation and Interpreting at the Beijing Language and Culture University.

Rachael K. Jones
Home is a House that Loves You
(Originally Published in *PodCastle*, 2017)
Rachael K. Jones grew up in various cities across Europe and North America, picked up (and mostly forgot) six languages, and acquired several degrees in the arts and sciences. Now she writes speculative fiction in Portland, Oregon. Contrary to the rumours, she is probably not a secret android. Rachael is a World Fantasy Award nominee, Tiptree Award honouree, and winner of Writers of the Future. Her fiction has appeared in dozens of venues worldwide, including *Lightspeed, Beneath Ceaseless Skies, Strange Horizons*, and *Nature*. Follow her on Twitter @RachaelKJones.

Claude Lalumière
Being Here
(Originally Published in *Tesseracts Nine*, 2005)
Claude Lalumière (claudepages.info) is the author of *Objects of Worship, The Door to Lost Pages, Nocturnes and Other Nocturnes*, and, most recently, *Venera Dreams: A Weird Entertainment* (a Great Books Marquee selection at The Word on the Street Toronto). He has published more than 100 stories, several of which have been adapted for stage, screen, audio, and comics. His books and stories have been translated into seven languages. Originally from Montreal, he now lives in Ottawa.

Rich Larson
Water Scorpions
(Originally Published in *Asimov's Science Fiction*, 2016)
Rich Larson was born in Galmi, Niger, has studied in Rhode Island and worked in southern Spain, and now lives in Ottawa, Canada. His short fiction appears in numerous *Year's Best* anthologies and has been translated into Chinese, Vietnamese, Polish, Czech and Italian. He was the most prolific author of short science fiction in 2015 and 2016. His debut collection, *Tomorrow Factory*, comes out in May 2018, and his debut novel, *Annex*, follows in July 2018. Find more at richwlarson.tumblr.com and support him via patreon.com/richlarson.

H.P. Lovecraft
The Shadow over Innsmouth
(Originally Published by Visionary Publishing Company, Pennsylvania, April 1936)
The Shadow out of Time
(Originally Published in *Astounding Stories*, June 1936)
Master of weird fiction Howard Phillips Lovecraft (1890–1937) was born in Providence, Rhode Island. Featuring unknown, extra-terrestrial and otherworldly creatures, gods and beings, his stories were some of the first to mix science fiction with horror. His inspiration

came predominantly from mythology, astronomy and the supernatural and gothic writings of such authors as Edgar Allan Poe. Plagued by nightmares from an early age, he was inspired to write his dark and strange fantasy tales; and the isolation he must have experienced from suffering frequent illnesses can be felt as a prominent theme in his work. Lovecraft inspired many other authors, and his most famous story 'The Call of Cthulhu' has gone on to influence many aspects of popular culture.

Angus McIntyre
The Hunted
(First Publication)
Angus McIntyre was born in London and now lives in New York, where he mistreats computers for a living. His short fiction has appeared in *Abyss & Apex* and *Black Candies*, and in the anthologies *Ride the Star Wind, Mission: Tomorrow, Humanity 2.0, Swords & Steam*, and *Principia Ponderosa*. His science-fiction novella *The Warrior Within* will be published by Tor.com in March 2018. He is a graduate of the 2013 Clarion UCSD Writer's Workshop. Find out more on his website: angus.pw.

A. Merritt
The Metal Monster (prologue–chapter IV)
(Originally Published in *Argosy All-Story Weekly*, August–September 1920)
Abraham Merritt (1884–1943) was born in Beverly, New Jersey. A writer of speculative fiction as well as an inductee to the Science Fiction and Fantasy Hall of Fame, Merritt wrote characteristic pulp fiction themes of lost civilizations, monsters and treacherous villains. Many of his short stories and novels were published in *Argosy All-Story Weekly*. His most famous novels are perhaps *Burn Witch Burn, The Ship of Ishtar*, and *Dwellers in the Mirage*. His writing was known for its excessive descriptive detail as well as the immense creativity of the alternative worlds he created.

Stephen G. Parks
Last Breath Day
(Originally Published on www.quantumtraverse.com, 2016)
Stephen G. Parks, a nomadic Canadian, once spoke with a wild bull elephant in Namibia for 5 minutes. Other life-altering experiences included working with the amazing students of the African Leadership Academy; releasing sea turtles in Malaysia; filming a documentary in the Kyangwali UN Refugee Settlement in Uganda; and having lunch with a giraffe in Kenya. Other than a few short stories on his website, www.quantumtraverse.com, this is Stephen's first publication. He hopes to have his debut novel finished soon. You can find him @stephengparks on Twitter.

Patrick Parrinder
Foreword: Alien Invasion Short Stories
Patrick Parrinder is President of the H.G. Wells Society and has written several books on Wells and science fiction, including *Shadows of the Future* which won the 1996 University of California Eaton Award. He is also the author of *Nation and Novel* (2006) and *Utopian Literature and Science* (2015), as well as being General Editor of the 12-volume Oxford History of the Novel in English. He now divides his time between London and Norfolk and is an Emeritus Professor of English at the University of Reading.

Sunil Patel

The Merger

(Originally Published in *The Book Smugglers*, 2015)

Sunil Patel is a Bay Area fiction writer and playwright who has written about everything from ghostly cows to talking beer. His plays have been performed at San Francisco Theater Pub and San Francisco Olympians Festival, and his fiction has appeared in *Flash Fiction Online*, *Fantastic Stories of the Imagination*, *Asimov's Science Fiction*, and *Asian Monsters*, among others. He has also edited fiction for *Mothership Zeta* and reviewed books and television for *Lightspeed*. His favourite things to consume include nachos, milkshakes, and narrative. Find out more at ghostwritingcow.com.

Laura Pearlman

Some Things I Probably Should Have Mentioned Earlier

(Originally Published in *Mothership Zeta*, 2016)

Laura Pearlman's fiction has appeared in *Shimmer, Flash Fiction Online, Daily Science Fiction*, the *Unidentified Funny Objects* anthology series, and a handful of other places. A full list can be found on her otherwise sadly-neglected blog, *Unlikely Explanations*. Laura lives in California, reads slush for *Escape Pod*, and has a Tumblr devoted to things her cats have dropped in their water bowl. She should probably get out more. Until then, you can find her at @laurasbadideas on Twitter.

Tim Pieraccini

Outvasion

(First Publication)

Tim Pieraccini has kept a cunningly low profile since publishing a short story in *Doctor Who Magazine* 25 years ago, busying himself making music videos, short films and one feature-length film, *All Heart*. He is still searching for a home for his fictional addition to the history of 60s music, *No Way to Beehive*. He lives in Hove, without animals or children but content with books, and has various fictions on the go at present, along with a projected book of feminist film criticism.

Robert Potter

The Germ Growers (preliminary–chapter II)

(Originally Published by Melville, Mullen, & Slade, 1892)

Robert Potter (1831–1908) was born in County Mayo, Ireland, a son of the local clergyman. He was an outstanding student of rhetoric and English literature at Dublin's Trinity College, later also delving into the arts. After gaining his qualifications, he followed his father's footsteps and upon becoming a clergyman he moved to Australia. *The Germ Growers* is the story of an interplanetary race that assumes human form and invades Earth to grow germs able to eradicate humanity. Science fiction enthusiasts have compared it to the later masterpiece *The War of the Worlds* by H.G. Wells.

Eric Reitan

Lovers at Dawn

(First Publication)

Eric Reitan, a philosophy professor at Oklahoma State University, has won numerous writing awards, including the 2014 Outstanding Writer Award of the Rose State Writers' Conference and the 2008 Crème-de-la-Crème Award of the Oklahoma Writers' Federation, Inc. His short stories have appeared in several venues, including *The Magazine of Fantasy and Science Fiction* and *Gamut*. His nonfiction books include *Is God a Delusion?* (named a Choice Outstanding Academic Title of 2009), *God's Final Victory: A Comparative Philosophical Case for Universalism* (with John Kronen), and *The Triumph of Love: Same-Sex Marriage and the Christian Love Ethic*.

Garrett P. Serviss
Edison's Conquest of Mars (chapters I–IV)
(Originally Published in the *New York Evening Journal*, 1898)
Garrett Putnam Serviss (1851–1929) was an American journalist, amateur astronomer, and science fiction writer. He studied science at Cornell and law at Columbia University. *Edison's Conquest of Mars* was commissioned by a newspaper in 1898 as a sequel to *Fighters on Mars*, an unauthorized, altered version of H.G. Wells's *The War of the Worlds*. The story was set in America and has been assessed as a competent commentary on American society at the time. It was Serviss's first of five science fiction novels, the remainder of which were considered to lack the flair of the first. He also wrote a short story and several non-fiction astronomy-themed pieces.

Jonathan Swift
Gulliver's Travels (part III, chapters I–III)
(Originally Published by Benjamin Motte, London, 1726)
Jonathan Swift (1667–1745), born in Dublin, Ireland, was perhaps the greatest prose satirist in the English language. His unique 'Swiftian' prose style, mixing irony, lighthearted humour and biting ridicule, inspired such later writers as John Ruskin and George Orwell. Unlike other satirists, his prose remained largely free of embellishments, rhetoric and affectations, and he opted instead for a plainer, common form. He is best known for his story *Gulliver's Travels*, and his hyperbolic essay 'A Modest Proposal.' Most of Swift's prose and poetry was published pseudonymously while he worked for the church in Ireland, and as a political pamphleteer during the Whig-Tory conflict in England.

Voltaire
Micromégas
(Originally Published by A Londres, 1752)
François-Marie Arouet (1694–1778), better known as Voltaire, was born in Paris, France. He was a highly prolific writer of the Enlightenment movement and a historian and philosopher who garnered controversy through his attack on the Catholic Church, advocating its separation from the state as well as freedom of religion and expression. His bibliography consists of over 22,000 works of all forms, including letters, pamphlets, plays, poems, novels, and essays. *Micromégas* and later *Plato's Dream* are seminal pieces in the history of science fiction as well as literature in broader sense.

John Walters
Dark Mirrors
(Originally Published in *Warrior Wisewoman 3*, 2010)
John Walters is an American writer, a graduate of Clarion West and a member of Science Fiction Writers of America, who recently returned to the United States after living abroad

for many years in India, Bangladesh, Italy, and Greece. He writes science fiction and fantasy, thrillers, mainstream fiction, and memoirs of his wanderings around the world. He currently lives in Seattle, Washington, with two of his five sons, precariously eking out a living as a fulltime freelance writer. You can find his blog at johnwalterswriter.com.

H.G. Wells
The War of the Worlds
(Originally Published in *Cosmopolitan*, 1897)
Herbert George Wells (1866–1946) was born in Kent, England. Novelist, journalist, social reformer, and historian, Wells is one of the greatest ever science fiction writers and along with Jules Verne is sometimes referred to as a 'founding father' of the genre. With Aldous Huxley and, later, George Orwell he defined the adventurous, social concern of early speculative fiction where the human condition was played out on a greater stage. Wells wrote over 50 novels, including his famous works *The War of the Worlds, The Time Machine, The Invisible Man,* and *The Island of Doctor Moreau,* as well as a fantastic array of short stories. *The War of the Worlds* is a seminal work in the alien invasion genre, and undoubtedly had a huge influence on later science fiction.

S.A. Westerley
What Survives of Us
(First Publication)
S.A. Westerley is one of Sheffield-based Spleeny Dotson's many alter egos. As S.A. Westerley he has an unpublished anthology of Golden Age style sci-fi, *The Speculators,* from which this story comes. Spleeny also produces radio comedy and drama for Sheffield Live radio. His sci-fi sitcom, *Accidentally Reckless,* is available on YouTube. Under his own name Spleeny performs stand up comedy and, not under his own name, he ghostwrites for money. Speaking of alter egos, Spleeny is somewhat involved in the career of embittered elderly pulp writer Foster Abraham, whose killer-hayfever beset works can be found at facebook.com/fosterabrahamarchive.

William R.D. Wood
Jars for Their Eyes
(First Publication)
William R.D. Wood traces his love of science fiction and horror back to a childhood filled with classic Universal Studios monsters, *Space: 1999* reruns, a worn-out copy of *Dune,* and *Heavy Metal* magazine. His work has appeared in *Nature, The Lovecraft eZine,* and the *3rd and Starlight* anthology, among other places. A good writing day often finds him at any of several favourite overlooks on the Blue Ridge Parkway deeply immersed in a new work of cosmic horror. Will lives with his wife and children in Virginia's Shenandoah Valley in an old farmhouse turned backwards to the road. Find out more at www.williamRDwood.com.

FLAME TREE PUBLISHING
Short Story Series
New & Classic Writing

Flame Tree's Gothic Fantasy books offer a carefully curated series of new titles, each with combinations of original and classic writing:

Chilling Horror Short Stories
Chilling Ghost Short Stories
Science Fiction Short Stories
Murder Mayhem Short Stories
Crime & Mystery Short Stories
Swords & Steam Short Stories
Dystopia Utopia Short Stories
Supernatural Horror Short Stories
Lost Worlds Short Stories
Time Travel Short Stories
Heroic Fantasy Short Stories
Pirates & Ghosts Short Stories
Agents & Spies Short Stories
Endless Apocalypse Short Stories

as well as new companion titles which offer rich collections of classic fiction from masters of the gothic fantasy genres:

H.G. Wells Short Stories
Lovecraft Short Stories
Sherlock Holmes Collection
Edgar Allan Poe Collection

Available from all good bookstores, worldwide, and online at
flametreepublishing.com

...and coming soon:

FLAME TREE PRESS | FICTION WITHOUT FRONTIERS
New and original writing in Horror, Crime, SF and Fantasy

GOTHIC FANTASY

For our books, calendars, blog
and latest special offers please see:
flametreepublishing.com